## APOLLO

*Bosnian Chronicle* | Ivo Andrić

*Now In November* | Josephine Johnson

*The Lost Europeans* | Emanuel Litvinoff

*The Authentic Death of Hendry Jones* | Charles Neider

*The Day of Judgment* | Salvatore Satta

*The Man Who Loved Children* | Christina Stead

*Delta Wedding* | Eudora Welty

# My Son, My Son

## Howard Spring

APOLLO

Apollo Librarian | Michael Schmidt || Series Editor | Neil Belton
Text Design | Lindsay Nash || Artwork | Jessie Price

www.apollo-classics.com | www.headofzeus.com

First published as *O Absalom!* in 1938 by William Collins
Sons & Co Ltd.

This paperback edition published in the United Kingdom in 2016
by Apollo, an imprint of Head of Zeus Ltd.

1 3 5 7 9 10 8 6 4 2

A CIP catalogue record for this book is available
from the British Library.

ISBN (PB) 9781784970772
    (E) 9781784970765

Typeset by Adrian McLaughlin
Printed and bound in Denmark by Nørhaven

Head of Zeus Ltd
Clerkenwell House
45–47 Clerkenwell Green
London EC1R 0HT

*For Eric Hiscock*

A few men and women who have played some part in the history of our times are mentioned in this novel. These apart, all characters are fictitious and all scenes are imaginary.

*And the king was much moved, and went up to the chamber over the gate, and wept: and as he went thus he said, O my son Absalom, my son, my son Absalom! Would God I had died for thee, O Absalom, my son, my son!*

## Introduction

William Essex rises from humble beginnings to become a successful dramatist and novelist. We get to know him rather well: he is the narrator of this novel. His friend Dermot O'Riorden, a reluctant Irish patriot, a talented joiner, founds a leading London furnishing emporium. When they first meet, both poor and aspiring, O'Riorden is 'sitting at a very dusty desk set in the middle of a small dusty room that was not so much lighted as dimmed by one small dusty window'. They become close friends, pouring out their hearts to one another. O'Riorden calls Ireland 'a stinking, starving little country that I'm glad to be out of'; but he also says, 'If ever I have a son [...] I'll dedicate him to Ireland'.

*My Son, My Son* – William's and Dermot's story – belongs equally to their sons, Oliver Essex and Rory O'Riorden. The boys grow up as friends in their father's shadows but, emerging into their own light, the very history that their parents have managed to circumvent lays hold of them. Fathers whose best-laid plans were for their sons, have no power to deliver them from their plans' consequences. Oliver and Rory are their Absaloms. Fathers provide, counsel, watch, regret, but cannot prevent. Of the mature women characters, only Livia Vaynol, a free and freeing spirit who arrives too late, gives the novel a romantic focus.

When It first appeared in 1938 the novel was entitled *O Absalom!* Two years before its publication, William Faulkner's masterpiece *Absalom, Absalom!* was published. *My Son, My Son!* kept only the repetition and, initially at least, the exclamation mark. Spring's and Faulkner's fathers could hardly be more unalike. If the books share themes – civil conflict, family, material, cultural and political ambition – they are worlds apart in form, texture and tone. Faulkner is a self-inventing modernist; Spring a social novelist in the English line of Eliot, Meredith and Hardy.

1937 had been a good year for English fiction. On publication, Spring's book succeeded John Steinbeck's *Of Mice and Men* on the bestseller list and outsold Daphne Du Maurier's *Rebecca* in its first year. Both these books have retained the limelight better than *My Son, My Son* and have not been out of print, where *My Son, My Son*'s hour has come and gone and come again as its themes return to topicality. In 1940 it was made into a feature film in the United States – where the book was extremely popular – directed by Charles Vidor and foregrounding the romantic themes. In 1979 it became an eight-episode BBC television series exploring the Irish dimension. Kate Binchy played Sheila O'Riorden, Frank Grimes Dermot and Gerard Murphy was Rory; Michael Williams was William and Patrick Ryecart Oliver. The two treatments are totally different, yet the book contains them both.

Howard Spring is a city novelist. Born and reared in poverty in Cardiff, his poverty is not rural but urban, of the slums. His is not Gaskell, Galt or Hardy territory. He has more in common with the worlds of Arnold Bennett and J.B. Priestley, writers whom he succeeded as an influential book reviewer at the *Evening Standard*.

The early chapters of *My Son, My Son* are set in and around my home town, Manchester. His first novel, *Shabby Tiger* (1934) is also set there. The locations – Deansgate, St Anne's Square, Palatine Road, even the Old Cock Inn – still recognizably survive. 'All the way from Ancoats to Hulme there was not a tree, not a shrub, not a twig to be seen.' Things have improved a little, but his world is familiar in outline. The action takes place a century ago, but the map of Manchester and its suburbs has not much changed. Many old buildings still stand, now put to different uses, or derelict and awaiting rehabilitation or the wrecker's ball. Hulme, where the protagonist endures his threadbare childhood and his mother works as a laundress, is improved but recognizable. The winter streets can still be 'full of writhing yellow fog'. Grey laundry hangs on lines, bullies are busy bullying, straitened families sprawl and multiply; 'there was a funeral now and then to thin us out'. Some once-posh neighbourhoods have come down in the world, but Didsbury today is still Spring's Didsbury, a place to aspire to.

Nellie Moscrop, whom William decides early on in his climb out of poverty to marry 'in cold blood', having realized how sick and how rich her father is, draws William's attention to the Manchester novels and writers. *Jane Eyre* 'began to get written not ten minutes' walk from here', and Mrs Linnaeus Banks's *The Manchester Man* was also local produce. William heeds her, but even then realises that the he is in transit through these streets that are like 'a small frozen furrow in the waste of the city', and that the people he uses to rise by he will eventually leave behind – apart from his intimate friend Dermot who rises in a different way and place. The narrator's candour is reliable and unnerving: he is without moral scruple, which makes time's judgement on him seem less gratuitous, more just.

William is attuned to social division. Having begun in poverty, he works and calculates his way out of it. His first job, in the novel's first sentence, is fetching washing for his washerwoman mother. He notices the differences between her clients; some considerate, others brusque. A knowledge of social division pervades the novel, a division based less on social class than on material possession. And William becomes increasingly aware of political division, between Britain and Ireland. Spring is a spare writer, his descriptive writing conveying a kind of uninsistent symbolism. The story moves forward in the characters' time and the country's history.

The little details are telling: whether a jam roll, Flynn's narrative of the Manchester Martyrs, or William's mother's funeral procession. Spring's London is less real than his Manchester, and when he writes Cornwall he has travelled a little too deep into Du Maurier country, leaving the real map behind.

Actual incidents and public figures tie the fictional elements to history. Spring insists on the reality of his novel. If someone leaves the action he will tell us – don't imagine they'll be back again. They leave for good, the way people do, the way things happen. He insists there is no design: this is life, plain and simple. The Irish home rule versus independence argument is conducted with increasing emphasis – Dermot's 'God damn England' becomes Sheila's 'God bless Ireland' – until we are in the heat of it. As if it was the book's specific prophesy, in 1996 its themes came to fruition in the huge IRA bomb that stunned Manchester city centre.

One aspect of Spring's realism was his commercial calculation. He dedicated the book to Eric Hiscock, author of the influential 'Whitefriar' column for *Smith's Trade News*, the source of information for the book world. Hiscock had a nose for bestsellers. His endorsement could make a book's fortune. Commercial calculation may have been on Spring's mind. It is always on William's mind as he climbs the social ladder and acquires the trappings of affluence. In a way, William is the prototype for the modern writer: a servant to his readers and his interests, knowing which side his bread is buttered on, and lacking the devil-may-care integrity that marks Hardy's and Eliot's protagonists. This corruption of artistic ambition is what the novel is about. It is an excellent novel because it makes no scruple in laying bare its narrator's existential compromise and the consequences it has.

*Michael Schmidt, 2016*

Part I

1

I liked fetching the washing from the Moscrops', and my mother liked washing for Mrs. Moscrop better than for anybody else. That was because Mrs. Moscrop always wrapped a bar of yellow soap in with the washing. There wasn't anyone else who thought of a thing like that.

The Moscrops' shop stood on a corner. The frontage was on the main road. To reach the bakehouse at the back you went down the side-street. The shop window looked very gay that night, especially as the streets were full of writhing yellow fog. It was a few days of Christmas. Chinese lanterns, some in long concertina shapes, some spherical, all lit with candles, reinforced the two gas jets which normally lighted the window. There was a long brass tube running the length of the window with half a dozen gas points sprouting from it like nipples, but only one at either end was ever lit. I suppose the Moscrops, like the rest of us in Hulme, had to think of pennies.

But that idea didn't occur to me then. Moscrops' was an oasis of light in the dingy slum, a lounging-place and *rendezvous* of the boys and girls, and on that particular night, with holly stuck into the tops of cakes, with coloured paper chains dangling in loops from one Chinese lantern to another, with "A Merry Christmas" hanging in separate silver letters from a string that was itself sparkling as though with hoar frost, Moscrops' looked as enchanting a window as a child could wish. There were loaves covered with crisp brown crust, buns oozing currants, Christmas puddings, cloth-covered, in basins, tall jars of biscuits, and bottles of sweets.

When I pushed open the door, a bell above it gave one

unresonant sound, more of a click than a ring, and there I was with the raw night shut out, the familiar, warm, foody smell all about me. Mrs. Moscrop, squat and rounded and friendly as one of her own cottage loaves, came in from the parlour behind the shop. "Oh, the washing!" she said. "It's not quite ready. Just go and talk to Mr. Moscrop in the bakehouse."

I went down the side-street and pushed open the bakehouse door. A lovely place! Lovelier even than the shop, warmer, more filled with appetising smells. Two deal tables ran down the length of it. They were as smooth as silk. Old Moscrop, shuffling about in slippers, with no coat or waistcoat, with his shirt-sleeves rolled high up and with a long white apron tied about his middle, looked as though he had been born in the place. His face was as creamy and pudgy as dough. All the rest of him was covered by a fine white film of flour. The door of the great oven was open, and I could see into its cavernous depths. Row upon row of loaves was within, some in tins, some standing in the brown armour of their crust. Mr. Moscrop had a wooden spade with an enormously long handle. With this he could reach right to the back of the oven. Sliding the blade under the loaves, he began to draw them out and put them on the two long deal tables. Some were for Mr. Moscrop's shop and delivery round. Others had been baked for customers who made up their own dough at home. Fanciful people pricked their initials into the top of the dough. Others wrote their names on pieces of paper and skewered them on to the loaves with matchsticks. These pieces of paper were now brown and brittle and would fall to bits if you touched them.

Mr. Moscrop cast an eye at me now and then, but he did not speak till all the loaves were on the tables. Then he pulled towards him a long jam roll, took up a knife, struck off an inch or two and pushed it towards me. In a voice as hoarse as though his throat were choked with flour, he said: "'Ave a pennorth."

The ritual was unfailing. The washing was never ready. I was always sent to the bakehouse. Mr. Moscrop always invited me to have a pennorth. Then I went back to the shop.

But now my heart gave a thump. Two boys were standing outside the window. I knew they would still be there when I came out. They were. I was burdened with that monstrous bundle, the week's washing of the Moscrop family assembled inside a sheet, with the four corners of the sheet tied together. I gripped the knot thus made with both hands. Only so could I carry the load, bending forward to allow it to rest on my bowed back. I was twelve years old, very thin and weak, and very much afraid of the two boys who, I knew, were following me. Presently they passed me at a light run, one in front of the other. Each gave a shoulder-shove as he went by, making me stagger. They vanished in the fog ahead. They would be waiting at the next corner, so, making the fog an ally, I doubled back and struck off down a side-street. I could get home by a detour. Presently, I heard them questing noisily, yelling the call with which they always assailed me: "Does your mother take in washing?" It went to a sort of tune, with a heavy stress on the first syllable of the last word, the "ing" trailing away and rising. I used to hear that call in my sleep. It haunted me everywhere.

Now they were on my trail. They had tumbled to my poor ruse. I turned swiftly to the right, down a dark lane between two sets of back doors. It was a fool's move, for it was a dead-end. I could hear them whooping through the fog and prayed that they would rush by. But they didn't. They felt their way cautiously down the entry and found me trembling, with my hands still clutching the big knot in the sheet, the bundle still on my back. I don't know why they persecuted me. Simply because they were young and foolish and I was helpless, I suppose. They tore open the bundle, scattered its contents in the muddy lane, leapt among them like mad things, chanting their song, and ended by pushing me down into the sorry mess, snatching my cap from my head, and making off with wild hoots of laughter.

How I hated washing! It seemed to dominate life in our house in Shelley Street. It announced itself in the front window: *Washing and Mangling done here.* It made itself felt in the narrow passage-way which always smelt of steam and soap-suds. It overpowered the kitchen where, everlastingly, washed clothes hung from lines suspended under the ceiling, from clothes-horses grouped round the fire; and where the smell of ironing seemed the accompaniment of all life. But most of all it inhabited the scullery where the copper was, with a fire beneath, and where my mother wearily boiled, and rubbed on the rubbing-board, and rinsed and mangled.

What a place it was, that dark little house that was two rooms up and two down, with just the scullery thrown in! I don't remember to this day where we all slept, though there was a funeral now and then to thin us out.

I was the youngest of the lot, the kid, the nuisance, too young to be of much use to the others either for work or play. They were glad to be rid of me; and, looking back to the conditions we lived in, I don't blame them for that. All the same, I felt it at the time. I could imagine the sigh of relief when the front door banged behind me. It made me turn in on myself.

One way of getting rid of me was often used in the summer. We had a small trade in herb beer, as a notice announced in our window alongside the one which advertised our activities in washing and mangling. I was often sent off to gather the herbs. A slab of bread and butter and a bottle of water were placed in a large basket, and, thus provisioned, I was expected to relieve the household of my presence for the best part of a day. I did so gladly.

It pleased me very much to turn out of the black fortress of Hulme and strike southwards along the Palatine Road that was not then the roaring tramway track it has since become. With the sky blue overhead and the road white with dust underfoot, I tramped along enthralled by the evidences that passed me of a world of unimaginable wealth and splendour. From their great houses that lined the road all the way between Fallowfield, Withington and Didsbury the kings of cotton came on their way to Manchester. Victorias and phaetons and barouches, coachmen with gloved hands and cockaded hats, footmen, gentlemen on horseback: all passed by along the road that was gay with hawthorn and cherry trees, laburnum, lilac and chestnut. Now and then, leaning back upon her cushions with a parasol above her head, some lady would be bound for the shops of St. Ann Square or Market Street, a lady so daunting with her great hat and flounced cape and lowered insolent eyes that it was impossible to conceive the circumstances in which her life was passed.

And there were the houses themselves to gaze upon and wonder at: big, square, stucco-fronted houses for the most part, each one standing splendidly in its own grounds, with conservatories looking like ornamental copies of the Crystal Palace, and stables, coach-houses and outbuildings in which you might have lost, and been no wiser, the four rooms of our house in Shelley Street.

Shelley Street! What mania was upon the builder when he so named that joyless, dingy alignment of brick traps! Byron Street and Keats Street and Southey Street and many another street blessed with the name if not the nature of poetry ran off the same black trunk of a high-road from which we branched. And to me, then, the names were nothing but names, and the name of Shelley Street evoked, as I passed the mansions of the rich, only a pang of bitterness and envy.

For, young as I was, I hated all the circumstances of my life. I hated the carrying of bundles of washing. I hated the turning of the mangle, and most of all I hated the close compression of a life that threw us all upon one another by day and night, and made us bite and snarl, and gave no one the chance to be alone. So that when I saw the fine rich houses on the Palatine Road, I burned to be as rich as the people who lived in them. I dreamed of a great room in which I might be alone, of a house full of servants whose chief job would be to prevent anyone from coming near me, of a park which would interpose itself between me and the touch and commerce of men.

I loved to go out on that job of gathering nettles and dandelions and the few other herbs from which our beer was brewed, because solitude could be had thereby. It did not take long in those days, even from the heart of Manchester, to reach flowery fields and hedgerows full of meadowsweet and ragged robin, nor did it take long to eat my bread and butter, swig my bottle of water, and fill the basket with herbs. Then there was nothing to do but wander here and there, lie for hours under a hedge, watch the swifts hurtling across the blue sky, and dream my unfailing dream of being rich.

It is incredible to me now that, then, I had never read a book. I couldn't read; I couldn't write. If I had been able to read, I should doubtless have been acquainted with many stories of boys like myself who had become cotton magnates or this or that, and whose first thought had been to make their old parents comfortable and relieve the want of their brothers and sisters. I was unaware that the morality of fiction demanded that of me; my dreams were crude and stark and centred upon myself. There was no one else in the picture. I didn't want anyone else in the picture. I wanted just me, comfortable, isolated from the demands and stresses of life.

It was because that foul range of dungeons miscalled a street was also called Shelley Street that a turn came to my career. In the pleasant rural part to which I had gone one day in my quest for herbs there was—and is today—an old church of red sandstone squatting in the midst of its graveyard on an escarpment from which you look down to the low water-meadows where the Mersey loops and twists. It is still a pleasant spot, and then seemed paradisal, for the city had not yet marched to within miles of it; and nothing met the eye save a comely house here and there, and tall trees, and the meadows where cattle were wading in the deep pastures.

I lay in the churchyard with my filled basket at my side, with a grey tombstone, fallen askew, to support my back, and with nothing to do but let the tranquillity of the day drift by till it was time to set out for home. The old man who came into my life at that moment was named Oliver—the Reverend Eustace Oliver.

Reverend enough he looked to me, pacing slowly through the grass among the tombstones, his long white hair reaching almost to his shoulders, his clothes black and austere, the index finger of one hand tucked within the pages of a book.

I scrambled to my feet with a feeling that this man, clearly a parson, owned this churchyard and that I had better get out of it. I was picking up my basket when Mr. Oliver put a hand upon my shoulder with a touch extraordinarily gentle and forced me back to where I had been sitting. Then he, too, with a smile at me, sat down upon the grass. "Don't run away," he said. "This is God's acre."

When I got to know Mr. Oliver better, I found him full of these phrases—what, I suppose, we should call today cant phrases—but he meant them all, and he was a good man.

I don't remember much of what we talked about that afternoon, except that he asked me my name and I said William Essex; and he asked me "How old are you, William?" and I said twelve; and he asked me where I lived and I said Shelley Street. Then he smiled again, and showed me the book he was carrying, and said: "I often wander down Shelley Street myself."

I didn't know what he was talking about, and said: "I've never seen you there, sir," and he replied patiently: "No, no. I mean I read Shelley. This book, you see—these are Shelley's poems."

He held the book out to me and I said: "I can't read, sir," and to that he answered: "Well, let me read to you."

It was a strange afternoon, and it ended magnificently in Mr. Oliver taking me to the kitchen door of the vicarage. He said to the cook, with his unfailing childlike smile: "Mary, feed my lambs," and Mary fed me on tea and bread and butter, raspberry jam and cake.

It was with no thought of Mr. Oliver's exalted discourse, but rather in the hope that the raspberry jam would happen again, that I contrived to be in the churchyard often during that summer. Sometimes Mr. Oliver appeared; sometimes he didn't; and even when he did, the lamb was not always fed. But the feeding was frequent enough to justify a going on with the experiment; and the upshot of it all was that out of cupidity on my part and a tolerant friendliness on his there arose an easy relationship between us which ended by his offering me employment. The wages were something ridiculous, but I was to have my keep, and Mr. Oliver said he would teach me to read and write.

He kept his word, and for three years I lived happily. There was plenty to do. I was the servant of every servant about the place. I helped the cook in the kitchen, lighting fires, cleaning cutlery with bath brick ground to powder, scrubbing tables, keeping the joints turning before the fire. I helped the old man who looked after Mr. Oliver's horse and garden, cleaning out the stable, carting manure to the garden dump, weeding the borders and raking the gravel of the paths, and occasionally even grooming the horse that was as old and grey and quiet-tempered as Mr. Oliver himself. I helped the sexton to keep the church clean; and in the first fury of my desire to be a good and useful servant, I even began to tidy up the tombstones, scraping with a nail the moss from the inscriptions. But Mr. Oliver wouldn't have that. He stopped me gently with a murmured remark about the unimaginable touch of time.

My lessons with Mr. Oliver were at no stated hour. At any time of the day he was liable to drop on me, snatch me away from my work, and take me to the copybooks in his study. I liked the winter evenings best, with the oil lamps lit in the brown room full of faded books and with a fire rustling and twinkling in the grate. The room looked upon open fields, and not a sound disturbed us save the occasional crying of an owl. Mr. Oliver sat in his easy chair by the fire, wearing comfortable slippers and smoking a long clay pipe. I sat up to the table which was covered with a red cloth fringed with little balls, and wrote or read aloud from my book.

I owe this to Mr. Oliver: that as soon as I could read at all—and I took to it with really remarkable speed—he kept me reading solid things. We began with the Old Testament; we read some Burton and Browne and some of the speeches of Burke, strange enough stuff for a boy, but it gave me an early sense of rhythm, of richness, a palate which was never easy afterwards with the second-rate.

I didn't realise it at the time; but what had happened to me was a chance in a million: I had acquired, and kept for three years, a private tutor of exceptional intelligence and skill at his job. Some whim had set him off; he was a bachelor and, I suppose, lonely; but having taken on the task, he did it thoroughly. He wrote a beautiful hand, and so do I to this day. He taught me something of geography. Never a place-name was mentioned but we must find it on the globe. He gave me a smattering of history and talked to me about the men and the happenings that filled the newspapers.

What is more, I had plenty to eat, and I had space and quiet. I slept in a loft over the stable, and, believe me, there was no hardship in that. It was a roomy loft with a window that looked over the fields. In the summer-time the river mists would be up, and I would see the cattle moving through them so deeply immersed that nothing was visible but their ridged spines like the keels of upturned boats floating on an opalescent lake. In the winter it was cosy in that loft, with three blankets on my bed of hay, and, above all, I was alone there. All the fabled joys of family life were taken from me, and I was happier, healthier and wiser in every way.

I worked hard. I was cleaning out the stable before seven in the morning, and what with my jobs and my lessons I had hardly a moment to spare till ten at night. My wages were ten pounds a year. Shameless exploitation of boy by wicked parson! Nonsense! What I owe to Eustace Oliver I can never repay.

At the end of the first year, he offered me my ten pounds. To a boy of thirteen, who had never handled more than a shilling at a time, it seemed an immense sum—a sum so immense that I could not accept the responsibility of touching it. There was nothing I could do with it. I could, of course, have given it to my parents, but the thought never crossed my mind. I saw them but rarely—more and more rarely as the year went on—and found myself wanting to see them less and less.

I needed no clothes. Though it was not in his bargain, Mr. Oliver provided them. I had plenty of food and a roof over my head; and, though I had by this time reached the point where I should have bought books if there were none to hand, I didn't need books either. There was all Mr. Oliver's library to explore.

So Mr. Oliver said he would bank the money for me and give me five per cent interest. And that was another piece of education for me. I learned that money I had no immediate use for had the delightful property of adding to itself with no effort whatever on my part.

"You see," Mr. Oliver explained, "if you had a hundred pounds out at five per cent, then at the end of the year you'd have your hundred with another five added. But as you've only got ten, that is one tenth of a hundred, you'll only get one tenth of the five pounds, that is ten shillings. But that is something, William, for the ten pounds plus the ten shillings will all be added to your next ten pounds, and then you'll have twenty pounds ten shillings all earning five per cent."

That was my first lesson both in mathematics and finance, and it seemed very good and wonderful to me.

I never had lessons with Mr. Oliver on a Saturday evening, for Saturday evenings were reserved for Mr. George Summerway. George Summerway lived in one of those fine stucco-fronted houses that were scattered about the church and vicarage. Like Mr. Oliver, he was a bachelor, but that was all, so far as I could see, that there was in common between them. Summerway was a huge, broad-shouldered man with a head overflowing with crisp black hair. He had a loud Lancashire voice that bellowed forth frighteningly from his florid face. He was always dressed with an overpowering elegance. He ran to tight trousers and sprigged waistcoats and a white beaver hat. You could see him driving up to town most days, managing the reins with an air, while a depressed-looking coachman sat beside him in the dogcart.

Throughout the time I lived with Mr. Oliver, he and George Summerway dined at one another's houses on alternate Saturday nights. It was on a Saturday night in the winter when I had served Mr. Oliver for two and a half years that he sent for me to the dining-room. The table was littered with the relics of the feast. George Summerway sat with one elbow leaning upon it, his chair skewed away, his legs sprawled out towards the fire. He was twirling a glass of port in one hand.

"Well, this is t'lad, is it?" he bellowed, as I stood timidly within the doorway. His face was flushed, and his curling black hair hung over his forehead. "Looks a skinny 'un to me."

"He's strong enough," said Mr. Oliver quietly. "I've been talking to Mr. Summerway about your future, William."

"Wants thee to go into t'cotton trade. Does that appeal to thee, lad?"

I'm afraid I didn't make a good impression. I stammered and blushed. The thing had been sprung on me too suddenly.

"We've taken him at a disadvantage, George," said Mr. Oliver kindly. "I'll talk to him about the idea."

"Ay, an' get him to learn to talk, too," Summerway shouted, swigging down his port. "Tha's got to shout in t'cotton trade. No place for dumb ninnies. And learn summat about figures, lad. Learn summat about figures, an' then us'll see."

That was all at the moment, but throughout the rest of that winter and during the succeeding spring Mr. Oliver conscientiously bent his mind to teaching me "summat about figures." I could feel that it was not a matter greatly to his taste. Often his hand would stray to some favourite volume, as though for once he would break the routine and diverge into paths more congenial. But he would put the book down with a sigh and take up a foolscap sheet ruled with cash lines.

We were occupied with this business of figures up to nine o'clock one May evening. It had been a beautiful day, and suddenly Mr. Oliver thrust away the work as though he were impatient with it. "That'll do for tonight, William," he said, and walked to the window to look out over the water-meadows towards the last flush of sunset that lingered in the sky. Then, as was his custom, he expressed his deepest emotion in a catchword. "The golden evening brightens in the west," he murmured. "Good-night, William."

"Good-night, sir," I said.

The next morning Mr. Oliver was found dead in his bed.

## 2

Mr. Oliver died on a Wednesday. Mr. Summerway told me to report to his office in Mosley Street on the following Monday. I disliked the idea of going home, but there was nothing else to do, so I went. Things were greatly changed since I had last been there six months before. There was no congestion now. My father had disappeared—had quite simply walked out of the house one morning and never come back. He is not exiled in order that he may dramatically reappear in these pages. He never did reappear. He was gone, mysteriously and for ever. My eldest brother, who was married, was now living in the house with his wife and my mother. There was no one else. My other brother had joined the army. One of my sisters had gone to "live in" at a large drapery store in the town; another had taken a position as "general." Concerning the third I could get no information whatever. "Ask no questions and you'll be told no lies," my mother said darkly; and to this day I have never discovered what happened to my third sister.

My brother was twenty-five years old and worked as a boiler-maker. He did not receive me graciously, and I don't blame him for that. His wife, whom I had never seen before, was a dark surly girl, big with her first child. They owed me nothing, and had no reason to want me about the place. I spent an intensely unhappy week-end, and when I set out on the Monday morning for George Summerway's office I made up my mind to follow what seemed to be a family habit: to disappear without a word.

I did so. I was fifteen years old, in good trim after three years of fresh air and generous feeding, but thin as a lath, dark as night, as all our people were, and as melancholy as hell at the sudden over-turning of my world. I had in my pocket thirty pounds, plus some odd shillings, my faithfully computed five per cents, and in a carpet bag I had a few clothes.

I was disappointed with George Summerway's offices. I had expected that so splendid a personage would conduct his affairs in splendid circumstances, but, though his own room was airy enough, the rest of the premises was dismal and dingy beyond what I should have thought possible.

"Report to Mr. O'Riorden," Summerway had said to me, and when I came in that morning out of the clear air of May I found Mr. O'Riorden before me, sitting at a very dusty desk set in the middle of a small dusty room that was not so much lighted as dimmed by one small dusty window. Mr. O'Riorden was himself small and dusty. When he stood up, I saw that already I was taller than he. He could not have been more than five feet two. He was as bald as an egg, and from the crown of his shining skull down to his chin his skin was of a dull parchment yellow. His clothes were black and formal, shiny with use. He wore paper protectors over his cuffs, and his silk hat hung from a hook behind the door. He looked at me from over the top of steel-rimmed spectacles, and said: "So you're Essex? Young and blooming. The good God help ye." He shook his head as though the sight of me filled him with intolerable sadness.

Having looked his fill, he took a snuff-box from his waistcoat pocket, sniffed vigorously at the brown powder, and said: "Ye'll work in the outer office. I'll introduce you to the clerks when they condescend to appear, the good-for-nothing limbs of hell. Ye'll do just what they tell you. Ah, Mr. Sloper, ye've decided to give us the benefit of yer presence?"

I find it difficult at this distance of time to recall the individual characteristics of Mr. Sloper, Mr. Sykes and Mr. Sayers, the three clerks, and that is probably because they had no individual characteristics. They called themselves the Three S's, and Mr. O'Riorden called them the Three Asses. My recollection is of three witless, cheerful blades who told the bawdiest stories of their nightly doings and whose clear eyes and guileless faces belied the saga of prodigal dissipation with which they regaled me and Mr. O'Riorden.

O'Riorden lived a harassed life, a buffer state between the Three Asses and Mr. Summerway. He called himself the confidential secretary and seemed, in practice, to be an overworked correspondence clerk, taking down innumerable letters in some shorthand system of his own and transcribing them laboriously in longhand into a carbon-copy book. Neither the typewriter nor the telephone was yet usual in such an office as that of Mr. Summerway, and for illumination in the often murky late afternoons we had crude gas jets singing dolefully in little wire cages.

I spent a futile and unhappy morning. It was soon apparent that George Summerway, who had the reputation of having never done a generous thing in his life, had done one for me out of regard for his old friend Mr. Oliver. There was no place for me, there was no need for me, in the office. I was to receive fifteen shillings a week, and I saw no means of earning it. But I provided great fun for the Three S's who were delighted to have someone to order about and who kept me busy washing their inkwells, dusting their desks and running their errands. When lunch-time drew near, Sayers's enterprise rose. He handed me a bottle and charged me to go to the dairy and buy half a pint of pigeon's milk, but when this time-heavy jest failed to get home, they left me alone, with nothing to do but mope idly about the shabby room.

At one o'clock O'Riorden came from his office into the clerks' room, the Three S's shut their heavy ledgers with triumphant slams, and four chairs were ritually arranged round the fireplace, though there was no fire in it. Sykes produced four cups from a cupboard, Sayers handed me twopence and a great jug and instructed me to fetch tea from a neighbouring restaurant, which was one small room, a couple of steps below street level, festering with steam and sweat and the smell of cheap food.

When I returned to the office, Mr. O'Riorden and the Three S's had produced packets of sandwiches and had already begun their lunch; and Sloper was asking: "Well, gentlemen, what is the subject before the meeting today?"

"That Woman," said Sayers, "is the End All and Be All of Existence; and when our fellow wage-slave William Essex has charged our beakers, I will begin the proceedings by asking you to drink to this toast:

*Here's to the girl with the bluest eyes*
*The darkest hair and the whitest—"*

"William," said Mr O'Riorden, looking at me uneasily over his spectacles, "haven't you brought any lunch?"

"No, Mr. O'Riorden," I said.

"Then you'd better come with me."

Mr. O'Riorden put on his silk hat, took me by the arm and led me from the room amid the ironical cheers of the Three S's. "Bravo, O'Riorden!" Sayers shouted, banging a cup upon a chair. "Bravo, the saviour of William's youth and purity."

We went to the stinking little restaurant from which I had brought the tea. Mr. O'Riorden's was not the only silk hat there, for silk hats at that time had nothing to do with income. Mr. O'Riorden opened his packet of sandwiches upon the table that was covered with flaking American cloth, ordered tea for both of us and some sandwiches for me.

"Ye'll take no notice of them three daft skites," he said. "They're all wind and blather and devil a bit of harm to 'em at all."

I thanked him for bringing me out, and finding him in a friendly mood I suddenly blurted out the truth about my loneliness, of the life I had led for the last three years, and about my resolve not to go home again.

"'Tis a hell of a thing," he said, looking at me compassionately and helping himself to snuff, "when ye're not aisy with yer own flesh and blood. 'Tis the worst sort of trouble there is, and only a fool tries to cure it. Mr. Summerway told me most there is to know about ye, but he didn't say ye'd not be having a roof over yer head."

"I could sleep in the office," I said, "till I find some rooms."

"Ach, to hell with that. What would ye say now to coming home with me? There's only me an' the missus and Dermot. There was Fergus, too. But Fergus is away out to America to join my brother who's doing a sight better than I am. So you can have Fergus's bed. You'll have to share a room with Dermot. He's seventeen."

I thanked Mr. O'Riorden fervently for thus removing a torment that had been in the back of my mind all day, but he silenced me with a wave of the hand, and the watery little eyes in his yellow face took on a pensive inward look. "It's queer the way things turn out," he said. "There was me and there was Conal—that's me brother in America—without a tail to the shirt of us. And off he goes to America to become a policeman an' off I go to England to become a rich man. For it was I that had all the learning there was between us, and he nothing but a pair of feet the size you could make tombstones of 'em. And now it's he that's rolling in money with a chain of stores the length of me arm, and me that's takin' the office boy home to pay a few shillings towards the rent. Ach, well; let's be gettin' back to see what them three young hell-rakers are after doing."

I lived with the O'Riordens for five years, and very happy years they were. To look at, Ancoats was not much better than Hulme, but it was better for me in every way. From the moment I stepped over the O'Riordens' threshold that first evening I was at home with them. I began on a satisfactory financial basis, which gave me status and did not make me feel like an interloper. I was to pay

twelve-and-six a week for my share of a room and my food, and
Mrs. O'Riorden was the sort of housekeeper who could do that and
make a small profit. She was a Lancashire woman who had worked
in a mill, but had no need to do so any more. She had a Lancashire
woman's pride in her house, and 26, Gibraltar Street shone, from
the whitened front doorstep to the brass knobs on the bed in the
room I was to share with Dermot.

It was this shining quality of the house that impressed me at
once. My own house had been dim and dingy; Mr. Oliver's house
had been dim with a sort of faded grandeur, but Mrs. O'Riorden's
house was a riot of gleaming surfaces. Mirrors and crockery, steel
fender and fire-irons, picture-frames, chests-of-drawers, linoleum,
all filled the house with twinkles; and it was a treat to see her tackle
the deal kitchen table with silver-sand and elbow grease, as though
she were determined sooner or later to coax a smile even to its dull
and unresponsive surface.

I have the clearest recollection of the great kindliness with
which I was received, of the absence of embarrassing questions, of
the simple frank acceptance of the fact that here was a boy whom
father had brought home because he wanted somewhere to live,
and somewhere to live he should have. I was taken upstairs to the
room that contained two beds: one that had been Fergus's and now
was to be mine, and one that was Dermot's; and then I went to the
scullery where already Mr. O'Riorden, who had taken off his coat,
waistcoat and collar, was making great play with soap behind his
ears. I took my turn, and then returned to the kitchen, which was
the living-room, and there found that Mr. O'Riorden had put on his
waistcoat, but not his collar, a pair of carpet slippers, an old jacket
and a smoking-cap with a rakish tassel. He looked a new, a more
comfortable, an altogether different Mr. O'Riorden. It was evident
that home was the place where Mr. O'Riorden was happiest, and that
he knew it.

The fire was burning brightly; Mrs. O'Riorden had lit a lamp and set it on the table where already she had laid an extra place for me. Mr. O'Riorden stood before the fire on the thick rag mat, comfortably warming his behind and keeping his back to the portrait of Queen Victoria, in a shining frame, wearing a crown and a blue sash, and the Order of the Garter, and a fat sulky frown. Mrs. O'Riorden, whose bosom was as comfortable as the Queen's, but who looked an altogether more cheerful and companionable person, was fussing here and there between the fire and the table.

We were waiting for Dermot, and soon he came in, a thin, rather pale-faced red-head, quite unlike either of his parents. His eyes were pale, and he had long gawky wrists covered with fine gold hair. He had fly-away eyebrows, rushing up like little opened wings. When he saw me, a stranger, they flew up higher, as though they would rush away altogether with surprise and agitation. He accepted me with the friendliness his mother had shown. There was a great courtesy about Dermot, cloaked in a great shyness. I never forgot him as he stood there that night, anxious to fly from the unexpected, constrained by his good manners to stand his ground and give himself to me in friendliness. He was working for a cabinetmaker, and as we shook hands I saw that there was a fine powdering of sawdust in his eyebrows and in the hair on his wrists.

We ate Lancashire hot-pot, and then we ate apple dumplings and then we all had a hot strong cup of tea. It was a satisfactory evening meal as Lancashire understood it; and for my part, though I've eaten the faldelals of the most famous restaurants since then, I don't know that I prefer them to that.

Washing-up was a communal activity. I carried the things to the scullery; Mr. O'Riorden washed them, Mrs. O'Riorden wiped them, and Dermot put them away. The white cloth was whipped from the kitchen table, a red one was put in its place, and Mr. O'Riorden took a book from the book-case. He sat on one side of the fire and Mrs.

O'Riorden, with a basket of darning, on the other. "Now, mother," said Mr. O'Riorden, "we've just got up to the death of Little Nell." He began to read.

I had read no novels with Mr. Oliver. I had never read a novel or heard one read; and I didn't hear much of *The Old Curiosity Shop* that night. Dermot made a sign with his head. I followed him into the scullery. He shut the kitchen door. "Let's leave 'em," he said. "They're happy. Come and have a look at this."

We stumbled down the dark path which cut the tiny garden into halves. At the end, Dermot said: "Stand still while I get a light." A latch clicked, a match was struck, and presently I walked into the small shed which leaned against the end wall of the garden. "This is my place," Dermot said. "What d'you think of it?"

I looked about me by the light of the lantern swinging from the roof. A work-bench almost filled the shed. There was just room to move round it. Shavings were everywhere, shavings and sawdust, and the air was full of the lovely smell of wood. There were hammers, planes, chisels, gouges, saws, and there was a glue-pot and a small oil-stove for heating it. "There's no screw-driver," I said.

"I never use screws," Dermot answered with a smile. "You wouldn't insult a lovely job like that with a screw."

He ran his hand lovingly over a piece of work that stood on the bench. It was a cupboard flanked by bookshelves, and the door of the cupboard was not yet on. It lay alongside the other work, with a rough scrawl of pencil markings upon it. Here and there gouges had bitten into the marks. A design was beginning to take shape. "For Father to keep his old Dickens in," Dermot explained. "It won't be finished before Christmas at the rate I'm getting on. No time. I ought to give all the time I've got to this sort of thing."

He moved about in the scanty room of the workshop with the light from the lantern falling on his high cheekbones and his freakish, fly-away eyebrows. He rubbed his hand caressingly up and down

the planks that leaned against the wall. "Oak. Ash. Walnut. Teak."
His voice sounded as Mr. Oliver's had done when he was reading a
poem. Suddenly he asked: "What do you think of William Morris?"

I had never heard of William Morris, and said so. Then Dermot's
pale eyes lighted up with a missionary fervour, and I began to think
that, if I lived long with him, William Morris was someone of whom
I should hear a great deal. But it was characteristic of Dermot that,
having flared like a rocket and shot his fire, he never mentioned
William Morris again except in the most casual fashion. But that
night, kicking to and fro among the shavings, feeling the edges of
his tools, rubbing his hand over his planks, and taking a gouge or
two at the design on his cupboard door, he preached the gospel of
William Morris with a hot and eloquent tongue. Beauty in every
home, each stick of furniture lovely and appropriate, every workman a craftsman glorying in his craft, loving his material, such
was the burden of the song into which Dermot broke lyrically that
night. He never sang it again, but I never forgot it, never had any
doubt of the joy he found in that little shed, or of the passion he
could impart to a thing that lay close to him.

It was a fruitful passion, too. Let me go ahead here a little and
say that during the five years I lived with the O'Riordens I saw the
furnishing of the house change under Dermot's hands. He finished
the book-case for his father; and after that, one by one, appeared an
oak refectory table for the kitchen, with bulbous legs, sumptuously
carved, chairs to match it, covered with leather which he stinted
himself to buy, and in Mr. and Mrs. O'Riorden's bedroom occurred
a bed of such gothic splendour that Mrs. O'Riorden declared she
was afraid to sleep in it: it looked too much, she said, like the bed in
which Henry the Eighth had murdered all his wives. These were but
the main waves of a tide of craftsmanship which Dermot let loose
upon 26, Gibraltar Street.

I had evidence that first night of another passion in Dermot's life.

Mr. and Mrs. O'Riorden had gone to bed when we came in from the workshop. They always went early. Dermot took a candle and preceded me up the stairs to our room. He had a way of moving with extraordinary stealth. I didn't hear his hand on the knob before the door was open and there we were in the bedroom. He put the candle down on a chest-of-drawers and began at once to undress. I stood looking about me in the unfamiliar roughly comfortable room. The light of the candle fell upon a carved frame that hung on the wall. I guessed that the carving was Dermot's work. There was a harp with broken strings, and there were shamrock leaves sprouting round the foot of a gallows. It was a strange, moving bit of work. The frame was round a piece of parchment on which three names were inscribed in red ornamental lettering. I read them aloud: Allen, Larkin, O'Brien.

Dermot was already in bed. "Ever heard of them?" he asked. I turned at the strange harshness of his voice and saw that he was sitting up, his eyes glinting green in the candlelight.

"No," I said.

"You'll hear about them some day. They were the Manchester Martyrs. God damn England. Put out the candle."

## 3

I shall not write much of the five years that passed over my head in Ancoats. They were happy years, as I have said, and they were profitable years. At the heart of them remains in my imagination the O'Riorden kitchen, and particularly the O'Riorden kitchen on winter nights. The chirping fire, the red cloth on the table, the lamp hanging by a chain above it, the heavy curtains drawn across the window, and the thick rag mat under foot: all these elements of that interior have pierced deeply into my mind as the trappings of a way of life that was solid, unambitious and good. It was not long before I was taking my turn with Mr. O'Riorden in the readings from Dickens. On most evenings Dermot would quietly disappear, and the rustling of the fire, the click of Mrs. O'Riorden's needles, and the solemn voice of the clock would be the only sounds to accompany our voyage with Magwich down the river or our breathless participation in that night of flood and fury that cast Steerforth upon the Yarmouth sands at the feet of David Copperfield. We would usually still be hard at it when, towards ten o'clock, Dermot would come in from his shed, his long hand brushing the sawdust from his coat, his long eyebrows quizzically raised as he asked: "Still at it? Why don't you learn to *do* something?"

He was all for doing, was Dermot, and in the course of the long walks which it became our custom to take together on Sundays he would sing of the time when his doing would be so effective that he would have a fine showroom in the heart of Manchester and everybody who knew what was what would come to him for beds and chairs and tables.

Grand days those were, walking in the flat green Cheshire countryside or upon the dark moors scarred with screes and gullies that we reached by taking a train to some Derbyshire station and then setting out whither we would. We would lie upon the purple heather with the blue sky above us and the sound of water tinkling in our ears, and Dermot would break the silence to damn England and to blether by the yard about Cuculain and the Dark Rosaleen and Davitt and Wolfe Tone.

"'Tis a throw-back ye are, Dermot," old O'Riorden would say if one of these outbursts took place in the house. "It's because ye've never seen Ireland that it's got ye by the nose. 'Tis a stinking, starving little country that I'm glad to be out of."

And Dermot would not answer, but his pale eyes would light up with their green flecks as on those nights when he came home late from some secret Irish conventicle with a flush to his pallid cheek and his fists clenched to show the knuckles white under the skin. If the old people were gone to bed and I were sitting up alone, he would say nothing of the business he had been at, but would rave of the old Ireland that was a land of saints and scholars, and, what meant more to him, of craftsmen and artificers who wrought in silver and in gold and precious stones. "If ever I have a son," he said one night, "I'll dedicate him to Ireland."

He had the better chance to catch me for his sermons because more and more I took to staying up when Mr. and Mrs. O'Riorden were gone to bed and getting on with my reading. That little kitchen library contained the whole of Dickens and of Thackeray, of George Eliot and the Brontës, a series of books called Great English Poets, and the plays of Shakespeare, which I had never embarked on with Mr. Oliver. I went through the lot like some base and indiscriminate drunkard to whom drink is drink, whether it be dregs or vintage. And there was not much that you could call dregs on O'Riorden's shelves.

Five good and happy years, and I didn't spend them in the service of Mr. Summerway. It was clear from the first that I was wasting my time there, for was it not my will to be rich, and how could I hope for riches in a situation where the next step up was occupied by the young and healthy Sayers who seemed set for half a century?

During those five years I worked in two other cotton houses, and in a shipping office, and in a draper's shop, and in an insurance office, but nowhere did I see that chance for a swift and spectacular ascent which was what I wanted. I began to be plagued, too, with an itch for fame as well as wealth, and it was inevitable that, as reading occupied so much of my time, I should think of writing as fame's portal.

I was seventeen years old when I sat down on a winter night in the cold bedroom of 26, Gibraltar Street and, using the freezing marble slab of the washstand for a writing-table, embarked upon a novel whose rich perspectives faded away into the distances of my mind clothed in all the circumstances of a Copperfield or Newcome.

That evening was notable because it was the beginning of long, gruelling work, and it was notable, too, because that was the first time I saw Sheila Nolan. I found that all the bright ideas that filled my head were spectres which retreated as I advanced upon them. They wouldn't be pinned down. It was a barren and humiliating evening. At nine o'clock Mrs. O'Riorden came to the foot of the stairs and shouted out to me: "Come down now, Bill. You'll be clemmed wi' cold up there. There's a cup of tea waiting for you."

I tore up the few wretched lines I had scribbled and went down. O'Riorden put A Tale of Two Cities back into the handsome book-case that Dermot had made and said: "'Twill be the same in Ireland some day. Mark my words. But to hell with it. My country's where I'm happy and where I'm let live in peace. 'Tis time Dermot was back."

And then Dermot came in, bringing Sheila Nolan with him. Dermot was nineteen then, and very tall, every hair of him red as a fox, but white in the face. Sheila Nolan was a dark slip of a thing: dark waving hair framed her olive face that had a moist red mouth and eyes as black as blackberries, and as glistening.

She was very shy that night, was Sheila, sidling in alongside Dermot as though she doubted her welcome. But she needn't have done that. Never in my life did I know anyone readier to love people than old O'Riorden and his wife. They saw how it was; there isn't often need to ask questions; and they took the girl to their hearts. We all sat round the table, drinking tea; and Sheila and Dermot were rather excited. Usually, when he came in from one of his Irish conventicles, Dermot's excitement simmered within him, for no one in Gibraltar Street was interested in his talk of saints and martyrs. But that night he had Sheila. He had met her often, it seemed, at the meetings. "And you should hear him talk, Mrs. O'Riorden!" she burst out, her eyes devouring Dermot. "Did you know you had an orator for a son?"

"Divil's a word we get out of him here," said old O'Riorden, "but a gift of the gab's not unusual in the family. If me father'd been paid a penny a yard for his eloquence, we could've bought up County Cork."

"The eloquence has missed a generation," said Dermot, who didn't often gibe at his father, even in fun, "Dad's a renegade. He's as good as an Englishman."

There was a bitter taste under the words, as though Dermot had found a new allegiance and had shaken the first grain of sand from under the foundation of the old. I think O'Riorden noticed it. He said nothing.

Dermot took Sheila towards the front door to say good-night. There was a lamp burning in the passage. From where I stood I could see them, the door being open. There was a bit of a scuffle. Dermot said in a voice we could all hear: "God damn England." I saw him seize Sheila's shoulders in his thin nervous hands and squeeze them tight. "Say it," he whispered, shaking her, his eyes flecked with passion. "God damn England. Say it!"

"God bless Ireland," Sheila said in her clear voice.

"That's better, my luv, that's better," Mrs. O'Riorden shouted. "You come and see us again."

"Say it!" I saw Dermot's lips form the words rather than speak them, and I saw Sheila shake her head. I never heard her damn England, or anything, or anybody, all the time I knew her. She was a grand girl, was Dermot's wife. They were married the next year.

4

When Dermot was gone I began to feel miserable in Ancoats. I missed his fierce whispered talks in the bedroom, the long walks into the country, the hours we passed in his workshop, with me lounging idly, drawing shavings through my fingers, Dermot planing and carving and constructing, moving every day nearer to the mastery that was at last to make his furniture famous. Dermot was getting somewhere. He was no longer an employed man. He had taken a small lock-up shop in Deansgate, Manchester, and filled it with his furniture. Sheila looked after the shop. Dermot went every day to the shed in his father's garden and worked there. They lived in two rooms in a street near Gibraltar Street. It was a small beginning, not much, you might think, to cause any dissatisfaction in me. But I knew Dermot. I knew he was embarked, and that he would reach what he was aiming for. I had an objective, too, but my scribbled exercise books were not satisfying things like Dermot's chairs and tables and sideboards. And I wanted money. I did not think my writing would ever bring me much. But money I must have. From the time when I was a child gazing at the houses of the rich, the craving for money had bitten deeper and deeper into me. As I saw it, you didn't need genius to make money. It was a matter of getting an Idea. You suddenly thought of something— something that millions of people would want once they saw it but which no one had thought of giving them before. I used to go about puzzling my head to devise such a thing. But thinking was no good. The Idea came to you: the thing was to see it when it was there under your nose.

There was a horse-omnibus at that time running between Manchester and Didsbury. I often travelled by it on a Saturday afternoon as far as the Old Cock inn, drank a glass of beer, and walked back along the Palatine Road into Manchester, turning over what seemed to me the unsatisfactory state of my affairs. During one of those walks I saw a funeral procession approaching me. It was in the winter after Dermot's marriage. The day was bleak and cold, and as I stopped to stand with bared head, as other people were doing, the moisture from the boughs of leafless trees fell upon my hair. It was a poor sort of procession: a hearse, with one small wreath of flowers upon the coffin, and a solitary cab behind it. The sleek black horses looked altogether too magnificent for what was evidently an inconsiderable corpse. It was my brother's face in the window of the cab that told me I was looking upon the funeral procession of my mother. Three women were with him, all veiled heavily in crape. I could not see their faces, but supposed that they were his wife and two of my sisters. A small girl sat upon the knees of one of the women and gazed with bright interest out of the window.

I stood there beneath the dripping trees, watching till the forlorn little procession was lost in the grey perspective of the winter afternoon. Then I went on my way, thinking with a strange impersonal sadness of the poor woman who had worked so hard and so long and was now hurried off the scene with the tribute of this shabby bit of pomp and circumstance. I remembered the look of strained despair with which she had gazed at the soiled and sordid linen I brought home from Moscrops' that night when the boys had trampled it in the mud. I thought of her, as I had so often seen her, spitting upon the hissing iron, wiping it upon her coarse apron, and bending her wearied spine over the ironing-board, pausing now and then to push from her temples the thin strands of grey hair.

When I reached All Saints Church in Hulme, I struck away to the left, visited by a sudden desire to look again at the house in Shelley

Street which I had not seen since the morning, years before, when I began to work for Mr. Summerway. The winter evening was closing in. The long main road stretched before me, grey and desolate. Byron Street... Southey Street... Shelley Street... here I was, looking down that brief and unappealing *cul-de-sac*. There were no front gardens. It was a short perspective of flat walls, pierced by doors and windows, rising straight from the pavement. Down at the far end a wan lamp had just been lit, and the lamplighter was lighting the other, in the middle of the street, as I stood there.

That lamp stood outside the house I had known so well, and as I watched the door opened and a man and woman came out. The woman was carrying a child in her arms. When they came to where I was standing I said: "Excuse me, but do the Essexes live at 28 now?"

"Essexes?" said the man. "Essexes? Never 'eard of 'em. I been livin' there the last two years."

Never heard of them! All her married life my mother had lived in that house, and so soon it was possible for no memory of her to remain. Though I hated the house, and though for so long I had consciously avoided it, nevertheless the thought that no one whom I knew was in it any more, that my mother was dead, and that my brothers and sisters were passed out of my knowledge, hung upon me like a cloak of lead. Dermot's marriage, too, I suppose, had something to do with it. I felt inexpressibly lonely and sad.

I walked on, my feet almost unconsciously following accustomed trails, and presently I found myself standing in what had once seemed so golden an oasis: the patch of yellow light in front of Moscrop's shop. It had always been a friendly place to me, and, impelled by a craving for company, I pushed the door. The well-remembered bell gave its unmusical "tang"; the warm familiar odour of new bread and spiced cake came to my nostrils. But the dear little squat figure of Mrs. Moscrop was not behind the counter. Instead, there was a girl whom I did not recognise, a plain and dowdy creature, who did not look any the more handsome now because she was trembling with fright.

The cause of her fright was on my side of the counter. He did not recognise me, but I knew him at once for one of my tormentors in days of old. He was one of the two who had pursued me into the alley—it must have been eight years before—and trampled upon the washing. The whole scene rushed back upon me; I savoured again the agony of humiliation, called up again the memory of the deepening tiredness of my mother's face when she looked upon the filthy mess that I brought home. Then I thought of the sad and meagre funeral that I had just seen, and of the long grey road that had led to so ignoble an end. I could hardly see the man before me, because of the tides of hate that surged suddenly into my head and clouded my eyes.

Of all this the young man was unaware. In a loud voice he was addressing the girl who shivered behind the counter: "And you can tell Mr. Bloody Moscrop that in future 'e can drive 'is own bloody 'orse—see? If you can call the spavined wind-broken, galled bloody creature an 'orse—see?"

The words fell like blows upon the girl. She clapped her hands over her ears and was near to sobbing.

"Dainty, ain't yer?" the man went on. "Yes, dainty an' religious, too. I know. Yer don't like my bloody language, do yer? An' I don't like this bloody job. Tell yer old man that. I won't be 'ere on Monday. Wot about a nice bit o' cake for a partin' gift?"

He strode towards the counter and made a grab at a fine Dundee cake. The girl grabbed at the same time, and the cake was crumbling beneath their pulling hands. Then the man lifted a hand to strike, but at that moment all the emotions that were tormenting me came to a head in a red fury. I had never struck a man in anger before, and instinct rather than science went into the blow. I caught him under the chin with all the weight of my body behind my fist. He went down with a grunt, and didn't move. There was an empty flour sack lying in a corner of the shop. I pulled it over his head, stuffed the cake in after him, and, without a word to the girl, who was now quietly crying, hauled him out on to the pavement. I remembered that I had seen Moscrop's hand-cart there. I lifted him on to it, and set off almost at a run for the dark entry that had been the scene of my old humiliation. I pulled him from the truck when I got there, dragged him to the far end of the entry, and then took the sack off him. He was groaning, but was not fully conscious. I could almost feel the rage running up my trembling arms and bubbling in my head. I pulled off his coat and his waistcoat and his trousers and every rag he had on. Then with my feet I rolled his naked body in the mud of the entry and jumped his clothes into the mire. I stood looking down upon him, with my hatred ebbing away. He sat up, and a last paroxysm came upon me. I took the crumbled cake from the sack, forced him flat upon his back again, and stuffed handfuls of the cake into his mouth till he choked and spluttered. Then I picked up the sack, threw it upon the hand-cart, and ran. So I worked out upon another the horror and loathing I felt for myself because my mother was dead, because for the last few hours I had felt her hearse heavy on my heart, and I knew that for eight years I had been a swine.

When I got back to the shop, old Moscrop was sitting in an armchair in the middle of it. The girl was still behind the counter, reading now. I could see at a glance that the book she held was the Bible. Old Moscrop had changed. He had always been a stout man. Now he was immense. He overflowed his chair like a Buddha. His eyes were hooded, and everything of him flowed downward in sagging lines. Under his eyes were blue sagging pouches; his flaccid cheeks sagged like a hound's flews; and his sagging belly rested on his knees. His arms were laid along the arms of the chair, and the hands, projecting beyond the chair's arms, hung downwards like broken fins.

He didn't stir when I came into the shop. Only the lids of his eyes went up, and he said in a voice that seemed to come whistling and wheezing out of a complicated series of tubes: "Well! William! Isn't it? William Essex?"

Even so few words seemed to exhaust him. His great chest heaved and he gasped for breath, the fins flapping helplessly over the arms of the chair. The girl pushed up the hinged part of the counter and came and knelt beside him. I recognised her now. She was Nellie Moscrop, the ugly shy little girl whom I used to see sometimes peeping from the parlour into the shop, always with a finger in her mouth. Or I would come upon her in the bake-house, and then suddenly she wouldn't be there. She disappeared like a rabbit down a hole when a stranger came. Not that anyone minded. She was so negative, insignificant. As she came out now from behind the counter I saw that she really had hardly changed at all, except to become bigger and ungainlier and, if possible, shyer. She had a shambling walk, and her big flat feet made me think of a cow wading through pastures. But she gave me a timid smile, and said "Thank you for helping me just now," and then to her father, she said: "This is the young man I was telling you about." Old Moscrop's eyelids went up again. A glint of thanks came to me out of his eyes, and his fins seemed to waggle appreciation of what I had done.

"You'd better come into the parlour, Father," Nellie said. "I'll light one of your pastilles."

Moscrop managed to raise one arm entirely from the chair and beckoned to me. "Under my arm, William," he wheezed. So I got hold of him under one arm, while Nellie took the other. We gently raised him to his feet, and there he stood for a moment, leaning on the two of us, feeling amorphous, boneless and very heavy. Then we began a slow, shuffling progress, through the raised flap of the counter, where Moscrop had to fend for himself, for he was a tight fit, through the lace-curtained parlour door, and across the parlour carpet to a red-plush armchair by the fire.

I had never before been in the Moscrop parlour. The first thing that caught my eye was an enlarged photograph of pleasant little Mrs. Moscrop. It was in a heavy oak frame over the fireplace, and it was the sort of picture you don't hang while the subject is alive. I knew at once that Nellie Moscrop, like me, was motherless.

We got old Moscrop into his armchair. Nellie put a cushion behind his head, and he remained still and exhausted. From a box on the mantelpiece she took a pastille, placed it on a saucer, and put a light to it. Heavy fumes began to fill the room, and Moscrop's large nostrils flared as he breathed them in.

"I'm afraid this isn't very pleasant for you," Nellie Moscrop said, "and I hate to seem to send you away after the way you helped me. But would you rather go now, and come back to supper? We have it about nine. The shop will be shut then, and I expect father'll be better, too."

I said that I had done little enough, and that I didn't see why I should worry her any further, her hands being full enough, and I should have gone and never returned if old Moscrop had not said, fighting to get the words out, and achieving at the same time a dreadful but gallant smile: "Yes—come back, William. Come an' have your pennorth."

I remembered his old friendly gesture—"There's a pennorth for you"—and gave him back his smile and said I would return.

I was glad I did. I was never sensitive about the feelings of other people, but I was soon struck by the utter loneliness of old Moscrop and Nellie. They were delighted to have a visitor and made much of me. The fumes of the pastille—ah! those fumes I was soon to know so well!—were gone, and Moscrop though wheezy, was articulate. I saw that Nellie had changed her dress, and her hair looked as though it had had some special brushing; but it was nothing much, anyway, poor girl; and her plainness and awful humility were as oppressive as ever.

It was a pleasant room. The fire burned bright and shone on well-polished mahogany surfaces. A gas jet, in a glass globe, was lit on either side of Mrs. Moscrop's photograph. There were lots of books in a solid mahogany book-case. They were all religious: a vast series of Bible commentaries, novels with a religious twist, the *Pilgrim's Progress*, Foxe's *Book of Martyrs*, lives of Christ and of St. Paul. But it was all very cosy. The Moscrops had always had the reputation in the district of being "warm" people, and I saw about me no reason to doubt it. When I got to know the old man better, he was fond of quoting a hymn verse to me:

'Tis religion that can give
Solid comfort while we live.
'Tis religion can supply
Solid comfort when we die.

A little observation convinced me that solid comfort had been the rule of Moscrop's life, and that he would have had very little use for any religion unless it could give him not only comfort but solid comfort when he came to die.

We enjoyed solid comfort that night. Nellie put a beautiful white linen cloth upon the table, with an ornate and complicated silver contraption in the middle. There were little vases sticking out here and there holding paper flowers, and above them towered three mythological creatures whose uplifted wings bore the weight of a tray containing apples and oranges. The china and cutlery were excellent. The silver kettle simmered upon a spirit stove; and the food was as good as the appointments and almost grossly plentiful. Moscrop asked a blessing upon it, and then insisted on hearing over again the story of the one blow which I struck in all my life. "I was terrified—terrified," Nellie kept on saying, "but Mr. Essex didn't seem afraid of him at all." Whether I had wanted to or not, it was clear that I had made an impression on the mind of Nellie Moscrop.

"What did you do with him, William?" the old man asked.

"Oh, I just ran him round a few blocks, and then dumped him out," I said. How could I tell the Moscrops that what I had done had no reference to Nellie at all, that a personal anger had overwhelmed me? And how could I tell the girl, anyway, that I had stripped the man naked and rolled him in the mire? One look at her was enough to convince me that such a story would send her shrieking from the room.

One look at her ... I can give that look now, and see Nellie as she was that night, so proud and so efficient, presiding at the teapot. She was dressed entirely in black satin which rustled in a matronly way when she moved. It swathed her arms to the wrists. It closed upon the base of her firm ungraceful throat, where a heavy cameo brooch pulled it together as though suspiciously guarding a portal. It fell flat in front and flounced out a little behind her when she walked, hiding her heavy feet. A thin gold chain was round her neck and the small watch attached to the end of it was tucked into her belt. Her hair was of a nondescript and unattractive brown, pulled down from a central parting and gathered into a "bun" on her neck. She was short-sighted, but did not then wear glasses, and this caused her, when she spoke, to peer at you anxiously with her kind and rather unintelligent eyes, above which a small frown gathered. The kindness, the gentleness of her face was its attraction; but she was completely lacking in the qualities which make a man look twice at a woman. She was twenty-one then, about a year older than I was.

"He's a bad lot, yon Ackroyd," old Moscrop said. "He's been driving the van for a month, forgetting half the customers, and coming back drunk as often as not. If he hadn't cleared out, I'd have cleared him. And now there's Monday."

He murmured "Christ's sake, Amen," over the table, and then waddled to his armchair. "Now there's Monday," he repeated, looking worried, "and no one to do the round."

Nellie put on a print apron and began to gather the supper things together and take them to the scullery. I offered to help, but she said: "No. Sit down and talk to Father. He doesn't often have anybody."

So we talked, and it was evident that the old fellow was pleased to spread out his little worries. His wife had been dead for two years. His own health was very bad. He could no longer do anything but supervise. He had a man working in the bakehouse. "It all takes a lot of money," he wheezed, "but Nellie's very good in the house. You don't need anyone to help you in the house, do you, Nellie?" he asked, raising his voice.

"No, no; I can manage very well," she called back amid the clatter of cups, and a brightness of relief appeared in his face, as though he had feared she might insist on paid help. I began to see that old Moscrop's "warmness" was something he would be careful to guard, and only the memory of his "pennorths" stilled the thought of miserliness.

"And then there's the man to do the round," he said. "That's more money. And no one to do it, anyway, on Monday. And what about you, William? What have you been doing all these years?"

I told him as much as I wanted him to know. He looked at me shrewdly. "You sound restless. You don't sound settled," he said.

"Well, Mr. Moscrop," I said. "If you mean by settled have I found the job I want to go on doing for the rest of my life, I certainly haven't. So far, I've gone from one silly job to the next and not liked any of them. I shall give up what I'm doing as soon as I find something that suits me better."

"What about doing the round on Monday?" he asked.

The question took me so much by surprise that I broke into a roar of laughter. The idea of driving a baker's van as the next step in the career of a man who intended to be very rich seemed gloriously comic. In the midst of my outburst Nellie came in from the scullery, wiping her hands on a cloth. She looked at me reproachfully. "It was my idea," she said. "I suggested it to Father. You'd live in, of course." Then she fled again, as though she had said something improper.

"Yes, live in," old Moscrop affirmed, his fins flapping on the chair. "We know each other, William. We can trust each other."

And suddenly I perceived that the old man and the girl deeply desired this to happen. They were lonely and helpless. My blow a few hours before had introduced me in the character of a hero. I should certainly come to them as a rather favoured being. Something in the situation suggested to my mind that it had advantages, and instinct urged me to say Yes. So I said: "Forgive my laughter, Mr. Moscrop. It was just the idea of laying a man out and then stealing his job. I'd like to come to you. I don't know anything about the work. But I'd like to come."

## 5

Thus it was that I became deeply acquainted with the solid comfort of the Moscrop household. It is all so long ago that I cannot remember which of the many foolish jobs I had been doing I gave up in order to work for the baker. Whichever it was, I did not bother about formality. I simply did not turn up on the Monday and that was that. I was sorry to leave the O'Riordens, but there was nothing to be done about that, either. I hired a four-wheeler cab, put into it the clothes and books that were my only property, except fifty pounds which I had in the bank, and rattled and jolted through the grim Sunday streets of Manchester. All the way from Ancoats to Hulme there was not a tree, not a shrub, not a twig to be seen. Soot-caked buildings, shut shops, the occasional cracked melancholy of a church bell, an air soaked with moisture, though it was not at the moment raining. I sat back in the musty damp of the cab, wearing my best clothes, which were thick honest ugly things, the waistcoat adorned with a gold "albert" from which a meaningless medal depended, my neck enclosed in a collar that stood straight up like a low white wall, a bowler hat upon my head. I listened to the clop-clop of the dispirited horse, and tried to persuade myself that this was the prelude to adventure.

Just as Moscrop's front window had seemed an oasis to me when I was younger, so Moscrop's house seemed that day. Goodness knows, there was nothing attractive about the outside of it. It stood on a corner. Some of its windows were in one mean street and some in another. It was bigger than other houses thereabouts, and that was all. But when I had paid the cabby and watched the decrepit growler fade away into the sadness of the dying afternoon I was able to forget all that was outside the walls of Moscrop's house.

Tea was ready, and Nellie made me leave my things in the passage and come straight in to eat. When she had carried the crockery to the scullery, she said she would show me my room. "You notice, William," said Moscrop, one lid lifting from the hooded eyes, "she says your room, not your bedroom. She's been having a high old time up there, shifting furniture and I don't know what all."

Nellie flushed and led the way upstairs. I followed with a suitcase in one hand and a bag of books in the other. My room was at the end of a short, oil-clothed passage. Now bedrooms had always till then been associated in my mind with a cold discomfort which you overcame by leaping into bed as soon as possible. Or, if you sat up, as I had done night after night in Gibraltar Street, you kept on your overcoat and pulled a quilt round your knees. I expected the same chill austerity to confront me when Nellie Moscrop opened the door at the end of the passage, but, to my surprise and delight, firelight dancing on drawn curtains was the first thing I saw.

"Why—!" I began, but Nellie hustled me into the room and closed the door. "Father doesn't know!" she said in an excited whisper. She stood there with the fireshine on her pale face, looking triumphant and a little disturbed, as though she had achieved something of an unparalleled daring. "D'you think it was wrong of me?" she asked. She stood before a chest-of-drawers, leaning back with her hands on the knobs, breathing quickly.

"Wrong!" I said. "Why, I think it's the most delightful idea. I've never had a fire in my bedroom in all my life."

"Neither have I," she said. "I mean, d'you think it was wrong not to let Father know?" She stumbled over her next words. "I wanted it to seem very welcoming. You deserve it."

And now I knew that blushes as well as flames were colouring her cheeks. "Thank you very much," I said. "It was a lovely idea—Nellie."

She said, "Oh!" and then "I must go," and went out very quickly. It was a fairly large square room. It was the best room I had ever had. The window, with its curtains hung on heavy wooden rings, faced the door, with the bed between. The fireplace was at the foot of the bed, with a good yard of passage-way dividing them. There was a little recess on each side of the fireplace. The chest-of-drawers was in one, and in the other was a table. This was fixed so that you did not face the wall as you sat at the table. The wall was on your left; you looked across the table towards the fireplace, and the gas jet was in the wall just over the table. Evidently the arrangement was not haphazard: it had been thought out. The only other furniture was a wicker chair with plenty of cushions on it.

I lit the gas and looked about me and congratulated myself on having obeyed my instinct of the night before. These were the cosiest private quarters I had ever struck. It remained to be seen whether I should have much time to spend in them. My hopes of writing soared. Doubtless, in the summer this window looked on a scene depressing enough, but now, with Hulme shut out, with my own walls about me, how I could get on with it! I began at once to make resolutions. I would buy my own coal and have a fire every night. A shilling a hundredweight, and a hundredweight ought to last for a long time if used only in the evenings. I would make my own fires and clear up my own grate. I wouldn't presume on Nellie's good nature.

In this happy, and hopeful mood, I put my few clothes away, arranged my books on the top of the chest-of-drawers, and sat down for a moment in the wicker chair to give myself a sense of proprietorship. Then I put a writing-pad and a pen on the table. Yes; it looked very workmanlike. I put out the gas and before leaving the room went to the window and raised the curtain. Grim and desolate, the Hulme street stretched before me, its few lamps blear in the winter night. Assuredly, here, if anywhere, a man who wanted a world must make one for himself. This one room, I decided, would do very well to be going on with.

When I got downstairs, I found that Nellie had finished the washing-up, had mended the fire, and placed old Moscrop comfortably in his chair beside it. A small table was against the chair, and on the table was Farrar's *Life of Christ*, with a pair of spectacles folded on top of it. Evidently Moscrop was settling down for the evening. His lids went up for a moment as I entered the room. "Well?" he asked.

"You're being too kind to me, Mr. Moscrop," I said. "It's a lovely room, and I'm going to be very comfortable in it."

"I'm glad," he said. "You see, William, I want someone we can trust. Since I haven't been able to get about very well, it's been one makeshift after another. We can't go on like that. Nellie and I have often talked it over and wished we could have someone to come in and live with us and look after things. But who was there? And then you came along. I think we'll get on all right."

"I'm sure we shall," I said. "You've put enough comfort in that room to chain me down for a long time."

"That's all Nellie's doing. And now I want you to do something for her. Just go along to chapel with her this evening. You're not doing anything?"

Nellie came into the room at that moment, dressed for going out, with a Bible and hymn-book under her arm. "It's a great loss to me," said old Moscrop, "but I can't attend the House of God as I used to. Sometimes in the summer. But these winter nights—no." He tapped his wheezing chest. "And after all," he said, "this is Hulme. I don't like Nellie coming home from the evening service alone."

The proposal took me aback. I had never attended a chapel in my life. Always, while I lived at Mr. Oliver's, I had attended service in church twice on a Sunday. Since leaving him I had gone nowhere. I was impelled to blurt out some excuse; but Nellie, standing there as though in no possible doubt of my compliance, weakened me. "Right," I said, "I'll go up and get my overcoat."

When I came down, the old man had put on his spectacles and opened his book. Nellie placed a box of matches and one of his pastilles in a saucer on the table. "Mind now," she said, "it's only in case. You're not to *imagine* you want it."

Then Nellie and I set out for the Wesleyan chapel. It was not a long walk, but it was a miserable one. The night was raw, oozing a cold dampness that seemed to search out our bones. Neither of us spoke. I slouched along with my hands in my overcoat pockets, and Nellie paddled in her ungainly fashion at my side with hers stuffed into an astrakhan muff.

The Oddy Road chapel was a large, soot-furred building that had the advantage of being the only place in sight that looked comfortably lit. And it *was* comfortable. It was almost reeking in comfort. A man with a professional smile was in the vestibule. He shook Nellie's hand and inquired about her father. He shook my hand and dazzled me with his smile. Then he opened a door covered with red baize figured all over with round-headed brass nails, and we went into the chapel. The building was cruciform. Two long aisles led down to the transepts that were on either side of the tall white stone pulpit. Behind the pulpit were the choir seats, rising in three rows, and above them was the organ. In front of the pulpit was a semi-circular carpeted space containing a communion table. Rails shut it in, and outside the rails was a step covered with thick red cushions.

I was horribly conscious of the squeaking of my boots as I followed Nellie up the aisle, which was carpeted with cocoanut matting. Along each wall of the chapel gas jets were burning in white globes and from the high ceiling depended two great rings of jets. I could hear the gentle singing of all that gas till suddenly it was extinguished by a low moan from the organ that shuddered through the building.

The Moscrop pew was the front one in the transept to the right of the pulpit. It was carpeted in red and had red hassocks and a strip of red carpet on the seat. Nellie knelt upon one of the hassocks and sank her head upon her hands. I did so, too; though I had nothing to pray about. I waited till Nellie sat up, then I sat up. She opened a little cupboard in the front of the pew and gave me a hymn-book and a Bible. I placed them on the ledge in front of me, and looked fairly about me for the first time.

The Moscrop pew seemed to me a dreadfully public place, poked out there under the nose of the parson, under the gaze of the choir, of the opposite gallery and of all the front seats of the chapel. The place was filling up. Noisy children abounded in the gallery. Down below family parties came by the dozen, nearly all the men holding silk hats in kid-gloved hands, all the women pictures of urban elegance in their furs and feathers. There was much kneeling and gentle rustling of hymn-book leaves, and over it all the organ maintained a sort of sonorous purring that was soothing and satisfying.

Just to the right of where I was sitting a door led into a vestry. A bald-headed steward in a frock-coat came through this, mounted the pulpit steps and placed some notices on the Bible, and at the same time the choir of men and women, old and young, came in up above. When they were seated, the organ fell to silence, and the silence spread through the building. You could once more hear the gas singing its gnat-like song, and you could sense an expectation that thereafter I was often to know. It was the expectation that always fell upon the congregation at Oddy Road when the Rev. Samuel Pascoe was to preach.

He came in through the vestry door which a steward held open, and mounted the pulpit steps: a man in his early thirties, dressed in formal parson's black, lithe as a greyhound, thin of face, but, as one could see at the first glance, vibrating with an athlete's fitness. His light brown hair was cropped close, and after standing for a few moments in prayer he swept round the congregation, which now filled every part of the building, a slow glance from dark piercing eyes. Then he gave out his hymn and read the first verse, and I liked the way he read it, with a full voice that made the poetry in it sing:

*Lord of all being, throned afar,*
*Thy glory flames from sun and star;*
*Centre and soul of every sphere,*
*Yet to each loving heart now near!*

There's a good tune to that hymn, too, and those people liked singing. The organist knew his job, and so did the choir, and so did the congregation. I'm no singer myself, but put me with a singing crowd and I'll let it go with the rest. And so I did that night, and so did Nellie at my side. Her voice was good, a clear soprano of no great power but extraordinarily true.

Then the parson prayed, and after that we sang

*O for a thousand tongues to sing*
*My great Redeemer's praise.*

That one has an even better congregational tune than the other, and it seemed as though the building would not contain the great volume of song that lifted to the roof.

But I don't want to recall every detail of that service. I'll go straight on to the slight shock I got when Mr. Pascoe announced his text. I know nothing about it now, for many a year has passed since I set foot in church or chapel; but it was a great moment then: the moment when the *pièce de résistance* of the service was about to be dished up. I can still see that evening's scene: everybody settled comfortably back in the pews, Bibles in hands, ready to turn up the passage when it was announced so as to confirm that there indeed, at the place named, were the words which the preacher proposed to expound. Nellie, like the rest, had the book in her kid-gloved hands, when there fell into the silence Mr. Pascoe's three words: "He made summer."

He dropped them out like three pebbles into water, each clear and articulate. He made summer! All about us were the stony wastes of Hulme, desolate as the stricken cities of the plain, and over Hulme lay the winter's sooty weeping, and the text was: "He made summer!"

It was a simple sermon on the theme of compensation. Here was Hulme. Here was winter. Yet—He made summer. Day follows night. Summer follows winter. And heaven follows Hulme. I remember he quoted Spenser:

> *Is not short payne well borne that brings long ease*
> *And layes the soule to sleep in quiet grave?*
> *Sleep after toyle, port after stormie seas,*
> *Ease after warre, death after life, does greatly please.*

And he quoted the text: "Now in the place where He was crucified there was a garden," pointing out that only John, the beloved disciple, had recorded that, because perhaps only John would know that a garden might help to assuage an agony. It seemed to me, then, and still seems, a beautiful thought.

I don't know how that sermon would affect me now; and, in any case, I shall not be such a fool as to try to dissociate the words from the man who said them, and the way he said them, and the moment at which he said them. I only know that at that time they affected me profoundly. The Rev. Samuel Pascoe could make you see things, and through the stifling heat that now was in the chapel my mind went out to the green fields of Cheshire and the wide strong reaches of Derbyshire, with the summer sun pouring down on lush grass or glancing among the sallies of the little moorland waterways. The preacher himself made summer in my heart that night, and when we sang the last hymn:

*For the joy of ear and eye,*
  *For the heart and mind's delight,*
*For the mystic harmony*
  *Linking sense to sound and sight*

I felt strong and uplifted and passed out unseeingly through the bobbing bonnets and silk hats in the vestibule.

## 6

I am not going on from this to tell you that a change came over my spiritual life from that night. Nothing of the sort. The significance of that night was that it was the first step towards my marriage with Nellie Moscrop. There was a warmth, a friendliness, about chapel-going in those days that appealed to me. Accompanying Nellie became a habit, and the habit landed me into marriage; but a good deal wars to happen before that.

To begin with, the morning after that Sunday service, there was the business of learning the bread round. There was room for two on the seat in front of the van. Wearing a vast overcoat and an almost square felt hat, and with a woollen muffler wound many times round his neck and a pair of woollen gloves on his hands, old Moscrop was heaved up alongside me and we started off. He was to accompany me till I got the round by heart, and as his immense body sagged across three-quarters of the seat, edging me to a precarious perch almost over a wheel, I prayed that that would not be long.

It wasn't. A few days told me all I wanted to know about that mechanical business. On the Thursday I did the work alone. The van was at the bakehouse door. The old man who did the night baking had helped me to load it. It was a bitter day. The damp and mists were gone and suddenly overnight a frost keener than I had known for years had fastened its jaws upon the city. The old horse, with his head down, was blowing little clouds from his nostrils on to the stiff ground, and when I had banged-to the double doors behind the van I did not look forward to the day's work with any pleasure.

Sitting up aloft there, I should be clemmed: no two ways about it. I stood beating my arms across my chest when Nellie came round the corner from the shop. Her arms were piled with clothing. She looked at me with that short-sighted puzzled frown that brought the creases to her brow, and said: "You're cold already. Put this on. It's years since we've had such a day."

She held up her father's overcoat, which certainly was big enough to go on over my own. But I didn't fancy wearing it, all the same. "What'll Mr. Moscrop do?" I said.

"Don't worry about that," Nellie answered. "He won't stir out on a day like this. Come along now."

She shook her head at me with a little reproving smile, and ungraciously enough I put my arms into the coat she held. Then she stood on tiptoe, for she was a short woman, and twisted round and round my neck a muffler as long as old Moscrop's; and then she handed me a pair of thick woollen gloves. My own were absurd kid-leather things, such as clerks liked to wear on Sundays. When I had staggered to the seat, I felt very much like one of the bundles of washing I used to haul through these streets. I said so to Nellie; and, trifling enough as the remark was, I realise, looking back on it now, that it was one of the few words I had ever spoken to her that were not mere formality. The little frown rubbed itself out from between her eyebrows, and her smile came strong and clear, puzzling me that so trite a comment should cause a face to light so gaily. Then I laid the whip gently along the old horse's flank, and off we rumbled on iron tyres that stirred up the barren bitter dust of the road.

Soon my breath was congealing on the woolly hairs of the muffler under my mouth, but my hands and body remained warm, though my feet felt as if they were clamped in icy fetters. I pondered on things in general as we pottered through the streets, pulling up at houses where women came to the doors with shawls about their heads and their teeth chattering, and at others where the open door at the end of the passage showed a kitchen shining with the brilliance of Lancashire housewifery and seasonably glowing against that disastrous cold. I began to think in a mixed, unsorted fashion of all the various lives I touched so lightly each day: the girl in the dressing-gown, who obviously had got straight out of bed to come to the door and whose brazen smile was at once inviting and repellent; the old woman, dirty-looking and grey-haired whom I had once glimpsed scuttling furtively about the back parts of this girl's house like one of the cockroaches that ran across the bakehouse floor when the gas was suddenly lit; the man with the grey, drawn face and the black-and-red check muffler, so cleanly-shaven, so horribly respectable and starved-looking, with his smile that was so polite and yet so frightened-looking. I knew already that he owed old Moscrop fifteen shillings. And there was the tiny woman, dressed always in white from top to toe, white ribbons in her hair, white satin shoes on her feet, who tore a piece from the loaf each day as soon as it was handed to her, put it into her mouth, and said: "Do this in remembrance of Me. I am the bride of Christ." And there were innumerable drab, featureless people, living on the verge of hunger, and innumerable cheerful, happy, commonplace people, dauntless in the stone wilderness of Hulme.

Driving up and down the little streets, watching the grey plumes of smoke rise so numberlessly over the houses into the clear cold blue of that winter day, I began to feel the fascination of all these lives, to realise that here under my hand and eye were tales without end, the very stuff of all those books that for so long I had wanted to write and had tried to write. I thought with amusement and contempt of the high-flown, fly-blown romances over which I had toiled in the O'Riorden bedroom, the far flights of fancy among classes and conditions of which I knew nothing at all. Here, in these little houses, were my subjects. These were my own people, the blood and marrow of my own upbringing, and an impatience stirred in me to be back at Moscrop's, to get to my room, and to begin some work that would matter.

I had not yet spent an evening in my room. Four nights I had passed with the Moscrops, one with Nellie at chapel, and three in polite but difficult conversation with the old man, whose asthma on one of those evenings had again struck him down into a sorry mass of flesh quivering and gasping over a burning pastille. I had asked Nellie to order a hundredweight of coal for me. She had done so, and the fire, I knew, was laid in my room, and the scuttle filled.

There were two bread rounds, morning and afternoon, and it was with great satisfaction that I put away the van and led the horse to his stable at the end of the second round. The cold had become more intense. The round coppery globe of the sun had plunged down in a violet haze at four o'clock, and now the sky was pricked with sparkling stars and a silent deathly cold was over the houses.

I went straight to my room and put a match to my fire; then I went to the scullery and washed myself; and then went in to supper. It was a meal that Moscrop enjoyed enormously. He loved to gossip, and any small details I could give him about the course of the day's work delighted him. He assured me again and again how pleased he was with the idea of having his right-hand man "living in," and for my part I pushed my questions as delicately as I could into the details of his business, on the score that there were all sorts of ways in which I could help him, apart from doing the round. I did not intend to content myself with being Moscrop's van-driver.

When supper was cleared away, Nellie put the small table, with the book and spectacles on it, alongside the big armchair: a sure sign that she was going out.

"Would you like to go with Nellie tonight?" Moscrop asked.

I looked at her questioningly; and she explained: "I'm going to class meeting."

"Class meeting? What class?"

"First class, my boy—the class of the Lord's redeemed," the old man said piously; and Nellie elucidated this more prosaically. "You see, every full member of the Wesleyan Church is what we call a class member. Every chapel has a number of classes, each with its own leader. We meet once a week, say prayers, sing a few hymns, and give our testimony."

"Oh, I see. But I'm not a member of the Wesleyan Church."

"But if you join a class you become one."

"I'd rather not—not now."

She looked crestfallen; and I thought I had better explain my refusal. "You see, I rather wanted to work tonight. I've lit my fire already."

"Fire?" old Moscrop looked up sharply, and I resolved to get this over once for all. "Yes," I said. "I hope you won't mind, Mr. Moscrop. I'm paying for my own coal. I like to work in the evenings."

"Work! Of course you can work," he grumbled. "Who's stopping you from working? But can't you work here? Isn't this comfortable enough?"

"It is, indeed," I said. "But it's rather private work, and I like to be alone when I do it."

"Private, eh? Not just studying. I'm all for a young man studying. I studied myself when I was young, and I'd like to know where I'd be now if I hadn't." His fingers waggled on the chair arms. Then he put his spectacles on his nose, and took up his book. "Well, run along," he said gruffly. "But it's very mysterious."

I thought I'd better out with it. "It's some writing," I blurted. "You see, I'm trying to write a book."

Dean Farrar fell plop on the old man's knees. One of his eyelids shot up. "A book?" he cried. "What sort of book?"

Now I was in a sweat of embarrassment. "Oh, I don't know," I said. "A sort of a novel, I suppose."

Then I noticed Nellie's face. It was lit up with excitement. She was gazing at me as though I had just been made poet laureate. "How marvellous!" she said. "A book!" She dashed to the book-case, pulled out a volume, and handed it to me. It was *Jane Eyre*. "*That* began to get written not ten minutes' walk from here," she cried excitedly. "Did you know that?"

"No, I didn't."

"Well, it's true. Charlotte Brontë had brought her father to Manchester to see an eye specialist, and they lodged in a street off Oxford Street. And while they were there she began to write *Jane Eyre*. Wouldn't it be wonderful if your book were as good as that!"

"It would."

"And there was Mrs. Gaskell."

"Yes."

"And the woman who wrote *The Manchester Man*. I always forget her name."

"Mrs. Banks."

"Yes. Mrs. Linnæus Banks. It seems to be all women who write novels in Manchester."

"Yes. It's time we had a man."

"Perhaps it will be you!"

"It will be."

I had never seen her so animated, but her excitement drooped a little at that presumptuous remark. She took up her muff. "I shall pray that it may be," she said. And she meant that very sincerely.

Old Moscrop said: "But what about the bakery when I'm gone?" And there it was, the cat out of the bag, all that he had been turning over in his heavy mind during the last few days suddenly revealed. Nellie flushed and went quickly away.

The fire in my room had sunk to a warm glow. I did not for a moment light the gas, but, pulling back the curtains, looked down the street. The lamps were no longer blear. They burned steady and unwinking in the iron cold, and above the rooftops the stars blazed.

There was the street, dingy and unimportant like a million streets in Birmingham and Newcastle, Liverpool, Leeds and London, a small frozen furrow in the waste of the city. Not a soul was visible. Not a footstep stirred. Everyone was gone to earth in the bitter cold like the beasts in a wood when the world is under snow.

I lit the gas and sat down before my paper, trying to bring them out from their little houses, to set them moving in some fashion of significance and beauty.

I heard Nellie come in; I heard her and her father go to bed; and still the scrawled and meagre words seemed dead on the paper. I sat back gloomily and saw a spider—the tiny sort of thing we call a money spider—appear suddenly upon the page and run quickly to the top edge of the writing-pad. He paused for a moment, peering over the precipice. I watched him breathlessly, saying to myself: "If he turns and runs back down the page, this book will be a success." He made up his mind, plunged over the precipice and ran along the table. "Damn you!" I cried to myself. "Damn you! It *shall* be a success whatever you do." Then I tore up all I had written, threw it into the fire and went to bed.

7

The farthest point of the bread round touched the comfortable suburb of Withington, and on a day in the following October as I was driving down a Withington street I was hailed by name. "Hi, Bill!" Dermot O'Riorden was leaning from a bedroom window. I pulled up, and soon Dermot came running down the short garden path. He looked younger and happier, and he looked prosperous. "Let me congratulate you," he said, "on giving up the odious job of pen-pushing. A baker is a craftsman."

"I'm not a baker," I said. "I'm a van-boy."

"Never mind. A baker's van-boy is worth a platoon of stock-brokers in any decent community. Can you spare a minute? Drive the bloodstock in here."

The house was square and solid, with a good front door, a bow-window on either side of it, and three flat windows on the first floor. There was a gate leading to a small coach-house at the side. I drove the van through, fastened the reins to a ring in the wall, and walked with Dermot to the front door.

"You're looking prosperous," I said. "This your house?"

His startled eyebrows took flight and his pale eyes laughed. "Prosperous, enough," he said, "but not so prosperous as all that, as you'd know if you took the trouble to look us up now and then."

It was a merited reproof. I had passed a sluggish winter and a lazy summer: chapel on Sunday nights, class meetings on Thursdays, too few evenings in my own room, and many, many evenings playing draughts and ludo with old Moscrop. Ludo was his favourite game. It was the most unprofitable stretch of time I had spent since that far-off day when I met Eustace Oliver. I had not even visited the only friends I had: Dermot and his wife and his parents.

"No," said Dermot, "this is not my house. This is a job I've been doing—the biggest job I've had yet."

I glanced about me. "It looks nice."

"Nice! Is that all you've got to say about the work of the finest furniture designer in Manchester? Nice! It's marvellous."

He ran his hand with a characteristic caress over the panelling of the small square hall. "Right," I agreed. "It's marvellous."

"And it all came out of having that little shop window in Deansgate. The chap who's just bought this house was passing by, saw the furniture, and stepped right into the spider's parlour. He's given me a free hand to do what I like here within the £500 limit. That gives me a bit of profit."

Dermot took me proudly round the house, and pointed out that he was doing decoration as well as furnishing. "Does anything strike you about it all?" he asked when we had walked through all the rooms.

"Clean, bright, airy…"

"Simplification. I'm cutting off the curls and getting down to the skull. I'm keeping my work as solid as anything Morris ever did, but I'm taking out a lot of the fancy work. Look at this table."

We were in the dining-room, and the table was certainly a lovely one. "D'you remember the one I made for my mother?" Dermot asked. "Those great bulging legs? I shudder now when I look at them. See the difference? This is just a table: solid, straightforward. Everything there is to it is due to sheer proportion. And believe me, that's perfect."

It was, so far as I could see. "I've taken out of there the foulest fireplace you ever saw," said Dermot, "and put in that simple surround of Dutch tiles. The walls will be white. I wish we could have some cleaner light than gas. We all shall, of course, soon. But I'm just a bit too soon for that. And I want to find a new name for myself. I'm not just a cabinetmaker any more. I want something to give the idea that I take over the whole show and make it beautiful. You see, I'm thinking of my new shop. I want a bigger place all to myself. How's this: Maker of beautiful furniture and decorator of interiors?"

Common enough now. Everyone is an interior decorator today. But Dermot O'Riorden was the first man I heard use the words and the first man I saw employing simplification, pure proportion, in place of a gaudy opulence.

"Hallo there! Anyone in?" a voice shouted from the hall, and Sheila walked into the room, carrying a basket. "The boss's lunch," she said. The boss bounded across the room and threw his arms about her. She was looking very happy and well, the black eyes dancing in her small dark face.

She shook hands and invited me to share the lunch. "There's enough for three," she said. "I'm trying to get some fat on this old skinnimalink."

But it was already more than time that I was off. I stayed long enough to express surprise that she was able to leave the shop. "You don't know the half our news yet," said Dermot. "You ought to keep in touch with your friends. I've got an assistant in the shop now that I'm out on jobs like this. Because, you see, this is only the first. And Sheila's got a house all of her own—haven't you—eh?" And he gave her a loving hug.

"You must come and see us, Bill," Sheila said. "Tomorrow night?"

Dermot gave me the address, and I said I'd be there. Then I went, leaving Sheila unpacking the lunch basket on the lovely table. I shouted back through the open window, as I turned the horse into the road: "I may bring a friend."

Now why had I said that? I turned to the right into Wilmslow Road, driving back towards Hulme, and I kept on asking myself: Why did the idea come to me to take Nellie Moscrop to see Dermot and

Sheila? And I had to say that it was simply because she had become so accustomed, so familiar. For the greater part of a year now she had grown on me like a habit. The chapel and the class meeting, one or two week-night lectures at Oddy Road, a chapel society or two. At one of them I had been induced to read a paper on the novels of Charles Dickens. It was a good paper. I still have it. I have read it recently and was not ashamed of it. I kept it because it was the first piece of writing I managed to finish. Nothing else had been finished. Both Nellie—very timorously—and old Moscrop in a brutal matter-of-fact fashion over the ludo board—inquired from time to time about the novel. It made the blood rush to my head. I hated to be asked about anything I was writing, particularly when it was going dreadfully; but I managed polite answers.

"Polite answers" about summed up my relationship with Nellie. I couldn't but be aware of her hovering and enveloping presence, particularly as her father again and again emphasised it.

"Cooking's not what it used to be, Nellie," he said one night as we all sat at supper.

The poor girl's agitation was at once extreme. She was a born housewife, and was touched to the quick. The frown deepened between her eyebrows, and without speaking she gave puzzled looks first at him, then at the excellent food on the table. Old Moscrop, who sat opposite me, allowed one eyelid to rise, then fall in a slow-motion wink. "I mean," he explained, "it's *better* than it used to be when you had only your poor old father to consider. Feed the brute—eh?—if I may coin a phrase—feed the brute."

At that, Nellie's confusion became greater than ever. She had nothing to say. There *was* nothing to say. I had myself noticed the gradually intensified attention she had given to the table.

It was not only that. She kept my room spotless. My metal pen-tray and inkwell were always being polished, and, though I had protested that it was not her job, she cleaned out my fireplace and relaid the fire every time I lit it. She insisted on my wearing extra clothing when the weather was very cold, and once, when I looked for my spare shoes, I found that she had sent them to the cobbler because one had a small leak.

When we went out together she spoke but little, yet I could feel the happiness in her heart. If by accident I touched her I was aware of the shock that went through her to the marrow. That night when I read the paper on Dickens she sat listening to me with glistening eyes as though I were a prime minister proposing some copper-bottomed scheme to secure the well-being of the nation; and when some misguided fool suggested that perhaps Miss Moscrop would propose the vote of thanks, she got on to her legs, trembled, and sat down, shaking her head.

Altogether, there was no doubt that Nellie was in love with me. I didn't feel even an egotistical pride that, without effort, I had achieved this miracle. It was hardly possible to conceive one human being less enthusiastic about another than I was about Nellie. And yet those words I had shouted to Dermot put the whole situation on a different footing. Hitherto, we had gone nowhere together save at her invitation. Now, for the first time, I was proposing to invite her. The words had come almost unconsciously to my lips. I remembered old Moscrop's question: "What about the bakery when I'm gone?" Was that it? The bakery was not grandeur, but it was a sort of security. It was a place where a man could be his own boss, and get down in comfort to other things which he might wish to do. I was not aghast at this sudden beam of insight into my own mind. I just shut off the beam quickly and drove home.

There was a snap of autumn in the air the next morning. When I had got the bread van loaded, I slipped into the living-room, to drink a final cup of tea before setting out on the round. It was another of the small domestic habits I had got into, and in which Nellie pampered me. Moscrop was pampered too. Everything was done for him in those days. I had been nearly a year under his roof, and bit by bit I had learned most of what was to be known about his business and had taken off his hands one responsibility after another. First under his direction, and now using my own intelligence, I was doing all the buying for the business, and deciding such matters as when a defaulting customer should be struck off the supply. Moscrop's asthma was going from bad to worse, and now the paroxysms seized him almost daily. It was small wonder that he got up later and later, and on that morning in October, 1891, when I returned back for my cup of tea, he was just sitting down to his breakfast. The *Manchester Guardian* was open on the table before him.

He looked up when I entered the room. "Parnell's dead," he announced.

"Oh," I said, for Parnell dead or alive meant nothing to me.

Nellie came in from the kitchen, carrying a teapot. "Wasn't he a bad man?" she asked.

"He was an adulterer," Moscrop exclaimed, his face going turgid with passion, "an adulterer, and a traitor, too."

One did not lightly use the word adulterer in those days in the presence of a girl like Nellie Moscrop. She placed the teapot hastily upon the table and retreated to the kitchen. When she returned with her father's eggs and bacon, I saw that her face was burning, and, as Moscrop was still glowering at the paper and looking as though he might burst out again at any moment, I said, to ease the tension: "Nellie, a friend of mine has asked me to have supper tonight with him and his wife. Would you like to come with me? He'd be glad to meet you. And his wife's a very nice girl. They're just about our age."

The crimson in Nellie's cheeks did not diminish, but now I knew it was not for the adultery of Mr. Charles Stewart Parnell. "I'd love to," she said. "May I, Father?"

Moscrop, too, forgot his rage. "May I, may I," he mimicked wheezily. "We've got a dutiful daughter, haven't we? Always wondering whether what she does pleases us, eh? Well, well, well. Do something to please yourself for once, my girl. And *this* pleases you, eh? I can see it does. Yes, I can see it does."

He wandered on heavily, driving her from the room again, and when we were alone he gave me one of his stupendous winks. "Bill," he said, "none but the brave deserves the fair, if I may coin a phrase"; and that drove me out, too. I wanted to offer him no chance to wish me luck, which he was clearly on the point of doing.

We walked all the way to Dermot's house that night. It is a good step from Hulme to Ancoats, where he was still living, hut interesting enough. Near as Hulme is to the heart of Manchester, Nellie's time was so closely divided between home and chapel that she rarely visited the great shopping streets. So we wandered through Oxford Street, and across the big open space of Albert Square to Cross Street, and went slowly up Market Street. Then we turned off to the left through the mean streets that led to Ancoats. It was all a grand adventure to Nellie. The mere thought of going to a meal with strangers was to her exciting and a little disturbing.

"D'you think they'll like me?" she asked nervously, as we turned into Dermot's dingy street.

"Good gracious," I said rather crossly, "why should they *not* like you? Always try to look at it like that. Don't get into the habit of looking down on yourself. Dermot and Sheila are intelligent, courteous people."

"Are they Catholics?" she asked, and the fear of the Scarlet Woman was in her voice.

"I don't know what they are. They've never mentioned religion to me, and if I were you, I wouldn't mention it to them. Anyway, here's their front door. Don't you think it looks a treat?"

Evidently Dermot was not going to hide under a bushel his light as a decorator. It was by now dark, but the light of a street lamp fell upon the door, painted an olive green that shone like silk, and decorated with a lovely brass knocker wrought in the conventional but always to me pleasing shape of a lion's head with a ring passing through the mouth. It was an agreeable door to find in that miserable little street.

Dermot and Sheila both came to the door full of welcome, and when they had drawn us into their sitting-room, even Nellie's reticence dropped enough to permit the exclamation to be drawn from her: "How beautiful!"

"D'you know, Miss Moscrop," Dermot laughed, "I believe it is! You see what Bill misses by giving the cold shoulder to his friends."

"And what we miss, too," said Sheila, "when he doesn't allow us to meet his other friends."

"You're full of blarney, the pair of you," I protested, "but this *is* a lovely room."

"Just advertisement," said Dermot. "I've got to stun my clients. Coming in and out of that bloody street, they get the full sense of contrast."

Nellie stared hard on hearing a forbidden word so gaily spoken, and Sheila said: "Dermot, try to be bloodless this evening, will you?"

Dermot gave a loud self-accusing laugh, crossed over to Nellie, and knelt before her with his head bowed. "Strike me, Miss Moscrop," he said. "Smite the devil out of me, if you think such words devilish. Anyway," he added gravely, "I'll say it no more. 'Twas not courteous."

The room we were sitting in had been stripped down to the plaster and painted white. "You'll forgive the fireplace," said Dermot. "That's the landlord's, and I can't touch it." The floorboards were stained and polished, and in front of the fireplace was the first white rug I ever saw in my life. The curtains, too, were a new idea to me.

They were of a rich material, deeply red, and what was strange about them in a cottage home was that they did not merely cover the window. They were hangings, not curtains. They hung in graceful drapery over the whole wall. One small low table stood in front of them, and on it was an earthenware pitcher containing white chrysanthemums. There were a few beautifully-made book-cases stocked with volumes whose bindings were all of vivid colours. The only other furniture in the room was a big billowy divan and two easy chairs; and the light was from a lamp, shaded with parchment-coloured silk, on a stand of finely wrought iron. Sheila went well with that room. She wore a long Pre-Raphaelite-looking dress of dusky red that suited the dark vivacious beauty of her face.

"The worst of these two-up-and-two-downs," said Dermot, "is that we can't have a dining-room. This is very nice to sit in, but we shall have to feed in the kitchen. I haven't tried to make that a work of art, because I shall be out of this as soon as I can. So come on now, and enjoy the beauty of contrast."

The contrast was striking enough, though Sheila's kitchen was spotless. The chairs and the table, which was covered by a red-and-white check cloth, were of Dermot's new simple workmanship, and everything superfluous had been swept out of the room. Sheila brought a steak-and-kidney pie straight from the oven to the table, and Dermot produced a bottle of wine from the dresser.

"This to grace a rare occasion," he announced, "indeed, two rare occasions. One, the return of William Essex to the friends of his youth; and, two, the receipt of Dermot O'Riorden of his first cheque. My client has paid up today, with a handsome testimonial thrown in." He held the bottle of Burgundy towards Nellie's glass. "Miss Moscrop, permit me."

Nellie, with a little panic-stricken gesture, placed her hand over the glass. "I'm a teetotaller," she said, in a small frightened voice. Sheila at once filled her glass from the water-jug.

"You, Bill?" Dermot asked.

"Yes. We must drink to the cheque."

"Now safely in the bank. It came by this morning's post, and before the morning was out I'd opened an account."

"And drawn ten pounds out of it," said Sheila.

"And drawn ten pounds out of it. But that doesn't alter the fact that the account's open. It's a grand moment, Bill, when you open an account. You must try it some day."

"I shall."

"D'you make anything out of your writing yet?"

"Nothing," I said ruefully.

"He doesn't stick at it, Mr. O'Riorden," Nellie exclaimed suddenly. "I do all I can to make him. I do *wish* he'd go on with it. He *could* do it. I know he could. You should have heard his paper on Charles Dickens." Then she shut up with swift embarrassment; and Sheila said kindly: "He will, Nellie. May I call you that? Don't try to rush him. Just leave him alone. Leave him alone when he doesn't want to write, and particularly leave him alone when he does. There; I sound quite motherly. Dermot, the cheese and biscuits are behind you on the dresser."

We drank to the cheque, and Dermot and Sheila drank to me and Nellie, and we then drank to them. It was all rather silly and childish, but happy and friendly, and when the two girls had put on aprons and carried the things to the scullery, Dermot and I went back to the sitting-room. He took out a tobacco-pouch and began to fill a pipe. "My latest vice," he said. "Haven't you taken to it?"

"No."

"Oh, you must," he said. "That's what's wrong with your writing. Come on; come and buy a pipe at once."

"No, no. Don't be daft."

"Daft! You'll thank me to your dying day. Come on, now. I insist on buying you a pipe out of my first cheque. You buy me something when you get yours."

"Good. That's a bargain."

He shouted to Sheila that he'd be back in a minute, and we plunged out into the short bleak street that was now full of a thin fog. The lights of the tobacconist's shop on the corner were an orange smudge till we were almost upon them. Dermot bought me the best briar pipe the shop had, together with an ounce of Smith's Glasgow Mixture, and I bought myself a red rubber tobacco-pouch. The counter of the little shop was strewn with cheap periodicals. Dermot took one up. It was called *Titbits*. "Stick that in your pocket and study it when you get home," he said. "That's how you'll make your money to begin with."

Then we wandered back through the cold foggy dark. It was not till we were just outside the door that Dermot said: "That girl's in love with you—madly in love with you. Did you know that?"

"Yes."

"So long as you know. She's a good girl. She's honest."

Sheila and Nellie were back in the sitting-room, with coffee on a little table. They sat on the big divan, and Dermot and I, smoking our pipes, on either side of the fire. Nellie watched my performance as though it were of unusual virtuosity, and Sheila chaffed me unmercifully, and pointed out the quickest route to the back-yard. But I didn't suffer any of the qualms I had been led to expect, and I don't think a day has gone by from that time to this without my smoking a pipe. Heaven help me! That night was forty-five years ago!

Forty-five years ago since Dermot drew that letter out of his pocket and said: "Oh, I was going to tell you, Bill. I got a letter from Fergus this morning. He's thriving in the States. Fergus is my brother, Miss Moscrop. He went out to join my uncle in New York. Listen to this.

"'My dear Dermot,—Why don't you chuck your fretwork and

come out here and join me? I've been asking you for years, but I'll never be able to make you realise what you're missing. The more I see of Uncle Con, the more amazing he appears to be. I simply can't realise that he and father were brothers. These stores of his are beginning now to push out of New York and he swears that in the next ten years he will have one in every town of over 50,000 inhabitants in the States. Next week I go to Chicago, where we are opening up the first outside New York. I wish to the Lord you'd come and help to keep the money in the family. I am—let me say it modestly—already Uncle Con's right-hand man, but there's room for you, too.

"'Believe me, Dermot, this is the life—incredible after Ancoats. But I'm getting used to it now, getting used to a house full of servants, getting used to seeing the old man signing 10,000-dollar cheques for charity.

"'One thing I can't get used to is Uncle Con's Irish republican mania. You know I've been a sort of confidential secretary to him for years now, and it's been an eye-opener. This country is riddled with secret societies. The old man is always meeting the maddest Irishmen, and the amount of his money that flows down that drain is beyond belief. There's a wizened little rat called Michael Flynn who's for ever to and fro between here and Ireland, and he never goes from this house without a wad in his pocket. Look out for this chap Flynn. He's in England now, and Uncle Con has given him your address. If he looks you up, I hope you will be more pleased to see him than I ever am.

"'But that's how it is, Dermot. It seems that in our family we can't have two brothers simultaneously devoted to Irish freedom. Father never cared a hoot about it, but his brother's mad, with a purely sentimental madness, because he'd no more go back to live in Ireland than he'd fly. And now there's you with Cathleen ni Houlihan and the I.R.A. on the brain, while all I ask is to be allowed to get on with the job of taking the O'Riorden chain of stores from here to the

Pacific coast. We'll do it, too, a darn sight sooner than you'll see a President running an Irish Republic.'"

"There's plenty more like that," said Dermot, "but that's enough. What do you think of my brother, Miss Moscrop?"

Nellie blinked at him short-sightedly, and the pucker deepened between her brows. "Really, Mr. O'Riorden," she said, "I know nothing about these matters, but your brother seems a very sensible man to me."

Dermot's eyes suddenly blazed with anger and contempt. "Yes," he said, clapping the letter down upon the mantelpiece, "very sensible."

Then, his voice rising to a shrill note: "D'you know nothing," he cried, "of the way Ireland has been bled and butchered and drained white by this damned money-grubbing Empire of yours, by the fat landlords sitting on their backsides in London, while the peasants haven't so much as a rotten potato to eat—"

Sheila jumped up and put her arms around him. "Dermot, my darling," she said, "not tonight, please, not tonight."

He sat down, white and trembling, upon the divan, muttering: "I'm a pretty host, am I not? I'm a pretty host," and at that moment there was a knock, which sounded furtive and discreet, upon the front door. Sheila went to see who was there, and a moment later returned with the strangest little gnome of a man I had ever seen. He cannot have been more than five feet high, and at first it was difficult to see him at all. A long double-breasted overcoat almost obliterated him and swept the floor at his feet. A woollen muffler was wound round his neck, and a black felt hat was pulled down over his eyes which at first were all we could see of his features, peeping brightly out from ambush.

"Dermot, this is Mr. Michael Flynn," Sheila said.

Dermot leapt to his feet and took the hand of the diminutive creature with what seemed to me to be almost reverence. "Mr. Michael Flynn!" he said. "Chester. The rising of '67. Clerkenwell gaol."

And it sounded as though he were talking of Troy and Salamis.

Michael Flynn was introduced to me and Nellie, and as he shook my hand I was astonished by the strength and fervour of his grip. He took off his hat, unwound the muffler from round his neck, and then pulled off his overcoat. He threw the coat down on the uncarpeted floor, and there was a hard sound as though the pocket contained metal.

There he stood, dressed in dingy tweeds, with a face like a small withered Shakespeare's. The little pointed beard was red; the hair brushed back from the great domed cranium was thin and dirty-looking; the eyes were bright and furtive as a weasel's. He pulled a pipe and tobacco-pouch from his pocket. "I may smoke?" he asked.

"Yes, do," said Sheila.

"And drink, too, I hope," said Dermot. He hastened to the kitchen for the Burgundy. The bottle was still half-full. We had been timorous drinkers. Dermot placed the bottle and a glass on a table by Flynn's chair. Flynn filled the glass, took a swig as though it had been beer, and wiped the back of his hand across his mouth.

"Ye've heard of me from your uncle?" he asked.

"We've heard of you from many people," Dermot answered, and Sheila nodded.

"I don't often need an introduction to patriots," said Flynn, "and now we can all be at home. Your uncle gave me your address, Mr. O'Riorden, in case I should need it, if ye know what I mean?"

Dermot nodded, his eyes bright. "I have never had a chance to do anything," he said. "I have done nothing but talk. I long to do something real."

"Perhaps you will," said Flynn. "But there's no need just now. I'm not in hiding tonight. If I was, I know I could count on Conal O'Riorden's grandson."

Dermot started in his chair. "You didn't know my grandfather?" he asked.

"Did I not!" Flynn demanded, his voice rising suddenly to a passionate note. "Did he not die in these arms with the front of his belly sticking to his spine? Ye've heard of the famine of 1845? Ye've heard of two million Irishmen, some of them rotting in the ground like the rotten potatoes that they couldn't eat, some of them flying overseas, driven out of the dear motherland that couldn't suckle her own children because the breasts of her were drained dry by the English parasites? Ay, ye've heard of that, but did no one tell ye that your grandfather and grandmother, too, died in a ditch—in a ditch on the roadside with the cold rain raining down and none but me to close their eyes?"

Dermot sat with his elbows on his knees, his chin in his hands, gazing exaltedly at the old man who had risen and was striding to and fro before the fire. "They keep these things from ye," he cried, his face fanatically shining. "What shall we do with Irish fathers who keep these things from their sons? I'm an old man. I'm seventy-six years old, and may the Mother of God help me to fight for Ireland to the last. I was thirty years old when the famine came, and never a day since then has passed but I've lifted up my hand against England."

Flynn was a great story-teller, and the story he told that night was one which, clearly, he had told many times before. He held us all spellbound with his picture of the quiet country life of men and women who asked nothing of God or man but the leave to work and eat a little food. "Never a bite of meat from year's end to year's end, Potatoes were good enough to keep life in the likes of us."

He made us feel the long wet sunless days that came with the autumn of 1845, the spread of the potato-disease that wiped out the food of a people, the settling down of winter with the famine-fever spreading through the land, and dysentery and starvation.

"We warmed our bellies at our little fires of peat, but, God, man, you need to warm a belly from the inside.

"And then," said Flynn, in a hushed dramatic whisper, "they began to die. Old men and old women and little children, dying up and down the length and breadth of a fertile land that God made to bear laughing harvests. But the only harvest was death's harvest. And when death grinned at the window, out they would go, shivering with ague, weak bags of skin and bone, indistinguishable from death themselves, to ask the food which they knew they would never find. They wandered to the towns, and there was no food in the towns, and they lay down on the pavements and died there. It was a winter not fit for dogs to be abroad, with death and pestilence riding in the fog, but up and down the land they went, dressed like scarecrows in a few old rags, crawling up the little bohereens to knock at cottage doors. But no one came from the cottages to give them food because there was no food in the cottages. There were only dead men and women—only citizens," Flynn burst out in a sudden gust of rage, "of the great Empire that was carrying Christianity to the heathen millions of the earth."

None of us uttered a word. The little man stood erect before the fireplace, holding us with his blue eye and with the ease of one accustomed to moving multitudes of people.

"It was in December of that year," he said, "that my father died— God give him rest eternal." He crossed himself, and Dermot and Sheila crossed themselves, too. Nellie, already shaken by meeting a man the like of whom she had never guessed at, noticed with dismay those three flickering gestures, those sketchy evocations of Calvary.

"He died in the morning," said Michael Flynn. "We were alone in the little cabin on the edge of the bog, he and I. I was his only son. My mother had long been dead. There was a bed of sacks in the corner of the cabin, and he lay there burning with the fever. There was no light but what came from the smoulder of the peat, and all night long I knelt by his bed and now and then dipped my finger in a cup of water to wet his lips. He was only fifty-five. He would have been a strong man in his prime, but there he lay, the skin clinging to his skull and the great eyes of him burning in their sockets. He was in his working clothes as he had first lain down, and at the same time he burned and shivered. I sat there in the lonely cabin and listened to the rising wind and the rain on the roof and at the window, and I thought of all the thousands who were dying in my dear land. They were dying like this in their cabins, and they were dying out there under the sky, these poor rent-paying beasts who could be left to rot to death now that they could pay their rent no longer."

Flynn paused again, and in the silence we heard that in Ancoats, too, the rain was suddenly beating on the window. He held up his finger. "Hush!" he commanded. "That is the sound I heard, long years ago, in the silence and loneliness of the night. And that sound, Dermot O'Riorden, was the sound of shot! It was the sound of battle. It was the call that from that day to this has been ever in my ears—the call to drive from a land that was never theirs the oppressors who doomed us to labour that they might live riotously, and when we could labour no longer doomed us to support as best we might the obscene death that their eyes must not be troubled to behold!

"When the little window whitened with the dawn, I stood away from the bed and looked out upon the new day that was coming over the bog. Grey and wet and hopeless it was, another grand day for the crucifixion of Ireland. I turned back to my father, and in that brief moment he was gone.

"I left him there, without burial, as so many thousands were left, and went out into the sad day. There was nothing to wait for now. My aim was to get to Cork and go to America. I had not gone far when I found a man lying in a ditch by the roadside, and that was your grandfather, Dermot. He was young—no older than I was myself—thirty, I should say; and when I bent down to lift him up

I saw that his coat had been thrown over a woman to keep her from the wet and cold. She was dead, but beautiful as she lay there with the rain falling upon her open eyes, and a look almost of relief upon her face. I sat in the ditch, and took the man upon my knees, and laid his head upon my breast. My body warmed him, and he opened his eyes, and at that moment there came along a man wheeling all that he possessed upon a hand-cart. He had a little brandy, and he poured a drop between the dying man's lips. He revived enough to tell us a story that we knew only too well: how he and his wife had wandered forth to seek food and had found nothing, how they had reached the end of their strength there in the ditch, and how they had lain there all night. He told us that two children had been left behind in the cabin, and he told us where the cabin was, and then he died. I laid him alongside his wife, and the man with the hand-cart and I went on together.

"He told me that he, too, was going to Cork, where he had a brother who was a priest. He was no priest himself, but a profane blasphemer who put into words the black curses that were in my heart. God grant him pardon and rest eternal." Again three crosses flickered through the room. "He had a little money which bought a bite of the food that was hoarded here and there, and that and his precious brandy kept the breath of life in us. We picked up the two boys and put them on the hand-cart, and we made Cork on the third day. We had walked through a graveyard, the like of which God grant we never see again."

Silence fell for a while, then Dermot said: "And one of the boys was my father?"

"He was. And one was your uncle. You have a brother, Dermot, not living in a house like this. He's living in a palace full of kow-towing servants and all the fat is flowing to his side of the plate. He doesn't like me. No, no—don't protest. I know it. But perhaps he'd think more of me if he knew what his uncle, Con O'Riorden, knows, and what you know now. But you needn't tell him. There are few amusements left for me now, and one is to think that that young man would not be in existence if I hadn't trundled his father to Cork on a hand-cart."

With the great story off his chest, Michael Flynn relaxed a little, filled his pipe, and sat down. We all breathed easier. In more matter-of-fact tones, Flynn told how he had left the two boys with the Irish priest whom he had never seen again, nor his blaspheming generous brother. "So you see," he said, "that's how I became a Fenian. That's how I was mixed up in the attempt to seize Chester Castle in '67, and in the great scheme for a rising in Ireland only a month later."

"Tell us about that," said Sheila breathlessly, and once again Flynn was launched on a tremendous narrative. "The snow defeated us," he said. "We reckoned all factors except the snow, for snow is not a thing you count on much in Ireland. We had the guns and we had the boys, and up and down the land we were to meet, but mostly in the defiles and gorges of the mountains. And day after day the snow fell, and it fell night after night. The fields were deep in it, the roads were impassable, and the drifts filled the meeting-places in the mountains. We had some grand commanders, men who had learned their job in the American civil war, but what could commanders do against the little feathery traitors that were mightier than all the police in their barracks?"

And so the great rebellion fizzled out with a few unco-ordinated shootings here and there, a few deaths, a few arrests, and all much as it was before.

Then the reckless old Fenian had come to Manchester. "Kelly and Deasy," he said. "Grand fellows they were. They had lain out with me in the hills of Antrim. They had been with me in New York. Ay, Dermot, time was passing. We were veterans. Twenty-two years had gone by since the famine, twenty-two years in which we had done much and suffered much. I know the climate of Dartmoor.

I know it well." He leaned back in his chair, smiling with reminiscent complacency through the smoke-filled room. Sheila got up and stirred the fire before he went on. "We go our different ways. Dartmoor was mine for a long time, success in New York was your uncle's. Mind you, he was not then the wealthy man he has since become, but already he was well-to-do and a power in the Irish movement. I went there as soon as I was out of gaol, and there I first met Kelly and Deasy. We worked together, and not long after the little traitor snowflakes had fallen in Ireland, Kelly and Deasy were arrested in Manchester.

"So to Manchester I came, and others came, too, but you may be sure we did not travel together. If I were here on such business as that tonight, Dermot, I would be asking you to hide me. But then I did not go to your father. No; I went to a patriot."

I watched Dermot's hands instinctively clench themselves, and the green flecks light his eyes; nor were those signs lost on Flynn, who had spent a dangerous lifetime in the reading of men. "Ach, lad," he said, "don't let it worry you. To some of us God gives the guts to suffer and, if need be, die; to others he doesn't, and that's all there is to it.

"Well, one by one we gathered in that house: Allen, O'Brien, Larkin, Condon, and a few others whose names I forget, and we made our plan to rescue Kelly and Deasy. It all seemed as easy as kissing the Blarney Stone. We knew that as sure as fate they'd be remanded and sent back to gaol, and so we'd post ourselves in a spot where the Black Maria'd pass, hold it up, smash it open, and rush the boys away.

"And so, some on one side of the street, some on the other, we waited, and sure enough there came the Black Maria as I'll see it to my dying day. I'll never forget the great horses tossing their heads up and down, jingling the bits and chains that shone like new silver, or the white foam of their mouths, or the red nostrils of them as I rushed out, brandished my revolver, planted myself in the road, and yelled: 'Stop, or begod, I'll blow lights through you!'

"Ye see, that was my job: to stop the van and keep the policeman on the box covered while the other boys smashed a way in to Deasy and Kelly. It was all to be so simple: a revolver shot in the lock, and out they'd come. Well, so they did, but the shot killed a sergeant, and that's why they hanged Allen, Larkin and O'Brien: three men hanged for an accidental death.

"I'd made my own plans for Kelly and Deasy and myself. We did some quiet dodging through the back streets till we came out almost on the very spot where the sergeant was shot. That was the last place where they'd dream of looking for us, and that was where I'd arranged we'd stay. There was a grand patriot there, an undertaker, who hailed from County Down, and he had three fine coffins in his window. The coffins were on trestles, and no one could see the air-holes in the bottom. We knew that house would be searched, and there we stayed in the coffins in the shop window till it was all over. Then he drove us out, still in the coffins, one one night, one the next, and one the night after that, and who would stop a coffin that was being delivered at the house of death? But we were delivered to friends far enough away, and I was not in Manchester again till the day the martyrs died. I mingled with the crowd that all night long—a dark November night—danced and sang before the prison. 'Rule Britannia,' they sang, and I skulked among them vowing my soul to the day when Britannia should rule no more.

"It was the Manchester martyrs that turned Parnell's thoughts to Home Rule, and now Parnell himself is dead. Do we regret it?"

"No!" Dermot shouted, and Sheila, sitting there white-lipped and fascinated, murmured: "No, not the likes of him."

"You're right, my children," Flynn said, standing erect once more, and, for all his little stature, dominating us with the concentrated venom of his looks. "Who wants Home Rule? Who wants to listen to a set of bloody play-boys larricking in the House of Commons and affording the great British public as much amusement as a pack of paid clowns? What sort of Ireland would Parnell have given us if he'd got his Home Rule? He'd have had his Irish Parliament, and what would he have been then? A good old Tory, sitting on his behind at Avonmore as comfortably as an English squire in Berkshire." The little man's voice rose high. "We who've been through the blood and fire, we who've seen our fathers rot, we who've toiled in English gaols and seen the flag fly up to announce our comrades' deaths at English hands—we don't want Home Rule. We want Ireland, all Ireland, nothing but Ireland, to be the home of our people for ever and ever."

There was a dramatic silence. I looked round the room, myself moved by the man's eloquence. Nellie sat staring at him as at some monster in human shape. Never before had she met a man who gloried in what she could but consider a life of crime. Dermot's face was painfully working. Sheila's countenance was rapt and lit. No one wished to break the quiet. It was broken by a sudden low cry from Sheila. She placed her hand to her side. Dermot at once leapt up and went to her. Flynn crossed the room in a stride and took her hand. "What is it, alannah? What is it, then?" he murmured.

Sheila looked at Dermot. "The child!" she whispered. "I felt him—for the first time. I felt him stirring."

"You will give him to Ireland," said Flynn simply.

Dermot stood up. "God damn England," he said. "We will give him to Ireland."

"We will," said Sheila. "God bless Ireland."

# 8

How long it is since I last saw Manchester! I don't suppose that even now it is a bright place at midnight, and then it was dead.

Midnight! When I told Nellie the time she nearly fainted. She had never before been out at midnight. Late hours and sin were almost synonymous in her mind. She rose hastily, and in the matter-of-fact atmosphere of departure the faint note of hysteria that had come upon the evening was dissipated.

Flynn said he was going, too. He wrapped himself up again into the unsightly bundle he had been when first our eyes fell upon him, and in the narrow passage-way, just as Dermot was about to open the front door, thrust his hand into his overcoat pocket. "Ye might like to see this," he said. "That's the revolver that shot the sergeant." The light from the lamp glinted on the metal. Dermot laid his hand for a moment upon the gun that had released two men and hanged three—a good revolutionary proportion, I thought—the gun that had produced the Manchester Martyrs whose names had stirred him the night years before when first I shared a bedroom with him. "Thank you, Michael Flynn," he said. "Give my love to my uncle. Tell him I'm a—a—patriot."

Then we were out in the street—Flynn and Nellie and I. The rain that we had heard dashing the window was gone, and it had cleared away the fog. The stars shone high and cold above the humble Ancoats roofs. Nellie walked between me and Flynn, speechless. I could feel her shrinking from the man, edging nearer and nearer towards me. The poor girl was terrified. Soon she took my arm. Her fingers gripped hard into my flesh. We passed out into the main road, no one speaking, our footsteps echoing hollowly on the pavements. Presently at a street corner, Flynn stopped, and instinctively we stopped too. He looked up at the majestic sky, and in a low vibrant voice said:

> "There's not the smallest orb that thou behold'st
> But in his motion like an angel sings,
> Still quiring to the young-eyed cherubins:
> Such harmony is in immortal souls,
> But while this muddy vesture of decay
> Doth grossly close it in, we cannot hear it.

God bless you."

His hand flickered across his breast, his fingers were raised for a moment as though it were his to bless, and then he was gone. The side-street shadows seemed at once to receive and annihilate him. I never saw him again.

Then, when we were alone, Nellie began to sob. Incoherent words tumbled out of her—the sinful lateness of the hour—her father all alone—that dreadful man with the revolver—that girl talking like that about a baby before it was born. Oh, it was all hateful, and they were all hateful people, and I must never take her to see them again. She clung to me and laid her head on my shoulder, and I patted her back with my one free hand and made comforting noises. A policeman strolled by with elaborate casualness, turned twenty paces on, and strolled back. I managed to propel Nellie across the road, into the side streets that led to Piccadilly. Once I had got her moving, things went better, but bitter sobs continued to shake her, and I hoped that, late as it was, there would be some sort of conveyance in Piccadilly. There was one hansom cab. I had never been in a hansom cab before. It was, to my mind, and still is, the most romantic of vehicles. To be in a hansom cab with a girl was, as a pure idea, dashing and debonair. And it was my luck to get into the hansom cab with Nellie Moscrop, a sodden bundle of misery and hysteria. It was with the greatest difficulty that I got her to use the cab at all. She had never used a cab—never in her life; and I think she had the gravest doubts concerning the propriety of what we were doing. But I got her in, the apron fell to, and off we went. It was a good cab, smart and well-kept, with a good horse who went trotting valiantly over the cobbles. I was able to appreciate all that, and to savour the bitterness of having this first experience diluted by the sorrowful presence of Nellie Moscrop.

So we drove through midnight Manchester, between the black crape walls of Portland Street, towering so high that the stars flowed over our heads like a river, along Oxford Street to All Saints, and so into the dark heart of Hulme. All the time, Nellie sat as remote from me as it is possible for one person to be from another in a hansom cab. She had regained some composure by the time we reached home, and, jumping out without ceremony, she opened the door and went into the house while I was still asking the driver to wait, as my money was indoors.

As soon as I followed Nellie into the house I sensed that something was wrong. The pungent smell of old Moscrop's asthma pastilles filled the place as incense fills a church. I had expected the old man to be in bed, but, on entering the sitting-room, I found him, gripping the arms of his chair, his whole body rigid, the veins standing out on his temples, and sweat pouring down his face. The wheezing of his laboured breath filled the room. Nellie and I stood before him in consternation, helpless and frightened. We had never before seen him in so shocking a paroxysm. For a long time he struggled to articulate, and at last gasped the one word: "Heart!"

"I'll get the doctor," I said, and thanked goodness the cab was waiting at the door. The doctor lived only a few streets away, and, as luck would have it, I hadn't to get him out of bed. He was just opening his gate as I drove up. He was a young man, scarcely older than myself, and he seemed very tired. "I've just come from a child-birth," he said. "They've got six already. God! Why do they do it?" He waved his hand comprehensively round the sleeping darkness of Hulme. "I must have a drink. Come in." His face was pale with weariness when he turned up the gas in his little den. He gave himself a whisky and soda. I declined to drink. "Then give this to the cabby," he said. I did so, and then we drove back to Moscrop's.

The old man was breathing more easily. The young doctor's boredom and tiredness were changed for smiling efficiency. "That's how it is, Mr. Moscrop," he said. "Gets you like a tiger, and then lets go almost as suddenly as it gets you. What's all this about your heart—eh? Let's have a look at you."

He got out his stethoscope, and while he was running Moscrop over I noticed that efficient Nellie had already let fresh air into the room, pulled the fire together, swept the hearth, and made everything as ship-shape as a captain's cabin. A sponge in a bowl of hot water suggested that she had been bathing her father's rigid and perspiring face.

The doctor himself helped me to put Moscrop to bed. When we came down, it was half-past one. "Come and take a breath of air," he said. "You might as well go to bed, Miss Moscrop," he added. "He's all right. There's nothing to be done."

In the street we walked for a while without speaking. Then he asked: "You a relative?"

"No, but I think I can call myself a close friend."

"You ought to know that the old boy's in a rotten way. Asthma's bad enough. There's nothing to be done about it, you see—not by a g.p. anyway. All the same, by itself it's only troublesome—though it's damned troublesome, as you have seen for yourself. But in this case it's not by itself. The old man's heart's in a frightful state. I needn't give you a lot of big words for it; but the fact is an attack like the one he's had tonight puts an enormous strain on the heart. He may live for years. He may pass out next time he has an attack. That's all. Cheerful life, isn't it?" He grinned at me under the gas lamp outside his door. "Sure you won't have a drink?"

"No thanks."

"Neither will I. Bed. Good-night."

For myself, I didn't feel like bed. I was thoroughly awake. I had never spent a more emotional night: first that madman Flynn, then Nellie's hysterics, and now Moscrop's asthma. Bed, indeed! I felt like walking and walking; but I knew that, whether Nellie had gone to bed or not, she would be keeping an ear open for my return. So I went back. She was gone to bed, and, as there was a good fire in the sitting-room, I sat down in the old man's big chair and pondered over the strange evening which had now shut down into a preternatural quiet.

One thing had been cleared up for ever in my mind. I had often wondered, seeing Dermot come home flushed and exalted from some secret meeting, just how much of the business was play-acting and how much was serious politics. Now I could have no further doubt that play-acting had no part in the matter at all. For good or ill, Dermot was meddling with something pretty serious. He was in touch with the actual plotters and makers of violence and treason, and his name as a "Patriot" must stand high, or a man so deeply implicated as Flynn would never have gone near him.

I was already impressed by Dermot's resolute grip upon the job by which he meant to live. Now I was the more deeply impressed by the knowledge that both he and Sheila were real beings, committed to possibly dangerous action, ranged on a side in life that had called for resolution and decision. In every way, Dermot seemed to me to be a man, as I had not yet begun to be.

I was used to these moods of dissatisfaction with myself—the moods in which I called myself a shirker, a good-for-nothing, and once again I administered to myself a stout dose of good resolves. The winter was coming on; I would read steadily, write regularly, get something finished and done with, whether it were done well or ill.

In this not unfamiliar mood of high determination, I rose to go at last to bed, and, rising, I knocked off the arm of the chair *Barnes on Revelation*, which evidently the old man had been reading when the paroxysm came upon him. But not only Barnes. A sheaf of papers had lain neatly under the book, and as I picked them up my eye ran over a page covered with pencilled figures. "Say £5,250," I read; then shamelessly read the whole thing through. "Learn summat about figures," Mr. Summerway had said to me long ago; and I had learned enough to see pretty quickly what it was I held in my hand. Moscrop had been figuring out the pros and cons of his earthly goods, and had arrived at the conclusion that he was worth "say £5,250."

It was a surprisingly large sum for a back-street baker, but the paper showed that he had made a few far-seeing investments. It would be a comfortable sum for a man to have behind him if he wanted to write. At that thought, I sat down again and pondered my position. In cold blood I made up my mind then and there to marry Nellie Moscrop.

The old man was anxious that the marriage should take place soon. I think he felt that he had not long to live. Nellie went about in a sort of humble pride. Our appearances together at the Oddy Road chapel were occasions of torture to her. At home, she lived in a whirl of stitching, making her own clothes with the help of a dressmaker who came in. As for me, I was married, God help me, in a frock-coat. I still have a photograph of that astounding outfit; a coat (with satin lapels) double-breasted across me, striped trousers, buttoned boots, and a silk hat. There I stand, in that yellow and melancholy memento, a flower in my buttonhole, Nellie holding on to my arm. It was a lilac-coloured dress she wore, and there in the photograph you see it, flowing down into a train. She is carrying a parasol, though it was winter then, and wearing a great cartwheel of a hat, piled with horticulture. That is old Moscrop on the other side of her, dressed like me, except that his clothes seem all width while mine are all height. On low stools in front of us three sit Dermot and Sheila O'Riorden. Dermot looks thin and pale and earnest. He is nursing his silk hat, and probably worrying about Sheila, because her time is drawing near. But she looks happy enough. She is the only radiant one there. Time, that has taken Moscrop and Nellie and Rory, has not dimmed the smile with which, I expect, she was thinking of Rory. It used to shock Nellie to the soul to hear Sheila say: "Oh, Rory, me darlin', don't kick, or don't flutter your wings, or whatever it is the dear Mother of God is lettin' you be at now." Usually, she talked English like me, but whenever she spoke to the child she would assume, or remember, this way of speaking, pressing her hands to her belly and gazing towards the future hung with merciful veils.

We were married by Mr. Pascoe at the Oddy Road chapel. No one but us five was present. When we got back to the house we found that Dermot had cleverly arranged to have presents delivered during the service. For me, already in place in my room, was a lovely writing-desk, smooth as silk, solid as stone, with no decoration whatever save an inscription in beautiful lettering round the edge on the top board: "Of the making of books let there be no end. D. O'R. In amicitiam. W.E." Of the long list of my books and plays there is hardly a word that was not written on this desk. For Nellie there was a dressing-table, also made by Dermot, the first of a famous design that he repeated many times.

A glint of sunshine fell through the clouds of Hulme as Nellie and I came out to the four-wheeler cab that was waiting to take us to Victoria Station. Old Moscrop kissed his daughter and said: "If I may coin a phrase, happy is the bride that the sun shines on." And that was all, except that, when we were both in the cab, Sheila's dark face with dewy eyes shining came through the window, and she said simply: "God bless you, Bill. God bless you, Nellie." We then drove off. It wasn't an uproarious business.

I had recklessly reserved a first-class carriage for our journey to Blackpool. Not that I had any lover-like desire to be alone at the earliest possible moment with Nellie, but I knew that she would be full of the embarrassed feeling that everyone recognised in her a girl straight from the wedding service. I hoisted the luggage up on to the rack: my suit-case and the solid leather one I had given her for a present. There it was, with the initials "N.E." staring down at me as a reminder of the irrevocability of what I had done—Nellie Essex.

The lights were already up in the great misty cavern of the station. When we drew out and at last got clear of the suburbs the day was fading over the lugubrious Lancashire plain. We had little to say to one another. We sat close together, my arm round her, all through the journey. It was quite dark when we got to Blackpool. The rooms we were to stay at for a week had been booked by old Moscrop, who was paying for the honeymoon. They were behind the front in a street whose silence and darkness when we came upon it, I carrying a suit-case in each hand, struck a chill to my marrow. The narrow-chested little house was called Mount Pleasant; and Mount Pleasant, when we reached it, was wrapped in aboriginal gloom. But the bell which raised a clamour in some remote fastness of the place called up a stirring of life. We heard slippered feet on linoleum, saw the coloured glass which decorated the door glow a faint yellow and ruby, as a gaslight went up in the passage. Mrs. Boothroyd opened the door, tall and thin, black and shining as a beetle's wing.

Boarders had been part of Mrs. Boothroyd's life too long for her to take much interest in us. Indeed, I felt all through the week that she resented our having stirred her from hibernation. Visitors to Blackpool were not customary in December, and all shortcomings she excused by saying "If it had only been in the summer-time, now—" as though in the summer-time Mount Pleasant were accustomed to blossom into delirious achievements of punctuality, comfort and convenience.

At the foot of the narrow stairs was a marble table that looked as though it had been made out of a tombstone, and on it were half a dozen tin candlesticks, enamelled in blue. "You'll always find your candle here, and matches," said Mrs. Boothroyd, imparting to the words a commentary on the unshakable efficiency of the Mount Pleasant machine. She lit the candle and preceded us up the stairs. "This is your room."

It was the sort of room one would expect. The washstand was another graveyard masterpiece. The linoleum was harsh and chill. The great double bed dominated the room, cold-looking as a snow-drift. There were lace curtains to the windows, and behind them Mrs. Boothroyd let the venetian blinds down with a bony rattle. "There," she said. "Don't you think it's nice?"

"I think it would be much nicer with a fire," I said.

"A fire? In a bedroom?"

Clearly I was entering regions of insanity where Mrs. Boothroyd found it difficult to follow. We eyed one another with hostility across the bed. "If it was summer, now—" she began.

"If it were summer we could do without a fire," I said, "but we'd like one tonight."

"Very well. But please remember I have no staff in the winter."

"If you'll show me where the stuff is, I'll light it myself. It's five minutes' work."

"I'll light it. It'll be a shilling a night."

"And worth every penny."

Mrs. Boothroyd retired. "Your supper will be ready as soon as you come down," she said at the door.

The house was infested with angels. I had noticed one in the passage—just simply an angel in an off-moment, engaged in an afternoon's untrammelled soaring. Elsewhere they were on definite jobs. Here in the bedroom was a whole posse of them giving a helping hand to Christian souls that were rising from bodies laid in decorous attitudes about the floor of an arena full of prowling lions. In the dining-room to which we presently descended there were no fewer than three illustrations of angelic usefulness. There was a white flock of them, some swooping like albatrosses round a sinking ship, others alighted gracefully in the rigging, looking down with encouraging glances at the distraught mariners who were clearly "In Peril on the Sea," as a caption informed me. A smaller picture showed an angel laying a friendly hand upon the shoulder of an old man at a graveside; and yet another depicted a soldier, prone on a battlefield, one hand thrown negligently across the neck of his fallen horse, the other extended to an angel who pointed upward with a coquettish "Come hither" look.

It was not a cheerful dining-room. The fire was a smoky smoulder, and over the mantelpiece was a card upon which embossed silver lettering said: "The Lord is the Head of this house, the unseen Guest at every meal, the unseen Listener to every conversation." I gathered an impression in the course of the week that, so far as the last clause was concerned, the Lord was ably abetted by Mrs. Boothroyd.

Nellie and I sat down to mutton chops seethed in grease, and to potatoes, and to the bread pudding which wasn't at all bad, and to lashings of tea. As we ate, we could hear Mrs. Boothroyd raking with incensed vigour at the fireplace above.

"D'you think you ought to have worried about a fire, Bill?" Nellie asked in a whisper.

"Of course I do. If you want anything in this world you've got to ask for it and see that you get it."

"I'm afraid it might make her not like us."

I laughed. "D'you care whether she does or not?"

"I like people to like me. That's all."

"I don't like 'em to sit on me," I said.

When Mrs. Boothroyd came down, puffing and giving a general impression of having stoked a liner, we were standing in the hall with our coats on. Nellie had asked to be taken for a walk by the sea.

"Remember I lock up at ten," Mrs. Boothroyd said shortly. With a grotesque attempt to be arch, she added: "I should have thought you'd want to get to bed tonight."

"We shall get to bed tonight. Make no mistake about that," I said. "And don't call us in the morning. We'll get up when we're ready."

I took Nellie's arm, and we went out into the cloudy night.

I'm no apologist for Blackpool, either as it was then or as it is now. I don't like the place—can't stand it at any price. Without its blatancy, it would be a bleak and miserable thing huddled in front of a grey and uninspiring sea. With it, it is the crown of a crazy, cowardly age that can't bear to be alone, or to be still, or to be silent. I didn't like it that night. There were, of course, no visitors at that time of the year. When we got down to the front the wind was blowing from the north. We turned and walked in the teeth of it towards Norbreck. There was hardly a soul stirring, hardly a light save from a pub here and there. We walked, bowed to the wind, Nellie's arm in mine, the sea, which was full, pounding in rhythmic reverberations on the beach to our left. We walked till we reached the inconsiderable rise of land at Norbreck, and then we halted, alone under the night, with the wind whistling and the sea lamenting. Nellie put both her arms around me and pressed her head against my breast. I got my arms round her too, and there we stood, clinging to one another. "Oh, Bill," she said in a smothered voice, hugging me tighter, "I do love you. I do love you so. We shall be happy, shan't we?—so happy!"

I did not answer, but pressed her closer to me, there on the cliff, with no light anywhere, and before me nothing but the sea, restless, dark and menacing.

## 9

The room which had been my bed-sitting-room became now my study. I moved into Nellie's bedroom, and that was the only change in domestic habits brought about by the wedding. I was afraid that Nellie would be possessive, that she would want me now to spend all my spare time with her and Moscrop, but nothing of the sort happened. Marriage gave her a certain amount of self-confidence. She let her father see that his growing disabilities made him a handful, that with him and the house to look after, she could not look after the shop; and that, if I had to look after the shop and superintend the business in general, I could not do the round as well. So a youth was engaged to drive the horse and van, and I, for all practical purposes, became the boss of Moscrop's.

When my day's work was over, Nellie would chase me away to my study. "Get on with your book," she would say, and old Moscrop would lift his heavy lids and say: "Ay, she'll make a great man of you yet, Bill."

But in my study, which I had managed to make cosy with bookshelves and a carpet, I was not working at a book. The paper called *Tit-bits* which Dermot had thrust into my hand that night when we met Flynn was occupying my attention. The sort of stuff it contained seemed so easy to write, and yet I think I tore up twenty efforts before I had completed one that I liked. It was called "Lodging-houses in Winter." My experiences among the Blackpool angels gave me the material. *Tit-bits* accepted it, printed it, and paid me thirty shillings for it. Pasted on to a board and framed in narrow black, that article hangs in my study today.

I suppose I am a sentimentalist, but I wouldn't sell for a lot of money that framed article.

From that moment, I began to make money by my pen. Once I had tumbled to the knack of it, it came easily. I could get a pleasant humorous twist into those skits and sketches, and they sold readily. Soon I was doing two or three a week. Dermot's advice had proved fruitful, but for years it kept me from the work I was made to do.

Made to do? Yes, I suppose so, for the itch never left me from the moment I began in the Gibraltar Street bedroom. It was there all the time, even when I was a rich and successful business man. For I became that, too. I must tell you about it.

There was great excitement at Moscrop's when that first cheque came. The old man advised the opening of a bank account, venturing to coin a phrase about saving the shillings and the pounds taking care of themselves. Nellie was as pleased and excited as though another *Jane Eyre* had come out of the purlieus of Hulme. But I remembered my promise to give Dermot a present out of my first cheque. I bought him a silver-headed malacca cane, and on a February night I walked round to Ancoats with it.

"You're just in time to see the grand performance," said Sheila, who came to the door. "Go right through now to the kitchen."

In the kitchen Dermot sat at the table on which were spread dozens of small pieces of carved boxwood. "Feel it," he said, pushing one across to me. "It's like ivory."

It was: a minute but lovely bit of carving.

"The very devil to do," said Dermot. "So small. I could have built a house in the time it's taken to make these."

"But what are they?" I asked.

"Toys for Rory," Sheila said with a happy smile, leaning on the back of Dermot's chair. "Just you watch now."

Dermot began fitting the pieces together. Each one was made with slots or dovetailing, and now they assembled themselves under Dermot's fingers. "It's an old English village, you see," he said, "every detail guaranteed true to the facts of the case."

The walls of the inn dovetailed themselves together; the roof slotted on. So did the lovely little dormers. From a tiny peg Dermot hung the separate inn sign. "Good, eh?" he said, engrossed in his job.

It was. I watched him, fascinated, a sudden turmoil in my mind. Here, I kept saying to myself, here at last was that great Idea which wise men recognised when it was under their noses.

Dermot went on quietly with his job, his eyes full of humour, his long deft fingers loving the wood. The church rose up, wall by wall, roof, tower and tiny flagstaff. He placed it on a piece of green paper, with the inn on the other side. Cottages rose round the inn, a vicarage sprang up alongside the church, and, decently removed from all else, there appeared a great house. As arranged there by Dermot on the green paper, it was a lovely and alluring toy perfect in detail, exquisite in proportion. "The great fun for children," he said, "will be not only in having this but in *doing* it. They love making things themselves."

Sheila roughly tousled his hair. "Rory, will you be listenin' to that now, ye spalpeen," she said. "Here's himself talkin' as though he had a dozen of ye and had spent a lifetime studyin' yer ways."

"Oh, that's all right," Dermot said confidently. "I know what children like. And this is so simply fitted together that any child can make it and unmake it."

He began easily to pull the lovely picture to bits.

"*Any* child?" I said.

"Well," he laughed, "any child that's lucky enough to have it, and that'll be Rory."

But I was thinking far beyond that now. "Dermot," I said, as he packed the pieces into a box he had made. "Let me take these home to show them to Nellie, will you? Rory won't be here for a month, you know, and he won't be fitting these things together for a bit after that."

"Go on then," said Dermot, "but mind what you're doing with them."

Then I produced the malacca cane and told him about the article in *Tit-bits*. He and Sheila were full of congratulations. We drank to it in a glass of stout apiece—stout which had been laid in because it was supposed to be good for Sheila then—but if they had known how far that article was by now from my mind! With the precious box under my arm I hurried away, my head swimming with grandiose dreams.

Harry Platts was one of the people I had met when doing the bread round. He had been out of work for a long time and owed us a good deal of money. I think he feared, when I called on him suddenly that night, that I had come to demand a settlement. When I said: "Look here, Harry, I want to put you in the way of earning a bit of money," his face brightened. I added expansively: "And you can consider that bread debt wiped out to begin with." At that he looked almost scared. "But Mr. Essex—" he began.

"That's all right," I said. "May I come in and talk to you?"

"Ay," he said with a grin. "T'missus is down at t'Salvation Army barracks prayin' for my soul." It was drink that had lost Harry his job. He was a moulder. We went into his cheerless little kitchen. I opened the box and took out all the pieces that went to make the village inn.

"Look here, Harry," I said. "I know nothing about the processes of moulding, but I do know that if you chaps are given a good model you can reproduce it in metal."

"Ay, that's so, Mr. Essex."

I handed him the bits of boxwood. "Are those good models?"

He fingered them carefully. "They are that," he said. "That's a champion job, that is."

"You could make the moulds, get them reproduced in quantity?"

"Oh, ay," he said. "That's a routine job to me."

"All those slots and things? You see, that's important. The reproductions have got to slot together as easily as these." I fitted the model together.

"Oh, ay. That's routine," he repeated.

"What metal would you use?"

"We'll have to think that over. There are plenty of light alloys."

"The lighter the better."

"Ay. What abaht brass?"

"Brass? You don't call that light?"

"Nay, Mr. Essex," he said, bursting into a laugh. "Ah mean the doin's, the spondulix. There are things Ah'll have to buy."

"Work it out," I said, "and call on me tomorrow. I'll let you have whatever's necessary."

That was how the business began which was known as "Easifix Toys." A week after that talk with Harry Platts I sat in my study slotting together again and again a dozen metal copies of the village inn. And, of course, Dermot was right. This was just what any child would love to do: to have the sense, when the whole village was spread before him, that he had *made* it.

That was the *appeal*, I said to myself, trying to think like a clever commercial plotter. And any child who had once discovered the joys of the old English village wouldn't want to stop there. We should have to go forward, once Dermot saw the point of the thing. Elizabethan town. That would be a one! Elizabethan Town, Set 1, the Playhouse. Elizabethan Town, Set 2, the Guildhall. Elizabethan Town, Set 3, Burghers' Houses. Why, you could make a dozen sets of that alone. Something progressive, irresistible, luring the buyers on.

Absolute accuracy, I mused, sitting down by the fire, just as in this first set that Dermot had made. Let the thing be educational. Perhaps schools would take it up. With a bit of archæological research, we might do actual cities. "Lincoln in the fifteenth century."

That sort of thing. Every detail good enough for a museum. And we could make a dash into the future. "The City of Tomorrow." Plenty of scope there.

I handled fondly the pieces that Harry Platts had made in a light grey metal that looked rather like the linotype metal of today. The things must be coloured, of course. Pantiles must be red and stone towers grey and cottage walls must have creeping plants upon them. Now who on earth could do that? Never mind. I'd soon find that out. Lord, what a lot of details there were! They'd all cost money. Never mind. This was not going to be a cheap toy. No cheaper than I could help, anyway.

It was just a year later that the one commercial traveller of the Easifix Toy Company went out on the road. He took the old English village with him. Not far from the bakery I had found a disused stable with a good loft over it. Harry Platts set up his end of the business in the stable. An office of sorts had been started in the loft. There, early that winter morning, Mark Harborough, the traveller, had a final consultation with me. He was a good man. I had thought often about how I should set to work to become rich, once the great Idea came. One point that had always been firm in my mind was: employ the finest experts you can buy. And so I bought Mark Harborough. I bribed him away from an old-established firm which he had served for ten years. His salary was to be the same as the one he was receiving; his commission was to be slightly higher. But the bribe went deeper than that. Once the Easifix Company had made a given profit for three successive years, Harborough was to be made a director, in charge of the sales staff which, with luck, we should then need. So long as I remained associated with Easifix Toys, we went on that principle: the highest reward we could afford at the moment, with the promise of even higher rewards for those whose efforts helped to make them possible.

It worked. In five years Mark Harborough was off the road, running his staff from the head office, and in ten years that staff was working the continent of Europe as well as England. When Dermot and I finally sold out of Easifix Toys, Harborough became the controlling shareholder and a very rich man.

But what could we know of all that, as we sat facing one another, sitting on hard wooden chairs in the office-loft that bleak winter morning! Harborough was thirty years old at the time, a thin, dark and strikingly handsome person with perfect manners and a natural gift for "getting on" with people. There was nothing about him of the rough-and-ready, rather bawdy good humour that was the stock-in-trade of most "commercials" of that time. His qualities went deeper than that. His bag, filled with boxes of toys, was on the table.

"Well, good-bye and good luck," I said. "And thank you for coming to us. You're taking a lot on trust."

"Thank you," he said. "I've worked for Wilbraham and Sugden for ten years. If I work for them for another twenty I'll still be where I am today. I've never had any means of laying my hands on a bit of capital, and till you employed me I didn't think I'd ever get into big things without capital. You've shown me how to do it. And now I shall do it."

He spoke confidently but without arrogance. We shook hands on it, and he climbed down the stairs. His smiling face had success written all over it as he gave me a final glance through the raised trap-door.

I heard Harry Platts come in to his work down below, and then I sat under the buzzing gaslight and made some anxious calculations on a writing-pad. Rent of premises, cost of metal, cost of packing, wages of Harborough and Platts and other workers, whole or part-time. It mounted up to a pretty penny, and it would be a long time before there was anything coming in. It was a good thing that I had faith and that Harborough had a worth-while incentive. No one else believed in Easifix Toys. Dermot thought it was an amusing pastime. Certainly he'd carve his little toys. It gave him something to do in the evenings. Especially now that Sheila couldn't go out. For there was Maeve to look after now. Not Rory, but Maeve. Oh, they were disappointed at first. But you couldn't be disappointed for long with Maeve about the home, with a black down on her head and her little monkey face puckered in a grin half the day. And there'd be Rory all right some day. Never doubt it. "It's waitin' till I've had some practice at motherin' he is, the spalpeen," Sheila would say, hugging Maeve to her breast, "and oh, you wee darlin', what could I want better than you to be goin' on with, if I was Queen of Ireland?"

So Dermot didn't go out much in the evenings, but carved away at his beautiful toys and his pale eyes lighted with laughter at my enthusiasm. "Ach," he said, "it'll be money for jam—if it comes off." And then, more gravely: "But, Bill, honest to God, man, I don't like it. There are you, putting your capital into this thing, and all I have to do is what I'd be doing anyway. And besides your capital, you're putting all this time and work. And yet you call me a director of your comic show, and we split fifty-fifty. It's not sense."

How often we had that out in those early days, sitting there in his kitchen, smoking our pipes as he worked at his toys! "It's the biggest sense ever," I argued. "These are the grandest toys ever made. They're bound to find an enormous market. You're making 'em. I'm reproducing them and selling 'em. Fifty-fifty's fair. You showed me an outlet for my capital that I'd never have thought of without you."

"*Your* capital, my hat!" Sheila mocked; and of course that was a sore point.

For it wasn't my capital at all. It was Nellie's capital, and though they never said a word, Sheila and Dermot, I could see, were shivering in their shoes lest I should pour it down the drain.

I was thinking of that as I followed Harborough presently down the ladder and walked through the dank morning streets of Hulme to breakfast. Alone with Nellie. There was no Moscrop now. Nellie's filial piety had put his portrait up alongside Mrs. Moscrop's. Of course there was no Moscrop, or there would have been no capital. In a sense, he brought his death on himself. It was at the time when first my head began to fill with the Easifix plans, a Sunday night in March. At teatime I told Nellie that I should not be going with her to Oddy Road that night; I should be working in my study. It was the first time since our marriage that I had stayed at home on a Sunday night.

"Eh, Bill? What's that?" the old man asked. "But Nellie can't go alone."

I didn't realise that they would both take the thing seriously. "Perhaps Nellie'd like to stay at home and read to you," I said. "It's a dreadful night." It was. All day long snowy-looking clouds had filled the sky, and now a sharp east wind was blowing.

"But I've never missed on a Sunday night—not for years and years," said Nellie. "And it's the chapel anniversary. Surely, Bill—"

"I don't see why we should go everywhere *together*," I said. I felt that very keenly, and spoke sharply—the first time I had spoken sharply to her since our marriage. She began to cry. Old Moscrop rose with an alacrity that was astonishing in a man of his size and condition. He put an arm around her and glared at me across the table. "You don't see why?" he demanded truculently. "Well, let me tell you, Bill, it's *expected* that a young married woman should have her husband with her."

The old man's sharp tone suddenly made me feel a stranger in the house—a dependant. And I said to myself that I'd be damned if old Moscrop should speak to me like that. "Because people expect a thing," I retorted, "it doesn't follow that it's common sense."

"It's common sense that someone should go to chapel with Nellie," the old boy declared stoutly, "and since you won't, I will.

The means of grace won't come amiss to me. Perhaps you will be so good, before you retire to your study, as to order a cab."

He sat down with dignity, Nellie mopped her eyes and fled upstairs. I put on my overcoat, walked to the cab-rank at All Saints and ordered the cab to be at Moscrop's at a quarter past six. The roads, you know, were not asphalted then. I noticed that the keen wind had stretched a film of ice on all the puddles.

The old man, who had not been out on a winter night for a long time, obstinately wrapped himself up in overcoat and muffler. He glared at me in a fierce "I'll show you!" fashion, and certainly it would be an Oddy Road sensation for a worshipper to defy his bodily ailments, arrive in a four-wheeler, and depart in the same reckless and spendthrift fashion. I saw them into the cab, helping old Moscrop across the pavement which sparkled with frost. "You needn't bother!" he exclaimed impatiently. "Get to your study. I'll manage." Both hostility and derision were in his tone. He was beginning to think that little enough was coming out of that study.

I did not see him alive again. He made an Oddy Road sensation all right. Half-way through the sermon he was seized with one of his paroxysms. I have pointed out before that the Moscrop pew was right against the vestry door. A couple of stewards got him under the arms and helped him into the vestry, gasping like a landed fish. If he had stayed there till the attack was over, he might have lived; but he managed to articulate the word "cab." A volunteer ran to the cab-rank and brought back the four-wheeler which would have been there, anyway, half an hour later. Moscrop and Nellie were got aboard, the old man fighting for his breath in the black wind that whirled round the corner. The hack that pulled the four-wheeler, nearly as broken-winded as Moscrop himself, went clickety-clack over the ice-bound road. He was turning the corner to Moscrop's front door when the accident happened. From my study I heard the sudden wild slither as the poor beast's hoof met an icy rut, heard the sound of the cab swerving as the horse tried to recover himself, heard the smashing blow as the cab went broadside-on into the street lamp at the corner.

When I got down, a few people had already gathered among the splintered glass on the pavement. The cabby was kneeling at the fallen horse's head. I helped Nellie out of the cab. She was frozen with fright. "Father!" was all she could say. She had noticed that his grim fight for breath had stopped. It had stopped for good. The shock of the collision had finished him off, as the doctor had expected some such affair would do.

I walked back through the murk of the Hulme morning after seeing Mark Harborough set off with the Easifix samples. The gas was lit in the living-room; the fire was bright; the breakfast was ready. Everything looked good, everything smelled good; but the sight of the room did not cheer me. Nellie sat at the table, reading her morning chapter from the Bible. I had persuaded her to see an optician about that frowning stare, and now she wore pince-nez. She put the silk marker into the book, shut it, and looked at me through the glasses. "I'll put the water on the tea," she said. Whenever I appeared she had some dutiful remark to make. "I'll put the water on the tea." "The joint's just done." "Can I sew those buttons on for you now?" But one thing she never did. She never came forward and threw her arms round me and hugged me and kissed me, as I had so often seen Sheila do to Dermot. And, of course, now she never would. Her father's death lay like a sword between us. She had not spoken of that matter, but in her complete submission there seemed to lurk reproach. Even now, nearly a year after the old man's death, she was in black from top to toe. She had taken, too, to wearing a vast cameo brooch that had belonged to her mother: a thing that depicted a maiden, vaguely Grecian, sitting beneath the drooping hair of a willow. She seemed to be doing all she could to add to her age and to bid good-bye to the fleeting joys of youth.

I had been unable to interest her in the affairs of the Easifix Company. Moscrop had left nearer six than five thousand pounds. He had died intestate, and Nellie was without a relative in the world. Every penny was hers, and I found it no easy matter to open the subject of throwing the money upon the waters in the hope of a goodly return. But once I had done so, she was acquiescent. That was her mood now in everything: acquiescence, resignation. Thy will be done. If I wanted the money, there it was. Was I not her husband? There were mornings when this attitude kept me awake at nights, shivering with apprehension. If she had heartily backed the gamble, I could more bravely have faced failure. But to lose the money of this spiritless woman would have cut me deeply. Every atom of my pride was engaged in making Easifix Toys a winning venture.

Nellie believed in feeding me well. She placed before me a plate containing rashers of bacon, a fried egg, and a fry-up of yesterday's surplus potatoes. I had begun to grow a moustache, and she handed me my tea in one of those monstrous creations, unknown to the present generation, called a moustache-cup. There was a china ledge to prevent the moustache from being waterlogged, though my own adornment was not of a size that made precaution necessary. A portrait of Queen Victoria, backed by the Union Jack, decorated the cup. This was the first I had seen of it; but Nellie was always doing me these small kindnesses, as though determined to fulfil all the duties of a wife.

I used the occasion to try to put some spirit into her. "Thank you, Nellie," I said. "This will do fine till we're drinking out of silver beakers. I hope that won't be long now. Harborough's on the road this morning."

"I shall pray for your success," she said austerely.

"Far better to work for it," I cried, but at that she shook her head.

"More things are wrought by prayer than this world dreams of," she quoted.

"Very well, then," I agreed, laying into a rasher. "You pray and I'll work. That ought to make a winning team. And I bet that within three years we'll be closing down the bakery, or, better still, putting it up for sale."

"You wouldn't do that!" she cried in alarm. "You wouldn't close the bakery!"

"Like a shot I would," I answered. "If Easifix turns out a success, why carry on with this? Why go on living in Hulme? It's never been my idea of paradise."

"I've always been used to it," she said. "And father was here ever since he was a boy. He remembered when there were green fields in Hulme."

"Well, there are none now, nor anything else that makes life worth living. The sooner we're out of it the better."

"I shouldn't like to leave Oddy Road. I've always attended there. I should like to go on there, even though you've given it up."

Now we were back at a sore point. I wiped my mouth with my handkerchief and pushed back my chair. "I'd better go and see that they're loading the van," I said.

I had given up attending Oddy Road. I don't know why. The wish to go there went as suddenly and inexplicably as it had come. The place no longer meant anything to me, and so I didn't go. That was all there was to it. So Nellie went alone. This was a real break, because Oddy Road meant so much to Nellie. It was half her life, and now it was a half I could not share.

## 10

Nellie did not like to see anything changed, but change enough soon came. Two years after Mark Harborough first went out, I had finished with Moscrop's bakery for good. It continued to exist, but an efficient man ran it. All my time now was being given to Easifix Toys. In the office over the loft I had a clerk, a telephone, and a routine. Once I had thrown off the bakery, I gave my time to mastering the three elements of any trade: buying raw material, making the product, and selling. Anyone of average intelligence, given the capital to start with, can do these three things, and I have more than average intelligence.

By the time another year had passed, the office had shifted to a couple of rooms in Oxford Street. Old O'Riorden came in as chief of the office staff. The manufacturing part of the business was housed in a new building that covered the whole of the yard in which our original stable had stood. Throughout all the time I was connected with Easifix, that building sufficed for our purposes. It was a good two-storey affair; and you don't want a great deal of room for toy-making.

We were all going ahead. Dermot had his fine new showrooms. They were under the Easifix offices in Oxford Street, and a sight they were, stored with the lovely furniture that carried out his ideas of strength combined with simplicity. They had never looked better than they did on a May morning in 1895 when even the sky of Hulme was like taut blue silk and in the grim and sooty soil of the All Saints churchyard a few shrubs were troubled for a while with a green dream of summer. We had only just moved into the new offices.

Reports coming in from Harborough were beyond all expectation; and I had come belting down from home full of energy and enthusiasm. I paused on the All Saints side of Oxford Street and looked across the road at the two first-floor windows with "Easifix Toys" lettered upon them, and at the large plate-glass expanse beneath them. Dermot had fitted the whole window as a dining-room. The furniture was teak. The upholstery was green leather. The carpet was sage-green. The electric-light fittings were all in wrought-iron, the work of a craftsman Dermot now employed; and the only picture in the room was a thing I had not yet got used to. It hung over the fireplace. Dermot's interest in ceramics had caused him to make a visit to Copenhagen. There he had drifted into an exhibition of paintings arranged by a Madame Gauguin whose husband was living and painting on a South Sea island. This thing had caught his eye—a thing of fierce burning colour: a pink beach, a Polynesian woman, a few palms—and he had bought it. There it was, a portentous thing to see in Manchester at that time. "It makes the room," Dermot had said the day before, "and what's more, it makes people stand and look. 'Pink beach!' they say. 'Nonsense!' And then they think: 'But the furniture's damned good,' and so I get 'em. But that picture's not for sale."

I dashed across the road, bounded up the stairs to the office, and shut myself in my own room, pondering on the case of Dermot. He was always a goad in my side, a bit ahead of me in everything. This picture was a case in point. I couldn't pretend at that time to like it, and I couldn't bear Dermot's easy laughter. "In ten years' time, my dear Bill, you'll probably be offering me a few thousand pounds for it."

There was his house, too. He had left Ancoats. The client for whom he had remodelled and furnished that place in Withington had failed in business. Dermot had taken the house over from him, furniture and all. He had moved in last week. "I don't want Rory to be born in Ancoats," he said, because now Rory was on the way—

once more. "And I want to show off, too," he added, his fly-away eyebrows going up in a grin. "I'm having a grand party to warm the house. Grand for me, anyway. There'll be six of us: me and Sheila, you and Nellie, and father and mother." He paused for an almost imperceptible moment; and added: "If Nellie'd care to come?" People were beginning to feel like that about Nellie now.

She came, though. I think she felt rather uncomfortable in Dermot's house. It was a great contrast to the cosy jumble of our own place. Dermot was passing through a mad phase of whiteness. The dining-room was panelled in white. There was a pair of candle-sconces over the fireplace, and between them the Gauguin picture looked exquisitely at home. "I can't leave it in the shop," he explained. "I'm always bringing it back and forth, and now, I think, it had better stay where it is." Six candles without shades burned in a row down the long table which Sheila had laid beautifully. "Not that I ought to be here," she said with a laugh. "The man's mad, asking people tonight, with Rory expected at any minute. Ach, ye young devil, I wouldn't be surprised if ye interrupted the party."

Nellie gave her a shocked and wondering look; but Sheila took her gaily by the arm and led her away to see the little Maeve, who had been put to bed.

Old O'Riorden turned up in a shiny frock-coat and stiff cut-throat collar, looking rather intimidated. Things had indeed changed for him since the day when he first took me home to Gibraltar Street, Summerway's new office boy, and Dermot was a gawky youth with sawdust in his hair. But Mrs. O'Riorden was not the person to be intimidated by anything. "Ah don't know why you can't live without all these faldelals, Dermot," she said, when Sheila's neat little maid had left the room. "Servants and candles, and yon picture that's like nothing on earth."

Dermot smiled benignly. "One of these days that picture may keep us all out of the workhouse," he told them.

"Time was," she said, "when the only picture you wanted was that thing with the names of the Manchester martyrs. That used to give me the pip, but I prefer it to yon."

"Ay, what's become of that, my lad?" old O'Riorden asked. "I'd be glad to know you'd put it behind the fire."

"Will you leave the boy alone?" Sheila demanded. "There was no place where it would fit in with his scheme of decoration. Dermot's an artist now, not an Irishman."

She spoke lightly. Was I mistaken in thinking there was a hint of bitter raillery behind the words? I glanced across the table, and saw what I had not seen for a long time: the green glint of anger and excitement flash for a second in Dermot's pale eyes. It was gone even as I looked, and Dermot answered easily: "Just concentrate now on the blessings here provided. I shan't discuss either of my two religions with unbelievers."

Sheila took Nellie and Mrs. O'Riorden away to the drawing-room, and we three men sat on at the littered table, smoking cigars. It was the first cigar I had ever smoked, and somehow that, too, increased the nagging sense of inferiority I felt in Dermot's presence. He produced them with an air, and invited us to drink port. I declined, but old O'Riorden took the wine gladly, holding his glass to the light and savouring the liquor lovingly upon his tongue. I couldn't have put up a dinner like this. I had no such home as this, and Nellie could never preside in it, as Sheila could do, even if I had one. And this was not coming out of Easifix Toys, either. Both Dermot and I were now making a little money out of it, but not much. Most of the takings were still going back into the business. All this comfort and comeliness of Dermot's was coming out of the work which primarily he wanted to do. That was where I felt a failure. Determined as I was that Easifix Toys should succeed and make much money, I still regarded it as a side-line. Writing meant as much to me as ever, though still I was doing nothing but fiddling little bits and pieces of work. Sitting there, chewing at a cigar which I failed to enjoy, I had another of those maddening urges to get on with my own job and worry it till I had broken its back.

These melancholy yet charming meditations were suddenly interrupted. Mrs. O'Riorden burst excitedly into the room. "Dermot! Dermot! Sheila's started! The baby's coming!"

This was where, according to the novels, a young husband should go to pieces. Dermot didn't. He got up and flung his half-smoked cigar into the fire. "Get her to bed," he said calmly. "Bill, go for the nurse. She was due to come in tomorrow morning anyhow. Here's her address. I'll go for the doctor. Dad, you— Well, you might as well stay where you are. Finish your port and cigar."

A moment later I parted from him in the street, he going one way and I another, and he seemed far more collected than I was. I pictured myself rushing back, dragging a palpitating and eager nurse, but the staid and middle-aged Lancashire woman whom I found at the address that had been given to me was not to be flustered. "Nay, tha needn't wait for me, lad," she said. "Ah'll mak misen a coop o' tea an' then ah'll be along. When did 'er pains begin?"

The question embarrassed me absurdly. "They're just begun," I stammered. "Ah well," she said, "she's got it all to go through yet. But tha needn't fret. Ah'll be along."

Half an hour after that, when the doctor and nurse were upstairs with Sheila, Dermot and I were in the small coach-house at the side of the garden. He had fitted it up into a lovely workshop. It was ten times the size of the old lean-to shed in Gibraltar Street. Nellie and the O'Riordens were gone. "You stay, Bill," Dermot said; and I recognised in the words the strength of our friendship and the need that was in him, despite his pose of calm. So there we were, as we had been on the night so long ago when first we met, the night when he had fiddled with the work he was doing, and had blazed out suddenly about William Morris, and then later about the

Manchester martyrs. I thought of those things as he moved about restlessly under the strong electric light, tinkering away nervously at a job that was on the bench. I sat on an upturned crate, smoking my pipe; and suddenly I said: "Did you ever see that fellow Flynn again, Dermot?"

"I did not," he answered, rather sharply; and then added: "The man's dead."

He took up a pencil and began to draw with smooth-flowing lines on a panel of wood; and then he threw down both pencil and panel and swung towards me with his eyes shining in his pale face. "It's all over, that," he said harshly. "I had to choose one thing or the other. I've got no use for windbags. I got sick of 'em, sick to death. What do they do but meet and talk and belch out the wind that's in their bellies? If I could have gone to Ireland, and worked for Ireland—in Ireland—and perhaps died for Ireland, I'd have done it. By God and all the martyrs, yes—I'd have done it. But I had to work for my living, and then I got married, and there's Maeve, and there'll be more. So what can I do? Go on being a windbag patriot? Not me! There was a time when I thought I'd be something else. But now I know I won't."

He sat on the bench and swung his long thin legs, and the light burned down on his red hair. "And there's all this," he went on, waving his hand round the room. "Sheila says I'm an artist now, not an Irishman. Well, I *am* an artist. No one's taught me to do a thing, but I can do it, and do it well; and by God, I'm going to do it better. You believe that, Bill, don't you?" he suddenly appealed, with a great need for comfort in his eyes.

"Yes, Dermot," I said. "I wish I could be as true to my job as you are to yours."

"You see," he went on, "wherever it came from, it's there. I know about these things. I know when a thing's right and when it's wrong, and when it's wrong I know how to put it right. I *knew*, as soon as

I saw those pictures in Copenhagen, that they were great pictures. Nobody I've met agrees with me—not even you, you dense old fool. But they will. And I not only know great things when I see them; I can *do* great things in my own line. Can't I?" he challenged me hungrily.

"Yes, you can," I said, and I meant it.

"Well then. I've had to choose what channels I should put my energy into. And I've chosen for good and all. But I'm no less a patriot for that. I'm no less an Irishman for that. I can still give something to Ireland. All that I should have liked to do can still be done. If I have a son, it shall be done. I am not satisfied, I shall never be satisfied, with the position of Ireland under the muddy feet of your bloody country. My son shall not be satisfied with it. He shall go to Ireland, he shall learn to be an Irishman as I am not, as my father is not, as my Uncle Con is not, doling out his dollars like all the other damned American-Irish who wouldn't come back if Ireland was a republic tomorrow. So now you know all about it. Now you know what I want most passionately in this world for my son." His rare pale smile lit his face. "And what about you, Bill?" he said. "What's your scheme for the next generation?"

I re-charged and lit my pipe before answering. "Well, Dermot, it comes to roughly what you want yourself. That is to say, I want to realise in my son all that I've missed myself. I've been poor in a way that even you have never known. I've been lonely and miserable and lacking in all that children should have in a decent world. If I have a son, I just want him to have everything. I'll work my fingers to the bone to give him every damn thing he asks for, and seeing him enjoying it I'll enjoy it myself and live my life over again from the beginning, but differently. Do you approve?"

He looked at me gravely, swinging his legs on the bench. "I don't know," he said. "You'll spoil him."

"I'll chance it. I'll give him a lovely life."

And so, Rory, and so, Oliver, we settled your destiny for you, Dermot and I, sitting there in that room at midnight, with the smoke from our pipes dimming the light, and the merciful veils of the future dimming our eyes.

But Rory was not born that night. That time it was Eileen; and when Rory was born I was not so excited about it, because Oliver was born the same night.

Before we were married, Nellie always called me Bill. After we had got back from Blackpool she began to call me William. I hated being called William, but Bill was too frivolous for Nellie when she had fully entered into a matron's estate. To everyone save Dermot and Sheila she called me Mr. Essex. "Mr. Essex says…" "Mr. Essex thinks…"

When little Eileen O'Riorden was three months old, and Dermot had resolved that Sheila must have a nurse for the children on whose room he was expending all his craft, I walked home from his house in Withington full of discontents. It was an August day, and the pavements sweltered. The nearer I approached to the heart of the town, the hotter I became, and when I turned left at All Saints and faced up the long street that led in the direction of home, my heart suddenly shrank within me. Everything was black and blistered, bone-dry and giving back the day's heat like a desert. Not a tree, not a leaf, not a flower anywhere in sight. In all the side streets I could see men in shirt-sleeves and weary women sitting on their doorsteps or on chairs which they had dragged out on to the pavements. Pale, pinched children squabbled or played in the dust of the gutters. Strident voices from upper windows were calling some of them in to bed. The thought of Dermot's home with its little garden, its few trees and bushes—not much, goodness knows, but so different from this—suddenly rushed upon me with a force which made me resolve there and then to have done with Hulme for ever.

In this mood I reached home, and walked into the living-room—the room that could be so cosy in winter with the curtains drawn and the firelight falling on polished wood and metal. But now, with the heat of the day imprisoned amid the plush upholsteries, with nothing but barren brick to be seen through the window, it struck me as intolerable. Nellie was reading with her back to the window. She got up as soon as I entered the room and said: "William, I'm going to have a child."

I felt neither glad nor sorry, simply surprised, so surprised that I said nothing. Nellie asked: "Aren't you glad?" and I said: "Yes, my dear. Of course. I hope it'll be a boy."

"I want a daughter," she said.

"Well, whichever it is," I told her, "don't let's have it born here. We're well off, Nellie, and we're going to be better off. Let's get out of Hulme—now—right away—and let the child have a start in fresh air with something beautiful to look at."

"But, William, I'd be lost. I've spent all my life here…"

I knew it all. I could have recited it for her; and I said no more that night. But the next day I wandered southwards along the Wilmslow Road. I came to a milestone which said "St. Ann's Square 5 miles," and that seemed to me a satisfactory distance. One wanted to be five miles from the heart of Manchester. I walked on again till I came to a little lane leading down to the Mersey, and just beyond that was a house standing back from the road at the end of a long narrow garden. A notice board said "To Let" and told me where I could get the keys. The agent wanted to accompany me, but I said I would rather see the house alone.

It was called The Beeches, and I knew I was going to live at The Beeches as soon as I had pushed open the front gate. It was a small friendly-looking house, and the length of its narrow garden gave it a remote and quiet air. So long was the garden that, though the two beech trees that gave it its name stood just within the gate, their shade was not daunting to the garden. The close-cut grass was thick and green; rosebeds had been cut in it and were full of blooms. The house was flat-fronted, of good red brick, with a window on either side of the porch and three windows above. Standing in the porch and looking back, I thought the road seemed a nice long way off, and the tall graceful beeches were both grateful to the eye and an assurance of privacy.

Before I had opened the door, I had begun to tell myself what I should do with the house. If there were no bathroom, one must be fitted. There must be four bedrooms: one for a maid, because Nellie would need a maid when she had a child to look after, one for the child, one for our bedroom, and one for my study.

As it happened, there were four bedrooms, and there was a bathroom. Under Dermot's advice, I had the place decorated from top to bottom before a word was said to Nellie. It was not till November had come that I made pretence of wanting to take her for a drive. She thought it mad extravagance, but I protested sternly against the way she was carrying on: straining her weak eyes over the sewing of baby clothes from morning till night. "I don't know why you don't buy the lot," I said. "We can well afford it."

"You don't understand," she said. "Catch me putting my baby into bought clothes. Men don't understand these things."

"I understand that it's time you took an afternoon out of this house," I protested, "and that's the cab. I can hear it at the door."

So we rolled in the musty old cab southwards along Oxford Street and the Wilmslow Road till we came to The Beeches. There we alighted. "Dermot's got a job on in here," I said. "Let's go in and see him."

I told the cabby to be back in an hour, and Nellie and I walked arm-in-arm for the first time up the long garden path of the house where Oliver was born. A few russet leaves still clung to the beeches and a carpet of them spread in gold and brown upon the lawn. It was a still day; it seemed to belong rather to late autumn than to winter. Chrysanthemums were still blooming before the front windows and under a tender blue sky the air was full of the sharp fragrance of burning leaves.

The house had an occupied look, for all the curtains were up. Though I had a key in my pocket, I knocked at the door and Dermot opened it. Nellie and I stepped into the little square hall, which looked more welcoming than I had hoped. Dermot had had a small stove fixed there, and the fire in it now glowed upon us through amber talc. There was room for a little table on slender legs, on which a vase of roses was standing, and for a book-case and an easy chair which stood now companionably upon the carpet beside the stove. Dermot lit the candles on the table. "D'you like this, Nellie?" he asked. "I'm working for a very particular sort of gent."

Then we went into the drawing-room. It was not yet furnished save for a table and a few chairs, but the fire was lit, and when we had drawn the curtains and produced lights the room looked inviting, especially as Sheila was there, kneeling at the fireplace toasting muffins. She had already prepared the tea.

We let Nellie into the secret bit by bit, and she rather grudgingly allowed herself to be persuaded. There was a Wesleyan chapel a few hundred yards down the road, and I think that helped. But Nellie was firm about furniture. I had for some mad weeks been contemplating a clean sweep of all that had been dear to the heart of old Moscrop. But we had at last to throw in the furniture to soften for Nellie the blow of removal. The one room that was completely new was my study. Dermot worked upon that with his own hands and made it beautiful. And when he had finished he took me to the door, landed a foot in my behind, and kicked me over the threshold. "There it is," he said. "Now work in it, you lazy devil."

On a May midnight in the following year when the beech leaves in the garden were in their loveliest green, I walked up and down, up and down, while a cold moon climbed over, and the leaves sighed and murmured, and a light burned steadily on in the window on the first floor. When they told me I could see Nellie and the child I crept upstairs with a heart near to bursting. I could feel it lamming my ribs, and it was not till I had left the room again that I realised I had hardly looked at Nellie. I brought out with me nothing but a memory of a small face with eyes serenely closed, and a little down-tufted skull, and a long thin hand, small and exquisitely shaped, into which I longed to pour the world.

A few hours earlier Sheila's third child was born, and that time it was Rory.

Part II

## 11

It was a hot June day. From the dining-room, while I ate my lunch, I could look down the long garden and see the perambulator in the shade of the beeches. I liked it to be there, where I could see it and think of Oliver's blue eyes gazing up into the wonderland of waving leaves, or of the green shade of the trees falling upon his closed eyelids, transparent and blue almost as the eyes beneath them. When I had finished lunch I wheeled the perambulator up to the front door, and Nellie took the child in and fed him at her breast. Then he was placed back in the perambulator, and I asked Nellie: "May I wheel him out this afternoon?"

She looked at me severely with her myopic eyes. "Can I trust you to be careful?"

"You can that."

"Well, don't be away for more than an hour or an hour and a half."

Those were the early weeks when Nellie was the despot of Oliver's destiny. I begged the boon of her as humbly as a prisoner might crave liberty from his warder.

A moment later I was pushing Oliver along the Wilmslow Road. It was the first time I had had him to myself. The pram was like a little gondola, hung high on big spidery wheels. It was stuffed deep with white bedding, and Oliver's face lay upon the frilled pillow like a peach on tissue paper. I suppose I was a picture of the typical proud father. I was wearing a brown Norfolk jacket and knicker-bockers and a straw hat. Imagine, too, my growing moustache. I was a tall, dark person, strong enough, but thin. I never considered myself handsome, and Nellie, certainly, was no beauty. I looked at Oliver's bloomy skin, and the round delicacy of his cheeks, and the milky blue of his eyes, and the fine proportions of his hands waving ecstatically at life, and I pondered on the mystery of beauty.

So I went down the Wilmslow Road towards Withington, putting my educational theories into practice. No baby-talk. "Trees!" I exclaimed as we passed beneath the green branches that hung over garden walls; and "Horses!" I said boldly as they trotted by. A drover went along with his cattle shambling in the dust, and I thought with contempt of the unenlightened who would say "Moo!" "Cows, Oliver!" I said; but Oliver's silken lids had fallen over his eyes and his head drooped sideways on his neck like a heavy flower on its stalk.

I had reached the gates of the large house called the Priory, when coming towards me from the Withington direction I saw Dermot, pushing a pram. He, too, was wearing the conventional "country" attire of the moment. Norfolk jacket, knickerbockers and straw hat. "I was bringing Rory to see you," he shouted when he was twenty yards away.

"I was bringing Oliver to see you."

Neither of us had seen the other's son. The prams came to a halt alongside one another, head to tail, under the trees that hung over the Priory wall. Dermot bent over Oliver's pram, and I bent over Rory's. Rory was awake, feet kicking, knuckles fumbling into his mouth, grey eyes looking earnestly up at the leaves above him.

"This beggar's asleep," said Dermot. "I wanted them to meet."

"Put your hand behind his back and lift him up," I said.

So Dermot heaved Oliver to a sitting position and held him there, and I held up Rory. Oliver opened his eyes, and the two children gazed at one another for a moment, with solemn scrutiny. Then Oliver's face puckered up in smiles, and Rory, after a doubtful moment, smiled too. They leaned towards one another, each dabbing at the other with unskilful and undirected hands. But soon their hands met and their fingers interlaced. They clutched, smiling broadly, till their dabbings drew them apart.

"Well, what d'you think of that?" said Dermot. "Shaking hands at one month! If these two don't make good friends no one ever will."

We wheeled the prams sedately about Didsbury for an hour; then Dermot went his way and I went mine.

Nowadays, of course, everybody keeps a snapshot record of his children's progress. But photography then was a more cumbrous and ceremonial affair. I have to rely on my memory for snapshots, and there is no lack of them. My visual memory is very good.

I am sitting at the window of my study, looking down the long garden. A year has passed since the day when Rory and Oliver met. It is a hot, still day, and an extraordinary sense of contentment is in my heart. On the desk at which I sit is a novel called *The Unkindest Cut*. Theoretically, I am writing. Actually, I take up the novel and look again and again at the title-page. "By William Essex." I can't get over it. I never have got over it: the excitement of seeing my name on a title-page; but that first time it was like an exaltation. The book had arrived that morning, and here let me say at once that it didn't do much except encourage its author. It was my second novel *Grind Slow, Grind Small* that gave me money and a reputation which, once earned, has never flagged.

Well, there I sat, dividing my wandering attention between the book, and the scrawled sheets, and the scene in the garden. A white semi-circular seat was under the beeches. Nellie and Sheila sat there, sewing, and our little maid was gathering up the tea-things from the table before them. The children were sprawling and shouting on the lawn. Maeve, who was now a beautiful and graceful child, Eileen, Rory and Oliver.

Maeve had ranged the three of them on cushions, forming a circle about her. There she knelt, scrutinising one face after another.

"Eileen is fat," she chanted. "Eileen is a fat dark baby. Eileen will be a fat dark girl. She will never be as beautiful as Maeve, because Maeve is an Irish queen."

"Maeve is a conceited little monkey," Sheila shouted. "You let other people tell you how beautiful you are."

Maeve went on unperturbed. "Rory is a dark fat baby. He will be a dark ugly boy, but Rory is a good boy. Rory is a better boy than Oliver. Oliver is more beautiful than Maeve. Oliver has blue eyes and curly gold on his head. He is the most beautiful baby I have ever seen. But I do not like Oliver. If I put my finger in Rory's mouth, Rory sucks it. But if I put my finger in Oliver's mouth he tries to bite it. But he can't bite yet because he is only a baby. But he will bite when he can."

"And I don't blame him," said Sheila. "Some people want biting."

Nellie said nothing, but even at that distance I could see that she was hurt and that her lip trembled.

It was a winter night, and I had come home tired. Winter or summer, whenever I went to town I walked there and back. I went up now to the Easifix works and offices only once a week. On the manufacturing and clerical sides the staff was excellent. They could do all that was needed to be done. For a number of years I had put all I knew into building up that business. I had no intention of spending my life on it now that I had obtained the men I wanted and trained them to do things as I wanted them done. But once a week I looked personally at the work of almost everybody employed in the Hulme factory and the Oxford Street offices. I never announced my coming, and no one knew on which day I would come. So everyone was kept up to scratch. I made a whole day's job of it and always got home in time for dinner.

Though I was fagged with the day's work, I walked home that night in a mood of excitement and exaltation. *Grind Slow, Grind Small* had been out for a week. Already it was evident that the book was going to have more than a moderate success. The reviews were enthusiastic. There was not a discordant note anywhere.

Dermot accompanied me as far as Mauldeth Road, but we had nothing to say to one another. I was full of my own thoughts and he, I knew, was pondering the biggest job that had yet come to him. A cotton king who had bought an estate in Hampshire and proposed to retire there had commissioned Dermot to go down and furnish and decorate the place. So we jogged along through the winter night, each busy with his own plans, Dermot pulling occasionally at the foxy-red pointed beard which he had grown during the last year.

We said good-bye at the corner of his street, and I went on alone. It began to snow, and soon I was powdered white in front where I met the drive of the storm. When I arrived at The Beeches, I stood for a moment looking across at the house. The two great trees were heavily mantled with snow, and the white road ran on immaculate as a highway in paradise. There was an extraordinary stillness in which the ear suggested to itself the gentle patter of the falling snowflakes. Lights shone from the windows of my house, friendly as a sudden gleam seen in a fairy-tale wood. I had never before felt such happiness on reaching home, such a sense of a haven awaiting me, and of the strength within myself to maintain a place or quietness and beauty to which those dependent on me might turn. And by that, of course, I meant Oliver.

At this time of night, he was being prepared for bed, and it was my turn to bath him. Since he had been two, Nellie and I had bathed him on alternate nights, and not for a lot would I have given up the privilege of lathering and sluicing that dimpled body. His hair had never yet been cut, and it stood out like a halo of spun gold round his brow.

But that night when I got in he had already disappeared, and the sound of shouting and banging from the bathroom told that the bath was already in progress. I bounced up the stairs two at a time and burst into the steamy room filled with a babel of noises. The tap was running, Nellie was scolding, Oliver was beating the water with his feet, banging the sides of the bath with his fists, and howling at the top of his voice.

"Here, whose turn is it to bath the infant?" I shouted.

Nellie dropped the sponge, turned to me with her most infuriating look of long-suffering patience, and readjusted the pince-nez that had been swinging by their little gold hook from her ear. "He was naughty," she said. "I told him that if he didn't behave I'd bath him and put him to bed at once. And he didn't behave."

That was the sort of logical syllogism of behaviour that Nellie loved.

"Sometimes children *can't* behave," I said. "It isn't in them."

"Then they must learn to have it in them," she answered.

We stood and glared at one another through the steam of the bathroom, quiet now save for the splashing of the tap. Sensing conflict between his elders, the child fell to silence and gazed with wide-eyed interest.

"It's my turn to bath him," I said doggedly. I took off my coat, hung it behind the door, and rolled up my sleeves. Oliver suddenly shouted: "Daddy's turn. *Said* it was Daddy's turn." He began to beat upon the water with his fists in furious glee.

"He's glad that you have defeated me," Nellie said quietly. "I did what I thought was right. Will you put him to bed?" And with that she walked dourly out of the bathroom.

I had never put Oliver to bed before. Soaping and rinsing him was all very well; but after that Nellie took over and performed the mysteries of powdering and clothing him and brushing up the halo of his hair. Well, I wasn't going to be defeated. I did all that I had so often seen Nellie do, Oliver all the time crooning with delight as though exulting in a male victory, and dabbing me in the face with his fists. At last I got him into his cot alongside our bed, kissed him good-night, and then, when I had washed, went down to dinner.

"Did you say his prayers?" Nellie asked.

"No, I forgot them."

She went frowning upstairs, and, standing in the little hall, I could hear her through the open bedroom door. "Oliver, say after Mummy: 'Gentle Jesus'…"

"Oliver not say."

"Oliver say: 'Gentle Jesus'…"

"Oliver NOT say. Daddy's turn. Daddy didn't say."

There was a pause, then Nellie said: "Good-night, then."

"Oliver NOT say goo-night."

I had slipped into the dining-room before she got down, and I was ashamed to look her in the face. Dinner was a silent meal, and when it was done she set off for her weekly class meeting at the Wesleyan chapel along the road. I pulled aside the curtain of my study window on the first floor and watched her go down the long white garden path through the snow that was still falling. She paused for a moment at the gate and looked back towards the house, as though she would for once give up her precious meeting and turn back to the child from whom she had parted in ill-will. Then she went on, a grey responsible figure, and as I turned towards the hearth in the lovely room that Dermot had made, my heart was riven with pity for the woman whose wandering steps out there were symbolical of her separation from all the things that meant so much to me.

I wonder if you will ever understand how I feel about pyjamas? When I was a child I always slept in my shirt. Worn day and night, it had to do duty for a week. Even when I was with Mr. Oliver I continued to sleep in my shirt. It was Dermot who said one night, soon after my arrival in Gibraltar Street: "Why don't you buy yourself a night-shirt?" I did so; and I wore a night-shirt then until I married. But I bought pyjamas to take with me to Blackpool, and, as that was a honeymoon, they were rather special pyjamas. Whenever I thought of sleeping in my shirt, a shiver of retrospective shame would get hold of me. I became absurdly conscious where night-clothing was concerned. My pyjamas became at first more and more resplendent, then the "froggings" of coloured silk offended me, and I entered the period of plain sumptuosity: rich silken materials, unadorned, with dressing-gowns to match.

A week before Oliver was five years old I went up to London to see my publisher. After lunch I walked alone through the West End shopping streets, looking for something to give Oliver for his birthday. In the window of a child's outfitters' shop I saw a suit of pyjamas: plain black silk. There was a little dressing-gown of black silk alongside them, with a broad silk belt that was finished off by a crimson fringe. I bought the outfit and took it back with me to Manchester. Travelling first, with the small parcel in my suit-case on the rack, I thought what fun it would be to see Oliver in that apparel, with the slippers of soft red Morocco leather that, also, I had bought. It would help me to think with more complacency of the small boy sleeping in his day-shirt. It would help me to kill and bury that small boy.

It was a warm May day when Sheila came with Maeve and Eileen and Rory to the party that was to celebrate the two birth-days. The children played together on the lawn for an hour before teatime; and when Sheila and Nellie were preparing the tea-table in the dining-room, I smuggled Oliver upstairs and dressed him in the outfit of which I had said no word to anyone. I washed his face and brushed up his hair. He looked delightful in black and scarlet, tall already for his age and as straight as a young tree. There were times when his beauty startled me, and that afternoon was one of them. His face, with its vivid blue eyes, full red lips, and crown of golden curls, was like the face of a Reynolds angel. His playing about in the garden had heightened his colour, and the joy of his new splendour brightened his eye. He was as pleased as Punch, and as proud as a pasha, strutting about the room, and examining himself in the long mirror, his hands thrust into the dressing-gown pockets.

"Now we'll show them how lovely you look," I said, and we went downstairs with his small hand in mine.

They were already at the table. Nellie blinked from behind the teapot, and asked practically: "Where did Oliver get those clothes from? And why is he dressed for bed?"

"Sure his father's showing him off. Can't you see that?" Sheila demanded. "Is this his birthday present, Bill?" and when I nodded, she took Oliver on her knee and asked: "And doesn't he look a fair treat?"

"He's forgotten his manners," said Maeve loudly, surprising us all. She was not a bit perturbed by the grown-up interrogation of our stare. Maeve was turning into a self-possessed young woman, as beautiful in her dark way as Oliver was in his.

"Just remember you're Oliver's guest, Maeve," said Sheila. "You shouldn't be finding fault with your host."

Oliver put an arm round Sheila's neck and looked triumphantly at the snubbed Maeve. But Maeve was not easily to be snubbed. "It's because we're his guests that I think he's forgotten his manners," she said. "He should have shown us before tea where to wash our hands and—and that. Instead of togging himself up like—like... Oh, what *is* he like? He's not like a boy. Ugly's like a boy." (Ugly was her name for plain, dark Rory.) "He's just like something that makes me laugh. Ha, ha!"

It was one of Maeve's remarkable qualities that she could laugh with complete conviction whenever she wanted to, just as a good actress can; and she laughed now, a long loud silvery laugh, pointing derisively at Oliver. She set Eileen off, and Rory, too, and in a moment all three of them had reached that uncontrollable state when they couldn't have stopped laughing had they wanted to.

Oliver glowered for a moment at the three faces contorted by laughter, his own face slowly reddening with passion. He leapt from Sheila's lap, tore off the dressing-gown and danced upon it in his red slippers. He pulled off the jacket of his pyjamas and threw that to the ground, too, and had laid hands on the girdle of his trousers, when Nellie picked him up and carried him kicking from the room. I leapt to open the door, and she gave me a bitter look as she went through. "This is *your* conceit, not the child's," she said in a low voice. "Your nonsense will ruin him."

Nothing would induce Oliver to wear his pyjamas and dressing-gown after that. "Rory laughed," he said with a scowl. It was the sight of Rory's puckered-up face of a merry little monkey that had been too much for him. For Rory was beginning to be more important to Oliver than any of us.

Miss Bussell's school was half-way between Dermot's house and mine. Maeve had been going there for some years, and now Eileen began to go, too. Sheila's nursemaid would set off in the morning with the three children and a mail-cart. This was for Rory to ride in when he was tired, but it was not often that Rory would admit that he was tired. He was short and dark, sturdy on his legs, with a growth of obstinate thick black hair, and those very dark blue-grey eyes that are smudged into some Irish faces. He was always merry and smiling, but there was a comical pugnacity about his square jaw and pudgy nose. He looked the sort of boy who would grow into a bruiser. Maeve's name for him had developed into Ugly-Mugly.

The maid left the two girls at Miss Bussell's, and then brought Rory on to The Beeches. She would take him back in time to collect the girls when school was over, and he would come again in the afternoon.

Oliver was always on tiptoe upon the low garden wall, peering over the iron railings that surmounted it, when Rory was due. He would dance with impatience at delay, and rush out of the gate as soon as his friend appeared. Morning after morning, sitting at my window, I saw the two of them run in from the road, come to a halt, panting, on the lawn, and shout: "Now!" They were like a whippet and a terrier, ready for fun.

They were aware that there was a war on. For weeks they played Britons and Boers, banging at one another with toy pistols from behind the boles of the beeches. Oliver loved to be an Englishman, and for days on end Rory had contentedly been a Boer.

We had reached the stage now, Oliver and I, of talking every night. The ritual was unchanging: the bath, prayers conducted by Nellie, a tale from Hans Andersen read by me, and then: "Let's have conversations." Oliver bounded up and down on his bottom in the cot as he propounded the formula. He loved conversations.

"Let's have conversations about Boers," he said one night. "What *are* Boers? Are they men?"

He looked at me with troubled young eyes, half-expecting to hear that they were fabulous monsters such as the fairy-tales told him about. I had always talked to him as gravely as to a grown-up, and I said: "Yes, Oliver, Boers are men just like me and Uncle Dermot. Perhaps braver than me."

"Why are we fighting Boers?"

"Because we are greedy. They've got something that we want to steal from them."

He continued to regard me with wide eyes, as though inviting me to continue this unexpected line of argument.

"You see," I said, "the Boers are simple Dutch farmers. They went to live in the country where they are now just because it was a good country for farmers, and we didn't mind that a bit. Then it was found that the country was full of gold and diamonds, and the greedy English wanted the gold and diamonds for themselves, so they picked a quarrel with the Boers so as to have an excuse to steal their country. And the Boers are brave men, trying to keep their country for themselves."

Oliver went to sleep murmuring: "The Boers are brave men," and the next day when the game was begun by Rory, who had for so long been so patiently a Boer, Oliver shouted: "You are English. I am a Boer."

Stocky little Rory stood suddenly still and defiant in the middle of the lawn. "I am not a damned Englishman," he declared. "I am an Irishman."

He glared fiercely at Oliver. They faced one another, grasping their toy pistols in their hot hands. Suddenly Rory fired, exploding the "cap" in the pistol loudly in Oliver's face. In accordance with the rule that whoever got in his shot first had won, Oliver obediently fell dead. Rory placed a foot on his chest and scowled at him. "Damned Englishmen," he said.

I concluded that Dermot had already begun the education of Rory.

## 12

I have pointed out that when you were walking along the Wilmslow Road towards The Beeches there was a lane that turned off to the right. It was very pleasant in those days. On the left was the high garden wall of a house, the red brick draped by the drooping branches of beech trees, and on the right you looked across parkland to a fine white stucco house. At the bottom of the lane were meadows through which the Mersey went a mazy twisting way between banks that had been raised very high to keep the floods out of the fields. From there I could see the red sandstone church at which my benefactor Mr. Oliver had ministered so long ago.

Not so long, either, when I looked at it in point of years; but when I went down to the meadows to play football with Oliver, it seemed an age since a boy of twelve began to sleep in Mr. Oliver's loft and to learn to read and write. A boy whose life was so different from Oliver's! There was always for me an intense satisfaction in that thought. It was difficult, looking up at the little eminence on which the church stood, not to snatch Oliver up and cry: "You shall have everything! Everything!" Because I was giving it all to myself through Oliver.

There was the question of football boots. It was in the winter after Oliver's sixth birthday. He occasionally went out alone now, little jaunts down the village street and back. One day he returned to tell us that there were football boots in the boot shop and that the smallest pair would fit him.

"What do you want with football boots?" Nellie asked. "When you go to play football, wear your oldest boots. That will be a good way to wear them out."

Nellie would never understand that there was no need to "wear out" everything. She disliked seeing clothes disposed of till they were threadbare, boots and shoes till soles were parting from uppers.

"But I want *real* football boots," Oliver protested. "How can I play real football without real boots?"

"You're having too much, my boy, that's what's the matter with you," Nellie said severely. "It would do you good to be without a thing or two now and then. How many boys d'you think there are in the world who've got what you have?"

"But if Daddy can buy me things, why shouldn't he?"

"All right. Wait till it's *you* who have to do the earning."

Nellie loved the boy with a passion that was deepened by her wonder that anything so beautiful should have sprung from her and me. But love to her carried with it a hard sense of duty. She had a Puritan fear of pleasure, and long ago she had reached the conviction that I was bad for Oliver. She never questioned my ruling in anything that concerned him. That, too, was part of her code. I was head of the household; my word was law; but before the law was promulgated she would try to have her say.

Oliver now gave me a downcast look across the table, and for once I was inclined to back up his mother's opinion. There was no doubt about it: he was more and more inclined to think that he had only to wish for a thing to find it in his pocket. I looked at him severely. "I had no football boots when I was a boy," I said.

And that very phrase was my undoing. I thought of the football I *had* played as a boy; the goal-posts chalked upon the end wall of a *cul-de-sac* in Hulme, the ball a tight-bound wad of brown paper, the players a handful of pale-faced urchins, and the consequence of the game for most of us a clip across the ear from our fathers for kicking our boots to bits. Oh, what would one not have given in those days for a field, a football, and a proper pair of boots!

As if the devil himself had put the words into his mouth, Oliver said: "If you had none when you were a boy, why don't you get some now?" and the idea of myself wearing football boots and playing with Oliver flashed so charmingly in my mind that within a few hours there we were, superbly booted, running down the lane that led to the Mersey meadows, dribbling and passing and banging the ball with satisfactory reverberations against the red brick wall over which the beeches drooped their winter arms.

It was a simple game we played in the meadow. We put down our overcoats for goals, and look turns at being goalkeeper. A few boys collected and joined us. The space between the coats was narrowed when a boy was "in goal," widened when I was. It was a grand afternoon. I shouted with the boys, got as excited as any of them; and when the light failed, and the evening air grew chill, Oliver and I pulled on our overcoats and walked along the uphill lane hand-in-hand under the brooding trees towards lamplight and firelight and tea and muffins, and there seemed nothing so crazy in the world as the idea that a boy shouldn't have all he wanted.

And who wouldn't be charmed to do anything for Oliver? He had a gracious way with him that went straight to your heart. We had extended the times of our intimacy. Instead of reading to him after he had been put to bed, I now had him in my study every evening between teatime and his bedtime, which was at half-past six. We had no prearranged way of passing the time. Sometimes we would talk; or I would read to him; or he would read to himself, or draw, sprawled on the mat, while I read. He drew very well, and I took care that there was always a good supply of paper and pencils.

By now, too, he had his own room. This was our second adventure in escape from old Moscrop's furniture. Oliver's room was very simple. His divan bed, a book-case to hold his favourite books, an easy chair to curl in, and a small chair against the table: that was all it came to. Nellie thought it bleak and uncomfortable. She wanted to load the walls with pictures, but I hardened my heart, knowing what sort of pictures they would be.

Well, that night after football Oliver was in a talkative mood. He roamed along the book-cases, and presently pulled out a book at random and looked through it, as he would often do, for a word he didn't know. It was one of our favourite games at that time. Endless "conversations" which he still loved, began with a word. I lit my pipe and waited for him. He brought the book to the hearthrug and lay full length at my feet, with his head to the fire. "Covetousness," he announced at last, boggling the pronunciation. "What does covetousness mean?"

"It means wanting what isn't yours."

"Like the English people wanting the gold and diamonds that belonged to the Boers?"

"That's right," I said. "That's a good illustration."

"Is covetousness wrong?" he asked, stumbling again at the word.

"It's like a great many other things, my dear boy. If you allow it to get the upper hand of you, so that you would even steal in order to have the thing you covet, then it is wrong. You see that, don't you?"

He nodded gravely, and I went on: "But you can say to yourself: 'I don't want that thing, because I should have to do something wrong to get it.' And so you kick your covetousness out of the home."

"But we won the war, all the same," he said. "You said we did wrong to steal the gold and diamonds from the Boers, but we won the war. So you can do wrong and win."

This startled me, and I said rather heavily: "You may win for a time, but in the long run it doesn't pay to do wrong."

"Well, how long does it pay? Do we get the gold and diamonds now?"

"It depends on what you mean by we. Some gentlemen with queer-sounding names will get them, no doubt. The rest of us will pay more for our tobacco and other things in order to pay for the war."

Then he wanted to know how tobacco could pay for a war. That was how our "conversations" usually went, ranging far indeed from their start. Soon I was trying to give him some idea of how everything that a country spent had to come out of the pockets of the people in the country; and then we were interrupted. There was a loud tattoo at the door, and Dermot's voice shouted: "May I come in, Bill?"

Rory was with him, and Rory rushed into the room, shouting: "Where's *The Cuckoo Clock*? I want *The Cuckoo Clock*."

"You want a smack on the bottom," said Dermot, his red beard bristling with mock anger. "Is that the way to dash into a gentleman's room, heathen that you are! Say good-evening to your Uncle Bill and to Oliver."

"I left *The Cuckoo Clock* yesterday."

"And what may the cuckoo clock be?" I demanded.

"The devil take you," Dermot said. "You to be calling yourself a man of letters and you've never heard of *The Cuckoo Clock*. Does the name of Mrs. Molesworth mean nothing to you?"

"My infant mind was suckled on the classics," I declared.

"So is *The Cuckoo Clock* a classic," Dermot answered; "and now let's have it, for this child will give me no peace till I've finished reading it to him."

"Rory took it home," Oliver announced.

"No!" said Rory. "We read it in your room, and I left it there yesterday."

"You took it home," Oliver repeated.

"He did not then, my young cock," said Dermot, "unless he lost it on the way, because I was there when he got home, and there was no book with him then."

Oliver looked Dermot full in the eye. "We'd better look in my room," he said.

*The Cuckoo Clock* was not on the table. It was not on the floor. "And it's not in the book-case," said Oliver. "You took it, Rory. I remember."

We cast our eyes along the books in the case. There was no *Cuckoo Clock,* but there was a book I had not seen before, and I thought I knew every book in that small library which I had myself assembled. The book that caught my eye had been covered in brown paper, and in gaudy lettering done in water-colour down the spine I read: "Adventures." Just that.

I pulled the book out. "This is a new one," I said. "Where did you get this from, Oliver?"

He leapt to take the book from me. I held him back with one hand, surprised at his sudden vehemence. "Here—steady!" I said. Then, as I began to flip over the pages, the colour drained from his face and he stood deadly still. I felt my heart suddenly hammer, and I wondered if I looked as pale as he did. *The Cuckoo Clock* I read at the top of every page as it flipped past my eyes. *Cuckoo Clock! Cuckoo Clock!* Liar! Thief! Oliver!

"This looks good," I said. "We'll go through it together. Well, Dermot, you've drawn a blank. Are you sure you didn't lose the book, Rory?"

Rory looked doubtful. "I might've done," he said.

The colour flowed back to Oliver's cheek. "You *must* have done," he cried; and for the first time in my life I could have struck him.

Dermot led Rory from the room. In a moment I tore the wrapping from the book, dropped it behind the book-case and threw the book into Oliver's easy chair, sticking a cushion on top of it. Then I shouted: "Just a minute, Dermot—a last chance," and when he and Rory were back in the room I pulled away the cushion. Rory's face creased in his ugly, attractive grin. "*I knew,*" he said, and went away happy with his treasure.

I didn't know what to do. I looked at Oliver for a moment, and he returned my look, level and unblinking. Then he smiled: the beautiful smile, confident of its power, that I had never been able to resist. I did not return it. I shook my head slowly and walked across the landing to my own room. I shut the door behind me and sat down before the fire.

I had often enough been a liar, as all men are liars; but I was appalled by the easy, winsome grace with which Oliver had lied.

Thief? I ransacked my mind, and could honestly say that never, so far as I could remember, had I stolen a thing. Had I been Ananias himself, and a professional pickpocket, I should nevertheless have felt at that moment as though a plank had been kicked out of the very floor of my life and I had glimpsed an abyss beneath.

For it was not enough that Oliver should be as good or as bad as I was. He *must* be better than I was. He was more than himself. He was myself, going on from the point where I had left off. All this had been implied in every thought I had had of the child. I felt face to face with some tremendous treason against my deepest faith.

I walked across the landing again to his room. There was a lamp hanging from a hook in the ceiling. Someone had come and lit it, and Oliver was beneath it, curled into his chair reading. The light fell upon his fair hair and the smooth childish curve of his cheek. He placed the open book face downwards on his knees and looked up with a smile. It was a smile so completely unconscious of offence that I was puzzled, almost baffled. I sat upon the hearthrug.

"Oliver," I said, "why did you steal Rory's book?"

"I didn't steal it."

"But there it was—in your book-case. You must have put it there?"

"Yes."

"And you covered it in paper and wrote 'Adventures' on it so that Rory wouldn't know it was his book."

"Yes."

"And you said that Rory had taken it away with him, though you knew he hadn't. Wasn't that a lie?"

"Yes, it was a lie. But I didn't steal the book."

"If that isn't stealing, what *do* you call it?"

He slid from his chair and came and knelt on the hearthrug at my side. "Don't you see," he said frankly. "I took it because it was Rory's. I love Rory. I wanted to have something belonging to Rory. Rory loves *The Cuckoo Clock*, so I wanted to have it."

There was the sound of water flowing in the bathroom. Nellie came into the room. "Bedtime, Oliver," she said, and stood waiting at the open door, looking like an affectionate wardress. He leapt up, and ran to her with unaccustomed alacrity. I said no more, but remained for some time sitting on the hearthrug, gazing into the fire. My heart felt strangely lightened. The explanation had been so ingenuously given that I accepted it without reserve. The child *could* not have invented so unusual a reason. He had done wrong, but in the motive itself I began now to see something that was not altogether unworthy. The more I thought of it the more it seemed to me that only someone out of the common, and rather finely out of the common, would have been trapped into offence by the very purity of his affections. Nevertheless, I said to myself, I had had a shock. I must watch Oliver more closely.

I was still in the room when he was brought in to bed. I did not read to him at night now that we had the afternoon interval together. The only bedtime formality now was prayers. A formality, indeed, I fear it was to me; but I knelt at one side of the bed as Nellie knelt at the other. All three of us sang the first verse of the children's hymn:

Gentle Jesus, meek and mild,
Look upon a little child.

Then we murmured together through the Lord's Prayer and that home-made particular prayer that every child seems to learn, asking God to bless all those people whom the child knows. After that Nellie slipped quietly out of the room. I rolled back the hearthrug, saw that the fireguard was safely in place, opened the window, and blew out the lamp. Then, with nothing but a faint fire-glow lighting the room, I knelt at the bedside and kissed him good-night. He felt warm and smelt delicious.

"And you believe what I said, don't you?" he asked.

"Yes, old boy."

"Then that's all right." He gave a great sigh, as though my good opinion were all that mattered in the world, and turned to sleep.

## 13

Maeve dragged a chair from the house down to the middle of the lawn. Her black hair that had in it a hint of blue sheen fell in a tangled wave about her shoulders. Her skin was white almost as alabaster. Never was there colour to the child: she was all black and white, save that her eyes were as blue as they were black and her lips were as red as coral. In her cheeks and brow there was no colour. I watched from my window her wild, undisciplined grace: the slender loveliness of her legs, the flowing gestures of her arms, ending in her shapely though dirty hands.

She sat in the chair, made a grab at chubby little Eileen and pushed her behind the chair. "Take up your shield," she commanded; and Eileen obediently took up a large saucepan-lid and held it self-consciously. Maeve sprang from the chair and looked at her younger sister. "For the love of Mike!" she cried. "You look like a black pudding. Give me the shield." Eileen meekly surrendered the saucepan-lid, and in Maeve's hand it became at once a shield. "See! Like that!" said Maeve. "Remember you're shield-bearer to the loveliest woman in Ireland."

She sat again, smoothed out her dress, threw back her head, and looked regal. "Captain of the guards," she cried. "My bronze-bladed spear!"

Rory leapt forward, and with a deep obeisance presented a long reed, which, for some reason of her own, Nellie kept standing, one of a bunch, in a porcelain jar in the hall. Maeve took the reed and held it as a queen might, with luck, hold a sceptre, "Stand on my left, Fergus MacRoy," she commanded Rory; and to Oliver she said with a curve of her long white hand: "Husband, stand on my right."

When Maeve sat, Eileen and Rory seemed of her own height. Oliver, standing on Maeve's right, out-topped them all. The summer afternoon's sun shone on the little group: on the red dress of queenly Maeve, who knew from childhood, what her colours'were; on the crumpled green of dumpy and earnest Eileen; on Rory, standing straight and stocky on Maeve's left, his honest eyes looking forward with great earnestness from beneath his tangled mat of hair and his broad low brow; on Oliver, slightly scornful of the game, slightly condescending, his shapely curly head on its slender neck bowed a little towards Queen Maeve.

"Now, this is what it's all about," Maeve chanted, "and if you want to read it for yourself you can do so in Standish O'Grady."

"I know it all," Rory interrupted. "I've read every word Standish O'Grady has written."

"So you would," said Maeve, "with father pushing him down your throat at all hours of the day and night. But that's no reason, Fergus MacRoy, captain of the guards, for interrupting your queen. Listen, all of you, to this: 'Queen Maeve summoned to her to Rath-Cruhane all her captains and counsellors and tributary kings. They came at once according as they had been commanded by the word of her mouth. When they were assembled, Maeve, from her high throne canopied with shining bronze, addressed them.'"

Oliver gave a supercilious glance at the empty air above Maeve's head. Unheeding the implication, while Rory gazed stonily ahead, Maeve went on in her rich and ringing voice that I could have listened to all day: "'She was a woman of great stature, beautiful and of a pure complexion, her eyes large and full and blue-grey in colour, her hair dense and long and of a lustrous yellow.'"

She flashed a scornful look at Oliver, as though daring him to comment upon that. Oliver returned the look with a smile which she refused to accept. "'Of a lustrous yellow,'" she repeated. "'A tiara of solid gold encircled her head, and a torque of gold her white neck.'"

"What's a torque?" Eileen demanded.

"For the love of God," said Maeve passionately, "what should a torque be, by the very sense of the words I'm speaking, but a thing to go round the neck?"

Eileen drooped her head in contrition. Rory turned and gave her his rare crooked smile; but added: "If we don't understand it, let's shut up. The thing is to feel it."

"'Her mantle of scarlet silk, very fine,'" Maeve proceeded, looking down with satisfaction at her red dress, "'was gathered over her ample bosom in the ard-regal brooch of the high sovereignty of Connaught. In her right hand,'"—shaking the reed—"'she bore a long spear with a broad blade of shining bronze. Her shield-bearer stood behind the throne. On her right hand stood her husband; on her left Fergus MacRoy, captain of her guards. Her voice, as she spoke, was full, clear and musical, and rang through the vast hall…'"

"Saying," cried Rory in sudden excitement, "'It is known to you all that there is not in Banba, nor yet in the whole world, so far report speaks truly, a woman more excellent than myself.'"

Maeve rose from the chair and threw down her reed. "Just because you know it by heart," she cried, "is that any reason for shouting and spoiling everything? You're just reciting it. I want to *act* it. Don't you know that it's silly tosh till it's acted? I was going to give you all parts."

Rory's face blanched and his fists clenched. "What d'you mean tosh?" he demanded, advancing his round little head as near as he could to Maeve's face. "It's poetry. You ask father. It belongs to the time when Ireland was the land of saints and scholars. Don't you call it tosh."

"You spoiled the acting," Maeve charged him.

"What if I did? You're always acting."

"So I am, then, and so I'll always be."

They glared into one another's faces, Rory with his fists clenched at his sides, Maeve tall, white and scornful. Eileen stood by perplexed, clumsily holding the saucepan-lid. Oliver, practically, recovered the fallen reed.

Slowly a smile spread over Maeve's face, and Rory's hands at that sight uncurled. "Of course I'm always acting," said Maeve, "and who wouldn't want to act lovely poetry like that?" She skipped merrily under the beech trees.

"It *is* poetry. Isn't it?" Rory demanded.

"Of course it's poetry, you ugly little patriot," said Maeve. "How couldn't it be when it's about a lovely woman called Maeve?"

I wasn't seeing so much of the children now because they were all by this time at Miss Bussell's. But that was a Saturday afternoon, and on most Saturday afternoons they were at The Beeches, because the garden there was better for playing in than Dermot's. Maeve at that time was always trying to get them to act: she was mad about acting. You would see her strike poses when she was all alone; but usually the game broke down on some silly quibble like the one that afternoon.

Dermot's children stayed to tea, and then Rory and Eileen set off for home. "Take care of Ugly and mind how you cross the roads," said Maeve to Eileen in a superior grown-up fashion. She was trying hard to be self-controlled, but I could see that she was jumping with excitement inside, for I was taking her that night to the Theatre Royal.

"I'll take care of Ugly," Oliver suddenly announced. "Let me go with him."

"And who'll take care of *you* on the way home?" Nellie demanded, appearing out of the house. "I think I'd better walk with you; then you and I can come back together."

Oliver's colour deepened. "I am big enough to look after my friends," he said.

"But Rory's as old as you are," Nellie argued obtusely; and I could almost see the answer forming in Oliver's mouth before he spoke it. "But don't you *understand*! I'm only pretending to take care of Rory, because I want to be *with* Rory."

He stood and glared at the uncomprehending adults to whom all his thoughts had to be explained.

"Very well," said Nellie. "But don't go farther than the Priory. And mind the crossings on the way back."

"Oh, as if I wouldn't," said Oliver; and he seized Rory's arm and hurried him away, leaving Eileen to toil after.

As soon as they were gone, Maeve clutched my hand and squeezed it frantically, all grown-up pretence vanished. "Oh, Uncle Bill! Won't it be lovely! Lovely! The first time I've ever been to a theatre!"

I patted her slender hand. "And lovely for me, too," I said. "This will be the first time I've ever taken a lady to the theatre. D'you know that?"

"No!"

"Yes! It's going to be a grand night for us both. But I wish it was the depth of winter."

"Why do you wish that?"

"Because that's the time for going to the theatre, and because we're going to have dinner first in a restaurant, and the winter's the best time for doing that, too. You go in out of the cold draughty streets and get a lovely slap in the face from the smell of soup and fish and meat and pastry and gaslight. Oh, yes. That's much nicer in the winter."

"We're *not* going to a restaurant!"

"Oh, yes, we are."

She was so excited that she didn't answer. She merely looked down appraisingly at her red dress. "That'll do," I said with a smile. "That'll do fine. I'll be proud to be with you. Now if we were in

London I'd put on a lovely white shirt; but I needn't do that in Manchester, not even for the stalls, where I've got seats. Not even for Henry Irving and Ellen Terry."

We had gone into the house and were climbing the stairs to my study, Maeve still hanging on my arm. "Oh, tell me about them," she said with a squeeze.

"Now what's the good of telling you when you're going to see them with your own eyes inside a few hours?"

"Well, tell me about the play," she insisted as we went into the study.

"Here's somebody who can tell you about that better than I can," I said, pulling Lamb's *Tales from Shakespeare* out of the book-case. "But I expect you've read this already."

"I have not then," she said, seizing the book and throwing her lithe young body into a chair. "It's all Irish stuff we get at home. You'd never believe—it's all wonderful or all woeful. Marvellous tales of Cuculain and the heroes, or miserable tales about patriots and potato famines. I'm getting sick of it, but Rory laps it up. And there's such a lot in it about hating the English. I don't hate you, Uncle Bill. Why should we hate the English?"

"I don't see any sense in hating anybody," I said, rather professorially.

"Well, then, I wish you'd ask father to give us a change."

"Ah, that's another matter. Get on with that while you have a chance."

So Maeve drew her long legs up under her on the couch and settled down to *The Merchant of Venice*. I filled a pipe, pulled a chair to the open window, and sat looking down the long front garden towards the beech trees.

"This will be the first time I've ever taken a lady to the theatre." Extraordinary! Before my marriage I had had little time for the theatre. I had gone occasionally with Dermot; less often with old

O'Riorden; but they were not enthusiastic. The old man preferred to have his feet on the hob and Dickens on his lap, and Dermot wanted to spend all his time with planes and chisels and gouges. Soon after marriage there came the time when I worked harder than I had ever worked before, harder than I have ever worked since: building up the Easifix Company all day, working on my books at night.

Then suddenly came success with both my endeavours. Easifix took up little time. The mornings were all I needed to give to my writing. In the afternoons I walked. The nights were mine to do with as I pleased.

It was at this time that I tried consciously to draw Nellie nearer to the things that were of my heart's desire. The very effort was evidence of breach. It must have been three years ago now—more than three years, for it was on a winter morning—that I said at breakfast: "There's a grand play at the Prince's Theatre this week, Nellie. What about going along there? We could have dinner somewhere first."

"I don't think so," she said. "I don't like the theatre."

"But you've never been. That is, so far as I know."

"No. I've never been."

"Then how do you know whether you like it or not?"

"Well, I don't approve of it, then."

She gave me the blank and dogged look with which I knew there was no arguing.

"Well, we could do something else. If we only had a bit of dinner in a restaurant. We might go on to a Hallé concert. You don't object to music, do you?"

"I don't see any sense in wasting money in restaurants," she said. "The food's nothing like so good as we get at home, and it costs about four times as much."

"I don't call it waste," I defended myself. "You pay for more than the food—the change, the service—all that."

"I hate eating in public, and I dislike waiters hovering about."

I found it difficult to be patient; but I persisted. "Well, if there was a Hallé concert you thought you'd like, we could have an early dinner here and go straight there."

She shook her head, got up, and began piling the breakfast things, a job she could never leave to the maid. "What would be the good?" she said. "I don't understand music, and I should feel out of place. Besides, I don't want to leave Oliver at night."

I knew this was the last time I should ever try to walk in step with Nellie. I would see it through. I strode over to the fireplace and stood there filling my after-breakfast pipe. "Nellie," I said, "just leave the things alone for a moment and listen to me."

She ceased her clattering and sat down. "What's wrong with leaving Oliver?" I asked. "We're fairly rich people, and so far as I can see, we're likely to get richer. If I wanted to do it, or if you wanted to do it, we could leave this house tomorrow and go into one twice as big, where there'd be room for a nursery-governess who'd have nothing to do but give all her time and thoughts to Oliver. Would you like that?"

She shook her head slowly.

"Why not? It would give you much more freedom."

"I don't want it!" she burst out. "I don't want women looking after the child. Can't you see that he's got too much already? Don't you know that you're ruining him by pouring into his lap anything he thinks or dreams of? I'll look after him myself. It won't do him any harm to see there's someone who's not gallivanting about and having this and having that. And I don't want a new house. I never wanted this house. I never wanted servants about me. I was happy where I was."

"Servants?" I raised an eyebrow, thinking of our one small maid; but it was no use. Had I been squandering our last few sovereigns on uniformed flunkeys I clearly could not stand more deeply damned in Nellie's eyes.

So I had never taken a lady to the theatre, which, I thought with a wry smile, sitting at the open window, was one of the pleasures of life that a civilised man should have pretty often. I had accepted the situation: that Nellie and I must rub along as best we could. After all, I had never pretended to love Nellie. I had nothing to blame her with. There was a lot with which I might blame myself. I had given her a great many things which, I saw with increasing clearness, she did not value in the least. She was stubborn, narrow, but, above all, she was honest and of integrity. She had a dislike and distrust of affluence which I now believe to have been grounded in reason. She didn't like the smell of riches, and I myself have more and more come to think that riches have a bad smell.

Well, there it was. We lived together; to the end we shared the same bed; we never quarrelled; and things might have been worse.

I looked across the room at Maeve's dark hair which, like a black drooping wing, hid her face bent over the conflict of Shylock and Antonio. Just such black hair as that, just such a healthy pallid face, had been Daisy Morton's. It was soon after that definitive talk with Nellie that I met Daisy. She would be in her middle twenties, I suppose, and she was beautiful and rich and had a quality of generosity that I have found in few women. I mean, her spirit came out to meet you, and you were aware of an absence of bodily prudery that was unusual and delightful. She was not the woman to expect marriage to follow a kiss. Not that I ever kissed her; but I knew in my heart that she was mine for the taking.

I never took Daisy to the theatre, but it was there I met her. I made the habit now of going every Saturday night, usually alone, sometimes with Dermot. It was Dermot who introduced me to Daisy Morton. She was an only child whose father, a cotton merchant, had died and left her all he had. Dermot had been out to Bowdon to overhaul the mansion in which old Sir Anthony Morton had been accumulating costly rubbish for half a century. Daisy gaily bade him sell, if he could get a cent for them, the lush Alma-Tademas and Marcus Stones that sprawled largely upon the walls, and to sweep away the combination of spidery knick-knackery and cumbrous pieces that made up the furniture.

She was interested when Dermot introduced us at the theatre. Novelists were not too common in Manchester then, though I believe they are now almost as numerous as knights, and my reputation had gone considerably beyond the boundaries of a local fame.

Daisy had read my books. She could talk intelligently about them. She criticised them with a good deal of common sense. She developed a habit of being wherever I was to be found. We had a few meals together at restaurants, and I discovered that I was dressing with unusual care.

She was so gay and happy, so full of good conversation, that I, who had known no woman well save Nellie and Sheila, was captivated by her company. It was so easy to envisage a life different from my present one—if Daisy were my wife.

For a couple of months I lunched with her one day a week—the day on which I went into Manchester to supervise the Easifix affairs. It was after lunch one day, when we were shaking hands outside a restaurant, that our hands didn't part. We could feel the hot currents of awareness passing from one to the other of us, and looking into her face I saw for the first time colour burning in her pallid cheeks.

She said: "Mr. O'Riorden has finished now up at the house. You've never seen it. Do come. Do come—now."

Her voice shook a little and I was never more certain of anything in my life than of the meaning of her words. I could go—and it would never be the same with me and Nellie again. I didn't go. I owed Nellie that.

Well, there it was. That's how things were with us.

Maeve threw down her book. "That's a big sigh," she said.

"Come along," I said gaily. "The cab will be here in a moment, and I'm going to take a lovely lady to the theatre."

Although both windows were down, the old four-wheeler smelt of mouldering leather. It was almost falling to pieces. It might have been the very cab from which, so many years ago, I had seen my brother's face looking out as he followed my mother's body to the grave. That was the night I had wandered into Moscrop's: the night I had knocked out the bully who was terrorising Nellie. So much had begun from that night. I sniffed the cab's odours with displeasure.

But to Maeve, lovely summer evening though it was, and all the circumstances hopelessly inappropriate to the theatre, the occasion was perfect. Hatless, she sat back in her red dress, her black hair falling about her shoulders, and watched the trees of the Fallowfield gardens wavering slowly past the windows. Her hands were in her lap, knotted, writhing with excitement. But her voice was unexcited when she spoke. "It's strange, isn't it, Uncle Bill, that I *know* how much I'm going to love the theatre tonight. I've never been, but I love the thought of it. I've been reading in *Villette* how Lucy Snowe went in Brussels to see Rachel act, and I've been reading everything else that I can find about actresses and plays."

I patted her hand. "Good. If there's anything you love very much, stick to it. Never let go till it's given you all it's got."

"I shall," she said gravely. "I want to be an actress. I *must* be an actress."

"Very well," I laughed. "One of these days I'll write a play for you."

She took me up seriously. "Will you? Really?"

I looked down at the blue-black eyes, earnest in the white oval of her face. I was surprised at their intensity. "Promise?" she demanded.

"Honest to goodness," I said. "I'll remember this promise."

"Thank you," she said. "You're a good man, Uncle Bill. I wish Oliver was as good as you are."

"But my child, my child," I protested, "he's got to be *better* than I am—much better."

She shook her head slowly, doubtingly.

"Why don't you like Oliver?" I challenged her suddenly. I had noticed her disapproval of him more than once.

"I don't know," she said, laughing it off. "Perhaps he looks too good to be true."

"Rory likes him."

"Oh, Ugly-Mugly likes everyone. Every night now when he's getting into bed he says: 'God damn England—except Uncle Bill and Oliver and all my friends.' And that means everybody."

"But it's a pity he says that at all."

"Oh, man," she said, relapsing into a touch of Irish that I loved to hear in her, "oh, man, it is that then. He gets it from father."

"It's a pity," I repeated.

"It gives me the creeps to hear it," she said. "'Twas but the other night I rushed downstairs and into father's room when he was sitting smoking his pipe and reading. 'Father,' I shouted, 'some day you'll have something to answer for.' He jumped up as if I had hit him, and stood in front of the fireplace with his teeth biting his pipe hard. He looked at me in a way he's never looked at me before—very pale and cold, and believe me, Uncle Bill, his eyes had little green specks in them."

I knew those little green specks. I said nothing.

"He said," she went on, "'If there's any answering to be done, I'm ready to do it.' So I just went out of the room."

Well, we had a meal, and Maeve enjoyed it because she wasn't used to dining out; but I didn't enjoy it much because I was thinking of pug-faced little Rory so carefully excluding his friends from his damnations; and of Dermot with the green flecks still lighting up his pale eyes, which looked so much lighter now that he had that red pointed beard; and of Maeve, growing so beautiful and talented—hadn't she told me that little story with real dramatic power?—and yet troubled so early by the madnesses of her elders. The Manchester Martyrs, and that brave fighting rat Flynn, and Dermot, and now Rory. A cold whiff of doom seemed to touch my spine. Why couldn't old quarrels die? There seemed to be always someone blowing on the coals. Politics…politicians…I hated them then; and today I hate them more: foul old men of the sea, astride the shoulders of the nations.

We went across the road and saw the curtain swing up, saw Irving and Ellen Terry walk the boards in the grand old theatre where now you can see nothing but shadows mouthing the inanities of little minds. So we progress.

I shall always feel a grudge when I think of the Theatre Royal going over to the "pictures." I have a personal sense that it should have remained true to the drama if only because there Maeve saw her first play, drew her first breath of the purpose of her life. But perhaps by now Maeve herself is forgotten: Maeve O'Riorden who flamed so splendidly and expired so soon. We do not long remember.

For myself, I have little remembrance of the play, but a most clear remembrance of a hot hand that hardly left mine all through the evening, of a small voice that whispered when I bent over her in the first interval "No, don't talk," and of a strange blow that suddenly hit my mind when I heard a voice speaking the words:

> Such harmony is in immortal souls,
> But while this muddy vesture of decay
> Doth grossly close it in, we cannot hear it.

What memory did they stir? And my thoughts rushed back to the fantastic Flynn pausing on an Ancoats street corner at midnight and reciting those words to me and Nellie. He had added: "God bless you," and then he disappeared.

So for the second time that night the thought of Flynn came back to me, and it was somehow with a foreboding heart that at last I found myself holding Maeve's hand among the jostling crowd in the gaslight outside the theatre. I looked down at her small form, and she looked up at me with a face illumined by more than the gaslight. "I'm so happy," she said, "so happy and so tired."

I got her into a cab and sat her upon my knee, with her head upon my shoulder. Although it was a fine summer night there was a nip in the late air, so I opened my coat and pulled it round her. She was asleep long before the cab reached Dermot's house.

Sheila came to the door and took Maeve from my arms. She looked rather strained and anxious, which was not usual with her. "Thank you, Bill. You're a dear to have taken her," she said. "Did she enjoy it?"

"It was the night of her life," I boasted.

Sheila opened the door into the drawing-room and said: "Good-night, Dermot. I'm taking Maeve straight up. Good-night, Mr. Donnelly."

A clear, pleasing voice from within the room said: "Good-night then, Mrs. O'Riorden, good-night."

"Come on in here, Bill," Dermot shouted, and I went into the drawing-room. Dermot and the man who was with him rose. "This is Kevin Donnelly, Bill. Mr. Donnelly, this is William Essex."

Donnelly shook my hand. "I've heard of you, Mr. Essex," he said in his pleasant silvery voice, "and, what's more, I've read one of your books. Only one. I don't get much time for fiction."

He looked a typical artisan. He was short and thick-set, dressed in comfortable homely clothes. His hair was rather thin, his moustache full and inclined to be ragged, his face as homely as his coat.

"Sit down, Bill," said Dermot. He mixed me a whisky and soda. Donnelly, who had an empty glass alongside his chair, declined another. He remained standing. "If you'll excuse me, Mr. O'Riorden," he said, "I'll be getting along. It's well past eleven, and I've got to get back to town. There's nothing more we can say tonight. But if you're of the same mind when the time comes, you can rely on me."

He shook hands, and Dermot saw him out.

"Well," said Dermot, when he came back into the room. "I'm glad you had a chance to meet Kevin Donnelly. What do you think of him?"

"He looks like a walking illustration of the dignity of labour, as understood by Ruskin and Carlyle," I laughed. "The very stuff of integrity. The firm, hard-working basis that makes it easy for parasites like you and me to keep on top."

Dermot looked at me queerly. "You wouldn't be on top for long if Donnelly had his way," he said. "D'you mean to say you've never heard of him?"

"Never. He doesn't look the sort of chap one hears of, does he?"

Dermot pulled at his pipe in silence for a while. "The conceit, complacency and ignorance of the English are beyond belief," he said at last. "There goes a man who has been working tirelessly, day and night, for years, nibbling away at the very foundation you stand on in Ireland, and all you have to say is that he doesn't look the sort of chap one hears of." He tossed off the remains of his whisky. "Well, well. You'll hear of him."

"At least, I'm willing to learn," I said. "Tell me about him."

"Well, he is by trade a printer, living in Dublin. When he's lucky, I suppose he earns about two pounds a week. He's married and has a small daughter. His family life is of extraordinary purity and beauty, I know. I've lived in his house for a week, and I've talked with many of his friends. I wouldn't entrust Rory to him without taking some personal care."

"Rory? What's all this?"

"I'm coming to it. I've lived with Kevin Donnelly and talked much with him. I've seen his library. Be flattered, Bill, that he's read one of your books. It's a compliment. He taught himself to read. Figure out what that means. And Bunyan and Cobbett are about the lowest point his reading touches. Figure that out, too."

"Thank you. He's read me."

"All right. His writing has the same punch as Cobbett's and that's all the worse for you—that is, if you're interested in keeping Ireland. Have you ever heard—no, I won't ask you. You've never heard of *Ireland Arise!* It's a little sheet that Donnelly writes and prints, and I myself don't know where he prints it. Neither does Dublin Castle, but it would like to. Donnelly gets nothing out of it. The Party funds provided the press and provide the paper. Donnelly does the rest, and the sheet circulates by the thousand. That sheet is one of the things that will help to blow Dublin Castle half-way to Holyhead. Even your bayonets won't stand against the logic of it much longer."

He paused to put a match to his pipe. "Well," he said, "that's your walking illustration of the dignity of labour. You never said a truer word, Bill. Add to this that Donnelly's an orator. Did you notice he had a beautiful voice?"

I nodded. "You've never heard him in full cry. The Party sent him to America a few years ago. One of his speeches charmed ten thousand dollars out of my Uncle Con's pocket. Not a penny for Donnelly, mark you—all for the cause. I've heard him talking to the Dublin toughs on a barrel alongside the Liffey and to the Wicklow farmers, standing on a haycart outside the very door of the village police-station. And he's irresistible every time."

"It's midnight, Dermot," I said. "I must be going home. But tell me first—what's all this got to do with Rory?"

"It's got this to do with it: that Rory's going to be brought up as an Irishman, as I told you long ago he would be. When the time comes, he is going to live with Donnelly in Dublin. I'll board him there, and Donnelly'll treat him as one of the family. He'll go to school in Dublin, and when he's old enough he'll go to the University there. And not Trinity College, either. Rory's going where he belongs, that's all."

"And when is this to come about?"

"I don't quite know. A couple of years."

"I'm sorry."

I stood up to go, and Dermot faced me, pale and angry-looking. "And why should *you* be sorry?" he demanded. "What the hell—"

I placed a hand on his arm. "Dermot, this is something we're not going to quarrel about. We're not going to quarrel—you and I—about anything. But perhaps it's just that I've got a general idea that the world's salvation isn't going to come so much from splitting up as from joining on. See? That's all. Good-night now."

He put out his hand impulsively. "Thank you, Bill," he said. "We won't quarrel—you and I—especially about this. But—just on general principles—God damn England."

## 14

It was Dermot who found Heronwater. I did not move about a lot. I don't want to intrude myself or my work too much into this book, but let me just say this: that by this time my reputation as a novelist stood higher, and my sales were greater, than I had hoped in my most cheerful dreams that they would be. But that seemed to me no reason for rushing away at once to set up house in London. My work had its roots in the North, so I myself stayed in the North, which I still hold to be healthier and more vigorous than the South; but Dermot's work took him everywhere. It took him to Cornwall during the week after my meeting with Kevin Donnelly, and when he had been there for a few days he wrote asking if I could come down and join him. He was staying then in Falmouth. I had been working hard, and welcomed the excuse to take a few days' holiday. I packed a bag and travelled to London, saw my publishers, stayed the night at the old Golden Cross Hotel, and left Paddington for Falmouth the next morning. It was the first time I had travelled into the West country, and once I had crossed the Saltash bridge, leaving Devonshire behind, and had entered upon the strange, riven countryside of Cornwall, with the railway passing over viaduct after viaduct, carrying us above chasms filled with dusky woods, and though tilted, angular pastures, and alongside the great white cones of the clay works that rose against the sky like giants' tents, and giving us here and there glimpses of a distant sea bluer than any I had known, and nearer views of unaccustomed vegetation: eucalyptus and palms and a profusion of hydrangeas: why, then I felt the North fall like a smoky burden from my back and a deep willingness for lotus-eating take possession of me.

Dermot was waiting at the station. Even a few days in that climate—days that had been all sunshine—had put a bronze veneer
upon his pale cheeks, and his red beard jutted forward with aggres-
sive healthiness. He was casually dressed. He wore no hat; his shirt
was open at the neck.

I had nothing but a handbag with me. I gave that to a boy to
carry to the hotel. Then Dermot and I walked together through the
narrow twisting street that led to the Market Strand, so narrow that
two carts had much ado to pass one another. There were a good
many windjammers at their work about the seas in those days, and
when we came down to the strand and the blue sparkling floor of
the harbour stretched away from my feet, it happened that one of
them was coming in under the white towering pride of her sail,
making for anchorage in the Carrick Roads. Already some of the
canvas was dropping from her, shouted orders came faintly across
the water, reaching our ears with the beauty and mystery of all
sound that comes across the sea.

Dermot waved his hand towards the harbour—that loveliest of
all British harbours—towards the great ship, and the little steamers, and the yachts that danced like toys upon the sunlit water,
hulls of yellow and red, blue and green, trembling above their own
shadowed loveliness, towards the green, distant land and the blue
enveloping air. "What did you know about that when you lived in
Gibraltar Street?" he said. "Is it any wonder Van Gogh went off his
head when he found the sunlight of Arles after the grey misery of
Brabant? I feel half-crazy myself. Let's get in and take some of those
ridiculous clothes off you."

The hotel stood just back from the strand, which was then a
more care-free place than you see today. It had no concrete pier
and clicking turnstiles and pierrot advertisements. It was just the
simplest sort of place for embarking and disembarking.

It was thence we embarked the next morning. Dermot was full

of mystery. "You don't think I brought you down here just to show you the scenery?" he demanded. "Get aboard."

I walked down the granite steps, past the wall hung with rags of seaweed and set here and there with iron mooring-rings, to the boat that rocked gently on the water. She rocked and she also shuddered, for she was that fairly new thing a motor-boat. An oily-handed customer, wearing a peaked white cap, was in charge of her. Dermot brought down a large luncheon basket, and then from under the cool sea-smelling shadow of the wall we shot out into the sunlight showering down upon the harbour.

"You don't see this place from the shore," Dermot shouted above the clatter of the engine. "Look at it now."

How often have I looked at it since! But always if I think of it when I am away from it now, I see it as I saw it then for the first time: see Dermot knotting a handkerchief upon his head and shouting: "You don't know what sunshine is till you get down here. Keep your neck covered, Bill!" See the grey old town rising above the water, street drawn parallel above street, the sunshine falling upon hundreds of flat windows that climbed up and up from the water's edge to the high blue of the sky. See the multitudinous craft, faltering under sail before the light summer wind, or driving purposefully under steam, or, like ourselves, roaring under the new power that soon would dominate everything. See the prospect open up, the water stretch away westward to the broad Atlantic and eastward to the lovely landlocked anchorage of the Carrick Roads. I see all that, and the little villages upon the shore as we speed by them: Mylor and Pill and Restronguet, and St. Just, glimpsed at the head of its creek, and over all the blue sky, beneath us the blue dancing sea, and the wind of our going cool to the feeling, as the hovering gulls were to the eye.

And then, when we came to the eastern end of Carrick Roads, to the view of the pillared mansions standing on its hill, the summit of the parkland that rolled smoothly down to the wooded fringes of the water, I saw that there was a way out of the roads.

"You can go right up to Truro," Dermot shouted, "when the tide's high. It's rising now."

And on the rising tide we went up the river, cool between the banks clothed with green fleeces of wood right down to the water's edge. The lower branches of the trees reached out over the water and were bitten off in a long straight line as cleanly as though the tide had had teeth.

No other traffic was on the water. We chattered on alone between the green cañon-walls. Here and there the water drove right or left into a creek where long-legged herons waded till our coming caused them to spread their wide wings and drift away with slow powerful beats. The river twisted and turned, boring deeper and deeper into the green heart of solitude and peace; and I said to Dermot: "Are we making for the end of the world!"

"Yes," he said. "And we're nearly there."

Another twist of the river and we were indeed there. Looking ahead as the boat chugged forward, I could see on the right-hand bank a small landing-place. As we drew nearer, it defined itself as a quay whose side to the water had been stoutly fortified by a wall of grey granite blocks. There were steps leading up to the level land that had been cut in the bank. A few sheds and outhouses stood there, and behind them the trees rose to the line of the blue sky.

"Look!" said Dermot. "Half-way up. Can you see the house?" You could just see it, deep among the cliff-side trees, and you could not imagine anything more peaceful, anything more free from strain and fret, than that house with the elms and oaks about it, and the water below it, and the high lift of the sky above it.

"That's it," said Dermot. "That's what I brought you to see." The engine was shut off. In perfect silence the boat drifted in to the steps. The boatman grasped a ring in the wall and we stepped ashore.

"Heronwater," said Dermot. "That's what they call this place. Lovely, isn't it?"

He strutted up and down the little quarterdeck of quay that was somewhat thrust out into the river, so that you could look up and down, comprehending the whole of the lovely reach in a glance to right and left. We sat on a log and lit our pipes, while the man brought up our luncheon basket.

"It's almighty quiet," said Dermot. "Just listen to it."

It was indeed a quiet that you could listen to, broken by nothing but a few harmonious sounds: the suck and gurgle of the green water at the foot of the quay, the low drooling of doves in the wood, the almost imperceptible murmur of wind stroking millions of leaves. And those sounds, filtering through the sunlight that burned down upon us where we sat, were good.

"And the name of the place isn't a cod," Dermot said. "There really are herons. Look at that one." The big grey bird ceased his slow cruising along the edge of the opposite wood, dropped his long legs, and came to a stand in the tide-ripples. "The place is for sale," Dermot added casually. "I thought you might like to buy it."

I nearly fell off the log. "Good God!" I said. "Have you had the cheek to drag me down here to make an idiotic proposal like that?" But even as I spoke I knew that the idea had hit at my imagination.

"Yes," Dermot said brazenly. "The thing's ideal. You'll never find a better place to work in. The house is quite small. We'll go and look at it by-and-by. I've got the key in my pocket."

"You're all wrong, my boy," I said. "I'm one of the few northern novelists who believe in staying in the North."

"Nonsense. And who wants you to leave the North, anyway? But you ought to vary it a bit. Have two places. Come down here when you feel like it. You're rich enough. I can't help knowing what you're making out of Easifix, and your books must be making a pretty penny."

I said nothing, but sat silent under the captivation of the place and the moment.

"Don't be afraid of the water," went on the tempter. "You're not dependent on the tides. If you climb up through the woods behind the house you find yourself on quite a good road. You can be in and out of Truro in no time. I suppose you'll be buying a motor-car soon."

"Hell!" I cried. "You *are* arranging my life for me! I suppose I'll have a motor-boat on the river next."

"I'd advise it, if you come to live here," said the boatman gravely.

At that I burst into laughter. It was too much. Dermot knocked out his pipe and patted me on the back. "Don't get excited," he said. "Let's have a swim. I've brought two bathing-suits and towels."

"You've thought of everything. I'm to miss none of the amenities of my estate."

"That's the idea, Bill."

He began at once to strip, and I followed his example. "I'll be making a fire, Mr. Essex," the man Sawle said, "an' you can have a nice cup o' tea when you come out."

"That's fine," said Dermot. "Come on, Bill. Did you ever imagine having anything like this on your own property?"

No, I said to myself, I had never imagined anything so heavenly. I stood on the edge of the little quay, the granite warm and sparkling under my feet, and looked down into the green enticement of the water. It was so clear that when Dermot suddenly let out a wild yell and plunged, I could see his white limbs going down and down till his fingers pointed upwards, rose and splintered suddenly the silver mirror of the surface. He trod water, shaking the drops from his red beard, and shouted: "Come on!" Then I was in after him, and we thrashed the water like schoolboys, and splashed one another, before settling down to serious swimming. I was out first, sitting on the steps, half in and half out of the water, watching him float on his back with his beard sticking up like a pennon. "Oliver will love this!" I shouted. He swung over and came over-arm towards me. "Of course he will," he said.

We stood with towels draped round our loins and felt the sun kissing our backs and the warmth of the fire that Sawle had lit warming our shins. We sipped hot tea and ate sandwiches, and then sat down with our backs to the log and our pipes going. It was a grand feeling: the relaxation of body and mind, the sun soaking into every pore, the utter silence.

In the afternoon we climbed the hill behind the quay by a narrow path twisting through the undergrowth of hazel. It led us to the house, standing on a cleared platform of land. The platform was a fine look-out. A stone balustrade faced towards the water, glimpsed through the trees. There was no attempt at a garden: just a big lawn, reaching back from the balustrade to the house. Behind the house the trees rose again, but here a good roadway had been cut, winding through them for a few hundred uphill yards till it ended in a fine pair of iron gates, with the name Heronwater wrought into them in delicate lettering. The gates opened into the high-road and along-side them was a notice board "For Sale." It offended me. I wanted to see it taken down at once. I didn't want anyone else to butt in and snap up Heronwater.

We turned and looked back down the drive. Not a stone or chimneypot was visible. I noticed that each side of the carriage-way was heavily planted with rhododendrons. That would look good in their flowering season. There would be other seasons. There would be winter nights, with the wind roaring down the gully of the river, and the trees moaning, and the water a dark confusion, where wind and tide contended. There would be a great wood fire, and me writing. I could come down with just one servant. But could you desert Oliver? Well, Oliver will be going away to school soon. So my imagination began racing ahead. "Come on," I said aloud. "Let's go and see the house."

The shingled roadway came round in a fine sweep to the front door which looked towards the balustrade. It was a plain and simple house, built of grey granite. Inside, it was roomy and comfortable and unpretentious. The entrance hall was panelled in oak, and one of the rooms that opened from it had a good fireplace that Dermot explained had been brought in from elsewhere. "Adam," he said. "This is the best room in the house. I can see you are already mentally pinching it and fixing it up for your own."

I admitted the charge. This was the room for those winter nights. Plenty of wall-room for books; plenty of hearth-room for logs.

"How much do they want for the place?"

He told me.

"Well," I said. "I hereby invite you and Sheila, Maeve, Eileen and Rory to be my guests here throughout August. The place won't be furnished, but I'll have enough done by then to make it livable. We've never spent a holiday together, Dermot. And Rory has never spent a holiday with Oliver. I'd like it."

"And so would I."

"We'll spend many holidays here together."

"There's nothing I'd like better," said Dermot.

And so it was that it became a convention for the O'Riorden and Essex families to spend August at Heronwater. The one of those holidays that remains most vividly in my mind is that of 1906, when Rory and Oliver were ten, and Eileen was eleven, and Maeve was fourteen, and I was thirty-five. Dermot was a bit older than I.

To begin with, there had been trouble with Oliver that year. He and Rory were still at Miss Bussell's, and on the last day of the term I allowed my walk to take me towards the school, so that I might meet him and walk home with him. But though it was past the time for school to end, I had not met him when I reached the school gates. I had seen other children walking homewards, so I went into the school to see if he was there. Miss Bussell saw me and called me into her private room, where Oliver was standing, flushed and defiant, side by side with Rory, whose forehead was creased by worry. He kept looking uneasily from Oliver to Miss Bussell and frowning in his queer grown-up way.

The white-haired old lady sat in her wicker chair, looking terribly perturbed. "I'm glad you've come, Mr. Essex," she said. "I'm rather worried by a problem of conduct."

Problems of conduct were dear to Miss Bussell's heart. She had plagued me with a good many of them—problems for which growing-up was the only cure. I sat down prepared to hear of another peccadillo.

"You know," said Miss Bussell, "I always give a prize at the end of term for some subject or other. I told the children last night that this term the prize would be for freehand drawing. They were to make their drawings this morning—anything they liked. Miss Dronsfield, who teaches drawing, examined the work during the lunch interval, and brought me Oliver's as the best. But she didn't notice what you can see for yourself if you look at this."

Miss Bussell handed me the drawing. She had ringed it with red ink here and there, and clearly enough inside the rings you could see where Oliver's pencil had failed to work over the incredibly light carbon tracing.

"I'm afraid," said Miss Bussell, in her prim, acid way, "that Miss Dronsfield hasn't seen this week's *Punch*. But I have. And all that Oliver has failed to do is sign his work Phil May."

I turned over in my hand the picture of the Cockney woman with her flaunting feathered hat and her tray of flowers. Miss Dronsfield must be a fool, anyway, I thought, to have imagined that a child would choose such a subject.

"Where does Rory come in?" I asked sadly.

"The incredible thing is," said Miss Bussell, "that Rory, who was sitting next to Oliver, swears that he saw Oliver do the drawing on a clear sheet of paper."

"Yes, I did," said Rory, going very white.

"Will you, please, Miss Bussell, leave them both to me?" I asked. She nodded her head and looked relieved. "I don't want to make a mountain of it," she said. "Naturally, the other children don't know."

"Let's walk home with Rory," I said when we got into the street.

Both the boys seemed glad to be out in the air, away from the magisterial atmosphere.

"Well," I said, when we had walked a little way, "it was cheating, Oliver. You draw very well. You could probably have got the prize without that sort of thing. Why did you do it?"

"Because I wanted to do something so good that Miss Dronsfield would always be saying: 'Remember that marvellous drawing that got the prize!' And that would make me work very hard."

"I don't see how that would help you. It wasn't your marvellous drawing that took the prize. What's wrong with saying: 'What a marvellous drawing by Phil May! I must try and do one as good'?"

"It wouldn't be the same thing," he said. "The point is, I wanted other people to expect me to do marvellous drawing."

"And as it turns out, other people will now wonder, when you do a decent piece of work, whether it's a copy or a tracing. Don't you think you've been a little fool?"

He sighed and looked martyred. "I suppose so," he said. "But I meant well."

"And what about you?" I said to Rory. "Didn't you see what Oliver was doing?"

Rory still looked white—more worried than Oliver, who seemed to see no reason why the matter should not now be closed. "I was putting myself on trial," he said. "I was hoping she'd cane me. She did cane a boy once."

I looked at him, mystified. "Supposing it was in Ireland," he said, the words rushing out of him, "and Miss Bussell was the police, and I knew something that would get Oliver into trouble, perhaps something they'd shoot him for—they do, you know. Well, then I'd have to tell a lie so as to be loyal, wouldn't I? If Miss Bussell hadn't asked me, I wouldn't have said anything. But she asked me whether I'd seen Oliver cheat, and suddenly I thought this was a trial, and I said No."

What could I say to the child, so white, so earnest and over-wrought? In my heart I said: "God bless you, Rory, and God help you," and to him I could only say: "I see. I thought perhaps it was something like that."

We left him at the gate, and Oliver and I walked home. Miss Bussell, I thought, had been up against something that would have surprised her had she guessed it.

What are you to do with a child when you catch him out in wrong-doing? You are aware of so many tortuous streaks in your own makeup, so many small things and great things that you have kept hidden, and which, if known, would make the moralists recoil, that to cast the first stone at your own child would cause you to stink of the Pharisee. Perhaps self-complacency comes into it, too. Whatever those things may be that the world knows nothing of, you are, on balance, a decent person, Well, so will the child be, no doubt. The theft of his friend's book? An attempt to bluff a silly drawing-mistress? Well, Academicians had been known to paint over photographs.

So I consoled myself as I walked after dinner that night over the hump-backed bridge that crosses the Mersey and on to Cheadle. There were so many things I could have done: all, it seemed to me, the inventions of human stupidity: I could stop Oliver's pocket-money, I could send him to bed early for a week, I could take away small privileges. If I were completely demented I could lock him in a dark closet, or I could use a stick on him. At the thought of this, I broke out into a prickle of sweat and my footsteps quickened.

But behind my attempts at gay self-assurance there was a trace of fear, for Oliver's misdemeanours were not spontaneous: they were worked out to the last detail. I remembered the case of *The Cuckoo Clock*; and I had found tonight, on looking for *Punch*, that he had carefully destroyed the traces of his small crime. The paper, which it was customary to leave lying on the hall table till the next issue appeared, was gone, I found it at last pushed below the rubbish of the dust-bin, and precaution had gone even further than that, for the Phil May drawing had been torn out, and doubtless burned.

So it was on the whole with a troubled mind that I returned home.

I was about to run straight upstairs to my study, as was my custom, when the drawing-room door opened and Nellie came out. It was twilight in the street, but in the house it was nearly dark: no lamps had yet been lit. She stood like a grey uneasy ghost in the doorway, and said: "What are you going to do about Oliver?"

"Do?" I said.

She went into the drawing-room, and I followed her. I sat down by the fireplace, but she would not sit down. She moved restlessly about the room for a while, then came to a stand at the window, her back towards me. She was a black silhouette between the drooping white of the curtains.

"Miss Dronsfield happened to be passing by," she said tonelessly. "I was in the garden, and she stopped to talk. She told me what happened at school, and said you knew about it. You might have told me."

"I didn't see that that would help."

"In what way do I help? Am I any help at all now? Do I matter?"

"My dear Nellie—"

She swung round, and demanded in a rising voice: "Why didn't you tell me? Whether I'm anything to you or not, you great man,

I'm the child's mother, aren't I? D'you think it doesn't matter to me that he's growing up a cheat and a liar?"

I had never known her so perturbed. She stood there at the window, grasping in her agitation a curtain in each hand, as though her emotion might overcome her and she needed support. "What are you going to do about it?" she insisted.

"I don't see that we can do anything except give the boy our care and love."

At that she laughed, almost hysterically. "Love!" she cried. "A pretty idea you've got of love! Do you call it love to bring a child up to think he can do what he likes without taking the consequences? Give him everything—more money in a week than I saw in a year at his age, more clothes than any child needs, presents, games, expensive schools, everything he fancies or dreams of—give it to him—that's your idea of love. Well, it isn't mine. Whom the Lord loveth He chasteneth."

She came away from the window and walked excitedly up and down the darkening room. "Oliver is my child," she said at last, "as well as yours. Bear that in mind. I know I'm nobody in this house. I know that the first thing you do when you come through the door is to dash up to your room as though I didn't exist. But so far as Oliver's concerned, I'm going to exist from now on. D'you hear?"

"What do you propose should be done about the present case?" I asked as calmly as I could.

She gave another of her strange hysterical laughs. "The present case! There's more in it than the present case. You love the child so much that you can't see what's going on under your eyes, I suppose?"

In her agitation, her spectacles swung off her nose and dangled from her ear. She brushed at them impatiently and swept them to the ground. "I have found Oliver lying and thieving, and not caring if other people are suspected of his thefts. I have said nothing about it. You have always made the child's upbringing your business, and now when he commits this crime in public, before his schoolfellows and teachers, you are going to do nothing about it."

"Crime is a heavy word," I said. "And as for his schoolfellows, they don't know what happened."

"Does that matter? Does your love only see wrong when it's found out?"

"Don't shout," I said impatiently. "You'll be heard in the kitchen."

"Do I care where I'm heard? The kitchen knows well enough what you think of me. You think I ought to be in the kitchen myself."

It was hopeless. Clearly, Nellie had for years been brooding on the gulf that there was no denying—the gulf across which we found it increasingly difficult to get at one another. And all this had surged up in her mind, complicated by her conviction that I was bad for Oliver.

I got up. "Quarrelling will get us nowhere," I said. "What do you think should be done about Oliver?"

"I think he should be thrashed."

"I don't."

"You haven't got the strength to do your duty."

"Put it that way if you like. If you have no other suggestion, I may as well go."

I went. In my room I drew the curtains but did not light my lamp. I sat in the dark, in no mood to read or to write. I heard Nellie's step pass the door, and assumed that she was going to bed. A moment later Oliver's voice could be heard, murmuring uncertainly, as though he had been awakened from sleep. Then the voice sharpened to a cry of protest: "No! Don't!"

I leapt from the chair, and as I hurried across the landing that divided my room from his, he gave a howl of pain. The door was open. Nellie had placed a lighted candle on the table. She had pulled back the bedclothes and stripped off his pyjama jacket. With her left hand she was holding Oliver face-downward on the bed. With her right she was lashing his back with a cane, "Cheat! Liar! Thief!" she cried. Her face was inhuman with cold fury. The child's cries were terrible. They tore my heart, and every blow seemed to bite into my own shrinking flesh.

I was across the room in a stride, and seized her wrist as her hand was aloft for another blow. "Stop!" I shouted. "Are you mad?"

She turned towards me, panting. "I am doing your work," she gasped.

Oliver had stopped shrieking when the blows ceased. He lay with his head buried in his arms, his body shaking with sobs. In the dim light I could see the weals livid on his skin. The sight raised in my heart a fury that almost blinded me. As on that night when the youth Ackroyd had terrified Nellie in old Moscrop's shop, I felt an irresistible impulse to strike. I tore the cane from her hand and swung it up over my head.

She faced me calmly, though her cheeks were ashen and her breast was stormy with effort and emotion. "Strike me," she said. "That's all it needs now—strike me."

My arm, lifted above my head, remained as though frozen, and then suddenly I felt the cane wrested from my hand. Oliver had leapt erect upon the bed. "Don't!" he screamed hysterically. "Don't hit my mother!" He lashed with the cane swiftly at my head, his face contorted with passion. I ducked, and took the puny blow on the shoulder. Then, as though all life had gone suddenly out of her, Nellie collapsed in a weeping heap upon the bed. Oliver threw the cane to the floor and knelt over her, fondling her and murmuring endearments. She cast herself full-length on the bed and took him in the crook of her arm. "Oliver! Darling—darling!" she sobbed, and he snuggled closer to her, crooning like a dove. "Mummy! Dear, dear mummy!"

I shook my head as though to clear it of illusions and went back to my room.

## 15

That was the first time that Nellie, Oliver and I were caught up simultaneously in an emotional storm. It was the last time. Following upon years of gloom and self-suppression, that adventure into aggression and assertion did Nellie all the good in the world. The next day the three of us were easier and friendlier with one another than we had been for a long time. It was a day of packing. We were leaving with the O'Riordens in the morning for Heronwater.

We had made that journey several times now, and taken two days over it. So we did that time. We were a regular caravan: four grown-ups, four children, our maid and one of Dermot's. As Dermot had guessed it would, Heronwater had grown on me. I was beginning to feel my roots in the North weaken. I was spending money on the place. Some day I should have to furnish a house according to my own taste. At The Beeches I hardly left my own room except to eat and sleep. It was still too terribly old Moscrop's house. And so it was that slowly I was gathering together at Heronwater the sort of establishment I wanted. I had taken a liking to Sam Sawle, the man whose boat we had hired when first we saw the place. He was a bachelor, fond of solitude, and, as I discovered, not prosperous. He was glad to find someone who could give him a regular wage and the sort of work he liked. He was handyman at Heronwater now. He kept the place clean and aired while I was away. He kept the lawn cut up on the look-out; he managed the electric lighting plant that had been installed, and kept the boats in order. There was a flotilla moored now on our little quay. There was the motor-boat which

I had bought from Sawle and christened *Maeve*; there was her dinghy; there was Oliver's sailing dinghy which he had named *Rory*, and Rory's sailing dinghy which he had named *Oliver*; and there was a light praam belonging to Dermot.

Altogether, Sawle had plenty to look after. I had had one of the outhouses on the quay made habitable for him. Its length had been split into two by a wall. In one of these rooms he cooked and lived, and in the other slept. He was a good man with the children. He was patient in imparting his great knowledge of everything to do with boats and small ships, and he had more knack than either Dermot or I in giving them confidence when it came to swimming. I thought of Sam Sawle altogether as one of my best investments. The Cornish holiday was one the children all looked forward to for months before it came; and it was always those activities with which Sam Sawle was associated that roused their liveliest expectations. He knew where the filthiest lug-worms could be dug for bait, and at what state of the tide to fish round the Lugo buoy, and he knew the captains of the great square-rigged ships that came into the Carrick Roads, and would sometimes get permission for the children to go aboard while the ships were still enchanted with the voyage that had ended. They would come back chattering of monkeys and parrots that the sailors had brought from abroad, and loved rolling grand names off their tongues; Antofagasta, Monte Video and San Francisco.

And there we were once more, the whole roistering tribe of us, clattering into the dark glass cavern of London Road station. We had a compartment reserved, but even so we were a jam. The children shrieked at the windows: "Good-bye, Belle Vue!" "Good-bye, Levenshulme!" "Good-bye, Stockport!" as the gloomy soot-smothered suburbs of Manchester slid by. They were all shouting except Maeve, who sat smiling secretly to herself. And I knew well enough what Maeve was smiling about. The children's thoughts were leaping beyond tonight and seeing already the green waterway, and the little quay, and the flotilla that Sam Sawle would have made all bright and gay; but Maeve was smiling because to-night came before tomorrow and tonight we would be in London.

It was going to be a great night for Maeve. Whenever I made one of these rare visits to town, I used the opportunity to call on my publisher. I had written to him a fortnight before telling him to expect me, and in reply he had told me that one of his novelists had written a play, that the "first night" would be the night when I was in London, and the author would feel honoured if I would accept the enclosed two tickets for dress-circle seats.

I had never heard of the author, but both Maeve and I had heard of the grand old lady who was to play the leading part. We had seen her in Manchester, and now we were to see her amid all the pomp and glory of a London first night. Ah, Maeve! No wonder you are smiling!

Maeve and I had dinner alone that night. Dermot and Sheila had disappeared on some errand of their own as soon as we had finished lunch at the Great Western Hotel at Paddington. (We always stayed there, to be ready for the 10.30 in the morning.) They had not returned at dinner-time. Rory and Oliver and Eileen were exhausted by a morning in the train and an afternoon enjoying such conventional delights as a look at Buckingham Palace and a walk in St. James's Park. Nellie put them to bed, and said she would stay and read in her own room in case any of them called. She tied my white bow for me, and said: "You look very nice, William," then went in, with her unfailing helpfulness, to see how Maeve was getting on. She brought her into our bedroom when she was ready. I don't remember what the child was wearing, except that there was a crimson flower in her hair and that her eyes were eager and she seemed anxious that I should find her pleasing. We went down the long, dim, heavily-carpeted corridor side by side, her white gloved hand resting on my arm. She was like a little queen. I noticed as she walked that she was wearing crimson shoes. Her head hardly reached to my shoulder.

We didn't dine in the hotel. I took her to the Café Royal, and she loved the gilt and red plush as much as I intended her to. But there was nothing of childish excitement and chatter about her. It was difficult to remember that she was only fourteen: she was grave and self-possessed, and I noticed what I had not noticed before: that the shape of her breasts was there to see. She looked the diners over, and said: "You're the nicest-looking man here, Uncle Bill. I love you in evening clothes. When your hair is all grey you'll be very distinguished."

"My God, Maeve!" I said. "You're looking ahead a long way."

"Oh, not so far. You're just beginning—just there."

She put a finger to the hair over my ears.

"I'm not!"

"You are. Just two or three hairs."

"Where's a mirror!"

There was no lack of them, and the one I looked in showed me that she was right. Maeve growing up—Maeve who was not born that night when we met Flynn, that night that seemed so little time ago—Maeve growing up, a young woman with ripening breasts, and I with grey in my head! I hadn't noticed either of those things before.

Maeve put her hand on mine. "Don't you like your grey hair?" she asked.

"I hate it."

"I think it's lovely. You'll have quite a lot of it by the time you write my play. It'll make you look very important, and we'll come here and have dinner before the first night."

"Is that another bargain?"

"Yes. And it all depends on you. You've got to write the play."

"I'll do it. Never fear."

She looked for a moment crestfallen. "Oh, man!" she said, "I don't fear so far as your part of it goes. But what about me? Father's not interested. He's not interested in anything except Rory and Fenians and all the silly old nonsense that I hate. How'll I ever be an actress?"

"And you still want to be, very much?"

"Oh, you know, you know!" she cried. "And haven't you encouraged me and taken me to all the lovely plays and said I must go after the thing I've set my heart on?"

I had, indeed.

"Well, come on, now," I said. "Let's see another lovely play—or one we hope is going to be lovely, anyway. And I'll speak to your father and see what we can do about it."

"You will? Oh, Uncle Bill, you darling!" And she sprang up, put her arms round my neck, and gave me a kiss. I felt as pleased as Punch, too. There were plenty of wenches sitting in the Café Royal, but there wasn't one whose kiss I would have changed for Maeve's. The waiter benefited by an extra shilling on his tip.

The play wasn't one of the high spots in our experience, and Maeve and I had done a lot of play-going together by now. But if the play wasn't much, the occasion was notable. We were wedged into the middle of a bright parterre of silks and feathers, jewels and caressing fans: a parterre from which an expensive perfume was exhaled and a light chatter of conversation floated. Looking sideways, I could see Maeve's dark head etched against the bulk of a dame whose flesh-creased wrists were all a-clinking and a-glinting with precious metal and stone, as the plumes of her fan slowly undulated before a face that had the staring insolent immobility of a figurehead. I was glad to see that Maeve was not daunted. I knew her well enough to be aware that she was deeply excited by this enclosing phalanx of men and women whose like she had not seen before, by the sparkle of a tiara here and there, by the high pitch of overbred voices, and above all by the expectant sense of the occasion: excited, but not daunted. It was not an easy experience for a provincial child, and I was pleased with her. Only, as the curtain went up, she placed her hand in mine, as she had done that time when first we went to the theatre together. I gave her a reassuring squeeze.

It was a poor play, only redeemed by the acting of the grand old lady whom we had come to see. Maeve applauded her madly when the last curtain fell; and then we were caught up in the press of departure. We had not got far from our seats when a hand tapped me on the shoulder. "Essex! One moment! I want you." It was Jordan, my publisher. The author of the play, it seemed, was one of my admirers. He knew I was in the theatre and was anxious to meet me. I tried to get out of it, but Jordan insisted. "Come on now. You're getting a dreadful reputation. You never meet anybody."

"I don't want to meet anybody."

"People are beginning to say you don't exist."

"So long as my books do…"

"Come on. Henderson is waiting in Mrs. Bendall's dressing-room."

It was a long "Oh!" that burst from Maeve that decided me. "This young woman wants to meet Mrs. Bendall far more than I want to meet Henderson," I smiled. "So let's go."

Maeve pulled her cloak about her and reverently trod for the first time the sordid sacred private ways of a theatre. We went up cold stone steps, and along cold stone passages where gas jets buzzed in wire traps; we passed shirt-sleeved preoccupied men and painted women, and presently Jordan knocked at a door on which was Mrs. Bendall's name. Then we were inside, in a jam of silks and feathers and broad white shirts, of fans and camellias, and high voices clack-clacking. Men and women were standing about with glasses of champagne in their hands, toasting the play, toasting Henderson, toasting Mrs. Bendall, toasting one another. Mrs. Bendall was sitting in an easy chair, with a little table by her side. She was not drinking champagne. She looked quiet and withdrawn, like a nice old grandmother. Her hair was white and now she had a lace cap upon it and a light lace wrap over her shoulders. "Where is my tea?" she was asking as we came into the room. Jordan introduced me and Maeve. Maeve curtseyed as though to a queen. "You dear child," said Mrs. Bendall. "You shall pour out my tea."

The teapot had been placed on the little table, and an attentive swarm of young men and women was waiting to be commanded to pour out. Mrs. Bendall waved them all away. Maeve poured out the tea and handed it to the old lady with a lovely grace. Mrs. Bendall placed the cup on the table, then put her left arm round Maeve's waist. She drew her close to the chair, took the cup in her right hand and held it to the child's lips. "Have a sip," she smiled. Maeve sipped and then Mrs. Bendall drank. "Perhaps I'll get back my youth and beauty by drinking where your lips have been," she said. "D'you think I shall?"

"Oh, madam!" Maeve cried with sudden passionate honesty. "If only you could!"

The old lady smiled sadly. "You mean that, dear child," she said. "You know, if I'd asked that of any of these young deceivers"—she waved her white hand round the noisy room—"there's not one of them but would have said, 'Ah, you're the youngest and most beautiful of us all!' Deceivers! Deceivers! I'm an old woman, and I'm very tired."

She sat quietly in her chair for a moment, then she said: "Now, you drink where *my* lips have been, and perhaps some day"—with a beautiful smile—"you'll be a great actress like Sarah Bendall."

Maeve took the cup in both hands as if it were a chalice and drank with her eyes closed. "I've asked God to do it," she murmured.

The old woman looked at her with wonder. "I didn't know," she said. "I didn't know it was your wish. But who can tell?" She turned to me. "Take the dear child away. I'm very tired." And as we were going she called: "Here! Take this," and tore a rose from a bouquet and placed it in Maeve's hand.

The next day we left the luggage at Truro to be sent by road to Heronwater. We continued our journey to Falmouth where Sawle was waiting with the *Maeve* and a dinghy in tow. The two maids, Nellie and Eileen got into the dinghy. The rest of us got aboard the motor-boat.

"Bags I steer!" Oliver shouted.

"No—bags I"—from Rory.

"All right." Oliver moved away from the tiller.

I had noticed a lot of that during the train journey. Oliver was being very kind to Rory, very self-effacing. Usually, he wanted to be the hero, the leader; but Rory's "loyalty" in the affair of Miss Bussell seemed to have made an impression on his mind. He did not even shout orders to Rory, as he was accustomed to do. That would not have been easy, anyway, with Sam Sawle sitting there in his neat navy-blue, with a white peaked cap, making suggestions in his gentle voice, that seemed to end every sentence with a caressing "midear." Sam was never known to "sir" or "madam" anyone. All the children, and Sheila and Nellie as often as not, were "midears" to Sam. Dermot and I were Mr. O'Riorden and Mr. Essex.

It was when we were half-way along the expanse of the Carrick Roads, flat as a pond and iridescent as a mackerel's back under the evening sun, that he said: "We've got a neighbour this time, Mr. Essex."

That was another thing about Sam Sawle: he was a part of every·thing he was associated with—not an outsider. Heronwater was "our house," the boats were "our boats," and "I think we ought to be thinning a bit of our woods," he would say. And now there was "our neighbour."

"Bought an old hulk, he have, and shored her up bang opposite our quay," Sam continued. "A regular crazy old zany. You never saw the like. I haven't been near 'e yet. I don't like the looks of 'e. He's about the deck all day as lively as a cricket. I must say he keeps her looking as pretty as paint. *Jezebel*, he calls her, and they say he calls himself Captain Judas."

"Sounds lively—Captain Judas of the *Jezebel*," I said; and I didn't like it. A neighbour was the last thing I wanted, and I hoped that Captain Judas would be as temporary as he was unwelcome.

We saw him as we turned into our reach of the river. The sun was still catching the trees high up over Heronwater, but the river was now in shadow. The shadow was deepest on the side where the *Jezebel* lay close in to the bank, herself a deeper shadow, for she was tarred dully all over. On the water side she was propped up with stout wooden posts, and all the masts had been taken out of her. We could see Captain Judas leaning over the bulwarks. There was little to be made out but black-clothed shoulders and a venerable head: white hair flowing down to the shoulders and a white beard flowing down to the chest. He remained immobile but appeared to be watching us intently. Only when the *Maeve*'s nose was turned in towards the quay did he let out a screech in a high childish voice: "Heronwater, ahoy!"

He tore a white handkerchief out of his pocket and waved it excitedly. The children were fascinated by his antics, and Rory could not be restrained from hailing: "*Jezebel*, ahoy!"

That worked like magic. Captain Judas threw open a port in his bulwarks, and, as sprightly as a cat, ran down a rope ladder to a dinghy that was fastened to the hulk's side. He leapt aboard and began sculling across at a great pace.

Nellie looked as though she were disliking the encounter. "You'd better go up to the house," I said, "and take the children with you."

Eileen fell in at her side readily enough, and with the two maids and Sheila set off up the path. Dermot and I, with the two boys and Maeve, awaited the coming of Captain Judas.

He handled his boat with great skill, weaving in and out of our little flotilla, and coming neatly alongside the steps of the quay. He shipped oars smartly and came ashore, bringing a painter with him. Not till he had tied his boat with a swift secure knot did he turn towards us.

He was a man of middle height. His shoulders were immense, but the arms that swung from them seemed disproportionately short and were finished off with small white hands. His feet, in spotless white canvas shoes, were small, too, and he had a light feline tread. The head was worthy of the shoulders, big and well-formed. We saw now that the long white hair that fell from cranium and chin was combed out finely and shone like silk. But you didn't get the full sense of Captain Judas till you looked him in the eyes. They were extraordinarily disturbing, looking out from the root of a thin-bridged nose whose nostrils had an outward flare, for one of those eyes seemed stone-dead, with that bluey-white opacity that you often see in the eye of a Welsh collie, and the other was sparkling with a light that to me at any rate did not seem sane.

"Good-evening, sir," I said. "So I have a neighbour now." I tried to sound more cordial than I felt.

"Good-evening, good-evening," he said in his high cracked voice, running his eye swiftly over our huddled rank. "Judas, my name. Captain Judas of the *Jezebel*. Introduce me."

"My name's Essex, and this is my son Oliver. This is my friend Dermot O'Riorden and his son Rory and his daughter Maeve. Sam Sawle here I expect you've met already."

Judas ignored the introduction to Sawle, but bowed stiffly to the rest of us as I mentioned the names. He was silent for a moment, then said with a grin that was not at all humorous: "Good thing there's a river between us. I hate people—hate 'em like hell. Every Tom, Dick and Harry. Every Moll, Doll and Poll. Every Sue, Prue and—what rhymes with Prue?"

"Well," I said, humouring the madman, "Lou, roughly."

"Thank you. Lou will do. Every Sue, Prue and Lou. Hate 'em. I didn't come over here to strike up acquaintance. Oh, no! Never get that idea into your heads. Don't flatter yourselves. I came to see what you looked like. That's all."

"Thank you," I said, and Dermot added: "Well, we'll be going. It's been a pleasure to meet you, Captain Judas."

"Oh, it has, has it?" he demanded. "Wait! Don't be too sure. Take it as a working hypothesis that I hate you all. That's where you always start with Captain Judas. Perhaps I'll change my views. Perhaps I won't. That's up to you. And d'you know why I hate you!"

He lowered his voice and crept nearer on his light feet. "Send those children away," he said. "They mustn't know."

"Go along, Rory—Oliver. Cut up to the house," I said. They went reluctantly, casting wondering looks behind at the prophetic face of Captain Judas. But Maeve lingered, her eyes round at the strange encounter.

"I hate you," Captain Judas hissed, "because you believe it. You've never inquired into the facts. Nobody ever does. You all believe it just because it's been handed down from generation to generation. But it's a lie! It's a lie, I tell you," he shouted in a rising voice. "I did not betray my Master!"

With that he rushed to the quay steps, unfastened his boat and in a moment was rowing like mad towards the now almost invisible hulk of the *Jezebel*. We stood there in uneasy silence, listening to the splash of his oars and the creak of his rowlocks, watching the white bob of his hair dancing over the darkening water. We watched him clamber aboard, and saw an orange square come to light in the side of the hulk. Then we slowly climbed the hill to Heronwater, and when we came to the grassy look-out I leaned on the stone balustrade and was annoyed to see that Judas's light was visible on what it had always pleased me to consider the uninhabited river.

For a wonder, I didn't sleep well; or perhaps it was no wonder at all. Thoughts of Captain Judas chased in and out of my mind, and I would no sooner fall towards sleep than I would start up from the thought that his one sound eye was boring through me like a gimlet. At six o'clock I got out of bed and put on a dressing-gown, intending to take a plunge in the river, and then to row in the dinghy till I was warmed up for an early breakfast.

To my surprise, Captain Judas was already astir. He was out on the river in his little boat, trailing a line behind him. "Damn the man!" I thought. "He's going to give us no peace. He's stolen our solitude."

I plunged into the water and swam out. I was within six yards of his dinghy, but he did not speak. He did not so much as glance at me. I swam back, dried myself and put on some clothes. Then I got into my own boat. I passed very near to him again, and politeness constrained me to say: "Good-morning. Fishing?"

There was a pocket-knife on the thwart. He took it up and sliced through his line, allowing all the tackle to drift astern. "Fishing?" he said. "No, sir! You don't catch *me* fishing. That skunk Simon was a fisherman. And the truth is not known about that man yet. But some day it will be. It's my belief that he did it. Or Andrew his brother. One or other of them."

I rested on my oars. Our dinghies rocked side by side on the silent river, smoking with morning mists. Captain Judas looked over his shoulder, searched the wooded banks right and left. Then he spoke in a low confidential voice: "There's not a soul in sight. I'd like to show you the evidence. Come aboard."

I looked dubiously at the poor crazy chap, in no mood to pry into his daft secrets. "You don't need to take too seriously what I said last night," he explained with a sheepish smile. "I mean about hating you. I have to do that sort of thing. Self-protection, you know. I can't have people nosing about my ship." He sank his voice lower still. "There's enough evidence aboard the *Jezebel* to blow the throne of Peter sky-high."

"I want to have a row," I said. "I'm a bit cold after my swim."

"My dear Mr. Essex," he protested, speaking quite sanely. "I know the duties of hospitality. My galley fire is lighted. My ship is warm. You shall have a cup of tea. And then—" with his lively eye glinting again, "you shall see the evidence."

He turned the nose of his dinghy towards the *Jezebel*, and I followed.

I was surprised at the order aboard. The long deck was spotless. We descended a stairway, and Judas explained how he had converted the below-decks of the ship into a home. A bulkhead cut off the rear portion which he used as a bedroom. Another cut off a part of the bows in which a useful kitchen was installed. Between these two, running from side to side of the ship and most of her length, was a room of splendid proportions. A fireplace was let into the side that faced the river. A window on either hand was cut through the ship's timbers, and a settle stood at right angles to each of these windows. On whichever you sat, there was the window to light you, a fire at your feet, a table before the fire, and a lamp hanging above it. On the opposite side of the room, the space between the ship's ribs had been fitted with bookshelves. There were hundreds of books, many of them abstruse theological works, some in English, some in German. Captain Judas pattered behind me on his light rubbered feet as I read the titles. "Nonsense, all nonsense," he muttered. "They've never got to the root of the matter. They haven't got the evidence. They'll all be blown sky-high."

I accompanied the captain into the galley where he made tea with an old-maidish neatness. He put the cups and teapot, with some biscuits, on to a tray, and then we went and sat at the windows of his big room. I imagined it would be a snug spot in the winter, when the fire and lamp were lit and the wind was blustering up the river.

But I should have preferred something other than the picture over the fireplace: a large reproduction of a painting of the crucifixion.

The windows were open on to the morning. The sun was getting up, drawing the mist off the river. Great scarves of it hung across the face of the woods opposite, like autumn cobwebs caught on brambles. I could see the façade of Heronwater through the trees, and Sam Sawle sauntering along the quay, taking the sense of the morning. Judas had chosen a lovely spot.

He was watching me intently. His one living eye was like the gimlet I had dreamed of. His small fingers were drumming on the table. Suddenly he said: "You are not a Roman Catholic, are you?"

I shook my head, and he looked relieved. With his arms folded before him on the table, he leaned across to me and whispered: "The Pope is on my trail. They've tried persuasion. They've offered to make me a Papal count. I've refused all that—turned it down flat. So now they'll try force or fraud. There are seven members of the Dominican Order who have been entrusted with this as a life's work—this business of laying hands on the evidence and destroying it. That was why I had to leave the Hebrides."

He poured me out another cup of tea. "You live a trying life," I said to humour him.

"You don't know the half of it," he answered. "The Archbishop of Canterbury, the Scottish Moderator, the President of the Wesleyan Conference, the head of the Baptists, whatever he calls himself— they're all one cabal when it comes to this question. But here I am. They don't know I'm here. And now I'll show you."

Long strips of cocoanut matting, laid side by side, covered the floor. Captain Judas rolled up the middle one and revealed a trap-door with a ringbolt. He pulled up the door and swung a lantern down into the cavity which ran right under the ship. "The bilge," he explained, "but as dry as a desert. Not a rat aboard this ship, Mr. Essex, not a bug, not a cockroach."

He was kneeling on the edge of the hole, and I looked over his shoulder into the faintly illuminated darkness. He took a rope with a hook on the end and lowered it towards a leather chest with an arched top. The hook caught in a ring, and, putting down his lantern, Captain Judas hauled with both his small white hands. Soon the chest lay at our feet. He shut the trap, rolled back the matting, and looked at me with cunning. He tapped the lid of the chest fondly. "Dynamite!" he said. "Enough here to blow the Pope off his throne. Descendant of Peter! This does for Master Peter!"

He locked all three of the doors: the one that gave upon the stairway, the bedroom door and the galley door. He shut the windows and drew the curtains across them. He hauled on a string that was fastened round his neck. There was a key at the end of it. He put the key into the lock and then paused dramatically, his glittering eye fastened upon my countenance. "In the name of the Father and of the Son and of the Holy Ghost. Amen." He pulled open the chest. It was stuffed with sheaves of paper, neatly tied with red tape, and Captain Judas plunged in his hands and tossed them out gaily on to the table.

"Take hold of them. They won't explode—yet," he chuckled.

I took up some of the bundles and read the superscriptions, written in a small beautiful hand. "Fishermen throughout the Ages—unreliability of—with special reference to recent fraudulent bankruptcy of Grimsby firm." "The Night in Question. (a) Where was Peter? (b) Where was Andrew the son of Zebedee?" "Judas, the Disciples' Cashier. Honesty of his Book-keeping Methods." "Suicide of Judas. Effect of Unjust Accusation upon Sensitive Soul. c.f. numerous cases throughout History."

There were other superscriptions that were just crazy: "The Cross, the Crux, the Crisis and Creation." "The Origin of Origen." "Pax vobiscum, pax Romanorum, packs of cards, packs of hounds." "Sketch of a method of approach to the Whole Matter with short cuts via (a) Bedlam (b) the House of Commons (c) the Curator of the National Gallery (vide Crucifixion pictures *passim*)."

There were scores of those dossiers. The trunk had been stuffed with them. I let them slide through my fingers, no longer reading the titles, somehow ashamed at having allowed myself to be drawn to this spectacle of a mind's disintegration. I should never now be able to look across the river and see the light burning on the *Jebezel* without picturing the old boy sitting thus behind his locked doors, gloating over these treasures of hallucination, or, bowed beneath his lamp, adding patiently to this babel of imbecility. And now to get out, as gracefully as I could.

I stood up. "A remarkable collection," I said. "This must represent years of research and writing."

"Ten years," he replied. "The ten happiest years of my life. Not a moment wasted. All tending to a point—and that point nearly reached. Whoosh! Bang! Wallop!"

He flung abroad his arms to indicate the suddenly disrupted pretensions of the Holy See, and smiled beatifically.

"Well," I said, "I must thank you, Captain Judas, for taking me into your confidence. You may rely on me."

He bowed with grave formality.

"And now I must be going. My people will wonder what's become of me."

He accompanied me to the door giving on the stairway and unlocked it. "Forgive me if I don't see you off," he murmured. I heard the lock click behind me, and could picture him refilling the chest, stowing it safely out of reach of the seven Papal desperadoes. I saw his curtain drawn an inch aside as I rowed away from the ship, and I knew he was watching me, wondering perhaps whether I looked the sort of man who would blow the gaff on his cosmic ambitions.

## 16

Now that I had broken the ice with Captain Judas, we knew no more of the mock ferocity with which he had greeted our arrival. Throughout that holiday the children were to be seen swarming like monkeys up the *Jezebel*'s rope ladder and making the ship their own. To live in a house however near the water is not the same thing as to live in a ship whose timbers are laved by the tide, and once old Judas had given the children a footing, they were soon all over him.

He had a telescope on a tripod fixed to his deck, and though the twistings of the river confined the view to our own reach, you would see Oliver, Rory or Eileen sitting at all times of the day on the chair which allowed the telescope to be used without fatigue.

It was Oliver who discovered that the old man could be coaxed beyond mere acquiescence. He invented the great game of the careened ship. The *Jezebel* had been sailing the seas for month after month. Judas, as Captain Morgan, had had a high old time, seizing treasure, causing captured crews to walk the plank, showing a clean pair of heels when a King's ship hove in sight. And now she had become so foul that she dragged through the water like an old dish-clout, and sailing her to a quiet beach, Morgan had run her ashore for a clean-up and overhaul.

I had not known how deeply Oliver had been reading in the annals of buccaneering, but he was all excited as he instructed us in our parts. He was a Greek hailing from Tiger Bay, Morgan's right-hand man, and Eileen must be an English heiress who has been spared, on some occasion when the decks ran blood, because she was worth a ransom. She had fallen in love with the handsome Greek, and was now ready to follow him to the ends of the earth.

"Why do you always have to be someone handsome?" Maeve asked sullenly.

Usually we left the games on the *Jezebel* to the three younger children, but that afternoon we were all there except Nellie. Captain Judas had invited us to tea. Nellie had not come because, she said, she had dinner for a regiment to look after. As a fact, it was because she distrusted anything so unusual as Captain Judas.

The tea had been a spartan affair, but Judas presided in his great room with considerable dignity. He lapsed occasionally. He regarded me now as a fellow conspirator, pledged to the ruin of Rome's pretensions, and mystified the other guests by occasionally tipping me a wink with his sound, fiery eye, pointing darkly in the direction of the bilge, and forming with his lips the words: "Whoosh! Bang! Wallop!"

And now tea was over, the girls had washed up, and we were all sitting on the deck above, listening to Oliver extemporising his game.

"Why do you always have to be someone handsome?" Maeve demanded.

Oliver flushed. "I can't help it. I *am* handsome," he declared.

Captain Judas clapped him on the back. "Of course he's handsome," he shouted. "The handsomest young cock that ever strutted on a deck." He caught hold of the boy and stood him between his knees. He gazed at him long and earnestly, ruffled the close golden curls of his head, and seemed to drink in an extraordinary pleasure from the steady glance that Oliver directed upon him from his blue, candid eyes. "Don't you be surprised," he said at length, "if you see this young man walking home some day. Yes—walking. Not rowing. Walking home from here across the water."

The children all looked baffled by this queer remark. Sheila, Dermot and I were embarrassed. We didn't know which way to turn. We felt that Judas was going too far; but he spoke with such simplicity and matter-of-factness that we could do nothing about it. In a moment he ended the difficult situation himself. He pushed Oliver from him gently, and said: "Well, get on with your game. Play while you can. They'll get you at last. So play now, play."

And we played. Morgan, his Greek, and the heiress remained aboard the *Jebezel*, with Sheila as an Indian girl of great beauty whom Morgan had picked up in the sack of a city. The praam, with Dermot and Rory aboard, the dingy with Maeve and me, were a couple of frigates that had come into the bay. It was our business to board the *Jebezel* and clap Morgan into irons.

It was a glorious engagement. From opposite points of the river the frigates converged upon the ship. Dermot was there first, and as he set foot upon the rope ladder old Judas leaned over the rail and yelled for a party to repel boarders. Rory tied the praam to the hulk's side and swarmed up the ladder behind Dermot. Blows from rolled-up newspapers rained on Dermot's head and shoulders, and above the shrill falsetto of Judas's shout rose a kind of Red Indian yodel which the Greek from Tiger Bay thought appropriate to the occasion.

While the battle at that point seemed likely to end in stalemate, Dermot firmly repulsed and Rory unable to get any higher on the ladder, I rowed the dinghy to the bows of the *Jebezel*. Keeping close in to the timbers, I was hidden from observation by the bulge of the ship's side. Once at the bows we were out of sight. We had a spare painter in the dinghy and there wasn't much difficulty in throwing an end over the figurehead that now loomed above us: the head and torso of a repellent woman with bulging eyes and flowing hair. When the two ends of the rope were fastened together, we had a practicable means of entry to the *Jezebel*. I swarmed up first, and found it easy to proceed from *Jezebel's* back to a point whence I could jump aboard. I raised a yell which caused the defenders to turn for a moment from their belabouring of Dermot. The brief respite enabled him to clamber through the open port in the bulwarks and drive the enemy towards me. A moment later he was joined by Rory and I by Maeve. We herded the whole crew towards the stairway and drove them safely below decks.

Oliver was dancing with excitement. "How did you get aboard?" he kept on asking; and Maeve twitted him: "That was one up on the handsome Greek! Brains are better than beauty."

"But how *did* you do it?" he persisted, so I took him up on deck and showed him.

"I'd like to try that," he said.

I climbed out first on to the figurehead and returned to the dinghy hand over hand down the rope. Oliver followed, unknotted the rope, and pulled it down. Then with the gravest concentration he did the whole thing for himself: swung the rope's end over the figurehead, knotted the ends, and swarmed aboard. He went through the process three times.

"You seem very keen on this," I said. "What's the idea? Are you thinking of burgling the captain some night?"

He didn't answer. He didn't look at me. He coiled the rope swiftly but neatly. "That'll do," he said. "Let me row you back." And all the way across the river he didn't look at me or speak.

It was very hot that day. After dinner we sat on deck-chairs on the lawn. You could just see the water darkling below, and the black curtain of trees hung before the opposite bank. Two orange squares bloomed silently down there on the darkness. Captain Judas, his boyish day-time relaxations behind him, would be toiling under lock and key upon his fantastic documents.

Nobody spoke. Farther along the terrace Dermot's cigar made a red spot in the dusk. Nellie and Sheila, doing nothing, leaning back, were between him and me. The children were gone to bed.

We didn't think of Maeve any more as one of the children. She came out from the house now, soft-footed across the lawn, and leant for a moment against the back of my chair. I could feel the fragrance of her breath on my head, and I put up my hand and stroked her hair.

"It's beautiful," she said in a voice that was part of the quiet loveliness of the moment. She took my hand and held it between both of hers. "Take me on the water," she said.

I got up, and we slipped together into the darkness of the trees. The rough, downward twisting path was invisible. She had put on a thick white coat and seemed to glimmer like a little ghost at my side. She put both her hands through my arm and linked her fingers. Her whole weight came on to me once or twice when she half-stumbled. The wood was full of the damp secret smell of ferns and of maturing things.

"I don't like the games—the sort we played this afternoon. I'm growing up."

"You're a sweet child," I said.

She protested eagerly. "No, no. I'm fourteen, and there's so much to do."

She clung to me rather desperately over a rocky bit of the path. "It's because no one cares," she said. "That's what makes me anxious. Nobody's starting me on anything. You said you'd speak to father about my being an actress. Have you done it, Uncle Bill?"

We came with a little rush out from the woods on to the flatness of the quay. It was lighter there. Her pale oval face, in which at night the eyes seemed quite black, looked appealingly into mine.

"Why, bless my soul, you tragic young woman," I said, "at your age I was chopping wood for a country parson, not bothering about a career. Don't fret, my dear. I'll speak to your father when the right moment comes."

Sam Sawle was sitting on the coping of the quay, smoking a pipe. He got up and came towards us. "You going out, Mr. Essex?" He spoke very quietly. It was the sort of night when a voice raised above a whisper sounded offensive. I nodded.

"What'll you take?"

"What about the motor-boat? We could run down to the Carrick Roads."

Maeve shook her head. "No. Not tonight. I hate the sound of a motor-boat at night up here where the river is quiet. Let's take the dinghy. I'll row if you get tired."

Sawle pulled the dinghy to the steps. "There'll be plenty of water for a long time," he said. "The tide's hardly full."

He fetched some cushions from his shack and arranged them behind Maeve as she sat in the stern. He pushed the boat out. The rim of the full moon, yellow and enormous, was just edging up above the woods and seeming to dim the radiance of Captain Judas's windows. A sprinkle of silver fell across the river in a trembling cord between him and us.

I pulled with leisurely strokes, listening to the musical fall of drops from the blades, the soft suck and gurgle as the boat nosed into the water.

"That's better," said Maeve. "That's the sort of sound to hear at night. I don't mind the old *Maeve*'s roaring when the sun's shining, but I hate it under the moon."

She trailed her fingers through the water and withdrew them quickly. "Cold! Cold!" she said, and tucked her hand inside her coat. She shivered slightly, and I asked whether I should return for a rug. "No, no," she said. "It's lovely. Don't talk."

That's what she had said that night in Manchester—the first time I took her to the theatre—when the curtain came down after the first act, and everybody but she seemed to want to chatter. More and more Maeve must have her silences.

The moon had climbed quickly. We could see the whole circle, softly effulgent, resting with its lower rim on the heads of the trees.

Judas's lights were hidden by a bend of the river. There was nothing but the water and the trees and the heavens swimming in misty radiance. From the banks there came an occasional cry: the throaty tremolo of an owl, the swift sharp piping of little coveys of oyster-catchers darting along at the water's edge. Here and there the wood thinned out, ran into bare patches of hillside upon which we could see the cattle couched in groups frozen to stillness beneath the dead light of the moon.

The river turned and twisted. Boring into the silent heart of enchantment we passed through cavernous glooms where the trees rose high and out again into moon-washed space, stippled with the dark shadows of bush and barn and rick.

Presently Maeve said in a low, thrilled voice: "Look! The swans!"

I allowed the oars to rest, and looked over my shoulder. I had thought we should soon be reaching the swans. I had seen them before, but not by moonlight. The bank on one side of the river dropped away, and there was marshy land threaded by runnels and pools and inlets that were now drawn in lines of burnished lead on the flat map of the land. On all that water the swans were resting: scores of them, some with their heads beneath their wings, some rocking sedately with their necks erect. There were large white birds, gleaming like icy figurings of beauty, and small brown cygnets that missed the superb transfiguration of the grown swans.

I took up the oars again, and slowly thrust the boat towards the fleet of birds. Some that were alert rose on the water, pressing down their black webs and reaching their splendid pinions up into the radiance of the moonshine. Then slowly they began to drift away before the approaching boat. Their unease communicated itself to the others, and long snaky necks were uncurled and raised above the rocking boats of the bodies. Soon all the swans that were near enough to have cause for fear were moving over the water. They seemed to glide without propulsion, mysterious beauty, slipping away through the moony texture of a dream.

Suddenly Maeve, who had been lying back, sat upright and clapped her hands in one loud explosive sound. Then the noise of wings broke the tranced quality of the moment. Some of the swans rose on the water and with trailing feet thrashed their way through the broken lights that quivered upon the ponds and inlets. Others rose above the water, and the creaking of their wings was a sound more thrilling than I had ever heard. It was astonishing, seeing them so close at hand, that such great bodies could be lifted clear; but soon six of them were up and climbing into the silvery luminescence of the sky. Instinctively Maeve and I lay on our backs to see a sight that was so unaccustomed. For a time we lost them, and then, when all other sound had faded away among the birds on the water, we heard far off but very clear the creaking beat of the pinions. We saw the swans, high above our heads, flying one behind another with necks rigid; and soon they passed, the incarnation of wild and inaccessible beauty, one by one before the face of the moon.

We lay there for a long time, not speaking, hoping that the miracle would recur; and at last Maeve said: "It doesn't happen twice. Let's go home."

It was very late when we tied up at the quay. The moon was high, and brighter and smaller. The tide had turned. We stood for a moment and watched how everything was obeying the water: the boats all swung round at their moorings with their noses pointing to the west, the moonlight yellow upon the ripples of their dancing, leaves and twigs hurrying by, and the water itself, with hardly a murmur, deep, mysterious, timeless, swinging to the sea.

Across the water Captain Judas's lights were burning yet, as though neither time nor tide could come between him and the spectres of his pursuit. Maeve with one hand pulled her coat closer about her. She placed the other within my arm and snuggled her body close to mine. "Thank you," she said. "I shall never forget tonight. I shall never have a lovelier night. I shall never see the swans again flying across the moon."

"Nonsense," I said, urging her towards the path. "You're going to see all sorts of lovely things, young woman. You talk to me in ten years' time, and tell me whether you haven't seen lovelier things than an old river showing a false face under the moonlight."

She shivered a little. "Ten years!" she said. "What a long time! I shall be twenty-four! I wonder what will have happened to us all in ten years' time: me and Rory and Oliver and you and Eileen."

"Why, child," I said, "that's easy. You will be a famous actress, making me more conceited than is good for me because everybody will be coming to my plays just to see lovely Maeve O'Riorden."

"Oh!" she whispered. "That would be beautiful."

"And Rory will be—let's see—probably his father's right-hand man in the most famous decorating firm in the world."

"Dear Ugly! His brain's full of banshees. He makes me afraid."

"And Oliver will be a curate with golden hair, and all the old ladies will love him so much that they'll put sixpence in the bag instead of threepence. And so they'll make him a bishop. Eileen, of course, will marry a nice man who keeps a newsagent's and tobacconist's shop in the corner of a village street. She'll have lots of babies and she'll steal sweets for them out of the shop when her husband's outside sticking up the news-bill. And so they'll go bankrupt and pay fourpence in the pound."

"Oh, you dear old silly, you do talk nonsense. And yet—I—I—do love you so."

And there was Maeve suddenly stopped dead in the path, in the pitch blackness of the wood, with both arms round me, and her head on my chest, which she could only just reach, sobbing her heart out! I let her stay there till the storm subsided, then, as we were near the house, I picked her up and carried her across the dew-drenched lawn. Everyone was gone to bed. I set her down under the light that was burning in the hall, and she raised to me a face that looked very small and white and tragic, tear-smudged. "Kiss me," she said.

I bent down and kissed her and tasted the salt of her tears. Then without a word she went draggingly upstairs. I sat down and lit a cigarette. I had kissed Maeve many times, but I knew I must not kiss her again.

I gathered that the outside world did not mean much to Captain Judas, but from time to time he went to Truro to see if any letters were addressed to him there *poste restante*. I was going up in the *Maeve* to do some shopping the next day and took him with me. He talked very sensibly all the way, and was full of information about the craft we saw at the town's quays, about their ports and cargoes. He had a word of commendation for the neat appearance of this ship and a growl of scorn for another's slovenliness. Only when the *Maeve* was in the narrow water between timber-yards on one side and flour warehouses on the other did he begin to show his nerviness. The warehouses stood up sheer from the water, and at open doors two and three floors up stood men powdered with flour from head to foot superintending the pulleys that were swinging the loaded sacks up and down.

He looked at them with apprehension. "Keep her out, my boy, midstream, midstream," he muttered. "A defective pulley, one of those sacks—whoosh! flop!—where am I then? Eh? An old game. They're up to all the tricks. But I know 'em. I know 'em. And when we get ashore keep away from the cathedral."

"Right you are, captain. I'm only doing a bit of shopping."

"And I'm only going to the post office. Mind you, I know nothing against this bishop—nothing definite, that is—haven't checked up yet. In the meantime, caution."

"You know, captain," I said, as we stepped ashore, "you've got a very noticeable appearance. Your long beard and long hair. Doesn't that rather give you away to 'them'?"

He chuckled knowingly. "You haven't got to the bottom of me, my boy. No, not by a fathom or two. There'd be something in what you say if I had always been like this. But I was clean-shaven and had hair cropped like a convict's when they—when—"

The old man stopped dead on the pavement. He turned to me a face that was blank save for the vivid light of his one sound eye. His mouth twitched. He tried several times to speak, and seemed to be tortured by an effort to remember something that escaped him. "It was—when—" he began again, and then leaned against a wall and passed his handkerchief over his brow. I saw that my remark had touched on something deeper than I had intended. I took his arm. "Tell me, captain," I said. "That Norwegian timber ship we passed. D'you reckon she'll get out on the tide tonight?"

"Tonight? Never! Lucky if they make it tomorrow, the rate they're going on." He was himself again.

There was one letter for Captain Judas. As we went chugging slowly homeward, he read it again and again. He had laid the envelope on a thwart, and I noticed that it was addressed to Captain Jude Iscott. I noticed, too, that printed across the top of the envelope was "The Mary Latter Comedy Company," and it was strange to me to think of old Judas being in communication with the world of the theatre. The Latter Company was well known. Maeve and I had occasionally seen them in Manchester. They toured the provinces with contemporary comedies—what one might call the best of the second-rate stuff that was sure of good houses. I couldn't help commenting on the envelope lying there under my nose. I prodded it with my finger and said: "I've seen these people, captain. They're pretty good."

He looked at me abstractedly, turning the letter in his fingers.

Then he said: "She doesn't know how difficult it is to get out here. She's arriving at Falmouth this afternoon, but how on earth is she going to do the rest of the journey?"

"Are you having a visitor?"

"Yes, my daughter—Mary Latter."

"Good Lord! She's your daughter? I've seen her act."

"I wish you hadn't, Mr. Essex," he said severely. "I don't approve of it. Babylonish whoring."

He continued to stare at the letter. "Flesh and blood," he muttered. "That's the trouble, Mr. Essex—flesh and blood. Strange deep things, your own flesh and blood. There's no turning back on that. I settled that long ago."

"I'll bring her from Falmouth," I said. Instantly, he was all polite deprecation; but I bore him down. I was on holiday. To run the *Maeve* into Falmouth was as amusing a way of spending the afternoon as any other. And, anyway, I wanted to talk to Mary Latter alone. The captain wished to stay aboard the *Jezebel*, to make all ready. Despite his daughter's Babylonish whorings, he understood the duty of hospitality. But he was full of old-fashioned notions about unprotected females. His daughter might not care to entrust herself to my hands. How was she to know that I was not some desperado, capable of anything. So I climbed aboard the *Jebezel*, and he wrote a letter which he gave me to read. My good friend William Essex…trustworthy…honourable…may safely entrust…

Armed with this introduction, I met Mary Latter at Falmouth Station that afternoon. A small trunk initialled "M.L." was all the identification I needed. I declared myself and handed her her father's letter. She read it and smiled. "The dear thing! Are you the novelist?"

"Yes."

"Then I'll shake hands again, just to say thank you. You've given me pleasure."

"And you me."

"Good. We're getting on well. How do I get to this hulk of father's?"

"You'll see. First, you'd better have some tea."

"I'd love it."

She was a friendly and intelligent woman, easy to talk to, with no demure pose of femininity. I judged she was rather older than myself. She had strong regular features which missed good looks. Her dark, purposeful face gave the impression of difficulties met and overcome. She was dressed in the spartan fashion of the time, with a straw "boater," a white high-necked blouse, and a dark skirt. Anything less suggestive of Babylonish whoring I had never seen. I smiled as I recalled the phrase.

"You are amused," she challenged me.

I told her what her father had said. "The dear thing," she smiled again.

We took a cab down to the Market Strand, left her small trunk there, and then walked back to some tea-rooms in the main street. It was a pleasant place, with a bay window from which we could overlook the harbour, full of steamers and little curtseying yachts and packets passing to and fro from Flushing and St. Mawes. She seemed tired. I poured her some tea.

"It's pleasant here," she said. "He should be happy. Is he happy?"

"I think so. I see him a good deal, and he seems to enjoy life—in his own way—you know?"

She sighed. "Yes. I know."

"There's a whole pack of us down there. I suppose we're good for him. Especially the children. They keep him busy."

"He always liked children," she said, and drummed on the table with her finger-tips, looking out over the colour and animation of the water. "He still—writes—at night?"

I nodded. "He told me all about that. He showed me his papers."

"We had a little house at Deptford," she began irrelevantly, "a pretty place with a magnolia tree against the back wall—one of the biggest I've ever seen—"

Then she stopped, with almost a blush on her dark, somehow weather-beaten-looking face. "I'm sorry," she said, again with that bright and kindly and courageous smile. "I was going to tell you the story of my life. So soon. Too soon."

"Let it keep till we're in the boat."

"I suppose it's the idea of seeing him again after so long. Five years."

I picked up the story bit by bit while Mary Latter stayed on the *Jebezel*. It began with the little house in Deptford, and the garden, and the magnolia tree, and the mother who was always there, and the young father there between voyages. A harmonium played a large part in it. Mother played it every night, and they sang hymns; and when father was home he played it and they sang hymns. "And it was very beautiful," Mary Latter said. "You know, I used to enjoy that exquisite sadness that only young children know anything about: the little dark parlour, with the window opening on to the garden where the magnolia tree was, and the blue summer dusk, and the melancholy hymns that made me think of father away on the sea. We always had the hymns last thing at night—just mother and I—I was an only child. Then I'd go up to my bedroom, and I could see the river, and in the winter there would be lights on it moving through the mist and the moaning of the sirens."

But the exquisite sadness would turn to joy when father's white cap with the bit of gold on it was on the harmonium, and father himself was there playing the hymns.

There was a mission chapel that they attended every Sunday, and sometimes on week-nights, too; and when father was home he often preached; and mother and Mary, sitting side by side, were uplifted into some incredible realm where God's especial favour and protection were over and about them. And in the little house at Deptford there were great wrestlings in prayer, father and mother and Mary all on their knees and father's voice ringing out into the dusk of the summer garden or filling the room when it was winter, and beyond the curtained windows the ships crawled bellowing through the mist.

"That's how I grew up," Mary Latter said, "in an atmosphere of hysteria and exaltation. When school was done with, such as it was, I just stayed at home and helped mother. We went on praying and singing our hymns, seeing hardly a soul except our two selves and on Sundays the people at the mission. She died when I was sixteen."

It was a blow to the girl brought up trammelled and dependent; and she failed under it. Her father, who had just obtained his first command, decided to take her to sea with him. "It was terrible," she said, "terrible. To think of it can still make me go hot all over." She shuddered as she sat beside me on the look-out.

She saw the old man for the first time as a sheer religious maniac. They were on a big square-rigged sailing-ship with a tough and godless crew. The old man, not so old then, had had the harmonium put into his cabin, and the hymn-singing went on. Sailing through a tropic night with the cabin door open so that the crew might have the benefit of what was going forward, he would play upon the harmonium and sing "I'm not ashamed to own my Lord," and "At the Cross, at the Cross, where I first saw the Light."

"And there was nothing perfunctory about the Sunday service," she said. "All hands had to be there and stay the course: hymns and prayers, and one of his impromptu sermons. It was ghastly, the atmosphere of mockery, that he was never aware of. They would parody the hymns, using obscene and blasphemous words; and cry out in the midst of his sermons; 'Alleluiah!' 'Glory to the Lamb!' all in derision and cruelty. His name, you know, is Jude Iscott, and they began to call him Judas Iscariot. The atmosphere behind his back was horrible: the laughter and contempt, the filthy gestures they would make with the tracts he compelled me to hand to them, all the muttering: 'Who sold Jesus for thirty pieces of silver?'"

She pieced it together very vividly, and I could see the big ship dipping across the blue, white-ridged sea, with her full press of canvas, and the young girl sitting before the harmonium that had been dragged out of the cabin for the service, and old Judas standing bare-headed with his hair and whiskers, iron-grey then, she said, blowing in the wind as he testified to God's love. And ranged below them would be the officers, decently sedate, and the ring of grinning faces, waiting for the chance to let go in a hymn. You can do anything with a hymn: I had heard the boys in Hulme. It must have been dreadful for the only woman aboard.

"You see, so long as I was ashore, I only met people who liked that sort of thing. Now, it was like being a missionary to cannibals. I was not heroic. I loved him and admired him, and he was a marvellous sailor, but I knew I could never make another voyage with him, and the thought of being all alone in the house at Deptford, for months on end, terrified me. I didn't know what to do."

That was settled for her. George Latter came aboard in Sydney and asked to be allowed to work his passage home. A couple of scoundrels had vamoosed, and old Judas took him on.

"Did you ever see George?" she asked. "We played together."

I shook my head.

"He was very handsome then," she said, "though he had been ill and was thin and white. He looked comically romantic. I was leaning over the rail when he walked up the gangway: a Byronic shirt showing the hollows under his neck, black ringlets, a tiny bundle on a stick over his shoulder. You never saw anything so Whittingtonian. The thought leapt to the mind. I remember the mate shouted: 'Here! We don't want hands for a bloody panto!'"

But the old man talked to Latter in his cabin, gave him a tract, and signed him on for the voyage home. Latter was the son of a wealthy mercantile knight who had already done all the Whittington business. George wanted to get away from it, and used the freedom from supervision that his first term at Oxford gave him to join a touring theatrical company. He had come with them to Australia, had fallen ill in Sydney and been left behind, penniless, to fend for himself. That was the whole of his brief and unremarkable story.

"And, of course, we fell in love on the voyage home," said Mary Latter. "I had never met anyone like him. When his strength and colour came back, he was the most beautiful man I had ever seen, and for that matter I've never seen a more beautiful person since—that is till—what d'you think?" She turned to me with her endearing smile.

"I know," I said. "Oliver."

"Yes. He's going to kill 'em. Well, you know, that's why I was moved to begin telling you things the other day in Falmouth, because The Firebird—that was father's ship then—ended that voyage at Falmouth. We got in late one afternoon, and at night George and I came up on deck and found the whole harbour swimming under the light of a full moon. I can see it now, especially the grey slate roofs of the town that looked like burnished lead, and I can feel the extraordinary hush of all that canvas stowed, and ropes tied, after months of straining and groaning and flapping. It was heaven. We decided then to slip away together the next day. We did. We were afraid to say a word to father. And I never saw Falmouth again till this week."

That was how Mary Latter learned the trade of the theatre— joining a travelling company with Latter, marrying him later, getting her experience as the old barn-stormers got theirs—not from academies but from doing the job.

"I have never been a very good actress," she said modestly, "but I do claim to know the game."

It was a thin life till Latter's widower-father died, unreconciled but happily intestate, and George Latter himself, never, I gathered, a strong man, died soon after. And so Mary found herself possessed of a considerable fortune, a profound knowledge of the knockabout life of touring theatrical companies, and a determination to run a company of her own. That was how the Mary Latter Comedy Company came into being, and its founder, a sound business woman, had not diminished but increased her fortune.

Some days after this conversation I brought Mary Latter's mind back again to the question of Captain Judas. She briefly sketched in the story of his decline. His proceedings aboard ship became more and more eccentric, and reports of his fervent evangelical services began to disturb the owners. They had no complaint about his seamanship, for there were few men who could get more than he could out of a clipper, but when he began to see in every albatross that followed his ship the visible encircling presence of the Holy Ghost, they called him up in London to give some account of himself. This to him was Paul before Festus, and all the board got out of the quiet little man dressed in respectable navy blue was a sudden and vehement call to repent while the acceptable day was yet with them.

And so it was that Captain Jude Iscott, to whom the name of Judas Iscariot had now stuck like a burr, found himself for a long time without a ship, then found himself passing from job to job on the down grade, and at last was to be found among the islands of the East Indies. It was there that it became customary to call him quite simply Captain Judas, his name and antecedents falling away and leaving him adrift among the islands, a fantastic and legendary figure. His long hair and beard, the apocalyptic shining of his eye, his undismayed conviction of a call to bring seafaring sinners to repentance, made him half-loved, half-feared, but wholly beyond the pale of sane if sinful men.

"What finished him," said Mary Latter, "was a mutiny."

Her first tidings of the affair were from a newspaper. It recorded the picking up of Captain Jude Iscott and a ship's cook in an open boat. The captain was unable to give an account of himself, but the cook had some garrulous tale of mutiny to tell. And then the little affair, which after all could not mean much to English newspapers, sank from sight. Mary did not even know what ship her father was commanding; it was not mentioned in the reports. It was merely recorded that the two men had been put ashore at Penang. So what did that woman do but resolve to go to Penang. You will begin to understand my admiration for Mary Latter.

"You see," she said, sitting there in the stiff formal clothes that she didn't change even for holiday, "I had just come into all that money. I thought a change would do me good. I was used to knocking about."

In English lodging-houses, yes. But Penang!

She told in her matter-of-fact way how she arrived in Penang, as though it had been Bournemouth. It seems that there was a hospital of sorts, and she learned that the captain and the cook had both been patients but were now discharged—gone no one knew where, except that they were supposed to be hanging about pending an inquiry.

Mary had plenty of money, and from her hotel—"you never saw such a disgusting place—and the food!"—she sent out well-paid scouts who, before long, brought in the cook.

"I was rather frightened. I never like black men." But the cook was a decent fellow, a Malay, not so black as Mary thought. His English puzzled her, but she wormed a story out of him. And, when all was said and done, it was a simple enough story of a piece of straight-forward cut-and-dried villainy. It was a small steamship that Judas had been commanding. He had an engineer, a mate of sorts, two hands and the cook. They were all villains except the cook. Every one was in the plot to steal the ship. The cook was invited to join the party, pretended that he would do so, and warned the captain. The captain replied by singing on the bridge a hymn in which he informed the world that he was "strong in the strength which God supplies through His eternal Son."

This did not prevent the plot from coming to a head that night. He was seized as he slept in his cabin, and was told to get into the boat. He resisted. He was frog-marched on deck. "Get in, Judas," the mate ordered, "and take your thirty pieces of silver with you." He tossed a contemptuous handful of coins into the boat. The cook attempted a diversion by the heroic method of rushing from the galley with a pan of boiling water which he threatened to hurl upon the mate. Before he could do this, he was knocked on the head by a member of the crew, and he knew nothing more till he woke in the boat. The steamer was out of sight, and, indeed, was never seen again under the name she had borne. There was no wireless in those days.

Judas was in the boat, too. He had been knocked on the head like the cook, and when he recovered he was raving. He picked up the coins from the bottom-boards and flung them into the sea, screaming to the dawn that was reddening the water that he had not betrayed his Master.

The poor Malay passed a few desperate hours. It was with difficulty that he prevented the captain from leaping overboard. There was no water in the boat and no protection from the burning sun. Both men suffered from the wounds in their heads, and it was only the odd chance of being picked up before that day was over that saved their lives.

Such was the Malay's plain tale, and such were the circumstances that finally tipped Judas's mind from extravagance to insanity. Mary Latter was taken to him that night by the Malay. The captain who had been teetotal all his life was in a dive behind the water-front, addressing an enthralled company on sin and salvation and denying that he had betrayed his Lord. He was very drunk.

Again her simple narrative gave me a clear picture of that extraordinary scene: the crowded, beer-stinking den, the buzz and ping of a myriad insects about the swinging oil lamps, the throng of evil faces catching the light as they pressed round the little wildly-bearded man with the blazing eye and burning tongue. Into the midst of this Rembrandt group strode without warning the stiff severe figure of the woman who had gone to Penang as though it had been Bournemouth. "They all looked struck silly." That was her sole comment on what must have been a superb moment.

It seems that she went up to Captain Judas, took him by the arm, and said: "Father, you come with me." He was helpless, and cried a little, and she and the Malay took him to her hotel and put him to bed. In the morning he was quiet and repentant and pliable. She told him he was going home on the next available ship. "But the inquiry!" he objected; and wherever she went she heard the same dismayed ejaculation: "But the inquiry!" "Damn the inquiry," said Mary Latter. "Let 'em come and hold it in London." And whether it was ever held, or what happened if it was, she never heard or cared.

"I couldn't do any more for him, could I?" she asked anxiously. "For years he was in a little cottage in the Hebrides till he became convinced that a few Catholic priests who went there for a holiday were emissaries of Rome, spying out his doings. Then he became crazy to have a ship again and live up a creek. So I let him buy the *Jezebel*. Don't ever mention money to him, will you? I'm sure you wouldn't, anyway. I like him to write his own cheques. It pleases him to do that. I pay a bit into his account every month. He bought the *Jezebel* out of it."

For the first time in all our talks together there was a slight break in the steadiness of her voice. "He keeps accounts," she said. "It's heart-breaking, you know. He has insisted on showing them to me. Every penny he owes me is down. It's all going to be paid back out of royalties when his book's published."

The lights sprang up in the *Jezebel*'s dark side. "I must go," she said. "If I don't, he'll start writing, and I want him to keep off that while I'm here."

When we left Heronwater that time, Mary Latter travelled with us to London. Captain Judas came into Falmouth to see us off. Sam Sawle was there to take the old man back in the *Maeve*.

All the others being aboard, Judas walked for a while up and down the platform with me and his daughter. He had nothing to say, but pathetically held on to an arm of each of us, keeping us on the move within the space of a quarterdeck. We had to get aboard at last; and when I leaned out of the window as the train was moving away I saw the little man as no more than a bent back and dejected shoulders, already shuffling off the platform, a different figure from the bellicose bantam who had confronted us on our arrival. He would be lonely. It was years, Mary said, since he had "taken" to anybody at all. He would draw his curtains early and get down to work.

I sat in my corner. Opposite to me was Mary Latter, Maeve next to her, with a hand through Mary's arm. That was a good piece of work! Mary had taken to the child, and I had allowed them to be much together before sounding Mary on the chances of her giving employment to Maeve. First there was the consent of Dermot and Sheila to obtain, and that was not difficult. They were both intelligent enough to know that a real bent, amounting almost literally to a calling, was rare in a child of Maeve's age, and that to give her her head was the course of wisdom. My own admiration for Mary Latter as a practical, ruthless and dependable woman was able to convince them that Maeve could not be in better hands.

Mary herself talked the matter over with me and Maeve as we walked our little quay one evening. "I hope you've got no nonsense in your head," she said severely to Maeve. "Don't think you're going to see your picture on post-cards. You won't while you're with me, anyway. Can you type?"

Maeve shook a frightened head. "Well, if you come with me you'll have to learn to. And to write shorthand, too. You'll have to write letters for me, and perhaps when I'm tired you'll have to read to me, and now and then, if you behave yourself, I'll let you come to the theatre and smell the place, and see how things are done, and get it in your bones. And perhaps in a year's time we'll put a little apron on you and a slavey's cap, and let you go on and say: 'The rector's called to see you, ma'am.' And if you can say that properly, perhaps we'll let you say something else. See?"

Maeve nodded again, speechless but happy. "Very well, then. So long as you understand. You'll have to learn as I did—just by doing it. How old are you?"

"Fourteen, madam."

Mary frowned. "Good gracious! You're younger than I thought. Never mind. I expect you've got more sense than I had at fourteen. Now run away to bed. You won't get much sleep when you're with me."

When Maeve was gone, she said: "Thank you for bringing the child to me. I like her."

"I think she's lucky," I said, "and—d'you mind my saying this?— I think you're lucky, too. I'm glad she's going to learn by knocking about. It's the best way."

"Yes," she said, "it's marvellous. They learn all we can teach them, and then leave us in the lurch."

## 17

It was at the beginning of September, 1906, that Maeve left us. We had a glimpse of her in the following April when the Mary Latter Comedy Company came for a week to Manchester. She had not yet set a foot upon the stage, but she was not the Maeve she had been. She had a calmness and confidence that were lacking when the theatre to her was no more than a dream. Now she was on the threshold. It was a matter no longer of contriving, only of waiting, and she was waiting with a fine self-reliance.

When August came she did not join the party at Heronwater. Mary Latter was going abroad for a month: France and Spain, Italy and Austria: "a regular gadabout," she called it: and Maeve went with her.

But the party was made up from an unexpected quarter. It came about this way. Dermot and I had been making a round of the Easifix works in Hulme, and we were walking home together when he said: "I'm sorry, Bill, but we shan't be joining you at Heronwater this year. You know what I mentioned to you some time ago—that night you met Kevin Donnelly—about Rory living in Ireland?"

I nodded grimly.

"Well, it won't be so long now before he goes, and I thought it would be a good idea if he saw something of Donnelly—got to know him in a free and easy way. There's a daughter, too—Maggie—a girl about Rory's age. I'm going to ask them both to spend a holiday with me and Sheila and Rory."

"And what's wrong," I asked, "with spending that holiday at Heronwater?"

Dermot's eye brightened. "You wouldn't mind? Or Nellie?"

"Nellie never minds anything. And as for me—well, if you're determined to send Rory off on this damned silly business, let's see him while we can. I'm fond of the little beggar."

Dermot stopped in his tracks. "Silly business!" he exploded suddenly. "Let me tell you—"

"No," I said. "Don't tell me. We don't argue on this. That's all there is to it."

Dermot took off his hat and wiped his forehead. The touch of opposition had made him sweat. His grey-green eyes were glinting. He took a pull on himself, put on his hat, and said: "I won't quarrel with you. Come on." He took my arm.

"Gladly," I said with a grin. "I'm proud to be seen walking down the street with so distinguished a figure. The lovely hat and all."

I think Dermot was looking his best at about that time, when he was approaching his fortieth year. He was very tall and thin. His face was long and fleshless and aristocratic, finished off with that provocative point of red beard. His hands, too, seemed to have incredibly lengthened. He had the longest fingers I have ever known on a man, and his wrists were beautifully slender. He dressed the part. He had taken recently to an immense black sombrero, and that day he was wearing a loose grey suit and a green tie. I hadn't seen Shaw then, but I think he and Dermot must have looked much alike at that time.

"There are two more things I want to tell you," Dermot said, smacking the side of his leg with a silver-topped malacca cane. "I'm clearing out of Manchester and I'm chucking this Easifix business."

"Clearing out of Manchester! But, my dear man—"

"And it's only a matter of time before you do, too. I give you another two or three years at most."

"But why—?"

"Because a good deal of my work's in the south now, and I want to expand it. I shall keep on the place here and leave a manager in charge."

He spoke with determination. Evidently he had worked out his details. "I've got premises," he said, "in Regent Street. I can't go in for a year. The lease isn't up till then. I want Rory to be away first."

He flicked a look at me, and his eyebrows flew up. "Comment on that, damn you," he seemed to say.

"And look here," he added. "This Easifix Company. You and I have drawn a tidy income out of it for years, and now I want to sell out and draw a lump of capital out of it. I advise you to do the same. It's becoming a bore. Now the thing's swimming along as it is, there's no need for me. Anyone can design the toys."

"What about your father?"

"Needless to say, it will be one of the terms of sale that he either retains his position or is retired on a pension. We can see that he gets a good holding of shares. And when I go he can have my house."

"You've got it all fixed."

"I have. Every point. What about you? Hadn't you better chuck it? You're doing very well out of your books."

"Three thousand last year."

"And your stock's rising. When you start in on these plays you talk about, it'll be five thousand before you know where you are. Oh, yes. You'd better chuck it. And go to London. And get yourself a car. They're reliable things now. I'm buying one tomorrow. And that reminds me. Our little crew will come down to Heronwater this year by road. I've been taking some driving lessons."

And so they did, but they took two days about it. Cars were, as Dermot said, getting reliable; but roads were not yet the glassy racing-tracks they were soon to become. Dermot wired from Bristol that the party had stopped there for the night and would reach Heronwater the next afternoon. I awaited them anxiously, for Heronwater was proving dull. That was the first time I had been there without a party. On the way down Oliver had missed his chattering companions, and was bored to distraction when we reached Falmouth at the end of the second day's railway journey. The trouble was, he was imagining Rory enjoying the excitements of a new method of travel. "What if the tyres burst?" "What if they go into a ditch?" "What if they arrive with an old horse pulling them?"—though all those glories were already fading into the dim annals of motoring.

And then, there we were, Sam Sawle manœuvring the *Maeve* to the quay. Captain Judas respectfully handing Nellie ashore. Nellie shuddering away from his unusualness and disappearing up the path with hardly a greeting. Oliver went straight to bed. Nellie was no sooner washed than she was fussing off to the kitchen. Meals to arrange for. This and that. The truth was she hated Heronwater. She couldn't swim and wouldn't learn to swim; she disliked being on the water; she was sure the children would be drowned every time they went out sailing in the *Rory* or the *Oliver*. And especially, I knew, now that there was no one there but our two selves, she hated the thought of sitting in the inimical quiet of the great trees that surrounded us and the water below us.

We ate a wordless dinner, and then I took a dinghy and pulled across to the *Jezebel*. It was nine o'clock and the light was fading. Judas's windows glowed. To my surprise, the rope ladder had been pulled indoors. That was something new. I let out a yell. "*Jezebel* ahoy!"

One of the windows above me opened cautiously and Judas's white mop came into sight. "Who's there?" he demanded.

"Bill Essex. Are you too busy to be bothered with me?"

"No, no!" he cried anxiously. "Oh dear no! One moment. One moment."

The window was shut, and a moment later Captain Judas peered over the rail. The rope ladder came down and I went aboard. Then the ladder was pulled in again. Judas took me affectionately by the arm and led me below decks, locking the door behind him. "Worse and worse," he muttered. "Don't think me inhospitable, Mr. Essex, but I've got to draw that ladder in now, for things are getting worse and worse. Sit down."

He pointed to a comfortable chair under one of the swinging lamps. "Smoke," he said, and when I had filled and lit my pipe he said, leaning towards me mysteriously: "It's leaked out!"

I lifted my eyebrows in interrogation and pointed with my pipe-stem down to the bilge. He nodded. "Believe this or not," he said. "A week ago I was upon deck when a dinghy came along. A woman sitting in the stern. A parson rowing. What d'you think of that for barefaced impudence! Not even bothering to disguise himself. There he was, collar and all. 'That's a nice-looking place,' he said to the woman. 'How'd you like to live there?' She shuddered. 'Probably full of rats.' Rats! Think of that, Mr. Essex—rats on the *Jezebel*! But, of course, that was all part of the plant. 'Looks all right to me,' said the parson, 'like a new pin.' See the cunning of the man! Flattery! Then he shouts: 'I wonder if you'd mind our having a look over your boat, sir?' Can you imagine anything more elementary in the way of a plot? Once have 'em aboard and where am I? Woman! A disguised man, I'll bet. My answer was to haul in the ladder, shut the door and go below, and the ladder's been hauled in ever since when I haven't been about to keep my eyes open."

"Quite right," I said. "Take no risks."

"No risks. That's the motto. And hurry on with the work. Finish. Publish. And then—Whoosh! Bang! Wallop!"

His face glowed. He beamed over the papers spread upon his littered table. "This is getting near the bone," he said, tapping the sheet he had been writing upon. "I'm sorry I can't let even you read it just yet. You forgive me?"

"By all means."

"There's one thing holding me up. I must learn Greek."

"But my dear Captain Judas, that's going to take you a long time."

"That has nothing to do with it," he reproved me. "Greek is necessary. I feel there are many clues hidden away in the original Greek, and therefore I shall learn it. I have sent to London for the necessary books."

He looked at me calmly, combing his long whiskers with his fingers. I knew that he would do it. His mania could overcome obstacles that, I realised with shame, I could never face in my sanity.

"I see now," he said, "that I was bigoted in my youth. I despised the wisdom of this world, not knowing how it might help me to the wisdom of the world hereafter. But it is not too late. I am only seventy."

He slipped his writing into a drawer and turned the key. "Now let me make you a cup of tea," he cried gaily. "Let us forget the wiles of the Pope and the President of the Wesleyan Conference and that poor fool who rowed by the other day. A Particular Baptist, I dare say. They'll all go up when the big wallop comes. What a sight! What a sight! Triple tiaras, mitres, birettas, silk hats, shovel boards and Salvation Army caps! All up in the air together. Ha, ha, ha!"

He pattered out into the galley and came back with cups and saucers and his inevitable biscuits. A few moments later the tea was on the table and we were talking sanely of sane things. He wanted to know whether I had heard anything of Maeve and his daughter, when Dermot was coming, how my own work was getting on. It was not till we were on deck again and he had let down the ladder, that he took my arm and whispered nervously, pointing across the river to Heronwater, where a single light showed amid the trees: "Is that the Master's room?"

"The Master's? Let me see: whose room is that? Why, it's Oliver's."

"I shall watch it every night," he said. "The Master's room! Some night he will come walking to me across the water."

I ran down the ladder and unfastened the boat. I was hardly aboard before the ladder ran up and the sound of locking doors came to my ears. It was a dark night. I rowed across the inky river, looking now and then over my shoulder towards the crack of light in Sawle's shack. The Master! The old man was beginning to give me the creeps. I was glad when Sawle, hearing the creaking rowlocks, came down to the water's edge with a lantern.

There was nothing to be done the next day till Dermot and his party arrived. Oliver was on edge for the unusual sight of a motor-car stopping at our gate. Nellie was in the depressed condition that always came upon her when she had to meet people she did not know. If Donnelly and his daughter had been visitors from Mars, she could not have been in a state of more acute apprehension.

Oliver and I spent the afternoon loafing near the gate, and at tea-time a cloud of dust and the honking of a large bulbous horn announced the coming of the party. The car was a big open one. It and everybody in it were whitened like the flour-workers on the Truro quays. Dermot sat at the wheel, his beard extinguished, with Donnelly, smiling quietly, at his side. Sheila, wearing a hat tied down by one of those great lawny scarfs that were all the go at the time, sat behind amid what looked like an immovable jam of children. When Dermot brought the car to a standstill and saluted with grave triumph, they unknotted themselves and were resolved into Rory, Eileen, and, appearing as it seemed from the floor of the car, the girl I knew must be Maggie Donnelly. If I had had any doubt in the matter, it would soon have been ended, for Rory, emerging out of the incredible confusion of that gregarious arrival, and ignoring everybody else, led the child straight up to me, holding her hand, and announced with a sort of shy pride: "This is Maggie, Uncle Bill. She's just as old as me."

"She's just as old-fashioned as you, anyway," I thought to myself;

and there was, indeed, something remarkably alike about those two children. They had the same serious friendly faces, the same straight eyes, grey and one might almost have said prematurely shadowed by thought, the same dark careless hair and pleasant irregular features. They stood there holding hands, very hot and dusty and excited, and Oliver swung carelessly on the gate, looking out of the corner of his eye at the little girl who had apparently this tremendous power of making Rory forget his friend. Then he leapt down from the gate, and, taking no notice of Rory, went straight up to Maggie. He planted himself before her, fresh and undusty, his hair golden in the sunlight. He offered her his hand and smiled radiantly. "I'm Oliver," he said. "Oliver Essex. Let me show you where to get a wash."

Maggie followed him politely, and Rory stood in the road, with a frown between his brows, kicking at the dust.

"Hi, Oliver!" I shouted. "Rory wants a wash, too," and at that Rory set off with a run and went into the house with the others.

Kevin Donnelly was a remarkable man. Everybody knows that now: everybody, that is, who knows anything of the recent history of Ireland. His name is on the page, among the martyrs.

But we, who could not foresee what was to come, had to accept into our midst a plain-seeming man who was not equipped with any halo of destiny or, indeed, with anything that we could see beyond a boundless good humour and wholesomeness. The most remarkable thing to us about him then was the way in which self-consciousness died in his presence. I have already described his short, thick-set appearance, the thin hair that was combed carefully across his skull, the big ragged moustache that adorned his homely face. But I had not till now seen the smile that was for ever breaking out, creasing little fans of laughter alongside his eyes, or heard his voice raised in song. There was something about him that instantaneously broke down, not your dignity, but any second-hand armour that had been pretending to be dignity. I have never known any man who could more decidedly, simply by being nothing but his unpretentious self, sweep away pretentiousness from his companions.

I had dreaded his meeting with Nellie, but there was nothing to fear. Donnelly was, among other things—among so many other things!—a simple artisan; and that was something Nellie understood. They shook hands, looked in one another's eyes, and I had an instant conviction that all was well between them.

Dermot had told me that Donnelly was a silver-tongued orator. His speaking voice was sweet and moving, and ever and again he would break into song. Unself-consciously as he did everything else, he would lift up his voice and sing a song through from beginning to end. If Maggie were by, she would join in and he would leave the main business to her, himself elaborating the harmonies.

And so I remember that holiday not least because it was a holiday of song. It began that night after dinner. We were all sitting in front of the balustrade, looking down upon the water, five grown-ups and four children, when suddenly Donnelly began to sing. He had a rich tenor voice, and he opened his throat and let the music flow out into the night. It was a comic song about an Irish horse-fair. It took us all by surprise and we listened a little uneasily, then with growing appreciation and finally with delight. When he had finished, we applauded, and he smiled, pleased that his efforts were well seen.

"Now then!" he cried. "Something we all know. Open your throat, Maggie, and the rest of you, too." And he led off into "Annie Laurie," and soon had us under his spell.

That was how the concert began, and before long we were wrangling like children to have our favourite tunes. Dermot started ed "On Ilka Moor baht 'at," and if you can't join in the marvellous harmonies of Ilka Moor, then you don't deserve a sing-song like the one we had that night. We were on the last glorious absurd verse—

"That's 'ow us gets wer oan back"—when I was suddenly aware of a rustling in the shrubs that lined the path to the river. The next moment, the white hair and beard of Captain Judas showed ghost-like against the gloom. He stood still, watching us breathlessly; and hardly had the last harmony faded across the river than, to my surprise, and to the consternation of those who had not seen him, he suddenly began to sing in a high cracked voice: "When I survey the wondrous Cross."

It was a dreadful moment, charged with the possibility of fiasco, but Donnelly whispered "Maggie!" and those two trained voices struck together into the hymn, strongly supporting and carrying forward the trembling reed of Captain Judas. Then Nellie began to sing, and then Dermot's bass threaded powerfully into the harmony. Soon we were all singing, the captain, pale still against the gloom of the tunnel, solemnly beating time with his skinny hand. The words rolled through the woods and across the water.

> When I survey the wondrous Cross
> On which the Prince of Glory died,
> My richest gain I count but loss
> And pour contempt on all my pride.

Donnelly knew the hymn and led majestically into the beginning of each verse. We sang it through to the end:

> Were the whole realm of nature mine
> That were an offering far too small.
> Love so amazing, so divine,
> Demands my life, my soul, my all.

The words died away in a falling cadence. Judas remained for a moment with his hand upraised, his head lifted to the dark sky;

then suddenly he was there no more. Donnelly rose. "That was beautiful," he said. "That was the most beautiful of all."

The party split up, drifted away to the house, Sheila and Nellie rounding up the children for bed. Donnelly remained, his elbows on the balustrade, his chin on his hands. I stood for a moment at his side. He seemed to be deeply moved. "Sorrow and love flow mingled down," he murmured. "Sorrow and love—mingled—always."

I think that, whatever had happened, I should have remembered that night and the disturbing irruption of Captain Judas, turning so suddenly the thoughts of all of us to that emotional key which broke up the party and sent us scattering this way and that, as though nothing further were now to be said. But I remember it the more poignantly because the hymn we then sang was the one which, years later, Donnelly's gaolers heard him singing the night before they led him out and shot him against a wall. It is now part of the Irish legend, Donnelly's hymn in the prison; and I have often wondered whether in his loneliness that night he thought, and perhaps gained some strength from the thought, of us sitting with him in friendship, and the quiet night, and the trees, and the river running to the sea.

With wraps over our bathing-suits and towels thrown like mufflers round our necks, we ran down the path to the quay the next morning. When Donnelly threw off his wrap I noticed the great depth of his chest, the breadth of his shoulders, the solid moulding of his legs. We all stood there on the edge of the quay, waiting to leap together. The sun rained down in a diamond sparkle on the water. "Now did you ever see a prettier sight than that?" Donnelly shouted. "The colours of 'em—like jockeys waiting for the flag."

Certainly we had come out very colourfully. Oliver was in the lightest blue, Rory in dark red, Eileen, who was standing there arm-in-arm with Maggie, was wearing green, and Maggie was wearing white. Sheila's bathing-dress was bright canary yellow and Dermot's maroon. Mine was a vivid scarlet, and Donnelly's was barred in red and white.

"Sure, we all look grand," Donnelly shouted. "But where's Mrs. Essex?"

"Don't worry about her," I said. "She doesn't bathe."

"In you go," said Donnelly, and as I leapt I was aware of the coloured figures leaping on either hand. I came up from the dive and lay over on my back. Then I saw that Donnelly had not dived. With his wrap once more about him, he was disappearing up the path. We were still in the water when he came back. He was dressed in flannel bags and an old white sweater. He went to Sam Sawle's shack and banged on the door. I came out and dried myself and joined them. "Mrs. Essex has no bathing-dress," Donnelly said, as though that explained everything. "She'll go in to Truro with Maggie this afternoon and buy one."

"But she doesn't swim," I said.

"There's fun to be had in the water without swimming," he said. "We're just going into that."

Sam Sawle managed to produce four barrels, and he and Donnelly tinkered about on the quay for the rest of the day. By sundown they had fabricated a fine raft, with rope loops scalloped upon its edge and a cocoanut matting floor. The next morning I was with them when they considered the question of mooring it. "There's a great chunk of concrete down there, with an iron ring in it," Sam said, pointing to the water just off the quay. "There used to be a mooring-buoy fixed to it."

Donnelly got into his bathing-suit, and we took out a long thin rope in a dinghy. It was coiled to run out easily after him when he dived. He filled his gorgeous chest, stood erect on the stern seat for a moment, then went down like an arrow. We could see his white limbs, ripple-distorted and as if themselves fluid in the water, fumbling about on the bottom. Then he shot up. His fingers splintered the surface. He hurled the end of rope aboard. Sawle caught it and knotted it quickly round a thwart. Donnelly took a great gulp of air and lay over on his back. Then with finny motions of the hands he paddled himself ashore. Sawle watched him with admiration. "I'd never worry about the children if they were out with 'e," he said.

Dermot had rowed up in the praam. "Hear that, Bill?" he grinned. "Lay it to heart, my boy; lay it to heart."

Sam Sawle fastened the thin rope to one that was as stout as a cable, and we hauled that with difficulty through the ring in the concrete. Then that stout rope was attached to the bottom of our raft, which we had launched with shouts of delight and which the children had christened the Kevin. And the Kevin made a glorious diving raft for the rest of the holiday. Donnelly himself rowed Nellie out to it, wearing the first bathing-dress she had ever put on in her life. She sat for some time on the rocking raft, looking at once pleased and distrustful. With infinite patience, Donnelly, swimming round and round the raft as confidently as a porpoise, with his sparse wet hair in thin black streaks upon the white of his skull, persuaded her to grip the scallops of rope, to lower herself into the water, to hang on, and to kick. Soon she was off and on the raft with confidence. But, more wonderful than that, before the holiday was over she had made the transit from raft to quay steps with a rapid anguished breast stroke, Donnelly at her side covering the distance with one powerful clip of the legs and reach forward of the arms. He was on the steps to help her ashore, to put a wrap about her, and to send her to the house with an encouraging word. Then with a leap like a buck, he dived far out, came up and trudgeoned across the water. Oliver and Rory watched him worshipfully. "Teach us that, Mr. Donnelly," they shouted. "Teach us!"

"Come on, then," he said, blowing the moustache away from his lips. "Dive in now, and come here to me." They flashed together from the raft, eager and emulous.

Dermot and I, tousle-headed, standing on the quay, looked at one another, towels in hand.

"All right, Bill?" he asked, quizzing me.

"Yes," I said. "It seems to be all right. Yes, I think so."

And I felt a bit ashamed that I had never bothered to teach Nellie that rudimentary breast stroke that had filled her with pride, that Donnelly had so easily dragged her out of the kitchen. I went up to the house wondering whether in a great many things I had not given up too soon with Nellie. But it was too late to start bothering about that now. I looked back across the river, and saw Oliver and Rory patiently following the shouted instructions of Donnelly. Leaning on the rail of the *Jezebel*, Captain Judas was watching them through a pair of glasses.

It was part of the Heronwater tradition that people came down to breakfast when they felt like it. Dermot was there, sitting at the long refectory table that he had himself made, and Donnelly, Nellie and Rory had appeared too. "Nellie," Dermot was saying as I entered the room, "I am an ambassador, charged by this sprig"— he waved his long hand towards Rory—"to make a request which he is afraid to make for himself. Namely, luncheon sandwiches for two."

"That's easy," said Nellie. "Why didn't you ask me, Rory?"

Rory slowly coloured. "Because there's a woman in the case," said Dermot.

"I know a good place for blackberries," said Rory, keeping his face down to his plate. "I've promised to take Maggie there. It's a long way. You have to take lunch," he added defensively.

"I know it," said Oliver, who had come into the room. "I know a short cut. I'll show you."

"We're going the river way," Rory said, his earnest pug face puckered. "We don't want a short cut."

"I'll take some lunch and go the short cut and meet you," Oliver promised.

Rory looked up, with the frown on his face deepening. "I'm showing her, not you," he said.

Oliver stood by the door, very tall for his age, beautiful with the golden brown of sun and sea on him, and a flush spread up his face to the very roots of his weather-bleached fair hair. Rory didn't want him, and had said so. "Very well," he said, and came and sat at the table, lordly and self-possessed. Rory looked at him with anguish in his ugly face, affection in his straight eyes; but Oliver's eyes were aloof. Rory's grappling for a contact came to nothing.

Oliver was on the quay when Rory and Maggie set off in the dinghy. He made it appear that he was there by accident. He kept his back to the departing boat and skiddled flat stones across the water. "Now, Oliver," said Donnelly when the dinghy was out of sight. "What about that trudgeon? Undivided attention. You'll beat Rory at it yet."

Oliver picked up another stone and skiddled it across the water. "I don't think I'll bother, thank you," he said, and didn't look round.

I had not yet done any writing at Heronwater. It had been simply a holiday place; but that day I found my mind in the jumping dithery state that meant I must sit down and sort out my ideas. Fortunately, I was deserted. Oliver and Eileen went off with Sam Sawle in one of the sailing dinghies, taking food, a kettle of water and a teapot with them. They would have a good day. Sam would land them on some beach where there was plenty of dry driftwood; they would make a fire, which was always a satisfactory thing to do; they would bathe, and then have one of Sam's "nice hot cups of tea," and altogether they would have the sort of generally-messing-about day that the district could so excellently provide.

Dermot and Sheila, Donnelly and Nellie went off in the *Maeve*, intending to make a day of it, too, with the Helford River for their destination. You see how Nellie was flowering? Nothing I could have said or done would have prevailed upon her to spend a day in the motor-boat; but there she was, and there was Donnelly, his rich voice rolling back over the water, as the boat disappeared round a bend, upraised in *The Wearing of the Green*. He certainly had a way with people.

I walked slowly up the path to the house. Never before had I had Heronwater to myself. I told the maids not to bother me with lunch, and sat down at my table in the long room that looked out on the lawn and the balustrade. I always enjoyed the actual physical business of writing, and I was in full enjoyment of the delightful process that morning, pipe going, mind easy, thinking how good a place Heronwater was proving for that sort of job, when a shadow crossed the window. I did not look up. I thought perhaps one of the maids had passed. But the shadow came again, and when I raised my head with some annoyance I saw that Captain Judas was pacing the lawn, his hands clasped behind his back, his whiskered chin sunk in meditation upon his chest.

I did my best to ignore him. Let him think I had not seen him. I went on with my work. But to and fro the shadow went. There was no putting it aside. I looked up with a frown, but though Judas must have seen me, I could not catch his eye. He was evidently determined to play the part of infinitely patient waiter; but my own patience was exhausted and my mind thrown off the track. I got up and went to the open window.

"Good-morning," I said crossly. "I was trying to get a bit of work done."

"I hope I haven't disturbed you," he said politely. "Not for worlds—"

"You seem to want to speak to me."

He combed his white fingers through the glossy white silk of his beard. "I want you to come to the *Jezebel* and see something," he said, looking nervous, like a child who fears its request will be refused.

"Very well. I must leave this now till after lunch. But look, Captain Judas, you must promise me: when I'm writing you mustn't hang about," I smiled as pleasantly as I could. "We're both writers—eh? How would you like to be interrupted just when the ideas are beginning to bubble—eh?"

The thought flattered him, and he began at once effusively to denounce his own dreadful manners. "Unpardonable, Mr. Essex. I'm going—at once. Some other time, when neither of us is in the divine grip—" And he began to make off swiftly on his tiny feet.

I climbed through the window, caught him up, and put my arm through his. "So long as we understand one another for the future," I said, "that's all right. Now what is it you want me to see?"

We were at the water's edge, and he waved me into his dinghy. "Wait," he said mysteriously. "I came this morning," he was all apology again, "because I saw everyone go but you. I can't often get you alone, and this is between you and me. Understand? I suspected it. Now I know."

We climbed aboard and went down to his big sitting-room. There was a litter of packing paper on the table. His long-expected Greek primer and lexicon had arrived. He stood me in front of the fireplace, cocked his head expectantly, and said: "Well?"

I was puzzled. I didn't understand what the bother was about. All I could see was that the picture of the crucifixion which had been over the fireplace was gone, and in its place was another picture, unframed, held to the wall, with drawing-pins. Upon this the old man's gaze was fixed. "Well?" he said again, rather impatiently. "Don't you recognise him?"

I looked more closely. It was a reproduction of a painting by Holman Hunt or Millais—I forget which—showing the boy Jesus in the workshop of Joseph the carpenter. The child stood there with his arms outstretched, and behind him on the wall was the shadow of the cross.

"Guard him well," Judas said solemnly. "And remember I am at your side. They'll see," he said in a sudden rising fury, "they'll see if I'm a betrayer."

"I don't understand," I said rather coldly, though I knew at once what shape the old man's mania was taking now.

"You don't understand," he said sadly. "Even you." He shook his head. "But I—I suspected it long ago, and when this came, wrapped round my books, I *knew*. Why should it have been sent to *me?*" he demanded, his excitement rising again. "It might have gone to anyone, but it came to me—to me. It confirms it. It confirms everything."

I looked hard at the picture. There was no likeness to Oliver, save the likeness of youth and beauty. What could I do? How tell this poor crazy chap that his sustaining dreams were baseless and abortive? I simply shook my head. "I don't understand," I said again.

"Well," he said, "guard his youth, Mr. Essex. Let him play. Let him be a child. Let him enjoy the happiness of this beautiful world. Now I know why I was sent to this place." His one living eye brightened and burned and he took on the strange apocalyptic look that visited him from time to time. "Let him be happy," he said. "His time will come again, his hour of darkness will descend, he will be betrayed. But this time they will know where Judas stands."

I stumbled up the steps into the sunlight. I couldn't listen to him any more. His was the only boat there. I got into it and rowed swiftly away. Let him stay there. He couldn't reach me again today. He was beginning to give me the creeps.

I wasn't in the mood to go on with my work. I went up to the house and got into a bathing-suit, then lay on the raft, sunning myself. Presently the sound of a propeller wove itself into the summer stillness, the gentle lapping of water, the rustle of leaves, the shrill cries of the oystercatchers darting in little orderly companies here and there. I rolled over and lay on my stomach, chin cupped in hands, watching the approaching ship. She was a small grimy-looking customer, carrying a high piled deck cargo of timber and flying the Danish flag. In a moment or two, as my raft began to rock in her wash, I saw her name, lettered on her black rounded stern: *Kay Kobenhavn*. On the bridge of the *Kay* of Copenhagen was an officer who with one hand was holding his white gold-braided cap and scratching a generous growth of the yellowest hair I have ever seen on man. It glowed in the sunlight like a great sunflower. The man was looking towards the *Jezebel*, and as he passed he pulled a string and a spout of steam projected itself into the still air and a hoarse scream, twice repeated, burst from the whistle.

I saw Judas rush on deck and wave frantically towards the *Kay* of Copenhagen. "*Kay* ahoy!" he shouted. "Jansen! Jansen!"

The yellow-headed officer waved his cap and replied, "*Jezebel* ahoy! Judas!"

"See you tonight," Judas bawled, megaphoning through his hands to the retreating stern of the *Kay*.

"Ja! Tonight!" Captain Jansen answered. Judas watched the ship out of sight, twisting her way up the river to Truro. Then he began to walk the deck on his small springy feet, very swiftly, very excitedly.

Jansen had a soft place in his heart for Judas. So much we soon discovered; and when I say we I mean Dermot, Donnelly and myself. We had to meet Jansen. Nothing else would suit Captain Judas. As soon as Judas's boat was returned that afternoon, he used it to come over and tell me what a great and wonderful man Jansen was. It was an incoherent narrative, and I could disentangle little from it except an impression that Jansen had known Judas in the days when the old man had all his wits about him, and had continued to treat him as a human being when a good many other people had ceased to do so. Jansen came once or twice a year to Truro with timber, and the friends then foregathered on the *Kay* and, I gathered with some surprise, dazzled Truro with the outrageous unconventionality of their conduct. I think it was the prospect of being present on one of these occasions, the opportunity to see Captain Judas painting Truro red, that made me accept the invitation at once and promise to bring Dermot and Donnelly.

We set off after dinner by road in Dermot's car. Judas was looking unusually spruce. His small shoes twinkled, his hair and beard looked electric with brushing, and his navy-blue clothes were as neat as a midshipman's. "You'll see!" he chuckled, sitting next to me on the back seat. "A Norseman! A Viking! A mighty man of valour!"

"Come on, boys," Donnelly shouted. "Get in tune for this nautical occasion." And he began to sing "As I was a-walking down Paradise Street, with a way—hey—blow the man down." We all sang as Dermot's car raised the dust along the quiet road, even Judas, not given, I had imagined, to secular melody, coming in with a reedy line here and there.

We parked the car in the timber-yard at whose quay the *Kay* was lying. Judas danced excitedly before us up the gangplank. "Jansen!" he piped. "Jansen! Where are you? We're here. I've brought my friends."

"Goom in! Ja! Enter. Entrez," Jansen's deep voice boomed, and Judas made his way before us to the cabin. Jansen was shaving. A bit of looking-glass was propped against a jug on the cabin table. His yellow mop flared above a white mask of lather. He stood up when Judas entered, and then I saw why he had been sitting down to shave. He was a giant, and he advanced towards Judas doubled up, as though he were about to spring, suddenly gathered the little man in his arms and hugged him to his chest. I expected to hear Judas's ribs snap, but Jansen put him gently back on to the ground as though he were something precious and stood there, bent over him, a grin splitting his frothy mask. "Ja," he growled. "Mein frent Judas, mon ami—ja? Amigo. Yes, yes. Goom in, señores."

He continued to growl in a variety of languages, as he grasped my hand and made the bones crack. "I resume now to shave myself. Asseyez-vous, messieurs."

He finished off the business with a large cut-throat razor, and his face was revealed a gleaming pink, hale as a child's, with a curling golden moustache, and with bright blue eyes, shining with extraordinary candour. He looked at Judas, sitting in a chair with his tiny feet barely touching the ground, grinned as though the spectacle pleased him, and began to growl: "Ah, mein frent Judas…" I thought he was about to rush to the little man and squeeze him again, but he merely punched him, saying: "You save my life? No?" He nodded to us: "Ja, he save my life. I relate to you cette conte-là. But not now. Nein. First, señores, we light—no?—ignite?—Truro. But now I wash. I give myself respectfulness."

He heaved the shirt off his back with one over-the-head pull, revealing a torso of golden bronze, rippling with muscle. Then he stepped outside the door, straightened, and we could see nothing of him from the shoulders up. I strolled through the door after him, and there he was, sluicing his face, neck and body from a bucket of water that stood on a tub. He turned to me, grinning: "Goot! Eh? To refresh the ideas! So!" His big white teeth gleamed in his ruddy face. He rolled the towel into a rope, slung it over his shoulders, and with an end in each hand sawed to and fro, grunting with pleasure.

He went back into the cabin and dressed, putting on a white shirt, a stiff white collar, a black tie, and a double-breasted navy-blue jacket. Finally he slapped his white, gold-braided cap at a slant upon his head. "Thus one is ready. Is it not, old captain?"

Judas beamed and nodded.

"Then we go."

He walked before us, folded up, till we got out of the cabin, then he straightened to his great height, which must have been six foot four, filled his lungs with air on the deck, and drummed heartily on his chest with both fists. He looked round with his white-toothed grin at Judas. "I eat you—eh? One—two—fini!"

Judas smiled as if he would have been only too pleased to provide a morsel for Jansen. He tried to slap his friend heartily on the back, but it was as near as nothing a smack on the bottom, so that we all got ashore laughing and made our way in good humour through the timber-yard.

Jansen ashore after a voyage was clearly a man of one idea. He leaned his great shoulders against the first pub door we came to, and we all tailed after him: Dermot, Donnelly, myself, with Captain Judas in the rear. Jansen picked Judas up and sat him on a tall stool at the counter. "So, my hero, I see you better," he said.

There was no one in the bar but a barmaid who looked like a clergyman's daughter. She put down a novel and served us with reluctance. "For the love of God," Donnelly whispered, "decide what you're going to drink, and stick to it. This man's dangerous." And aloud: "A John Jamieson, miss, please." Dermot and I ordered whiskey too, Jansen rum and Judas ginger-beer.

The barmaid murmured as though it were a litany: "One Jamieson, one Haig, one White Horse, one rum, one ginger-beer." Donnelly paid; we took up our drinks and made for a table in the corner of the room. We were seating ourselves when Jansen banged his already empty glass on the counter, had it refilled, and then joined us. It was not that he wanted to dodge standing his turn; he stood his turn with the rest of us; but he drank twice for every drink of ours. In between rounds he would, as it were, stand himself one and throw it off at a gulp.

There were five rounds that night, in five different pubs, so that Jansen had ten rums, which, as I understand these things, is pretty good going. He drank them, too, and Donnelly drank his five John

Jamiesons, which is more than Dermot and I did. After the first two, we developed the technique, which was cowardly but efficient, of leaving the greater part of the drink in the glass. Even so, the very atmosphere of the pubs, and the hilarity of Jansen, and the frequent song-bursts of Donnelly, gave the evening a somewhat unusual texture for me, and woven against that background was the epic which Jansen, after four or five drinks, began to develop.

The affair which made Judas a hero in his eyes had happened, it appeared, the best part of twenty years before. Jansen was a ship's boy, making his first voyage. He insisted, in the pubs as we sat smoking our pipes, and in the quiet streets as we wandered from one bar to the next, on elaborating every detail: his boyish misery, the rotten food, the kicks and cursing, the gradual demoralisation of his whole being, so that when in the North Atlantic the gale burst upon his ship he had nothing left, no reserves, nothing but sheer funk, terror.

He certainly learned everything about the sea that first voyage. He took refuge in the galley at the height of the storm. "I am afraid. Ja. I shiver. There is nothing—rien du tout—but a few little bits of sail left up there; and I am afraid, sick in my guts, that the captain say: 'Goddam you! Go and fix them sails.' So I hide in the galley."

The ship was wallowing, soggy, full of water. The galley floor was awash, and the galley walls shuddered under the thump of the waves. The next thing Jansen knew was that there were no galley walls to be thumped. The galley went, and he with it, choking and spluttering as though he were already done for. He was slammed by the rush of the wave against a hatch coaming, hung on, and when the wave had passed over, he saw the mainmast lying across the deck, snapped off at the foot, holding to its stump by a sinew or two and trailing its peak in the sea. It had smashed the captain and two men in its fall. The mate yelled to him to get a hatchet and help cut the wreckage free.

"And now, señores, I am not afraid. I am brave. Ja. I run to get the hatchet, and then I am in the water. Like that." With an undulating motion of his huge outspread hand he swept a cork off the table and sent it spinning across the room.

So Jansen was spun into the North Atlantic, the only man of that crew to come out of it alive. He was washed against the floating galley, clung to it, and five minutes later saw the ship vanish in the grey water of the storm. "But my life, it is—how?—enchanted? charmed?—si, señores. I am a charmed life. There is the ship with my hero!"

He slapped Judas's knee. The little captain looked at him affectionately, and kept his eyes modestly averted from the rest of us.

The floating galley, with Jansen clinging to it more dead than alive, was seen from the ship, but in the terrific weather no boat could be lowered. Jansen told his story well. Now he was down in the trough, gazing up despairingly at the glassy, dark-green, white-flecked wall whose tattered and toppling summit shut out from view all else that was in the world. Then the wall slipped its whole weight and bulk under him and his frail ark, and lifted him up and into and through that dither and surging of its crest. Thence, for a moment, he would see the ship, and wave with the last of his ebbing strength, then down again he would plunge into the black gulf flecked as if with snow by ten million bubbles.

In one of those seconds when he was uplifted by the water and was gazing with all hope and all despair in his eyes he saw a man poised for a second on the ship's rail, then saw him drop off into the boiling of the waves.

"It is my little captain—ja—so small—so big a hero—eh? But he is not then a captain—no—he is no one—no long hair, no whiskers."

Judas self-consciously combed his beard with his fingers and sipped his ginger-beer, as Jansen threw the eighth or ninth rum down his throat and reached the climax of his story. For a time, no sign of the rescuer. Upon the crest, his eyes searching the tormented water; down into the trough, with hope dying and his breath sobbing; and then Judas's face breaking suddenly through the white fringe of a wave.

"Ah! Just so little a man, señores; but his face is like the sun coming out of the night. I lean over and grab him—so tight!—and pull him on to the galley. I feel I am saving him, for already I am so big, and already he is so little. Then he fastens his rope round a plank of the galley, and we are in tow. Ah, señores, just a little rope, no thicker than that"—he held up his thumb—"with all the Atlantic ocean rushing over it, but I am no longer sobbing, because the little rope is tied to the galley."

"Praise the Lord," said Judas suddenly, "and forget not all his benefits." Then he began to sing:

*Throw out the life-line, throw out the life-line;*
*Someone is sinking today.*

He leaned back in his chair, with his eyes closed, holding his glass in his left hand and beating time with his right. The barmaid, who, here, was not so disdainful as the clergyman's daughter, contemplated his performance for a while in silence, then said sympathetically: "You'd better be taking Dad home."

"I think so, too," said Dermot, dexterously concealing his full whiskey glass behind a jug; and we all clattered out into a night which was very dark though the sky was starry.

Jansen was as firm on the ground as an oak. "Now you all come back to the *Kay*—ja?—and we make some grog."

We turned down this proposal with vigour.

"Then my hero will come and spend the night with me—eh, Judas, mon vieux?"

There could be no objection to that, since Judas would find the grog no temptation. We watched the tall figure of Jansen mount the gangplank, his head appearing for a moment among the stars. He stooped and took Judas under the arms as though he had been a child, and held him aloft for our inspection. "You see him—eh? Now you know why I shall do anything for him. Ja, *anything*. Now I make the grog. Buenos noches, señores."

We saw him bend double and go into the cabin. Then Dermot started up the engine. The night air blowing in our faces was good, and Donnelly opened his throat and sang:

*If you're the O'Reilly men speak of so highly,*
*Gorblimey, O'Reilly, you are looking well.*

The *Maeve*, with the luggage aboard, was ready at the quay to take us to Falmouth, and Oliver, Nellie and I were at the gate to see Dermot depart with his overcrowded car. They went off in a halo of dust. Donnelly, sitting on the back seat, had Rory on one side of him and Maggie on the other. One of his arms was round each.

We made our way down the path winding through the wood, which already was touched here and there with red and yellow, and got aboard. The *Kay* was going by, outward bound. Jansen, on the bridge, blew his whistle, and Judas came out to wave. They exchanged farewells across the water, and when the *Kay* was round the bend we, too, shouted good-bye. Judas fluttered his handkerchief and then rushed below, as though the sight of so many friends leaving him were more than he could bear.

All the way home that time Oliver nagged about motor-cars. When are *we* going to have a car? Can't we afford a car as well as Uncle Dermot? Think how nice it would be to save all that journey into Falmouth and go straight to Truro by road.

"I like going in to Falmouth," I said.

"So do I," said Nellie. "For goodness' sake, Oliver, give over whining for everything you fancy. How many boys d'you think get the things you have? Rowing-boats and sailing boats and I don't know what. D'you think your father had these things when he was a boy?"

"There weren't motor-cars when father was a boy."

"And we got on very well without them," said Nellie. "Nasty smelly things they are, anyway. I shouldn't like to eat bread delivered in those things."

Oliver flushed. No one had ever told him in so many words the story of the Moscrop bakery, but from things he had heard he had put the facts together, even to my inglorious employment as vanboy. I knew it was a topic he did not like. I watched his flush with amusement—a flush so beautiful on the skin that was golden brown like one of old Moscrop's loaves. "You needn't bring that up," he said.

There! Now it was out! That was the first time he had allowed his resentment to escape in words.

"Bring what up?" Nellie asked sharply.

"You know what." Oliver squirmed on his seat and looked desperately unhappy.

Nellie looked at him, the holiday colour draining from her face. "You little snob," she said venomously. "If you're referring to the work your grandfather did all his life and that your father did when he was a young man, then I only hope you'll do something half as useful when you grow up."

Oliver's colour deepened. He did not answer, and Nellie went on, after a shocked, wondering silence: "Well, I never did? I never expected to hear that you were ashamed of your father. Let me tell you this, my boy; if you're half the man your father is, then some woman will be lucky."

This was very handsome of Nellie. She was not in the habit of paying me compliments; but also it seemed to me rather amusing. Oliver was being a little fool; no doubt about that; but Nellie, I thought, was taking it with rather a heavy hand.

"Well, Oliver," I said, "you seem to have discovered that your grandfather kept a baker's shop and that I drove his van. Tell me, honestly, d'you think that matters a damn?"

"William!" Nellie exclaimed.

"Do you, Oliver?" He looked slowly from Nellie's outraged face to my amused and smiling one. He shook his head.

"Good!" I said. "Because there it is. If you don't like it, you can lump it."

Part III

## 18

Nellie cocked her short-sighted eyes up to the sky and said: "The nights are drawing in."

I had accompanied her down the long garden path of The Beeches. She paused at the gate and said, "I shan't be long." She patted my arm, gave me a wan smile, and trotted away to the right, to the Wesleyan chapel.

She was warmer in her manner towards me. I was forty. She was a year older. We had been married for fifteen years. Each of us realised the limitations of that companionship. Nothing had ever set it on fire; nothing had given it glory. During the last couple of years its comfortableness had deepened. I think perhaps Nellie was glad to have me to herself. Dermot and Sheila had gone to live in London, taking Eileen with them. Maeve had left Mary Latter. She had lapped up all that Mary Latter had to teach her, and now she was playing her first part in a London theatre. I hadn't seen her in it. I should have to run up to town soon. Her work, when I had seen her once or twice with the Latter Company in Manchester, had surprised and thrilled me.

Rory was in Dublin. I knew less of him than of the others. He had written occasionally to Oliver, but now Oliver was away at school, so I didn't see even letters.

I leaned on the gate, looking up and down the empty road. Autumn melancholy was upon the suburb and upon me, too. There was a faint wind in the beeches over my head, and they sounded dry and done. A few yellow leaves spun through the beams of a street lamp, that was contending with the twilight. Down in the meadows, where I had been accustomed to play football with Oliver, the white mist would be crawling across the fields, as I had so often watched it crawl when, a boy, I looked out through Mr. Oliver's study window.

An inexpressible sadness settled upon me. I felt that a phase of my life was ended. Oliver gone. The one family in Manchester that had meant anything to me gone. Nellie was still there, sensing my trouble, being maternal. I wondered what she would say if I tried to carry our relationship, after a long cessation of intimacy, beyond the realm of sad male and comforting mother-woman. We still slept together and served each other in the office of a blanket. That was something. There was a nip in the air tonight.

I walked back to the house with a pipe in my teeth and my hands in my pockets. There was not even work to do. I had finished a novel a week ago—my twelfth—and I was loose-ended and aimless, a prey to harpy-emotions that came crowding out of the nostalgia of the October twilight. I felt an urgent desire to tear up my roots, have done with Manchester, and match myself against some environment that was new.

In my study I looked at the eleven novels in the elegant case that Dermot had made for them—leather-bound presentation copies from my publisher. He could afford them too; he had done well out of me. Soon the twelfth would stand beside the eleven. Then the case would be full. I had not noticed that before. It seemed to me an omen.

Leave novels alone for a bit. After all, I had nothing more to say about Manchester and the people who lived in it. Those twelve books would be a sufficient monument so far as that part of my life was concerned. The critics said I had done for Manchester what Arnold Bennett had done for the Five Towns. I had: and more. I had stayed on the spot and worked with the material under my eyes.

Prowling about, restless as a beast in a zoo cage, fiddling with this and that, I knew suddenly that I would write no more novels about

Manchester. I wanted to leave the place; I wanted to go to London. Maeve was growing up. Time I thought about that play for her.

The corners of the room were full of shadow and I was ruminating in my easy chair when I heard Nellie's voice calling from downstairs. "William! Are you there? Can you spare a moment?"

I went down and found her in the hall with a big gaunt parson. "Oh, William, this is Mr. Wintringham."

I had seen his name on the chapel boards: the Rev. W. Wilson Wintringham. He was over on some special business: anniversary services yesterday, a lecture on "The Message of Whitman" tonight. You were no good at all to these chaps unless they could dig a message out of you. It appeared that there had been a breakdown in transport arrangements. The Rev. W. Wilson Wintringham had to get home that night and the car which was to take him to the railway station at Wilmslow had not appeared.

"I thought if you were not busy tonight—" Nellie appealed.

I told the Rev. W. Wilson Wintringham that I would be pleased to take him to Wilmslow. I would have been pleased to take him to Jericho or anywhere else. A blow in the fresh air was just what I needed, and since taking to motoring a year ago I had come to like it more and more. Far too much to employ a chauffeur, though that was what Oliver wanted me to do. "But Uncle Dermot's got a chauffeur now." Well, he can keep him.

Mr. Wintringham thanked me in a sort of consecrated *basso profundo* which caused his Adam's apple to bob up and down like an egg in an old brown stocking. I invited him to take a whisky and soda—"the sort of drink Whitman would have appreciated, I'm sure, Mr. Wintringham"—but he declined, and Nellie urged me to make haste or we would miss the train.

I got out the car—an open four-seater—and off we went, Nellie beside me in front, the Rev. W. Wilson Wintringham nursing his despatch-case full of the message of Whitman in the back.

"And what do you think *is* the message of Whitman, Mr. Wintringham?" I shouted, as we turned left by the squat old church at Cheadle.

"Well, generally speaking, just brotherly love," Mr. Wintringham's bass roared over the engine.

"And how's brotherly love getting on in this old world? I suppose you're in a position to keep an eye on these things?"

"Rather!" he agreed heartily. "Reports from the foreign field, you know. I think you'd be surprised if you knew how the evangel of love is catching on in the world, if you'll allow me to put it that way."

"You think the reign of universal love and peace is appreciably nearer?" I asked, feeling like a junior reporter conducting an interview.

"No doubt! No doubt!" I could almost hear the gristly knob rasping up and down in his throat. "I predict that the next ten years will see an extension of Christ's Kingdom on earth that will surprise those who are not watching the signs. It's a blessed thing to be young today, Mr. Essex. The young will see signs and wonders. The poets were not mistaken—Whitman, Browning—"

"Oh, Browning. His message is that it's good to sing in the bath."

The Rev. W. Wilson Wintringham laughed suddenly, disconcertingly, like a horse neighing. I could feel his breath on my neck. "Well, here we are," I said thankfully.

We were lucky in not having to wait to see him off. The train drew in as we reached the platform. A moment later we were watching the red tail-light receding and diminishing in the bloomy dusk.

A great orange disc of moon had climbed into the sky. I fixed a rug round Nellie's knees and got in beside her. "Nellie," I said, as soon as we were off, "I've finished with Manchester. I've got nothing more to do here. I want to get out."

She gave a tremendous start. "Get out! But, William, we're so comfortable!"

"Yes, I know—too comfortable."

"Well, I call that downright ungrateful to Almighty God," she said, as though the Adam's apple had got into her throat. "Too comfortable! You should give thanks for your blessings, not cry them down."

"Nellie," I answered, "there are two things to be said to that. One is that your religion tells you to shun comfort like the plague. Sell all that thou hast. Not peace but a sword. That sort of thing. And there's this: that if I give thanks for my blessings, I'll give them to two people: to your father who accumulated the capital that allowed me to start in business and to myself whose darned pig-headed determination kept me writing till I wrote something worth reading."

She fell into a sulky silence for a while, then said: "You never think of me. You just announce what you're going to do."

"Do you remember," I said, "a long time ago I announced that we were shifting from Hulme to The Beeches? Don't you think it's been a good thing that we did?"

She made no answer. "Very well, then," I continued, "be reasonable. You will be consulted about the house we are to live in and everything else that concerns you, but leave Manchester I must, or I shall perish. You'll like London."

"London!" she breathed. "London! But I'd be terrified. You don't understand. You must not take me away from here."

"Don't let's talk about it any more just now," I said. "Think it over quietly."

I felt that the slight advances she had been making to me lately were chilled. She sat silent and resentful at my side. We came through Cheadle and turned left into the road that led straight home.

I gave the car an extra turn of speed. The full harvest moon shone down on the road and over the dark hedges and the fields sleeping at either hand. There is a path that comes through those fields. I had often used it myself. It brings you straight on to the road. There is no pavement. And that night came two lovers, oblivious of all save themselves under the enchantment of the moon. Oblivious of the car, a brutal thing that could not exist in their fairyland.

Straight out into the road they walked, arms wrapped around each other, and only then, caught in the sudden blaze of headlights did they pause, wrenched back to the world of sense. Then they stood stock-still while my heart cried: "Oh, poor young fools! Leap! Backwards or forwards. But leap!" and Nellie's hand went to her mouth, smothering a cry.

They did not leap. They dithered now forward, now backward. On me, then, the decision fell, and I drove the car full pelt between them and the hedge through which they had come. I suppose it was all a matter of three seconds, and already joy was springing up in me at having missed them, when I found that the car was not coming round on to the road again. There was a tearing of shrubs and saplings, a sudden remembrance, piercing me like a knife, that the hedge hid a sharply-falling bank. Then we were through the hedge, and my mind was recording everything with a dreadful slow-motion exactitude: the bonnet sticking its snout into the earth half-way down the bank, the end of the car lifting, poising, dropping forward, the car sliding with us beneath it for a little way, then coming to a standstill. I raised my arms, trying foolishly to lift the weight that oppressed us; I tried to move my legs, and agony forced a cry from me; I called "Nellie! Nellie! Are you all right?" but there was no answer, and when I ceased to shout and struggle in order to concentrate all my attention on listening for her breathing, I fell into panic, for there was no breathing, no movement, no sound at all, except the sound of men shouting and of hands rasping on the fabric of the car as it was seized and lifted.

A fractured thigh for me. A broken neck for Nellie. They said she must have died instantly. A statement was taken from me in hospital, but I could not attend the inquest. Dermot came down from London and made the formal identification. Dermot and Sheila arranged and attended the funeral in the Southern Cemetery. It was a long time before I saw the grave. Early in the new year I hobbled out of the nursing-home, whither I had gone from hospital. My new car was waiting for me, with a chauffeur at the wheel. I did not think I should want to drive again in a hurry, so here was Martin, a pleasant-looking youth enough, but wearing that impassive mask that chauffeurs have. Oliver would be pleased, anyway.

The amenities are beautifully considered at the Southern Cemetery. There is a monumental mason's where you may back your fancy, letting it range from a simple marble "surround" to a variety of angels: angels with heads bowed in sorrow, angels erect and triumphant bearing rewarding wreaths, angels kneeling with hands joined in prayer, and just angels, ready to do for a fee paid to the monumental mason a mercenary watchman's job of standing guard till judgment day. Next to the monumental mason's is an excellent public-house, where fortitude may be acquired before the cemetery is entered and sorrow assuaged when it is left.

The car stopped at the cemetery gates, and in the drear winter afternoon the marble angels shone, reminding me of that far-off day in Blackpool when Nellie and I considered the pictured angels on the walls of our boarding-house. I remembered, pottering among the graves with a stick in each hand, how that night she had taken me walking and how we had reached the cliffs at Norbeck and stood there holding on to one another while a sullen sea thudded on the beach and the wind howled round us in the dark.

I wondered whether I could have made life happier for Nellie. I had done all that the copybooks ordered. I had given her a home and supported her handsomely in it. I had given her a child that a mother might be proud of. I had been monogamous. Yet, walking through that flat expanse, under the grey lowering Manchester sky, with the monuments of the innumerable dead strewing the ground as far as the eye could reach, I reflected that I might easily have been a worse man and a better husband.

Dermot had told me how to find the grave amid that afflicting wilderness of graves, and it was with a shock that my eyes fell presently upon a humble piece of marble bearing the name Nellie Essex. At first, my mind, bemused by reverie, merely felt surprise that so soon Nellie should seem so much at home among the dead. Already the lettering looked old, the grave unkempt, as though it harboured an habituated and domestic ghost. Then I realised, with a catch of the breath, that I was looking at my mother's grave.

I had not known her Christian name. To my father, and to all of us children, she was always "Mother" when she was anything at all more than someone to be casually addressed. I had not seen the grave before. It seemed to me unbearably poignant that in such a place, at such a time, I should learn the simple secret of her identity, of the one thing that had been hers alone, her name. It was all she had, and no one had bothered about it.

Standing on the path, leaning on my two sticks, I gazed for a long time at the grave, then turned, walked a pace or two, and there, on the other side of the path, was the mound of clay that I had come to seek. Here, also, lay Nellie Essex, unrecorded as yet in marble, sleeping beneath the sodden remnants of the flowers that pity had heaped for concealment of the crude fact of burial. Broad white satin ribbon, stained by the earth into which the rain had beaten it, was draggled among the flowers. There were a few black-bordered cards, with the writing already indecipherable, anonymous valedictions.

Standing there in the path with a stick in each hand, I could almost touch the two graves of the women who, both, had been Nellie Essex. They had not known each other. At most, perhaps, in years gone by the younger Nellie Essex had been accustomed to hear her mother speak of Mrs. Essex for whom, in kindness, a bar of soap must be wrapped with the week's wash.

Washed…washed…washed… Sweeping through the gates of the New Jerusalem, washed in the blood of the Lamb.

I went slowly away, leaving to their sleep side by side two women who had loved me and whom I had not loved.

That was a Saturday afternoon. There was a letter waiting for me at the nursing-home when I got back. "Dear Uncle Bill"—I glanced at the signature—"Maeve." She was coming to see me tomorrow. "And you've got two things to thank for the pleasure—first, Livia; and, secondly, the intelligent management of this theatre which doesn't put the play on on Mondays. That gives us a lovely long week-end. I wonder when all managements will be so sensible and save poor actresses from nervous breakdowns? Livia is bringing me in her car. Man! She's a fiend of a driver, and that's just as well—there'll be so much more time to spend with you. The Sunday trains are dreadful. We shall start as soon as it's light, and you will wake up with burning ears, for we shall be talking about you all the way. Livia isn't doing this for me—oh dear no! She's dying to meet you. She's read all your books, and I don't think she quite believes that I know you. How wonderful to be a Person, whom mere people want to know! However, I live in hopes. It'll come!"

Well, that was a pleasant letter to get. I didn't feel quite so lonely now. I had my own room at the nursing-home. A maid came in and pulled the curtains, shutting out the prospect of bare boughs and evening mists. She switched on the lights, and the primrose walls and pale green curtains seemed to draw closer and more comfortably about me. My fire was going well, my tea was brought in.

Livia... That would be the girl Dermot had told me about when he was up for the funeral. I remembered that he had seemed a bit hurt. He and Sheila and Eileen were living at Hampstead. There was plenty of room for Maeve, but she preferred to live alone—"or rather with a girl—Vaynol—Livia Vaynol," Dermot said. There was a snap in his voice.

"He's jealous, Bill. Take no notice of him," Sheila said. "It'll do

Maeve all the good in the world to make her own friends and live as she wants to live. After all, she's had four years of knocking about with Mary Latter. She's no fool."

"She's only eighteen," Dermot objected.

"And how old is Rory? You've pushed him out into the world."

Dermot's eyes sparkled angrily. "Is there any comparison between the two things?" he demanded. "Rory's with a responsible man."

"He's not where we can descend on him in ten minutes as Maeve is," Sheila persisted. "Livia's all right. She'll do Maeve no harm."

There was no more said at the time. Livia Vaynol, I gathered later, was not much older than Maeve—twenty or so. She was an orphan with a little money: just enough to allow her to contemplate with humour a series of failures. She had scrounged a small part in the Mary Latter Company. That was where Maeve had met her. But she was not good enough. Then she had been in the chorus of a musical comedy and had hated it and left. She had dabbled with writing. She had, indeed, had a few short stories published in magazines. Now she was trying both to compose songs and to do what Sheila vaguely called "designing." "You know," she said, "she just draws shapes—squiggles—that look as if they meant something, but I can't see what. Dermot says they're good. He admits that much. He says that some day he may take her up for carpets and hangings and that sort of thing. Exclusive designs. The fact is, the poor child hasn't discovered what she wants to do, and she's not going to sit down and just live on her little income. I like her for that. And she's so good-humoured about it all—never discouraged."

Well, that was Miss Livia Vaynol; that was all I knew about her.


"My dear, what a woman you are!"

Maeve had come impetuously into the room. Crippled as I was, I couldn't get up quickly, and she stood looking down at me, holding both my hands in hers, as I sat in my chair. She was wearing a close-fitting little coat of grey astrakhan and a round hat of the same material. Her face was as white as ever, but the black eyes that had a hint of blue in them swam with pleasure, and her mouth was very red. Her hands gripped mine tight, and her body, which had grown tall and flexible, swayed above me with an emotion that I could feel passing into her hands. I wondered if she would kiss me. She didn't.

She sat down at my feet, leaning against the arm of my chair. "You poor dear," she said. "I'm so sorry."

"Don't let's talk about that. Tell me about your journey. And where is your friend—my admirer?"

"It was a wonderful journey, I suppose, as those journeys go. But I hate motoring, you know. It doesn't make me sick, thank God, but it's such a waste of time. Except that I was coming to see you." She gave my knee a pat. "That made it bearable."

"And when am I to see Miss Vaynol?"

"Oh, Livia'll be up in a moment. She's seeing that her precious car's all right."

"Tell me about your play." I tamped down the tobacco in my pipe, and Maeve sprang up to get the matches from the mantelpiece, struck one, and held it while I puffed.

"Oh, the play's grand," she said, sinking down to the floor again, "and I'm on in every act. Five minutes in the first, then a really important scene lasting for eleven minutes in the second, and off and on a lot in the third. It's a marvellous chance."

"And you're making good use of it. I know. Just hand me that book."

She brought the book from the table. "See," I said. "Here's what *The Times* says: 'Miss Maeve O'Riorden is a new actress who brought to the part of Henrietta Shane a talent that gave us both a fine performance and, what is more important, the promise of better work in the future.' And here's the *Telegraph*…"

"Oh, Man, that's sweet of you—to bother with my old cuttings," Maeve cried, jumping up and looking at me with her eyes shining.

"Well, look at the book," I said. "See what lovely stout leather binding it has! See how many pages! I had it specially made. And look at the title-page, written in my own best hand: 'Maeve's Progress.'"

"Oh, you shouldn't! You shouldn't!" she cried.

"Oh, yes, I should. See, they're all here. This is the very first. It crept into an Accrington paper when you were on your first tour with Mary Latter. Whitby, Aberdeen, Edinburgh, Carlisle, Birmingham. I've got your whole career taped out. Look! Here's one from a Cape Town paper—that's Mary Latter's South African tour."

"You darling!" she said. "Are you so much interested in me—in my career," she corrected herself with a blush, "as all that?"

"This is only the preamble," I laughed. "Wait till we come to the important chapter: 'Maeve O'Riorden in William Essex's plays.'"

She took the big book in her slender hands, placed it upon the carpet, and turned the leaves. "There's a terrible lot of pages," she sighed. "I wonder shall we fill them all?" She lifted to mine the eyes swimming with emotion in her white face. "No one cares so much about me as you do," she said. "You've wanted this from the beginning, haven't you, as much as I have?"

"My dear, I've wanted it as much as I've ever wanted anything, except perhaps to see Oliver doing things that will make me as proud as you do."

"Oh, Oliver." She got up and placed the book on the table. "And what is Oliver going to do?"

"I don't know. He's away at school now."

"Yes, I know. He's fifteen, isn't he?"

"Yes."

"Older than I was when I went off with Mary Latter."

"You mean—?"

"He's having a jammy life, isn't he?" She shrugged her shoulders with a faint dislike, then turned eagerly at the sound of footsteps on the stairs. "Livia!" She opened the door, and Livia Vaynol came in. "This is Uncle Bill," said Maeve, "or, if you want to be reverent, William Essex."

Livia Vaynol was the first woman I knew to wear short hair. As she came into the room she pulled off a leather motoring helmet and at the same time shook her hair free from constriction. The shake was hardly necessary, for the hair seemed of its own accord to ray out suddenly into a nimbus of spun gold round her head. I think that hair, which had its own startling quality of vitality, was the first thing anyone noticed about Livia Vaynol. It was the colour of corn, a gold that was almost white, yet sparkling and gathering to itself any light there was. Livia knew all about the attractiveness of that hair, and I was afterwards to discover that her favourite hat, whenever the occasion made it possible, was the simplest thing, fitting close to her head like a skull cap, allowing the hair to flow out all round it. Always the hat was of rich velvet: sometimes crimson, sometimes deep blue.

But at the moment there was no hat: there was nothing but that sudden apparition of the golden hair, so immediately impressive that I did not at once notice the broad white brow, the eyes that had the blue colour of a cornflower, the compassionate mouth, and the way the whole face fell down to the small pointed chin, so that it was shaped like the petal of a rose.

She was wearing a stained leather jerkin, and below that a tweed skirt and brogues. Her clothes seemed altogether too utilitarian for so decorative a person. We shook hands, and I said: "Miss Vaynol, you look like a fine flower in a jam-jar."

"I've brought a suit-case with me," she said, "containing one or two porcelain vases."

Her red mouth opened in a smile, revealing the even whiteness of her teeth.

"Yes, Uncle Bill," said Maeve, "you needn't worry about that, if you're thinking of taking us out to dinner. Livia's a dressy young piece, though you'd hardly believe it to look at her now."

"It certainly is my intention to take you out to dinner," I said.

"Do you remember the first time I did that? The night we saw Irving and Ellen Terry? It seems a long time ago."

"Ages."

"And we drove home in a four-wheeler. You were asleep in my arms, with my coat pulled round you."

"The child hasn't forgotten it, Mr. Essex," Livia said. "It's a memory she treasures like a pearl. She's told me about it. Don't blush, Maeve, darling. I'd be as proud as Punch to have famous men tucking me up in their coats. I was brought up among stockbrokers. They never called themselves that, of course. They were 'in the City.' Wonderful life, isn't it—buying something you've never seen from someone you've never met, and selling it for more than you gave for it to someone you've never heard of. Wonderful fellows. I've written a song about them. Like to hear it? You shall, anyway."

Maeve, clearly, was used to the oddities of Miss Livia Vaynol. She was unsurprised by this sudden threat to break into song. For my part, though the time was to come when I should hear Livia's songs before anyone else, I was perturbed when Livia's voice broke into the silence of that Sunday afternoon in Victoria Park.

Livia's voice was not good for singing, but the words amused me, and I congratulated her.

"Oh, a trifle," she said airily. "First-fruits. You see the idea? Chorus girls with top hats, marching to and fro across the stage, carrying attaché-cases. There's much more to come. I have great schemes for this young woman, Maeve O'Riorden."

"But Maeve's an actress, not a singer," I protested. "'Pon my soul, Miss Vaynol, I've set my heart on making Maeve an actress for years past, and we can't have you butting in and turning her into a ballad-singer."

Livia made a gesture that I was to get to know as characteristic. She raised both hands to the golden fluff-ball of her hair and threw them up sharply as though she would toss the bright bubble into the air. "Poof!" she said. "An actress isn't just a solemn hussy reciting someone else's words. An actress must learn to do everything. She must dance, she must sing. Hasn't Maeve told you about the dancing and singing?"

"No."

"Oh, you don't know half the tricks we're up to. Yes, the child's working. Singing, tap-dancing, everything. We'll make her an all-rounder yet."

I looked at Maeve questioningly. "It's all true, Uncle Bill," she said, "and I'm loving it. Can't you imagine a big musical show, with every-thing for a leading lady?—singing, acting, dancing? I'd love that."

Livia Vaynol patted her on the head. "Beware of this man," she said in sepulchral tones. "I can see what he thinks is your Destiny. Sudermann, Ibsen, Strindberg. Perhaps even Shaw. Perhaps even himself. God alone knows. We'll beat him yet."

Then she laughed merrily and once more sent her hair flying with a "Poof!" "Anent tonight," she said. "Let us be practical. Where do we sleep?"

"Ackers Street," said Maeve. "Don't forget I'm an old trooper. I know some rooms—"

"Ackers Street be damned," I said. "You will both stay at The Beeches."

For the first time since I had left it to drive to Wilmslow with Nellie and the Rev. W. Wilson Wintringham, I sat in my study. The girls were to share the bedroom that Nellie and I had used for so long. They were there changing now.

A maid had been left in charge of the house until I made up my mind what to do about it. I knew that I would not live in The

Beeches again. There was no reason why I shouldn't have left the nursing-home some time ago; but I was comfortable, well looked after, and there was room to spare. I might as well remain in the place till I left Manchester for good.

We hadn't all been able to squeeze into Livia Vaynol's car, so Martin had brought mine round. He was waiting now to take us to the Midland Hotel to dinner. I had not changed. Though I could get about now well enough with my sticks, and hoped to discard them soon, changing was a bore in my condition. I sat there waiting for the girls, as I had sat waiting for Maeve eight years before, that day when she and Rory had quarrelled in the garden about Standish O'Grady and his "poetry."

I could hear, my door being open on to the landing, the girls laughing and talking in that room which for so long had known only the grim uncompromising presence of Nellie. The bedroom door opened, and Livia Vaynol came out alone. As I watched her cross under the landing lights, unselfconscious, not aware that I was watching her, her beauty came upon my heart with almost a physical shock. She was very tall and moved with a slow stateliness. Her dress was of blue velvet decorated with small stars of silver tinsel. I can't decide to this day whether such a scheme was childish and a little tasteless. I only know that Livia carried it off, that the little stars seemed as she walked to wink against the night-blue fabric of the dress, and the pale globe of her hair was suspended moonily above the whole midsummer-sky creation. Her bare arms shimmered like milky ways.

I tried to get up, but at that moment she saw me, crossed the room in a few quick strides, and placed both hands on my shoulders. I think she must have felt the tremor which passed through me. She smiled, and said: "Please—don't get up."

She crossed over to the fireplace, where the light winked and danced on the stars of her dress. The book-case that Dermot had made to contain my novels was over the fireplace. They were all there now. The last had arrived a few days before, but it was not yet published. Livia ran her slender fingers along the titles. "What lovely editions," she said. "I know them all." And then, turning towards me: "I'm really very proud to know you. I suppose a lot of people tell you that?"

"Not many. I don't know many people."

"Forgive me for acting like a child when I first met you. I'm like that. One can't be serious all the time, and I'm particularly liable to go silly when I meet someone I'm a little bit nervous of."

"Yes, I realised that."

"You would, of course."

"But you seem quite self-possessed now. And very lovely. D'you mind my saying that?"

"Why should I?" she asked frankly. "If you really mean it."

"I do."

She sat down in a chair facing mine and crossed one knee over the other. The folds of velvet flowed down in regal lines from the hard round point of her knee. She swung her blue velvet slipper gently up and down and considered me thoughtfully. Her regard was so calm and inscrutable and prolonged that I found myself shifting uneasily in my chair, and I wondered whether I was blushing like a schoolgirl. Presently she said: "When I put my hands on your shoulders just now, you trembled. Why was that?"

What answer I should have made to that extraordinary question I do not know. But at that moment the bedroom door opened. Livia put a finger to her lips and whispered: "Here's Maeve!" There was something conspiratorial about the gesture, something suggesting confidences between us that no one else must share, that gave me a queer thrill of satisfaction and pleasure.

Livia rose as Maeve came into the room and went to meet her with a frank smile. Now that they were both in their evening clothes, I saw how much taller than Maeve she was. Maeve had not changed her preference for crimson. Her dress fell in straight lines, giving her all the height it could, and this she had enhanced with a Spanish comb stuck in the back of her hair. But even so Livia out-topped her.

Maeve put her arm through Livia's, and they stood there side by side, the crimson smouldering against the night-sky blue. "You're lucky to have two such handsome wenches to take to dinner, Uncle Bill," Maeve said; and as I got slowly to my feet I felt that that was true. "Nothing like it will be seen in Manchester this night," I said. "Get your cloaks and let's be off."

We all three sat in the back seat. Maeve's arm was through mine, and on the other side I could feel the warmth of Livia Vaynol's thigh. We had not gone far when something familiar in the appearance of a cyclist who shot past us, head down, hatless, rather dishevelled-looking, caused me to twist and try to look through the small back window of the car. "Surely—surely," I murmured, perplexed, "it can't be!" but at the same moment Maeve's grip on my arm tightened and she exclaimed: "Uncle Bill! Did you see that? Wasn't that Oliver, or am I dreaming?"

I told Martin to turn back home. As the car pulled up at the gate, Oliver was wheeling his bicycle up the long garden path. "Stay here, my dear," I said to Maeve, "and you too, Miss Vaynol. I shan't be long."

"No, indeed, I shan't stay here," Maeve exclaimed. "Good gracious! Boys don't appear suddenly like that from a school miles away unless something serious is up. We'd better see what's the matter. Where is Oliver's school, by the way?"

"Fifty miles away. And hard going. Come, then."

Oliver stood under the light in the hall, his face pale and drawn, his golden hair wind-blown about his forehead. He was wearing no hat or overcoat, and his clothes were mud-splashed. He was altogether a dreadful apparition. From childhood—and he was now fifteen—he had been finicky about his clothes. I had never seen him in such a condition. It struck me to the heart. The girls in their bright cloaks and I in my careful clothes stood round him in a wondering semi-circle. He was wearing flannel bags and an old tweed jacket. He thrust his hands into the jacket pockets and grinned at us rather sheepishly. "Hallo, Dad! Hallo, Maeve!" he said. "I feel rather—ashamed. You all look so gay."

"This is Miss Vaynol," I said. "My son Oliver." The formality of it struck me as absurd.

Oliver and Livia Vaynol looked steadily at one another, and I had a strange feeling of exclusion—that Maeve and I were both excluded from that regard. Colour had ebbed back into Oliver's cheek. His long hand made a conscious gesture as he brushed back the hair from his forehead. A smile came into his blue eyes. Then, to my surprise, he put into words the thoughts that had occurred to me when first I saw Livia Vaynol come out of her room that evening. "You look like a moon-girl, Miss Vaynol. 'With how sad steps, O Moon, thou clims't the sky.' You'll find that in Palgrave."

This was all absurd, monstrous. "Oliver," I said, "your presence requires some explanation." I took him by the arm, and led him towards the stairs. "Maeve, would you mind putting in a call to this number?" I gave her the number of Oliver's school. Then he and I went up the stairs to my study. At the turn of the landing I paused and looked down. Maeve was at the telephone. Livia Vaynol stood as if rooted to the ground, watching Oliver's dragging progress. He smiled down at her, but she did not return the smile. She just stood there, one hand holding her cloak about her, watching him.

"That's a marvellous girl, Dad," he said as he came into the room.

"Sit down," I said, unable to keep irritation out of my voice. "Would you rather discuss now what has brought you home, or wait till the morning? You must be exhausted."

"I'm very tired," he said. "I've been riding for hours. I came through a lot of rain."

"You mean you don't want to talk tonight? I can understand that. Hadn't you better go straight to bed?"

"I'm very hungry," he said, "and I'd like a bath."

"Then you'd better have a bath quickly, and come with us. We're going out to dinner."

"Oh, may I?" he cried. "I didn't expect that. That's very good of you."

The fact was, I didn't want to let him out of my sight that night. I remembered the strained look of his face under the lamp. It was no time either to harass him or to leave him to his own devices.

"Well, get along and bath," I said. "And remember, we discuss this first thing in the morning, seriously."

He looked relieved, nodded, and went to the bathroom.

While he was bathing the telephone call came through. I told the headmaster that Oliver was at home, and begged him to excuse discussion of a grave matter by telephone. I would bring Oliver to school myself in the morning. The headmaster sounded grim, and reluctantly he left it at that.

The girls were hovering, restless and disturbed, about the hall. I took them to my study, where there was a fire. "What a beautiful boy!" Livia exclaimed, as she sank into a chair.

"Don't waste your sympathy on *him*," said Maeve with sudden surprising sharpness, and coming over to my chair she knelt at my feet and took both my hands in hers. "You poor darling," she said. "It's you—you look so worried. As if you hadn't had enough to put up with lately. I do hope it's nothing serious. Oh, dear! I couldn't have a moment's peace with Oliver. Forgive me for saying that?"

I nodded, squeezed her hands, and gazed rather miserably into the fire. We said nothing more, just sat there, till Oliver came into the room. With the happy ability of the young, he had recovered his poise and his looks. His face was shining; his hair, which he wore rather long, had been brushed and brushed till it glistened in the light. He had put on a suit of grey flannel with a double-breasted jacket and a bright tie and brown shoes. He at once addressed Livia Vaynol as though there were no one else in the room. "Father says I can come out to dinner with you!"

She did not answer him, but said to the rest of us: "Well, shall we go?"

She got up, and Oliver sprang to help her with her cloak. My leg had stiffened a little. Maeve helped me to my feet.

I was at The Beeches at nine the next morning. Maeve was in my study. "Isn't Oliver up yet?" I asked her.

"No. Livia has just taken breakfast to his bedroom."

"He's fortunate."

"Very," Maeve said dryly.

Oliver was sitting up in bed, with a bright tousled head. Livia Vaynol was sitting on the edge of the bed, watching him eat, and he was doing that with great heartiness. She rose as I entered. "Is this the inquisition?" she asked sadly. I nodded, and she went dragging from the room.

I sat down in that easy chair wherein, so long ago, I had concealed the copy of *The Cuckoo Clock* which Oliver had stolen from Rory. The memory came back to me with a stab, and I feared to open the matter which had brought me there. Oliver did not help me. He went on delving into the shell of a brown egg.

"Livia prepared this breakfast, all by herself," he said. "She told me. It's good."

"Livia?"

"Miss Vaynol. She said I was to call her Livia."

I allowed that to pass. "Well—?" I began lamely.

"It was Grimshaw," he said. "I've told you about him. I don't like him."

"Yes, you've told me about him, and I've met him. Don't you remember—last half-term? He was put on to explain to parents some of the work his form was doing. I thought he was intelligent. He's a scholarship boy, isn't he?"

"Yes. His father's a butcher in Wigan."

"You should feel at home with him, seeing that your father was a baker's boy in Hulme."

Oliver flushed and glowered. "Well, go on. What happened between you and Grimshaw?"

"He's always getting at me."

"Getting at you? As I remember him, he's a small weak boy."

"Yes, that's it. He thinks no one will hit him."

"I see. There was a fight?"

"Not exactly. He was getting at me again, and I saw red, and before I knew what I was doing I kicked him—"

"You *kicked* that poor wretched child?"

Oliver burst out explosively. "Well, don't you understand? I didn't mean to. He makes me see red. It's the way he gets at me."

I summoned up the image of the small, spectacled Grimshaw, evidently with a waspish tongue that knew how to get under Oliver's skin.

"Well?" I prompted him again.

"We were standing at the top of some steps—you know, the steps that lead down to that little courtyard behind the gymnasium. I kicked him in the shin and he went backward down the steps. Rawson was there, and he said: 'Christ, Essex, you've killed the little sod.' He lay quite still at the bottom of the steps, with blood on his face."

I felt sick, took the tray off the bed to give myself something to do, and then sat down again.

"Well, everybody came crowding up. They took him into the san., and old Foxey"—who was Fox the headmaster—"went tearing along there. I hadn't moved off the steps, and when Foxey came back he said as he passed me: 'Come to my study in ten minutes.' I couldn't face it. That's all."

"I see. That's all. Without knowing whether Grimshaw was alive or dead, you cleared out." (But I didn't imagine there was much the matter with Grimshaw, or Fox would have told me on the telephone.) "I am returning you to school this morning," I said. "What do you say to that?"

"I'm glad. I ran away just like I kicked him—without thinking; but now I want to face it out."

My heart gave an irrational leap of gladness when Oliver said that, fixing candid blue eyes upon me. I didn't pause to consider that there was no option, that he would have to face it out whatever his views might be. "I'm delighted to hear that," I said. "That's the first decent spot in a rotten business."

"But you do believe, don't you," he pleaded, "that I just acted thoughtlessly?"

"I must believe that, if you say so."

"And you won't tell Livia what happened?"

I didn't want to spare him everything. "I should be ashamed to," I said. "You'd better dress. We leave here at ten."

The interview with Fox was not easy. He was not a very intelligent man; he had one or two half-baked social ideas, and I had found before this that in conversation he worked them to death. He was, or said he was, proud that most of his scholarship boys were tradesmen's sons, and on every occasion he rubbed that in by a loud insistence on all his boys being treated alike. Why there should be any need to labour the point, why a butcher's son should not be as estimable a young animal as a stockbroker's or some other artful dodger's, I could not make out.

Fox sat back in his big armchair and swung his pince-nez in a fashion which I think he must have observed in some statesman. "The fact is, you know, Mr. Essex, that Oliver think's he's *somebody*."

"In itself, that's a good thing to imagine," I said. "So far as I can make out, the trouble in this case is that he's not a big enough somebody. Young Grimshaw, I gather, has the secret of making him feel small—a nobody rather than a somebody."

"Yes," Fox consented, with a satisfied smile, "I have observed that my faith in tradesmen's sons is more often justified than not. In the case of Grimshaw, there is certainly a gift for the telling phrase that a boy from any social stratum might envy. But what I mean," he continued, putting on the pince-nez and looking at me over them with a preposterous solemnity, "is that Oliver seems to assume, because he is the son of a distinguished man, that he may, shall I say, take it out of a boy less fortunately circumstanced."

"I entirely disagree," I said. "I don't think that has anything to do with it. If it had been the Prince of Wales, Oliver would have kicked him just the same. Don't let's get all wrapped up in theories about it. The facts are simple: there's a boy with an annoying tongue; Oliver couldn't stand his tongue, lost his temper, and kicked him. Now, whatever the provocation, it is agreed that kicking is a dirty trick, and what to me seemed worse than the kicking was the running away without discovering what were the consequences of the kick."

"As you know, they were fortunately light. A bruise on the shin, a superficial cut on the head, a brief fainting."

We were interrupted by a knock at the door. It was the father of young Grimshaw, who had received an alarmist report and seemed relieved that his son was little the worse. Mr. Grimshaw was a sturdy, hale-looking chap, and I gathered the impression that he was a better man than his son was likely to be. He shook hands with me without hesitation. "Ah've bin talking to yon young beggar of mine," he announced to me and Fox, who seemed rather colder with tradesmen than with their scholarly offspring, "an' Ah've told 'im if 'e can't keep a civil tongue in 'is 'ead Ah'll put 'im into t'butcherin'. 'E always was a one for lip. 'E's tried it on wi' me once or twice an' Ah've given 'im a clip in t'lug. That soon stops 'im. Ah reckon your boy won't be 'earin' much more from 'im, Mr. Essex."

I thanked Mr. Grimshaw for this very generous view of the matter, but explained to him that perhaps Mr. Fox could hardly be expected to see it in so simple a light. "I think when you came, Mr. Grimshaw, our conversation was just about to reach the question of what disciplinary action it might be necessary to take."

Fox swung his spectacles and pursed his lips gravely, but Grimshaw burst in heartily: "Nay, it'd be a bloody shame if a boys' rumpus led to all sorts of 'owdy-do…"

Fox interrupted stiffly: "It is Mr. Essex's son who is now in question, Mr. Grimshaw. If you will please allow us…" and he rose and steered Grimshaw out of the room. "Well, don't do anything daft," I heard that forthright man expostulating as he disappeared down the corridor.

And Fox, I soon gathered, for all his pretended judicial weighing-up of the matter, was not going to do anything daft. There was some question of my joining the governing body of the school. I suppose my name would have looked well on the prospectus. Anyway, when I asked point-blank: "Do you want to expel Oliver, or would you like me to remove him from the school?" there was a lot of tut-tut-tutting and deprecation of over-hasty action. Some added discipline, no doubt, would meet the case. When I left, I was wondering not whether Oliver was good enough for Fox, but whether Fox was good enough for Oliver.

Oliver himself, in the school courtyard, was explaining to a group of admiring fellows, including young Grimshaw whose head sported a star of sticking plaster, that this was his father's car and his father's chauffeur.

## 19

There was a time when the idea of spending six months or more out of England, with plenty of money and no one but myself to please, would have fascinated me. Now it would fascinate me no longer. I had done it, and I was glad to be home again.

I had got rid of The Beeches, passed the winter in a quiet London hotel, taken Oliver to Heronwater for his Easter holiday, and then, when he was back at school, set out. I had found a house on the Spaniards Road, overlooking the Heath, and Dermot was to see to its furnishing and decoration. This was the end of old Moscrop. He had been in my life since I could remember any life at all. Now he was going.

I felt as excited as a child as I paced the platform of Victoria which was bustling and cheerful in the May weather. I had never been abroad before. There would have seemed to Nellie something a little immoral in going abroad, and so long as Nellie was alive the idea of going abroad alone had not entered my mind. And as my thoughts turned back to Nellie and to the grey streets of Hulme and to the flat depressing acres of Manchester's Southern Cemetery, I saw Livia Vaynol, vivid and disturbing, hurrying along the platform. Maeve followed her slowly, and slower still came Dermot, more like Shaw than ever in foxy-red tweeds, and Sheila, a little out of breath, looking, I noticed for the first time, a shade on the stout side, sedate and matronly. I glanced from her to Maeve, and "Good God!" I thought, "Maeve must be twenty, and Sheila might easily be a grandmother."

"Quite a deputation!" I mocked them, but in my heart I was glad they were there, glad there were a few people in the world to whom it seemed to matter that they would not be seeing me for six months or more.

The doors began to slam, and I got into my compartment and leaned from the window. Livia pushed a dozen newspapers and magazines through to me. Sheila and Dermot shook hands, and as I leant out to wave, Maeve suddenly stood on tiptoe and kissed me. "Good-bye, Uncle Bill," she said. Then Livia Vaynol pulled her aside, crying, "Me, too!" and as the train gathered speed, through the scabby back-yards and tottering chimneypots beyond the station I sat back in my corner thinking, as though there were no such person as Maeve in the world: "Livia kissed me."

I had no scheme, no time-table. I stayed where I liked as long as I liked and then passed on. By land and sea I visited most countries in Europe and some in Asia, and in Constantinople I decided suddenly to take a ship home. I had avoided tourist routes, and whenever possible had travelled on cargo boats. I did so on the homeward journey. There was one other passenger on the ship, and we met at dinner in the captain's cabin. The captain introduced us— "Mr. William Essex, Mr. Josef Wertheim"—but, so far as I was concerned, there was no need for the introduction. I should have known Josef Wertheim anywhere. His fat, pale, dark face, bald head and brooding melancholy eyes were familiar to anyone who saw the newspapers and weekly magazines. I could well understand his presence on that ship. To avoid publicity would be a grateful thing to Wertheim.

There was a small saloon on the ship, and after dinner we sat there and talked. I had a whisky and soda at my side, and smoked a pipe. Wertheim was a teetotaller but a large cigar was rarely out of his mouth. His reputation was tyrannical; it was said that he worked his artists to the bone. He had a genius for finding them everywhere: the latest Spanish dancer, the coming world's champion heavyweight, the biggest giant and the smallest midget, jugglers, trick cyclists and troupes of equestrian acrobats: it didn't matter to Wertheim what they were so long as they were the best in the world. I asked him if he had been scouring Asia for exotic talent, and he said No, he had been visiting his mother who, I gathered, lived in a small house in a suburb of Constantinople. He spoke of her with deep affection, and I felt a sympathy for the man, guessing a childhood which, for all its difference of environment, had been much like my own. Looking at Wertheim's burly rigid body that seemed to move, when it moved at all, all of a piece, I had difficulty in envisaging the days of which a hint dropped here and there, of his young body lying on his father's raised feet, thrown into the air, twirled barrel-wise, the father back-down on a carpet strip, a small sister collecting the offerings of a niggardly street audience.

The recollection did not move Wertheim to mirth. He never smiled. He merely let the story drop out in a few hints, then struck the bell at his side. To the steward who answered he did not give a look; he merely indicated without words my empty glass.

He asked me what I thought of *Reach for the Sky,* the musical show which he had on at the Palladian. When I said I hadn't seen it, he apologised with grave courtesy for having taken up so much of my time with talk of his affairs and began to draw me out about my own books. He had read a number of them, and showed an understanding of life in the North of England that surprised me. He had put on several big shows in Manchester, and confessed that Manchester audiences frightened him. If you could get past them you were all right.

I said that I felt I had said everything that I wanted to say about Manchester. I wanted to settle in London and try my hand at a play.

"A play," he said, looking gravely at the glowing end of his cigar. "That is something now." He pondered, and added: "I have never done a play. That would be satisfying. Musical shows, circuses, boxing—yes, all that is amusing, and with wisdom one makes much money. But a play—that might be to make money and to satisfy something here—eh?" He tapped his enormous chest. "I have thought I would do it some day."

"You have only to make it known, Mr. Wertheim," I said, "and you'll have a hundred young men of genius on your doorstep every morning."

"Ach, I know, I know," he exclaimed, throwing out his hands in a wide gesture of despair; and I thought of all the stories that were told of the sorrows of Wertheim. He could hardly stay at an hotel, it was said, without the chambermaids turning out to be chorus girls in disguise, anxious to display the beauty of their legs when they brought up the morning tea.

It was not till the last day of the voyage that Wertheim reverted to this conversation. We got on very well together, chiefly, I think, because we kept out of one another's way all day, and met only in the evenings. He was as lethargic bodily as he was alert mentally. He liked to spend most of the day in his bunk with a pair of horn-rimmed spectacles on his nose and a book in his hand. After dinner we talked till midnight and became very easy and intimate with one another. It was on the last night that he said: "You know, Essex, I have been thinking about what you said—all those young men of genius on my doorstep with plays in their pockets. Well, here you've been, on my doorstep for days and you haven't tried to interest me in that play you're going to write." He got up to go to his bunk and laid his heavy hand on my shoulder. "I like that. You let me see that play when it's ready."

He went off with his heavy shambling walk, and I went to my cabin to give a look at the skeleton of the play on which I had been quietly working since I got aboard.

We came into London river at night. Wertheim at once went ashore, but I slept aboard. I had told nobody I was coming home, and the next morning I walked happy and unembarrassed about London

which still had for me the lure of novelty. It was a grey and lowering November day, but any day was good to be home on, and the
only thing I lacked was agreeable company for lunch. With that
idea in my head, my footsteps automatically made their way up
Regent Street, into Oxford Street, and through Orchard Street to
Baker Street. In a turning to the right was the house where Maeve
and Livia shared their flat. What more could I ask, to complete
the benediction of homecoming, than the company of Maeve and
Livia at lunch?

I climbed the stairs to the top floor, and knocked at the door of
the room I had visited several times before going away. It was a long
room with a large skylight. Receiving no answer to my knock, I
pushed open the door and saw Livia standing before an easel under
the skylight. She was wearing a green overall. The nimbus of her
hair shone, as improbably round as a dandelion clock, in the light
that fell from above. With a brush full of sepia water-colour she was
"squiggling," as Sheila would have called it: producing upon paper
pinned to a large board a series of flowing and somehow curiously
related curves. Maeve was not in the room, and though I had been
telling myself all the way to the flat that I wanted to take Maeve and
Livia to lunch, I was aware of a leap of gladness at finding Livia alone.

"Good-morning," I said, and Livia whirled round in surprise.
Then, seeing me, she stuck her brush into a pot and hurried across
the room. "Oh, the brown man!" she exclaimed, putting a hand
on each of my shoulders and looking me up and down. "What a
bit of holiday will do! Thinner, if anything. And greyer—but most
handsomely grey. And brown as a gipsy. You look like a handsome
colonel just back from service in the East—little clipped moustache
and all."

"Thank you. That's the first time anyone has called me handsome, and I must say I like it."

"Well," she qualified, pulling me into the room and taking my hat and coat, "at least you're thin. I always feel that if a man can't be truly handsome, thinness is the next best thing."

There was a healthy fire burning and an inviting divan stretched before it. I sat down, and Livia produced sherry. She sat at my side. "You know, this is really very charming," she said. "I had no idea you were homeward bound, much less home."

"I only got into the Thames last night, and I slept aboard."

"Then I must be the first person you've called on."

"You and Maeve. I called on Maeve, too, you know, though she isn't here. I wanted to take you both out to lunch. But I seem to be interfering with some work." I glanced towards the easel.

"Oh, that! Poof!" And Livia gave that comical push to her hair that had amused me in Manchester. "You wait till you see your house," she said mysteriously.

"Have you been allowed to trespass?"

"I've seen one or two things. I have even," she added proudly, "designed one or two things—the curtains."

"Well, I'm glad to know that," I said, genuinely pleased. "I suppose Dermot commissioned them?"

"Yes. He liked some of those things," waving towards the easel, "and got me to do them on linen. They look nice."

"I'm sure of it. I hope he paid you well."

"Seeing that it's an 'exclusive design by O'Riorden,' for which he'll charge you, I hope you won't think he paid me *too* well," she said with a little malicious grin.

"I shall be really glad to have something by you in the house," I assured her. "And now, what about lunch? Is it any use waiting for Maeve? Will she be in?"

"She will not," said Livia. "The show she was in ended last week. She'd worked all the year with hardly a day off, and now she's taking a holiday. She's earned it."

"Oh! Is she gone away?"

"To Ireland. She's visiting her brother."

"Rory. How's he getting on?"

"I know nothing about him. I've never seen him, you know. All I can tell you is that Maeve's potty about him. They write to one another two or three times a week, and not long ago I was present at a pretty little row between Maeve and her father. She wants the boy to be brought back."

I sighed. "Yes, I know all about that. It's an old, old story now. Well, let's lunch alone. Café Royal?"

Livia got up and shook her head. "Oh, no—please," she said. "I've just got you back after months of wandering in the wilderness, and now you want me to share you with a crowd of chatterers. Let's have lunch here. I was just going to put out my own. There's so much I want to know—where you've been, what you've seen, what you've done—"

I followed her into the kitchen. She put a cloth, glasses, cutlery, on to a tray. "Here, fix the table in the studio. I'll knock up an omelette."

She knocked up an omelette very efficiently, and with that and a crusty French loaf and butter, followed by fruit and coffee, we made a good meal.

"Light your pipe," she said.

I did, and felt at ease and at home. Livia carried the dishes into the kitchen. I liked that. I detest seeing the *débris* of a meal lying about a room. While she was away the sky, overcast all day, darkened. Besides the skylight, there was one window in the room. It looked on to nothing but a tumble of roofs and chimneypots, and upon that wry landscape a heavy leaden rain began to fall. It rattled on the skylight, and, looking up, I could see it sliding past, giving me the impression of being under a little stream in spate.

Livia came out from the kitchen. She had shed her overall and was wearing a grey skirt and a red woollen pullover that fitted closely to her body. She reached up to a cord and pulled a blind that slanted down across the face of the skylight. "I can't stand seeing this sort of weather," she said, "and I can't stand seeing the stars or the moon through that skylight. I always shut it out at night. Maeve laughs at me. But I hate to feel an immensity above me when I'm shut in. Now this one," she added, pulling the curtains across the window. "Ugh! Those grey roofs under the rain!"

She threw some coal upon the fire and then sat down on a comfortable chair over to my right. "There!" she said. "Isn't that better? Isn't that cosier and more human?"

The room was filled with a comfortable dusk, livened by the leaping flames. "Now," she prompted me. "Tell me of strange cities and marvellous seas."

I would much rather have told her how glad I was to be there, how enchanting I found her company; but I repressed that desire and did my best at a lively travel lecture. When I told her of my meeting with Wertheim she became excited. "There's a man to know, now," she exclaimed. "What a thing it would be to design for a show by Wertheim! Stage settings, dresses—couldn't something marvellous be made of it?"

"Poor Wertheim!" I laughed. "No wonder he looks pale and sad and travels on cargo boats. Everybody wants to use him or to be used by him. You want to design for him. I was dying to talk to him about a play, but thought it better policy not to. And above everything else, I want him to see Maeve act and give her a good push off."

"Let's think of something for Oliver while we're at it," she chaffed me. "What can Wertheim do for him?"

"I don't know yet that Oliver has any talents Wertheim can use. You and Maeve have. I have. But what about Oliver? Tell me, how did you get on with him?"

During my absence that summer Dermot had looked after Oliver's holiday. Rory had remained in Dublin; Maeve's play was still running; so the party at Heronwater was small: Sheila and

Dermot and Eileen, Oliver and Livia Vaynol. I gathered from letters I had received that Oliver had invited Livia.

"Who wouldn't get on with him?" Livia now asked. "I think he's the most marvellous person for getting on with that I've ever met. Perhaps, after all, Wertheim isn't his man. You ought to put him into the diplomatic service."

Once she was launched, she talked for a long time about Oliver. There was one adventure that evidently remained vividly in her mind. Oliver had taken her out in the *Maeve* after dinner, and though Sam Sawle had warned him about tides, he had made a mess of things. He had taken the boat up the Percuil river on a falling tide—a mad thing to do. They had thrown out an anchor and gone ashore in the dinghy.

"It was a marvellous night," Livia said. "There was a huge moon, and you know up that river in the evening it's as quiet as the grave."

"It would be," I said, "with the tide falling. Certainly no one in his senses would be there to disturb you at such a time."

Livia looked up sharply. "You sound cross."

"He seems to have been inconsiderate," I said, aware that I was feeling very cross indeed. I didn't want to hear the end of the adventure, and yet for the life of me I couldn't leave the subject alone.

"I suppose while you were ashore the last of the tide went?"

"It was all right for the dinghy," Livia said. "We rowed alongside the *Maeve*, and there was water under us, but the *Maeve's* pretty heavy. She was on the mud. We had to get back ashore. It was lucky there were plenty of rugs."

"Lucky! It sounds providential," I said, and again across the darkened room, with the rain tap-dancing on the skylight and the fire flickering, Livia looked up sharply at the tone of my voice.

"Providential," I repeated. "To provide for. To cater. To prearrange."

"You mean, you think Oliver—"

"Well, one doesn't usually, when going for an after-dinner run, provide for a night out," I said bluntly. "You must have been there all night. You'd get no more water up that river till the morning."

"No," she said tartly. "The tides come twice a day." She fluffed her hair and shook her head as though she were annoyed at my persistence. "Naturally, we were there all night. It's possible to make yourself comfortable. The hillside's covered with bracken, and what with that and the rugs, we were quite well off under some bushes. There was a moon. It was hardly dark at all, and we were warm." She seemed to be talking to herself now, to be re-living and re-enjoying an experience.

"It must have been very upsetting for Dermot and Sheila."

"I suppose it was."

"I know pretty well where you must have camped. Do you know that if you climb up through those fields you come to a road, and that on the road you find houses with telephones? Oliver could have got through to Heronwater. He knows all I'm telling you. He knows all that country like the back of his hand. I suppose Dermot had his car there?"

She nodded.

"Well, it would have been easy for him to get to you by road."

"It sounds more and more—providential," she smiled.

But I didn't like it. The more I heard of it, the less I liked it. I put down my pipe, walked across, and sat on the arm of her chair. She turned her heart-shaped face up and smiled at me. "You know, Livia," I said, "this seems to me to have been a rather foolish adventure."

The smile faded from her face. She got up and left me stranded awkwardly on the arm of the chair. Colour mounted to her cheeks as she faced me from the hearthrug. "I don't think it was foolish," she said. "I'm not a child. I know what I'm doing."

"But Oliver's little more than a child."

"Is he?" Her brows went up, and there was in the question a

depth of meaning that shocked me. "He must have done a great deal of growing without your noticing it. I apologised to Dermot and Sheila for the uneasiness I caused them, and I'm sorry for that. But for the rest, I regret nothing that happened—nothing."

The strength of feeling in that repeated "nothing" made my heart bound. I slipped down into the chair she had vacated and lit my pipe. The rain had ceased, and in the sudden silence of the room there was a vibrant tension. Livia broke it by harshly rattling the curtains back from the window, revealing the wilderness of wet gleaming roofs, and letting the skylight blind run back with a snap. Daylight flooded the room, dimming the electric lamp that was still burning. Livia knocked up the switch with a defiant flick, and as the cold calm daylight gave everything solidity and proportion again, and the dirty sparrows fluttered and chattered in the roof-puddles, I felt as though I had awakened from a nightmare full of implications that were the more horrible because they were so illusive and ill-defined.

"Let's have a look at you," I said, and I was pleased with what I saw. Oliver had said he would whistle across the landing when he was ready and he had whistled, and I had gone to his room to see him in his first dinner-jacket. To reach his bedroom, I had to go through his sitting-room, and opening out of his bedroom was a bathroom. It was a convenient arrangement. He need disturb nobody, and nobody need disturb him. I wanted that house at Hampstead to be something final. I didn't want to be always on the shift, and, while providing for myself, I had provided for Oliver. Here, surely, was a useful and necessary part of the machinery for his living. Soon he would go to Oxford or to Cambridge. He would decide what he wanted to do with his life, and here, during the vacations, and afterwards when he was done with the university, he could get on with preparations for doing it. I imagined a young student of law or medicine, or perhaps a young writer, thanking his stars for this excellent provision of quiet and privacy.

Nothing was lacking. There was a comfortable desk, well-furnished: stationery, pens, ink, blotter. The bookshelves, which on two sides of the room went half-way up the wall, had been beautifully made in Dermot's workshops. I had spent some thought in filling them. There was all sorts of stuff that I believed was calculated to stir a boy's imagination, give him hints, open gates. At sixteen something should be happening to a boy's mind. Sometimes, when Oliver was out, I would go into the room hoping to find open on the table or left lying on a chair some book that would give me a hint of the way his mind was tending. How I should have taken such a hint, fostered it, blown it to life! But so far, all I had found were books I had not bought, novels with garish pictures on their shiny paper covers: Guy Boothby's *Dr. Nikola*, Richard Marsh's *The Beetle*, that sort of thing. These and such-like seemed to be the whole of Oliver's reading, and there were plenty of weekly journals lavishly illustrated with racehorses and lovely actresses. Since Oliver had come home for the Christmas holiday there had been no other signs than these of mental stirrings. He liked to loll in his large chair with his feet on the desk, the Heath spread before his gaze, and an occasional cigarette in his mouth.

Time enough, time enough, I consoled myself. Here, in these surroundings, he will find himself one of these days. And what were you doing at sixteen? Well, I was lodging in Ancoats with the O'Riordens. I was earning my living. I was catching the flavour of Dermot's enthusiasms. I was eating my way through all the good stuff in old O'Riorden's book-cases. I was dreaming of making a fortune; I was beginning to scribble.

Can you imagine Oliver doing any of these things? No, nor do I want him to. Time enough for that. But all the things you were not doing at that age he is doing already; dressing up to the times, smoking, making eyes at girls. I wondered how far he was going with that.

Oliver turned round proudly from his dressing-table. He was shooting up in the most astonishing fashion. He must have been five foot ten, slender, graceful as a young tree. He had given himself a lot of attention. His longish curly hair was gleaming from the brush. His blue eyes had an almost childish diffidence as he stood there asking: "Well, will I do?"

"Let's have a look at you," I said. "Yes. You can wear evening clothes with anybody."

"Who's coming tonight?"

"Your Uncle Dermot and Sheila. A man named Wertheim—I've mentioned him to you, haven't I?—and his wife. I don't know her. She's an actress. They're the only people you don't know. Then there'll be me and Livia Vaynol, and you and Maeve. Are you ready to come down now?"

"Yes. D'you know what I was thinking as I dressed?"

"What?"

"Something you'd never guess. Something you've probably forgotten."

"Well?"

"Do you remember when I was very small and you bought me a suit of black pyjamas? You came upstairs and dressed me in them. It was a birthday or something and Maeve was there to tea, with Rory and Eileen. We went downstairs hand-in-hand, and everybody laughed at me."

"I remember it very well. You never wore those pyjamas. Never. Not once. Good money wasted. Well, no one will laugh at you tonight."

"Rather not! I think I look pretty good." He surveyed himself in the mirror. "Yes."

"Come on, then. We must be downstairs when people come."

We went out through his sitting-room, and I detained him for a moment, holding his arm. "You find this all right? You can work here?"

"Top hole," he agreed.

"I see you have been doing some reading. What is it this time?"

I picked up the book lying face downwards on the desk. It was another of the prolific Mr. Boothby's—*The Beautiful White Devil*.

"You seem to like this chap."

"He's jolly good," he grinned. "I wish you could turn out books like that."

"How do you know what I turn out? Have you read any of them?"

"I've tried."

"But not got far?"

"Not very." Abruptly changing the subject, he said: "By the way, guv'nor, Christmas is coming. I wish you'd give me a good cigarette case."

"Gold? Jewelled?"

"Don't twit me. Something decent. Something you can offer people. You don't mind my smoking, do you? I'm not doing much."

"So long as you keep it in reason. Were you really thinking of tonight?"

He nodded.

"Well, put this in your pocket. It's full. I make you a present of it now."

I handed him my gold cigarette case.

"Oh, no," he protested. "I can't take yours."

"Take it. I don't mind offering people a cigarette from a yellow cardboard packet. If they don't like it they can lump it."

He put the case in his pocket. "Normally, of course," he conceded, "I think you're right. But when one's wearing evening clothes it's rather different, don't you think?"

I grunted, and we went downstairs together.

*

Dermot walked up and down the drawing-room, poking out his red beard inquisitively at this and that. He walked with his hands behind him, body bent forward, almost prodding with the beard. Occasionally he passed a hand over a table, fingered a curtain, stood back from a picture.

"D'you remember those first things I made, Bill?" he suddenly demanded. "Those bookshelves for father, that dining-room table with the atrocious bulgy legs for mother? God! How I've got on! How I've got on!"

"Let him stand up on a chair," said Maeve. "He's going to crow."

"Something to crow about, my girl," said Dermot, "and don't you forget it. And don't misunderstand me. When I say 'got on,' I'm not thinking of filthy lucre. I'm thinking of the mind—the soul—the imagination—all that." He gestured vaguely with his white, long-fingered hands. "They don't know what they're talking about, this generation that gets everything done for it."

Sheila smiled at him affectionately, and patted the hand of Maeve who was sitting on a footstool at her feet. "Let him be," she said. "It's just the way of him. He always was an orator."

There was a lot of grey in Sheila's hair. She was making no pretence of being a young woman. She was dressed like a matron. Her face and figure were stoutening, but her eyes remained grave and beautiful. She held out her hands to the flames.

The two girls were excited at the prospect of meeting Wertheim. "How does one tackle a rich Jew who has everything to give away that one desires?" Livia asked. "Does one say: 'O Jew! Rich as thou art, the talents of thine handmaiden will enrich thee still further if thou wilt deign to employ them?' Is that the line, or something more direct and slashing: 'Look here, Ikey-Mo, my designs are pretty hot and there's money in 'em?'"

"When you see Wertheim," I answered her, "you won't think much of either of those lines. And here he is."

Dark, unsmiling, immense, Wertheim came into the room with his wife clinging to his arm. Clinging is the word. I had heard that Wertheim had married an actress, and, as I came to know the story later, the facts were these. Josephine Robbins was a New York girl who worked in a big store. It was the first of the stores founded by Dermot's uncle, old Con O'Riorden. Josephine was stage-struck, worked like the devil, and at last found herself in the front row of the chorus. There she stuck. She had a lovely figure but the plainest and most homely face you could imagine. Nor had she any talent for anything but dancing, and she was no good at that except in a regiment. But Wertheim saw her, fell in love with her, and married her. He said she reminded him of his mother. From that moment, she wanted to forget that she had ever been a "chorus lady." Nor did Wertheim want to remember it. So it was that Josephine's clothes were always of the demurest, her deportment of the most serious. She was Josie to Wertheim; he was Jo to her; and they were a devoted and happy couple. She came into the room that night holding on to her mighty man like a slender and undistinguished bear-leader whom you would hardly notice in the presence of its sulky-looking powerful charge.

This was the first dinner-party in my new house. I was anxious to make it a success, and, frankly, I was anxious to put everyone on good terms with Wertheim. I was careful when I made the introductions to mention the things about them that would interest him.

"This is Dermot O'Riorden, my oldest friend. Perhaps you've seen his shop in Regent Street?"

Wertheim nodded his head. "We have, haven't we, Josie? Very expensive. Very expensive. But very lovely."

"This room is done by Mr. O'Riorden," I explained. "Everything in it."

"Not everything," said Wertheim, advancing to look closer at a winter landscape by Vlaminck over the fireplace. "Not this—eh?"

"Well, I chose it," Dermot said, "and induced him to pay a lot of money for it. I got on to these fellows early. They didn't cost me much."

"And there's something else that he chose but didn't do," I said, displaying the curtains. Wertheim gazed at them hard, making with his hands passes in the air that the decoration of the curtains seemed to suggest. "Yes. That is good now," he admitted. "That *is* good. There is a sense of design here. Something original. I could imagine this done on the grand scale. In the theatre—eh? Curtains—very important."

"They are the work of Miss Vaynol here," I explained and was rewarded with a "God bless you, my child," look from Livia.

"We meet all the talents," Wertheim exclaimed, shaking hands.

"Including Maeve O'Riorden, the actress," I said. "She trained with Mary Latter, and was all through the run of *Mid-Winter Harvest*."

"Yes, yes. We saw it three times, didn't we, Josie?"

Josie nodded. She seemed to have no other role than that of agreeing with her husband. Seemed to: but as I got to know her better I found that she was his most effective dragon, too, and that no nuisance could come at him that had not first overcome Josie.

"A charming piece," said Wertheim, "and we remember your part very well, Miss O'Riorden. And this, no doubt," he added, bearing down on Sheila, who had shyly kept aloof, "is Miss O'Riorden's mother. I can see that. I can see that this is what Miss O'Riorden will be like in a few years' time, if she is lucky."

"Jo!" said Josie sharply.

"Yes, Josie?"

"Control your emotions."

"There!" he exclaimed with comical despair. "She thinks I am too much of the East. She has been reading Disraeli and Queen Victoria. Ah! When will they let us have a play about that: Disraeli, Gladstone and Victoria. Poetry, prose and the heart of a woman.

There's a theme for you, Essex! And this—this Phœbus in black trousers—whose son is this?"

He took Oliver by the hand and gazed earnestly into his smiling and lightly flushed face.

"Mine," I said simply.

"Ach, God!" said Wertheim, dropping Oliver's hand and lifting his eyes to the ceiling. "To be young and beautiful! I never was either."

I sat at the head of the table, with Wertheim on my left and Mrs. Wertheim on my right. Next to Mrs. Wertheim sat Oliver with Livia beyond him. He was very attentive to Livia all through the meal, exchanged hardly a word with Mrs. Wertheim and scarcely a look with Maeve who was opposite him. Poor Maeve, I am afraid, was left disconsolate, for she was sitting between her father and Wertheim. Wertheim recurred to the subject of the French Impressionists of whom Dermot had a splendid collection, some in his flat, some in the gallery he had opened at his Regent Street shop. This was a matter on which Wertheim was deeply informed, and the pair of them talked over Maeve's head in the most shameless fashion. At last, Dermot threw even the pretence of courtesy to the winds. "Here, Maeve, change places with me," he said, upsetting the arrangements I had carefully made; but now everybody seemed happy: Dermot and Wertheim swopping stories of the men they had known in the Paris studios when you could pick up dirt cheap pictures now declared to be masterpieces; Maeve and Sheila hobnobbing the more happily because they saw little of one another in those days; Livia and Oliver exchanging heaven knows what quiet sweetnesses; and Josie Wertheim and I.

She astonished me by saying: "Jo tells me you are going to write a play for him. I want him to do plays, you know. The big showman business is all very well, but I think he's got more in him than making a nice background to show off girls' legs."

This was pretty good from Josie, whose own adorable legs, though I did not then know it, had been her fortune. But Wertheim interjected a growl: "Essex, don't let her run down the loveliest things God ever made—a woman's legs. They kicked me into Park Lane."

Josie waited till he was deeply immersed with Dermot once more, then said: "Seriously, now that his mind's turning to this, help me to keep him up to it. He's talked a lot about you lately. He's spent his life finding new things, and now that he's thinking of the legitimate stage, he won't look at the men who've had a long list of successes. He'll find a new dramatist. It might as well be you. How is the play going? What do you call it?"

"It's finished. I don't know yet what it will be called."

"You're a quick worker!"

"Oh, no, I had six months' holiday. The thing was working in my head all that time, and bits of it had got written. During the voyage home I roughed it out. Since being back, I've been completely undisturbed and I've had nothing else to do."

"Would you like to tell me what it's about?"

I did; and Josie said: "You must call it *Every Street*."

"That's splendid! That fits it perfectly."

"Are you free tomorrow?" she asked, rummaging in the handbag which she kept on her lap. She produced an engagement book. "Eleven o'clock?"

I said that would suit me.

"Very well, then." She made a note in the book. "Bring the play with you."

I liked her intense practicality. I liked the way I found her the next day, sitting in an anteroom through which one reached Wertheim's study that looked out on to a garden in which a plane tree held up its bleak winter arms to the sky.

"You won't be disturbed," she promised, opening the door and allowing me to see Wertheim's back, as he stood, hands behind him, brooding through the window upon the grey, grisly day; and I knew that we were indeed safe enough from any intrusion, with Josie posted on guard.

I had imagined that Wertheim and I would have an hour's talk about the play, that perhaps I would read a bit here and there, and that then I would leave it for him to turn over in his mind. I hadn't known my Wertheim. He sank into a great leather chair by the fireside, a cigar in his mouth, and commanded me to read. I hadn't read two sentences of stage directions for the first act before he exclaimed sharply: "No!" and proceeded at once to let me see how little I knew about the facts of the stage.

"Essex," he said, "a friend of mine received a manuscript which began: 'The curtain rises at the moment of dawn. A cock is crowing on a dunghill. Nearby, a hen, with busy cackling, lays an egg. Enter a farm servant who picks up the egg.' Now try to *see* your stage and everything that's done on it. I think we'll have to alter those directions to read like this…"

So we were at it from the word Go. Lunch was brought in, and I stayed to dinner, and after dinner we were at it again. It was eleven o'clock when I called a taxi and set out for the Spaniards Road. In my pocket I had a sheaf of notes; in my mind an immense respect for Wertheim. He had been through that play with a small comb. He refused to suggest a word of dialogue. That, he said, was my job. But he was ruthless in insisting when he thought dialogue must be cut. He could will himself into the audience, see the thing, and hear the thing, as from a theatre seat, and I knew he was right. It was an exhausting, illuminating day. "And now, Essex," he said, laying his heavy hand on my shoulder as we came through the anteroom where Josie was reading a novel, "now we're on the way to making something of it."

And we were. *Every Street* went on in the following spring—1913— and ran till the war broke and killed it. But by then Wertheim knew what Maeve could do, and that was the important matter.

## 20

W hen I look back across the gulf of horror—the world's horror and my own—to the years before the war, that April of 1913 shines with an especial radiance. It seems now as though there was something fatal about it, as though we were all too happy. The gods couldn't put up with it. Maeve, I think, was the only one in whose heart there was a premonition.

There we incredibly were, she and I, dining in the Café Royal, redeeming the ancient vow that we would dine together on the night when she was to make her first appearance in a play I had written for her. We had to dine very early, so that she could go on to the St. John's Theatre, where *Every Street* was to try its luck. That was a thing we had not thought of in those days—how early that dinner must be—for we had been very innocent in matters of the theatre. We were learning. We had had difficulty in getting away. Everybody had wanted us: Jo and Josie, Livia, Sheila and Dermot, Rory and Maggie Donnelly. They were over, those two, on the first visit they had made to England since Rory's Irish apprenticeship.

But Maeve and I had got away. We should all meet at supper, anyhow, to count our laurels or lick our wounds. We leaned back on the red plush, with coffee before us. I gave Maeve a cigarette and lit it for her.

"Nervous?"

She shook her head, and asked in her turn: "Happy?"

"Very—but with a fearful joy. Shivering in my shoes."

"You did really write *Every Street* for me?" Maeve asked, suddenly clapping a hand over mine and looking into my face.

"Yes. Isn't Annie Hargreaves your part—down to the bone?"

"I'm very pleased with it. Oh, Man, I'm so glad—so proud—this moment has come at last. But, you know," with a valiant smile on her colourless face across which the scarlet of her lips made a vivid mark, "I didn't think that when the moment came you'd be engaged to another woman."

"My dear—" was all I could say.

She suddenly stubbed out her cigarette. "Let's go."

If my engagement to Livia was painful to Maeve, it was incredible to me. It had happened so suddenly. It was on the night that I have written about, when I had a few people to dinner, that I knew I loved Livia. I had loved no woman before. I suppose I had come as near to loving Maeve as a man can come while yet feeling use and wont in the way, and an affection too level and kindly for passion.

When we went into the drawing-room that night after sitting for a while over our cigars, I was conscious that the first face I looked for was Livia's and that the first face Livia looked for was Oliver's. He walked straight up to where she was sitting, took the cigarette case from his pocket, and sprang it open expertly. She took a cigarette; he lit it for her, and she patted the settee on which she was sitting. He sat down beside her, plucking with a dandy gesture at the knees of his trousers. "Phœbus in black trousers." That wasn't bad, Wertheim.

Oliver had drunk no wine; I did not permit that; but his face was flushed and excited; his eyes shone; and the curls of his hair seemed almost to radiate vitality. No one, I thought to myself, could fail to be aware of his extraordinary physical attractiveness; and on the thought my mind pulled up with a jerk. Physical? That was the first time I had qualified, even in the secret thoughts of my heart, Oliver's attractiveness.

But what else did I know of him but the envelope that met my eye? I faced that squarely, and admitted that we had grown apart.

When he was a child, I grew down to him. I did not stoop down to him. There was no condescension. It was a growth, as though I had been endowed with the happy faculty of shedding my years. I enjoyed our games as much as he did, and the happy explorations of ideas that he had called our "conversations."

There had been no "conversations" for a long time. It seemed to me that the time had come when my growth downwards towards Oliver's mind must cease, and contact must now be established by his reaching up to me. He was on the verge of young manhood; I was ready, I was aching, to improve the first signs of his wanting me on wider, manlier terms. But there was no sign. Oliver the child had been my comrade. Oliver the youth had receded far from me. I saw him with sudden shattering clarity as beautiful, commonplace and vain.

It is a fearful thing when one love wars with another. Watching him and Livia, hearing no word they said, seeing the understanding in their looks, their smiling acceptance of one another that tortured me with implications of secrets, experiences shared, I felt my heart turning over, because I knew then that I wanted Livia Vaynol for myself, and that my desire for her, and nothing else, was depreciating Oliver in my eyes.

I knew that night, as I had theoretically known long enough, what it was to desire a woman. Liking, affection, even the brief stirring of passion that sweeps you into bed: since Nellie's death I had known all those; but this was irrational, tyrannical, the dark fusing of body and mind in the desire to possess.

Dermot was quizzing Josie Wertheim about a legend that had come to his ears that once, when she had been gardening at Wertheim's country cottage, she had chased down the village street, long garden fork in hand, a girl who had tried to intrude into the quiet of Wertheim's week-end. "One jab and four punctures," Dermot cried ecstatically. "How could a girl with such a spread of stern hope to get into a chorus? What a forkful of ham!"

"It was four jabs and one puncture," Josie corrected. "That just shows the nonsense that gets about."

Wertheim was telling Sheila about his mother in Constantinople. She was listening with her beautiful serenity, as though she and the mother were contemporaries and Wertheim a small boy.

I sat down beside Maeve. She put her hand over mine, a gesture she had used since childhood. "Well, Man," she said, "it's a lovely house, and it was a lovely dinner, and I thank you very much and hope you'll be happy here."

"I'm sure I shall," I said, and I told her of the play I had written for her and of Josie's encouragement.

"Does that please you?" I asked, patting her hand and looking down at the whiteness of her, rising out of the crimson velvet dress. Never any colour. White, sloping shoulders—perhaps a thought too thin—and the neck lifted up proudly between them, bearing the snow-white face, with its resolute little chin, its eyes that were both blue and black, like damsons, its red shapely mouth. Her hair was as black as coal, with no blue in it at all.

"Dear Bill," she said—she did not call me Uncle Bill any more—"it pleases me very much, but now the idea of having me in the play has got to please Mr. Wertheim—hasn't it?—if he likes it."

"If he likes it, there is one condition on which he can have it," I assured her. "And that is that Maeve O'Riorden plays Annie Hargreaves."

"You've always thought of me, and thought for me. I should never have been on the stage if it hadn't been for you."

"And you still think being on the stage is the right thing?"

"Oh, Man, how can you ask!" The look and tone made me feel happy that there was something I had done about which there could be no doubt.

"Livia seems pleased with herself," Maeve suddenly remarked, bringing my thoughts back to the focus round which they had been swaying. I looked across the room. Oliver had said something which left on his face a smile hovering between impertinence and doubt of its reception. Livia responded by reaching up a hand to tousle his hair. The whole scene bit into my mind: the long white arm, the sudden shift of the half-exposed breast, the fingers, sinking in Oliver's curls, the light of affectionate raillery on Livia's face. My hand gripped hard on Maeve's, and she looked up with sharp surprise.

"Tell me," I said. "What do you think of Livia?"

The surprise deepened on Maeve's face. Her dark brows for a moment contracted and brought out a puckered frown that made my mind leap incongruously to a thought of Nellie. Then Maeve said: "She's wanton."

"Good God!" I cried. "What an old-fashioned word."

"There are more modern ones," said Maeve, and she got up at once to go and talk to Josie.

I threw the end of my cigar into the fire and walked across the room. Oliver rose from the settee. "I think perhaps Sheila would like a word with you," I said. "You haven't seen much of her this holiday."

He went away, exchanging a bright smile with Livia. I sat down at her side, aware that my heart was knocking and that I should have difficulty in controlling my voice. I was overpoweringly aware of her; of the perfume of her hair, of the long white lines of her arms, meeting now in hands cupped in her lap, of the swell of her breasts and the shape of her legs, emphasised by the hands pressing down the rich material of her dress, stretching it tight across her thighs.

"I should like to drive you home tonight," I said, and to me the words had a choked unnatural sound. She appeared not to notice that. "I had arranged for a taxi to call for me," she said.

"For you and Maeve?"

"No. Maeve's going home with her people for once."

Then the room and everyone in it seemed for a moment to black out. I was aware only of Livia's hands lying in her lap, of her calm voice saying: "Maeve's going home with her people for once."

I was hardly conscious that it was myself speaking when I said: "Taxis have been sent away before now."

"Or even shared."

The words brought me to myself again with an extraordinary sting of hope. "You mean—?"

Her only answer was a clear ringing laugh. For one dreadful moment I thought she was going to tousle my hair as she had tousled Oliver's. Then a parlourmaid came in and announced: "Miss Vaynol's taxi."

She got up. "Good-bye. And thank you a thousand times. A lovely evening."

Wertheim and the play kept me busy throughout that holiday of Oliver's. I didn't see much of Oliver except at meals. We went to a pantomime together, but it was a poor thing compared with the Manchester pantomimes; and once or twice we walked together on the Heath. But we never got near one another. He was at a stage which baffled me. I could not meet him on a child's ground any more, because he was not a child; and he did not seem to have advanced a step towards meeting me on my ground.

Walking among the gnarled thorns with their winter-rusty haws, watching the grey squirrels nip from bough to bough, I thought his eyes were as bright, unresting, as theirs; and he was as difficult to get hold of.

"You'll be finishing at school in a year or so, Oliver."

"Good egg."

"What about the university? Have you thought about that? Have you any reason for preferring Oxford to Cambridge, or for not wanting to go to either?"

"Pogson's going to Oxford."

"Yes, but you?"

"Oh, I dunno. Is it a point to settle just yet?"

"Well, I'd like to see ahead a bit. There's the possibility that that sort of thing may not interest you at all. I don't think one should go to a university just for the fun of it."

"You mean the place should be kept for the good old swotters?"

"Well—I mean if we knew what you wanted to do, we could settle the best way to go about it. You might want to do something which made the Manchester College of Technology the place for you."

"Oh, God forbid! Manchester! Have a heart."

"Well, the law? Medicine—?"

"Isn't there plenty of time to make up my mind?"

I had to leave it at that.

The path dropped sharply into a little hollow, a basin carpeted that December afternoon with sodden leaves, brown and yellow, and filled with mist in which the tree trunks were twisted gnome-like. A youth, with his checked cap knocked askew, was sitting on a fallen trunk, awkwardly clutching his girl, whose hair was radiant with a dew of pearls. We plunged down so suddenly upon them, lost in their wraithy world, that the girl looked up with sharp surprise and fear in eyes like a fawn's, then buried her face in the boy's neck. I hurried on, striking out at the leaves and flints with my stick, and as we reached the farther lip of the hollow Oliver momentarily paused, looked back, and I felt that if I hadn't been there he would have stopped and stared. Well, there was *something* he was interested in.

He continued to spend a lot of time sitting about in his room. I noted that Oppenheim's *The Mysterious Mr. Sabin* and Bram Stoker's *Dracula* were added to his library. Occasionally Pogson called for him with a car. They would smoke a cigarette or two in Oliver's room. There would be a lot of guffawing, and then off they would go. If I asked Oliver at dinner where they had been, he would reply: "Oh, we just belted about. Poggy can make her go!"

Pogson, pimply, with a downy upper lip, was a brewer's son. I didn't like him. He was at Oliver's school and was leaving at the end of the summer term. He looked to me as though he should already have left.

How much Oliver was seeing of Livia, where he saw her, I never inquired. She turned up at St. Pancras to see him off when the holiday was over. I was surprised to see her there. He introduced her proudly and proprietorially to Pogson whom she stared at as though he were a slug she had found unpardonably intruding on her cabbage at dinner. Oliver looked hurt, and whispered: "He's Pogson of Pogson's Entire," as though that were almost equivalent to being Hodson of Hodson's Horse. "I don't care a damn whether he's entire or in little pieces," said Livia warmly. "Of the two I should prefer the latter." Oliver's blue eyes turned sulky, but she was very sweet with him and he went away, happy and smiling, with Pogson's loathsome countenance—Hyperion and the satyr—craning out above his through the carriage window.

Livia and I walked together out of the station, steamy and echoing with an incoming train. It was the first chance I had had to speak to her since the night of the dinner-party. I could have made a chance, but I had carefully refrained from doing so. I had told myself that I would wait till Oliver was gone, and now Oliver was gone—he was gone no farther than the tunnel beyond the station, but he was gone—and there was Livia at my side.

I said to her: "I've been working over a play with Wertheim."

"Yes. Maeve told me about it."

"Wertheim and I have done all that's possible together. I must finish it off alone now. I can do it in a fortnight."

"Good. I hope it will be a whacking success."

"I shall take it down to Heronwater tomorrow. I've never been there in the winter. Would you like to come with me?"

"You'd never work with me about the place."

"Oh, yes, I should. I can do all that's necessary by working between nine in the morning and one o'clock. Authorship, you know, is one of the soft jobs, though authors like to pretend that it's arduous."

We stood beside my car, exchanging this banal chat, while my heart was beating so furiously that I wondered whether it could be heard by Martin, standing there with his face politely averted.

"I've heard a lot about the pains of creation," said Livia, keeping the game going.

"All nonsense. A professional writer who can't turn out a thousand words in a few hours is a bad workman. And think what that means. A thousand words a day; three hundred and sixty-five days a year. Give the poor hard-working chap the sixty-five days to play with—that's two months' holiday a year, and he still produces 300,000 words! Enough to fill three novels—more than anyone has a right to ask the public to accept. No. The successful novelist is on a soft option."

"Well," with a little embarrassed laugh, "thank you for the inside information. Wasn't that Pogson child loathsome?"

"I'm beginning to be troubled altogether about Oliver's friends."

She cocked her head up at me sharply. "Do you want my companionship in Cornwall to see whether I'm worthy? I'm not sure that I ought to come, anyway. My reputation's bad enough as it is."

I took her by the elbow and led her along the pavement, away from the car. "Would it help to regularise the position if we were engaged to be married?"

She came to a halt, and gave a restless shake to her body. "Oh, send that blasted car away," she said. "We can't talk about these things walking like a couple of fools in front of all this—this ghastly—"

She helplessly waved a hand at the monstrous, the monumental, ugliness of the station façade.

So I sent Martin away, and we walked out into the hardly more inspiring atmosphere of the Euston Road, where the buses roared by and the taxis honked, and we were beset on either hand by that filthy and unco-ordinated thoroughfare. A grey gritty wind was blowing, and a sky of blotched unpolished pewter pressed upon the roofs. We walked towards Marylebone.

"For the best part of last year," I said, "I was gallivanting about the loveliest places in Europe. If you had been with me, I could have proposed to you on the pont d'Avignon, or on the ramparts of Montreuil, or in an olive field looking over the Mediterranean, or beside a lake in Sweden, or on the shores of the Bosphorus. As it is, I propose in a gritty January wind in the Euston Road, with those awful caryatides holding up the church across the street."

"Listen, Bill," she said, taking my arm snugly, "cut out all the pretty things, and look at the grisly facts. I wanted to like you from the beginning. You remember—when you were in the nursing-home in Manchester and I motored Maeve up?"

I nodded.

"Well, I did like you. I knew your work, and I liked that. You didn't have much to say that day, you know. You were not brilliant, and I liked that, too. I loathe talking to people who try to make every phrase sound as though it's the one good thing Oscar Wilde forgot to say to Whistler. I couldn't live with a person like that."

"That's lucky for me."

"But, you see, that was just an elementary first impression. After all, we were only together for a few hours, and then Oliver came along."

"And that altered things."

"That altered things."

"Are you—are you—in love with Oliver?"

"I think all day about his beauty. I don't know whether I'm in love with him or not, but he obsesses me."

"Have you seen much of him this holiday?"

"Very little. I'm not so bad as Maeve thinks." She said that rather bitterly. "I have tried to do without him."

We walked on without speaking for a while, and facing into the dour gritty wind I thought suddenly of a night long ago when Dermot and I had sat up late under a swinging lamp in his workshop, arranging the fate of our sons who were not born. "If I have a son," I said, "I just want him to have everything. I'll work my fingers to the bone to give him every damn thing he asks for, and seeing him enjoying it, I'll enjoy it myself and live my life over again." The words rattled dryly in my memory like the soiled scraps of paper rasping dryly along the gutter in the wind. I found no comfort in them. Now Oliver was asking for Livia, and I was not enjoying it.

Was he asking for her? Well, here was a point where Give, Give, Give, came to an end, and I began to question the demand. That Oliver was infatuated was clear. That night on the Percuil River. The excited glances that I had caught between him and Livia. But what did it all come to? Calf love. Hay fever. The traditional explanations marshalled themselves obediently to my aid. Let him wait, find a woman of his age.

Or was this the one thing that mattered? What if the truth were this: that I might with impunity have refused him all those advantages—those superfluities?—he had till now enjoyed, but that here was something come at last which I should refuse him at his peril? At my peril? At the peril of everything there had ever been between us? I wouldn't allow myself to work it out. Not then. I have worked it out since, walking again in imagination that arid road, with the ghosts of Maeve and Rory and Oliver blowing beside me down the bitter wind. And the ghost of the man I never knew; for if our deeds determine anything, the fourth ghost, too, was predestined from that day.

It seemed a long time since either of us had spoken. We walked on, with her hand resting on my arm, a contact which I found unbearably dear, unbearably precious. Once she removed it, and I took it and put it back, and patted it, and said: "Let it stay there."

She was tall, I think I have told you, and free-striding like a fawn, and that day she was wearing a brown skirt and an astrakhan coat and hat, Russian-looking. The wind had whipped colour into her cheeks, and I suppose the colour was heightened by the agitation of the moment.

At last she said: "I didn't know you were so serious about it," and the words were rather hoarse and strained, as though the constriction of my own throat had communicated itself to her.

"I have never been so serious in my life," I said unsteadily. "I'm terribly in love with you, Livia. I've never loved a woman before. Do you believe that? I've never known any of the things that I imagine marriage to mean."

"It's a hell of a fix," she said with a shaky laugh. "Why do you think I shall be able to give you the things you've lacked?"

"Oh, don't ask me to reason about it. My first marriage, believe me, was completely reasonable."

"You don't know me. You don't know what a bad lot I am."

"Don't say that."

"I must say it. At least let me be honest. Let me stand up and shout in your fool's paradise."

"No, no. Take me or leave me. I'm willing to take you."

"I'm terribly susceptible to men. There! Now I've said it."

"I didn't hear it."

"The more fool you."

"Will you marry me, poor fool as I am?"

"If I married you, it would be because I liked you and because you were a very distinguished man. I'm vain. But you see, I'm honest. Oh, God," she added, "I wish you weren't Oliver's father!"

"Can't you forget Oliver, or think about him differently?"

"I don't know *how* I think about him. Why don't you wait? We're in a tangle. It will clear itself up if you give it time. Why don't you? You see, you offer such tremendous inducements. It's a pressure upon me. I don't think it's fair."

"I'm sorry," I said. "Forgive me." I called a taxi, and set her down a few moments later at the door of her flat. She looked shaken and excited, standing there waiting to wave to me as I turned the corner into Baker Street.

Martin drove me down to Heronwater the next day. How different from the first journey! We had gone by train from Manchester. Nellie...Sheila...Dermot...all the children...maids...luggage. What a business! "Good-bye, Belle Vue!" And, of course, it was summertime, holiday-time, time without a care. How different!

"A bad day, sir," Martin said, when I came out to the car after a very early breakfast. It was. The Heath was a cheerless place under the rain; the sky seemed to be on top of our heads. All England lay under the weeping; the day got no better, no worse, as we went westward.

I didn't sit with Martin, as I usually did; I sat behind, looking through the streaming windows at flooded ditches, and bare dripping trees, and villages that flashed by with their shoulders greyly hunched, and the downs, dull as slate, losing their heads in vast convolutions of creeping mist.

The whole world seemed inimical, and Cornwall, when we came to it in the last washed-out dregs of daylight, was a forlorn and fabulous province that seemed to resent intrusion. I had wanted to put up at Plymouth, but Martin made it a matter of pride to reach Heronwater that night. His headlights reached out into the gloom and through them the incessant arrows of the rain rushed from darkness to darkness. I pulled down the blind in front of me, wearied by their hypnotic attraction, and then it was as though I were in a dark box, hurtling through chaos.

The wind got up, strengthened quickly, and hurled the rain against the windows in gusty, pebbly handfuls. I could feel the push of the wind on the car, sudden powerful blows that made me uneasy despite her great strength and weight. I was utterly lost, completely confounded, and when, now and then, the lighted window of a cottage or the sparsely scattered lights of a hamlet shone briefly through the dark glass, there was no comfort in them, but only a will o' the wisp eeriness from which I was glad to be flying.

I gave it up; I left it to Martin; despite the now bellowing wind and the undiminished ferocity of the rain, I must somehow have slept, for the crunch of the tyres on gravel, the gentle sliding to immobility, jerked me up like a blow. Martin's face was at the open door of the car—a face that, even after those gruelling hours, seemed unchanged save for a smile of quiet pride. "We're here, sir," he announced. "She's a grand car."

"A grand car would have been precious little use without a grand driver," I said. "I'm glad we didn't stop at Plymouth. Thank you."

The door was open, and Sam Sawle was standing there under the light. "Bring me my gum-boots and oilskin," I shouted. They were always kept just within the door. Sam brought them out and I stepped into them right away. "Glad to see you, Mr. Essex," he said.

"And I'm glad to see you. I'll be in in a moment. Put the car away, Martin, and get something hot into you."

I squelched across the wet lawn to the stone balustrade. I wanted to see my Cornwall on this winter night—the first winter night I had spent there. I rested my hands on the cold stone that I had always known honey-mellow, warm and ripe with summer. The rain pattered on my oilskin. The wind roared through the dark gulf into which I looked: roared through the leafless trees, roared over the dark water that I could not see. I looked up and could see the tortured branches, a darker black against the blackness of the night, lashing and thrashing, and no star shone upon their frenzied dance. But down on the water that I could not see, incredibly calm amid the mad carnival of the elements, two orange squares of light lay side by side, and I wondered what riot of emotion was stirring the brain of Captain Judas this night behind those placid faces.

I turned to go back to the house, then stood as if rooted to the ground, leaning back, gripping the wet balustrade with both hands thrust behind me. I had seen her looking white and tired, waving to me as I turned into Baker Street. The day's apocalyptic journey seemed to have set a gulf between that moment and this that could not easily be bridged.

"It can't be you!" I said foolishly, and indeed in the hissing of the rain and the howling of the wind, in the intense darkness of that spot on the topmost edge of the falling wood, it was hard to make out the features of the face that glimmered whitely before me.

"Yes," said Livia.

"But, my child—my dear—in such a night! What are you wearing?" I reached out my hand and felt the fragility of the dress, sodden with rain, gummed to her body.

"I'm being melodramatic." Her laugh was low and provoking. "I wanted to surprise you. Have I done it?"

I took her suddenly in both arms and drew her to me, straining her to the creaking armour that I wore. She threw back her head, and I crushed my mouth upon her wet mouth, and upon her hair and her throat. She was dripping like a dryad, and I kissed the rain out of her eyes. Then I picked her up and waded awkwardly in those great boots of mine through the wet grass. She was easy to carry for all her weight. I put her down in the porch and saw that her eyes were starry. "For God's sake, go and change," I said. "You'll catch your death." The rain had sleeked her like a seal. She kicked off her soaking shoes and ran upstairs.

I took off my gum-boots and oilskin, and Sawle brought me some slippers. I was dazed by what had happened. I followed Sawle into my study. A log fire roared; the curtains were drawn; I felt elated, like a child that has come on some uncovenanted pleasure.

"When did Miss Vaynol come?"

"She's been here some time, Mr. Essex. She came by train to Truro and then on by car. She's been having a fine laugh, saying give her trains any day to beat cars on a long run."

"You shouldn't have let her go out, dressed like that."

"I don't have the dressing of her, Mr. Essex, and as for going out, I didn't know she had gone."

"Well—right. You've got this place looking very comfortable."

"And a bath ready for you, too, but by the sound of things someone's got it before you."

Bless the girl, let her have the bath. I was dry enough. I went up to my room to wash, and while I did so Sawle unpacked my bag.

"Well, how do you like winter visitors?" I asked him. "You're not used to this."

"I'll manage, Mr. Essex," he said confidently, "though I didn't expect two of you. I thought there'd just be you to look after, and I reckoned Martin and I could do that between us, cooking an' all. But when Miss Vaynol come, that was a different story. 'I reckon you can take the cooking off my hands,' I said to her."

"Quite right. And what did she say to that?"

"She said 'So long as you cook the breakfast, I'll do the rest. I'm a poor getter-up.' Well, that suits me. I reckon I can knock up a bit of breakfast."

"I'm sure you can."

"As for dinner tonight, I cooked most of it, but Miss Vaynol did some fancy bits."

"For example?"

"Well, I roasted a shoulder of lamb, and she made onion sauce.

Then I thought you'd like some bread and cheese, but she said biscuits and cheese, with what she calls Charlotte russ to come first. She's been a long time messing about with that. She pinched some of the best brandy for it. And she said perhaps she'd better make the coffee. I was surprised to find her so keen on playing about in the kitchen. She wasn't like that in the summer when she was here—when you wasn't, you know, Mr. Essex. Mrs. Essex, now—I could understand that. She was always a one for the kitchen." He looked at me shyly. "I was sorry about that."

It was only then that I remembered I had not seen Sawle since Nellie's death. "She was all right, was Mrs. Essex," he said. "And didn't that chap Donnelly know how to bring her out!"

He hovered round for a while, turned down the sheets of the bed, then made off, announcing that his shoulder of lamb would be just about done.

I sat down in a chair and listened to the tumult of the storm. Now that Sawle's slow steady voice was gone there was nothing else to listen to: the rain dashing with an angry hiss at the window, the wind raving in the trees. But now I could listen without disturbance, with comfort even, savouring the rich contrast of the wild weather without and the peace within—the peace and the sure, unobtrusive companionship of Sawle and Martin. And Livia.

She was already in the study when I went down. She was standing with a bare arm white on the mantelpiece, a foot on the fender, looking into the fire. She was wearing that dress of night-blue fabric sown with silver stars which she had worn in Manchester. The train flowed over the hearthrug in lovely lines.

When I entered the room she turned, her face lighted by a welcoming smile. "It's more than a year," I said, "since I first—and last—saw you in that dress. I'm glad you don't throw away your clothes too quickly. I shall always love you in that."

She kicked her train into position and glanced down her slender body appraisingly, to the tiny slippers peeping from beneath the hem of the dress. "My own design," she said, "my own make. I think I could earn a living as a dressmaker."

"There seem to be so many things you could earn a living at," I said, passing her a glass of sherry.

"Yes; and I stick to none of them." She sighed. "You see, I'm inconstant." She raised her glass. "Here's to constancy. There's nothing I admire more."

"Here's to Livia, and constancy."

Sam Sawle entered and announced: "The lamb's on the table, Mr. Essex. Eat it while it's hot."

"How I love servants who are not flunkeys," Livia whispered. I agreed with that. We went in to dinner.

I filled my pipe and settled in a big chair by the study fire. Livia poured out the coffee which stood on a small table between us. A tall standard lamp with a shade of loose-hanging primrose silk shed a soft light to augment the light of the flames leaping in the chimney. Now and then a sharp hiss of rain upon flame reminded us that the storm was not over, but the wind had ceased to buffet. It had fallen to an occasional rumble in the throat of the night.

"Ever since I bought Heronwater," I said, "I have imagined what it would be like to come down here in the winter, work all day long with no one but Sam Sawle to look after me, and to spend long evenings, tired out, sitting alone under this lamp, reading all the books I ought to read. Well, here I am under the lamp. But I am not alone. Why?"

Livia sipped her coffee. "Of all the men! Didn't you invite me?"

"I formed a painful impression that my invitation had been refused."

"But I've told you, I'm a very inconstant and changeable woman. You must learn never to take me at my word. If I had accepted, you might even now be enjoying your heart's desire—reading all those books that one ought to read but never does: Grote's Greece, Gibbon's Rome, Motley's Dutch Republics, oh, and those dingy little rows and rows of bound volumes of the *Spectator* that go for thirty shillings the set in the second-hand bookshops... Poof!" She tossed her fingers at her hair. "May I have a cigarette?"

I gave her one, and lit it. "Well, now that the preliminary is achieved, tell me—why did you change your mind and come?"

She drew in the smoke, exhaled it in a slow deliberate plume, considering my face thoughtfully. "You are one of those men who will not accept the accomplished fact. They must have all the reasons. Was that not an accomplished fact, in the garden, when you held me in your arms? Oh, dear! I have never before been hugged by a man in oilskins. I should hate to be a sailor's bride."

"You are not serious," I said resentfully.

Livia got up and threw her cigarette into the fire. "Serious!" she cried, suddenly dead white with seriousness. "Why should I be serious? Is there anything to be serious about? Isn't it self-evident that when a girl has to choose between a schoolboy of sixteen who will probably be nothing, whom she knows to be as conceited as the devil and as greedy as hell—when she has to choose between that and a famous wealthy man, I ask you, isn't it self-evident that she'll choose the man? Let her do it without worrying her for reasons. What reasons can there be? One would think you were afraid of what Oliver could do against you. You're not, are you?"

"No," I said. "It's not a question of fear—"

"Right. So long as you're sure of that. Here I am. I'm yours. It's your job to keep me now you've got me."

I had risen, too, and I put my arms about her and felt her head sink on to my shoulder. She began to cry without restraint. I held her close and whispered comforting words to her. My heart was smitten to see her so distressed. "Don't keep on w-worrying me about r-reasons," she sobbed. "I want to b-be fixed—safe."

"You'll be safe. You'll be safe," I murmured, "as safe as love can make you."

She looked up at me with eyes brimful of tears. "Oh, Bill! I do like you so much. If I loved you, it would be wonderful."

"You will. You will," I promised her.

She managed a smile, reached up her lips to be kissed, and said: "Let me go to bed now. I'm tired out."

In the morning there was no sign of the storm. The rain had ceased, the wind was gone. I looked from my bedroom window through the trees down towards the river. The trees were snared in nets of mist. The air was still and full of the drip and dribble of falling drops.

I went about my affairs with a head buzzing with thoughts of Livia. I commended to myself everything that I had done. It was excellent all round. She had said she wanted to be safe. She should be safe. What greater safety could there be than in marriage to a solid established person like myself? As for me, I wanted the woman—wanted her in every sense of the word. She obsessed my imagination as no other woman had done. The way she walked, how she looked, the way she spoke, the way her hair sat on her head and her hat sat on her hair; everything about her, the great things and the little things, had taken on for me the magical and momentous proportions of obsession. There was no arguing about it.

And Oliver? Well, it was best for Oliver, too, I comfortably assured myself. The idea of Oliver at sixteen being in love with a girl of twenty-one was monstrous, absurd. If I helped to cure him of premature notions romantic, so much the better.

I went down to breakfast and found Livia there before me, already busy with coffee and eggs and bacon. She kissed me, rather dutifully I thought. "Now," I teased her, holding her tight, "a warmer kiss than that."

She sat down at the table. "You're lucky to get a kiss at all," she said, "coming down to breakfast at this hour. Shall I pour you some coffee? I thought I should have to go without seeing you."

"Go!" I said in dismay. "What do you mean—go?"

"Clear out. Partir. Vamoose. Abscond," she replied, buttering a roll. "Can you spare Martin to take me in to Truro?"

"But why Truro at this time of day?"

"Because the train to Paddington stops there."

"But today! The first day of our engagement? I thought we'd get about—see things."

"You see! I told you you'd do no work with me about! No. As soon as I'm gone, you'll settle down to your work. Please. Look what a lovely wretched day it is! Perfect for work."

"Will you make a habit of running off just when I want you?" I asked miserably.

"I'm the most impulsive creature in the world. I don't make habits. So you see, you'll never be just one of my habits. That should be gratifying to a husband."

She said it charmingly, but I was inclined to sulk. She shook a finger under my nose. "William Essex," she said, "you're no end of a great man and all that sort of thing; and I've told you frankly that, in getting me for a wife, that has been useful to you. But—I'm not allowing my great celebrated man to sulk and frown over what I choose to do. I won't have that any more than if you were a Covent Garden porter. Now, what about Martin? My bag's packed, and there's just time to catch the train."

I ordered the car. She gave me a much warmer kiss than the first one, and a moment later she was gone.

I had never formulated the thought, but deep in my mind, whenever I had considered the question of a second wife, had been the idea of someone completely different from Nellie. Well, it looked as though I had got what I wanted. And this very property of airy lightness, of incalculability, strangely charmed me as I made my way to my study and straightened out the notes for Act I of *Every Street*.

"You can see across the river now, Mr. Essex," Sawle said as I was getting up from lunch. "You can read Captain Judas's announcements."

I slithered down the path to the landing-stage. The black hulk of the *Jezebel* loomed up through the still murky night. Painted in scarlet upon the planks of the hull I read: "The Great and Terrible Day of the Lord cometh." "Sheep—rejoice! Goats—ah-ha!"

I didn't like that last grim chuckle. The old man seemed to be smacking his lips as he contemplated the discomfiture of the unredeemed. I had intended to call on him, but this new turn was not encouraging.

"Have you seen much of the captain lately?" I asked Sawle, who had accompanied me to the water's edge.

"Not so much, except when he was hanging overside painting that up."

"It's a long time since I saw him."

"Ay, but he saw plenty of Oliver last summer when you wasn't here. They were as thick as thieves. There was a night when Oliver didn't turn up. Got stranded. You may have heard of that, Mr. Essex?"

I nodded briefly.

"Well, we were all pretty well worked up. Old Judas heard about it overnight—that they were missing. We didn't know till the next day, but the old madman was out all night. What d'you think of that? Out all night, rowing about in a dinghy at his age! It was moonlight."

"Yes, I heard so."

"Well, he rowed from here to the Percuil river. Right down the roads, round by St. Mawes Castle, and right up the river! At his age! He was pretty well done up, I can tell you. And he found Oliver all right. What d'you think of that? Animal instinct, I call it. They took him on to the *Maeve* and gave him a ride back, towing his dinghy behind their own. I was down here when they come in. He stood up in the bows, waving his hat and shouting 'The Lord's anointed cometh! We have found the Lord's anointed.' Mr. O'Riorden said he'd like to do the anointing with strap oil."

"It might have been a good thing," I conceded, and Sawle grunted, "Ay, maybe."

We gazed across the water at the enigmatic shell of the *Jezebel*.

"It was a pretty poor party altogether last year," Sawle said at last, "without you and Mrs. Essex and Rory and Maeve. I missed Maeve. They tell me she's becoming quite a famous woman."

"She's getting on."

"She's all right, she is. She's a grand 'un. I missed her most. And I wouldn't mind seeing that Mr. Donnelly again. He was a caution. They say Rory's living with him now in Ireland. That's a funny idea."

But I was not prepared to discuss the humour of that idea with Sam Sawle. "I think I'll pull across and see Captain Judas," I said. "He's bound to find out that I'm here, and he'll expect me."

I pulled the dinghy across the water in the utter stillness of the hushed, grey afternoon. There was no sign of life aboard. The ladder had been hauled in. The windows were fastened. The day was so quiet that I didn't like to shout, and as I hesitated there, looking up at the frieze of gulls that decorated the rail, I made up my mind to suggest to Judas that he should arrange a bell, with the pull-rope hanging overboard. "You see, if anyone tries to surprise you by swarming up the rope, that will automatically ring the bell. If they're unwelcome visitors, you can easily slash the rope and drop 'em into the river." I'd put it to him like that.

I had to shout at last, sending the gulls wheeling and crying, and my voice echoing down the misty tunnel of the river. Then Judas came, his hair and beard seeming more abundant than ever, his eye more glittery, the caution with which he peered over the rail as great as a most nervous beast would use, fearing an enemy presence.

"Essex here!" I shouted, standing up in the dinghy with one hand on the *Jezebel*'s side, and gazing upward at that wild apocalyptic headpiece, white against the grey ambiguity of the sky. The anxious face cleared, and the voice came down to me as thin as ever, but warm and welcoming. He threw open the port in the bulwarks, dropped the ladder, and a moment later I had scrambled aboard. He pulled up the ladder and closed the door, then took me by both hands. He didn't come much higher than my shoulder, but there he stood like some game bantam, fierce yet joyous, driving his one piercing eye into my face. He was, as always, impeccably clean; a triangle of white handkerchief protruded from the breast pocket of his navy-blue jacket.

He had heard of my travels, and when he had taken me below he was all agog for news of the ports I had visited. The rest of my story didn't interest him, but Havre and Marseilles, Stockholm and Copenhagen, Constantinople and Naples: all these were evidently bells in his head and they rang old tunes that he was glad to hear.

This was the first time I had been aboard the *Jezebel* in the winter, and I praised the captain's quarters sincerely. The big room was as cosy as the snug of an old inn, with the fire burning brightly and the cushioned settles on either side of it inviting to repose.

"I think I could work better here than across at Heronwater," I said.

"Ay, one can work," he agreed. "But when will the work end? There is so much—so much. I did not get on very well with the Greek."

I expressed my sorrow, and assured him, without seeing how it could comfort him, that I knew none of it.

"But now it's going better," he said. "I am in league with the enemy."

He looked at me craftily. "Light your pipe and listen," he said; and he told me how he had bought book after book, but the cursed language would not yield its secrets. So in Truro he had looked out a curate who was glad to augment his doubtless wretched stipend by giving him lessons in Greek. This had been going on twice a week now for a year. "Poor fool, I think. Little do you know whom you are entertaining unawares! But I sit there quietly and suck his brains, and it's all high explosive—all dynamite." The captain chuckled in his beard. "Woosh! Bang! Wallop! But," he added despondently, "it's slow work."

He had decided that he must make his own translation of the Greek Testament. He produced his work, which had not yet advanced very far into the first chapter of the first Gospel. Already, it appeared, he had discovered enormous discrepancies between the Greek and the accepted translation, and it was not for me to inquire whether the mistakes were possibly his.

"Matthew, Mark, Luke, John," he said. "But where is Peter? Not a word did that fellow commit to paper. Peter! Fishmonger! Probably he couldn't write. But we'll see. We'll see. We'll get him yet. Old Judas is on his trail. Ta-ta to the Triple Tiara. Excuse me a moment. I'll make a note of that. It's a good heading for a chapter."

He wrote for a while in a book that he took from his breast pocket, then asked: "And how is the Lord God? Has He announced the date of His Second Coming?"

I looked at him coldly, and he shook his head. "It has not been revealed unto him," he murmured; and then, with that quick birdlike agility of his, he leapt to his feet, putting the whole matter from him. "Tea!" he cried. "Come and see the galley." And, as sane as any man in Christendom, he proudly pointed to the good work he had been doing with the paintbrush, making the walls of his galley shine.

In this happier, less exalted mood, we sat down to tea, looking out through the window at the winter-grey river, where a few white gulls dipped and flashed, and at the close-congregated skeletons of the trees on the opposite banks. It was then that I suggested the bell-pull to him. He discussed the idea very intelligently, pointing out that to bring the rope through the deck to a bell in his sitting-room, he would have to bore a hole in his deck and that would let in the rain. But he could overcome this difficulty, he said, by fixing a wire to the rope and passing the wire through the deck. That would need only an infinitesimal puncture. And, so keenly did the old man's mind welcome anything to keep it in the realm of sanity, by the next day he had carried through the whole scheme. Being on the river in my dinghy, I saw him at the root of his ladder hauling on the rope and through his open window could hear the clear answer of the bell.

It had been my idea to be at my desk every morning at nine, to work till one, to spend the afternoon out of doors, and to read every night after dinner. But things didn't work out like that after all. I began each day by writing to Livia. I found that there was an immense amount to say; the letter usually took an hour to write. Everything I had done and seen, the progress of the work; it all had to be told. I felt it was only half realised till it was shared with Livia. And when the letter was written I couldn't get Livia out of my mind, so that it was not before eleven o'clock that I could begin work. Thus it came about that there was no reading, after all. I had to make up after dinner for the dilatory morning.

Livia replied regularly every day. Every time I read one of her letters, I had that feeling: that it was a reply. She never opened out, never let herself go; she just took my points and answered them or commented upon them. She was glad the weather was not too bad. She was delighted that the play was making progress. She was dismayed to find that writing to her was interfering with my work. So her letters went: always short, always subscribed "Yours with much love."

There were only two points that were, so to speak, from Livia to me. "By the way, Maeve finds the flat rather small. She has decided she ought to have a place of her own. I told her, of course, about us. You wanted that, didn't you? Yours with much love, Livia."

That was one point, and I felt, somehow, I would rather have told Maeve myself. I ought to have told Maeve myself.

The second point was this. "By the way, I have just received a letter from Oliver, and it is pretty clear that he knows nothing about our engagement. Will you tell him, or shall I? Personally, I'd rather you did. Yours with much love, Livia."

"My dear Oliver,—Livia Vaynol and I are engaged to be married…"

Dreadfully abrupt! "You may be surprised to know that Livia and I…"

"My dear Oliver,—I have noticed that ever since you met Livia Vaynol you have felt affectionately towards her, and I think, therefore you will be pleased to know…"

Pleased! My God! Would he be!

"It is now more than a year since your mother died…"

I tore that up, too.

"My dearest Livia,—You said that by being here you would make it difficult for me to work. I wonder if you realise how much more difficult your being away makes it! If you were here, I could look up and say to myself: 'There she is—sitting in that chair—reading that book.' And then I would bend over my work again and get on like a house on fire. Or I would know that you were on the river, or gone into Truro to buy chops for dinner, or were giving Captain Judas a taste of heaven.

But as it is, I am unable to get through an hour without asking myself a hundred questions. Is she up yet? Is she brushing that lovely, absurd, adorable, altogether delicious *poofy* hair? Is she going shopping in Oxford Street? Oh, God! Let her be careful at the corners! Don't let her be run over! Is she thinking—just one small crumb of thought spared for that humble sparrow, her bloke—is she thinking of him, working on his play, doing everything he knows to make it good, so that when the crowds get up and cheer on the first night, Livia will be pleased?

Oh, my love, do believe that all day long and every day a thousand, a million, loving, absurd and tender thoughts of you fly about in my head. God! What a fate for an eminent novelist—to be an aviary! That's what I am, my love, a crazy cage filled with cheeping, chirping, fluttering thoughts of Livia Vaynol. You could still the whole riot with a kiss; but there you are, so unaware of your power to soothe me that you think your being away keeps my mind easy. Absurd delusion! I shall know no peace till I am home again and my love in my arms.

I'm glad you haven't told Oliver of our engagement. I intended to do so myself, but have now decided that it would be better to wait till I see him again. There's no reason why he should know at once. The Easter holidays are not so far off as all that. Don't you agree?

The play goes well. After all, having written it once, and having talked it over so thoroughly with Wertheim and made such sheaves of notes, there's little to be done but write what is already clear in my mind. I sent Wertheim the first act, and he is very pleased with it. The second goes to him today. The third I begin to write tonight. I find writing at night here is delightful. Not a sound but the fire and an occasional moan of wind. Whatever time it is when I finish, I go out for five minutes' air before turning in to dream of Livia, and my fellow scribe Judas has always outstayed me! This morning, it was one o'clock. His lights were burning steadily. What concentration there is when everything is focused to a point of madness!

But hurrah! and three big cheers for the glorious sanity of my love for Livia Vaynol!

For ever and ever your lover, servant, husband, BILL."

"MY DEAR BILL,—Yes, perhaps it would be better if you told Oliver when you next see him. How good to know that you find Heronwater so congenial to your work and that Mr. Wertheim likes the first act! I'm sure he'll like the second, too, and that you'll soon be through with the third.

I find it hard to believe that my being with you would make all that difference, and you may rest assured I'm very careful of buses!

Poor Captain Judas! What a sad case he is! So sane at times, and terribly fond of Oliver. He seems to idolise him.

Maeve has found a flat and moves out tomorrow. She asked if we would be getting married soon. In that case, she would have stayed on and kept the flat after I had left. But I said we should not be hurrying things. Don't you agree? Yours with much love, Livia."

"My dear Father,—I'm afraid this letter will disappoint you because it is to ask whether I may be permitted not to come home at all in the Easter holidays. You know that Pogson is leaving school when we break up for the summer, so this coming holiday will probably be the last when he will have much use for me. I mean, when he goes to Oxford he will meet older people, and after all he's two years older than I am.

His people have a place in Scotland, and Pogson would like me to go up there this hols. There would be no point in coming south first, as all Pogson's people will be picking him up here and going on by car.

The point is, Pogson's people have a yacht up there in Scotland, and Pogson always goes up in the Easter hols, and helps to overhaul her for the summer because he's a practical seaman and likes doing these things himself. It's not as though he couldn't afford to have it done for him if he wanted.

I should very much like to be up there in Scotland with Pogson and to see this yacht and learn something from Pogson about over-hauling a yacht. It's a steam yacht, and I only know about small sailing and motor-boats. Pogson says we might even cruise a little in the yacht if the weather is fine and if his people agree.

If you agree to this, would you be so kind as to have my dinner suit sent on when I give you the address, as Pogson says they dress for dinner, and you will know, of course, how much money you ought to send me, and you might give me a hint about the scale of tipping when I discover what staff Pogson's people keep.

There is one matter I am ashamed to mention, but must do so. I think I should take the gold cigarette case that you were so kind as to give me. Unfortunately, I pawned this during the Christmas hols, being rather short of money and not wishing to bother you. Do you think you could get it out and send it on? I should like to send you the money, but am rather short. You will find the pawn-ticket in an envelope marked 'Pawn-ticket' inside the cover of a book called *Across the World for a Wife* by Guy Boothby in the top left-hand drawer of the desk in my room.

I gather from your last letter that it will be about the time of the Easter holiday that your first play will be going on in London. I should have liked to have been present to have seen it, but I have no doubt it will survive long enough for me to have that pleasure in the summer hols or even at Xmas.

Well, that's all except to say how deeply sorry I am about the cigarette case, but you will, I am sure, appreciate the importance of me having it.

Love from OLIVER."

I was back in Hampstead when Oliver's letter came. I went at once to his room and found the envelope labelled "Pawn-ticket." Then I went to town and redeemed my cigarette case.

"MY DEAR OLIVER,—I shall naturally be disappointed at not seeing you during the Easter holidays, especially as I was looking forward to your being present when *Every Street* goes on. However, this seems an opportunity that shouldn't be missed. You will have a chance to learn something about engines and to be with new people. Both those things are worth while.

I shall send on your clothes and some money. As to the tips, ask Pogson about it. There's no need to make any pretence of being accustomed to staying in houses that keep large staffs. I have no doubt Pogson is an intelligent fellow and will understand.

I have rescued the cigarette case from pawn, and you can have it any time you repay me the amount I paid to the pawnbroker. Let me make no bones about it: I was disappointed to find what had happened, though glad you told me. When you are short of money, let me know, and if the purpose for which you want it is intelligent, you know you can have it. And I'm not stingy, either, in interpreting the word intelligent. But don't start borrowing, whether from pawnbrokers or anyone else. Meantime, I'm afraid you'll have to imitate my degrading habit of offering fags from the packet. Alternatively, you needn't, for some time, offer them at all.

You see what a moralist and skinflint I am becoming! But there it is.

I've had a very good time down at Heronwater, working on the play. Captain Judas came to breakfast with me on the morning I left, and impressed upon me at least a dozen times that I was to send you his love.

Accept mine, too, and believe me always your devoted FATHER."

So that was how it was that the Easter holiday went by without Oliver's knowing anything of my engagement to Livia.

## 21

W e started early from Heronwater, and Martin was able to make better time than on the journey out. We were at home by four, and I at once rang up Livia. She asked me to call for her and to take her out to dinner. When I reached her flat she was dressed, all ready, and was sitting down at an open grand piano. She went on playing, and nodded to me to take a chair. Her face wore a deeply concentrated expression. Now and then she tried a phrase over again, and then again and again. Presently her hands dropped to her lap. "Composing," she said with a smile.

"Another of your accomplishments."

"Yes, but please don't say it like that: as though it were something like the water-colour drawing that Victorian misses were taught. *Polite* accomplishments they were called, weren't they?"

"I believe so."

"Well, this isn't at all polite. It's a song. I just thought of the phrase 'When it's with you, it's wonderful.' And now the tune's coming. Don't you think that's a good phrase for a sentimental song?"

And she began to play again, singing in a low, crooning voice:

*With anyone else it's just comme-ci, comme-ça,*
*I can take it or leave it, but when you are there*
  *It's wonderful!*
*When it's with you it's wonderful*

She got up brightly. "Well, that's that! I'll finish it some day. Perhaps I'll sell it to Wertheim—let him make it the theme song of one of his big shows. And so the play is finished! Help yourself to a cigarette."

She waved her hand towards a silver box on the mantelpiece. Resting alongside it was a letter, addressed in Oliver's unmistakable handwriting. It rather jolted me, seeing it there.

"You're still hearing from Oliver," I said casually.

"I shall be glad when he knows we're engaged," she answered briefly.

I didn't light the cigarette. I crossed the room and put my arm round her waist. She lifted her face to be kissed, as though she had just remembered it. I sat in a chair and pulled her down on to my knee.

"You told Maeve that we were not in a hurry to get married. You asked in your letter whether I agreed. I don't." I kissed her on the eyes. "My sweet, what is there to wait for? Let's be married soon."

She twisted the lapel of my coat in her fingers and shook her head slowly. "My dear, I'm so terribly afraid you'd be sorry." She did not look into my face as she spoke.

"Is that really the reason?" I asked. "If it is, put it out of your head right away. But is it?"

"It's one of the reasons."

"And what is the other?"

"Oh, I want to be certain," she cried, springing up. "I want to feel that there's no *doubt* about it." She had taken the letter from the mantelpiece, and on the emphatic word "doubt" she tore it across and threw the pieces into the fire. Then she came and sat on the arm of my chair and stroked my hair—very grey now, I thought, an ageing man's hair. But she spoke kindly, as though to assure herself as well as me. "You *can* make me love you, Bill—can't you—can't you?"

"My dear," I said, taking the restless hand and holding it between my palms, "I can give you my love. That's all. And I can wait till you're ready to take it."

"You old darling," she said, and slipped on to my knees and put her arms round my neck. "Let's wait, shall we? I'm sure I'm going to be terribly fond of you. Where shall we have dinner?"

Maeve wrote to me. "DEAR BILL,—Congratulations on your engagement. Rehearsals of *Every Street* begin tomorrow. I suppose you'll be there? If so, would you call for me and take me along? It's only a sentimental idea, but I feel I'd like to take up my first stroke on your play in your company. After all, we've had this play in mind for a few years now, haven't we? Besides, I want you to meet someone here at the flat. So come early. And I want you to meet the new flat, too! You'll be surprised! I am, I assure you. I never expected to live in such luxury. I've had to take a five-years' lease on the place. That takes us to 1918. Goodness knows what may have happened by then! But, as I have a twenty-first birthday not *inordinately* far ahead, Daddy has anticipated his present by furnishing the flat for me out of the most lavish resources of Messrs. O'Riorden's most lavish Regent Street shop. Hence the dazzler you're in for! But, anyway, shouldn't the leading lady in William Essex's gread play be living like a someone? Most certainly! And it is a grand play, Bill. I've been in plenty, and I *know*. Wertheim let me read the whole script, and I loved it. I love him, too! The dear man is risking twenty pounds a week on me! What do you think of that? And, like all my other blessings, it comes from you, dear Bill. Love from MAEVE."

I thanked Wertheim in my heart. But to him it would be just business. "How do you *keep* all your great stars?" I asked him once, knowing the legend that his players never deserted him. "Like this," he said, with no smile on his big pale face, and jingled the coins in his pocket. Well, I hoped he'd find Maeve good value. I believed he would.

Maeve's new flat was in Bruton Street. I walked up two flights of stairs and found a door, painted a deep peony crimson, with the name "Maeve O'Riorden" on a neat brass plate affixed to it. I rang the bell, and stared, struggling with recollection, at the portly, rosy dame who opened the door.

"Nay, don't look like that," she said. "Tha's forgotten me, Mr. Essex."

"Just a minute," I said, "don't tell me—yes—why, Annie, I'd have known you anywhere, in a hundred years' time. You haven't changed a scrap."

Annie Suthurst smiled delightedly. How long ago was it since Dermot and Sheila had taken that house in Mauldeth Road? Oh, dear! It must be the best part of twenty years ago, and Annie Suthurst, a young widow who had gloriously lost her husband in the Boer War, was their first maid. She was with them right up to the time when Dermot moved to London, and that intimidated her. "London, nay, that's a daft place. I'll not go to no London with thee," she declared firmly. "And now here I am, Mr. Essex," she explained, leading me into a small hall. "Ah've coom after all. But on'y because Miss Maeve were so set on it. Ah wouldn't've coom for anybody but her. An' London's nowt to get excited about when tha's looked at it once. Ah reckon nowt to Oxford Street. It's nobbut Market Street, Manchester, a bit wider."

So chattering with the delightful animation of an old hen glad to be back with a lost chick, Annie Suthurst kept me standing there, giving me time to look about at the fine carpet on the floor, the engravings on the wall, the hat-rack and seat for callers. A nice, useful little hall, with all the doors painted red like the one I had entered by, and the walls and carpet grey.

Maeve came out proudly to meet me. "Isn't it lovely?" she asked, and when I said that indeed it was, so far as I had seen it, she took me round to see all the rest. Her own bedroom, "with two beds so that I can put up a visitor," and with just a little sideways peep over the garden of Berkeley Square. "Not much now," said Maeve, drawing the deep-red quilted curtain to look at the bare trunks of the planes and the dun winter grass, "but how good that's going to be for tired eyes when everything's green!"

"May Maeve's eyes never grow tired," I exclaimed piously; and Maeve said: "At least until they're as old as Mrs. Bendall's. You remember, Bill?"

Oh, yes, I remembered all right. Mrs. Bendall was dead now, but I remembered the dear old lady and the tiny Maeve pouring her tea.

"See," said Maeve, and opened a drawer. There was a little cedar-wood box inside, and in the box lay the dusty petals of a rose. "That's the rose she gave me that night. And look at this." She handed me a card which was lying under the brown shrivelled petals. "From Sarah Bendall to Maeve O'Riorden, with love." In an old woman's large staggering handwriting.

"Do you think I had a cheek?" Maeve asked. "I wrote to her as soon as we got to Heronwater that time, and told her I should always keep her rose. So she sent me this to keep with it. I've never told a soul till now. It's my good-luck casket. It's been on all my tours with me. Sarah Bendall's love in a little box. What a lucky woman! Sarah Bendall's love, Mary Latter's training, and Bill's play to play in!"

She shut the little box with a snap and replaced it in its drawer. Then we continued our tour. Annie Suthurst's bedroom. "The only room in the house that hasn't been new-furnished. Daddy tells me that when Annie first came to us in Manchester she brought her own bedroom furniture. She said, 'That's t'bed Ah went into when Ah were wed and that's t'bed they'll carry me out of to my coffin.' She brought it all along again. She dislikes these distempered walls, so I'm going to give her a wallpaper with rosy wreaths."

We stood on the threshold and peeped guiltily at Annie's *lares*. A double bed with brass knobs as big almost as pineapples at head and foot. Such a bed as Sairey Gamp must often have come across in the course of her professional sojourns. But there had been no need of a Sairey for Annie Suthurst. An enlarged photograph in a stout oak frame of the late Private William Suthurst—curling moustaches, curly-brimmed hat upturned at one side, a young face for ever fixed in its hopefulness while Annie went marching on—hung over the head of the bed. A plain white cotton counterpane. There were three books on a three-legged table by Annie's bed, and I ventured to tiptoe in and peep, for I can never resist the temptation to see what people are reading. The Holy Bible, Charles Dickens' Christmas stories, and Conan Doyle's *The Great Boer War*. Great! Good Lord! How! Why?

There was a fire burning cheerfully in Annie's grate, for this was sitting-room as well as bedroom, with a sagging wicker chair alongside it, and a hassock on which, clearly, she would like to "put her feet up." On the mantelpiece a clock, a magnificent clock, comprising both timepiece and a pair of rearing stallions in metal that was faked to look like bronze. A little plate at the base of the clock: "To William Suthurst, on the occasion of his marriage, from his friends on the warehouse staff, Heywood and Atkinson, Ltd." On either side of the clock a blue china vase, containing faded paper flowers. The vases, I guessed, were wedding-presents, too. There was a sewing-machine under the window. Every Lancashire housewife liked to have a sewing-machine.

"This room," I said to Maeve, "would make me cry, if I didn't know Annie."

"Yes," said Maeve, "Annie's wonderful. All her ghosts are tame now. She's happy with them, and stronger because of them."

"You're lucky to have her. I'm so glad. When you said in your letter that you had someone to show me, Annie was my last guess."

Maeve opened the door of her sitting-room. "Annie, indeed!" she said. "No. Here's my surprise."

Rory came forward with a smile lighting his face, and farther into the room stood Maggie Donnelly.

"Well, Rory, my dear boy!" I placed both my hands on his shoulders. It was easy to do. He had not very much grown upwards like Oliver, whose eyes now looked at me almost from the level of my own. Rory looked up at me. He had grown outwards, like a young oak, like a young bull. His shoulders seemed strong enough to batter down doors, his wrists were as thick as mine and his hands large and capable. The serious grey-eyed face had not changed much, except that it was, if anything, more serious, save now when the old shy smile set little crinkles fanwise about his eyes. I put my hand into the untidy tangle of his hair. It was like harsh wire.

"This is Maggie Donnelly," he said rather timidly. "You'll not have forgotten her since she was at Heronwater."

"I haven't forgotten her," I declared, "but it would be small blame to me if I didn't recognise this for the same young woman."

And that was true enough. She, too, had retained the old gravity that sat so well upon her as a child, that accorded so excellently now with her grey eyes and dark brown hair. But, like Oliver, she had grown upwards. She had a strong, resolute look, but was tall and beautifully feminine, with long legs and narrow hips and young swelling breasts, and a complexion that was full of sunny colour.

"This is my first time in London," she said, in a voice which I had not remembered to be so attractive. "Father sends you his love, Mr. Essex. He's never forgotten Heronwater and Captain Judas and Captain Jansen."

"It was a good time," I said wistfully. How far away it seemed! They had all been children.

"I'm staying over Easter," Rory said. "It'll be grand meeting Oliver again. Now that I've got a job and am more or less self-supporting, we'll have lots to talk about."

"I'm afraid Oliver hasn't got so far as thinking about a job yet," I said. "And what's your job, Rory? You make me feel a very old man."

"Nonsense," Maeve broke in sharply. "You're one of the youngest men I know, Bill. Don't get stuff and nonsense into your head. Don't you think he's looking beautiful and young, Maggie?"

"He's not a day older than Dad," said Maggie, "and Dad can work us all and play us all off our feet, can't he, Rory?"

"Ay," said Rory, with devotion in his eyes. "And shame us all with the risks he takes."

"Well," I said, pulling out a cigarette case—it happened to be that gold one which Oliver had coveted—and offering it to Rory. "And what is this job of yours?"

"I don't smoke, thanks, Uncle Bill. Well, I shan't begin working till this holiday's over, and then I'm going in as a learner at the printing works, where Mr. Donnelly works. Printers are useful in Ireland just now—aren't they, Maggie?"

Maggie nodded. "Yes. But Mr. Essex doesn't want to hear about the discontented Irish," she smiled.

"I'm sorry," I said, "you won't meet Oliver, Rory. He's not coming home for Easter. I wish you had let him know you were coming. Then I'm sure he'd have changed his plans. He's going to some people in Scotland."

"But—" Rory began, his face clouding; then: "Ach, well. There'll be another time."

"Maggie, come and put on your hat," said Maeve. "Uncle Bill's going to take us all to lunch." She led her away to the bedroom.

I walked across the room to look out of the window, which, like that of the bedroom, gave a glimpse of Berkeley Square. With my back to him, I said: "I'm sorry, Rory. You mean, Oliver *did* know you were coming over?"

He came to me impulsively and put his arm through mine, looking down with me into the garden. "Ach, now, that's nothing at all," he said. "It's a good chance for Oliver. Scotland doesn't offer every day. Now isn't Maeve the lucky one, with this flat, and this bit of a view and all?"

"God bless the boy! He's got the jargon of a stage Irishman!"

"And why not?" Rory grinned. "You just wait a bit now, and all Ireland will be a stage. You'll see."

After lunch Rory and Maggie left us. "She doesn't know the first thing about London," said Rory, "and all I know is what I learned those times when we were on the way to Heronwater. We'll have a grand afternoon."

They went out together, Maggie half a head taller than he. "Poor young things," said Maeve. "They seem terribly fond of one another."

"Dear, dear! And how many decades does Maeve give these deplorably young creatures?"

"I know I'm being silly," she smiled. "Actually, I'm only four years older than Rory. But they make me feel sad, all the same. They are so terribly in earnest, and terribly in love, I think, though they don't know it. I hope they won't know it for a long time. I don't think a pair of babes like that ought to be up to the neck in a 'cause.' D'you know, they were actually arguing last night as to whether a certain house in Dublin was or was not a safe place to hide rifles in? It makes me impatient. I hate it all. They have a doomed look, those two."

"Your father was up to the neck in it," I said, "at Rory's age. I was fifteen when I knew him first. He's a little older than I am—a couple of years, I think. He'd be seventeen or so. He was mad to avenge the Manchester martyrs and all that sort of thing. Sheila was in it, too. They've grown out of it. I expect Rory will."

"Do you?" she said briefly. "Then you don't know Rory as I do. And father's grown out of it? Yes; he's grown out of it as Abraham did when he laid Isaac on the altar."

"But God intervened," I cheerfully reminded her.

"Good old God," she said gloomily. "Can you see Him intervening today? I can't. Bill, my dear, I don't like the world we're living in. Lord Roberts blowing off hot air, the Germans blowing off hot air. I've a feeling that anyone who places a sacrifice on the altar today has got more than an even chance of finding that God isn't intervening this time. The sacrifice is going to be snatched up. Thank you very much for a nice burnt offering. And a fine sort of author you are, allowing your leading lady to get into this state of mind half an hour before rehearsals begin. Come on. You ought to be ashamed of yourself."

And now those rehearsals in a dreary hall in a back street were over, and the later rehearsals at the St. John's Theatre were over; and Maeve and I got up from dinner in the Café Royal and walked out into Regent Street. The street was agleam with light, the pavement jostling with walkers, the road noisy with traffic.

"Sorry, my dear," I said. "I gave Martin the very second to draw alongside here. I hate to see you jostled tonight of all nights."

"I'm all right," she said, "but d'you know what I want you to do? When we get in, just talk to me all the time till we reach the theatre about that night at Heronwater when the swans flew across the moon."

"I will," I said, "it was a lovely night."

"It was the loveliest night of my life. Their wings sounded so strong. They were creaking like wicker. I can always hear it when I think about them. Ah, here's Martin."

"Sorry, sir," Martin apologised, "half a minute late. Miss Vaynol stopped me just along the road."

Unexpectedly, Livia was sitting in the car. I had arranged to meet her at the theatre. Now, as we climbed in, she exclaimed: "I just couldn't resist being here to waylay Martin and accompany the important man to the theatre. You forgive me, Maeve darling?"

"No swans, Bill."

"No swans."

"Swans?" said Livia, as the car swung into the traffic eddying at the Circus. "What are you talking about?"

"Shall we tell her, Bill?"

"No," I teased.

"Just one of our secrets," Maeve explained with a laugh. "It goes back a long way."

"I'll bet it does," said Livia with sudden venom that took me by surprise. "You've been barmy about Bill all your life."

Then silence, horrified, all three of us looking at one another in the dim light of the car, dim light cut up by wheels of greater light as lamps and street signs flashed by. Maeve, always white, seemed to shrink into a shadow even of her little self. Livia, usually vibrant, seemed as though her words had snapped some spring in her, so that when she, first to speak, said "I'm sorry," it was a tiny sound.

There was another long silence before Maeve said in a quick passionate voice: "All right, then, you might as well know it, Bill might as well know it. I have loved him—always—always. And that's the difference between you and me, Livia. I know what I want. I hope you do this time. Do you? Do you?"

Livia did not answer. Then we arrived at the theatre.

It was all right. From the rise of the curtain, almost, I knew it was going to be all right. Wertheim had made me write the opening sentences seven or eight times. Every word had to tell. The first ten minutes of a play, he insisted, are tremendously important. You have to fight against late-comers and the apathy of the audience. You must get 'em quick. And as I sat in my box with Livia and Rory and Maggie Donnelly, I knew that we were doing that. There was a laugh in the first line, and we got it. The audience was anxious to settle down; it was chiding the blundering late-comers. Soon there was that grand satisfactory silence which means that everyone in the theatre, from the stalls to the back of the gallery, is gripped by the play and is intent on every word.

I relaxed, I allowed myself to look about. In a box opposite were

Dermot and Sheila and Eileen, with Josie Wertheim. Wertheim himself, a stout, uneasy ghost, was now standing at the back of the box, now vanished. I next caught sight of him materialised suddenly on an end seat in the stalls; then he was gone again, to appear at the back of the circle. I had heard of his first-night peregrinations to sense the temper of the house and to test the audibility of the players. Towards the end of the first act, the door of my box opened quietly and his soft heavy hand rested on my shoulder. It remained there as the curtain fell, and I felt it grip a little till the applause started, then it relaxed, and he joined in. It was applause well deserved. The company had put the act over beautifully, and Maeve, it seemed to me, had fulfilled all our expectations. I joined in the clapping; Rory and Maggie followed my example rapturously, and Livia more decorously.

I need not go through all the incidents of that evening. Even today, *Every Street* is well enough known. I am told I have never written a better play. It was a success from the start. When the final curtain went down the audience remained to cheer and cheer again. It was a demonstration to warm any author's heart, to still any qualms. Wertheim, his pale broad face faintly flushed, was there to hustle me down to the stage, and first I faced the audience in the midst of the smiling, weary, gratified company, then with Maeve alone. I took her hand and felt it give mine a warm, reassuring pressure. "This is it, Bill," she whispered. "This is the moment after all these years. Now say something. It'll never come again—this first night of your first play." And still holding her small warm hand, the hand that had lain in mine when she and I so long ago had seen Henry Irving and Ellen Terry in Manchester, I told the audience just that: how I had taken Maeve to her first play, how I had seen her grow up loving the theatre; how I had promised that some day I would write her a play, and how this was the play. And when a loud voice from the back of the gallery shouted: "And a damn good 'un, too," and the audience roared with laughter and started to applaud anew, I realised that I had, stumbling on it unwittingly, said the right thing.

Wertheim thought so too. Grasping me by the shoulders when I moved into the wings, he exclaimed: "God, Essex! What a story! Every paper in London will print it. You're a fox." There was no fox about it. It all happened simply and without premeditation; but it was, nevertheless, as Wertheim predicted. Every paper printed the story. Some called it a "romance of dramatist and actress" and printed photographs of me and Maeve. Reporters were sent to interview both of us, and though I had said all that was to be said, we had to say it over again, and it was printed over again. This "romance" atmosphere did the play a world of good and kept the theatre full till *Every Street* settled down to run on its own merits.

Wertheim bore Maeve triumphantly away, his arm round her waist. "Jo, control your emotions," said Josie severely. The other actors and actresses were gone. I was left alone on the stage and loitered there for a moment, feeling unreal and deflated. Through the chink between the curtains I could see that the house was already empty and the lights were going out. God! What a place for moralising an empty theatre is! I shook myself, and made my way to Maeve's dressing-room.

It was seething with people. There was hardly a soul I knew except Livia and Maggie, the Wertheims and the O'Riordens. My entry nevertheless was the signal for shouts of welcome, cries of felicitation, back-slapping. "You've done it, Essex." "Never felt more certain on a first night." There was a lot of drink flowing, and I was toasted, and Maeve was toasted, and a man I had never seen in my life lurched up and said: "I always said you had it in you, ole boy."

"I always thought it was the dead that attracted the vultures," said Livia, taking my arm. "The legend needs revising."

We made our way through the mob to where Maeve was sitting.

Rory, flushed in the face and trying not to look self-conscious in evening clothes, stood beside her, pride and happiness shining in his eyes. Dumpy little Eileen—poor Eileen who would never look distinguished in any circumstances—stood beside her chair; and suddenly it rushed upon my mind with a burst of poignant memory that exactly thus had I seen Maeve sitting and those two children standing by her on the green grass at The Beeches when she played at being Queen Maeve holding her high court. Oliver had been there, too, tall and beautiful and supercilious, the only one who had not entered into the game's spirit.

It was almost as though the thoughts in my mind struck a responsive chord in Rory's heart, for he said: "I'm sorry Oliver's not been here tonight, Uncle Bill. He would have enjoyed the play. Maggie and I did—immensely. And we're so proud of Maeve."

It made me feel very lonely—that all these O'Riordens were there and no one of mine—and I turned to get my arm, for reassurance, through Livia's. But Livia had moved nearer to Maeve, and was saying "It was a good performance. Very creditable, Maeve."

Maeve did not answer. She could afford to let such tepid praise go. People known and unknown were besieging her, pressing her to drink, which she would not do, giving her invitations, praising her. She sat there with an aloof dignity which suddenly made me think of Mrs. Bendall. And then I laughed aloud, because I was *sure* that Maeve was thinking of the old lady, and, little chit, trying to act like her. "May I pour out your tea, madame?" I twitted her. "And if I did, would you give me a rose?"

She looked up with a smile.

"Tea?" said Livia.

"You wouldn't understand," said Maeve. "It's just another of our little secrets."

## 22

From my side of the Heath I could reach Dermot's house by walking across Parliament Fields. My play had been running for about a month. May had come, and soon Rory and Maggie Donnelly would be returning to Dublin. I had seen a great deal of them, and now I was walking among the greening hawthorns to Dermot's house where I was to meet them once more at tea.

It was a beautiful day. The sky was blue; a lark went up from the grass; but, still, in those days four o'clock of a May afternoon was four o'clock, not three as it is now, and there was a bite in the wind. So I was glad when I was in Dermot's study, up on the first floor, where a fire was burning, and some of his loveliest things were collected. He had never sold the Gauguin, the first good picture he had ever bought. It hung over the fireplace, the only picture in the room. I stood at the window, looking down the short garden. Grey squirrels were swinging through the branches of the trees that grew inside the garden wall. Beyond the wall the setting sun made the new green of Parliament Fields shine celestially bright.

I turned to see if Dermot had finished reading the letter which was in his hand when I came into the room. It gave me a pleasant feeling of superiority to see that he now used spectacles for reading. My eyes were as good as ever; but then my hair was grey. Dermot's was still ruddy. It had darkened from the fierce red of his youth. Sheila called it "Titian," and Dermot wore it abundantly.

There he sat, one long elegant leg over the padded arm of his easy chair. He took the spectacles from his nose, placed them and the letter on a little table beside him.

"It's from Uncle Con," he said.

Uncle Con—one of the two small boys whom that old fanatic Michael Flynn had pushed into Cork on a hand-cart during the famine of '45. The other, Dermot's father, my own old friend, had been dead these two years; but Conal O'Riorden, who must have been of a great age, still lived, and, I gathered from Dermot now and then, still flourished. Most of his business affairs had been handed over to Dermot's brother; for many years Uncle Con had been digging himself deep into United States politics.

"He's all awake, the old man," said Dermot. "He can see what's coming."

"And what is coming?" I innocently asked.

Dermot leapt lightly to his feet, and faced me, back to the fire, head outthrust. "For God's sake, Bill! What sort of a world do you live in?" he demanded. "What sort of a fool's paradise? Here's an old codger of eighty or thereabouts, living five thousand miles away, and he's more alive to the realities of the world than you are with all the facts under your nose. Haven't you heard the treasonous hounds yapping for this past twelve months?"

It was a long time since I had seen Dermot lit up. He was lit up now, his face pale, the point of his beard quivering, his eyes flashing their old sparks.

"Well, seriously, I haven't been paying much attention to all the hot air that's been blowing off in Ulster. I suppose that's what you mean?"

"Hot air! Hot air be damned!" Dermot shouted, clenching his fists. "As for Asquith's Home Rule Bill, you know what he can do with it so far as I'm concerned. 'It recognises no Irish nation.' That's Arthur Griffith, and that's me, too. The Liberal Party and that dirty dog Redmond can keep their Home Rule Bill till they learn the elementary meaning of words."

He struck a match, suddenly threw match and cigarette into the fire, and waved his hands in the air.

"Then why the outcry?" I asked mildly.

"Who's making the outcry? Carson and Co. This miserable, stinking pretence of Home Rule has set a quarter of a million people squealing, running to sign a Covenant. A Covenant! It tells the government: 'Go to hell! We shall defy you. We shall take up arms against you. We don't believe in law and order unless it's our law and our order and suits our book.' And they've got permission—permission, mind you! They're not doing it in a corner—they've got permission to arm and drill. Have you never heard of the Crimes Act of 1887?"

"Never."

"You wouldn't. Well, listen to old Con." He took up the letter from the table. "'Arms are pouring into Ulster every day. Bonar Law, I see, declared that rather than be ruled by Nationalists, the Unionists would prefer to be ruled by a foreign power. Germany, I suppose. My dear Dermot, things are pretty dicky between Britain and Germany at the moment. The Germans over here open their mouths freely. And these patriotic Unionists are willing to demonstrate their unity by splitting away and invoking the aid of their country's most powerful and dangerous Continental enemy. Why doesn't Asquith use the Crimes Act of 1887? Innumerable Irish patriots have been gaoled under it for so-called seditious utterances. Is this army that the Unionists are gathering seditious or isn't it? Of course it is. Gaol 'em.'"

"Gaol who?" asked Rory, coming into the room at that moment with Maggie Donnelly.

"These damned Carsons and Craigs and Smiths," Dermot shouted. Rory did not shout. He brought a chair for Maggie, and when she was seated, turned to his father with a quiet smile. "Don't bother about them," he said.

"Don't bother? D'you want to read this letter from your grand-uncle?"

Rory shook his head. "No. I've no use for American-Irish

patriots—only for their cheque-books. And don't bother. These people will be dealt with when the time comes. Won't they, Maggie?"

Maggie nodded. "We are not asleep," she said.

They staggered me—these two whom I had looked upon as children. Suddenly old Con O'Riorden's dollars seemed mean, and Dermot's shouting seemed futile and theatrical. With a sure thrust of knowledge, I felt myself in the presence of authentic players in whatever tragedy Ireland might be staging. It seemed as though Dermot and I were infants in the presence of two resolute adult intelligences. We were babblers of words. Here were two who had done with words and understood the nature of action.

This flashed through my mind as I stood there at the window with my back to the fading light, watching the little group about the fireplace. Rory, so short alongside his tall father, took Dermot by the elbow and propelled him towards his chair. It seemed to me an almost symbolic action. "Keep out now, please. You let me in for this. Well, I'm in it up to the neck. There's nothing more that you can do but let me go through with it." That was what I read in it.

"Uncle Bill?" Rory invited me. I joined the others round the fire, and tea was brought in. Maggie Donnelly poured; and she and Rory talked a little, quietly, of Ireland. A few heroes loomed through their words: Jim Larkin and James Connolly and the Countess Mackievicz. And they talked of the poems of MacDonogh and Plunkett; and there were hints of Rory in a green uniform marching and drilling in the Wicklow mountains with others of an organisation called the Fianna, of which that afternoon I heard the first word. And all they said was said with gravity and resolution, and each seemed to lean for support upon the other, so that the words Maeve had uttered a little while before came back to my mind.

"You see," said Rory finally, "what it comes to is this. If, because of a beggarly Bill like this they rear up and shout, what will they do when we demand the freedom that alone will satisfy us? We have tried for it by fair means; but now armed force has been made the issue, and not by us. But since it has been made the issue, we shall not be caught unprepared. Isn't that it, Maggie?"

And again, Maggie Donnelly, watching him out of her grave grey eyes, nodded her head like a sybil.

Suddenly I thought of Oliver, and of his gold cigarette case and of "Pogson's people," and I could have fallen on Rory's neck and cried.

Maeve came, with apologies for being late. She had been to a dancing-class. Dermot rang for more tea. "Why dancing?" he asked testily. "You'll be wearing yourself out, girl. Your business is straight acting. Why don't you stick to it?"

"I'm not so sure about that," said Maeve. "I don't know what my business is. I'm young, and I've got time and energy. I want to learn everything."

"I've wanted that all my life," Dermot grumbled, "and I haven't succeeded."

Maeve turned to me. "One of these days, Bill, you'll have to write me a comic part," she said. "Have you noticed how well the Hargreaves' party goes in *Every Street*?"

"I have indeed," I praised her.

"So has Wertheim. He's mentioned it several times. Something might come of that."

The Hargreaves' party came into the second act of the play. It was the sort of scene you might imagine at a party in any suburban house, provided the family had a daughter like Annie Hargreaves. She had been strictly brought up, in a family that shunned the theatre; but for years she had been secretly visiting and loving the music hall. Called upon to entertain the company at the party, her reserves suddenly broke; and, sitting at the piano, she gave impressions of all her loves—Maidie Scott and Vesta Tilley and Fanny Fields and Marie Lloyd—singing their songs. They were, of course, thoroughly bad imitations, so that coarse words and hinted depravity came across unredeemed by the wit and genius of the players.

It was a grand scene; I was proud of it; but it was an impossible scene without an actress who could suggest poor Annie Hargreaves' sad belief that she was "getting it across," being outrageous and audacious, while, in fact, she was filling the room with mounting horror. It is while she is representing Maidie Scott singing "If the Wind had only blown the Other Way" that Annie suddenly realises that the silence does not denote admiration, but something more grim than she has ever before experienced, and on a great jangling discord at the piano she breaks into tears and rushes from the room.

Maeve perfectly achieved the mingling of comic and pathetic that the scene called for, and I was not surprised that her work there had caught Wertheim's especial notice.

"So you see," she said, "when he puts on a big musical show, I might get a good part in it, and a part like that would mean singing and dancing and comic acting and all the rest of it. I just want to be ready, that's all. But, dear Bill," she added, leaning across and putting her hand over mine, "it'll be a long, long time, I hope. I want your play to go on and on, making lots of money for all of us."

"You'll be wearing yourself out," Dermot repeated.

"Leave her alone," said Rory. "She'll do it, because she's like me. Don't you think she's like me, Maggie?"

"The spit an' image, in everything but looks," Maggie confirmed.

"Oh, looks!" Rory laughed. "Maeve bagged the lot when looks were being handed round in this family. When I was a kid, they used to call me Ugly."

"Ugly? Why?" Maggie demanded. "You're not ugly—you're just—well—solid—like a mountain."

"Ach, woman!" Rory protested, shrugging his shoulders.

"Ach, woman!" Maggie mocked. "You learned that from Father."

"What didn't I learn from him?" And Rory's face lit with the fire of a disciple naming his beloved captain.

Oliver was back at school; Rory and Maggie were back in Dublin; *Every Street* had settled down to my satisfaction and Wertheim's; and I had a lot of time on my hands.

Oliver had enjoyed himself at the Pogsons' Scottish house. The theme recurred in his letters after he was back at school. "Pogson's people ran to a butler, and it was most amusing being addressed as 'sir' by this reverend person. There was quite a big staff altogether, and the house looked like an ancient castle, though Pogson says it was built by his grandfather. Most of the stone, though, came from an old house that used to stand on the site and that Pogson's grandfather bought so that he could pull it down.

Poggy very decently told me all I ought to know about tipping," Oliver went on, "and even offered to make me a loan, but I didn't accept much. The grounds are extensive. We overhauled the engines of the yacht, according to plan, and in the last week, with the captain aboard, took her out for a day's run. It was very interesting to look back from the sea to the romantic turrets of Pogson's house.

By the way, as I shall be seventeen in a day or two, and you will no doubt be sending me my accustomed gift, I wonder whether you could make it a *really good* book on steam yachts—something that gives a useful idea of first cost, subsequent cost of upkeep, management, etc.

By the way, I haven't heard from Livia Vaynol for some time. She used to write to me pretty frequently, so if you should chance to see her perhaps you'd be kind enough to give her my greetings. I think your attitude about getting the cigarette case out of pawn was quite right, and I will repay you this money as soon as I can, as I should like to have the cigarette case very much."

\*

I have never found it difficult to do nothing, and a successful drama-tist is even more fortunately placed than a successful novelist when it comes to that. The play was written, and really it had taken me very little time to write it, and now Maeve and seven or eight other people had to work six nights and two afternoons a week to fill my pockets, while I could afford to do nothing at all for a long time. An unsuccessful writer has a dog's life; a successful one has the softest job on earth.

This seemed to me the perfect opportunity to further my acquaintance with Livia. When I look back, it seems remarkable that I should have to put it like that; but, though Livia and I were engaged to be married, the extent of our relationship still amounted to no more than acquaintance. I was able now to see her every day. We always had either lunch or dinner together; we went to theatres, and—what was new for me—to a great many concerts. Her own compositions were jingles that could at most hope to be popularly whistled, but she had a deep hunger for music.

But though we were so much together, we got nowhere. I could not pretend that there was any depth of cordiality in her feeling. We were just two people who had a fondness for the same ways of spending time, and spent it together.

I bought Oliver his book on steam yachts, though I did not see that it was going to be of much use to him. Certainly, I could not run to a steam yacht, and there seemed little prospect of Oliver's doing so for a long time to come. Livia was with me at the time. "For Oliver," I told her. "I must post this at once. It's his birthday tomorrow. He's seventeen."

"Cupid, I suppose," she said with a laugh, "was ageless. But if he had grown like the rest of us, he'd have been marvellous at seventeen."

"I don't think Oliver's so marvellous," I said rather sourly as we left the shop. "I should like to see his mind clinching round something."

"Oh, well," she said gaily, "if you're talking about mind—"

"I was impressed by young Rory O'Riorden. In a way, I hate to see so young a boy eaten up by political ideas. But I couldn't think of Rory as a boy. He's become quite a personage. Did you meet him?"

"Casually. I hadn't much chance. He was staying with Maeve."

No; I suppose Maeve would not have encouraged an acquaintanceship between Rory and Livia. The less those whom Maeve liked saw of Livia, the better Maeve was pleased. She would have liked me to see less of Livia. She would have liked me to see nothing of Livia.

When I had left Livia at her flat and was driving home, I asked myself why it was that Maeve's judgement, which I was prepared to respect in most matters, had no influence with me here. Maeve would have liked to marry me; let me face that frankly; but I knew that her dislike of my association with Livia sprang from more than that. Friendly at first, she had come on deeper acquaintance to dislike Livia herself.

But it was not a matter of respecting Maeve's judgement, or my own judgement. Judgement didn't come into it. Nothing came into it except that Livia's looks and ways and voice were things I loved when I had them, sickened for when they were absent.

Her ways? Her ways included that odious encounter with Maeve on the first night of *Every Street*, and they included flippancy whenever, struggling as I was in an emotional situation that was beyond my depth, I tried to get solid ground beneath my feet. Ought I to have felt humiliated because I permitted these things? Perhaps I ought; but I didn't; and, going over my position as I had done again and again, facing even the fact that Livia had me, to use the crude effective expression of childhood, on a bit of string, I saw that humiliation didn't enter into the matter any more than judgement did. No, indeed; I felt nothing so base as humiliation when I thought of Livia.

All I wanted now, with time on my hands, was to spend as much of that time as I could with her. And then things so turned out that she had not much time to spend with me.

It was towards the middle of June that I had taken her to lunch, and at another table in the restaurant was Wertheim, splendid and iridescent in a silk suit that shimmered like a peacock's plumage when he moved. A gorgeous creature was with him, and it amused me to see her make her way steadily through cantaloup, cold salmon, strawberries, ice-cream and iced coffee while Wertheim ate a few pieces of dry toast and drank a glass of Evian water. He went to the door with her when the meal was over, conducting her as ceremoniously as though she had been a queen and he a humble viceroy who had been accounting for his corner of territory. She gave him a condescending smile from gorgeous eyes shining from under a wide hat-brim and held out a languid white-gloved hand. Then he hurried to my table, sat down, and wiped his forehead with a large silk handkerchief. "The bitch!" he said. "She would never have got me if Josie had not been away. I will *not* employ her!" He flicked a crumb off the table, and so the exquisite creature was disposed of.

"But you," he added, "I want to see you. Where can we talk?"

"Would I be in the way?" Livia asked. "There is my flat. I'll take you there and then clear out."

"Good, good," Wertheim agreed. "Let us go there, and you stay, too. At my house we should be pestered. You see—" And he waved a hand towards the door through which he had bowed his beauty.

"Shall we walk?" Livia asked mischievously when we were in the street. It was a sweltering day; the pavements were burning. Wertheim held up his stick to a passing taxi. "I never walk," he said. And, indeed, when I came to think of it, I had never seen Wertheim on his legs unless he were inside a building.

When we got to Livia's flat, he sank, shimmering in his silken suit, into an easy chair, and asked permission to light a cigar. "Do, please," said Livia, "and you light your pipe, Bill."

Wertheim carried a silver cigar-piercer on one end of his

watch-chain. As he ritually adjusted this to the cigar, he said, without looking up from what he was doing, "What d'you think of these revues, Essex? I suppose you've been seeing some of 'em?"

"Yes; I've seen a few, and I like them. I like their speed and colour, and some of the sets were magnificent."

"Well, I've never done a revue," he said, "and I want to do the best one there's ever been. *Reach for the Sky* was all right in its way, but there was too much of the old musical comedy about it." He lit his cigar, blew out a long streamer of smoke. "Something different from that. A bigger chorus than anyone's ever put on—all picked girls—all beauties. Lovely dresses. Lovely sets. Good songs. The dancing'll have to be superb. The leading lady'll have to be able to sing anything—sentimental song, comic song, and she'll have to be an *actress*. And she'll have to be able to dance. I want to get going. I want a book, and I want ideas about people new. I don't want the old gang. I don't want Doris Trent."

"That was Doris Trent you were having lunch with?"

"Yes."

"I thought so. She's extraordinarily beautiful."

"She is. And that's all there is to her. She's welcome to a job in the chorus, though her legs are on the thin side. Ever seen 'em?"

"No."

"I have."

He smoked for a while in silence, then said suddenly: "Look! Tell me if you think this is crazy. You know, you've put me in touch with an interesting set of people. Look at Maeve. That girl's versatile. There she is doing a magnificent piece of straight acting in *Every Street*, and in the middle of it she plunges into that party scene. It shows a grand sense of comedy. I don't know, but I think there's my leading lady. Now there's her father. I like that man. I've had a lot of talk with him. I've been round his workshops. He's got the best business of its sort in this country, and yet you find him playing about with planes and chisels as if he was an apprentice. He's got a marvellous sense of modern design. I want to use it. He could do me some grand sets."

"A family affair?"

"Yes. Here's Miss Vaynol."

Livia leaned forward in her chair, her eyes shining. "Do I come into it?" she whispered.

"You'll have a chance to come into it," he said. "O'Riorden tells me you design dresses, and he likes them. Well, what he likes is all right, I should say. When we've got some idea of the book, and the sort of dresses it will call for, I want to see what you can do. Mind," waving a fat finger at her, "I'm making no promise. It's a chance—if you can take it."

"And do *I* come into it?" I asked, smiling.

Wertheim looked at me in his sulky way for a long time. "I don't know," he said. "You're the dark horse. I'd like you to, because I've liked working with you on your play. But I don't know. I wondered about the book. Does it appeal to you? D'you think you could do that sort of thing?"

"Oh, Bill, yes, yes. Let's keep it all in the family!" Livia cried excitedly.

I shook my head. "No. I don't see it, Wertheim. I'd like to think of myself as a man of all the talents—novels, plays, revues—but I don't see it. It's not up my street at all."

"Thank you for knowing your mind," said Wertheim. "It's rare."

And when, a long time after that, *Choose Your Partner* went on at the Palladian, I had had nothing to do with it. The book was written by Clive Seymour—brilliantly—and most of the songs, as well as the dresses, were Livia's. But I felt glad, all the same, that I had been present at that small conference of three which first discussed the spectacular affair that blazed through the war years, that produced songs that soldiers whistled and sang and played on gramophones in trenches and dug-outs, that made a bright, remembered patch between stages of the cross for untold thousands of men. How strange it would have seemed to me then could I have foreseen what was to be a common spectacle no long time hence: the earthy burrow, the guttering smoky candle, the rifles and equipment leaning against the wall, the table of planks and boxes supporting the gramophone on which weary eyes are strained from tired faces. *"When it's with you it's wonderful."*

And every man thought of the "You" his own heart meant, as he recalled the Palladian spotlight dropping its blue-white cone on Maeve, stock-still as if bewitched in its moony circle, Maeve wearing the strange white hieratic dress with one red rose that Livia had designed, Maeve singing out into the dark hushed white-face-crowded auditorium, in that husky voice she used for giving enchantment to this song, the words that Livia had written: *"When it's with you it's wonderful."*

"Oh, Man, I hate it, I hate it! What must they think! So many of them going back tomorrow—tonight!"

"Dear Maeve! I know. I know."

"I can't go on doing it. They send me letters—flowers…"

She went on to the end.

So there it was. High summer of 1913 was on us, and my dream that Livia and I might do this or that—go to Heronwater, go abroad, perhaps even get married—faded out. Now she was a different woman. Now she had a job for her talents. Now it seemed she didn't want me at all. I might call at the flat and take her out for a quick lunch, and she seemed grateful; or, at the end of her long day, I might take her out to supper; but she wouldn't linger. She would want to go home, repeating some wise maxim about early to bed.

She had succeeded in striking the imagination of Wertheim, and she was making the most of it. She began on that first afternoon when Wertheim opened the matter which was to end so brilliantly in *Choose Your Partner*. When the conversation slackened, she sat down at her grand piano without a word and began to sing and play.

> *All by myself the night seems long,*
> *And the stairs are hardly worth climbing.*
> *But when it's with you, it's wonderful!*
> *Climbing to the moon and the stars*
> *Up golden bars.*
> *With anyone else, it's just comme-ci, comme-ça;*
> *I can take it or leave it, but when you are there*
> *It's wonderful!*
> *You pin the stars on the wall,*
> *And if a star should fall*
> *It's just a tear*
> *Of joy because you're here,*
> *Because you are wonderful,*
> *When it's with you, it's wonderful,*
> *The most wonderful thing in the world.*

I know something about what makes a play or novel "go"; but the psychology of the popular song baffles me. Looking at these words as I have set them down now in print, I can't see what's in them; but I know, and everyone who lived through the war years knows, that in some strange way they insinuated themselves into the hearts of lonely, stricken, harassed men and women. The tune was almost dirge-like, and there was more in that to me than in the words—some deep quality of loss and longing that was to match itself with the years so soon to come.

But though, to me, there seemed nothing to be excited about when Livia sang the song that afternoon, the effect on Wertheim was instantaneous. His head went back in his chair, his eyes closed, and when Livia had finished he said, without opening his eyes: "Sing that again. I want to imagine how it would sound with a proper voice."

"Thank you, sir," said Livia saucily, and put out her tongue towards his unseeing face. Then she sang the song again.

Wertheim walked over to the piano. "Now me—please," he said.

Livia got up, and Wertheim entrusted his great shimmering bulk to the fragile stool. But there was nothing bulky about Wertheim's fingers. Even to my untutored ear, the song gained from his playing. He made it more caressing, extracted a moving undertone of lament.

He got up from the piano, smiling. "We had better have lunch together tomorrow, Miss Vaynol," he said. And to me: "You see, our talent begins to assemble itself, Essex. Eh? What do you think of this song?"

"I'm afraid I'm no judge of such things."

"I am. That is why I invite Miss Vaynol to lunch tomorrow."

## 23

Livia was gone away. Oliver would be home soon for the summer holidays.

I had called at Livia's flat unexpectedly and found her packing.

"I'm off," she said, trying hard to be casual.

"Off?"

"Yes. Holiday. I've worked hard for six weeks—harder than I've ever worked in my life. You don't grudge me a holiday, Bill?"

"No—but—"

"But I ought to have told you. Well, see, there's the letter. I should have posted it at Victoria this evening."

"But—" I began again.

She stood up, and I thought she looked tense and strained.

"If I had told you, there would have been arguments, persuasions—wouldn't there? I didn't want to tell you why I'm going. Oliver will be home soon."

"I see."

"I wonder whether you do! Oh, don't stand there looking anguished! I'm trying to *help* you. I'll write to you. I'm going to a tiny place in France where no one ever goes but me."

She stood there looking at me, white, defensive. There was nothing to be said except that, of course, I would come to Victoria and see her off.

The next evening I walked on the Heath with Dermot.

"You're looking as cheerful as a sick monkey, Bill," he said. "You ought to come to Ireland with me. It'll do you good."

"Ireland? Oliver'll be home in a day or two, and I thought of taking him down to Heronwater."

"Have a change. Bring Oliver, too. Come to Dublin." I thought the matter over, and liked the sound of it.

"Maeve, of course, can't come. What about Sheila and Eileen?"

Dermot's face darkened. "It's a terrible thing to get middle-aged, Bill. There was a time when I could have said to Sheila: 'Let's go to Ireland and buy a couple of guns and pot at the first people we see coming out of Dublin Castle,' and, begod, she'd have done it. You remember her when we were engaged to be married?"

"I remember the first night you brought her home. She was a darling, and she was shy, and you tried to make her say 'God damn England,' and she wouldn't. I remember all that."

"She wouldn't say it, but that didn't mean a thing. And then there came the time when my work took all my energy, and I had no use for the merely mouthy patriots. She didn't like that, Bill. You didn't know, did you?—but there was a stretch when Sheila and I found one another hard to live with. It was just then."

"I didn't know."

"Ah, well; that's over, thank God. Now it's all the other way about. And, of course, that's because it's not me, but Rory. That's why she won't be coming to Dublin with me. She won't meet Donnelly; she won't see the life Rory's living now."

"And you think that's just middle-age and a terrible thing? Maybe it's wisdom."

"Well, it's why I'm going to Dublin alone—unless you'll come."

"I'll come. I'd like Oliver to see Rory again."

Oliver and Pogson tumbled out of the train at St. Pancras and came along the platform arm-in-arm. Pogson's pimples were no better. His voice was an absurd bass amid the shrill chattering of his companions. He was, as usual, overdue for a shave. Oliver never knew, physically, an awkward age. He was as tall as Pogson, nearly six foot, looking extraordinarily well after the summer term. He was hatless. His fair hair was rather long, brushed in a glistening undulation across his forehead. His face was tanned, making his deep blue eyes look very attractive. He never lost the power of startling me. I saw him now so infrequently that there was always some change, some accession to maturity, that made him a new picture. I saw him that day as a man—a young man, but a man, and a man of such beauty that people turned their heads to look at him.

A new and splendid motor-car was drawn up in the road between the platforms. The chauffeur saluted Pogson, who, with Oliver, made ecstatic exclamations about the beauty of the car. They examined the gadgets, the dashboard fitments; then Pogson said to the chauffeur: "I'll drive her. Didn't know there was a new car."

He climbed to the driver's seat, the chauffeur opening the door for him, and thence called to Oliver: "Well, I'll be looking you up!"

He drove off masterfully, and Oliver stared at the lovely car till it was out of sight.

Martin was doing some repair job to my car. "We'll go home by tube," I said. He looked crestfallen.

What on earth was the matter with me? It had given me pleasure to emphasise the difference between Pogson's seigneurial departure and our democratic ride in the tube train. Not so long ago I should not have thought it possible that anything which caused Oliver to look crestfallen would give me pleasure. I should not have thought it possible that the idea of spending a holiday alone with Oliver would cause me uneasiness. But I was aware of being pleased that we were going to Dublin with Dermot. Maeve working, Sheila and Eileen taking their holiday elsewhere, Livia away: there would have been no one but me and Oliver at Heronwater, and I was glad that that was not to be. As the train jolted northwards, we sat side by side, saying little, and I thought of the times when we had so much to say, when a word—any word—was enough to start "conversations."

We got out at Hampstead station and walked home—up the hill, past the Leg-of-Mutton pond, past Jack Straw's Castle.

"Come along to my study as soon as you're ready," I said. "We'll have tea there."

He went off to his own rooms carrying his suit-case. It was pretty heavy. He had carried it up the hill, effortlessly, splendidly upright.

He came down presently. He had taken the trouble to change completely. He was wearing a grey flannel suit, a blue shirt and a crimson tie. He threw himself down into an easy chair and dandled a neat brown shoe. The tea-table was between us. He balanced a cup of tea in his hand, and his eye roved round the room. It came to rest on a photograph of himself, standing on a low book-case.

"You haven't had me done lately," he said, nodding towards the picture and smiling. The white teeth gleamed in his sun-browned face.

He didn't give me time to reply, but went on: "I asked Mother about that once—you know, the annual ritual."

He was referring to the visit he had made to a photographer every birthday during his mother's lifetime.

"She said it was because you were sure I was going to be a great man and you wanted a record for my biographer."

He smiled again rather mockingly. I had, indeed, said that to Nellie in a fond half-seriousness. The record of Oliver's years was carefully put away in my desk.

"We've missed quite a number of years now," he said, "and I'd like a new picture. There's a practical reason for it."

Then his laughing impudence suddenly broke down. "Honestly," he said, his colour mounting, "I want to give a picture to Livia Vaynol. I'm terribly fond of her." He said it with a rush.

My heart gave a thump. I had not expected him to make that avowal.

He went on: "She hasn't written to me all this term. She used to write."

Then for a moment he could again say no more. He put down his cup, and it clattered shakily on the table. At last he said: "I've wanted to talk to you about this, but it hasn't been easy. Of course, you think I'm only a boy. I'm not. I feel quite grown-up…"

He stumbled again, confused, unable to find the words he wanted.

"Oliver," I said, "listen. Don't think that I misunderstand the feelings of a young man. I know how sincere and real they can be, and what pain they can give. But they pass. They change. I'm sure of this. Otherwise, I could never tell you what I have to tell you now—what Livia herself has asked me to tell you—she and I are going to be married soon."

My voice sounded like that of someone talking in a dream. "She and I are going to be married soon." So matter-of-fact. I had often pictured the moment when I should say those words to Oliver. I had arranged the scene in my mind. Now the words were out, suddenly, without frillings. I had often imagined, too, what he would say and do: go very white, perhaps, shout, protest. He didn't do any of these things. "I feel quite grown-up," he had said; and before that, at the station, he had struck my imagination suddenly as a man. He answered as a man. There was one sign of emotion: he moistened his dry lips with his tongue. Then he said: "I knew you were very fond of Livia. What you say doesn't surprise me. But I think you are making a mistake."

Only when he had spoken the words very calmly did I see from the colour in his cheeks, and from a pulsing vein in his neck, that he was deeply affected.

"What do you mean—a mistake?" I said, half-rising from my chair. Then I sank back again. No. This wasn't a thing I could argue about. I leaned forward towards him across the table, sought to put my hand on his knee. "Oliver, do please understand—" but he rose and looked down at me, very composed, very haughtily lovely. He put my own thoughts into words. "We can't discuss it, can we? We have nothing to say to one another."

He took a cheap gun-metal cigarette case from his pocket, opened it, and held it towards me. I shook my head, and sat staring at the ground. Oliver put a cigarette between his lips, snapped the case to with affected indifference, and walked out of the room.

Eight o'clock was our time for dining. I found myself fussing into the dining-room at a quarter to eight to inspect the table. I wanted everything to be perfect for Oliver. I rated the parlourmaid because a salt-cellar was slightly tarnished, and sent her skipping to burnish it quickly. I rearranged the flowers, fiddled with the cutlery. My heart was crying in my breast. I could see, as though I should never cease seeing, that poor little gesture with the cheap cigarette case. I was wondering whether he had rushed away to cry, once the door was closed behind him.

Just before eight, I went up to bring him down. He was not in his room. I shouted "Oliver!" and he replied from the bedroom: "Yes. Come in."

I went in. He was in bed, sitting up with a dressing-gown over his pyjamas.

"Hallo!" he said, smiling brightly. "Want me?"

"My dear boy, you've forgotten the time," I said, speaking with the same false brightness that had been in his smile. "Aren't you coming down to dinner? Got something good there?"

"Not bad," he said, tossing across to me the paper-back he was reading. It was Fergus Hume's *Mystery of a Hansom Cab*. "It's a thing Poggy gave me."

"It's jolly good," I said, finding myself for the first time anxious to discuss the queer books that Oliver chose to read. "Of its sort, I should say it's very good indeed."

"Oh, well, I haven't got much to finish it, then I'll shut-eye. I'm dog-tired."

"But don't you want any dinner?"

"No, thanks. Not a bit hungry." Again the bright glassy smile.

"Well, what about a tray? Shall I have something sent up?"

"Oh, no—no, really."

"Well—"

"Don't bother about me."

"I'll tell them to be very quiet, then. Oh, and look, I wanted to give you this." I pulled the gold cigarette case out of my pocket.

"No—please! I know how you value that. Besides, I've got this one now. Poggy gave it to me. I've taken quite a fancy to the old thing." He took up the gun-metal case from the table beside the bed. "Sure you won't have one?"

I shook my head, and stood there foolishly holding the gold case in my hand for a moment, then slipped it into my pocket.

"Well, I'll tell them to be very quiet."

"That's awfully good of you. Good-night." He turned to his book, dismissing me.

I hesitated at the door, fiddling the knob in my hand. "See you at breakfast?"

He looked up quickly, as though he had thought I was gone. "Oh, breakfast!" He smiled again, and this time I thought there was something hard and mocking in it, something which said to me: "Ah! I've got you jumping now."

"Breakfast," he said, considering it. "Well, now, that is an occasion for a tray. Ask 'em to send it up."

I couldn't stand the thought of dinner. I told them to take it away. I couldn't stand being in the house. I called Martin and he drove me to town. I ate in a crowded restaurant and stayed there till the show was nearly over at the St. John's Theatre. Then I collected Maeve and drove her to her flat in Bruton Street. It was a very hot night. Even at midnight the streets had no coolness. Maeve was tired and rested her head on my shoulder. "Nothing will kill your old play, Bill," she murmured, "not even this heat. Sometimes I wish it would. Oh, dear. I'm so tired."

Annie Suthurst was at the flat, fussing round with eggs beaten up in milk. "Now you get out o' t'place quick, Mr. Essex," she admonished me. "I'm going to put Miss Maeve to bed. Wearin' 'erself out, she is, I'm not 'avin' 'er stoppin' up half the neet chin-waggin' wi' you."

"Nonsense, Annie," Maeve smiled, gulping down her milk. "I don't see Mr. Essex so often as all that. We're going to have a good old jaw."

But we didn't talk much. Mostly, we sat in her darkened room, with the window wide open, and listened to the murmur of the London streets which is never wholly hushed, and watched the leaves of the plane trees in Berkeley Street, still as if cut out of metal, with the light of the street lamps shining on them. Then we went out and walked slowly round the square, and Maeve put her arm through mine, and when we got back to the door of her flat she said: "Feeling better?"

"Yes."

"I'm glad. I could see there was something wrong with you."

It was two o'clock. A little wind crept round the corner and Maeve shivered slightly. She looked up into my face, as though wondering whether I would give her my confidence. I remained silent, and she shook her head.

"D'you remember old Dobbin, Bill, that poor dumb brute in *Vanity Fair?*"

"H'm."

"So long as you do." She slipped her hand from my arm and ran upstairs.

A letter from Livia at Tour des Roches in Provence came in the morning.

\*

"Here I am, down on the farm. How you have taken me on trust! You didn't even know that my father came from these parts, did you? Well, he did. But I needn't now tell you the story—after all, a very simple one—of how he found himself in London teaching languages, how he captivated a girl with a bit of money, and how they both died a few years ago, so that the bit of money—such a little bit!—is now mine. My mother's brothers were stockbrokers, which is why I decided to live alone!

There, you trusting one! Now you know something about me! And here I am on my uncle's farm which has a little white tower at one corner, and in the tower are two little round rooms, one on top of the other. The bottom one is a sitting-room and you climb from it to the bedroom by a ladder. These two rooms are now mine, and from either you can look out at the rocky hillside behind the farm which, with my tower, gives the place its name.

It's all very, very nice, Bill, though at the moment very warm, and if you want a pretty good picture of the sort of life it is, read Daudet's *Lettres de mon Moulin*.

I didn't tell Mr. Wertheim that I was leaving London. If you see him, let him know that I do not intend to be lazy—after a day or two. I shall get some good ideas for dresses out of these Provençal villages, and I'm going to work hard on songs.

I expect Oliver is at home now. Have you told him? Give him my love—if you think you ought to. I shall stay here at any rate till the school holidays are over. Love, LIVIA."

"If you think you ought to." It was not an easy question to decide after a wretched sleepless night. I refilled my coffee cup, and was twiddling the letter in my hand when the parlourmaid, looking flustered, came into the room.

"Have you taken the tray upstairs?" I asked.

"Yes, sir. I was just coming to tell you, sir. Mr. Oliver isn't there."

"Isn't there? But he said he'd have breakfast in bed. Has he got up? Have you seen him about?"

"No, sir. And I've asked everybody. Nobody's seen him. There's this letter, sir."

She handed me the letter, addressed to me in Oliver's writing. I strove not to seem excited. "Let me have some more toast. And— yes, and some more coffee."

When she was gone I opened the letter.

"MY DEAR FATHER,—I am now just over seventeen years old—old enough to know my own mind. I feel much too old to be at school. I am tall for my age, much taller than most boys, and this makes me feel uncomfortable. I should feel worse if I went back to school now that Pogson is gone. In any case, I should have asked you to let me spend a year in private study or something before going on to the university, but now it may turn out that I shall not go to the university at all. You may not want me to, and if I find a satisfactory job, the university may not be of any use to me. For I am going to try and find something to do. There is no need whatever for you to worry about me. As I told you last night, I am a man now and I have no doubt at my age you were looking after yourself. I've got one or two things in mind, though unfortunately I've never been brought up to do much either with my hands or my head. I will let you know what I am doing as soon as I have got something. I know a boy leaving school ought to give a term's notice, so I'm afraid I've let you in for £100 or so; but I shall doubtless be able to pay this back, with what you paid the pawnbroker for the cigarette case, one of these days. I was very interested, as you know, in steam yachts, and for some time I have stinted myself by paying into what I called my 'yacht fund.' This now proves to be fortunate because I have £10 by me which will keep me for a bit.

Yours, OLIVER."

Not a word of Livia. Not a word of his real reason for leaving home. I brushed impatiently past the parlourmaid bringing in the coffee and toast, and went up to Oliver's rooms. The sitting-room, the bedroom, the bathroom. This was to be the place where Oliver and I would find one another again. Working in my own room, I was to know that here a young and eager spirit was unfolding near me.

I knew in my bones that Oliver would never live under my roof again. He never did.

Suddenly the house with its servants and superfluities, its too many rooms, its wanton waste in provision for circumstances that could never be, seemed hateful to me. I sat down in Oliver's chair and buried my head in my hands.

When I got up, I felt worn and haggard. I noticed a heap of charred paper in the fireplace. The drawers of the desk were open. Evidently he had been having a clean-up. I went over to the fireplace and stirred the ashes with my toe. Here and there, on uncharred fragments, my own handwriting appeared. Letters. It looked from the size of the pyre as though there had been a good many. It looked as though he had burned every letter from me that he had hoarded since he was a boy.

Part IV

## 24

Dermot and I stayed at the Hamman Hotel in O'Connell Street—the great flat-fronted building that was doomed to death by bombardment and by fire. "I was in a house on the other side of the street with the Free State Army. The Hamman had been burning for a long time when I saw the whole façade, in one solid piece, lean slowly outwards, hang suspended for a moment, crash into the street. Then the flames roared to the sky like hell let loose."

That was how it was described to me by a man who saw it. And as the flames roared, those who had been in hiding there fled, to be shot down like rats smoked out of a hole, shot down by the men who had been their comrades.

The sense of such things to come hung like a doom about the beautiful filthy city. It was early in August when we arrived and late in October when we left. For three months I lived with the sense of being in a dream that must have an evil waking.

We saw a great deal of Donnelly and Rory and Maggie; but it was queer not to know when you would see them. Oftentimes, we had arranged to meet one or the other at this place or that, only to find, if it were Rory, that Maggie would turn up and, with some evasive explanation that explained nothing, let us understand that he was suddenly needed elsewhere. If it were Donnelly, Rory might turn up and tell us that Donnelly thought it "safer" not to be seen anywhere that day.

There was an air of mystery and conspiracy that made men look twice at their neighbours before opening their mouths. Once, when I was walking with Donnelly, he whispered "Keep straight on," and as I did so he turned to the left and disappeared. Two men were walking towards me, and when they came to the corner they turned the way Donnelly had gone and I heard their boots on the pavement breaking into a run. I kept straight on, as Donnelly had told me to do, and presently, to my surprise, he stepped out of a tobacconist's shop ahead of me. Smiling, he said: "It's good to know the back doors."

Donnelly was now a widower. He lived in a small workman's cottage, "two up and two down." He and Rory shared a bedroom. The sitting-room was jammed full of furniture. There were bookcases revealing the tastes of a scholar, a large pigeon-holed desk, a piano, and, as though the place were not congested enough, a huge bird-cage. It must have been six feet long and three feet high, and in it budgerigars kept up an endless billing.

Here we gathered one night—Donnelly and Maggie, Rory, Dermot and I—for one of those festivals of song that Donnelly loved. It was a hot night. The curtains were drawn back from the open window. Maggie played, and, care-free, Donnelly put back his head and sang. We all sang: ballads and music-hall songs and hymns—anything with melody that came into our heads.

The window was a bay, and sitting within it I could see along the street. A youth came unhurryingly towards the house, and as he passed raised his hand and threw something through the window. Whistling, he passed on.

Donnelly pounced upon the stone, gave it one glance, tossed it through the window into the scrap of front garden, and said: "Quick!"

What followed was a matter of seconds, each, evidently, having rehearsed a part. Maggie shut the window and drew the curtains. Donnelly leapt to his desk and took out a lot of papers. Rory in a stride was at the bird-cage, pulling out a false bottom. I should say it was fifteen seconds at the outside before the papers were in the cage, the false bottom slid to, and Donnelly was saying "Right!"

Maggie sat at the piano, heartily hammered out "Annie Laurie," and the concert began again. We were not through the first verse when there was a knocking at the door. Donnelly went to open it. Maggie continued to play, and the budgerigars kept up their billing.

Two men, branded with the inescapable look of having been detectives from their mothers' womb, came in, bustling Donnelly before them. They gave me and Dermot scowling looks and said: "Get out!"

We went.

Late at night, Donnelly joined us at the Hamman for a good-night drink. We were relieved to see him. He said nothing about what had happened, expecting us to understand from his presence that the budgerigars had kept their secret.

For the first time in my life I saw bloodshed. I saw the great frame of Jim Larkin reared up over an immense throng of men and women. I heard his great ranting voice playing all the tricks of the demagogue upon the responsive instrument that could so easily be supplied by a city where twenty-one thousand families were living in one room each. I saw the crowd sway and wilt as the police charged and belted into them. Dermot seized my arm. "For Christ's sake!" he shouted, and pulled me out of the mêlée. We bolted ignominiously with the crowd that was melting down side streets and alleys. Three were left dead upon the ground.

It was a distressful city, full of distressful sights. The ragged unemployed, locked out by masters who would have no truck with unions, wandered like wolves about the streets, gathered in knots upon the Liffey quays, crowded into Liberty Hall where Maggie helped with the soup kitchen.

"Soup! My God, it's guns they want, not soup," Dermot cried; and soon we were to see the guns, too.

We were to see the Citizen Army at Croydon Park, marching and counter-marching; we were to see Donnelly, dressed in the uniform of a high officer, walking with a sprightlier step, glancing with a harder eye; and Rory, wearing an officer's uniform, too, putting his ragged squad through work which he seemed to know like the back of his hand. He roared at them and cursed them and cajoled them, and they grinned and sometimes answered back, and looked as though they loved him.

I glanced at Dermot, standing by my side, his beard quivering, his eye glistening. "Well," I said, "how do you like it?"

For the first time in my life, Dermot had no answer. He took my arm and walked away, beyond words.

In the evening of that day we called at Donnelly's house, and there he and Rory were, in civilian clothes, indeed with their coats off and their shirt-sleeves rolled up, eating their supper as though they had come in from a day in the country.

They had nothing to say about the day's events at Croydon Park; they were discussing the prospects of a hurling match. Maggie came in. "Well, and what's the woman been doing all day?" Donnelly demanded heartily, leaping up and laying a place for her at the table.

"Learning to put on bandages," she said.

"Come and see some architecture," Dermot said. They were lovely houses, built with the decency and restraint of Georgian times. We did not linger, but passing quickly by, we could see here and there the exquisite proportions of a fireplace, the exciting beauty of a moulded ceiling.

We did not linger because of the stench of offal in the streets, because every other window was broken, and the doors were sagging on one hinge or gone altogether, and the doorsteps were occupied by foul old women and the pavements by bawling cursing children. Hags and harridans leaned from windows, mumbling or screeching, and the stamp of hob-nailed boots echoed on the uncarpeted stairs. The lovely Georgian houses were the foulest slum I had ever seen. "Holy Oireland!" said Dermot, his voice between a sob and a jeer.

There were days in the Wicklow mountains: there was a day at Howth Head, when all five of us lay in the heather and said nothing and looked at the blue sky and the blue sea and the white gulls wheeling between. Then we had tea at a cottage, boiled eggs and bread and butter and honey; and everything was so beautiful that I could not believe this was the world wherein Donnelly might suddenly vanish from my side, and Rory shouted his young throat hoarse on the parade ground, and there were dead people lying where the police had charged them, and beauty decayed to the filthiness of slums, and Maggie was learning to put on bandages.

I left the others sitting at their meal, and went out to the field behind the cottage whence, once more, I looked at the sea with the westering sun striking it to a dance of sequins. As I stood there, Maggie and Rory came round the angle of the cottage, holding hands. The fierce sunlight was in their faces, dazzling them, so that for a time they did not see me. They were not speaking, but as they walked the face of each was instinctively drawn to the face of the other. They came on slowly, handfast, looking at one another, confidently, steadfastly, with the wide shine of the sea behind their heads and the sun lighting their faces. Then they saw me; their hands fell shyly apart; and I thought of what Maeve had said: "They love one another, but they don't know it yet." Ah, well; they knew it then.

A letter reached me from Oliver, sent on from Hampstead.

"MY DEAR FATHER,—You will be pleased to know that I am at work. The first thing I did was to lay my case before Pogson, who was very decent and insisted on my staying at his house for the night. All his people were away. They had gone to Scotland, but fortunately Pogson had one or two things to see to in town before joining them. This meant that he had three days to spare, and he very decently wrote at once to his father, asking if there was any sort of job for me in the office. Mr. Pogson replied, enclosing a letter which I was to take to the head clerk of one of the departments in Holborn. Pogson went with me, and it appeared that the letter said I was to be given some sort of job to be going on with till Mr. Pogson came back, when he would more fully go into the matter.

Pogson had to go the next day, and I found some lodgings in Camden Town, but I enclose no address because this is not the sort of place you would like to be seen in. When I have got on, perhaps a different view may be taken of the matter; but the chief thing is I have made a start, though I have very little money and this year I must do without a summer holiday.

Mr. Pogson was away for six weeks, and sent for me when he came back. Of course, he remembered me from the visit to their place in Scotland and from hearing Pogson speak about me. He asked me what I was doing and I said just miscellaneous clerking, and he said perhaps I had better carry on with that and he would see how I shaped. But he was very decent and asked if I was happy, and when I said 'Yes' he said that was the main thing, and there was no reason why anyone working for Pogson's should be otherwise.

So I am very much where I was when I started, but I do not regret the move I made and am determined to keep my shoulder to the wheel though things are tight at the moment.

Your son OLIVER."

I had arranged to leave Dublin in a day or two, but I did not wait till I got home. I at once enclosed a five-pound note in a letter, addressed to Oliver at Pogson's in Holborn, congratulating him on the courage he had shown in setting out on his own, and wishing him luck. I suggested that, now that he was a wage-earner, he might feel differently about living at home, and said that, in any case, I should be glad to see him at Hampstead whenever he cared to call.

There was a letter awaiting me when I got back. It said that he would feel happier in Camden Town if he did not have the occasional contrast of Hampstead, and that, having left home, he wished to rely wholly on himself. The five-pound note was returned.

Livia had got back to London while I was in Dublin. In my letters I had said nothing to her about the turn things had taken with Oliver. It was a matter to speak of personally, and I decided to call at her flat on the day after my return and take her out to lunch.

But first I must see Oliver. I would not attempt to speak to him: no good would come of that. But my heart was yearning to see him again—yearning the more deeply because for so long now I had been in the company of Dermot and Rory, a sad observer of Dermot's pride and pleasure in his son.

Only to see Oliver; that was all; and the next day at noon I was pacing Holborn on the side opposite the polished granite façade of Pogson's Limited. It was the first day of November, but warm and serene still with an aftertaste of autumn. For a long time I paced up and down, scanning the face of everyone who left Pogson's. All were of interest to me, because all were the faces of men who might know Oliver, who perhaps worked alongside him, who possibly had come out even now from talking to him.

At last I crossed the road. Perhaps it would be a good thing to loiter on that side till I caught sight of Oliver, then quicken my pace and meet him with a start of surprise. "God bless me, boy! Fancy meeting like this! I'd forgotten you worked in Holborn. What about some lunch?"

Two prosperous-looking men came out of the office together. I approached them. "Excuse me, but I wonder whether you know a new clerk here, named Essex, and whether you have any idea what time his lunch hour is?"

The man I addressed raised a supercilious eyebrow and spoke to his companion. "*Do* you know all your new clerks, Pogson?"

"No. But there *is* a fellow named Essex—friend of Philip's; but God knows when his lunch-time is. I don't."

So this was Pogson, laughing so disagreeably at the idea of knowing anything about a clerk's lunch-time, dismissing Oliver as a bit of a nuisance foisted on to him by his son. He turned a cold shoulder to me and held up his rolled umbrella for a taxi.

And then again I was overcome with fear at the thought of meeting Oliver. I felt that if he came out at that moment and found me loitering there, I should die of shame. The five-pound note returned to Hampstead recurred suddenly to my mind; I felt a hot blush surging to my cheeks, and hurriedly I crossed the road again. There was a bookshop opposite Pogson's, with a short corridor, book-lined, leading to its door; and standing there, pretending to browse among the books, I could keep an eye on Pogson's entry.

Then I saw him. Clerks had been coming out in twos and threes. Oliver came alone. He came very slowly down the short flight of steps that led from a swing door to the street. He was without hat or overcoat, and the mild autumnal light that filled the street shone upon his curly hair. He stood there for a moment very erect and debonair, tapping a cigarette upon his nail. If I had expected to find someone crushed and humiliated, I was disillusioned. Upon most of the faces that I had watched come through that door there was the inescapable impress of servitude. Quick, furtive, white-faced men, rushing as though at once they were glad to be out but anxious to waste no time, fearing to be late getting back.

But Oliver stood there in his good-looking clothes, unanxious and unhurrying. He looked content. I felt that all my solicitude was needless, and this, which should have pleased me, was the bitterest ingredient of the moment. What I was looking at was a handsome, well-clothed young man, who appeared to be in need of no one's help or pity, who looked, indeed, uncommonly well satisfied with himself and the beautiful day about him. He jerked up his left arm, with a gesture I well remembered, to consult a wrist-watch, looked up at the sky, turned to the left, and began to walk slowly down the street.

Well, I had done what I set out to do: I had seen him. What now? Nothing. There was nothing I could do. I had come prepared to be abundant in everything he needed, and it seemed he did not need anything. It seemed he did not need me.

I watched the tall slender young man going down the street, with the sunlight on his hair; and I felt as though my own youth were walking away, visibly before my eyes. I could feel the tears stinging at the back of my eyelids as I stood there, with some volume, which I had not even bothered to look at, foolishly in my hands. At that moment an absurd phrase stood out as though written across my brain, sprung suddenly from those far-off evenings when the curtains were drawn in Ancoats and I read from Dickens to old Mrs. O'Riorden. "In our children, my dear Copperfield, we live again."

Do we! Oh, my God—do we!

My hands were trembling as I shut the book and put it back in the book-case. I felt as though I had endured all that I could endure that day; but, in an obsession of self-torture, I crossed the road and followed Oliver along the pavement. Presently he paused under a clock hanging out over the street and began to look about him. Evidently he was expecting someone. "Under the clock." I paused, too, and obliterated myself as well as possible against a shop window. Whom could he be meeting? Pogson would be at Oxford now.

Suddenly I knew—knew in my bones the interpretation of the happy face that I had watched lifted to the sky, the poise of a man content as though the world had no more to give him. I saw her come, bustling happily along the crowded street, still beautifully bronzed from her long stay in France, her hair bleached like a ripe harvest. I saw how, instinctively, each held out both hands, and, when the hands had clasped, how they stood there looking into one another's eyes. Then Livia called a taxi, and they came in it along the street towards me, and I turned my back like a felon who must conceal the crime of existing.

I wondered whether Livia would tell me that she had met Oliver. She did. I rang her up and asked whether I might look in for tea.

"Don't be so humble, Bill," she said. "Of course you may look in for tea. Look in any time you like. You sound dreadful. Have you just come from the dentist's?"

"I've just had a bit of a shock."

"You poor sweet. Come and tell me all about it."

She looked heart-breakingly beautiful when I called. "Full of the warm south." Golden-brown. And she was charming to me. She put her arms around me and held up her face with her mouth pursed like a bud for me to kiss. When I sank my face upon hers, her hair smelled warm and sunny, like new hay.

"Sit down," she said, "and let me make a fuss of you. You look tired out. What's the matter with you? I thought you'd been having a holiday? I suppose it's all this business of Oliver leaving home?"

"You know about that?"

"I do, indeed. I've just been having lunch with him. Why on earth didn't you let me know about it?"

She was so casual, she was taking it all so much for granted, that my heart began singing. I pulled out my pipe and filled it, and leaned back in the chair, feeling happier than I had been all day.

"I didn't want to disturb you with a thing like that while you were on holiday."

"Well, you let me in for a nice disturbance when I got back. There was a letter waiting, from Oliver, telling me the whole rigmarole. He asked me to ring him up at the office, and when I did so, suggested lunch together. So we had lunch together."

"I hate to criticise anything you do; but do you think it was wise to meet him?"

"I don't see why I shouldn't. There's no harm in standing a decent meal to a poor young devil trying to pig along on an office boy's wages."

"I suppose not. But you've been so deliberately avoiding him since we became engaged that I'm a bit surprised."

She smiled brilliantly. "Well, my resistance broke. I had to see him. And I thought he looked a most creditable step-son, though he's as great a fool as ever. I told him so, and advised him to go home."

"And what did he say to that?"

"He said he was every inch as good a man as you are, and seeing that you had made your way in the world, he saw no reason why he shouldn't do so, too. In short, he was beautifully cock-a-hoop."

I smoked in silence for a while, then said: "He didn't leave home, you know, merely because he felt stifled and wanted to earn his own living. He left because of you. He left the night I told him we were engaged. He told me frankly, as he had a right to do, that you meant a great deal to him. Did that come up? Or would you rather I didn't ask that?"

She got up and walked nervously about the room for a moment. "No, please don't ask that," she said. "I can manage Oliver all right. Don't worry."

## 25

Oliver wrote:

"MY DEAR FATHER,—I'm afraid that after all I must let you have my address, because there are so many things I need. When I left home I could take no more than my suit-case would hold. Now I am particularly in need of clothes. Would you be kind enough to send all the clothes I have, not forgetting my dinner suit? Pogson will be home soon for the Christmas vacation, and he may want me to go out now and then. Indeed, he has several times written, suggesting a few dinners—just he and I in the West End. I am rather looking forward to this, as I have never done it before. So please send the clothes. The studs and cuff-links are in one of the drawers of my desk. I rely upon you not to look me up here. I am all right.

Your affect. son OLIVER."

I packed everything myself, and when I had done and stood there looking at the empty wardrobe and chest-of-drawers—drawers gaping, wardrobe doors swung open, litter of papers and odds and ends scattered about the carpet—I felt desolate. There was so little of Oliver left once his clothes were gone.

Annie Suthurst rang me up, trembling with wrath. "Look 'ere, Mr. Essex, when's Miss Maeve going to 'ave an 'oliday? She's fair worn out, an' I don't know 'ow you expect flesh an' blood to stand it, wot wi' night shows an' matneys an' Lord knows wot all. You see she gets an 'oliday."

I had no opportunity to answer. Annie slammed on the receiver.

An hour later I rang up Maeve. "What's your idea of a holiday? Wertheim is announcing a 'slight indisposition' and your understudy's going on tonight. The world's yours for a week."

Uncomplaining Maeve gave a gasp of pleasure. "Oh, Bill, you're always thinking of me! I've only got one idea in my head: a busman's holiday. Let's have a nice long dinner together, and then go and see a show. What about the Palladium? Harry Weldon *and* Little Tich. Can you beat it?"

"Very well, so long as you let me prescribe for the rest of the holiday."

"Go on, doctor."

"Pack off to Heronwater in the morning. It's lovely there in the winter. Take Annie Suthurst with you, and Eileen, too, and do nothing for a week. I'll telegraph right away to Sawle. Agreed?"

"It'll be heavenly. And tonight?"

"I'll call for you at half-past seven."

We dined at an obscure restaurant. It had to be obscure, because a paragraph in the evening papers had announced Maeve's "slight indisposition," and it would not have done for her to be recognised merrily feeding out. She was very happy, like a child on a day off from school.

Only over the coffee did she become suddenly grave. We had an alcove to ourselves in that fusty, amusing little restaurant; and not many people were there, anyhow. As soon as Maeve turned to me and placed her hand upon mine I knew she was going to say something serious. I could always tell from the gravity of her white face, the intense blue-blackness of her eyes. She pushed aside the little pink-shaded lamp, pulled an ashtray towards her, and knocked the ash off her cigarette. "Do you think it necessary for Mr. Wertheim to change his name?" she asked.

"Why on earth should he?"

"He's going to, anyway. He came to see me this afternoon—to see if I really were ill. He's an awfully kind person, I think."

"I think so, too. He's a grand man."

"Well, he stayed there talking for an hour, and said the most extraordinary things. He said we should be at war before this year was out."

She looked at me with the deep wells of her eyes troubled. "Is it very terrible, a war, Bill? You see, I know nothing about these things. I can't remember a war, except in a vague sort of way the Boer War. And that seemed to mean nothing except wearing buttons with generals' photographs. I can remember their names: White, Methuen, Gatacre, Buller."

I pressed her hand gently. "It means more to grown-up people, my dear. It meant more to Annie Suthurst, didn't it?"

"Yes, of course."

"But tell me: what was Wertheim getting at? What makes him think there'll be a war?"

"Oh. I don't know. He just sat there—you know how immense and unstirring he is—and looked into the fire and talked as if he were prophesying. He made my flesh creep. Of course, he's always on the move, all over Europe and Asia, watching things and thinking, and he is very wise."

"I'm sure he is."

"Well, he says things are approaching a smash-up, and he predicted it would come this year. And that's why he's going to change his name. He says anyone with a German name will have a terrible time in England before the year's out. So he's going to become an English citizen and change his name by deed-poll to Worthing."

"Extraordinary."

"D'you think so? D'you know, Man, while he was talking I couldn't help believing every word he said! He was so queer, mixing up his business arrangements with all this visionary talk."

"How did he do that?"

"Well, he said that the war would be a terrific one, and that when there was a terrific war on, people would want big bright shows. And so he intended to have this new revue of his ready down to the last detail."

"Extraordinary," I repeated; and yet, looking up from the bright circle projected upon the table by the pink-shaded lamp, looking up into the dim spaces of the badly-lighted restaurant, full of eddying smoke-wreaths, I felt suddenly a tremor of the spine. From five thousand miles away, old Con O'Riorden had predicted this same thing; and now Wertheim, the cosmopolitan wanderer and watcher, and, I was by now half prepared to believe, the sensitive medium, repeated the warning.

"And Wertheim thinks it's coming this year? Where are we?"

"1914. Sounds like any other year, doesn't it? I wonder whether it will ever sound different? You know, there are dozens, hundreds of years that mean nothing, and a few that sound different. 1066. 1660. 1837. I wonder whether 1914 will ever have its own special sound?"

I signalled the waiter for the bill, and, standing up, pinched her ear. "Let's try and believe that Wertheim's all wrong," I said. "Let's try and believe that things are all right with a world in which we may see Harry Weldon and Little Tich on the same bill."

Maeve got up, gathered her bag and gloves, and smiled valiantly. "Yes," she said. "Let's try."

I said, when we came out of the Palladium: "Tired, my dear? Shall I call you a taxi?"

"No, it's so lovely, let's walk. Come with me as far as the door. I don't want you in tonight. Annie will riot if I don't go straight to bed."

So we set off to walk to Bruton Street. It was a dear frosty night, with a sharp wind blowing and a glitter of stars above the roofs.

Maeve put her arm through mine and we hit up a good pace, thread-ing our way through the crowds. Suddenly I felt Maeve's gloved hand constrict sharply upon my arm. I looked down in some sur-prise. (Maeve's head was hardly higher than my shoulder.) She had almost stopped in her tracks; and then, aware that I had sensed her perturbation, she quickened her pace again. But I had followed the direction of her eyes, seen what she had seen. On the other side of the street, clearly illumined by the light of a street lamp, were two young men in evening clothes: Pogson with an opera-hat askew, and Oliver, hatless. Pogson leant against the lamp, his hands in his trousers pockets, his chin sagging; Oliver stood by him, one arm through Pogson's, looking from him to a pair of girls wearing immense hats and skirts foaming with frills. As I interpreted the situation, Pogson's collapse had held up a procession of four.

"Stay here," I said to Maeve. But Maeve would not stay. She still held to my arm as I crossed the road. Oliver looked up, saw us coming, and made a not ungraceful inclination of the head to Maeve. But she seemed frozen at my side, and looked at him like death.

"Poggy," Oliver said, shaking Pogson's arm gently, "my father."

The young women at that word took their skirts in their hands and faded with gentle susurration round the corner.

Oliver continued to shake Pogson, whose opera-hat had now slipped to a more precarious angle at the side of his head. "My father," he repeated.

Pogson looked up, stood up, levering himself forward from the lamp by pressure from his shoulder-blades, pushed back his hat, and recognised the presence of myself and Maeve. His hand fum-bled towards his hat. "G'evening," he said. Then he relapsed upon the lamp and said no more.

A taxi cruised by and I held up my hand to the driver. "Do you know Pogson's address?" I said to Oliver.

"Yes, sir. I'll see him home. I'm perfectly sober."

He certainly was. He even looked fresh, debonair. He and the driver helped Pogson into the cab. They drove away.

Maeve and I continued our walk to Bruton Street. She had said no word from the moment she caught sight of Oliver, but the intensity of her grip on my arm was maintained all the way home. Even when we reached her door she kept her head averted and said nothing. I knew that she would not trust herself to speak because her voice, like her eyes, was full of tears.

I continued my walk, alone, round Berkeley Square, trying to fake up an interest in the vigour of the night, the black etching of the bare plane-tree boughs against the stars, the beautiful ironwork of some of the gates, and the old extinguishers fixed alongside them. But my mind wouldn't focus on any of these things. I wandered on past the Berkeley Hotel into Piccadilly, where the walkers now were few. It was past midnight. I turned left towards the Circus, and all the way, walk as I would, that recent encounter possessed my mind.

"Yes, sir." Somehow that stuck in my gizzard more than anything else. More than the women. More than Pogson's deplorable condition. The icy formality of it was like a stab in the heart, for never before had Oliver so addressed me. It labelled me a stranger; it showed me the fence and told me to keep on my own side of it.

Well, for God's sake—what was I going to do about it? Was I going to allow a seventeen-year-old boy so coldly and resolutely to put me out of his life, to bring to nought so much hoping and striving and loving? Suddenly I was besieged by a multitude of recollections sprung from the days of Oliver's utter dependence: Oliver in the bath, so soapy that he slipped through my hands like a trout; Oliver so small that I could put my hands under his armpits, heave him aloft and drop him on to my shoulders, his legs clutched round my neck, drumming my chest; Oliver, wearing his new football boots, a diminutive figure in a red jersey, looking comically inadequate between the goal-posts; Oliver in the porch of the boarding-school when I delivered him there for his first term, looking at me vanishing towards the turn of the drive which would hide me from him, waving, waving, frantically, as though he could not, dared not, sever the tremendous bond that had held us so close for so long.

A taxi crawled along the roadside. I stopped the driver, gave him Oliver's address in Camden Town, and told him to hurry.

"I rely upon you not to look me up here."

Rely on what you like, my boy: I can't let all that go, I can't see so much that was so good founder so miserably.

Pogson, I knew, lived at Sydenham. It would take a taxi a good time to get there. I could easily reach the house in Camden Town before Oliver got back. I did not wish to intrude on him in the house: I could understand his wishing me not to see the sort of place he was living in. Not that he need have feared to shock me. I had known Shelley Street, Hulme, and Ancoats. And this street in Camden Town was not unlike a Hulme street when we reached it. Under the moonlight, lying like silver rime on the slate roofs, giving one side of the street a brightness almost of day, the other an almost solid blackness, the long thoroughfare stretched its lifeless uniformity. Every downstairs window was a bay; every upstairs window was flat; and the smokeless chimneys cut at precise intervals into the cold radiance of the sky like turrets on the long precision of a prison wall.

It was one o'clock, and in all the length of the street there was no stirring save the dry rustle of paper in the gutters and the occasional prowling of a cat between the bright clearing of the moonlight and the sinister thicket of the shadow. Not a window anywhere was open; linen blinds were down, and the white light gave to the window-panes a subaqueous and insubstantial quality.

In this dead and moonstruck cañon I waited for Oliver and from the first I knew that I waited in vain. Something in the very air of the place smote a chill to my heart and told me that I might as well expect to encounter warm flesh and blood in the craters of the moon.

The driver and I, by unspoken consent and compulsion, spoke to one another in grave quiet voices. He asked me, on a note of surprise, if this was the place, and I said it was. I told him we might have some time to wait, and gave him a sovereign. I remained in the car; he got down and began to beat his arms gently across his chest. There was frost in the air; you could see it glittering on the roofs like a dusting of mica. We had drawn up at a corner, alongside a little general shop. I pointed out to the man the house where Oliver lived, and asked him to let me know if a young man in evening clothes arrived there. I was feeling overpoweringly sleepy, worn with emotion, and feared that I might fall asleep in the car.

And that was what I did. I was aware of nothing more till the driver was shaking me gently and telling me it was four o'clock.

"No one's come to this 'ouse, guvnor," he said, "an' the world's beginnin' to wake up."

I stumbled out of the car, feeling drugged and stupid, and there was not much sign of the world's awakening. The moon was gone, and the touch of frost. The morning was raw, damp, and utterly black. But presently the sound of a hob-nailed boot echoed along the pavement.

Then here and there pale lights appeared at upper windows and behind fanlights. Against the pewter of the sky the paler grey of smoke wavered from chimneys.

"Early risers 'ereabouts," the driver volunteered, speaking out loud now that the mystery had gone from the world and its grey misery had returned. "I don't reckon it's any good 'angin' around any longer. I could do with a drop of 'ot coffee."

I agreed that there was nothing to wait for. I could picture the boozed magnanimous Pogson. "An' Essex better stay the ni'. Goo' ole Essex."

So we drove to a coffee-stall, and then the driver took me home to Hampstead. And for all the hobnails that had echoed through Camden Town, it was still dark when I got into bed and fell heavily asleep.

## 26

That was in January of 1914. When May came, Oliver's birthday month, I, not having seen him in the interval, was sorely tempted to write to him and send him a present. But I thought of the five pounds I had sent him from Dublin, and of how it had come back, and that made me hesitate. Livia, I suspected, had been seeing Oliver a good deal, but I only questioned her about it once. Then she answered rather testily: "Of course I don't see him every time he cares to ring me up. But I can't help seeing him now and again, can I?—an occasional lunch…"

Being convinced that she knew at this time more of Oliver's mind than I did, I resolved to take her advice about this business of the birthday present. I called at her flat and found her up to the eyes in work, designing dresses for the revue with which Wertheim was now pressing forward. She kissed me dutifully, and was not very cordial, and asked me to sit down and smoke while she continued with her work.

I lit my pipe. "Does it disturb you if I talk while you are working?" I asked.

"So long as it's just prattle. Then I can say 'H'm' or 'Ah' as the case may be. Nothing serious, please."

"But it is serious. I want to talk about Oliver. He's eighteen this week."

She put down her pencil and lit a cigarette. "Yes; on Friday."

"I wonder whether this might be a chance to get in touch with him again—whether a present and a letter might help. Have you seen him lately? Have you any idea what his feelings about me are now?"

"Bitter," she said briefly. "I don't think anything you could do would help—at the moment."

Then I burst out, formulating a thought that had been niggling in the back of my mind for a long time: "Why is it that he's turned against me because I'm going to marry you, and yet is so friendly with you, though you're going to marry me?"

Livia crushed out her cigarette and stood up. "After all," she said lightly, "I am the bone of contention."

"Contention!" I almost shouted. "What contention is there about it? For God's sake, let's get married and settle this wretched business once for all. We should have been married months ago. Once we're married, Oliver will come to his senses. The way things are now is bad all round."

I got up in my agitation and paced across the room, paced towards a long mirror hanging on the wall there, and pulled up short, suddenly appalled at my own reflection coming to meet me. Gaunt, almost haggard with the anxiety of the last six months, a thin man with hollow cheeks and face too deeply lined, the hair at the temples turning from grey to white, elsewhere from dark to grey. And I thought of the golden-haired boy, knocking a cigarette on his finger-nail outside the office in Holborn, sauntering with the self-possession of a young confident god to keep an appointment under the clock.

I turned, abashed, to Livia, who was watching me as though she divined the thoughts that were burning up my mind. I wanted to say: "You don't love me. You have never loved me. You love Oliver, and he loves you. And that is right. That is as it should be." But I did not say that. I could not say it. Instead, I took her suddenly, hungrily, into my arms, as I had never taken her before, all the thwarting I had endured from her stimulating a desperate wish to possess her. She remained for a time rigid, almost resistant. Then my heat melted her. Her body relaxed and she gave me kiss for kiss. She herself threw off the overall she was wearing and thrust my hand up under the loose jumper to the warm flesh of her straining breast. She pressed herself against me, limb to limb, each limb alive and passionate. So this is Livia! This, at last, is Livia! She said huskily: "Lock the door." When I turned from doing so she was already pulling the jumper up over her head.

In her sleep Livia turned over. When I woke up I was gazing at the great dandelion clock of her hair. My nose was almost nuzzling into it; the warm hay-like smell of it was in my nostrils. Gently, so as not to wake her, I pulled down the bedclothes to delight my eyes with the sweet spectacle of her back, brown and silky. With my finger I traced the ridge of her spine, then ran the flat of my hand down her body. I could reach to the incredibly smooth skin behind her knee. Then up her thigh my exploring hand came, on to the slight convexity of her belly. She stirred, half-woke, pressed my hand into her flesh, then raised it till it was cupped round her breast. There she squeezed it again, sighed with happy exhaustion, and slept. Holding her thus, I, too, fell asleep once more.

When I woke for the second time, the room was dusky, I was alone in the bed. The frame of the window showed like a dark cross behind the tissue of the curtains. The corners of the room were quite dark. I lay on my back, happy, relaxed, flooded with a sense of well-being.

The door opened, Livia pressed down the switch which lighted a rose-shaded lamp on a table at the bedside. She pushed the heavy curtains across the window. The room looked delightfully warm and intimate. Livia wheeled in a tea-wagon, with a kettle hissing over a spirit-lamp, cheerfully tinkling china, and a plate of muffins under a silver cover. She sat on the edge of the bed and poured water into the teapot.

"You'll catch cold like that, you old Esau," she adjured me, as I sat up in bed naked as I had slept. "Put this on."

She draped a ridiculous wisp of a dressing-gown round my shoulders. But I was not in the mood to feel a fool. I felt a conqueror. I laughed happily, and Livia laughed with me. She leaned over, put her arms round my neck and her lips to my ear. "I daren't look you in the face while I tell you," she whispered. "It was wonderful."

I held her tight while I whispered back: "Why wouldn't it be, my sweet? It was the first time ever with a woman I love."

As I held her there, I could feel that under the dressing-gown she had nothing on. I pulled her arms out of the sleeves, and she sat up, her golden torso emerging from the blue silk held tight by the girdle.

"That's my idea of Hebe," I said. "Now pour the libations."

She sat like that on the edge of the bed, giving me tea and muffins, now turned sideways to me, with one taut breast in profile, now full on with both the rosy peaks directed towards me. Now and then I reached out a hand to touch the softness of her flesh; to press gently the domes that stood out so white, so beautifully blushed with pink, upon the tan of her body. The clock ticking quietly on the table under the lamp was the only sound we could hear save our own muted voices and the gentle chatter of the kettle-lid. The world, and all the cares of it that had pressed upon me so heavily of late, seemed very far away. The clock said six-thirty.

"My sweet," I said, "I had no idea I had slept so long."

"You slept for nearly an hour after I got up. I bathed before I made the tea."

I put my arm round her waist, pulled her towards me, and buried my face between her breasts. "You smell divine."

"It's the bath salts."

"It's Livia-Hebe, Hebe-Livia."

"And what does all-conquering Jove propose to do tonight?" she asked, sitting up, one hand pressed to the bed on either side of her.

"What is the good of being a god if you cannot pull strings?" I asked, and took the tassel of her girdle, and pulled.

*

I have said before that Livia was good at making omelettes. It was at midnight, when I lay drowsily between waking and sleeping with her in the crook of my arm, that she suddenly sat up and said: "I'm going to knock up some omelettes. I don't know about you, but I'm starved."

I grunted: "I don't know whether I'm starved or not, and don't care. I'm just happy."

"D'you realise that we went to bed without any lunch, that tea was a long time ago, and that we had no dinner? Omelettes, I say."

She leapt out of bed and pulled me by the hair. "Come on, you too. Put on a few clothes. It's cold."

We went into the kitchen, which a gas-fire soon warmed, and while Livia made the omelettes I laid the things on the red-and-black-checked cloth of the kitchen table. I loved doing it—laying knives, forks, plates, cups, saucers, so intimately for me and Livia. She swooped upon the table, removed the cups and saucers, replaced them with tall thin amber glasses, and produced a bottle of hock. "We're not going to let the occasion down with tea," she assured me. "You get on uncorking that."

I applied myself to the corkscrew, and as the cork came away with a plop, I started upright. "What's that?"

Was it a knock, or had the sound of the cork merely made me imagine it? But Livia had heard it, too. She turned out the gas-ring, and in the cessation of its singing we heard the knock again.

Whoever was at the door could not hear our voices in the kitchen, for the sitting-room was interposed, but instinctively I spoke quietly. "Who on earth can it be at this time of night? Better ignore it."

Again the knock, louder, insistent.

"Let 'em knock," I insisted. "They can't see the light in here." But Livia, without speaking, shook her head. She had gone white, and her hand, holding a fork, clattered suddenly against the side of the gas-stove. She remained silent for a moment; then she said: "It's Oliver. He won't go away. I'll have to let him in."

As she spoke, she regained her self-possession. The colour came back to her face. She laid the fork smoothly on the side of the stove. She whipped quickly from the table everything that suggested a meal laid for two. Knife, fork, plates, glass: all went at high speed to their places. Even as she thus swiftly worked, she said: "Get into the bedroom. Take the key with you, and lock it inside."

I felt crushed, deflated, humiliated. To have to conceal from Oliver the intimacies of my own life, to have to cut barbarously short the happiest experience of my manhood! I could not get into the bed. I felt absurd, outraged, in the clothes I was wearing: nothing but a collarless shirt, a pair of trousers and an overcoat. I huddled unhappily into an easy chair.

Now Oliver was in the sitting-room, on the other side of the door near which I sat. There was a hint of arrogance in his tone. "You take a lot of rousing, Livia."

"My dear, forgive me," she said. "I was in the kitchen cooking some supper, and the gas-ring in there sings enough to drown the last trump. And, anyway," she added, with anxiety in her voice, "look at the time! It's half-past twelve. I should have been in bed an hour ago if I hadn't such a lot of work to get through. I don't expect visitors at this hour."

There was a long pause; then Oliver said: "Can you put me up for the night? I've got nowhere to go to."

"But, my dear, what do you mean? Why can't you go to your rooms?"

"Because I couldn't pay the rent last Saturday. I've bluffed along between then and now, but tonight the old slut showed me out. Said she didn't want any shabby-genteel toffs sponging on her, and I could call for my things when the rent was paid. Nice, isn't it?"

I could imagine the defiance, the bravado, in his eye. I heard the rasp of a match as he lit a cigarette.

"But you shouldn't have let things reach such a pitch," Livia said. "You silly boy, I could have paid your rent."

"You've paid enough," he said; and that told me what I had long suspected. "You'd have been paying for a long time, perhaps, because I've lost my job. Otherwise, I could have paid for myself."

"But I knew nothing about that. I didn't know you were working out your notice. They have to give you notice, haven't they?"

There was a long, significant pause. I could imagine Oliver sitting there, his hands dropping between his knees, the flick of cigarette ash to the carpet as he burned his boats and answered brazenly: "Not always. There were circumstances which made it impossible for me to insist on my rights."

"I see," said Livia in a tiny voice. "You mean you had done something which caused you to forfeit your rights?"

"Oh, for God's sake!" Oliver burst out testily. "What sort of life was it, anyway? I'm not sorry to leave it. Old man Pogson made me sick. I never heard such pi-jaw. If it hadn't been that I was a friend of his son—a friendship which he must now insist should end forever—God! Anyone would think I was a thief. A piffling ten bob that I'd have put back at the end of the week—"

I could swear that Livia was on her knees before him now, such pleading and reproof were in her voice. "Oh, Oliver, my dear, my dear! Why did you do it? It was so little—such a foolish little bit of money that I could have given you twenty times over."

"No!" he said sharply. "I'm sick of sponging on you. I've had enough of it."

"But what will you do?"

"Find another job. There must be plenty of them."

"I'm not sure that it will be so easy—now."

"You mean Pogson won't give me a reference? I shan't ask the old swine. I'll say I've never had a job before. I look young enough."

"But until you find another job?"

"Couldn't I stay here?"

"You see how illogical you are, my dear. You said that you were sick of sponging on me. The little money you wanted wouldn't have made any difference, but now you want my time and privacy. They're far more important."

There was a moment's silence; then Oliver spoke again—now in a new, caressing voice. "I'm sorry, Livia—my dear, my sweet. God, I'm useless! I know—don't think I don't know. I can't understand why you put up with me; but please, please don't turn me down now I've been wandering about town all night, trying to think of some way without troubling you, but there wasn't any—not any at all. Let me stay tonight. We'll think of something in the morning. We'll see some of your friends: that chap Wertheim—people like that. There must be work."

Livia seemed to ponder. There was silence for a long time. "You'd better have some supper," she said at last. "I was just making my own. Go into the kitchen and eat it. I feel too upset to join you. Then you can sleep on that couch. I shall get up at eight and expect to find you gone. Make some breakfast before you go if you like. I shall meet you at the Café Royal at one o'clock for lunch. Do you agree to all this?"

Her voice was brisk, almost stern; then suddenly I heard sobs—heart-rending weeping. She had broken down completely, and I could picture her sitting there with her body shaking, her eyes streaming.

"Livia—my sweet—my darling—"

"Go away!" she almost screamed. "Don't touch me. Get out. There are times when I hate you."

I heard the reluctant shuffle of Oliver's feet towards the kitchen, and a moment later Livia was at the door of the bedroom.

I unlocked the door; she locked it again behind her. I held out my arms to her, but she shook her head impatiently and climbed miserably into bed. We dared not speak. I pulled the clothes up round her shoulders, tucked her in, and stood for a moment looking down at her still shaking body. Then I put out the light, went back to my chair, and, huddled in my overcoat, tried vainly to sleep.

In the morning I heard Oliver moving about in the next room. It was a grey overcast day. The bedroom seemed cold and cheerless. I was aware of having dozed and wakened and dozed again throughout the night, of having felt cold, of pulling the overcoat about me. Now, as I stood up, my bones seemed to creak. My teeth suddenly began chattering. I felt an old man. The mirror did not comfort me. A strained, tired face, hollow-cheeked, stubbled with grey, stared at me and caused me to recoil in disgust. I felt rather sick and very hungry.

Livia slept. I tiptoed to the bed and looked down at her. She lay on her back with one bare arm out—flung over the bedclothes. The black dry stains of tears were on her cheeks. She looked extraordinarily defenceless and pitiful. I had never seen her sleeping face before, for when I had wakened up in the bed yesterday afternoon her back was to me. There was not a line on her face. It was young, untrodden by the years. So golden she looked to me, but gold unminted, lacking the stamp and superscription of time. Tears which would make their channels now made only stains. Suddenly as I watched her she smiled, turned on to her side, and sighed. But she did not wake.

There had been silence without for some time. Oliver, I guessed, had gone into the kitchen to make some breakfast. Now I heard the sound of his feet crossing the living-room. I held my breath as the handle of the bedroom door turned softly. But the key was turned. "Livia! Darling!" Oliver whispered. I imagined he must hear the beating of my heart as I stood there a few inches from him, picturing the fair head bent listening at the keyhole. "Darling! Darling!" he said again, as though this time he were ecstatically exclaiming to himself, not calling Livia. Then he went. I heard the outer door of the flat pulled to behind him, softly.

I dressed quickly then, gave a last look at Livia who was still sleeping and murmuring now in her sleep, and went out of the flat. I could not bear the thought of her seeing me as I then was.

I took a taxi to Paddington Station where I was shaved and then had a bath. I went to the hotel dining-room and ordered breakfast. With hot coffee and food in my stomach I felt better. I resolutely chased away the ghosts that could not but haunt me in that room: for this was the room where, often enough, we had all sat down to breakfast together: Nellie and I, Dermot and Sheila, Maeve, Eileen, Rory and Oliver, all on tiptoe, with the ten-thirty to Falmouth waiting without. Chase them as I would, the ghosts closed in on me. Suddenly I felt utterly miserable in that room, utterly abandoned and alone. I called for my bill and went gladly out into the street.

It was still only half-past eight. By nine o'clock I was back at Livia's flat. She was at breakfast, looking as fresh as though she had come with perfect sleep through a night that had held no disturbance. She kissed me, but there was in the kiss none of the passion that she had shown when we lay together the day before. She inquired politely if I had breakfasted, and when I said I had, she sat down and tapped the top of an egg.

"Livia," I said, "if I were to get through now on the telephone to Martin he could have the car here in an hour, with all I need for going away. Could you be ready in an hour?"

She laughed merrily. "My dear Bill, you look so grim! What is this you've been thinking out?"

"That it's high time we were married. We can go down to Heronwater, find the nearest registrar, and have done with it."

"You old Puritan," she mocked me, complacently excavating the egg. "Do you feel you must make an honest woman of me?"

"For God's sake be serious, Livia," I burst out. "I want to make a happy woman of you, and a happy man of myself. We can't go on like this. There's no sense in it. It's not fair to me. It's not fair to Oliver. Don't you realise that it's playing the devil with my life, with everything I worked for and hoped for, when Oliver gets into the sort of trouble he's in now?"

"You don't suggest, do you," she asked with dangerous calm, "that Oliver's stealing to entertain me?"

"No no! Don't twist what I say. But the boy's all to pieces. He's upset, restless, loose-ended. I don't suppose he knows what he's doing or why he's doing it. If we were married, he'd have to come to his senses. We could take him in hand between us, get him back on the rails. Perhaps we could get him off to a university. Let's have this thing settled now. If you won't marry me at once, let's have an understanding about when we shall marry. Give him something concrete and settled."

"Are you thinking about him or yourself?"

"I'm thinking about both of us, and about you, too. We're all three of us at a damn awful loose end that's no good to any one of us."

"I'm not," she said with exasperating calm. "I've got work and to spare for Wertheim, and—"

"Oh, damn Wertheim!" I exploded unjustly. "I wish you'd never met Wertheim."

"That's very egotistical, Bill. It would have been nice to have me entirely dependent on my celebrated husband. I decline to go round with all those horse-faces who are smashing windows and tying themselves up to the railings at Westminster, but I'm all for women's rights when I'm the woman."

I could have ground my teeth in exasperation, but forced myself to keep calm.

"Will you marry me," I asked, "when you have finished this job with Wertheim?"

"Yes."

Somehow the answer surprised me', and I was surprised, too, to find that I was sweating. I took out my handkerchief and wiped my forehead.

"When will that be?"

"I should be through in two months' time—say the middle of July. I'll marry you in August."

It was incredible. We were talking as though we were arranging to go somewhere for the shooting. I could hardly believe it as I walked through the May morning across Portman Square. "I'll marry you in August."

## 27

I saw Livia's tears again that night. She rang me up and asked me to take her out to dinner. "I want to tell you about Oliver," she said.

He had spent the morning in a public library, answering advertisements for clerks. At lunch-time he appeared at the Café Royal, very spruce—"you know, Bill, his hair was shining, and his eyes were so blue. And his clothes—I don't know how he's kept them so perfect in that awful Camden Town house."

"You've seen it, then?"

"Yes, but he doesn't know it."

"So have I."

We were silent for a moment, thinking of the long, grey vista of that satanic street.

"It's amazing," said Livia, "how bright and shining he keeps. He commands attention, you know. I've never been to a restaurant with any man who brings the waiters hovering more quickly, without a word, without a look." She smiled, evidently recollecting many such occasions. "Were you like that when you were Oliver's age?"

"I had never been into a restaurant at Oliver's age, and if I had gone, I should certainly not have known what to do about waiters."

"I couldn't help admiring him," Livia continued. "If I had been where Oliver is now—without a job, without a penny, at odds with everybody—why, I should be utterly crushed."

I didn't hurry her. I let her tell her story in her own way, and soon she got past this bright façade to the grim facts. Oliver was quite sure that he would soon get work. In the meantime, he was, as she had said, without a penny. She had tackled the matter in the business-like way I should have expected of her: told him he must pay his landlady what he owed her and keep the rooms as a base for job-hunting. She had promised to give him two pounds a week as long as he needed it. He had smiled. "Not give, Livia—lend." Very well, then: call it a loan. And how much would he need to clear up the present mess? He thought five pounds would do, and produced from his pocket an IOU for that amount, already signed.

It was then that Livia got out her handkerchief and cried furtively. "You see, he had it ready. He *knew* that he was just there to raise the money."

She took the IOU out of her bag and handed it to me, blinking back her tears. I indignantly tore it to pieces and dropped them into the ashtray. I took her hand and caressed it. "Livia, you mustn't, my dear, you mustn't do this. Oliver is my responsibility. As long as he needs money he shall have it—from me. Will you let me do this?"

"You really want to?"

"Desperately. God knows I want to do it. It's little enough. But you must not let him know it is from me."

She dabbed at her eyes and tried to smile. "Very well," she said, and added, looking at me queerly: "You don't deserve two bad eggs like me and Oliver."

I was walking along Regent Street the next day—a fine blue and white day when I should have felt in the best of spirits. But I didn't. A definite date had been fixed for my wedding, and not so far ahead. That should have made me gay enough, or at any rate should have lifted the feeling that wherever I moved a grey fog moved with me. I looked up at the clouds thin as lawn veils on the blue; I was conscious of the frolic wind blowing the women's skirts and livening the air I breathed; but all the same, the thought of Oliver was more powerful than all other thoughts, and it darkened my mind.

Across the street was the long frontage of Dermot's shop, now, as always, an attraction to loiterers. It was full of lovely things: furniture, fabrics, pictures, glass, porcelain, all unique. I lingered for a moment, letting my thoughts go back to the shop in Manchester, where the Gauguin, daringly exhibited after Dermot's first visit to Copenhagen, had caused so much head-shaking; the shop over which were the offices of our toy company. It all seemed very long ago; it seemed to belong to a golden time, when life had more difficulties and yet was easier, the time before one was middle-aged and feeling it.

I crossed the road and went through the swinging glass doors. Within, all was silent, the feet treading a deep-piled carpet. There was not in Dermot's shop anything of the roar of the market, the hullabaloo of the vulgar popular "emporium." Down long vistas the eye travelled, resting on lovely and expensive things, staged superbly. The assistants looked like attachés, the managers like ambassadors. A swift, silent lift, whose door was a grille of beautiful wrought-iron, took me to the topmost floor where Dermot had his office. It was the sort of office Dermot would have. It was beautifully carpeted. Every stick of furniture had been made not only in his own workshops but by his own hands. It was cosy and intimate without being crowded, without fuss. The linen curtains were Livia's work. A Monet landscape was over the stone fireplace where, despite the warmth of the day, a fire was burning. Dermot sat before the broad expanse of his desk, but there was not a paper on it.

He jumped up and greeted me with outstretched hands. "Well, trying to catch me out again?" he demanded, waving his long bony hand towards the workless desk.

"I'm just looking for company," I said. "I suddenly felt lonely as I was passing the shop, so I came up."

He looked at me sharply, the point of the beard raised, the acute nose almost visibly scenting. I knew that little which I did or thought was concealed from that penetrating intelligence. He laid a hand on my shoulder with an affection he had not shown for a long time. "You know, Bill," he said, "since you came to London you've never been happy—not really happy."

He was aware that Oliver had left home, though we had never discussed that matter. He was aware—but I am not sure how deeply aware—that all had not gone smoothly with me and Livia. His awareness of these things, his sense of the long bond between us, was in his eyes and his voice and in the sensitive fingers that rested now on my shoulder. "Old friend," he said—and he had never used such an expression before—"old friend, it would do you good to talk about this and that."

He spoke into the telephone on his desk, asking for coffee to be sent up. He gave me a cigar—"the sort we use," he grinned, "when the deal is of over a hundred pounds"—and we took the coffee out on to a little balcony to which you stepped through his window. There were a couple of cane chairs, and a painted iron table, and a few tubs with bay trees and flowering plants. We were lifted up over London: a grey, smoking plain of roofs ran out before our view, punctuated with spires and towers and domes. The noise of the street came up muted and almost melodious.

We sat in silence for a while, then Dermot said: "I've got nothing to say to you. I'm here to listen. Go on now. Talk."

And I did. Diffidently at first, then with gathering confidence and relief. A wonderful relief. This was what I had wanted. Too much had been bottled up in me. At the end of an hour I felt much better, happier even.

"And you've been keeping all this to yourself," Dermot said then. "Well, I guessed most of it."

"And I've told some of it to Maeve," I said. "You know, Dermot, look back over my life as long as I can, I've had only three friends: that old parson Oliver that I've told you about, and you and Maeve."

"Maeve," he ruminated. "But you want to marry the Vaynol woman. Well, that's how life is, and I'm not going to argue with you about it. But marry her—for God's sake marry her quick. Don't wait till August. And then there's Oliver…"

He ruminated again, turning up the point of his beard and nibbling it thoughtfully with his teeth. "You can't have him wandering about at a loose end like this, Bill. It's damned demoralising. Taking a weekly dole from a woman… God in Heaven, man! Rory'd shoot himself first."

I winced at the harsh truth of those words and Dermot put a hand over mine—that was Maeve's trick, too. "Sorry, Bill. That slipped out. You send the young fool to me. I'll give him a job. Have you seen the young sparks strutting about downstairs? I always insist on looks. He's got looks, anyway. Yes; send him to me."

"I can't send him." Hateful to have to admit that.

"No, of course not. Well, look, I'll advertise in the *Daily Telegraph*. See that this woman calls his attention to it and makes him answer. We'll hook him that way. And marry the woman! Marry her quick!"

We got up and wandered back into Dermot's room. He picked up a newspaper from a chair and slapped the open page with his fingers. "See that? God damn England! Another nail in her coffin."

I took the paper and looked down the column, Dermot standing there bristling at my side. I read of the Amending Bill to exclude Ulster from the operation of the Home Rule Bill.

"Marvellous, isn't it?" Dermot snarled. "All the pukka sahibs, all the best people, all those officers at the Curragh who took the oath of loyalty to the king have told the king where he gets off. We do what we're ordered to as long as it's something we want to do, see, Mr. King? But don't you step on our toes. Remember, we've got the guns. That's the stuff to give the disloyal Irish. That's the way to teach 'em loyalty, eh, Bill? So along comes this lovely Liberal Government, with the blessing of Mr. Bloody Redmond, and says:

'Dear Boys, we wouldn't offend you for worlds. If you want Ulster left out, it's all one to us. Yours is the last word.'"

I thought he would have spat. Certainly he would have spat if he had been a spitting sort. But he just bristled. There was an almost palpable electric emanation of anger from him.

"But is it the last word?" he demanded, his eyes shining with fanatic light. "I'll tell you this, Bill: it's the last word necessary to do one important thing, and that is unite the south. They haven't loved each other too much, believe me. But love isn't necessary now. They've all got something to hate, and that'll work just as well. Love for the same thing never makes allies. It's always hate for the same thing."

"And when the fight's over the allies have nothing left but their hates. I'm not much of a politician, Dermot, but that's why I expect there'll be hell in Southern Ireland for a long time to come."

"But a lot will happen in the meantime. Rory'll see a lot happen in the meantime."

"I expect he will," I said.

All very well for Dermot to say: "Marry the woman at once." The woman would not be married at once. But Dermot's scheme for Oliver worked well enough. Livia told me that Oliver had found in it a matter of rejoicing because he imagined a personal score. He wrote to the box number under which the advertisement appeared, and when a reply came from O'Riorden's he at first shied away. Then the idea lit him up. "But imagine! Getting a job off his own best friend! That would be something, Livia, eh?"

And Dermot told me of the interview at his office: Oliver look-ing—"Well, you know, Bill: not Angles but angels: like one of those kids, perfectly dressed by a modern tailor."

It was a comfort to me to know that Oliver was working for Dermot and not for Pogson, and that Dermot encouraged rather than frowned upon the old name of Uncle Dermot, hoping through this intimacy to lead Oliver into confidences that might be twisted at last towards a reconciliation with me. But there he was not successful. He confessed as much to me sorrowfully. "Charm! Begod, Bill, he's as charming as a spring morning; and then at the first sign of the cloven hoof when I drag in your name he hardens over like a winter day."

I was still hopeful that time would cure that, and as the summer deepened I felt altogether happier, confident that a way would open out of the dead end into which my affairs had drifted.

Dermot thought that a definite effort should be made to bring me and Oliver together. "You've never seen the boy, Bill, except the time you talked to him on the pavement with his boozy pal. That was hardly a time for opening hearts. Now you must meet at my house."

So he invited Oliver to dinner at Hampstead, not letting him know that I would be present, and he did not invite Livia. It was a Sunday night, so that Maeve might come, and Sheila and Eileen were there. Just a family gathering which Dermot hoped would do the trick.

It was not a success. When I went into the drawing-room Oliver was already there with all the O'Riordens. He kept his self-possession marvellously. A quick shock of surprise flashed over his face, and then was subdued. He rose with easy good-humour, and shook hands. His grasp was warm and firm, as of a friend. It affected me queerly, for Oliver and I were not accustomed to shaking hands. "Good-evening, sir," he said, and as he uttered that formal word which I detested I could have sworn there was a light of mockery in the candid blue of his eye.

I looked beyond him to where Maeve was sitting, and saw that with both hands she was gripping the arms of her chair, as though to force herself to remain in it. I could see that the moment was for her one of agony and suspense. Actress as she was, she had not mastered the moment with the almost insolent nonchalance of this smiling boy.

All through the evening he called Dermot "Uncle Dermot," and addressed the others with easy familiarity. For me he reserved that chill formal word, speaking to me only when I spoke to him. They all tried hard to keep the tone of the occasion friendly and happy-go-lucky, as though nothing unusual was happening, except that once, while we were at dinner, Maeve took my hand beneath the cloth and squeezed it with affectionate reassurance.

When Sheila, Maeve and Eileen got up, Oliver said: "Will you all excuse me if I go now? I have an appointment in town."

They politely demurred, but he went, with charming apologies and insistence. Three-quarters of an hour later I asked if I might use the telephone, and rang up Livia's flat. There was no answer. I devised in my mind a score of reasons why there shouldn't be.

It was in June—on Sunday, June 21—that this humiliating dinner was given by Dermot. Perhaps the adjective is not a good one. Grieved I was, and hurt and sorrowful, but even until the end I felt no humiliation from anything Oliver did to me. No more than I felt it from what Livia had done and was yet to do.

We talked for a long time after Oliver had left us. Not one of them referred to what had happened. But there was in the manner of all of them an added solicitude, a deepening of the customary kindness, that was comforting.

It was a warm night. We had all trooped up to Dermot's study on the first floor, because thence we had a view over the Heath. The curtains were pushed right back across the open window, and we sat round the window in a semi-circle of chairs. Not a breath was stirring. The sky was a lucent green, full of light, but light thinned out to the last tenuity. The room was in darkness. Dermot was smoking a cigar, I a pipe, Maeve a cigarette. Eileen, who did not smoke, was sitting on a footstool with her head resting on Sheila's lap. Sheila was knitting a garment for Rory.

It is one of those clear pictures that the mind takes in and keeps for ever, unaltered through the ruin of years. I see it in every detail; the glowing points of cigar and cigarette, the clear green light of the sky over the Heath. I hear again the silence, emphasised for a long time by the click of Sheila's needles, broken at last by Maeve saying in a low voice: "The longest day. From now on we go downhill."

"I sincerely hope not," said Dermot, shattering with a laugh the solemnity that had come upon us. "I'd rather go for a holiday. What about you, Bill? Can't we join forces at Heronwater this year? I'm ready to set off in a week's time."

"My forces, I'm afraid, will be small," I said. "But I'd like to come. There's nothing to keep me in London at the moment. Perhaps Livia will come—at any rate when she's finished the work she's doing. She said that would be in the middle of July."

"'We should still be there," said Dermot. "I'm for making it a long holiday. I'd like to stay on well into August. What about you?"

"That would be fine," I said. I did not say what was in my mind: that as Livia and I were to be married in August, we could get married at the church of St. Just, buried in its pit of trees alongside the little lost creek. I should like Dermot and Sheila and Eileen to be there. But with Maeve in the room, her white face glimmering in the dark, her eyes fixed on the clear swim of light out over the Heath, I said nothing of that. "I'd like that," I said.

"I shall be glad when I can take a long holiday with you all again," Maeve said, not drawing her glance back into the room. "How long ago it all seems, Bill dear, since Mary Latter came down to visit Captain Judas, and we saw the swans flying across the moon, and you launched me." She got up. "I must go. I hate longest days. I hate endings and things that suggest endings to come." We all got up.

"Walk across Parliament Fields with me, Uncle Bill," she invited. "I'll get on to the tube at Hampstead station."

"I'll get Martin to take you down in the car," I offered.

"I wouldn't bother him. Let the man enjoy his Sabbath," she said. "But walk across the fields with me. It's on your way."

So I walked across the fields with Maeve. There were many people about in the warm evening, under the wonderful light which still pulsed thinly in the sky. "I shouldn't feel tragic on such a night," she said, "but I do. 'From now on we go downhill.' What a thing to say! What a daft, mad thing!"

I saw her on to her train and walked slowly home. The Crown Prince who was heir to the Austrian throne was thinking that night of his forthcoming visit to the Province at Bosnia. He set out to keep his appointment two days later.

Livia promised to join us at Heronwater as soon as she was able. Probably in about three weeks' time, she said. Dermot and Sheila, Eileen and I, travelled on Sunday, June 28th. Martin had gone on with my car a few days before, taking the luggage of both families—if you could call me a family. We travelled that Sunday in Dermot's car, he driving. We took it easy, knocking off on any excuse—for mid-morning coffee, for lunch, for tea. There were not many cars on the roads in 1914; it was a lovely day; and we were all in the best of spirits. Ahead of me, things looked clearer than they had done for many a day. I felt that Oliver would be safer, working under Dermot's eye. I told myself that before I came back this way again I should be married to Livia. I began to think of the work I should take up when she and I were settled down with the winter ahead of us.

I was ready to be pleased with everything on that day of high June as we sped along the roads that had not yet been denuded of their country air, of their hedges and elms, their foxgloves, honeysuckle and meadowsweet. "What have we done to this chap, Sheila?" Dermot demanded. "I could almost take him for Bill Essex, that little Manchester snotty we used to know."

Sheila, sitting in the back of the car with me, her hat tied to her head with a veil knotted under her chin, for the hood was down, turned her smile upon me and said nothing. Sheila didn't need to say anything. She was happy when those about her were happy, and she was happy now. Her grey eyes were deep with content. Her mouth was a sweet and lovely line. The hair that escaped in wisps from under her veil was grey, but she was a desirable woman still.

The cathedral bells were calling to evening service as we threaded our way through Truro's ugly streets. Half an hour later we were turning into the gravel drive, winding through the trees, catching the smell of the river we could not see. Dermot pulled up. "There!" he exclaimed proudly, dropping his hands from the wheel. "The slowest time ever made between Hampstead and Heronwater. That's what I understand by motoring."

We clambered out of the car, and as we stood there stretching our legs on the gravel a wheeze of rusty music came drifting up from the river. I turned a questioning eye on Sam Sawle who had come out to greet us. "That's Captain Judas, Mr. Essex," he explained. "He's been holding a service on deck every Sunday evening this summer. That's his harmonium you can hear."

We all crowded to the balustrade and looked into the dense foliage that ran downwards. We could not see the *Jezebel*, but soon we heard the captain's voice upraised, a thin reed of sound running with the harmonium's wheeze:

*Praise ye the Lord, 'tis good to raise*
*Your hearts and voices in His praise.*
*His nature and His works unite*
*To make this duty our delight.*

"Donnelly would like that," said Dermot. "He'd be down there singing."

"He do go through the whole thing proper," Sawle said. "All the hymns and prayers, and a short address. And in the middle of the prayers he do shout his own 'Halleluiahs!' and 'Praise be's' and then he reads the announcements and takes a collection from himself."

"And what announcements does he make?" I asked.

"Always the same one, Mr. Essex. 'The great and terrible day of the Lord is at hand. The date will be announced from this pulpit in the near future.'"

We looked at one another without speaking as the singing came to an end and Judas's voice rose and fell across the water, calling upon his God.

"The poor man," said Eileen quietly, and started towards the house. We all followed, somehow subdued.

But we did not feel subdued in the morning. How good it was, after all the doubts and agonies I had endured during the past few months, to be standing there with Dermot in the utter simplicity of that morning hour! We stood on the edge of the landing-stage, looking at the water sliding and whispering by. There was still a trace of the night's mist, but the sun was gaining strength, with promise of a long day of blazing heat. A heron flew high overhead, with slow, lazy strength, but there was no other living thing to be seen and none heard save the birds twittering in the woods. Nothing stirred on the black hulk of the *Jezebel*. The dinghy, the *Maeve* and the two sailing boats curtseyed on the sliding river.

The moment was too perfect for speech. Without a word, Dermot and I slid into the water, swam round the boats, and then came ashore. A quarter of an hour later we joined Sheila and Eileen at breakfast. There was that marvellous fish a John Dory, which Sawle had somewhere procured, and a fine cold ham, with bread and butter and marmalade and jam and plenty of tea and coffee. Sawle had resolved on a good start for the holiday. I asked him if there was a newspaper in the house and he said that Martin had been in to Truro and had doubtless brought one back. Martin came in at that moment with the *Western Morning News*. Dermot brusquely snatched it from him. I didn't bother. This was no time for newspapers, with Sheila handing me a cup of tea and Eileen piling John Dory upon my plate. Only when I had taken the edge off my hunger did I ask: "Well, what's the world doing?"

"Nothing that matters to us," he said. "Getting ready for the week's cricket and racing. Oh, and an Austrian grand duke was assassinated yesterday while we were so comfortably driving down here. At Sara—Sarajevo. Ever heard of it?"

"No."

"Neither have I."

"Put down the paper and get something into you," said Sheila. "They're always assassinating people in those places."

"Well," said Dermot, tossing the paper across the room. "No news is good news."

Livia joined us on Saturday, July 18th. That was the day Oliver's holiday began. A week before this, Dermot had said to me: "There would be no harm in giving Oliver a chance to join us here. I don't think it's likely he'll come, but anyway I shall write and tell him to take a fortnight's holiday. What do you think?"

I was anxious to try anything that offered a hope of coming to terms with Oliver. I asked Dermot to point out to him that Livia would be coming on the 18th, that there were two sailing dinghies longing for work, and that the weather was glorious. All this Dermot threw out as coming from himself.

He received an answer from Oliver thanking him cordially for the holiday—"which really I don't deserve after so short a service"—but saying nothing about Cornwall, nothing about his intentions in any way.

"That seems to be that," said Dermot ruefully.

On the 18th I took the *Maeve* in to Falmouth to meet Livia. I might have sent the car to meet her at Truro, but I liked fussing about with the motor-boat, especially now that I no longer touched the wheel of a car. I was glad at any time to run over to Falmouth, to do shopping, to pick people up, or for any other purpose.

Livia looked worn out. She explained it by saying she had been working too hard. She was glad it was all over. She had done all that Wertheim wanted of her. "And I'm not sorry to get away from him, either," she said, lying back on the cushions as I manœuvred the boat away from the pier and made out for the open water of the harbour. She looked round at the sparkling blue of sea and sky, the green hills that sloped down to the sea, the gaiety of the multitudinous craft sailing and steaming about us. "Oh, it's so peaceful," she exclaimed, breathing deeply of the lively air. "You simply can't believe in war with all this about you."

"War!" I exclaimed in surprise. "What on earth is there to go to war about?"

"It's Wertheim," she said. "That's what I meant about being glad to get away from him. I expect he's mad."

"That man's got war on the brain," I soothed her. "As long ago as last January he was talking about it."

"Well, he says it's here now—a matter of weeks."

I laughed, suddenly and loudly, out there on the wide water of Falmouth harbour, and at the sound Livia's face cheered. She looked almost grateful for that quick spontaneous guffaw. "Thank you for that, Bill," she said. "You've no idea how that man has got on my mind. It's that business at Sarajevo—I expect you read about it in the papers."

"Yes, some grand duke or other."

"But remember," she said swiftly, "he was the heir to the Austrian throne," and in the way she had at once picked me up I sensed Wertheim's tuition.

"But, good Lord," I exclaimed impatiently, "what have Austria and Serbia got to do with us?"

"That's what I wanted to know, and Wertheim was terribly convincing—with pepper-pots and salt-cellars and pieces of bread—you know, showing how the whole thing was going to work out. He says that Russia will simply *have* to back up Serbia, and Germany won't have Russia butting in, and France will rear up as soon as Germany moves a man or a gun. I wanted to know what all that had to do with a chap being shot in Sarajevo, and he just looked pitying and said 'Nothing, my dear Miss Vaynol, nothing at all. They've been ready for a long time, and what we heard at Sarajevo was only the starter's pistol.'"

I felt my face becoming as grim and drawn as Livia's had been. Suddenly the sunlight seemed to dim. There was just a grain of possibility in this nonsense of Wertheim's. I could imagine him sitting there with Livia, immense, impassive, convincingly demonstrating the end of the world with pieces of bread. "But dash it all!" I cried irritably, "what do other people think? What are they saying in London?"

"Does it matter what they are saying in London?" Livia asked, suddenly contemptuous. "No, I've heard this only from Wertheim. Everybody else is playing about as usual."

We had shaken off most of the traffic, for now we were in the Carrick Roads, and I let the *Maeve* go all out. "Well," I said, "war seems a long way from here, and until it's a good deal nearer I refuse to talk about it."

Ahead of us a steamer was making her way on the rising tide up the river to Truro. "What flag's that?" I asked Livia.

"Danish."

Something familiar in the cut of the vessel teased my memory, and suddenly I remembered the night when Dermot and Donnelly had accompanied me and Captain Judas to Truro. Now we were near enough to verify the guess. Round the counter of the ship, which was heavily laden with timber, I read the name of the *Kay* of Copenhagen, and on the bridge I had a glimpse of the tall figure and sun-tanned Viking head of Captain Jansen.

"I've met that chap before," I exclaimed. "A friend of Captain Judas."

"And how is that poor old fool?" Livia asked without much interest.

"Madder than ever. Announcing the coming of the great and terrible Day of the Lord."

"Like Wertheim."

"Give Wertheim a rest," I said, almost savagely.

At the head of the Carrick Roads we swung right, well ahead of the *Kay*. There was plenty of water in the river and very little traffic. The *Maeve's* engine was in beautiful form. The richly wooded banks, broken occasionally by pasturage coming down to the water, swung past us. A heron or two flapped lazily away at our approach. All the lovely panorama of that most entrancing river unfolded itself, reach after reach; and speedily we were turning the last spit of land. I slowed down the engine, pointed the *Maeve's* bow to the landing-stage, and saw that Dermot, Sheila and Eileen were all standing there, gazing across at the *Jezebel*. At the same moment I clearly heard the bell sound in the *Jezebel's* living-room—the bell which I had myself persuaded Judas to install. A small motor-boat was alongside the black hull of the ship. A man sat at the engine which was boxed amidships, and a tall stripling stood up with his hand on the bell-pull. We were a good way off, but something familiar in that spruce upright figure started my heart beating quicker. I looked at Livia. Her face had gone white. "He must have been on my train," she said tensely, "and he's hired a boat to bring him on from

Truro. He rang me up last night. He said he was going to do it but I thought he was fooling."

"But I'm glad," I said, "glad to have him. We'll all have a great holiday."

She looked at me wearily. "Will you? Oh, Bill, you fool! He hasn't come to give you joy. He's come so that his presence may taunt you. He's not calling on Judas for fun. He's going to stay with him."

I couldn't believe it. "Stay with Judas! With us on the other side of the water? It's monstrous, impossible!"

"Oh, no, it isn't," she said; and then savagely: "Why couldn't he go somewhere else? Why the hell can't he leave me in peace! I told him not to come."

She was trembling, her knuckles white as she clutched the gunwale. I had stopped the engine, and in the silence the bell in the *Jezebel* clanged again. Oliver's clear, unmistakable voice rang out over the water. "Judas! Ahoy there, Judas! Come on! It's me—Oliver."

I picked up my glasses from a thwart and saw Judas appear and look over the rail. This was the first time I had set eyes on him that holiday. His always meagre face, which was all I could see, appeared to have shrunk. His cheeks seemed to have caved in, his head to be all wild white hair and whiskers. It was the face of a far-gone fanatic. I saw it light up when he caught sight of Oliver standing there in the boat, hailing him insolently. "Ho, there, old 'un! Don't keep the Master waiting!"

With trembling hands Judas lowered his ladder. "Coming, my Lord, coming," he quavered.

Oliver picked up a rucksack from the motor-boat, slung it on to his shoulders and climbed the ladder. The motor-boat started up and went back towards Truro. Oliver must have been well aware of the *Maeve* out in the river, of the little knot gathered on the Heronwater quay. He did not spare a glance for either. As soon as he was aboard, Judas pulled up the ladder, and they disappeared.

The *Maeve* chugged slowly in to the landing-stage. Sheila and Eileen had disappeared. I felt that they had not wanted to see me in my discomfiture. But Dermot was still there, and under pretence of helping me ashore he wrung my hand hard.

"The worst yet, Bill," he muttered.

I nodded, unable to speak; but worse was to come.

In the morning, before any of us were up, the *Rory*, which was Oliver's boat, was shifted from her moorings on our side of the river and tied up under the shadow of the *Jezebel*.

Dermot, who had walked down to the landing-stage with me, was livid with rage, and Sam Sawle, who had come up to the house to tell us what had happened, stood beside us, grave and concerned. He asked if he should row across in the dinghy and fetch her back. I pretended to consider this for a moment, then said: "No, the *Rory*'s his boat. He can do what he likes with it."

I turned on my heel and walked away, Dermot following. I could feel him fighting to keep back the words that were bursting to his lips. He did not succeed. "The bloody little whippersnapper…" he began.

I held up my hand. He was silent for a moment, then fired forth again: "He's sacked! I won't have him! Sacked! He can go to hell."

An hour later he was still sitting on the landing-stage, smoking morosely, glowering across the river at the *Jezebel* and at the *Rory* ducking and curtseying alongside her.

There were times during the following week when I could have cut and run. The situation was agonising, only made possible by a touch of the absurd which Dermot lent it. He wrote to Oliver telling him that he was no longer in the employment of the firm of O'Riorden and enclosing a week's wages. Sam Sawle was sent over in the dinghy to deliver the note. He was asked aboard and found Oliver in undisputed command of the ship. Judas was in the galley, cooking. Oliver threw himself into an easy chair, read the note, and shouted: "Judas! Pen and ink."

The old man came trotting out of the galley, wiping his hands on an apron, and deferentially produced all that Oliver demanded. "That's all," said Oliver, and Judas bowed and retired.

Oliver winked at Sawle. "Sit down, Sam," he invited easily. "There's an answer to this."

"I'll wait on deck," Sawle said.

The letter he brought back contained the money which Dermot had sent. "I don't need this," Oliver wrote. "I am well provided for here, and in any case I do not accept your notice to leave the service of the firm of O'Riorden. You give me no reason connected with my work, and if you persist I shall bring an action for unlawful dismissal."

Dermot went white with fury. "Can he do that? Can he do that?" he demanded.

I knew no more of the law on that matter than he did, and he was for rushing at once to Truro to consult a solicitor. I dissuaded him.

"I'd rather you let it drop, Dermot."

He was contrite at once. "Sorry, Bill, sorry. Just my damned personal pride."

How much Dermot had told Sheila and Eileen I do not know. They were aware that Oliver and I had parted, but I had no reason to believe that they associated Livia with that. Nevertheless, they were difficult and restrained with her. Some intuition was at work that made them treat her with the considered courtesy shown to a guest rather than with the equal comradeship that the rest of us enjoyed.

One day we all packed into the *Maeve* and went to Molunan beach. Everything should have been perfect. It was heavenly weather, with the level blue of the sea stained here and there with patches of violet deepening to purple. The gulls were dropping in cackling companies on to the water, sure indication of the presence of fish, as Eileen reminded us. She told us of how Sam Sawle used to manœuvre the boat over spots where the gulls had descended and how the lines always came up with a catch. "I've known all of us—me and Maeve and Rory and Oliver—to be pulling them up one after another as fast as we could go," she said.

And the recital of the names—me and Maeve and Rory and Oliver—knelled like a litany of lost days, of days incredibly far, days filled with peacefulness and youth and hope not yet stained by any doubt, so that Dermot and Sheila and I, catching one another's glances, and each seeming instinctively to note that the others were recording the absence of three out of the four children mentioned, all dropped our eyes again to casual things, feeling a little damped, perhaps a little older.

We anchored the *Maeve* off the beach and, in two companies, went ashore in the dinghy, taking our lunch things with us. Dermot and I scoured the beach for dry driftwood, and built up a fire ready for the match. Then we all bathed, and I suppose bathing from Molunan beach on a day of high summer is one of the things most calculated to make you forget the sorrows of the world. With my toes gripping and curling into the hot loose sand, with the silky blue of the Cornish sea reaching away under a dazzle of sunlight, and the blue arch of the sky too ardent to be looked upon, I stood for a moment drenched in light and warmth, watching Livia and Sheila and Eileen running down to where blue and yellow met in a white embrace of foam. Then Dermot came from behind his rock; we ran to join them; and with a great shout we all leapt upon the water and thrashed round the *Maeve* and back again.

"That's enough for me, Bill," Dermot shouted. "I'll see to the fire."

He ran up the beach, and the others followed him. I remained swimming slowly just beyond my depth. I could see down through the crystal water to where the light wavered in cool patterns upon the yellow sand. I could see here and there the pallid rays of a starfish, a frond of seaweed undulating to minute and unguessed currents, responsive as a polar needle to invisible compulsions. Then there came the sight I had hoped to see, the sight of all others most fascinating in those waters: a horde of tiny silver fish, swimming in a long thin procession, ten or a dozen abreast, like a small marine army on the move. Endlessly they went by, never changing their formation, wheeling now to the right, now to the left, but always precise, regimented, moving as by a common will. A small cloud drifted before the sun, and the water, still pellucid, turned grey. And the silver fish turned grey. I could see them still: a grey endless army, moving to some unknown encounter across the grey floor of the sea.

The fire was blazing, and the kettle of water which we had brought was "singing," when I ran up the beach. They had all quickly dressed. Sheila and Eileen were unpacking a lunch basket. "Let me help," Livia said. "Give me the plates and things. I'll lay them out."

"Now you sit down and make yourself comfortable," Sheila answered. "We can manage this."

Livia turned aside with a groan. "Oh, God!" she muttered, and threw down the cigarette she was smoking and crushed it with her foot in the sand.

When we had eaten, we leaned back relaxed against the rocks. Dermot and I were smoking our pipes. Eileen sat between us. Sheila and Livia lay extended at full length on the sand at our feet, their eyes closed. Suddenly Eileen exclaimed: "Look! The *Rory*! That must be Oliver!"

Livia at once started up. "Oliver! Where?" Then she seemed to be overcome by confusion.

It was like that all through the week. Wherever we went Oliver appeared. Judas we never saw. The report which Sam Sawle brought back after taking the note to Oliver was the only hint we had of his activities. One night we saw his friend Jansen come down by water from Truro and go aboard. That night, till a late hour, we could hear the Dane's great voice booming, and song and laughter coming over the river.

Oliver we saw constantly. After the first few days his natural good looks were enhanced by the sun. The deep bronzing of his body made the blue of his eyes and the white of his teeth remarkable, and his hair was bleached and wind-blown. I was near enough to him often to notice even such particularities. He would appear before us almost, it seemed, out of the blue, and with nonchalance be unaware of our presence. He had arranged a diving platform, hanging on loops of rope over the *Jezebel*'s side, and it was ten to one that if any of us chanced to be near the boat he would ostentatiously appear, wearing nothing but the bathing slip that showed off magnificently his six feet of splendid golden body, and would dive, and swim by with insolent unconcern.

I knew that all this was aimed at Livia, and it had its effect. She became irritable and moody and at last professed herself unwilling to join our outings because, she said, she could not stand the situation which Oliver had forced upon us. But she continued to accompany us until the Friday. We were all going to Helston that day, a fairly long trip, and Livia at the last moment—actually when some of us were in the boat and the rest stood by the dinghy loaded with lunch and bathing things—shouted to me that she did not feel up to coming. Sam Sawle was sitting in the dinghy, holding her to the landing-steps, and Livia stood there on the steps shouting across the water to me: "No, Bill, really I can't. I don't feel up to it. I must rest."

Sam Sawle looked over his shoulder towards the *Maeve*, waiting for my instructions. Dermot, who was aboard with me, looked at me hard and said: "Sam can manage the *Maeve*. Stay with her."

I shouted: "I'll come ashore, Livia. I shouldn't like you to spend a lonely day."

Her voice came very clear over the water: "No, no. I won't have that. I'm not going to spoil your outing."

Dermot looked towards the *Jezebel*, and said quietly: "Stay with her."

I hesitated. Livia ran lightly down the steps and put her foot on the dinghy's bow. She pushed the boat out. "Go on, Sawle," she said.

Dermot looked grave, but he did not speak again. "All right, Sam, come aboard," I shouted.

Only then did Dermot take his eyes from my face, as though a tension had relaxed, an important decision been taken. From me his gaze turned to Livia who, with a wave in our direction, had swung round and started up the path to the house. In a moment the bushes hid her. Dermot continued to gaze for a while at the spot where she had been. Then he said: "Gone."

We in the *Maeve* had no sight of Oliver that day. We did not get back to Heronwater till just before dinner-time. Livia was waiting for us at the landing-stage, gay and full of fun, eager to know all that we had done and seen. She said that the rest had done her good. "Tomorrow," she said, "I'd like to do a lot of shopping in Truro. Could I have the car quite early, Bill? I'd like to be there by ten."

I was delighted to find her in such excellent spirits, and told Martin to have the car ready. She wrote down a list of things that we all wanted: tobacco for me, wool and knitting needles for Sheila, and so on.

In the morning she was gone without my knowing it. I had been on the *Maeve* with Sawle, overhauling the engine, and when I got back to the house I was just in time to see the car disappearing towards the road. It was a pottering morning. We had made no communal arrangements. I went back to the river and sat there smoking, and presently Dermot joined me, bringing a newspaper. We talked desultorily about the tension that all through the week had been growing between Austria and Serbia. It didn't seem a very serious matter to us.

"Wertheim is sure there'll be war," I remarked, as though I were talking about the dead certainty of a cricket fixture.

"There'll be war all right between Austria and Serbia," Dermot said. "The Austrian ultimatum expires today."

He, too, spoke as though we were discussing the antics of some remote species, unrelated to any concerns that might touch us. Then we said nothing more about it. He stretched himself in the sunlight on the short turf of the landing-stage, and I sat there, smoking, idly glancing now at the newspaper, now at the river, beautiful at the top of the tide.

The sound of engines came through the drowsy morning and presently the *Kay* of Copenhagen, having finished her affairs at Truro, steamed round the bend, making for the sea. Jansen on the bridge set his whistle screaming as he drew near to the *Jezebel*. Captain Judas appeared on his deck, not aproned as Sawle had described him, but beautifully dressed, as I had been accustomed to see him. He stood with his hand raised to his cap in salute as the *Kay* went by: went by, though I did not know it then, a coffin-ship wherein all that I had hoped for and worked for was interred. Livia and Oliver were aboard the *Kay*. Livia had made her decision at last... The bone of contention... She wrote to me when they reached Copenhagen.

But that day I knew nothing of this. I wondered vaguely why Oliver had not appeared alongside Judas, but that question did not worry me for long. The *Kay* was an object of interest, as any ship was on the quiet river. I watched her out of sight, and then turned again to the blissful, mindless contemplation of sky and river.

# 28

As that Saturday drew to its close we all knew—Dermot and Sheila and I, and even little Eileen—that the thin crust I had been treading for months had caved in. Lies, evasions, deceptions, hopes and fears: all were ended. There was even, at first, crazy as it sounds, a sense of relief. I knew now where I was.

It was at noon that Martin rang up from Truro to ask whether Livia had come back some other way. She had told him to stay with the car near the cathedral till she rejoined him, and there he had waited till anxiety caused him to make his inquiry.

I was up at the house when the telephone bell rang, and I answered it myself. As soon as I gathered what Martin's worried voice was saying, my heart gave a great hurting thump in my breast. I knew in that moment that Livia would not come back.

"Don't wait any longer," I said; then hung up the receiver and stood there in the cool shadowed hall, looking out to the dazzle of sunlight beyond the door. Sheila passed slowly by, a white figure on the vivid yellow gravel. I called her name quietly. She came into the hall, blinking at its shadows, and then exclaimed: "Bill! What's the matter? You look ill!"

I had the bowl of my pipe in my hand, the stem between my teeth. I did not realise till she spoke that the stem was clattering. I put the pipe down unsteadily on a table. "That was Martin, ringing up from Truro. Livia hasn't turned up at the car."

"Perhaps there's been an accident?..."

"No. I don't think we shall see Livia again."

"My dear!" Sheila took my shaking hand in both her hands

and held it tight. Unshed tears were shining in her eyes.

"I shall survive it," I said, and gave what must have been a ghastly smile. "Have lunch without me today, there's a sweet. Tell Dermot what I think has happened."

"I suppose—Oliver?"

"Yes, I suppose so."

What was the sense of doing what I was doing—using my study as if it were the lair of a wounded beast, now sitting in my chair, with the curtains drawn, now restlessly striding up and down, now peeping through the chink of the curtains to see whether the sunny commonplace world still existed outside? Of course it did. "You're not the first fool to be duped," I told myself, "nor will you be the last." But what difference did that make? I was a fool, and duped.

At four o'clock, Dermot came in, bringing a tray of tea. "I'm damned if I'll eat that here, like a sick child petted in the nursery," I said. "Take it out into the sunshine."

Dermot took the tray out to a table near the balustrade, where Sheila and Eileen were at tea, their bright clothes shining against the dark green foliage of the wood.

That was better, and they had the sense not to pity me, though I guessed pity in the quiet respectful demeanour of Sawle and Martin throughout the rest of that wretched day. It was not till Sawle said to me, late in the evening: "Shall I bring the *Rory* across the river now, Mr. Essex?" that I saw in that one word *now* how completely they had weighed up the matter.

Martin was there with us on the landing-stage. He had been tinkering, like the rest of us that day, with the *Maeve's* engine. I hated to think that these two men, whom I liked and respected, should be standing there shut away from me by an absurdity of convention. "Yes, bring her across," I said. "You seem to think my son is gone."

Sawle nodded.

"And I expect you and Martin have been having a guess about why he is gone?"

"It's not our business, sir," Martin chipped in. "But we naturally couldn't help coming to certain conclusions."

"Will you keep them to yourselves?" I said. "I would thank you."

It was all very terse and formal, but they seemed glad I had spoken. It established something between us; and I was not sorry for that when Martin, within six months, and Sawle within a year, had been killed, the one on land and the other at sea.

And we were now moving swiftly to the killing days. Even then, on that Saturday ten days before England and Germany were at war, Dermot and I refused to entertain the thought which, from this point and that, had tried to slip into our lulled minds. But on the Monday Wertheim rang me up. He said he wanted Livia to return to London at once.

"She's gone from here," I said, "and left no address."

I felt myself going hot as I imagined Wertheim's heavy, intelligent face registering this news and his mind commenting upon it. There was not much that escaped him. "Hard lines, Essex," he said. "I mean the holiday won't be so good for you now." I knew well enough what he meant.

"Look!" he added. "*Every Street's* coming off. Yes, right away. I'm going ahead with that musical show. I shall want Maeve for that."

"Why have you decided all this so suddenly?" I asked him.

"Suddenly! Where do you live, Essex—on this earth or in the moon? Don't you even read the papers? Haven't you seen that Austria and Serbia are at war—or will be by tomorrow, anyway?"

"Yes, but surely that's all very remote?"

Something that sounded like a groan of despair shuddered over the line and into my ear. Then Wertheim hung up.

And the next day Serbia and Austria *were* at war; and on the Saturday Russia and Germany were in it; and on the Sunday Dermot came to me looking very grave.

"Bill," he said, "that damned man Wertheim is right. I'm going home. I've got a business to look after."

"Everybody is making very sudden decisions," I grumbled. "When are you going?"

"Now—as soon as I can get away. Sheila's packing."

We looked at one another irresolutely. There was nothing to say, but there was a tension in the air. Martin appeared driving Dermot's car round to the front of the house, and Sawle came through the front door carrying a suit-case. These trivial things moved me. More than the prognostications of Wertheim or the gathering strain that had been manifesting itself in the newspapers, the sight of Dermot's car appearing like that, unexpectedly, ready for departure, the sight of Sawle carrying out the bags, imparted a gravity to the moment. Sudden destruction of carefully made plans, swift severance of friends: these things I understood, and these things were being caused by the shadow that was spreading from Austria.

Dermot took my arm and drew me towards the path that led down to the water. We stumbled over the flinty way, through the green umbrage, as we had so often done before. We came out into the light blazing on the river. We stood for a moment looking about us, silent in the utter peace and indifference of the summer afternoon.

"We've had some good times here, Bill," Dermot said. "I shall remember them. The children. I shall remember all the fun we've had here with Oliver and Rory."

"And Maeve. There was a summer night I rowed her up the river, and there was a full moon, and we saw swans flying across it— strung out they were in a line."

"I was thinking particularly of Oliver and Rory," Dermot said.

"It's all behind us now, you know, but I'm glad it's there to think of. We had some good times with them."

"Yes, we had."

"The whole damn world is falling to bits, Bill. Did you know that? This is the big thing. This isn't the Boer War this time."

I didn't answer, and after a moment he said, as though it took some saying: "Bill, you've often heard me say 'God damn England.' Well, now I say 'God help England,' and that's a prayer."

I looked at him, moved and surprised. He was standing with outthrust beard, his face pale, the cheeks twitching, not looking at me, looking across the water at the *Jezebel*, but I don't think he was seeing it.

"I'm glad to hear that, Dermot," I said. "This isn't a bad country."

"This is not a bad country," he echoed. "I've spent my life here, and I know. If this country is in it—and I don't see how she can fail to be—she's going to need her men. I'd like Rory to be one of them. And begod," he flashed, "we could have it out with you afterwards."

"You mean that? You'd like Rory—?"

"I do."

"You're too late, Dermot."

"Like you, Bill."

He said it without anger, in no way as a taunt. It was a simple statement of the truth.

Dermot had taken me down to the river so that we should face this truth together: the truth that we had lost our sons.

That summer, in its fullness and in its autumn decline, was the loveliest I had ever known. I do not think this is an illusion, a nostalgic looking-back to Paradise lost. I have the clearest remembrance of day after lovely day, of evening after evening in which the light prolonged itself into blue magical dusks, and of splendid dawns arriving as if out of some inexhaustible benevolence. The summer and the autumn seemed to be the work of a God who must surely be very pleased with a creation he favoured so deeply.

It was unendurable, this weather. Had thunder and lightning and blasts that stripped the trees come on that Sunday after Dermot had left I should have rejoiced in the sense of the appropriate, but when I awoke to the house empty of my friends, and saw the sun shining through the window, and heard the green stately indifferent trees gently rustling their wings, I felt abandoned and desolate.

When I got downstairs I asked Sawle and Martin to have breakfast with me. They diffidently did so, but it was not a success. It was stressing the abnormality of the moment.

But to be alone was torment. I went down to the landing-stage and sat there smoking my pipe, looking at the woods rising up behind the *Jezebel,* touched here and there with a rusty streak of brown, a patch of yellow or red, the first diffused sparks of the flame that would soon be running from one end of the wooded river to the other. It was heart-breakingly beautiful there, with the silky blue of the sky stretched over the woods, and the light raining in dancing drops on the water.

The boats stood over their blue and white reflections on our side of the water. We shan't want them again, I thought. They stirred memories that were wounds; memories of that visit when Nellie was alive and the boats were new, and the children saw them for the first time. "Boats! All our *very* own?"

I thought kindly of Nellie and her timid faithful ways, and I made a mental note to tell Sawle to get rid of all the boats except the *Maeve* and her dinghy. They hurt me too much.

Then I fell to wondering where Livia was and what she was doing; and I thought of that night in her flat when I had awakened and counted the little bony peaks that punctuated the ridge of her spine, lying like the main range of a delectable country that I had been permitted so briefly to invade and possess.

At that I got up and shook myself. This way, I should go melancholy mad. I rowed out to the *Maeve*, took her down the river, and when I reached the Carrick Roads let her go all out, racing across the tranquil water where the gulls dipped and screamed, racing through the heartless perfect day from the loneliness and desolation that settled again grimly on the thwart beside me when the engine's clamour subsided to a purr and the *Maeve* slowed towards the white bob of the moorings.

All through the Monday Sawle and Martin went gravely about their affairs. We three existed there in the isolation of Heronwater as if in a vacuum. We saw no other soul that day. The weather again was hot and still. The very trees seemed to be as motionless as though all their energy were absorbed in the expectation of some mighty event. Martin had gone early to Truro and brought back all the newspapers he could buy. They echoed with the marching of armies. Serbia, Austria, Russia, Germany, all were astir. Germany had invaded Luxembourg. Moving west.

Till that day, no word of the war had passed between me and Martin and Sawle. But when I went out after breakfast Martin was hovering anxiously near the door. "D'you think we're going to be in this, sir?" he asked.

"Yes," I said. He went away with thoughtfully pursed lips and squared shoulders.

And on Wednesday morning we knew we were in it. Martin asked: "Shall we be going back to London soon, sir?" and I knew what he meant. If I were not going back, he would be going without me. His worried face cleared when I said: "Yes, we're going back today. As soon as you can get things ready."

There was no reason now for me to remain at Heronwater. Some voice which I knew had no sense in it had urged me to stay there till I had heard for good or ill whether Livia would come back.

Now I knew that she would not come back. Her letter from Copenhagen had reached me that morning.

She did not call me "Dear Bill." She did not call me anything. I could imagine the debate she had had with herself as to what, in the new circumstances, she should call me. So she just plunged straight into the letter like this:

"I am doing this because I must. You asked me once whether I loved Oliver, and I said I did not know. I think I was lying to myself even then. I have loved him from the moment I first set eyes on him, though, God help me, I expect little profit from it. But I have learned not to expect profit from love, and I have loved more than one man. I think it was the utter safety you offered me that I could not stomach, for I am too young to feel the need of safety. If I have done you wrong, it is not in robbing you of the marriage you expected, for that would have been small comfort to you, but in ever allowing you to expect it. For that I ask your forgiveness.

LIVIA VAYNOL."

That was all. The letter was addressed from a Copenhagen hotel. I saw no reason to answer it.

It was from Wertheim that I learned of their Odyssey. He was frantically trying to get Livia back to England. Every day he wrote and telegraphed and telephoned, threatened and cajoled. "Soon! Soon!" he shouted to me one day. "She says 'soon'! My God, what does soon mean to me?"

I have never before seen Wertheim excited. Josie was with us. "Control your emotions, Jo," she admonished him. "I don't know what 'soon' means to you, but to me it means when one or the other of them has got it out of the system. Not a minute before."

She was a wise woman, was Josie. When she heard that they were making for Paris she nodded her head. "Now we shall see," she said. "In Paris that young man will see something of the war: men marching, bayonets, girls cheering. That is going to mean something to a young man without a job. And he's had her for three months now."

Josie was right. It was soon after this, at the beginning of December, that Wertheim said: "She's back. She's brought him with her."

A day or two later I saw them. I was crossing Waterloo Bridge on a raw blustery afternoon, darkening towards twilight. The wind was combing cold ripples into the river, and water, air and sky were alike chill and foreboding. Coming towards me from the north side was a marching company of men, such as one saw then at almost every hour of the day: newly-attested men, not uniformed, marching to a station to set out for a training-camp. This was a mixed and ragged lot. A military band went before them, blowing heartily into the dank air, and they stepped out to it bravely enough: short men and tall, toffs and ragged hobbledehoys, men in caps, men in bowlers, men in felt hats, some neatly overcoated, some in threadbare coats. I could not have overlooked Oliver: no one could have overlooked him. He was the tallest man there and he carried his body straight and his head high. He had neither hat nor overcoat, and wore new blue tweeds. They struck me, because I had never seen Oliver in tweeds before. His fair hair was lifted by the light wind. Some obstruction ahead caused the column to halt, and as they stood there marking time, he did not look to right or left but kept his head up and his eyes fixed far ahead.

I felt my throat contract with emotion. The brave music. The boys marching. Oliver! He had halted very near me where I leaned on the cold parapet of the bridge. If I had called his name he would have heard me. But I dared not. I dared not risk the sightless, unacknowledging turn of those blue eyes. The sergeant at the head of the column shouted "Forward! Quick march!" and the music and the men diminished on my hearing and my vision into the murk of the afternoon. I stood there in the wind whistling up from the river till the high golden head was gone from my sight and the last far notes and drum-beats merged with the customary drone of the city.

The encounter emphasised my loneliness. I continued to walk across the bridge feeling sucked and dry and withered. I was very lonely indeed. Oliver, Livia, Martin, Sawle: all were by this time gone. I could have found the companionship that these men had accepted. I was forty-three. There were men of my age dyeing their hair, swearing to a youth that had passed them, scrounging a way into the army by one deception or another. I could have done the same. But I did not do it, or at any time feel an inclination to do it. Later, my reputation as a writer got me work with the Ministry of Propaganda, and I wrote much that I remember neither with pride nor pleasure. There is no need to go into any of that now, but I write this to show that I had an occupation of sorts while the war lasted. But at that time I had not even this shadowy consolation.

I had been suddenly overcome by the absurdity of a man in my position, with no family and no hope of a family, owning two large houses. I tried to sell the Hampstead house, but failed to do so. But I couldn't live in the place. It had become a mausoleum. I had all its furniture, and all the furniture from Heronwater, put into storage, shut up both houses, sold my car, and for the first time since I married Nellie Moscrop all those years ago I was without the responsibility of a home.

During those friendless, hideous early months of the war, when everybody about me seemed buoyed up by an enthusiasm—an hysteria?—which I was unable to share, I lived in a small obscure hotel, rarely venturing out, because I equally disliked the "God bless you, Tommy" scenes of the day-time streets and the sepul-chral crawling about of people in the darkened thoroughfares of night: the most hateful confession, as it seemed to me, that man has yet made on the earth. I could not stand it when lighted windows, the loveliest symbol of peaceful men dwelling quietly about their hearths, were put out.

Living thus alone, with no responsibilities, seeing no one but a few shabby strangers, doing no work, brooding upon the defection of Oliver and Livia and the more impersonal but bitter and obsessive tragedy of the war, I fell into a morbid condition of body and mind, a hypochondria in which I felt myself to be deserted by all the world, though I was deliberately concealing my whereabouts from those who could have helped me. I was hugging my griefs to me, inviting them to kill me, and they nearly did.

My walk that afternoon on which I saw Oliver was typical of the sort of thing I was doing at that time. I had been over to the south side of the river because it was unlikely I should see there anyone I knew. I had wandered about among mean streets, filling my mind and my eyes morbidly with the flaming posters that invited the sheep to the sacrifice. I lunched meanly at a greasy little coffee tavern where the tables were covered with scabby white American cloth. I was piling the agony on to myself in every way I could devise. The encounter with Oliver was the last thing needed. When he had marched by, the wind seemed shrewder, the world more bitter and I made my way to the back-street hotel that was my lair in a spirit of mental and physical hopelessness which I savoured like an opiate.

After dinner I was the sole occupant of the lounge—a dimly-lighted decrepit place with a handful of fire crumbling in the grate. An old black-beetle of a waiter came sidling in now and then, God knows why, flipped at this or that with a napkin, and sidled silently out again. Presently I gave a violent shiver, and pulled my chair nearer to the insufficient fire. That did me no good, and the next time the black-beetle crawled in I asked him to bring me whisky, hot water, sugar and lemon. There was no lemon, but I compounded a grog of sorts, drank it and went to bed.

I slept badly. The shivers returned, so that at last I dragged myself out of bed and spread my overcoat on top of the eiderdown. Then I slept, and when I woke in the morning I was drenched with sweat. All through the day I slept and woke in fits and starts, and the only thing I was conscious of was the lightness and apparent largeness of my head that seemed like a balloon eager to lift my body out of the bed and float it away.

I awoke out of one of my dozes to find the day gone and the dreary room lit by a bedside lamp. I was aware that people were in the room, but I did not know that they were a doctor and Annie Suthurst. This had been achieved by a piece of detective work on the part of the hotel manager. It was characteristic of that wretched little hotel that the play-bill of *Every Street* still hung in the hall, though the play had been off for some months and Wertheim's great musical show was settling down to its success. The manager knew that I was the author of *Every Street*, and, being alarmed about my condition, he decided to ring up someone who might be supposed to have an interest in me. He found Maeve's name in the telephone book, and she was just setting off for the theatre when news of my illness reached her. So Annie Suthurst was sent for a doctor, under whose sedative I slept calmly that night, and awoke in the morning weak, clear-headed and feeling very foolish.

Repentant, I think is the mood I was in when Maeve and Annie appeared soon after breakfast-time. I felt like a child who has been consciously playing the fool. It was over: there would be no more melodramatic nursing of sorrows.

But that didn't help me with Maeve. There I was, haggard and unshaven, in that frowsy room, and Maeve without stint told me what she thought of me. I had worried my friends unpardonably; I had caused her profound anxiety at a time when she ought to have had her mind on her work—"to say nothing," Annie Suthurst broke in, "of draggin' you round 'ere after t'theatre last night."

I think Maeve had not intended to say anything about that, and in fury at my learning that she had rushed to the hotel with the paint hardly removed from her face, as soon as the show was ended, she exclaimed: "Shave him, Annie. He's disgusting."

"I will an' all," Annie said, delighted; and ignominiously I had to submit to her ministrations, thankful that I used a safety razor. She sponged my face and brushed my hair, and I felt so much better that I managed a sheepish smile. "I could eat something," I said.

I was allowed nothing but hot milk and dry toast, and then, Annie having miraculously made the bed and pillows comfortable, I was told to go to sleep again. Happy to be commanded, to be, after that morbid aberration, in competent hands, I did as I was told.

Three days later, when I had got back from a tottering walk with Maeve in a spell of winter sunshine, she raised the question which she had already settled for me.

"Where are you going to live now? You can't stay in this place."

I said I would think about it. "I've been thinking for you," she told me sharply. "It's high time someone did. There's a furnished flat on the floor below mine. It'll be empty at the end of the month."

"Thank you. I'll go into that. Who'll look after me?"

"Annie Suthurst, of course. My place doesn't take all her time."

"I'll speak to her."

"I've done the speaking, and taken the flat, too. All you have to do is go to Brighton and get some fresh air. When you feel well, come back. The place will be ready."

I kept the flat as long as the war lasted. When Maeve was dead, Annie remained with me.

I didn't like the look of Maeve. I got back from Brighton on a crisp January afternoon, and she was at the station to meet me. For the first time since I had known her there was colour in her cheeks, or rather on her cheekbones: a pinkish suffusion that at first I put down to the sharpness of the air. Then I reflected that I had known Maeve in every sort of weather for years on end, and never had the matt pallor of her skin, which was healthy and attractive, shown any change of hue. I looked at her again, and thought her eye too bright, and when we shook hands her hand seemed dryly hot.

She seemed to be affected intensely by the hectic atmosphere of the station. It was full of jostling men in khaki, and sad-eyed women who did nothing to hide their misery, and women bravely bright, talking of ordinary things. There was a knot of private soldiers, cheerfully boozed, singing songs to the accompaniment of a mouth-organ. The organist, an old sweat with his cap pushed to the back of his head, revealing a fine oiled quiff, looked old enough to have tasted the Boer War, and the songs of that war seemed to be his favourites. He played "Dolly Grey" and "Soldiers of the Queen"; and then one of his mates said: "Give us 'When it's with you.'"

The player didn't find it easy; the song hadn't yet got fully into that triumphant swing that swept it over England and France; but the men made a go of it, and Maeve shuddered. "Come on!" she implored, dragging on my arm. "Come and see your flat."

As we went the station echoed to the deep, spaced coughs of a departing train, and the cheers of the men, and the called good-byes of the women.

It was inevitable, as we lived in the same building, that Maeve and I should occasionally take a meal together. At last we developed the custom of always lunching with one another, sometimes in her flat, sometimes in mine. It depended on the caprice of Annie Suthurst, who treated us both as children subject to her discipline. On a Wednesday in March, when lunch was over, and Maeve, on the point of departing for a matinée, stood at the door with her face framed in grey fur, upturned about her ears, she said: "If you want to see Oliver, be at Charing Cross about half-past three." She closed the door quickly and ran down the stairs.

This was the first time she had mentioned either Livia or Oliver. I was not aware that she knew anything of their movements, nor do I know now whence she obtained this information. I put on my overcoat and walked to Charing Cross, with my collar turned up about my ears, as Maeve's fur had been, for it was a day of cutting wind. At least, I told myself that was why my collar was up, but why, also, was the brim of my hat pulled down in front? That was not a fashion I was accustomed to. I admitted an instinctive attempt at disguise. I had come to spy on my son, as I had spied on him that day in Holborn, and throughout that long bitter night in Camden Town.

The wind was harsh and gritty, the sky was as hard as flint, as I crossed Trafalgar Square under the façade of the National Gallery. When I came out into the Strand a policeman was holding up all traffic, and men and women were lined deep on the pavement outside the station. I took my place with the rest and watched the long procession of the ambulances come into the Strand. I had never known such a silence in a great city. The policeman stood with his arm still as the arm of a signpost. The men took off their hats. The white vans with their blood-coloured crosses filed out one by one. The drivers had a rigid look, taking no notice of the crowd standing there. Ten, twelve, I counted; and then something happened to the head of the convoy, and everything slowed down, stopped. It was an infinitesimal delay. In a second or two all was in motion again, but in that brief suspension of movement, breaking into the utter silence, there came from the van that stood half in and half out of the station gateway one deep groan, followed by a choked-back sob. Like a winter wind suddenly moving through frozen branches, a swift responsive sigh passed through the crowd, and men and women looked into each other's faces, and shuffled their feet, like the helpless spectators of some supreme tragedy.

When the ambulances were all gone, and the crowd was fluid again, I passed into the station with that groan still in my ears, and all the devils of imagination showing me the proud head that had been held so high on Waterloo Bridge lying as low as Oliver's feet.

But that was never to be his fate.

When I saw him that afternoon there was already a change from the boy whose eyes I had seen looking ahead with intensity of speculation as he marched with his comrades. Now he was here, in the present moment, and enjoying it. It was Livia whom I saw first. She was better dressed and better looking than I had ever seen her. Her cheeks glowed with health and happiness, and with a possessive pride that she did nothing to conceal she looked up now and then into the face of the man who overtopped her by several inches.

He had grown a small golden moustache. The exercise of the last few months had broadened and toughened him. His blue eyes gleamed out of a face that was tanned by weather. Brown boots, shining like chestnuts, were laced up his calves, and the skirts of a well-cut overcoat swung as he strutted. I could not avoid the word: he was strutting; and when private soldiers passed and saluted the single pip he wore upon his sleeve, a little cane that he was carrying in a gloved hand went negligently to his cap. He was enjoying himself. He was enjoying those salutes though he never looked at the men who gave them. He was enjoying having Livia there to look upon his glory and, in turn, to be looked upon as an adjunct to his splendour.

I was proud of him. How, even then, I would have outdone the father in the parable who, when his son was yet a great way off, ran! How I would have run, and abased myself before this young, jocund Mars whose body, pink and soapy, I had held in my arms, whose love had once been as unquestioningly mine as the sunshine and the rain! But I knew that I could as soon call back Nellie from the grave as hope to see those blue eyes smile at me, as they were smiling now at Livia, not turn to cold indifference.

So I lurked behind the bookstall, with my collar up and my hat-brim down, and saw two other youngsters dressed as he was, but with nothing of his size and presence, join him, and selfconsciously salute Livia, and stand there talking and casually returning salutes. Then they all made for the barrier, passing so close to me hunched furtively there that the skirts of an overcoat brushed the back of my legs, sending a shiver of excitement through me. I turned when they were gone, watched their backs disappearing through the barrier, and knew that I was looking my last on Oliver before the war swallowed him—to fashion him into what unknown similitude? I could feel the blood pulsing in my temples and overworking my heart. I pressed towards the barrier and stood there looking down the vista of the train until all the emotional activity that was strewing the platform alongside it was separated out into those who were aboard and those who were left standing to see them go.

I did not see him again. The station was filled with the deafening shrillness of escaping steam. That stopped. The engine strained and panted beneath white spreading clouds that obscured the roof, and I saw Livia Vaynol running as if to escape into the city from a scene that was unbearable. I turned my back as she came through the barrier. She did not see me as she hastened away, not smiling now, but with loneliness and desolation upon her unmasked face.

## 29

That was in March, 1915. In memory the year is strewn with fragments like bits of wreckage seen on a beach long ago. The Dardanelles, Tipperary, Rupert Brooke, go easy with the matches, S.S. *Clyde*, Keep the Home Fires Burning, put one of these saccharine tablets in your coffee, it's as good as sugar, we're lucky to get coffee, anyway. When it's with You it's Wonderful, It's a bit thick: if you work in an office everything's gone from the shops by the time you get home, we'll have rationing soon, I suppose, If you were the Only Girl in the World, Defence of the Realm Act, Let the great big World keep turning, put that light out, George Robey, Violet Lorraine, Maeve O'Riorden, When it's with You it's Wonderful, casualties, shells, casualties, *Lusitania*, white feather, if a German raped your sister, PUT THAT LIGHT OUT, casualties, casualties, blessed was it in that dawn to be alive, no fraternising this Christmas, some say Good Old Jerry, CASUALTIES, men in bright blue suits and red scarves hobbling through the parks, being led through the parks, being wheeled through the parks, It's the blind ones I can't stand seeing; My dear, you don't *have* to look at them, PUT THAT LIGHT OUT!...

We had got used to everything. We had got used to the ambulances, to the men in blue, to gas warfare, to the trains departing full of spick and span youngsters with polished buttons and the trains arriving full of men caked with mud, cluttered with uncouth accoutrements, who rushed from the stations as though rushing upon life, to seize it frantically for their few permitted days. There's nothing you can't get used to. It's the new thing that shakes you up. And the new thing came.

Dermot rang me up on Monday, the 17th of April, 1916, and said he was coming round to have lunch with me and Maeve. Maeve, for once, had not intended to have lunch. She had been out in the country on the Sunday, had come home early, and gone to bed, complaining of being tired. Annie Suthurst had brought me a message in the morning saying that I must lunch alone, as Maeve wanted to spend the day in bed. But when she heard that her father was coming, she got up and came down to my flat. "Don't ask me how I am, Dutch uncle," she exclaimed defensively as she came through the door. "I'm just suffering from ten years of overwork. That's all. I shall get over it."

She sat sideways in the window-seat, so that she could get a squint into Berkeley Square, where the leaves were unfolding on the plane trees, delicate and beautiful against the brown prickly maces of last year's fruit. Those leaves outside, and on the round polished table in the middle of the room, a cut-glass bowl full of daffodils, reflected as if in a peat-dark stream.

"Leaves," said Maeve, "and flowers; and yesterday there were lambs—white tottery things—so lovely. We saw them in a meadow that went down to the Thames."

"Who were *we* this time?" I asked.

"Oh, you wouldn't know," she said wearily. "I only met him myself on Saturday night. Someone brought him round to my dressing-room, and he *besought* me to come out with him on Sunday." She got off the seat and stood up, looking out of the window. "You never saw such a boy," she spoke over her shoulder. "He looked about sixteen, with blue eyes and smooth round cheeks. He's been out once, and he's going again today. In the Air Force. I wished him luck, and d'you know what he said?"

I shook my head.

"He said: 'I've lasted longer than Freddie and Bunnie, anyway, so I feel lucky.' Freddie and Bunnie lasted a week. They were at school with him a few months ago."

I almost wished she would cry, or show some emotion. But she went on in a flat voice: "When he saw those lambs, he said: 'Christ! Isn't that pretty? My mother'd like to see that.' He'd borrowed someone's car for the day and was awfully proud of his driving. He insisted on a big hotel for lunch and ordered champagne. He wasn't very used to it. It made him talk about Bunnie again. He said: 'Those lambs made me think of something Bunnie said. It was the first time we ever saw anti-aircraft shells bursting. Bunnie said: "That's a pretty sight—like white lambs in a blue field." Old Bunnie was a bit of a poet. Or d'you think that was a dappy thing to say?'"

Suddenly I stopped her. "For God's sake, Maeve, shut up," I shouted. I hoped it would be like a slap in the face. It was. She spun round in surprise, looked at me for a moment dreadfully hurt, then collapsed into my arms and cried. I let her have it out, then led her back to the window-seat and sat her down. Presently she became calmer.

"Look, my dear," I said, taking her hand and fondling it, "d'you think you ought to do all this promiscuous going about with men? It's such a strain. I know how you feel, and what you hope to do for them; but you can't go on being the pillow for everyone's sorrowing head. Your work's enough."

"The work's a fraud, a swindle," she said sadly. "Oh, Man! You don't know how I feel standing there singing that song that makes me everybody's woman. Because, you know, that's what it comes to. They think I look so marvellous—oh, God knows *what* they think and dream about me. And then you can't avoid meeting some of them. And what are you to do? What are you to do?"

What could she do? I knew she was living as she would never have wished to live. Her life was being fevered by a hundred casual contacts that could mean nothing for her but wear of nerve and body. No comfort, no tranquillity. She was racketing about: suppers after the theatre, dances, lunches, dinners, week-end jaunts like the one from which she had just returned, giving bits of herself, tearing herself to tatters for strangers, because they were strangers, who lived in the shadow of death.

Presently she smiled and patted my hand in the old affectionate way. "Don't worry, Bill," she said. "It's the penalty of being a famous woman. It's the penalty of having a Bill Essex at my side making me a grand actress through all these years. You see, the poor boys are bucked to pieces at having personally met Maeve O'Riorden. It's something for them to swank about. And you needn't worry about my virginity. I can look after that, for what it's worth."

I had not heard her talk so recklessly, thoughtlessly, before. It was the back-kick of her stifled emotion. There was nothing more I could say. I could only think; and as we sat there in the window-seat waiting for Dermot to come, my thoughts were just two words: "Dear Maeve! Dear Maeve!"

Annie Suthurst put the coffee on a table in front of the window-seat. It was a big seat—room for us all. When Annie was gone Dermot put on his spectacles and took a letter from his pocket. "I haven't shown this to Sheila," he said. "She'll know soon enough."

He unfolded the letter and handed it to me. Maeve hitched herself up close to my side and read with her chin resting on my shoulder. The letter was from Rory.

"MY DEAR FATHER,—I wouldn't be such a fool as to post this to you in the ordinary way here in Dublin. We don't trust the Castle, you know, and just now, I think, they're particularly busy steaming open letters. A friend I can trust is crossing to England and will drop this into some inconspicuous letter-box.

Well, I think I ought to let you know that before long now anything may happen. I'm only having a guess. I know you think I'm no end of a person in the movement, but I'm small beer really, and I'm kept pretty much in the dark. But there's something in the air, more marching in uniform than usual, more attacks on public buildings. You know we do that as an exercise, everything except the actual shooting and rushing the buildings. In that way, we've taken half Dublin over and over again! The Castle does nothing about it. One of these days the fools will be surprised.

Well, there's so much of this sort of activity, we're being keyed up so keenly to concert pitch, that I reckon they're going to use us soon. There's plenty of ammunition flowing in. I know that.

Another thing that makes me feel we are on the verge of something is this. Donnelly is so gay and yet so secretive. Of course, he's at the heart of things. He's away attending conferences all day and half the night, and he's singing at the top of his voice. But not a word out of him. I've tried to get a hint, without being insubordinate or impertinent, but he won't give me a word. Except once. He said: 'Rory, my lad, there was a damned good English soldier called Julian Grenfell. He was killed, and he left a poem that's a glory.' Then he recited the poem right through. It ended: 'If this be the last song you sing, sing well, you may not sing another, Brother, sing!' Then he said: 'Remember that, Rory, and keep your rifle clean.'

You know, my dear Father, last August I was with the multitude that followed the body of O'Donovan Rossa to his grave at Glasnevin. I was one of those who fired the volley over his grave—the grave of a martyr. It was a scene I shall never forget. Padraic Pearse was there, wearing his uniform, and he spoke with his hand on the hilt of his sword. He said: 'I hold it a Christian thing, as O'Donovan Rossa held it, to hate evil, to hate untruth, to hate oppression, and, hating them to strive to overthrow them.'

I thought, as I heard those words, that they were the very heart and soul of all that you yourself have ever taught me. I shall go into battle remembering them and remembering you.

One thing more. I hope to come out of this alive. The chances that Donnelly will do so are slenderer than mine. If our attempt is made, and if it should fail, no mercy would be shown to Donnelly. I have learned to love him, Father, and I wonder if you know that I love Maggie, too? She is so brave and patient and uncomplaining. I shall marry her some day however this matter turn out, but if Donnelly should be taken from us I shall marry her at once.

Give my love to my Mother. Kiss Eileen. Kiss Maeve.

RORY."

The sheet trembled in my hand as I put it down on the coffee table. For a moment no one spoke. Then Maeve said to Dermot: "Well?"

He sat still, looking straight before him, one hand outspread on each knee.

"Well—are you happy?" Maeve demanded more sharply.

Still Dermot did not move. She got up and moved across the room till she faced him. "I ask you," she said, her voice rising shrilly, "are you happy now? You've got what you worked for. Does it please you? You—you *bogus* creature! You're on a level with the white feather girls who hound other people on to satisfy their bloody instincts. Two generations of you—your precious Uncle Con living in luxury five thousand miles away, and you—you— And what does it come to, all you've done between you? You've killed Rory, that's all. You've killed Rory! You've killed Rory…"

She broke down hysterically. Dermot put his hands before his face and murmured weakly: "Don't, Maeve, don't!"

I got my arms round her shoulders and led her, weeping, upstairs to her own flat. When I came down again Dermot was gone. Rory's letter lay on the floor. I picked it up and put it into a drawer of my desk.

So you see, when the new thing came—that Easter Monday rebellion in Dublin—Dermot and I were not surprised. It flamed into the headlines of the newspapers, it staggered the unsuspecting English public; and few people knew what a pitiful, bungled, lamentable affair it was. Few guessed that a little group of professors and aspirant politicians and poets had been haggling and chaffering, ordering and countermanding orders, deciding to proceed, deciding to withdraw, for a week before the outbreak, and that when at last some sort of decision came to their vacillating minds, it was too late. The heart was gone out of an army that had been ready to spring; and only a remnant paraded on the fatal morning when the visionaries at last set out on their brief pilgrimage to the grave.

One of the remnant was Michael Collins, a thick-set play-boy with a wing of black hair tumbling over his brow, almost unknown, but destined to learn that day and in the few days that intervened before Padraic Pearse handed in his sword that not thus must Ireland be fought for. Not with windy proclamations and the pretence of uniformed might. No more marching save the stealthy march at night of two or three; no more parades save the parade of the faithful few rendering account in secret; no more uniforms save the pulled-down brim of the black felt hat and the uniform steel of eyes that looked along the barrels of trusty guns. Get out of the daylight, burrow, get underground. All this became clear to Collins and to one other of the remnant who paraded on Easter Monday—Rory O'Riorden.

On Monday, May 1st, Dermot brought me the letter that had come from Rory. It had been written on the Wednesday night of the rebellion week.

"MY DEAR FATHER,—This has been a great and terrible day. On Sunday we were all at sixes and sevens. A parade had been ordered, and was countermanded. This caused a good deal of heart-burning, and the men began to get angry and to damn leaders who didn't seem to know their own minds. I saw nothing of Donnelly all that day—he was confabbing at Liberty Hall—and I have not seen him since. I wonder whether I shall ever see him again.

Then we were called on to parade at 10 on Monday morning.

It was a grand Easter Monday, bright and sunny. We did not know what we were paraded for, but some of us had a good guess. All the officers wore their green uniforms; many of the men were in uniform, too. The streets were full of people strolling about in the cheerful holiday weather. They did not take any more notice of us than usual, because they are so used to seeing us marching here and there. My battalion is the 3rd of the Dublin Brigade, and we were commanded by Commandant Eamon de Valera, a pallid spectacled man who hasn't much to say.

Well, there we were at 10 o'clock in the familiar Dublin streets. De Valera marched us off, and when we reached our objective, we didn't play at taking it as we have done in the past; we entered upon it. It was a place called Boland's bakery, and as soon as we were there I realised that the decisive moment had come. Boland's bakery commands the road by which troops would have to pass coming from Kingstown Harbour to Dublin. We were there to stop them. That was clear.

They gave us plenty of time to dig ourselves in. No one disturbed us all through that day. When night came and nothing had happened, an extraordinary sense of unreality came over me. This couldn't be true. We knew by then that Pearse had taken the Post Office in Sackville Street—just walked in as we had done here— and that there he had established his headquarters and proclaimed the Republic. We knew, too, that other important points had been occupied; things had gone as they were intended to go, and yet there we were in Boland's bakery, a handful of men, looking through the windows into the quiet street, and nothing was happening to us. I couldn't believe that the Republic was here—actually here in Dublin—proclaimed by Pearse, with Pearse himself as President. I kept on telling myself: 'Now you have a country and a ruler, and you are a soldier sworn to defend them,' but the silence, the inaction, as though the enemy were treating us with contempt, made me feel cold and queer. I imagine De Valera realised what I was thinking.

As the light was fading and I was sitting at a window looking unhappily into the empty street, he passed by and clapped a hand on my shoulder. I looked up, and his eyes glinted at me through the spectacles and down his long nose. 'It'll come,' he said. 'It'll come.' That was all, and he continued his rounds to another room.

We didn't all remain at Boland's bakery. We were ordered to occupy other houses round about. On the Tuesday we seemed a more ridiculously small army than ever, for I was now in a house with only two other men. We took all our ammunition up to the attic. A skylight from there opened on to the roof. There was a useful parapet to serve as a breastwork. Lying flat on the roof, we could rest our rifles on the parapet and get a good shot down into the street. I was in command. The other two men were named Clancy and Deasy. Clancy was a huge fellow, a docker, who swore everything 'by the Mother of God and Jim Larkin,' and Deasy was a thin dark slip of a chap who swears he's been a detective in London, but I think he's a good liar. Anyway, he kept on throughout the day telling us we were all daft.

'Would you listen now to them bloody guns?' he suddenly broke out, and by this time there were guns enough. We could hear artillery roaring and the loud explosive shock of bursting shells. 'It's off the face of the map this city will be blown,' said Deasy. 'I'll obey me orders with the bloody rest, but whoever organised this shooting-match was daft from his mother's womb. Can the poor bloody bhoys stand up to the likes of that artillery? Begod, it's assassination we should be going in for. Every sod in the Viceregal Lodge. Shoot 'em in the back. Let 'em send out relays. Shoot 'em down. Every bloody one. In the back. That's the war we want.'

Clancy told him to shut his gob, and I thought they'd be getting to blows. We were all lying on the roof, with our rifles by our sides. I decided to change the arrangement. I ordered Clancy to remain where he was, and to call us if anything happened. Deasy and I climbed down the ladder from the skylight to the attic.

All through the day we remained there, listening to the tumult of artillery elsewhere in the city. Nothing happened to us. We took turns on the roof throughout the day and night, two hours on and four off. De Valera visited us several times, but save for that, Deasy, Clancy and I were alone in the empty house.

It was nerve-racking, this inaction. Donnelly, I knew now, was in the Post Office with Pearse, James Connolly, Thomas Clarke, Joseph Plunkett and others. I thought of him all day long, and as the artillery crashed I prayed God he would come to no harm.

In the course of the day we had evidence that the Post Office garrison was holding out, for a leaflet reached us, signed by Pearse, saying that nowhere had British troops broken through the Republican lines.

Deasy and Clancy slept well on Tuesday night. I did not sleep at all.

Now we come to the morning of this day on which I write. The clamour of the British artillery greatly increased, and it sounded as though hell were let loose in the direction of Sackville Street, where Donnelly is. I had made this arrangement for us three men. All the ammunition we had was taken up on the roof. There were three rifles. Deasy and Clancy were not strangers to me. I knew that Clancy was a magnificent shot and that Deasy might waste ammunition. So the orders were that if fighting came our way, Clancy and I should do the shooting. Whichever emptied his rifle first should drop it and pick up the third. Deasy, lying on the roof, would see that a dropped rifle was immediately loaded and placed ready to hand.

So far as I remember, it was at about half-past three that Clancy shouted from the roof: 'Mother of God and Jim Larkin! Sojers!'

My heart thumped. I leapt up the ladder, Deasy following at my heels. I took up a rifle and crouched, peering over the parapet. There at last was the enemy—men in khaki, coming unsuspectingly up the road. It was, somehow, so different, when you saw the men there, from anything you had imagined. It held me and Clancy spellbound, so that we just crouched and watched, the triggers under our fingers. Then suddenly it all became real. From another house along the street there came the sharp crack of a rifle, and one of the soldiers in the road turned round very slowly on his own axis, then quietly folded up in the road. Clancy said: 'Poor sod!' and pressed on his trigger. A second soldier fell. Then I fired, and there were three dead lying in the road.

My dear Father, I cannot tell you of all that has happened this terrible afternoon. The fight went on for hours. Hundreds of British soldiers were killed and wounded. Clancy was killed. During a lull, he lifted himself to peer over the parapet, but by then our position was too well marked. He slid back on to the roof with not so much as a groan. Deasy took his place.

The weight of numbers told at last. We were all withdrawn from the outlying buildings and are now back at Boland's. We gave a good account of ourselves. We can hold on to this place for a long time.

A man has to sneak his way back into the city tonight. He has promised to get this letter to a friend of his, a seaman who is crossing on a Liverpool boat. It is to tell you that all is well with me, and that I am happy. I have done what you wanted me to do.

Pearse's proclamation which reached me yesterday says: 'We have lived to see an Irish Republic proclaimed. May we live to establish it firmly.' We shall do that, and then all this will not have been in vain.

Love from RORY."

When I had read the letter I could not look Dermot in the face, for I knew, as he knew, that by then Pearse had handed in his sword. It was not easy to make some of the men obey his order to surrender. The 3rd battalion, which still held Boland's bakery, was stricken with consternation. Some smashed their rifles rather than hand them in. Among those who did so was Rory O'Riorden.

## 30

Rory had told his father in a letter that if Donnelly were executed he would marry Maggie at once.

Donnelly was executed. He sang to the last. Some of the prisoners prayed. At least one of them used his last night on earth to be married. Some of them uttered brave words, and some passed in a bitter silence the disillusioned remnant of their days. Donnelly sang, and it is known that in later years one of the ablest and bitterest of the Irish rebels was one of Donnelly's warders. He had been converted to the cause of a man who could sing like that.

So Donnelly sang till the moment when a bullet shattered the song in his mouth and crumpled him under a wall in a Dublin gaol: but Rory did not marry Maggie then. Maggie, her hands red with days of bandaging, was with a surrendered battalion. She was discharged by her captors; but Rory was one of the thousands who were sent to English gaols. He went to Frongoch where one of his fellow prisoners was the play-boy with the wild wing of black hair flapping on his forehead. Like prisoners at all times and the world over, the men of Frongoch found their means of communicating with the world without. It was late in 1916 that Dermot received a letter from Rory containing the phrase: "I am bound to Michael Collins by the most solemn and fearful oath."

The page fluttered in Dermot's nervous fingers. "I hoped it would be ended when Donnelly died," he said. "Michael Collins... I've never heard of him."

"There was a time when I had never heard of Kevin Donnelly. Do you remember? It was the first time I had ever taken Maeve to the theatre. I brought her home in a cab, asleep. Donnelly was there."

"Yes," said Dermot. "I remember. It's no good shooting one or shooting a dozen. Another one or another dozen crops up. Michael Collins…" He mused for a time upon the new name that destiny had written upon his page. Then he folded the letter and went away. He looked old and very tired.

That was on an autumn afternoon. When I had left Dermot I walked in the streets that were beginning to fade into a bloomy dark, bought an evening paper, and took it into Gunter's teashop. I spread it open and my heart gave a bound as I saw Oliver's face looking at me from the page. I hardly dared read the letterpress. Killed in action? Wounded? The fearful and familiar possibilities of the time assailed me. Then I saw beneath the picture: "Captain Oliver Essex, V.C."

The room had been swimming. Now things took focus again. I came back to life. My tea was being laid before me. I filled my cup, drank, and then read the paragraph. It announced that the King had conferred the Victoria Cross upon Captain Essex, M.C., Croix de Guerre. "The action which earned Captain Essex the highest award for valour took place during the Somme offensive, which still continues. A machine-gun, entrenched in the edge of a wood, was taking heavy toll of our troops. Three efforts had been made to rush the wood and take the gun, and every one of those who made the attempt fell dead or wounded. Captain Essex had been advised to retire to a dressing-station, as he had been twice shot. One bullet had glanced across his forehead, leaving a wound which filled his eye with blood; another pierced his right hand, striking from it the revolver which was his only weapon. He declined to retire, and announced that he would make a single-handed effort to capture the gun. Armed with a Mills bomb held in the left hand, he walked without haste towards the wood. It seemed as though his life was under Divine protection, for he was able to advance within throwing distance before he was again wounded. Literally as he threw the bomb a third bullet struck him—in the face; but the bomb found its objective; the gun was silenced, and Captain Essex's men rushed forward and took the wood. They thus straightened out a sag in the line and allowed the day's victories to be consolidated. It was only when he had personally seen his men entrenched on their new line that Captain Essex consented to retire to a dressing-station.

"Captain Essex is the son of the famous novelist and dramatist, William Essex."

I looked at the picture staring at me out of the paper. It was of no Oliver that I had ever known. A remark that Wertheim had made came back to my mind: "Phœbus in black trousers." And I thought of the rosy jocund Mars who was Oliver as I had last seen him. That was eighteen months ago that March day when Livia Vaynol had rushed by me unseeingly, and the tall boy in his brand-new kit had been so debonair and proud. This was neither of them—not Wertheim's boy nor the boy I had then seen. The moustache which I had then noticed for the first time was fuller. The hair, which he had always tended to wear long, was cropped and wiry-looking. The eyes were incredibly hard, staring straight out of the face with a fanatic and inhuman regard.

"God! Doesn't he look a killer!"

It was almost as though my own reluctant heart had spoken. Then I saw that two young officers at a table next to mine were considering the same picture that had captured my fascinated regard. The face of one of them teased my memory. At last I placed him: he was one of the two or three who had joined Oliver at the station on the afternoon I had just been calling back to mind. He laughed uneasily. I saw that he was now wearing the uniform of the Air Force. "A killer all right," he said. "I was with his mob for a time before I transferred. God! He was a tough nut. He was doing the rounds one night and found a sentry asleep on the firing-step. He just stayed there till the chap woke up—a solid hour. Then he took a grip on the feller's coat at the chest with his right hand, held him up, and buzzed him a straight left in the teeth. 'Let that teach you. And now report me,' he said, and walked on."

"He might have court-martialled him."

"That wasn't Essex's way. He preferred hitting."

"Well. He's a damned good soldier. Good luck to him."

"Oh, he's a good soldier all right. But I didn't like him. Something about him—I don't know. He *enjoyed* it. I've seen him as bloody as a butcher with his white teeth laughing."

"Well, if there are medals going, that's the sort of chap to have 'em. At any rate he's not a G.H.Q. wallah. They have a roster there for D.S.O.s. You take your turn. Even if you do nothing but order the stationery. Some Distinguished Service."

I looked at the youngster's chest, innocent of ribbons, paid my bill and went out. It was almost dark. I walked round Berkeley Square with the Air Force man's phrase vivid in my mind: "Bloody as a butcher with his white teeth laughing." Oliver! Twenty. Twenty last May. Captain Oliver Essex, V.C., M.C., Croix de Guerre.

It was a fortnight later that Maeve said, as she was leaving for the theatre: "Oliver will be at the Palladian tonight."

"Oliver?"

"Yes. Didn't you know he was on leave?"

I shook my head.

"Wertheim told me. He's invited Oliver to a box."

Wertheim would. He was a showman. He knew the publicity value of personalities, and for the moment Oliver was a personality.

"Will you be there?" Maeve asked.

"Not much good trying to get a seat at this time of night," I said. "The show's always booked up for weeks ahead."

"I should like you to be. I've got a stalls ticket. I took it for a friend and now she's rung up to say she can't come after all." Maeve laid the ticket on the table. She stood by the door, holding the knob with one hand, swinging her gloves in the other. "You do want to see him, don't you?" she asked.

I nodded, unable to speak.

"It's a long time since you've seen him. He's changed, you know. I met him this afternoon."

"Changed?"

I suppose some dying flame revived in my face. Maeve abandoned her poised-for-flight air and came into the room. "Sorry, Bill," she said. "I don't mean in that way. I don't know at all. We didn't mention you. I mean he *looks* different. He looks—well, rather frightening. I suppose it's his wounds. There's a scar that lifts his left eye and another that gives a small twist to the end of his mouth. When he laughs his face looks contorted—a bit sinister."

"Where's he staying?"

"With Livia Vaynol, I suppose."

"Why don't they marry and have done with it?" I burst out.

Maeve looked at me patiently. "I'm not in the confidence of either," she said. "I'm not particularly in anybody's confidence. Even you don't exactly open your heart to me, do you? Never mind. There are plenty of parties and rides in cars and dances, aren't there?"

She smiled a little bitterly. I got up and put an arm around her. "Maeve—my dear—I'm sorry—"

She pushed me gently aside. "It's all right, Bill. I'm not complaining. But I'm so much in the dark about the whole lot of you. I don't even know what you think about Livia now. Would you marry her still, if you could?"

"I've put that all out of my head, my dear. She'll never have me while Oliver's above ground."

"I said if you could," she persisted.

"If I could—yes," I said.

She took up her gloves from the table and slowly drew them through her fingers. Then, saying nothing more, she went.

What an incredibly different Maeve it was I looked at a few hours later! And what incredible circumstances they were in which I looked at her! How, at this distance of time, get down on paper that atmosphere of the great war-time show? Outside, the city lurked in its shadows, shrinking the vast sprawl of its body as deeply as possible into the night's obscurity. Within, the lights blazed. "Joy, whose hand is ever at his lip, bidding adieu." Here, if ever, one understood the meaning of that line. True, there were plenty whose joys seemed likely to endure; but their serenity threw the more sharply into focus the hundreds of faces that one knew were looking their last on lovely things.

I entered the theatre just before the rise of the curtain; just in time to catch the animated buzz of talk that contended with the music of the orchestra dashingly dispensing the opening airs of *Choose Your Partner*. From floor to gallery in a vast overpowering *bourdon* the voices rose, and already the air was heavy with the blue smoke of tobacco. There was a sense of expectancy, an eagerness to clutch at the coming hours of gaiety and brightness, that perhaps we shall never know again.

I took my place between a Cabinet minister and an officer whose shoulder strap was decorated with a baton crossed by a sword. The lights dimmed, the curtain swung up, and the piece began with the customary swirl of legs. You couldn't beat Tiller girls for that sort of thing: that precise regimented prancing, that rhythmic swaying of twenty bodies as one, that dipping forward of necks bearing feathered heads. And as they pranced and swayed, arms interlocked, making of themselves a barrier behind which nothing could be seen, the principals of the show came one by one, and one by one were revealed by the twenty dancing girls breaking into two walls of ten, leaving a gap for the principal to emerge.

Each came in his own way: the leading comedian with a leap and a smile; his lugubrious foil with a frightened shamble; but there was never any doubt whose show this was. Maeve appeared last of all. The dancing girls parted their ranks; and this time kept them apart, standing still. And there was Maeve, with that intensely black hair, that white face, those red, red lips. She wore for that first appearance the dress that Livia had designed: the dress of white stiff icy lines, decorated with one crimson rose in which, later, she sang the song that now was in a million mouths. She didn't come forward. She just stood there, strangely still, and the dancing girls closed their ranks behind her. As the house rose and cheered, clapped and stamped and whistled, she looked, to me who knew her so well, intolerably lonely and somehow dedicated.

It was a long time since I had last seen the show. I had forgotten how hard Wertheim was working her. In scene after scene, with song, and dance and dialogue, she was the focal point, the personality on which all pivoted, and she threw herself into it that night with a self-abnegation that I did not remember to have noticed in her rendering of the part before. Do you think it strange that in such a production as this—light, frothy, bubble after gay bubble— a woman could literally be *giving* all that was in her? Then you have understood neither Maeve nor the nature of an inspired artist. I felt as I watched her that all the passionate sorrow that was in her heart, all the grief for dead men and for those who were about to die that I knew obsessed and burdened her, was here transmuted into the provision of the most perfect moments which she had it in her to create. This was the only assuagement she could offer to those on the dolorous way, and she offered it with every particle of her art and every fibre of her being.

Only once did she come on to the stage alone, and that was when

she sang *When it's with you, it's Wonderful.* The song preceded the fall
of the curtain at the end of the first part of the show, and I knew it
was now I should see Oliver. Maeve had told me how for some time
Wertheim had been working a new trick—turning a spotlight for a
moment here and there upon members of the audience so that the
song seemed to be personally addressed. Maeve hated it. "Oh, Man!
It's bad enough, that song, without seeing some poor face shining
at you and drinking in the words. There was one in the stalls, with
a great red scar across his forehead. I dreamed about him. I dream
about lots of them."

The curtain went up and there she was, on the stage that was
darkened of all light save the blue cone that fell upon her white, still,
lonely figure. The stiff satin folds of the dress seemed to have icy
edges. She was very remote and withdrawn, and the silence of the
audience as her small, faintly husky voice floated out into the dark
of the auditorium emphasised this. All the thousands there who
for an hour and more had been teased and titillated and shocked
into laughter and charmed with superb arrangements of form and
colour were now intent and withdrawn, held lightly in the hollow
of Maeve's little hand.

She didn't stir. She stood in the attitude I have called hieratic,
her arms hanging down, her hands cupped together before her, her
eyes closed.

*All by myself the night seems long,*
*And the stairs are hardly worth climbing,*
*But when it's with You, it's Wonderful.*

It was on that third line that Wertheim's spotlight rayed through
the dark of the theatre, found a box, and lighted up the face of Oliver.
He must have been recognised by hundreds of people. His photograph had been in all the papers. The illustrated weeklies had run

him—"Captain Oliver Essex, V.C., dining at Frederico's." "Captain Oliver Essex, V.C., with Miss Livia Vaynol. A happy snap in the Green Park"—all that sort of thing; but so deep was the enchantment of Maeve's singing that not a sound broke the silence of the house.

There they were: the two who had played together on the lawn at The Beeches, the two who had swum and sailed and wrangled at Heronwater: Maeve twenty-four, Oliver twenty, each famous now, each the sort of personality that in those fevered and distraught days could bring the thousands to gape. On each a spotlight rested: on Maeve a blue and softened ray, on Oliver a harsh white light that made him blink. But between them was a great space of darkness.

I could see that Livia Vaynol was sitting at Oliver's side. I could see that what Maeve had told me of him was the simple truth: there was something frightening about Oliver now. I turned my glasses upon the remembered face, and it held little that I could remember. The upward pull at the side of one eye, the downward pull of the mouth, had changed the whole aspect of the face grotesquely, and everything of youthful softness was gone from it for ever. What had been good looks of a most melting sort had been changed to a startling mature beauty, scratched, damaged and half-effaced, sinister even, as Maeve had said, but daunting by its harsh rigid composition of lines that all had meaning. I watched him blink with annoyance, take up his cap from the floor of the box and hold it before his eyes. The action showed another wound: a livid scar that ridged the back of the hand.

Maeve sang on, and now she opened her eyes and looked at Oliver, seemed to be singing to him alone. And now and then, over the top of his cap, Oliver looked at Maeve.

*When it's with You, it's Wonderful,*
*The most wonderful thing in the world.*

The song ended, the curtain swung down, and pandemonium broke loose. Half the crowd shouted "Maeve! Maeve!" and half shouted "Essex!" The curtains parted and Maeve appeared. People waved their programmes, waved their handkerchiefs, stood on seats and shouted "Maeve!" "Essex!" "Essex!" "Maeve!" The house lights were still dimmed. The spotlight remained upon Oliver's box. He sat for a long time, impassive and unsmiling, till someone shouted "Three cheers for the hero!" He got them; and then stood up, unsmiling still, and raised a hand in a stern greeting to the mob. Then he turned and bowed stiffly towards Maeve. She dropped in a curtsey, then blew him a kiss, which set the house howling with delight, and then the curtain fell. The lights came up in the auditorium. Certainly Wertheim knew what a hero was worth.

At the final curtain, Maeve gathered up the bouquets—the bouquets which would contain the notes that broke her heart. Proposals of marriage, invitations to dine, to dance, to fill in this way and that the brief interlude between one slice of hell and another. Invitations, too, from the War Office *embusqués* and the meat contractors and little Dolly Daydream officers whose unsullied uniforms were worn on adventurous inspections of mills and factories and workshops. Maeve was a giver—a giver without stint—but she knew where to give.

Her dressing-room was cluttered with flowers when I went round, and cluttered with the customary mob of men and women. The bright spot was burning again on her cheek. She was at once animated, gay, and dead tired. But no one there save myself seemed to notice the tiredness. They all had their demands to make on her spirit and vitality and she denied them nothing. I put my arm through hers and drew her aside. "Come along home," I said. "Leave all these people for once."

I don't know what she would have answered, but at that moment Wertheim came bustling into the room. With him were Oliver and

Livia Vaynol. I only noticed then that Oliver's very uniform was no longer the uniform of the stripling I had last seen. He wore it as though proud of its shabby distinction: the leathern patches on elbows and cuffs, the old dim stains of use and weather. He spoke to no one, he smiled at no one, but the chattering crowd in the room instinctively parted to give him passage.

I saw that he had something of an *entourage*. As well as Livia Vaynol, three or four men and women came in behind him. One of them, I now saw, was Pogson, metamorphosed, but not so completely, so incredibly, as Oliver. Pogson looked fitter, less gross and loathsome. He was the breezy officer, monocle in eye, laugh ready and hearty.

The last thing I had expected was that Oliver would appear in the dressing-room. I cursed Wertheim in my heart for bringing him: he had known I was there. The situation was beyond me, but not beyond Maeve. Oliver must have seen me, but she gave him the opportunity to appear not to have done so. She slipped quickly in front of me and went to meet him with hand outstretched. Other people closed in behind her. I was able to maintain a decent pretence of being obscured. But between heads, over shoulders, I was able to see all that happened.

Maeve greeted him radiantly, as though he were a long lost lover. She had never looked more charming. "I'm so glad you came round," she said. "I hoped you would."

Oliver looked round for somewhere to lay his hat, contemptuously moved aside a bouquet or two, and put it on the table. "It was a good show," he said brusquely. "I congratulate you."

"Oliver, old boy, introduce your pals," Pogson said. "I've never met Miss O'Riorden, you know." He screwed the glass into his slightly bulging eye and ogled Maeve.

"Oh, yes, you have, Poggy," Oliver answered, "but you wouldn't remember it. You were tight—leaning against a lamp-post."

He said it without a smile, cuttingly, cruelly; and Maeve said: "If we met, we certainly were never introduced, and I'm sure I don't remember even the meeting. So do your duty, Oliver."

"Major Pogson," Oliver said briefly, and introduced the other people who were with him. One of them was a Pogson, too—one of "Pogson's people." But Oliver looked as if he didn't give a damn for Pogson's people now.

"Look, Maeve," he said. "I want to take you out to supper. Can you manage it?"

"But I'd love it!" Maeve cried, clapping her hands.

"Bravo!" Pogson shouted. "We'll make it a party. Livia, Polly, Jack—are you all on?"

There was a delighted chorus of approval. Everyone was "on."

Oliver looked at them with the cold, almost insolent, stare that seemed to be now his customary expression. The lifted eye and the slightly twisted lip gave it a sort of savage authority. He picked up the cloak that was over the chair near which Maeve was standing. "This yours?" he asked curtly.

She nodded, and he put it around her and took up his cap. "Come, then. I've got a cab outside. Excuse me, Poggy, I don't feel like a crowd tonight."

Again the crowd opened for him. Maeve put her hand on his arm. "Good-night, Livia," she said.

I had thought of Livia at the moment when Oliver was putting the cloak round Maeve's shoulders. I wondered if she recalled the occasion that flashed to my mind: that night when first she had met him—a wet and muddy schoolboy in disgrace. While he changed, she and Maeve and I were waiting for him—waiting to go to dinner at the Midland Hotel in Manchester. Then he came, and while Maeve helped me to my feet, for I was lame, he took up Livia's cloak and put it round her shoulders.

As this memory invaded my mind, I watched her face, saw her eyes narrow, scrutinising Maeve and Oliver with the wary vigilance of a cat. Oliver seemed unaware of the scrutiny. He seemed unaware of Livia. But Maeve saw all. She must have seen the spasm of hatred that shot across Livia's face when she said "Good-night"—a spasm instantly suppressed as Livia "poofed" at her hair and turned with a quick laugh to the others of the party. "Well, are we going on anywhere?" she asked.

The other Pogson—not Oliver's "Poggy"—a prosperous-looking beefy chap in full evening kit, said: "Well, I'm damned. That's what I call a bit thick. He's doing the God Almighty all right, isn't he?"

Poggy said: "Well, I leave him to it, for one. A, he's earned it, and B, you don't catch me across his path."

He buttoned up his stylish British warm—a resplendent garment so bright that there was a hint of salmon-pink in it. "Well, I'm for bye-byes. Won't hurt us for once."

The other Pogson and the all but anonymous Jack and Polly stood sulky and undecided for a moment, then they all drifted away, Poggy asking over his shoulder: "You staying here, Livia?"

"For a while," she said; but I could see that this was only a ruse to be alone, to have done with them. She didn't want Oliver's crowd: she wanted Oliver; and now that these others were gone she could go, too, to wonder what had happened: to make what she could of the fact that Oliver had walked out as though she didn't exist and as though Maeve existed in a very lively fashion indeed.

I didn't go home at once. I wandered through the darkened streets: darkened, that is, of lamplight. But there was a full moon that cast shadows. It had an effect of great strangeness. You didn't expect to see the pale wash of moonlight lying along one side of a street in the middle of London; the darkness of shadow on the other. You had looked up sometimes, and there, far above the roar and dazzle of the streets, alien and remote, was a moon impotent to leave its silvery impress. But now, there it was, quietly triumphing over the blare and gabble that had been obliged for once to efface themselves.

My wanderings brought me, at about midnight, into Bond Street. It was there that I noticed the long fingers of the searchlights feeling their way across the sky. I paused to watch them for a few moments. Beautiful and damnable. Then the bark of anti-aircraft guns broke out. I could see nothing of the prey those lovely tentacles of light were trying to seize, the intruder at whom those watchdog guns were barking. But he was there. A bomb crashed...another. They seemed a long way off, but I might as well get a roof over my head. Not that a roof would be much good if the fellows up there...But somehow one irrationally preferred to be under a roof. It would keep off splinters, anyway.

I turned into Bruton Street, and there was Livia Vaynol. Impossible for me to avoid her, or for her to avoid me. We were face to face. Indeed, my hat was off, I had said "I beg your pardon" before I saw it was Livia.

She gave a little uneasy laugh, glanced up at the sky. "It looks as though I ought to be getting home," she said.

"It's a longish way, isn't it? You're welcome to a chair in my flat and a drink till this is over."

She hesitated a moment, then: "Thanks," she said, "but I think one's as safe in the street as anywhere, don't you? I'll just plod along."

"Sure?"

"Yes. D'you know what I've been doing? Keeping on the shadowed side of the street so that they"—she jerked her finger upwards—"shan't see me. I didn't know I was doing it. It's just struck me. What extraordinary things our minds do! Well, good-night."

She turned into Bond Street, and I went on down Bruton Street to my flat. What on earth was she doing here? I wondered. Waiting for Oliver, I suppose; waiting for Oliver to bring Maeve home.

I mixed myself a drink, lit a pipe, and sat there with no light but the dim fire-glow, thinking of Livia waiting in the street, waiting for Oliver. The Oliver, I guessed, who would now mean so much more to her: the hero, the man of the moment. And I found that I was thinking of her without emotion, without love, without so much as the pity one would accord the discarded mistress of a comedy. It seemed incredible that I had told Maeve a few hours ago that I would marry Livia if I could. Now I knew that I had been lying—lying to her, lying to myself, to keep alive a romantic notion that now dangled before me with the sawdust dribbling from its punctured artificiality. All very well, I saw clearly in that disillusioning morning hour, with the guns still barking beyond my window, all very well to cherish the notion of love lying like the Sleeping Beauty this more than two years dead but ready to be awakened by a kiss. But what if the Sleeping Beauty is really a lovely lifelike corpse that crumbles to dust at the breath of reality? And I knew that that was what had happened, that those few words in the street, that confrontation that had not quickened my pulse, or speeded my heart, or tied my tongue, called the emotional bluff that I had been playing on myself too long.

The raid lasted a long time. More than one airship came over that night. I felt undisturbed, aware of nothing but a sense of the hopeless boredom of this war that had gone on too long, A war that brought you to this senseless level of a beast crouched in the dark of a burrow. My only concern was for Maeve. I couldn't go to bed till she had returned. Presently the gunfire died to a receding mutter, and I lit my lamp and took up a book. At about three o'clock I heard a taxi stop in the street. Then there was Maeve's step on the stair. It stopped outside my door. She tapped and came in.

"Late hours, sir!" she said with mock gravity. Her eyes were dancing. All her face was animated.

I knocked my pipe out into the fire that had withered to a few warm ashes, and yawned. "I was just going to bed."

"You weren't by any chance waiting up for me?"

"Well—"

She came right into the room, put her arms round my neck and kissed me. "Good-night," she said. "I've had a lovely time."

Oliver and Maeve made an even more attractive pair for the picture-papers than Oliver and Livia had done. "Captain Oliver Essex, V.C., and Miss Maeve O'Riorden, the popular star of *Choose Your Partner,* as our camera man saw them supping somewhere in Soho."

There was plenty of that sort of thing. They looked well: Oliver's upright six-foot-one clothed in rusty uniform, Maeve quite absurdly small-looking beside him, but exquisite in face and clothes.

They were everywhere together. "You see," Maeve said to me with frank pride, "I'm *someone.* Who's ever heard of Livia Vaynol, except a few people in the theatre? It flatters him to be seen about with Maeve O'Riorden."

I suppose that was how she did it. Oliver had been given a temporary job at home. It seemed to leave him plenty of leisure for suppers, dances, dinners, charity matinées and all the flim-flam of the time.

One day I ran into Dermot, and he said: "What the hell's all this about Maeve and Oliver? What's going on? Don't these emancipated children tell parents anything nowadays?"

He had a cheap and scabby paper crushed in his hand. He opened it out and jabbed a long finger at a picture of Maeve, wearing very little—one of *Choose Your Partner*'s publicity pictures. Underneath was the line: "Rumour has it that pretty Maeve O'Riorden has chosen her partner," and a few paragraphs lower down it was innocently stated that "Captain Oliver Essex, V.C., hero-son of famous novelist Essex, is much seen nowadays in company with Maeve O'Riorden."

"Well, what's it all about?" Dermot repeated. "Damn it, Bill, I don't have to pretend to you. I don't like Oliver—V.C. or no V.C. And what about that Vaynol woman?"

"Say what you like about her. That won't hurt me now."

He looked sideways at me sharply. "Good! I'm glad to hear that. Sheila'll be glad too. Has Oliver chucked her?"

"I'm not in Oliver's confidence," I said bitterly. "But it appears that they don't any longer go about together."

"And he and Maeve do?"

"Yes."

"Well—do you like it?"

"Romantically, it should be perfect. Children of lifelong friends join hearts and hands. But I hate it. I hate it like hell."

We were walking on the Embankment. We stopped and looked at one another, with the gulls cat-calling overhead and the grey river sliding by. Dermot leaned his elbows on the granite parapet. "Neither do I like it," he said slowly. "No good will come of it. As sure as that river is flowing to the sea."

He looked despondently at the water for a moment, then said: "Bill, will you speak to her?"

"I?"

"Yes. It's a damned hard thing to say, but honest to God I think she looks up to you more than to her own father. You see, she's— she's never forgiven me for Rory." He took hold of the sleeve of my overcoat and appealed to me: "Will you do this for me now? We don't want anything to go wrong there, do we—either of us?"

I promised him that I would speak to Maeve.

But I put it off. Again and again I put it off. Maeve and I had been shifted by the war into different worlds. We rarely met now at lunch, as we had been used to do: there were so many other claims on her time. There was nowhere else where I might meet her. I did my job each day at the Propaganda Ministry—Information I think they called it—and at night I was glad enough to withdraw into my own thoughts. Thank God, the war caused me no physical discomfort, and if I live to see another, I shall do my best to ensure that that causes me no discomfort either. I shall always escape to the best of my ability from the enterprises of lunatics. I had enough to eat and drink, there was a fire to sit by and a lamp to light, and I made the best of these things as a refuge from the boredom, depression and exalted lunacy of the time. At night I hardly ever left my room. I discovered in myself an aptitude for the life of the recluse; I looked forward with keen expectation all day to the curtained, lamp-lit evening. I was writing a book which I did not think would ever be published, and which, indeed, never has been published; a simple record of the life about me. Read now, it has the quality of a fantastic nightmare recalled in the disillusioning light of day.

Withdrawing thus more and more into the quality and condition of an observer of events in which he refused to participate, I found for the first time that even Maeve had drifted a little outside the orbit of my concern. That arid little contact with Livia Vaynol on the night of the air-raid had left me feeling extraordinarily contented, like some Christian from whose shoulders there has dropped an emotional burden which he sees with a gasp of pleasure and surprise he had for long been carrying without reason. Now I was free. Now I could hug my seclusion not as one who escapes from what he fears to find but as one who knows all that is to be found and from it turns gladly aside. In this state of mind, I allowed the weeks to drift by, and forgot my promise to Dermot. Or, if I remembered it, I said to myself that Maeve was not the girl to make a fool of herself. She had no reason to love Livia Vaynol. If she found Oliver so easily detachable, I couldn't blame her for detaching him. She would know how far to go.

# 31

On a morning of early January, 1917, I was awakened by a banging on my bedroom door. I sat up in bed with a start, sniffed the frosty air, and got back into the blankets, deciding that the noise was an imagination of dream. The banging came again, more urgently. "Who's there?" I shouted.

"Me—Annie."

I stepped out of bed into the piercing cold. The bedside lamp showed me that it was five o'clock. I slipped on a dressing-gown and opened the door. There was Annie Suthurst, clutching a shapeless garment of red flannel across her chest and looking more upset than I had ever seen her.

"Eh, Mr. Essex! Ah'm that scared. Miss Maeve hasn't coom home. Ah can't get a wink o' sleep."

Her fear communicated itself to my own heart, but I said reasonably: "She's often late, Annie. I expect she's dancing."

"Dancing! Don't be daft, man! Who'd be dancing at five in t'morning?"

It didn't seem unusual, in that strange hectic world from which I was withdrawing more and more. But I let that pass. "You'd better make yourself a cup of tea," I suggested.

"Tea! Ah've done nowt but drink tea all t'neet."

"Well, perhaps you'll make me a cup," I suggested.

"No need to mak' it. Pot's on t'hob."

So I went up to Annie's room, more and more affected by the concern in her face. "Now you'd better go to bed," I said when I had drunk the tea. "You can do no good by sitting up. If there's anything to be done, we shan't be able to do it for a few hours anyway."

"Ah'll not go to bed," she said obstinately. "Ah'll sit here till Ah know what's happened to Maeve. No good, Ah reckon."

So we sat there together, in that room containing the memorials of Annie's long-dead husband, and we passed the time by playing draughts. Our pretended absorption in the game did not prevent us from keeping our ears skinned for every murmur of sound from the dark, bitterly cold street.

Maeve came in at seven o'clock. She looked dead tired, yet excited, almost exalted. She threw her hat and coat upon Annie's bed, then sat on the bed herself. "For the love of Mike, Annie, give us a cup of tea," she said. Then with a pale smile: "I find you two in very compromising circumstances."

Neither Annie nor I spoke. Annie fussed about, making a fresh pot of tea. I looked at Maeve, trying to decipher the mood of excitement that was on her. The silence made her uneasy. She got up and walked about the room for a while, then burst out: "Oh, why do they send troop trains away at such a godless hour of the morning!"

"Troop trains?"

"Yes. Trains with troops in them. You know, men who are going out to be killed, wounded, shot to bits. You ought to go and see them some day, Mr. William Essex. You ought to see all sorts of things, you damned old mole, shutting yourself up night after night, hiding from real things. Oh, I know it's all horrible, contemptible, a complete breakdown of all the lovely things that keep the world cushy for you. But all the same, you ought to see it. It's happening, you know, however much you shut your eyes."

The colour that I disliked had come back to her cheeks. Her eyes were burning. I remembered the time when she had stood before Dermot, shouting: "You've killed Rory! You've killed Rory!" So she stood before me now, her hands clenched at her sides. Then the strength seemed to go out of her. She sank into a chair and murmured: "I've just been seeing Oliver off."

"Get her to bed," I said; and Annie nodded like a wise old hen over Maeve's bowed head.

That was a Sunday morning. I went back to bed, but I didn't sleep. At nine o'clock Annie, who had had no sleep at all, brought me my breakfast in bed. "You'll need it, Mr. Essex, after a neet like that," she said, as though I, not she, had kept vigil. "Miss Maeve's sleeping, an' Ah'm going to let 'er sleep an' all." She nodded grimly, and drew the curtains, letting in the light of the pale frosty morning.

"Tell me as soon as she's awake," I said.

I knew a man who would lend me a car, and as soon as I had had breakfast I went and borrowed it. I had not driven for years, but I would chance that. There was not much traffic on the roads in those days when petrol was hard to come by. I drove the car back to Berkeley Square and waited for Maeve to wake.

It was two o'clock when Annie came to say that Maeve was sitting up in bed, having breakfast. She looked intolerably small and fragile, propped up by pillows, nibbling a piece of toast.

"This is the first time I've seen Maeve O'Riorden in bed since she was so small that there was no thrill in it."

"Was I a lovely baby, Bill?" She stretched out her hand to lay it on mine. I put it firmly back on her lap.

"You keep that hand to help some food to your mouth. You look half-starved."

"Oh, Man! Svelte...vivacious...you'll never make a gossip-writer." She obstinately put her hand on mine again. "Mr. William Essex, it occurs to me that I was rude to you last night."

"Last night, indeed! You've lost your sense of time, my girl. And if you were rude, you're going to atone for it. Have you any engagements today?"

"As it happens, no."

"Marvellous!"

"Isn't it?"

"Yes. And if you had, you would have had to cancel them."

She raised her eyebrows in a question.

"Because your Uncle Bill has got you booked for the rest of the day. When you've finished breakfast, dress up warm and report to me."

She came down sheathed in a coat of blue-grey fur, with dark blue violets pinned at her breast. The collar went up as a cosy-looking background to the dark hair on which a fur Cossack hat was pulled down.

"Good! You'll need all that. It's an open car."

"Then put a muffler round your neck," she ordered.

I did so, and, plentifully swathed, we went down to the car. It was three o'clock. The sun had already lost its strength and was declining, an orange disc, towards the horizon of roofs. The frost, which it had not wholly vanquished all day, was getting the upper hand.

There was no wind. The cold air tingled in our faces as we drove westwards. It was a small two-seater car, and Maeve snuggled comfortably into my side, under the rugs.

Neither of us said a word for a long time. I think she knew what was in my mind: to have done for a while with words, with gadding, with rushing, with all the fevered circumstances in which she had been living. We were together, and we comforted one another by being together, with the wind on our faces, and the hedges slipping by with the tall leafless elms rising out of them and etching their lacy patterns on the pale winter air.

After a long time Maeve said: "Miss Maeve O'Riorden presents her compliments to Mr. William Essex and begs to know whether his prolonged silence denotes continued resentment."

"Resentment!" I snorted. "I know you too well, my dear, to be resentful. I know what these months are meaning to you—what you're doing and suffering. But don't let's even talk about it. Just for these few hours."

She smiled gratefully and gave a long relaxing stretch of the body. The sun went down; the frost sharpened its edge; the western sky became a rich smother, damson in colour, velvet in texture. An owl, with short stubby-looking wings, drifted silently, ahead of the car, from an elm on one side of the road to an elm on the other.

"'The owl, for all his feathers, was a-cold,'" said Maeve. "Bill, these are fine feathers, but I'm a bit shiversome. What do we do about that?"

"You should eat more food," I said pedantically. "However, I'll deal with that."

We were under the shoulders of the Berkshire downs which ahead and to our right loomed up darkly against the sky's last light. I stopped at the next village we came to. There was an old coaching inn on the high street, and I remembered that once, driving back from Cornwall, Martin had stopped the car there and we had eaten a famous dinner. I didn't know how the war had affected the place, but I had had it in mind as our objective, and it did not fail us. The landlord seemed surprised to have any custom at all, outside the bar. He spoke disparagingly of his resources, but said he would do his best. He led us to a small room where a fire was burning and a lamp hung by a hook from an immense black beam as thick as my thigh. The red curtains drawn across the windows gave us a fine sense of intimacy. Presently two old-fashioned silver covers were set on the table. Under one were thick hearty rashers of ham grilled to a golden brown, flanked by potatoes thinly sliced and fried. The other yielded half a dozen fried eggs, and this was a meal with which we were well content. We drank beer. I had never seen Maeve drink beer before. She boasted that it was one of her chief accomplishments, raised the large silver tankard to her red lips, and smiled happily at me over the top. It was a joy to see her eat, heartily and well, here in this quiet room, where we were scores of miles from anyone who could say: "Shall we dance?" or "Where are we going on to now?" or "Do let's fix something for lunch tomorrow."

The landlord looked in and asked: "All right, sir?"

"Excellent. They're not starving you down here."

"We manage," he said. "There's a nice bit of cheese..."

"A nice bit of cheese is the cue I'm longing for," said Maeve.

It was good Stilton, and when we had done we had that feeling that now is the time to draw in a chair to the fire and talk. So we did that. I lit my pipe and gave Maeve a cigarette, and as she lay back with her feet to the blaze, blowing a small smoke-ring through a large one, I said: "So Oliver's gone back?"

She nodded. "I knew it was coming, but I didn't want to bother you with it, Bill. You don't mind, do you? It would have been— no good, you know."

"Yes. I see that. Would you like to tell me anything about Oliver? You've been seeing a lot of him."

"Every day. You know how it started, don't you? That night you were at the theatre? I wanted to take him away from Livia. Because you wanted Livia."

So that was it! Of course that was it, you fool! Couldn't you see it without having it put into words? And I hadn't wanted Livia after all. I couldn't find a word to say. I was suddenly aware of myself as a black selfish incubus, obscuring the clarity of three young lives: Oliver, Maeve, Livia; and myself now wanting, now not wanting, an ageing inconstant interferer, sending all awry. I licked my dry lips before I could speak again.

"You succeeded. You certainly had all Oliver's attention."

"I succeeded!" she said bitterly. "Only too well. I had no idea he'd be in England all this time. I thought it would be a short leave, and back he'd go and little damage done. Then he got his home job, and what could I do? I had to go on with it. You can't cut a man off because his leave's been lengthened. Not even in these days when everybody seems more or less mad."

"Didn't you *want* to go on with it? Wasn't it—agreeable?"

She got up and began to pace the room in agitation. The flush came back to her cheeks. She threw her cigarette impatiently into the fire. All the old restless symptoms that I had hoped to banish for this one day broke out again. I rose and put my arms about her shoulders and tried to calm her. "Maeve...I'm sorry...I didn't want to talk about upsetting things. Let's leave this now. Let's make this one day of peace."

She put me aside. "Sit down," she said. "It's no good trying to shut things up. Let's have this out, Bill."

She pushed me down into my chair, then said: "I know I made a mistake. That's what made me angry with you this morning. Because I'm angry with myself, see? You don't love Livia. You don't want Livia."

I shook my head miserably.

"You've been a long time finding it out," she said.

"I didn't think you knew."

She almost snorted in her impatience. "You didn't! Does it take much finding out? Does a man who loves a woman and is pursuing her spend all his leisure time stewing in a flat? For God's sake, Bill, give me credit for a little common sense. And there I was landed with Oliver for weeks and weeks. He wouldn't go back to Livia. Heavens, no! There you are: grand theatre, isn't it? Heroine's generous gesture recoils on her own head. How do we go on from there? You're a playwright. Tell me."

What was there to tell? Abased, I had nothing to say. Presently Maeve sat down and lighted a cigarette, more composed. "Don't think I've been suffering," she said, "except from a flat feeling that I had made a fool of myself. You've done a great deal for me in your time, Bill, and here was the golden opportunity to do something for you. It wasn't nice to see it wasted. But Oliver's not bad."

I looked up at that more hopeful note. She smiled at me like someone encouraging a despondent child. "Light your pipe," she said. "No, he's not bad," she went on, "You know I never really liked him, but at least I've liked him better this last few weeks than ever before. He's more real now. There's something rather terrifying in his realness. At times I felt frightened with him. He would be silent and brooding for hours together, melancholy-mad. But at least he's not the little boy in black silk pyjamas. You remember that odious little boy?"

"I do."

"Well, he's dead, believe me. Oliver's on his own feet now."

"Tell me about this morning. You frightened Annie Suthurst out of her wits."

"I ought to have let her know," Maeve apologised. "I didn't intend to be out all night. The train went at six. I'd promised Oliver to dance after the show. We danced till about two, and then when I wanted to go home that Pogson man proposed that we should all go on to Oliver's hotel. There was quite a party of us. It was four o'clock before we knew where we were, and then Oliver said he saw no sense in going to bed at all, so we stayed there till it was time to go to the station."

I remembered my promise to Dermot, and I asked point-blank: "Does Oliver want to marry you?"

"They all do," she said wearily, "but I suppose I'm not a marrying sort. Hadn't we better be getting back?"

I packed her up in the rugs. We had not been travelling half an hour before she was sound asleep, her head resting on my shoulder.

A week later Oliver was reported missing, believed killed. A few days after that he was reported to be a prisoner. During the days between the two reports Maeve was in a daze. She had cut out a great many of her promiscuous engagements and lunched with me every day. We were lunching together when a man I knew at the War Office rang me up to give me the first news that Oliver was safe. Maeve broke down and cried. Then she put her arms round my neck and kissed me. "Oh, Bill," she sobbed, "I couldn't have borne it if he'd been dead. You pretend to be so cold and restrained, it breaks my heart to look at you. But you love him so much. It would have killed you. You do love him, don't you?"

"So much," I said firmly, "that I wish to God we were all twenty years younger. I might make a better fist of things. I haven't been a conspicuous success, have I?"

"Oh, you dear, you dear. I can't bear to hear you say that." She was in my arms, her eyes, swimming with tears, a foot from my own. "Everything's gone against you since Nellie died."

"I've been my own fool and made my own folly."

"Don't, don't! I couldn't stand it if life made you bitter. It could all have been so different. I love you so much."

Her head sank on to my shoulder, and my grip about her tightened.

At that she thrust me away. "But now—it's too late."

She strained her tear-marked face back from mine and gazed at me wildly. Then she ran out of the room and up to her own flat.

Towards the end of February I received a letter from Dermot. It contained some trivial message which he asked me to pass on to Maeve. After breakfast I ran up to her flat, and went straight into the sitting-room. The door leading thence to the bedroom was open, and I could see Annie Suthurst standing outside the door of the bathroom which opened off the bedroom. She was bent down in a listening attitude, with her ear to the door. Her face was drawn and haggard. Presently she saw me and beckoned me to the bathroom door, putting her finger to her lips to enjoin silence. I heard the sound of a faint moan, followed by painful retching.

Annie took my arm, walked me through the bedroom to the sitting-room and then sank into a chair. She rocked to and fro, stricken with grief. "The same yesterday morning, Mr. Essex. God help us! Oh, Miss Maeve! Miss Maeve!"

The man whose car I had borrowed to take Maeve for a drive was Sir Charles Blatch, a physician who lived in Wimpole Street. Blatch, like myself, was a member of the Savile Club. We had nodded to one another occasionally, and then one day he sat in a chair next to mine in the smoking-room and began to talk. He knew my books well and confessed that he had seen *Every Street* more than once. I have always found it difficult to resist an admirer, and Blatch was frankly that: an admirer of my own work and of Maeve's. When we had talked for a time, I found that he wanted me to do something for him. He had written a book. I was on my guard at once. They were to be met so often, these people who flattered your work and then asked you to read theirs. But somehow I couldn't take Blatch that way. He was an honest man. He spoke so diffidently about what he had written and seemed so sincerely to value my opinion that I consented to read his manuscript.

I liked the book, and I liked the way it was written; and I was able to arrange with my own publishers to publish it without alteration. The book had a modest success, and Blatch was very pleased about it all.

There was a chapter on euthanasia. Blatch was a believer in it. He wrote of the many men coming back from the war, doomed to a maimed and tortured life, who would prefer to end their days rather than live on as grim wrecks of the men they had been. "Uneasy ghosts," he wrote, "tethered by the frailest threads to the ruined habitations that once were those proud mansions their bodies, how gladly many of them would welcome the hand at once courageous and pitying enough to give them release."

Our friendship warmed a little, though it never became really deep. He invited me to dinner at his house in Wimpole Street. He was a rugged, thick-set fellow with strong hairy hands and a clean-shaven granitic face. He was a widower, and his only son was serving in the Air Force. There wasn't much in his life to make him cheerful, and he wasn't. He was not pessimistic or depressing: sombre is the word for him. He was strong as an oak, and his character seemed as umbrageous.

There were no other guests, and after dinner we sat in his small oak-panelled library with a decanter of whisky on a table between us. Like me, he smoked a briar pipe. He was a good talker, and he liked talking shop, but as it was not my own shop I didn't mind that. He got on to euthanasia, which was something of a bug with him, and from that to suicide.

"Have you read Richard Middleton on the subject?" he asked.

I recalled that Middleton had himself committed suicide, but said that I had not read the essay he referred to. He took a blue volume down from the shelves and flicked over the leaves with his powerful stubby fingers. "Here you are: 'We can forgive a man for booing or creating a disturbance in the theatre of life, but we cannot forgive him for going out with a yawn before the play is over.'"

"That's true enough," Blatch said, sitting back in his chair with a finger still in the pages of the book, "barring 'with a yawn.' It's not only boredom that leads to suicide. Frustration, more often, I should say."

He seemed to consider this for a while, then put the book on the table, pulled at his pipe, and said: "I should feel completely frustrate if Roger were killed." (Roger was his son.) "My wife's dead, I have no other relative in the world. You can tell me there's my work. Well——" Then he dismissed the work with a wave of the hand. "No. It wouldn't do. I couldn't live without a sense of human continuity.

"Mind you," he said with a smile, pushing a tobacco jar towards me, "I'm not contemplating suicide, even in the eventuality I mentioned. But, as a possibility, it can't be dismissed. And," he said, looking at me narrowly, "if it ever came to that, I should be the only man, I should think, who exemplified in his own life two things I believe in: that in certain circumstances a doctor should be allowed to take life, and in certain circumstances a man should be allowed to take his own."

He had gone too far to draw back. He saw that as soon as the words were out of his mouth. "Dangerous ground—eh, Essex?" he said.

"Very," I agreed. "Shut up if you want to; but, if there's a story you want to get off your chest, here I am. I understand the importance of confession, and I can be as dumb as a Trappist."

He told me the story: of his early life of poverty in Birmingham, of the struggles of himself and his mother after his father had died. There was a little back-street shop in the story, and there was the indomitable courage of the boy and the woman, his taking at last of his medical degree, and all the wild storm of hope raised thereby.

"Now—don't you see, Essex?—now she was going to have everything—comfort, growing at last to affluence: servants, a carriage, God knows what. You know how dreams go when you're young. But all she got was inoperable cancer, agony…"

Blatch poured himself another whisky, drank, and put the glass down with a steady hand.

"I gave her the means to die," he said.

Neither of us spoke for a moment, then Blatch continued: "It took me a long time to do it. She begged me to do it, and at last—well, I did it." He paused. "And I got away with it."

"Suicide," he said after another thoughtful pause, "mind you, not any suicide—not any weak-willed chucking down of a bearable burden—but suicide of the sort I'm thinking of is simply saving someone else the trouble of administering euthanasia. And," he added with his rare smile, "I'm not speaking as a certified medicine man: only as a private disreputable philosopher."

Well, that was Sir Charles Blatch. That cold Sunday morning when I called to borrow the car I found him alone in his library, standing with his back to the fire, reading a letter. "Talk of the devil," he said, "or rather of a close friend of the devil's—" He went on reading. "Excuse my reading this. It's only the hundredth time. It's from Roger."

When he had finished, he said: "This young devil has met your Maeve O'Riorden. He talks about hopes of leave and says"—Blatch read from the letter—"'We must go again to see that show *Choose Your Partner*, so as soon as I give you a date, book seats. Book for every night I'm home if you like. We've got all Maeve's songs for the mess gramophone, and I just can't make the chaps believe I once took her out to dinner. You never knew that yourself, did you? Well...'"

And as Blatch read on, I was able to identify this Roger. I could see Maeve looking through the window into Berkeley Square, talking to me over her shoulder. "You never saw such a boy. He looked about sixteen, with blue eyes and smooth round cheeks." I remembered, too, how Maeve had told me that Roger, seeing some lambs, had said: "My mother'd like to see that." So Blatch's widowerhood was very recent. It had been last April that Roger took Maeve driving. Well—last April—nearly a year. He'd been lucky for an Air Force boy.

"I should like to meet this Maeve of yours," Blatch was saying. "She seems good value."

"She is," I said with conviction. "She's tearing herself to pieces for these boys."

"Well, introduce me some day, will you? I'd like to know her."

*

The thought of Blatch was in the back of my mind as I stood looking down at Annie Suthurst crumpled in a chair. I took her by the shoulders and shook her gently. "Annie! Pull yourself together! Remember, Maeve wants your help now more than ever she did. Are you listening to me?"

She nodded her grey head. "Well, I've got to go out now. Remember, Maeve's in your charge. Do nothing to upset her, and for goodness' sake don't let her know that you suspect anything is wrong. Can you manage now?"

She got up and began to put her face to rights. "Yes, Mr. Essex."

"Good. I shall be lunching with her. Get out of the room as soon as you can. I want a good talk with her. I'll let you know if there's anything you can do. We'll manage this between us."

"Eh, Mr. Essex, it looks to me like summat that's got to manage itself this time."

Uncomfortable words! They were in my head as I sat at the table facing Maeve a few hours later. She was pale as usual, but quite composed. I thought that she had given if anything more than customary care to her appearance. Her dark hair reflected like polished metal a beam of light from the window. The lips were very red on her white still face. Annie put coffee on the table and slid out of the room, giving me an admonitory look from the doorway.

"Have you heard," Maeve asked, "that Livia's gone away?"

I poured out her coffee, shaking my head. Livia's movements seemed of extraordinarily little importance to me then.

"Yes; she's gone to France. Joined some nursing unit or other. Tired of waiting for you, Bill."

"Oh, I don't think that. I don't imagine that she has any more use for me now than I have for her."

She looked at me gravely and said: "So wasteful! So wasteful! What a bad schemer I make. My parts should always be written for me."

"Perhaps they are," I said sententiously.

Her face brightened. "You mean predestination and all that. What must be will be. D'you know, Bill, I'd like to believe that. Do you believe it?"

"It's one of those things you could argue till Doomsday. I don't see how you can ever reach a solution. I'd like to believe myself that I had occasionally by my own free will turned a corner here and there."

She looked crestfallen. "It would be such a comfortable doctrine," she said, " that whatever I did had been prearranged and was unalterable—that I couldn't personally be blamed, *whatever* I did."

*Whatever* I did. God forgive me for the blindness of my heart. There was something tragical in her stillness, in the way her beloved mouth let drop those words; but all I did was to say: "My dear child, I cannot imagine you doing anything very terrible."

"Very terrible—I wonder? Bill, why do you call me your dear child? You've always thought of me as a child, haven't you? I wonder why you should think me a child and Livia a marriageable woman? Have I ceased to please you as I've grown up? D'you prefer to think of me always as a little girl snuggling into your coat?"

"Maeve, my sweet…"

"No, no. Don't protest. I shouldn't blame you if…"

She turned away suddenly, her eyes full of tears. "I just wanted you to tell me that I haven't disappointed you," she sobbed. "You expected so much of me, I know."

I sprang out of my chair. "Disappointed me?" I shouted. And I knew that in all the sad tangle I had made of my life, Maeve stood clear and uncomplicated, the one thing that had never given me a pang, the one presence in which disappointment could never be felt. I crossed the room to her and took her in my arms. "Maeve, my love," I said.

She looked up at me in wonder. "My love," she whispered. "You've never called me that before…my love…"

"Let me call you that always. My love…my love…my love."

I tried to get my face upon hers. She forced her head backwards, away from me, gazing deep into my eyes; and suddenly I saw a look of horror born into her face. She gave a little cry and dragged herself free. She sat down and buried her face in her hands, moaning.

"My love, my sweet," I besought her. "What is the matter? Maeve, I love you. I love you."

"I have loved you always," she murmured, "and I have known I loved you ever since the night we saw the swans flying across the moon. So free…so beautiful…"

"Look at me, Maeve. Look at me now, my dear one, my lovely one."

"God help me, Bill," she said in a sobbing whisper, "I love you so that I could lie down and let you walk on me and the child that's in me."

"I know about that; don't be afraid about that."

"It's not that I'm afraid of. It's you. You didn't want Livia till Oliver wanted her. You didn't want me till Oliver wanted me. What is it about you that seems to prey on young lives? There was something…in your face… It frightened me."

"My dear, you're ill. You're imagining things. God forgive me if my face could bear anything but love for you."

"No, no! It's the look that Oliver's got now—hungry—a look that wants to consume lives. It was the look he had that night… You know that night I told you about? I lied to you. We went back alone to his hotel. This is Oliver's child. You can't have me. Christ! You can't pretend to be the father of your grandchild."

She reached a hand out blindly across the table, and I took it and as blindly stroked it. Presently she raised her head and I could have cried at the wreckage of her face, especially when a pale wisp of smile waked like a ghost amid its desolation. "So there we are, Bill," she said. "There we are." She lifted her free hand and let it fall with a little helpless gesture.

"Maeve, we must talk about this child. What are you going to do? How can I help you?"

"You can't help me. I expect you think I'm a pretty fool."

"God forgive me if I think of anything except how to help you."

"You can't! You can't!" she repeated. "But you do understand, don't you, Bill? You don't despise me?"

"Despise you?" The tears were stinging my eyes. "Could anyone in the world despise you if they knew you as I do?"

"There have been so many of them," she said in a low, rapid voice turning her face away from me. "They've all wanted it, even the ones who were too nice to say so. Some of those were the hardest: they looked so dumbly miserable and hungry. I tried to be everything to them—except that. And I felt it wasn't fair. I felt like a rich man who gives and gives so long as giving won't hurt him. So many of them have died, and I thought what a little thing it would have been, after all. They have been like waves battering me. You know that line in the Bible, Bill—*All Thy waves and Thy billows have gone over me.* I've wakened up in the morning like that—feeling battered and defeated: the gay Maeve O'Riorden, having such a lovely hectic time. Ask the dirty little gossip papers. You'll find it all there—my frivolous, heartless career..."

I stroked her hand. "Hush, my dear. Don't go on with this."

But she went on rapidly: "You know, it had to come. There would be a wave too many. I should be undermined. Well, it happened with Oliver. We danced and danced, and then he asked me to go back to his hotel to have a farewell drink. We went to his room. He didn't say a thing, but just locked the door and stood leaning against it looking at me. He looked frightening, with those wounds of his twitching. I knew what he wanted. I said: 'No. No, Oliver. Please!' He went on looking at me. Then he laughed. 'My God!' he said. 'You women!

You take the cake. You hand us white feathers, you raise hell's delight in our hearts with your leg-shows and lascivious songs, and you expect the whores in the red-lamp houses in France to do the rest for you. There you are then. Good-night.' He flung the key down at my feet and started to undress. It was horrible, filthy, and yet it was true. 'You know, you ought to be a bishop,' he said. 'Bless the banners and hand out tracts on purity. Sublimate your passions, lads, by sticking Germans in the guts. And if you want a nice clean change from that, listen to the Lena Ashwell party singing *A long, long Trail,* or when you're on leave hear Maeve O'Riorden intone *When it's with You, it's Wonderful.* There's the key. Aren't you going?'

"And I couldn't, Bill. I stood there, fascinated. He had taken off his tunic. He kicked the key towards me. 'Go!' he said. 'Go, or by God—' Then he sat down in a chair with his head in his hands and began to sob. I went across and put my hand on his hair, and—and that was it."

"Thank you for telling me." The words sounded idiotic as I looked at the white wreck of Maeve. "Don't think about it any more. Let's consider the present."

"There's only one thing to be done at present. That's go to bed, or I shall be no good tonight."

"Ought you to go on? Shall I ring up Wertheim?"

"Only to wangle a ticket. I'd like to be there tonight. He'll find you a place. Come round and bring me home afterwards. Will you?"

"Shall I try to get a cab?" I asked.

"No. Let's walk."

She put her hand on my arm, and we jostled through a little crowd clustered at the stage door. One man said simply: "Thank you, Miss O'Riorden." Another stuck a book and pencil under her nose. "D'you mind, Miss O'Riorden?"

"Come on," I whispered. "Don't let 'em bother you." But she

stopped and signed the book and showered smiles on the people pressing round her. "I hate to disappoint them," she said.

Then we were free. She took my arm again. "You and your opera-hat!" she teased me, looking up at me overtopping her small fragile figure. "You big important man! You don't frighten me any more."

"Was I ever very frightening?"

She gave my arm a sharp little hug. "Not so very," she said.

We walked in silence for a while, then she said: "Well, well. That's that. That's over now. Was I all right, Bill?"

"Lovely."

"No one would have guessed?"

"Guessed? Oh, that... No, no. No one."

She was very quiet after that, her little hurrying footsteps trying comically to adjust themselves to my long strides. I don't remember that we exchanged another word till we came to the front door. It is those footsteps I shall always remember—like a child's footsteps trying eagerly to keep up.

I have said that her flat was above mine. At my door I said: "Good-night, Maeve. Unless you'd like to come in for a moment. A drink or a chat?"

"No... No, Bill... Bill...?" She took the lapel of my coat and began to twist it in her fingers, looking up into my face. "Say—what you said this afternoon." She whispered: "Say 'My love.'"

"Why, Maeve, my love, my darling," I said, and bent down and took her in my arms. "Sleep well, my love."

I watched her go slowly to the turn of the stairs. "Good-night," I called.

"Good-night. Good-night, Bill. Good-bye."


At seven the next morning Annie Suthurst came knocking at my door. One look at her distraught face set my heart racing. I did not wait for her to speak. She could not speak: she just stood there with her shaking lingers fumbling at a shaking mouth. I pushed past her and ran up the stairs, through the sitting-room to Maeve's bedroom. She lay with one long white arm hanging out of the bed. Her head was fallen a little to one side. The face, framed by the black hair, looked childish and hurt and puzzled.

At eight o'clock I rang up Sir Charles Blatch. He answered the telephone himself, and seemed surprised at my vehemence when I asked him to come round at once. "Yes—urgent—most terribly urgent."

I met him outside the door of my flat, and led him to the next floor. I had told Annie to stay in her own room. Outside the door of Maeve's bedroom I paused. "You have wanted to meet Maeve O'Riorden," I said. I opened the door softly. "There she is."

He went in alone. I shut the door behind him and waited for him in the sitting-room. He joined me about ten minutes later, and sat down beside me on a divan. His big rough-hewn face was moved as though Maeve had been his own child. "Poor little thing," he said, "poor little thing. She looks so small." He sat with one hand spread palm downward on each knee and looked thoughtfully at the floor between his feet. "You know, Essex, in all my practice, that's the first suicide I've seen. You'd think she'd died in her sleep."

"Yes," I said, not looking at him, "if she'd had a weak heart, say. I suppose if she *had* been quietly seeing a doctor—keeping it to herself—for the last twelve months or so, and he had warned her that her heavy work at the theatre, with all this dancing and dining and sleeplessness thrown in, was very dangerous—if she had been seeing, say, you—then you wouldn't be surprised to find she had died in her sleep?"

He gave me a shrewd sidelong look. "No," he said at last, "it would be in the usual course of nature to expect it."

"And in those circumstances, of course, there would be no diffi-culty about granting a death certificate?"

He got up, stood looking down at me, fingering his chin thoughtfully. "I have no record of the case on my books," he said, "because I was charging her nothing. She never came to my place in Wimpole Street. I always saw her here. It was purely a friendly arrangement, because I'd taken such a personal interest in her ever since you introduced us—about a year ago, wasn't it?"

"Yes, about that, I should say."

"You wouldn't have got my car out of me, you know, if I hadn't liked her so much."

"No, of course not. I couldn't have expected it."

"And I grant this death certificate the more readily because I was present when she died. What time did she get home from the theatre last night?"

"Just before midnight."

"She must have been taken queer almost at once, because it was immediately after midnight that you rang me up ... Oh, damn this pretence, Essex, I *was* rung up just after midnight, and I didn't get in till seven. No one on God's earth knows where I've been, and it may as well have been here. I saw her die as I warned her she would die ..."

He strode unhappily about the room. "If she were a nobody ... but she isn't. Think of the stink in the papers ..."

"I had thought of it. And I thought of our talk about suicide. She had good reasons, Blatch."

"The poor child. Tell me some day. Not now, not now. Well, I'll spill no mud on her corpse ... It was veronal ... Who else knows?"

"One old woman who was devoted to her. I'll answer for her, Blatch."

Suddenly he asked with difficulty: "Was there a baby behind this?"

I nodded. He wiped perspiration from his face with a large silk handkerchief. "I was—thinking of Roger," he said. "He tells me he's been about with her."

"It wasn't Roger, Blatch. I knew about Roger. That was a year ago."

"The leave before last. Well, thank God for something." He held out his hand. "Essex, I'm going to commit a crime, and you're conniving at it. Let us both be proud. It will be as decent a piece of work as will be done in England today."

He left me then, and I braced myself for the long ordeal of the day. First, to ring up Dermot…

NOTE.—It would have been impossible to give these particulars if Sir Charles Blatch were still alive. He died soon after his son Roger was killed in 1918. The circumstances of his death were such that it was necessary to hold an inquest at which a verdict was returned of "Death from Misadventure." The posthumous book in which he advocated euthanasia, excused suicide in certain circumstances, and told fully the story of his mother's death, created a sensation. He left no relative, and so no one will be injured by the disclosure here made.

The person to be consulted was Dermot, to whom I had confided the facts only after Sheila's death, which took place in 1930. He offers no objection to this publication.

Part V

## 32

Annie Suthurst asked: "Will you be going out tonight, Mr. Essex?"

I shook my head. "I don't think so, Annie. No: I really don't think I could stand it. They cheered and went mad when the war started. Now they cheer and go mad because it's ended. The two things don't make sense to me."

"It's like Mafeking night," said Annie. "That didn't make sense to me."

It wouldn't. Annie's husband had not lasted as long as Mafeking night.

"I'll make you a nice Lancashire 'ot pot," she said. "When you've 'ad that, just stay in by your own fire and read a book."

And that was what I did, while the dervishes were loose without. When I went from the dining-room to my study, I found the curtains drawn, my chair pulled up to the fire, and my slippers on the fender. There, alongside the chair, was the little table with my pipes and tobacco jar and spectacles. Annie looked after me well.

Too well by a long chalk, I thought, as I settled into the chair. She's making a regular old codger of me. I'm only forty-seven.

I put the spectacles on my nose, reflecting sadly that not so long ago I had exulted because I could do without them and Dermot couldn't.

Well, forty-seven. And turning into a bit of a misanthrope. Feeling more at home in the winter than in the summer, because in the winter there are firelight and drawn curtains and one's own company. Grey now, not only in that spot over the temples that

Maeve used to find attractive, but all over; and putting on no weight with the years: thin as a thread.

Annie came in with coffee. "Now, don't you get up, Mr. Essex."

But I got up, peering at her querulously over the spectacles. "Damn it all, Annie Suthurst," I said, "what are you trying to turn me into! Why shouldn't I get up? Is the creaking of my old bones so distressing to you?"

"Nay, don't harass your carcass, Mr. Essex. Ah'm sure you've got plenty to do in that old office of yours all day long. A rest at neet won't hurt thee. Now, sit down wi' a nice book. Ah'll not worry thee again."

The fact was, of course, that Annie would always spoil me because she had never got over the miracle, as she thought it, that Blatch and I had achieved between us. The shame that had been averted from the memory of her dear Maeve... Annie had proved utterly reliable. Not even to me had she ever mentioned what had happened. We had stood side by side on that day which now seemed far off; that blustery day of late winter when Maeve was buried. On one side of the raw gash in the earth, to which the small body that a week before had been so gaily dancing had already been committed, I stood and held Annie's arm, and on the other Dermot and Sheila stood side by side, not touching one another. Dermot's head was up and his beard thrust forward and the eyes stared out of his pale face beyond and through us all. Sheila alone of us looked steadfastly down into the grave, even after the clods had begun to fall, lost, it seemed, in some reverie stretching back through the years, perhaps to that day when the old Fenian Flynn had held us with his wild eye and wilder tales, and Sheila had cried out suddenly that the child was stirring in her.

And now the child lay there, having herself been quickened with child; and as, with Annie still clinging to my arm, I broke away from the people now putting on their hats and talking together— Wertheim, and Blatch with that baby-faced son Roger of his, and a few other officers on leave, and boys and girls from the *Choose Your Partner* company—I thought not only of Maeve but of that other life, life sprung from my life, so that a part of me seemed to have died with her and to have been buried there that March day without hope of resurrection.

It all surged upon my memory as I sat in my room that Armistice night and listened to the jubilation. Even in the staid precincts of Berkeley Square the merrymakers came in arm-linked bands, shouting, blowing upon trumpets, singing the songs to which four years—four such years!—had given the sanctity of dire association. All through the evening the songs came up to me: *Tipperary, When it's with You, it's Wonderful, Till the Boys come Home.*

There would be that, too. Oliver would be coming home. Around the chill of my heart a faint warmth awakened at the thought. Livia...would he want Livia now? Would Livia want him? I saw nothing there. And Maeve was gone. Did I remain? Did I count? I had yet to find out. I had written to him at his prison camp when Maeve died. Twenty months ago. There was no answer. I waited for six months, then sent him food and tobacco. There was no answer.

There was a ring at the door of the flat. I heard Annie Suthurst shuffle out from her bed-sitting-room and break into cries of pleasure. She came bustling into my room, so overcome that she forgot to knock at the door. "Coom in, Mr. Rory. Coom in."

Yes; it was Rory. "I'll see you later, Annie," he said, seeing that she hovered there, making ecstatic noises, unwilling to take her eyes off him. "You pop along for a moment. Well, Uncle Bill?"

He stood grinning in his old diffident, deferential fashion. He was wearing a not-very-good-looking navy-blue suit, and with his big hands, grey eyes and rough black hair, with his short stocky body bearing down firmly on his feet, he looked like a young officer of the merchant marine ashore for the night.

Our hands met in a hard grip. "Sit down," I said. "You don't change much, Rory."

"No, so Maggie says. She says I just—deepen." He smiled deprecatingly. "You don't mind having one of His Majesty's convicts defiling your home?"

"I was longing for someone to talk to, and I don't think there's anyone I'd rather talk to than you. How is Maggie?"

"As well as can be expected," he said grimly.

I knew he was referring to Donnelly's death, and that made me think of Easter, 1916—of Rory lying behind the parapet of a roof, picking his man, watching him twist and fall and shudder to stillness. Strangely, I had not thought of that till his remark brought it to mind. And looking at him now—at the great width of his shoulders and the steadiness of his hands lying in his lap like rocks—I still could not see this Rory as that Rory. I took my mind from the whole matter.

"You'll be able to marry Maggie now," I said.

"We are already married. She is staying at Father's house. We thought there was no need to make a fuss, so we just got married, and we came across when it was all over."

"I wish you joy, Rory. Maggie's a fine girl."

"She is that," he said emphatically. "But that's no reason why she or I should know anything about joy. It doesn't matter about being a fine girl and having a fine country to live in. You can be any sort of damned scallywag so long as you kiss the boots of the British. Then you might find some joy. But Maggie and I don't expect much joy. That's why we came to see Father and Mother and Eileen. You never know."

"So you're still in it? You're going back?"

Even as I spoke them, the words sounded flat and without meaning. The answer was there in Rory's resolute pugnacious young face. He did not permit himself the indignation that I deserved. He said simply: "Yes. We shall go back. There's a lot to be done."

He would neither smoke nor drink. He sat hunched into his chair and told me something about Donnelly. Maggie had been allowed to see him in gaol. "She told me," Rory said, "that they didn't cry. There wasn't a tear between them. He wanted to know all she had been doing that Easter, and when she told him, he said: 'That's a good girl. Do the same thing next time. Because there will be a next time, and a time after that, till the last time comes. Then all these times won't matter any more. And now kiss me.' So she kissed him and came away."

"He was a good man," I said.

"He was the best man I have ever known," Rory said, "the best and the bravest. The sort of man I should like to be." He added after a moment: "So you see, we shall go back."

"Yes, I see that."

I puffed my pipe in silence for a while, feeling diffident and humble in Rory's presence. His utter single-mindedness had that effect on me—of making me feel more humble than I felt with anyone else. I said suddenly, impulsively: "Rory, you don't have to wait to be the sort of man Donnelly was. You're the same breed, and as good a man as Donnelly any day. You know, I've watched a lot of boys grow up in my time, and you're quite the nicest boy I know."

The colour mounted to his cheeks, but he turned off the embarrassing moment with a laugh: "Ach, Uncle Bill, you're thinking of that old poem, *The Whitest Man I Know*. To hell—no, I'm not that sort. But thank you all the same. I believe we do understand something of one another, you and I. Otherwise, I couldn't say what I'm going to say now. But I came to say it, so here goes. Thank you for what you did for Maeve."

"But, my dear boy, I did nothing. I..."

His grey candid eyes were looking me through and through. I hesitated, flustered. "I don't know how you did it or exactly what it was you did," he said. "But, you see, I know that Maeve committed suicide. And I know that no one knows that—not even Father and Mother."

I felt perspiration trickling on my forehead. I wiped it away with a handkerchief, got up and poured myself a drink. There was utter silence in the room, broken only by the light tinkle of the decanter against the whisky-glass.

"She was going to have a child by Oliver."

I had taken a drink, and turned to face him as he said this. His head was sunk into his chest; his underlip was thrust forward and his eyes seemed to have shrunk to little points having the hard grey glitter of granite. Now I was seeing the Rory who had crouched behind the parapet, finger on trigger. Now a cold breath of doom seemed to be in the room with him. Sitting there, still hunched up and unmoving, he said: "She wrote to me from the theatre the night she died. She must have scribbled the note in an interval and given it to someone to post. I was already back in Ireland then. She told me what she was going to do and why she was going to do it." He added simply: "You see, we were very fond of one another, and I was proud of Maeve. We told one another everything."

He glowered at the fire for a while, then went on: "I said nothing to my friends. They'd know soon enough, I thought. I waited for the row. I expected the papers to be full of it—the inquest and all that. And there was nothing—nothing except that Maeve was dead, and all the columns of praise. Then I knew that somebody had cooked it, and I guessed it was you."

I broke in eagerly: "Yes, I—"

He interrupted me with the holding up of one big hand. "Please! Say nothing. There must have been a doctor concerned. I can see that. I don't want to know. I only want to thank you. I'm glad you did it. I should have hated..."

He broke off, frowning. Presently he said: "I did you an injustice. At first I thought in my bitterness that what you had done was to save Oliver's skin. I apologise for that. You did it because you loved Maeve. Always and always. Those are Maeve's words: always and always. I want you to know that, too. She always loved you, and believed that you loved her but that you were too blind to know your own heart. It's a pity. I wish you had married Maeve. So much would have been so different. Because now..."

He got up, leaving the sentence unfinished, but my own heart finished it for him. *Because now Oliver and I have a matter to settle.*

He shook hands, and I went out with him to the landing. Still the shouting and tumult came up from the streets. "Armistice!" he said. "Now you'll be able to give all your attention to the wild Irish."

I stood there till I heard the street door bang. I never saw Rory again.

## 33

Now that the long futility of the war was over, I remained in London for many months. I would never again open that big house in Hampstead; my flat would do well enough. I had taken an affection for the place. It was quiet, a good bolt-hole for one who had no more use for public occasions. There was the night, for example, when *Choose Your Partner* came to an end. It was late in the February after the Armistice, and, as it happened, the night was the second anniversary of Maeve's death. Wertheim was anxious for me to be there, but I wouldn't go. It was a grand occasion, I heard. Men who had known the show during leaves were there singing all the old songs with tears in their eyes. Wertheim went on to the stage at that moment when, before the interval, it was customary to sing *When it's with You, it's Wonderful.* He reminded the audience that Maeve had died two years ago; then they stood in silence for her, and instead of the song being sung by the girl who had taken Maeve's place, Wertheim had Maeve's picture thrown on a screen, and, looking at it, the audience sang the song in unison, *pianissimo.* I suppose it was all very moving, but I had no use for that sort of thing any more.

I had a queer feeling that I had Maeve under my own roof. Once, when I was going to bed in the early hours of the morning, I heard light footsteps running up the stairs to the flat above mine. Just so I had many times heard Maeve run by, coming home late after the theatre. The steps were so like hers—so delicate and dancing—that my heart gave a great thud. I opened the door on to the stairway. The footsteps were still audible, and I stood listening to hear a key in the door above and the opening and shutting of the door.

But I heard nothing except the steps, which ran lightly for a time and then stopped. There was no other sound.

I never heard them again, but I listened for them every night.

I was listening for other footsteps, too. I wanted to get away. After more than four years spent continuously in London I wanted to open up Heronwater again. But I stayed because I feared that Oliver might come and find me gone.

"Why don't you go out and get some fresh air into your lungs?" Annie rated me. But I wouldn't go far; a turn round the Square, down perhaps as far as Piccadilly, then left into Bond Street, my feet unconsciously hurrying as I neared the corner of Bruton Street.

"Any callers, Annie?" I would shout.

"Callers! Tha's not been aht o' t'house five minutes."

The streets were full of emancipated men. Lorry drivers still wearing old British warms or long khaki overcoats, young flâneurs ogling the girls in Bond Street, not anxious, evidently, to settle down yet to the dull routine of earning a living. On a morning when already there was in the air a premonition of the spring that had not yet come, a 'bus conductor hung out by one hand from his 'bus to shout to a man he recognised on the pavement: "Wotcher, cocky! Better than the old Menin Road!"

"Not 'arf it ain't!"

So here and there I saw them, the men who had come back; and soon the spring itself was in London, filling the kerbside baskets with anemones and mimosa, daffodils and tulips. And now my walks became a little longer, and as I went up the stairs to my flat I did not shout to know whether there were any callers. I knew there were none, that there would be none. Then I called on the firm that had stored my furniture and arranged to have a man sent down to put everything back into Heronwater, to air the house, and make it habitable again. I remembered that I had last seen it when waiting on there with Martin and Sam Sawle: waiting irrationally through a procession of superb autumn days to see whether Livia Vaynol would return. And then her letter had come from Copenhagen. Now, before returning there, I was waiting again: waiting this time to see whether Oliver would come back. I reflected bitterly that I had done a lot of that lately: a lot of waiting to see whether I was the sort of person to whom the young came back. Well, it looked as though I wasn't.

I rang up Dermot at his shop and told him I was coming to see him.

"About time," he said, "but all the same, make it short and sweet when you get here. I'm busy."

I hurried off, and in Bond Street ran into Eileen. Eileen at twenty-four was good to look at. She had never got over her comfortable dumpiness, but happiness and good-nature made her face a thing that, so to speak, put the top on that lovely May day. And she had good reason to be looking happy that morning. Her hand was laid on the arm of a tall, handsome boy whose hatless head was a tangle of dark brown curls. "Hallo, Uncle Bill!" she greeted me; and looking up shyly at her escort: "This is Guy Langdale. I don't think you've met him. This is William Essex, Guy."

I liked the boy. I liked his frank blue eyes and his firm handgrip; but I was not so sure that I liked the excessive respect of his tone, as he said: "I'm delighted to meet you, sir." Established...honourable...OLD...That's what he thought me.

We loitered there for a moment, talking commonplaces, and I noticed that Eileen was very well dressed and that her happy face was happier than ever. Well, good luck to you, Eileen, I thought, as I walked on. There hasn't been too much luck coming the way of Sheila's children. I had heard about young Langdale. He had gone to work for Dermot in 1914, looking after the art gallery which was part of the establishment. He was something of a painter himself, but I had gathered that Dermot thought highly of him as a business man, too. He had joined the army in 1916, and now here he was, back again. Yes,

Eileen, the young come back to the young. I wish you a good innings.

A girl took me up in the lift, and she was just a girl. She wasn't a jolly tar, or a brigadier-general, or a grenadier of the Inkerman period. She was just a girl in a white blouse and a black skirt. "Merely not to be vulgar is so distinguished," Dermot had once explained.

My entrance startled him out of a reverie. He was sitting with both hands spread out on a perfectly clear desk, sitting bolt upright, gazing before him with the end of an unlit cigar chewed to ribbons in his mouth. A portrait of Maeve, by Guy Langdale—not a bad one, either—was on the wall before him. He didn't seem to be looking at that, or at anything, though it may well have started his reverie. His face was haggard.

"You look as if you want a holiday, my boy," I said.

"Well, since we're exchanging compliments, Tyburn Tree is just round the corner. You look as though you were recently cut down."

He fell into a kind of irritable brooding for a while; then said: "I don't like the damned news from Ireland."

"I haven't noticed anything in particular."

He snorted impatiently. "You wouldn't. You haven't noticed that what used to be peaceful police-stations are now forts, with steel plates instead of windows, with sandbags and barbed wire. You haven't noticed that, despite all this, these police-stations are being burned down, and policemen shot, and that those who are not shot are resigning. Resigning, my boy, with the fear of God in their hearts, though a lot of 'em are pretty near the age for pensions."

"Well, because a lot of bobbies are resigning…"

"Bill, you're the most maddening fool. Don't you know that Ireland has been governed by policemen as long as anyone can remember, and that the smash-up of the police force means that government is being destroyed all over the country districts? Soon there'll be no government left except in a few big towns. And what happens then? Something will have to take the place of the police.

It won't be anything nice, believe me. Ireland isn't gallant little Belgium, and I can't see you bloody English getting sentimental about her, but, of course, this all means nothing to you. You haven't got a son out there."

He leapt up at that and put his hand on my shoulder. "Sorry, Bill. That slipped out. Let's say no more about it."

A telephone shrilled on his desk. He took it up and listened. "Speak to Miss Eileen about it. She's got the whole matter in hand."

"There's no Miss Eileen to speak to," I said. "I met her in Bond Street in pleasant company."

Dermot threw up his wrist and consulted his watch. "She said she'd be in at eleven. It's two minutes past. She must have come in on your heels. She's a business woman."

He went over to the telephone. "For the next half-hour put *all* inquiries through to Miss Eileen. Tell her I'm not to be disturbed till eleven-thirty."

"There you are," he said proudly. "What d'you think of that? And that will be *done*. One thing the war did. It taught me I had a jewel of a business woman under my own roof. She's my under-strapper now in everything. I'm making her a director. Was she with young Langdale?"

"Yes. Looks a nice boy."

"He's got his head screwed on the right way. I shouldn't be surprised if he's a director, too, before long. Or does that strike you as too mercenary a wedding present?"

"It strikes me as a good thing that one of Sheila's children should be plain bread-and-butter."

He nodded his head in agreement. "And now what the devil have you come to disturb me about?" he demanded.

"This is May," I said. "In a month's time Heronwater will be in order again. Neither of us has had a holiday for nearly five years. Come, and bring Sheila."

"And what about my work? Now that this damned war's over and business is picking up a bit."

"Excellent experience for Eileen."

"She could do it. But that would mean we should be there with no children... Just you and Sheila and I..."

We looked at one another, and suddenly the idea of being at Heronwater with no children struck us both with all its significance. Of course, they were no longer children, anyway; but, even so, they were gone. Maeve dead, and Rory married, and Eileen leaning on the arm of her tall beautiful boy; and Oliver God knew where.

We were silent for a while. I pulled at my pipe and Dermot jerked his unlit cigar from one side of his mouth to the other. "I wonder," he said at last, "whether we've had our best times, Bill? There was one time I always think of—when Donnelly was there. That was a houseful? You and Nellie and Oliver—"

"And you and Sheila and Rory and Eileen—"

"And Donnelly and Maggie—"

"And Sam Sawle and Martin. They were good fellows—"

"Yes, and that old madman Judas over the river and his husky Viking friend in Truro. Remember him?"

"I do that. It was a good time. But Maeve wasn't there."

"Wasn't she?"

"No, no. She'd gone off with Mary Latter."

"She had so. I'd forgotten that."

"Well," I said, "you'll come? We'll do our best, eh?—three old stagers."

"Yes. I wonder what's happened to old Judas? Ever hear of him?"

"Not a word. We shall see."

He was still in the land of the living, and that is the only reason why I write of that holiday—to give some account of Captain Judas at that time.

Dermot drove us down. One of Sheila's maids and Annie Suthurst had gone on in advance by train. We should need no one else. Dermot would look after his own car and I could look after the *Maeve*, which had been overhauled. She and her dinghy alone were left of our little fleet. I sat at the back of the car with Sheila, thinking of the time when Dermot had first come by car to Heronwater. Oliver and I had waited for them at the gate, and there was Sheila, little Maggie Donnelly on one side of her and Eileen on the other, young and radiant with a great chiffon scarf passing over the top of a large hat and tied in a bow under her chin. Her dark hair was white with the dust of the Cornish roads, for it was an open car. Now, so that she might lean her head back more comfortably in the big close saloon, Sheila wore no hat at all, and her hair was white not with Cornish dust but with the sorrows of the short twelve months that had seen the imprisonment of Rory and the deaths of Donnelly and Maeve. Something was gone out of Sheila. Her face was still kind and thoughtful, her smile ready to encourage, but when there was no encouraging to be done and you caught her face unawares, there was an inward brooding which suggested a life counting over the past and not much concerned with the present. Maeve had been the child of her heart; and sometimes I had an uneasy feeling that the very intensity of her thinking about that loved girl would tell her the truth, that she would suddenly say to me: "What really happened to Maeve?" So that I was never now completely at ease in Sheila's company.

We came to Heronwater in the evening, to the abiding peace and beauty that had smiled on unchanged through the agonies and convulsions of a continent. Sheila said she would rest till dinner-time, and Dermot and I walked out to lean on the warm stone of the balustrade where, that winter night when the rain hissed through the darkness and the wind volleyed like guns, Livia Vaynol had come upon me with the brimming cup that was so soon to be spilled.

Then we went down the path to the water. It seemed as though the very leaves we had left were still upon the trees, and in our scrambling descent we recognised the very pebbles we knew so well. We came out upon the little quay of level greensward and looked upon the river drifting out on the first of the ebb. "Change and decay in all around I see." Never were words less appropriate. All the visible world seemed to mock by its calm stability the change and decay that were in our hearts alone.

"Nothing seems altered," said Dermot, breaking a long silence. "Not even the *Jezebel*."

Not even the *Jezebel*. There she was, the ugly old black hulk, shored up under the opposite bank, looking as she had looked when last I saw her, that day when Judas was waving good-bye to Jansen as the *Kay* steamed by carrying, though I knew it not, Oliver and Livia to the beginning of their momentous adventure.

I didn't seek out the old man then; indeed, I didn't know if he were aboard. We went back to the house, where Annie Suthurst was happy to be serving Sheila and Dermot again, and we had dinner, and then we sat in deck-chairs on the lawn, glad to do nothing after the long journey. Glad just to sit there and see the sunset smouldering behind the trees and to listen to the rooks settling noisily in for the night. Dermot held Sheila's hand, and I saw them suddenly very clearly as people whose youth was finished, being kind and understanding with one another because they had done much and endured much together.

The next day I took the dinghy and pulled myself across to the *Jezebel*. Hanging down her counter was the rope I had urged Judas to fix so long ago. I hauled upon it and heard the peal within the ship's timbers. Presently a woman's head leaned over the rails, and a voice cried delightedly: "Why, Mr. Essex—!"

It was Mary Latter, looking old and drawn. I knew that she had given up the stage. Her company still toured, but she did not tour with it. I had heard that she was settled in a flat somewhere in Kensington. She dropped the rope ladder overboard. I tied up the dinghy and climbed to the deck. "Well, this is delightful," she said. "I haven't seen a soul for a week."

A querulous voice came up the stairway. "Who's that, Mary? Have a care, my girl, have a care. Don't go letting every Tom, Dick and Harry aboard."

She took my arm. "Come down and see him. He's in bed."

It was a nice little bedroom that the captain occupied. The walls were painted white. The windows were flung wide open and the daffodil-coloured muslin curtains fluttered in the fresh morning air. Captain Judas was sitting up in bed, with pillows piled behind him. Spectacles were on his nose and his small thin hand held a book. He looked tiny, a mannikin, in the big bed, with his hair and beard combed and glistening like fine silk.

"It's Mr. Essex, Father," Mary said.

I gave him my hand and was startled by the dry fragility of the claw he placed in mine. He looked at me long and earnestly over the spectacles, and asked: "Have we met before?"

"Yes, yes, Father, of course," Mary explained patiently. "Mr. Essex from Heronwater."

"It's a long time since I've seen you, captain," I said. "Before the war. Four and a half years."

"The war," he said, speaking to himself rather than to us, "the war... They came upon me with swords and bows, and their spearmen rent me in sunder."

He let the book fall on the bed and his eyes shifted to the window, to the far green bank and the sunlight spilling on the water. He seemed to forget us altogether; Mary took my arm and drew me out of the room. "Go up on deck," she said. "I'll bring you some coffee."

She came presently and put the coffee down between us. "What a dreadful thing," she said, "young Maeve O'Riorden dying like that. It must have been a ghastly shock to you. Oh, dear! I am glad to have someone to talk to, even about horrible events like that."

"Tell me about your father," I said. "He looks much frailer."

It was the sort of story I should have expected. Even down here in this dreaming backwater of the world the madness and hysteria of the war had raged. The queer and incomprehensible became sinister and portentous. Judas's innocent lights became signals—though to whom or what God alone might tell. No one living in those parts, save me and Dermot and the children, had ever been permitted to board the *Jezebel*; and the most fantastic rumours spread as to the devilries that were hatched there. It was a quiet harbourage for spies; it housed a printing-press whence sedition was propagated; a German submarine had come up the Carrick Roads and an officer, getting into a collapsible boat, had been rowed at dead of night to the *Jezebel*. There were those who saw this with their own eyes.

One night bucolic policemen went aboard, armed with a search warrant, and all old Judas's pitiable secrets were laid bare and trampled beneath uncomprehending feet. His queer scrawls in Greek, because to the policemen they were meaningless, took on the meaning of codes and ciphers. Excited, they turned the neat ship upside down. As the old man, hauled from his bed, alternately whined and cursed, padding after them in a night-shirt, they found the way down to the bilge, heaved up his chest of writings, and gloated over that fantastic discovery. They could make nothing of it all, and that fed their deepest fears and suspicions, and Judas, feeling his very soul outraged as these harvests of his fantasy were pawed and pored upon, was at last hauled off to gaol till the whole suspicious farrago should be elucidated.

"Nothing came of it," Mary Latter said tiredly, "except that he became—madder—than ever."

She took him to London, and he lived with her all through the war. "And then he wanted to come back, so I let him. He's quite happy here, you know, in his way, and well able to look after himself. This illness now is nothing to worry about—just influenza. He'll be up and about soon. I'll stay till he's quite fit."

"Did he get his papers back?" I asked.

"They all came back most neatly done up with sealing-wax and red tape after the war. But it was too late. He didn't know what they were and burned them all. It was a pity, because it was all harmless enough. You see, it had given his mania an outlet for ten years and more. Then the continuity of the thing went, and now there's nothing. Except your son."

"My son!" Her words nearly startled me out of my seat.

"Yes," she nodded. "He still believes… Well, I expect you know what he believes."

"But he hasn't seen Oliver since before the war."

She looked at me curiously. "Oh, yes, he has."

"But—when?"

"I wasn't here at the time. It was just after I'd brought Father back. Your son must have been just demobilised. He came down here and stayed for a week. Father wrote me a most exulting letter and— borrowed some money for the first time in his life."

"I'm sorry."

"Don't worry. I'm a rich woman."

"Yes—but—that's not the point."

"Please forget about it," she said. "I shouldn't have told you."

"You don't know where—Oliver—is now?"

She shook her head. "I know that he writes to Father, but I've never seen any of his letters."

I went down to say good-bye to Captain Judas, but he was asleep, his little face, framed by the white of hair and whiskers, sunk in the pillows, his two claws lying fraily on the counterpane.

*

We had not been long back from that holiday when I got news of Oliver's whereabouts. It was a hot July night—no night for eating in town, Dermot said; so he took me off to Hampstead. I still had no car of my own, and Dermot insisted on driving me home. He came up to the flat to have a drink, and a few minutes later Annie Suthurst brought in a card: Captain Dennis Newbiggin, M.C. There was no address. "Show him in," I said.

"I'll be going then," said Dermot.

"No, no; sit down a minute. I expect I'll soon get rid of this chap."

Captain Dennis Newbiggin wore brown suede shoes and a neat suit of navy-blue, with a double-breasted jacket and a regimental tie. His hat, which had somehow eluded Annie, was a grey felt with a spot of bright plumage fixed into the band. He held this in his left hand, and tucked under his left arm was a silver-headed malacca cane of unusual strength and weight. The head itself was heavy, and the whole thing had the appearance of a weapon—a knobkerry. The captain held out his right hand, from which the middle finger was missing.

I didn't like the look of the fellow, though it was difficult to say what was wrong. He was a shade—well, flash. I shouldn't have called him jannock. He looked fundamentally a tough; yet he tried to get away with pretty airs; a little toothbrush moustache, perhaps too much oil on his abundant, well-brushed dark hair. He looked about thirty.

I shook his hand. "Pleased to meet you, Mr. Essex," he said.

"Sit down, Captain Newbiggin," I invited him. "Still a captain?"

"Well, no. Been out of the old mob now, you know, for some months."

"Ah! This is Mr. O'Riorden, Mr. Newbiggin."

Dermot gave him a rather distant nod.

"You'll have a drink?"

"Just my time for a gargle. No, no—please don't drown it. Thank you."

He tossed off the almost neat whisky and wiped his moustache with a handkerchief drawn from his left cuff.

I looked at him expectantly, and he took out a morocco-leather pocket wallet and extracted a card from it. This he handed to me. "I wondered if I could interest you in this little business, Mr. Essex." He grinned. "It's a bit short of capital."

Dermot got up. "Perhaps I ought to be going."

"I'd like you to stay," I said, "if you can spare the time. This will interest you."

I handed him the card:

NEWBIGGIN & ESSEX

MOTOR-CARS

NEW AND SECOND-HAND

DEANSGATE      MANCHESTER

Dermot sat down and considered Mr. Newbiggin more carefully.

"The poor must live, you know, Mr. Essex," Newbiggin said cheerfully. He took from his pocket a thin gold cigarette case and held it towards me and Dermot. We shook our heads. "D'you mind if I do?" He flicked a light from an ornate lighter, let the smoke ooze slowly through his nostrils, and said: "We stuck together, Oliver and I. We stuck it for a long time before we were both pipped at Arras in '17. Then we had hell's delight organising escapes from a German prison camp. But we never got away with that. All the same, we got away with some high old times together, one way and another. Paris leaves…" His eyes became meditative.

"And you're still sticking together?" I prompted him.

"Well, we parted for a time. You know, back in the dear old homeland, after two years on the Western front, and the best part of another two lodging with old Fritz, and a bit of gratuity in our pockets...well, it wouldn't be human, would it, Mr. Essex? Boys will be boys. As a student of human nature—I speak as one who's read your books, Mr. Essex—you realise that?"

"Realise what?" I asked him coldly.

"Well, I mean, we decided to part company for a month or two and each shake a loose leg while the dibs lasted, and then get down together to a spot of work."

"You mean you got through your gratuities and then tried to start a business, presumably on borrowed capital?"

"That's the size of it, sir; and believe me capital is damned hard to come by. We're living pretty near the bone."

There was some truculence in this last remark.

"Did my son ask you to make this call?"

"Well, not exactly, but I figured it this way. Here I am in the gay metrollops trying to raise a bit of money—and believe me it's cost me a Savoy lunch and no end of drinks today to get nothing at all—and I say to myself 'What about applying to the fountain-head?' After all, a son's a son, and a father's a father." There was silence for a moment before he added, gazing round the room, "You don't look short of a bit."

No one spoke and Newbiggin shifted uncomfortably in his chair. His legs were stretched right out in front of him. I noticed that the sole of one of the natty suede shoes was worn nearly through, and that took my eye to his coat cuffs, always another symptom. The whiskers had been trimmed down neatly with scissors.

Poor devil, I thought. And yet he's a scoundrel. I feel it in my bones.

"Well, anything doing?" he asked jauntily. "A couple of hundred would see us on velvet."

"I won't say No off-hand," I said. "I'd like to communicate with Oliver, and perhaps with some accountant up there to give me a report on the business."

"For God's sake, Mr. Essex, do nothing of the sort," he implored me, suddenly completely genuine. "Oliver'd blast the skin off my back. He'd walk his legs down to the knees before he'd ask you for a penny. Don't say a word to him. He'd get in a hell of a temper, and I can't handle him when he's like that."

"Then the idea was—?"

"To get a bit of capital and work it quietly into the company without saying where it came from. See the idea?" He added brightly, fingering his gay tie, "If you could see it like that?"

I shook my head.

"Oh, well…" He got up and held out his maimed hand.

"Another drink?"

"Righty-o. Just to show there's no ill-feeling."

He tossed it off, and I went out with him to the landing. "Not a word to Oliver, eh?" he said.

"All right."

"Fact is," he confided, "I was his batman. He's bloody good to me."

I shook his hand, slipping a pound note into it. He looked at it in astonishment. "Thank you, sir," he said, with a sudden humility that made me feel sick. He raised his hat with the spot of gay plumage and went away.

"Well," said Dermot, when I got back to the study. "That was pretty amateur."

"Yes."

"I suppose he would have liked it in pound notes. What would the odds have been on Oliver seeing it then?"

"Have another drink?"

"No, thanks. I'll be going. Will you look Oliver up?"

"No. Well, not yet. I'll see."

"He'd walk his legs down to his knees." So even Newbiggin knew that, the cheap little skate. I could imagine the scene: "Well, what about touching the old man for a bit? He's got plenty." And the wounds in Oliver's face twitching, pulling up the side of his eye, pulling down the side of his mouth, as he told Newbiggin he'd blast the hide off him if he mentioned the old man again. This Oliver of whom I knew nothing, this man who had been scorched and twisted by war, changed into something whose anger the likes of Newbiggin did not care to face. He was removed from me as far as the East is from the West. I had had no commerce with him since those incredible days when he lounged through life in the company of Mr. Guy Boothby, his deepest longing being to possess a gold cigarette case and a book on the management of steam yachts. What could I do to bridge the gulf between that far-off puerile figure and the formidable man who now was Oliver? Nothing.

Ever since leaving Manchester I had continued to read the *Manchester Guardian*. It was towards the end of the following winter—in March of 1920—that I came upon a paragraph in that paper which threw the next beam of light upon Oliver's affairs. It was a report of bankruptcy court proceedings, and the Official Receiver was frank about the affairs of Messrs. Newbiggin and Essex. Books, he said, had been improperly kept insofar as they could be said to have been kept at all, and the whole conduct of the business had shown a reckless disregard for customary commercial procedure. He was not sure that the condition of things disclosed did not merit the investigation of another court; but in view of the splendid military record of one of the partners he would give them the benefit of the doubt and assume that ignorance of business practice had led them to their present position. The inquiry was closed.

It was this which led me at last to visit Manchester. Perhaps now was the time…

I went one afternoon towards the end of March, travelling from St. Pancras by the route that goes switchbacking through the

Pennine Chain. There was snow in the gullies of the high hills, and frequent water tumbling in white spates among the leafless woods. There were enfilade glimpses down the length of dale after dale, and I wondered why, with all this remote loveliness to choose from, men herded themselves in great cities. Perhaps this sort of thing would be welcome to Oliver now. Perhaps he had had enough of the lone and desperate hand and would be willing to rest, if only for a while, in some place like this, or at Heronwater. Then, when he was rehabilitated, when the stink of war was out of his life, we should see...

So I pondered as we roared along the valleys, and through the tunnels, and over the viaducts of that romantic land, and shot out at length on to the Cheshire plain and the thickening agglomerations of Manchester suburbs.

I took a room at the Midland Hotel, and when I had rested for a while I was taken in a taxicab to Didsbury. At the White Lion Hotel I dismissed the man and walked on down the Wilmslow Road. This was sentimentality. Well, so be it. I walked on down the Wilmslow Road.

I wanted to recapture, if I could, the Oliver I had known. Here was the house called the Priory, at the corner of Fog Lane, where, nearly a quarter of a century before, I had met Dermot wheeling a perambulator to meet the one I wheeled myself. The trees had been trailing green branches over the wall, and there for the first time Rory and Oliver had looked at one another, clasped one another's hands, smiled in one another's eyes. The sunny scene was extraordinarily clear to my imagination, though now it was not sunny, and the trees were not green, but clawed with skinny fingers, dewed with fog, in the light of a street lamp.

I had not paused; the memory had come back, rounded and complete, as I passed that spot and continued my walk along the road—that road between my house and Dermot's—which held more

of my youth than any place on earth. This way all the children had
come to Miss Bussell's—Miss Bussell who had so little understood
what she was up against that day when Rory had lied to make trial
of his courage. This way Maeve had run and danced, eager to reach
The Beeches and play out on its lawn her infant imaginings.

I passed the stone which said "St. Ann's Square 5 Miles," and the
village shops, and so presently I came to The Beeches. It was not
at all changed. The winter branches of the trees drooped weeping
in the misty evening air; comfortable lights were geometrically
imposed upon the darkness at the end of the long lawn. That one
on the left, on the first floor, marks the room where Oliver slept;
behind that bright pane on the right had been my study where,
night by night, we had come close together in our "conversations."

I thought of Nellie, peering about short-sightedly in those rooms,
and of her queer cantankerous faithfulness, and of how, since her
death, I had known little joy.

So pondering, I turned into the lane that runs down to the
river meadows. It was dark and cold, but imagination livened it
with Oliver's small presence running at my side, wearing his first
prized pair of football boots and thudding the ball with satisfying
reverberations against this brick wall which now was nothing but
a shadow cutting the darkness of its top into a sky only less dark.

Down here at the end of the lane there was not a soul. I did not go
into the fields, but leaned on the stile by which we had been used to
enter them, and in the darkness and silence listened to the whispers
that came across so many years. Then, indeed, with yesterday held
in the hollow of my hand, and all its details intimate and complete
before my regard, it seemed that no power could destroy what then
had been, that I had but to come face to face with Oliver to know
him once more in all the glad out-flowing of love from one of us to
the other. In the intensity of my desire, I leaned my head upon my
hands there on the stile and groaned for my son.

I did not go back the way I had come, but followed the lane where it turned to the left. It climbed here to the rising sandstone hill on which stood the church and churchyard where so long ago I had first met Mr. Oliver. There was a jagged rip in the clouds over the square church tower and through it a star or two looked down like bright eyes gazing with compassion into an abyss. Here I was back not at Oliver's childhood but at my own. I did not know that I was looking at it for the last time, that already the happenings were in train which, in their consequences, would make abhorrent any return to the place where Oliver and I had known and loved one another.

I was not sure where I should find Oliver. I would begin my search in the morning. As for this cold and foggy night in Manchester which was now upon me, there could be no better way of passing it than in the brightness of the Palace Theatre which was presenting a musical show. I do not remember what the show was. What remains in my mind is that during the interval I saw Mr. Dennis Newbiggin again. I was in the stalls, and by the time I had struggled through to the bar at the back of the house, the place was a welter of people trying to get to the counter, talking at the tops of their voices, filling the air so thick with smoke that it was difficult to see from one side of the room to the other.

It was this confusion which permitted me to escape the notice of Newbiggin. He and a friend had entered the fray early. They were struggling back through the forward-pushing crowd, each precariously maintaining the balance of a full tumbler. They managed to seat themselves at a table, and I stood with my back to them, unable to move, and obliged to overhear.

"Well, cheers, captain."

"All the best, old son."

There was the smack of tumblers on the table-top.

"Don't forget," said Newbiggin's friend, "send us a line. I don't say I won't join you myself."

"You're a b.f. if you don't, laddie. Think of it: an officer and a gentleman once more, with a quid a day guaranteed. Are you making that?"

"Am I hell-as-like."

"There you are then. And that's only the half of it. I've had it on the strict Q.T. that the pay's nothing to the pickings. Had a letter yesterday from that young brother of mine. He's joined the Black and Tans. Them's the rankers. My lot—the Auxiliaries—all officers and gentlemen. But these Black and Tans, you never saw such a bloody lot. Khaki coats, with black trousers and caps. Well, this kid of ours wrote to me. Half a tick; here's his letter. 'Thumbs up. Went into a pub yesterday for a drink with Johnny Buckle. When it came to paying we hadn't got a brass farthing between us. "What now?" says I. "Watch your uncle," says Johnny. He went out into the street and was back inside five minutes. He slaps a pound note down on the counter, and I notice that he strips this off a wad of three or four. "Christ, Johnny!" I said. "That's all right, kid," he said, "it grows on the citizens. You just go out and pick it." I haven't tried this yet, but perhaps I shall.'"

Newbiggin's voice had dropped to a conspirator's whisper as he read this letter. In a louder voice he said: "The Black and Tans only get ten bob a day, so p'r'aps you can't blame 'em."

"And, of course," rejoined his companion, "you officers and gentlemen in these—er—"

"Auxiliaries."

"You'd never be naughty boys like that."

"Well, laddie, it's a case of exploring possibilities. Anything's better than this lousy town and the lousy life I've been having in it. Just to have a whack at the bloody Irish will be something. Christ! It'll be fun to have my fingers on a gun again."

"You won't be sorry to see the Major, either."

"Sorry! Boy, we're life partners. If he hadn't been in this, I don't suppose I should have been either. God, he's a card. Says he's going to win a few more medals shooting the eyes out of Irish potatoes."

"Well, I think it's a pity."

"A pity? What the hell d'you mean?"

"Essex could be doing something better, if he wasn't just a cat on hot bricks with his nerves all shot to bits."

"D'you know anything better than money for jam?" Newbiggin demanded.

The bell buzzed, cutting off the answer. The bar slowly cleared, and at last I was able to get a drink. I felt I needed it. I didn't want to see the rest of the show. I slowly drank the whisky in the empty, smoke-fouled bar; then claimed my hat and coat from the cloak-room and went back to my hotel through the mirk and drizzle and tramway clamour of the streets.

When I got back to town, I rang up Dermot and asked him: "Do you know anything about these Black and Tans and Auxiliaries that are going to Ireland?"

"What's the matter with you, Bill? Are you developing a political conscience?"

"No, tell me: d'you know anything about them?"

"Yes, Bill, I can tell you in a nutshell: they're the last nail in the English coffin over there. They're the dirty scum and off-scouring of England sent to demonstrate what this government thinks of the rights of small nations, and by the time the demonstration's ended there'll be no need for any more Irish Martyrs. Not foreign imports, anyway. We'll start making our own. We're like that. But what's our damned distressful country got to do with you?"

"Oliver's joined the Auxiliaries."

Dermot didn't answer that. There was a silence; then I heard the receiver click back on to its hook.

## 34

I had been writing for an hour. The room was full of the extra-ordinary silence that accompanies a fall of snow. The scratch of the pen over the paper, the flames in the grate flapping like little blown banners; that was all I could hear. I laid down my pen, crossed the room, and drew the curtains. The snow was still falling. It was deep in the street, and every corner and crevice on the face of the building opposite held its small white burden. I watched a taxicab crawl by soundlessly and foot passengers with coat-collars round their necks, hands thrust into pockets, breasts whitened, boring head-down into the eddying fall.

The old childish picture of fairyland; but, letting the curtain fall back, I thought of Rory and Oliver.

Was the weather being cruel like this in Ireland? Were they lying out in the hills, pursuing and pursued? And who the pursuer, who pursued?

Now, indeed, for a year I had been taking an interest in the old feud, blown in those days to so hot a flame, that Dermot for many years would have liked to impose upon my notice. No need to impose it now. I could not take up a newspaper without tidings of slaughter and atrocity. We had seen "Bloody Sunday," when four-teen British officers were shot in their beds in Dublin, and by way of reprisal machine-guns had that same day been fired into a crowd at a football match. The war had crossed to England. Warehouses blazed in Liverpool. In the environs of Manchester burning hay-stacks lit the night.

In the south and west of Ireland no man could close his eyes at night in the certainty that he would open them in the morning. The midnight gun-butt thudding on the door, the masked face, pistol, petrol, crowbar, bomb, the frantic rushing of lorries through the dark with cargoes of down-crouched desperate men, finger on trigger, ever alert for the down-crouched men in the ditch whose finger might be first; the swift ambush, desperate mêlée, unpitying death, and the eye of morning opening on the smoke going up from homes made desolate: these were the way of life and death in Ireland then.

For the most part, it was a nameless warfare, a warfare of nameless heroes and nameless villainies. But here and there names percolated into the newspapers, attached to the leaders of wild guerrilla bands. And so once, and then again, and then more often, appeared the name of Rory O'Riorden, a man to reckon with in the parts about Cork.

He had written once to Dermot:

"MY DEAR FATHER,—This is a restless and unsettled life, but for the most part I am in and about Ballybar. You perhaps know the reason for that and think it sentimental enough. But I have never forgotten the story you told me of how your father and my great-uncle Con were trundled on a barrow from Ballybar to Cork, their father and mother being left dead in a ditch, in the time of the great famine. This little Ballybar, then, is the place we hail from; and I took some trouble to be appointed to help the operations in those parts. I don't know that I need this association to strengthen my arm against the bloody tyrants who are now exposing themselves in their true colours for all the world to see; but I do know that I cannot pass a cottage without thinking 'Perhaps from that very cottage they crawled out to die' or lie ambushed in a ditch without the thought that the parapet on which my rifle rests perhaps rested the head of those two poor people who were starved to fatten a landlord's belly.

Well, I suppose you think that's enough Fenian jargon, and so it is. I only wanted you to know that I am up to the neck in the good work and enjoying every day and every moment of my life. I rarely sleep in a bed, but the weather's dry and the stars are lovely, and the boys I have with me here are all I could wish them to be. God give us Ireland soon. The dear boys deserve to live in peace in their own land under their own flag."

Tonight, the weather would not be dry and the stars would not be lovely. I paced the room, thinking of Rory, transferring the scene here to the countryside of Cork, imagining an immobile figure, with snow on the drawn-down peak of his cap, standing in the sheltering angle of a building, a cold revolver held in a cold hand. Waiting for the rumble of the expected lorry, knowing that the man out there, lying in the snow with his ear to the ground, would catch its farthest rumour; knowing that men like himself, tough and reliable, were immobile shadows behind tree and telegraph post and barn-end; hearing then the rumble grow to a roar, the roar to a shriek as the headlights thrust their yellow swords into the dithering snow, as the first revolvers cracked, and the sawn-through tree crashed in the lorry's path, and a machine-gun opened its deathly stutter.

And from Dermot in his cold poor bedroom in Gibraltar Street, gloating upon the names he had carved of the Manchester Martyrs, through the incursion of Flynn and the coming of Donnelly, step by step a doomful lunatic logic seemed to run right up to this imagined moment when the firing dies down and some figures spill red upon the road and others are black running dots disappearing upon the white face of the land. Perhaps from farther back than that; perhaps to some unimagined future.

The telephone bell shrilled, bringing me back with a heart-thump to the moment: to nine of a snowy March night in 1921. It was young

Guy Langdale. He had married Eileen in the autumn and they had a small house at Richmond. He was speaking from there in great agitation. Could I come at once? Yes, he knew it was a foul night and an unusual thing to ask; but could I pack a bag? They could give me a bed for the night.

"But what is it, man? What's it all about? Is Eileen ill?"

"No," he said testily. "I'd be ringing up a doctor, not you. It's not Eileen—it's Maggie."

"Maggie? Is she with you? You mean Rory's wife?"

"Yes. Rory's dead. Now will you come?"

I put down the receiver and looked dazedly about my familiar room. Just there Maeve had stood that day, confronting Dermot.

*You've killed Rory!... You've killed Rory!*

God help you, Dermot, now.

I went by Underground from Charing Cross. The chill and hideous station, my fellow passengers steaming and smelling of damp clothes, the glimpses when we came above ground of the white and desolate country, deepened the mood of dejection in which at last I arrived at Langdale's house.

Guy himself opened the door and led me to a small room at the back which he used as a study. I took the slippers from my bag and put them on. A scared-looking maid bore away my wet shoes and snowy overcoat.

"That girl looks frightened to death," I said.

"I'm not surprised," Guy answered. He poured me a drink. "It was she who opened the door. Maggie collapsed on top of her. She crossed to Holyhead on last night's boat and travelled south today. How she managed it all I don't know. This poor girl was alone in the house. She had no idea who Maggie was, and Maggie was in no condition to explain. She just staggered into the hall, sat in a chair, and fainted."

Guy went on to tell me that he and Eileen had luckily returned home at that moment. They brought Maggie round and put her to bed, talking wildly. It was some time before they gathered from her broken and desperate words that Rory was dead.

"Strange creatures," I said. "Rory himself told me how stoical she was about her father's death. She saw him in prison just before they shot him, and they seem to have talked like a pair of Romans. And now—"

Guy looked very tired. He took a drink himself before he answered. "You know what these people are—forgive me, I'm speaking dispassionately. I've never seen Rory or Donnelly, and this is the first time I've set eyes on Maggie—you know what they are when for years they've been sleeping and waking for a cause. I think I can understand it. I can understand that anyone dying as Donnelly did would leave a feeling of exaltation behind him. 'O Death, where is thy sting?' But this time it isn't like that. We don't know yet what it is, but there's something terrible on that girl's mind. She's haunted."

"Had I better see her now?"

"In a moment. Let me finish. We sent for the doctor, but he was a longish time coming. She was delirious. She kept shouting 'I betrayed him!' and then your name began to come into it. There was a lot of babble about Essex. That's why Eileen wanted you to come. We thought there was something she wanted to tell you, and that if you were here and she became sensible it might help. But now she's asleep. The doctor's been and seen to that. He says she should sleep till morning. There's another thing. We gathered that she came to Eileen because she dared not go to Rory's father. She couldn't face that. So you see," said Guy, his knuckles white as he clutched his glass, "someone has to tell O'Riorden that his son is dead." He added after a while: "Eileen and I agreed that it would be hateful to telephone the news. And she's in no condition to see his father. And frankly I loathe the job. Will you do it? Will you see him in the morning?"

It was on a March morning four years ago that I had rung up Dermot to tell him that Maeve was dead. I looked bleakly at young Langdale who loathed the job. Well, young fellow, you haven't known Dermot since he was a pale lanky red-headed youth with sawdust on the fine hairs of his wrists. "All right," I said. "I'll tell him. Now let me see Maggie."

There was a fire burning in the bedroom and one dim lamp. Eileen sat in an easy chair at the bed's head, her eyes red, her face crumpled by weeping. She was leaning forward, a ball of hand-kerchief grasped in her hand. Maggie looked the calmer of the two, all the stress eased out of her face by sleep. There were black smudges under the eyes and the cheeks were more hollow than I remembered. Both hands were lying out over the counterpane, folded very peacefully one upon the other. She was wearing a wedding-ring.

I took Eileen by the hand, led her out on to the landing, and shut the bedroom door. "Go to bed, my dear," I said. "It's past eleven."

She turned and clung to Guy and began to cry afresh.

"Get her to bed," I said, "and go yourself. I'll call you if Maggie needs you. I'm used to sitting up all night."

Guy took her away, her body shaken by sobs. I went down to his study to get a book I had left there. Presently he joined me, put the decanter, a soda siphon and a tin of biscuits on a tray, and carried them up to the bedroom. Then he went, the door closed softly, and I was left alone with Maggie.

I made up the fire and sat in the easy chair by the bedside, looking at the peaceful folded hands with the wedding-ring: the ring upon the hand of the little girl who had tumbled out of the car with Rory at the gates of Heronwater so long ago. Soon every sound died in the house, and I nodded a little in my chair, and then I slept. It was two o'clock when I woke. Maggie still slept on, but she had changed her position and now lay on her side, with one hand under her cheek, her face towards me. She stirred, and smiled, and then muttered "Ach, Father!" as though deprecating some playful nonsense. Back, now, beyond her present terrors; back beyond her father's death, in some happy return.

I watched her intently, but she did not speak or move again. I did not sleep any more, but put on my spectacles and read the book I had brought with me—brought with me, indeed, so far, for it belonged to the days of Gibraltar Street, to the youth of my friendship with Dermot. And so my mind wandered to Dermot, sleeping, no doubt, and unaware that already he was in a day of darkness.

At three o'clock I pulled back the curtain and looked out of the window. The snow no longer fell. The garden glimmered in the night, cold and pallid under a few stars. Standing there with the small warm room behind me and the inimical expanse of night reaching endlessly out, my mind murmured the words I had been reading.

*Still are thy pleasant voices, thy nightingales, awake;*
*For Death, he taketh all away, but them he cannot take.*

Not the nightingales...Donnelly, Maeve, Rory...Oh, not the nightingales!

I wonder.

I was travelling back to Richmond with Dermot and Sheila. After a day and night of snow, the sun was shining; the sky was tenderly blue. But the roads were dreadful and so we were travelling, as I had travelled the night before, by Underground. Sheila sat between me and Dermot, not speaking, perfectly still, her gloved hands lying in her lap, her eyes fixed on the window opposite. The train ground and screeched over the rails.

There was nothing dramatic in the moment: it was just misery:

black, hopeless misery. Dermot, when I called upon him, had been surprised to see me so early. He was busy at his desk, opening letters with a paper-knife.

"Why, Bill, what's dug you out at this godless hour?"

"Rory is dead," I said. "He has been killed in Ireland."

The paper-knife tinkled to the smooth parquet of the floor. For a moment Dermot said nothing. He sat there examining the backs of his long white fingers extended on the desk. Then he said, as if speaking to himself: "God damn England. And God damn Ireland. And God damn every country that thinks its dreams are worth one young man's blood."

In my heart I said "Amen," and say it still; but I said nothing to Dermot.

He got up stiffly and came and stood with his hands resting on my shoulders. I looked into his eyes. There were no green flecks in them now. There was only a great depth of misery.

"That leaves Eileen," he said. "Just Eileen."

"Yes. You'd better come and see her. I've been at her house all night. Maggie is there. She brought the news."

"I must tell Sheila."

"Yes."

"Come with me, Bill."

So we jolted and jerked by Underground to Hampstead, and when we reached the house he said in the hall: "Just sit here by the fire. I'll see her alone. Can you come on with us to Richmond?"

I nodded, and he went on up the stairs.

I sat there for perhaps a quarter of an hour, and then he came back with Sheila, who was already dressed for going out. She was white and stricken. She looked at me as though to say that she would speak if she could, but she couldn't; and so, with no word spoken, we filed out of the house.

*

Maggie was sitting up in bed. She was alone when Dermot and Sheila and I went in—sitting up with a white shawl cowled over her head, held at the breast by her thin ringed hand. She was in possession of herself; her hysteria was ended; but a world of woe looked from her grey eyes.

While Dermot and I stood just within the doorway, Rory's mother crossed the room and kissed Rory's widow. It was a cold perfunctory kiss, and suddenly I knew that Sheila's heart was burning with hate for Maggie. I knew, too, that Maggie felt this. She turned upon Sheila a shy propitiating glance which seemed—to me at all events—to cry aloud in the room: "I know! I know! And I don't even ask you to understand. I don't blame you."

Tears grew in her eyes, flowed out on to her cheeks. She wiped them away and said: "I mustn't cry."

"It doesn't do much good," Sheila said. "I've lost two children, and I know."

"No," said Maggie. "No good at all. I've lost a father and a husband. I know, too."

She was composed after that. Eileen and Guy had come in, and we all sat round the bed. She told us of Rory's death. "They came to a house we used sometimes. The whole place was surrounded. There was no getting away at all. They shot him down."

Just those few bare words. She had no more to say.

"What became of—of his body?" Sheila asked.

"The boys would see him buried at Ballybar," Maggie said. "I couldn't stay."

"I should have liked to attend the funeral," Sheila said in a low voice. "Couldn't you have telegraphed to us?"

"Oh, Mrs. O'Riorden, you wouldn't have liked it," Maggie burst out. "'Tis a terrible country. 'Tis half burnt to the ground and the bridges blown up and the roads with trees cut down across them. You don't know the waste…"

Sheila muttered to herself: "The waste…I know it…" and at that the tears welled up in Maggie's eyes again.

Dermot took her hand. "Lie down now," he said, "and try to sleep. We'll have another talk later."

Eileen stayed in the room with Maggie. The rest of us went downstairs. Sheila's eyes were hard and rebellious. That was the only visit she made to Maggie.

A few days later I called alone, and found that Maggie was up and dressed. She was well enough to be left; Eileen and Guy had gone to town. So I took her out to lunch, and then we went for a walk in Richmond Park. We had not been walking for long when she put her hand shyly on my arm and said: "Rory was very fond of you."

"I believe he was," I said, "and I'm glad of it."

"Do you think I was—good enough for him?"

"I knew Rory well enough to know this: that he wouldn't have chosen anything second-rate."

"His mother thinks I'm a coward—that I ran away."

"I believe she does, but I should think it's difficult just now for Rory's mother to be as fair as she usually is."

Suddenly Maggie sat down on a seat and buried her face in her hands. "I *did* run away," she sobbed. "I did. I did. I *was* a coward."

I tried to comfort her. "My dear, who can blame you? What you told us the other day—it must have been terrible. You have been through so much, and with that at the end of it—"

"Oh, that—that was all lies. It wasn't like that at all. It was far, far worse than that. Listen—"

Most of the boys worked all day long in the fields. Mick Slaney drove the butcher's cart and Ken Conroy was at the sawmill, behind Doonan's garden. There was a well in the garden, but some time ago a false bottom was put in, just above water-level. They kept their guns and ammunition there. Ken Conroy was a slip of a chap. He could stand in the bucket, holding the rope in his hands. Then they would lower him, and he would fetch up the guns a few at a time. They kept a tarpaulin sheet over them in the day-time. Doonan got his water from the priest's well, and Father Farrell very well knew why.

At night the boys gathered in the barn to get their orders from Rory. They came one at a time, three minutes between each arrival. A loft ran over the extent of the barn. It was very big. All the walls were wooden, and at one end there was a false wall. The planks that made it were as old and crazy as the rest of the building. One or two of them were loose and you could squeeze through into the secret chamber that was no more than a yard wide but a good twelve yards long. One of the boys always lurked outside. When he thought it necessary, he pulled a piece of tarred string that even in daylight was invisible from a few yards' distance against the tarred side of the barn. The pulling caused a cotton reel to dance on the table before which Rory sat. Then talk ended and the dim light was extinguished till the cotton reel rattled again.

Every man, at every meeting, had to show his gun to Rory, demonstrate its cleanliness and efficiency, check over his ammunition. This was the time, too, for bringing in cotton-wool, lint, splints, bandages, iodine, which Maggie kept with scrupulous care and cleanliness in a box at the end of the long room. She had there, too, a few elementary surgical instruments; scissors and forceps and so on; and a spirit stove and saucepan for boiling water to sterilise them and to wash wounds.

Sometimes she spent a whole day with her patients who lay on straw mattresses. Sometimes she came to cheer an hour or two of the night. Sometimes it was possible for Mick Slaney to take them, hidden under the bloody sacks in the floor of the butcher's cart, to some place where they could get better attention than here. And Tuohy, the butcher, knew about that.

There was nobody in Ballybar who didn't know all that was

going on. And if in the day-time, when there might be strangers about, they were surly to the stocky, grey-eyed deep-shouldered young man who worked in Donohue's grocery, there was policy in that.

A law-abiding, decent little place was Ballybar while day-light lasted; but strangely empty of young life at night. Then, one by one, at three-minute intervals, a shadow here and a shadow there detached itself from the darkness of the country night till all the shadows were hung like bats in the darkness of Rice's loft.

Then there was no surliness to the young leader.

"Slaney!"

"Yes sir."

Slaney laid revolver and ammunition on the table. Rory examined them carefully, approved them, pushed them back.

"We have long suspected Sir George Winter of giving information to British soldiers. Yesterday he was seen in conversation with a major of the regular army and with a captain of Auxiliaries. These men had three lorries of troops drawn up in the road outside Sir George Winter's house. Sir George walked down his drive with them and was heard to give them directions for avoiding an ambush. He shook hands with them and said: 'Good luck to you, boys. I wish it was your ambush and that you could wipe out some of these swine. This place is a nest of them.'"

"I suppose Pat Hickey was working in the hedge," Slaney grinned.

Rory frowned. "Conroy!"

"Yes, sir."

"You have heard what I said to Slaney?"

"Yes, sir."

"Well, Slaney supposes things. I want this job done by a man who supposes nothing and can keep his mouth shut."

He held out his hand, and Conroy pushed across revolver and ammunition.

"Sir George Winter will give no more information to the enemy. After dinner, he sits in a room on the ground floor, and he never bothers to draw the blinds. I suppose he thinks God Almighty is looking after him. When you have taught him better, pin this on his front door."

Rory handed Conroy a rolled piece of paper on which was printed: "DON'T OPEN YOUR MOUTH TOO WIDE."

"That's all."

Conroy saluted and went.

"The rest of you boys can go. There's nothing else tonight."

One by one, at intervals, the shadows detached themselves from the barn and disappeared by a dozen routes into the darkness.

Maggie and Rory faced one another across the table in the dim light. "Let's have a look at Dan," Rory said.

Maggie took up the lantern and they went to the end of the long chamber. Dan O'Gwyer, lying on his pallet of straw, grinned.

"Well, how's this feller?" Rory asked.

"Ach, to hell with keepin' me here," said O'Gwyer. "Let me be now. I want to be hobbling about again."

"You'll stay here, Dan, my boy, till you're told to go. If the wrong people see you hobbling they'll want to know what made you hobble. Let's see his leg, Maggie."

Maggie unrolled the bandage, and held down the lantern for Rory to examine the bullet-wound that went through the flesh of O'Gwyer's calf.

"That looks all right. Fix him up again. You're going on fine, lad. Don't think I'm keeping you here for fun. I want you, and plenty more like you."

"I'm ready, when you say the word."

"That's the chap. You being well fed?"

"Ach, they're stuffin' my guts fit to bust. How's Mary Clarke? She's not about with Slaney?"

"Ach, now, don't you be worrying about Mary Clarke. She's a good girl and she thinks you're a hero."

O'Gwyer grinned. "So I am then."

"And now I'll read to you a bit."

O'Gwyer settled down quietly on the straw, the pin-point of his cigarette glowing in the dusk. Rory took up a book and began to read:

*Queen Maeve summoned to her to Rath-Cruhane all her captains and counsellors and tributary kings...*

"He was very quiet on the way home," Maggie said to me, "and seemed to be thinking a long way back."

The next day a lorry-load of Black-and-Tans drove into Ballybar. A few stayed in the lorry; the rest clattered into Donohue's grocery and demanded drink. Rory served them and when they had had a drink or two they began to serve themselves. The sergeant in charge asked, with no particular show of interest: "Is there a chap called Sir George Winter in these parts?"

"Yes; lives four or five miles down the road."

"Seen anything of him lately?"

"No. I don't get about much."

"What sort of feller would you say he was? Is he liked about here?"

"Oh, yes; I should say so."

"This is the nearest place to his house, isn't it?" the sergeant persisted.

Rory considered. "Yes, it would be, unless you went across country."

The sergeant took a pull at his drink. "News seems to travel slow round here, young feller."

"All the wires are down," Rory pointed out reasonably.

"You haven't heard that Sir George was shot dead last night by some bloody skunk, have you?"

"Good Lord! That's a bad do."

"It's going to be a bad do for this bloody village if we find a gun in it," the sergeant declared savagely. "There's one thing. Sir George shot back. I hope he hit something. Have another drink, lads, and then get on with it."

The Black-and-Tans laid their hands on the first bottles they could reach, drank deeply, and then got up with a clatter of arms. "This place first," the sergeant ordered.

The scum got busy. With rifle-butts they smashed and hammered. They swept bottles from shelves and stamped the broken glass underfoot as they poked at cupboard doors, pulled open drawers, scattering the contents to the floor, tried to pull up the floor itself. From a search they passed to wanton wrecking. They knocked the pictures from the walls, tore down curtains, tramped upstairs and hacked the beds to pieces. Rory accompanied them upstairs. Maggie was sitting in an easy chair in one of the bedrooms. A lout, unsteady with drink, advanced upon her. "Boys, look what I've got!" He laid a hand on Maggie's shoulder, then found a painful grip on his own. He swung round to find himself gazing into Rory's cold grey eyes.

"Maggie, get out into the street," Rory said. When she was gone, he released his grip. "If you want to rip up the chair get on with it."

The chair was ripped up, and in the interests of thorough search gun-butts were swung against walls, smashing down the plaster lest some hiding-place be behind.

Half the men had by now gone downstairs and were drinking what was left of the liquor. They took some bottles out to the lorry. Then the last of them staggered and stumbled out into the cold light of the dying winter day.

"Any more, Sarge? Shall we do another house?" one of them demanded.

The sergeant, none too steady himself, looked at them contemptuously. "Christ!" he said. "And we won the war! Get into the bloody lorry."

They began to pile themselves in when Maggie, who was standing by Rory's side, felt his hand clutch her arm with a sudden painful pressure. "O God!" he said under his breath.

Limping round the corner at the village cross-roads, unsuspecting messenger of doom to all the boys at Ballybar, came Dan O'Gwyer.

"The fool! The fool!" Rory groaned.

Too late, Dan saw that he had walked into a raid. Father Farrell's house was there on the corner. Dan lurched towards the deep embrasure of the doorway, hoping to obliterate his fatal being. The sergeant, emptying a last bottle, let the bottle drop to the ground. "What the 'ell!" he cried. "Come on, some of you."

Rory and Maggie moved forward with the rush of Black-and-Tans. Mick Slaney was there, too, and Ken Conroy, and most of the lads. When they came to the priest's house, the door had been opened, and O'Gwyer stood there with Father Farrell's arms about him. You could see right into the little hall, with the ebony crucifix on the white wall at the back. The priest's hair was as white as the wall. From his hale, ruddy face blue eyes looked out fearlessly at the sergeant's. The sergeant seized O'Gwyer and with one strong heave landed him sprawling in the road.

"Where did you get that bloody wound?" he demanded.

O'Gwyer lay face downwards at the cross-roads in the darkening evening and did not answer. Mary Clarke came running up from Tuohy's where she worked, and when she saw Dan lying there she let out a great shriek. A soldier struck her across the mouth, and she fell to a quiet sobbing, with a shawl drawn over her head.

"Have a look at that wound," the sergeant ordered.

"Pull his pants off. That's the quickest way to get at it," a soldier suggested; and they pulled off O'Gwyer's trousers and left him naked from the waist. Then the bandage was savagely pulled off, causing the wound to bleed.

"Can you beat that!" said the sergeant. "That's a bullet-wound. In there. Out there." He jabbed with his finger at O'Gwyer's leg. "Still bleeding."

The Black-and-Tans stood in a circle round the prostrate man, clumping their rifle-butts restlessly into the ground. Outside them the villagers stood in a wider circle, gazing at the naked legs and the ooze of blood. And round about them all was the quiet countryside, fading swiftly to dusk, a few bare elms, a few rooks, cawing homewards. The priest's servant lighted a little lamp in the hall, and the crucifix stood out plain.

Suddenly the priest spoke. "That's an old wound. You've broken it open by brutal treatment."

"New or old, it's a bullet-wound," said the sergeant. "What the 'ell d'you know about it, anyway?"

He stood up and faced the priest truculently. "If you know it's an old wound, p'raps you know when 'e got it, and 'ow."

The old man said deliberately, "He got it while defending his country from drunken barbarians like you."

The sergeant struck him hard in the face, and the men with the rifles closed in menacingly.

Father Farrell bent over Dan O'Gwyer. "Get up, my son," he said, and helped the boy to his feet. "Come into my house." Leaning on the priest's arm, the boy, keeping his face, for shame of his nakedness, buried in the old man's shoulder, limped towards the open door.

The sergeant leapt before them, raised his stout arms, standing there outlined against the light in the hall. "I'm going to have that man shot. I advise you to stand aside from him."

The women in the crowd set up a wailing, and the men with the rifles stood back, half-way across the road, their fingers itch-ing on the triggers. The priest's voice said calmly: "If you must shoot, shoot."

"Gawd 'elp you," said the sergeant. He sprang away from the door. "Men," he shouted. "Don't shoot the parson. Fire!"

The rifles cracked; the flames were apparent on the darkening air. Father Farrell and O'Gwyer fell together, crumpling very slowly beneath the crucifix.

Following the shots, there was a moment of intense silence. Then the women knelt in the road and their wailing filled the air. The sergeant said curtly: "Get back to the lorry."

The men of the village took up the bodies and carried them from the hall into the priest's bedroom. The women followed. Only Rory and Maggie remained to go back in the trail of the soldiers to the lorry which still stood outside the grocery. Maggie was crying quietly. Rory's broad shoulders were rock-like, stubborn, his eyes hard as grey granite. The men clattered into the lorry. The sergeant climbed up last into a seat alongside the driver. The lorry was vibrating, ready to be off along the road that was now lost in darkness. The headlights flamed out, revealing nothing at the cross-roads but a black smudge that must have been O'Gwyer's boots and trousers.

"Get some more drink in by tomorrow," the sergeant shouted. "We'll be back about the same time."

Rory gazed at the bragging brute without speaking. The engine roared suddenly and the lorry moved off. The men in it began to sing.

Rory took a handkerchief from his pocket and gave it to Maggie. She looked a question; he nodded grimly and slipped into a ramshackle shed in the grocery garden. He hastily pulled away the pile of junk that hid the switch. His hand on the switch was as steady as a rock; his eye watched Maggie through the small window. She knew what to look for. As soon as the headlights touched the blazed tree she dropped the handkerchief.

The explosion of the mine lit the night, shook the village. There was still no haste in Rory's step as he walked to the spot where the remains of the lorry lay half in and half out of the crater. He looked contemptuously at the dead and drove away the women who would have cared for the wounded. "Go!" he said. "As far as you can. As quick as you can. It's our turn now." All the boys were gathered round. "And if any of you want to go too, do it now."

All the boys stayed. They got the guns out of the well behind the sawmill yard that night.

By midnight most of the women were gone from Ballybar. The boys gathered in the grocery. There were twelve of them. In addition, there were Rory and Maggie. Rory told them that this would be their last fight in Ballybar. "For some of us, perhaps for most of us, it will be the last fight of all. I shall call it a good fight if you leave three men dead for every one of us that dies. Five of you will stay here with me and Maggie. The other seven will occupy Tuohy's house opposite. I have his permission. He's too old a man for this sort of thing. He's gone and taken his wife and Mary Clarke with him. Slaney, you'd better take charge opposite. Pick your six men."

Slaney picked his men, and Rory shared out the ammunition. "Don't waste it," he said. "Let's hope they come late. If they do, keep them in play till dark. Then get away if you can. You can go to the barn, or you can disappear into the country. Those of you who can, will meet me at the waterfall at ten the next night. This is the end of things here, and I shall have fresh orders by then. If I am not there, you will know where to go for your orders."

He paused for a moment in his pacing of the room, and stood there with his wide shoulders hunched, his head bowed, his eyes troubled. "Of course," he said, "we needn't wait for them. We needn't have this last fight. We could clear out now. But I want to stay. This is war, and wars are won by killing the enemy; in no other way. They will come back after what has happened tonight, and we shall be ready to do our job in circumstances that give us a good chance. That's all."

Slaney and his six men picked up their guns. "When you go in," said Rory, "put heavy furniture against the front door. Fill the passage with it. Jam up the back door, too. Put mattresses to the windows and shoot between them. I'll tell you what I'm going to do here, and you can do the same if you like. I shall send my best shot—that's you, Conroy; take your gun and get ready—to find a window that overlooks the back of this house. Don't waste a shot unless someone really looks like getting in that way or tries to fire the place. I'll keep three men up here on the first floor; Maggie and I and another will shoot from the ground floor. There are three Mills bombs for each party; no more. If they force a way into the ground floor, let the men there retreat upstairs. Let the enemy have the bombs as they follow. There's nothing more, except that you'll fight better with food in your bellies. See to that, Slaney."

Rory shook hands with Slaney and his six, and they clattered away down the stairs, a grim rain-coated cohort, with black hats slanted over their foreheads.

When they and Conroy were gone, Rory got his men to work, barricading doors, masking windows with mattresses. Not till everything was done did he send Maggie and three of the men to sleep. He and another sat up till five, then changed the watch.

But for all that happened in Ballybar that night, the whole party might have slept. The grey winter dawn came, with none of the customary activity of the village. No carts creaked along the street; there was no sound of the opening of little shops. Rory removed the mattresses from the ground-floor window and swung himself over the sill. To the right and to the left the road stretched with not a thing upon it, and only here and there from far-scattered houses did a plume of smoke rise into the cold air. Slaney shouted cautiously from across the street that all was well with his garrison; and passing to the back of the grocery, Rory had a reassuring glimpse of young Conroy who had cut no more than a peephole into the boarding of an isolated loft.

Maggie made tea, and they breakfasted on that and bread and jam; and after breakfast the four men of Rory's command, as if acting by some agreement, all went upstairs to the upper floor. Rory took Maggie in his arms. The two pairs of grey eyes met, and held for a long time.

"Well," said Rory. "I'm a bright sort of husband, am I not?"

"I had a bright sort of father, too," she said.

"Here am I with a lovely young bride, and this is all I can do for her: give her bread and jam for breakfast and guns in the afternoon."

"You darling! You don't know what you've given me. You'll never know."

"Oh, yes; I know all right," Rory said, "because I know what you've given me. We've just swapped hearts." He put his head down on her breast. "There! I can hear it! That's my old heart, ticking away in there."

She kissed the thick tangle of his hair, then lifted up his serious face with both her hands. "What a fraud I feel," she said. "Oh, my darling! You ought not to be doing this. You ought to be doing lovely things. You were brought up on dreams, weren't you? Oh, I know them all. The land of saints and scholars; Dark Rosaleen. And this is what we give you. Oh, God! How you must hate this country!"

"Ach, my dear, you must never talk like that now. It's easy to hate what needs a helping hand. It's easy to pass by on the other side. And dreams? Ay, I've had them, too. When all of us children played with Maeve and Ireland was a country of lovely queens. But now the dream's cold day-light, and the queens are girls like Mary Clarke. But don't think that there's any room in my heart for regret. Promise me that, my love: if I'm killed, don't think that I died regretting the easy things I've missed. I've had you, and I've had the boys, and we've all had some grand times."

"And if we—get out of this, you'll love me for ever and ever?"

"Dear Maggie, eternity is now. There's no past about it and no future. It just *is*. And that's how my love is for you."

"And mine for you," she whispered. "Kiss me now."

So they kissed for the last time, straining body to body, as though they could not let one another go. Suddenly, he went rigid in her arms, his whole being concentrated on listening. He put her gently from him, and said quietly: "They're coming." Mulligan, who was to share with them the defence of the ground floor, came running down the stairs.

"You shoot kneeling, Mulligan," Rory said. "I'll fire over your head. Maggie'll keep a spare rifle loaded for either of us. It's a pity this isn't a bay window. We can only see 'em when they're right in front of us."

"And they can only shoot us from right in front," Mulligan grinned. "I prefer that."

But there was no shooting for a moment. They heard the lorry stop a good way off—perhaps at the entrance to the street.

"They don't like the look of things," said Rory. "Everything's too quiet for 'em. They're afraid of a trap. It would have been nice if they'd stopped the lorry right between these two houses."

They kept their eyes to the slit that divided the mattresses. It allowed them to see little more than the house Slaney occupied. Presently, appearing soundlessly upon that little field, like shadows creeping upon a screen, came two Black-and-Tans. They moved cautiously, close under the walls of the houses, their rifles in their hands.

"Slaney can't see 'em," said Rory, "but I expect he can see a couple on this side," and to confirm the words came the sudden *crack! crack!* of two rifles. Almost at the same moment, two shots, fired from the first floor, thundered through the grocery. One of the men opposite spun round, fell, and began to crawl away on hands and knees, slowly fighting each inch of the way. The other began to run back swiftly the way he had come; he suddenly fell headlong and lay still. The crawling man passed him, moved slowly off the screen of vision.

"Poor devils," said Rory. "They've just been sent out to see where we are. Well, now they know. Let's sit still for a bit and see what strategy they employ. As a rule, they've got as much as a mad bullock."

Twenty minutes passed; then the lorry roared loudly. They heard it charging down the street. When it came into view, there was no one in it but the driver. He swung the lorry round sharply, ran it nose first almost into the wall of the house next to that which Slaney occupied. Rory's garrison was too interested in this manœuvre to fire. By the time they had recovered from their surprise, the driver had leapt from his seat and lay flat on the floor of the lorry.

"What the hell!" said Mulligan. "I don't see it."

"Wait a minute," Rory advised him. "I'm beginning to get the idea. We're going to have a real fight today, my boy. There's someone with brains out there who's thinking about saving his men's lives."

Presently, four men came at a rush. They appeared so swiftly on the narrow screen that only one shot rang out from the grocery. It missed. Then the men were under cover of the slewed-round lorry, and with boots and rifles they began to beat down the door of the house. It took them less than half a minute. Then they were inside. And no sooner were they in than, at disconcertingly infrequent intervals, others rushed up, one at a time, past the protecting lorry, into the house.

Soon there were a dozen men in the house next door to Slaney. Suddenly, from its upper floor, a volley was poured upon the grocery windows. Rory, Maggie and Mulligan heard the bullets thump into the mattresses. One sang between them and buried itself in the wall. For a second there was consternation, and in the room upstairs, no doubt. In that second, the driver of the lorry leapt to his seat, put his engine in reverse. Instantly, bullets spattered the cab of the lorry. An answering volley came from across the street. The man worked with the fury of fear. He got his lorry away.

"Take it easy," said Rory. "We can rest a bit. Now they'll repeat the manœuvre on this side of the street. We'll have to leave it to Slaney. We're fighting brains this time, my boy. These men will all be under cover. They'll have endless ammunition, and they'll be able to plug at us all day from both sides of the street."

They waited for a long time. The stillness that had been on the street at dawn came back, punctuated at rare intervals by a rifle-shot, trying pot-luck at Rory's garrison. Then there came again the roar of the motor-lorry. But this time there was no surprise in it. Six shots rang out almost as one from Slaney's house. Rory and Mulligan, gazing through their slit, saw the driver crumpled over the wheel, saw the lorry swerve crazily, crash into the front of a house, and come to a standstill.

"Now the brains of that organisation can do some more thinking," Mulligan grinned. "Holy Mary! Will you listen to that?"

"That's the thinking," Rory said grimly.

A machine-gun had begun to stutter in the street. Slaney's house was getting it. The gun sprayed from the ground floor to the upper windows. No one dared appear at those windows then. At the same moment, men could be heard smashing down the door of the house next to the grocery. The horrid yammer of the gun ceased, and in the silence Rory could hear men trampling in the room beyond the wall.

"That's simpler," Mulligan said, crestfallen. "Why didn't he do that with us? Seems easier than all the business with the motor-lorry."

"Because he's realised what I'm always trying to drive into you:

that you don't waste ammunition if there's any other way. The man with the last shot wins."

"And what the hell are we to do with our shots now?" Mulligan demanded. "Sure we can sit here gazing at one another across the streets of Ballybar till St. Patrick's Day."

"Just do what I'm doing," Rory chided him. "Watch those windows opposite, and as soon as you see a movement, shoot. You'd better watch the bottom window. I'll take the top."

"Ach, the hell of a lot of movement we'll see. They'll all be after having their dinner. I can…"

Mulligan swung round, and looked at Maggie with a pained, surprised look on his face. It was so sudden and comical that she was about to laugh, when she noticed a red hole in the middle of his forehead. His knees doubled under him; his rifle clattered to the floor. At the same moment, Rory's rifle spoke. "I got him," he said grimly; then turned to Mulligan. "Don't leave him there," he said. They carried him to the room at the back. Rory picked up Mulligan's rifle and laid it carefully on the table. He looked at his wrist-watch. "Make some tea for the boys," he said. "It's noon."

Maggie took the tea upstairs. When she came down she began to rummage in a cupboard. Rory said testily: "What are you doing there? Come and load the rifles."

"I'm looking for a bandage. Somers is shot through the right wrist. They didn't want to tell you. He's no more use, I'm afraid."

"If he's no more use, leave him. You must help what is of use. Load the rifles."

Maggie loaded the rifles. "Now kneel down where Mulligan was and shoot at anything you see."

Maggie knelt, and shot, and saw a man fall half out of the window.

And so the battle went on. Desultorily, at long intervals, the rifles cracked, each side wary. At three o'clock there was a trampling on the stairs. "Clancy's dead."

Rory wheeled round. "Then for God's sake what are you doing here? If Clancy's dead and Somers is useless, you're the only man left up there. Get back, and send Somers with messages if you must send them."

He went back to his window, stood once more sighting through the slit between the mattresses that were drilled like a target at the end of a day's shooting.

"Notice what's happening over there?" he muttered.

"Yes. I noticed it a long time ago."

There was firing from only one window of Slaney's house, and that was slow and infrequent. "One rifle, I should say," Rory said grimly. "Well, we've notched a good few."

The afternoon wore on. There was a moment when Rory recognised the face of the last man holding out opposite. It was Slaney, bandaged about the head. He continued to shoot, steadily, unhurriedly.

Towards three o'clock there was shooting in a new quarter. Rory, grimed and red-eyed, laid down his rifle. "Hear that? They're shooting behind Slaney's house. They'll try to rush him now."

There was silence on Rory's side of the street. Barney Day, who was holding the room upstairs, ceased firing, as he, too, waited to hear the upshot of the attack on Slaney. It came swiftly. One, two, three detonations shook the street. "He's given 'em the bombs," Rory muttered. No other sound after that came from Slaney's side of the street. The last explosion shook the mattresses down from the upper window. No face appeared at it.

Rory shouted up the stairs, and Barney Day came running down. He was in his shirt-sleeves and one of the sleeves was red.

"You hurt?" Rory asked him.

"Ach, it's only a fleabite. I can shoot."

"Well, it looks as though it's you and me and Maggie now. How's Somers?"

"Bad. He's groaning."

"We'll stick it out till dark. Then you'd better slide away into the country and take Somers with you. How d'you think we've done?"

"Not bad at all. We've give as good as we took."

"I think so. That's fine. Well, get back now." Day started off towards the stairs. Rory recalled him with a gesture, and held out his hand. "Well, Barney...in case..."

"Good-bye, Rory. At dark, then, it's each for himself?"

"That's it. Good-bye. You've made a good fight."

About ten seconds after that Barney was shot through the heart, and just as the light was giving out Rory was shot through the leg. He fell in a heap, groaning, a kneecap smashed to pieces.

Maggie knelt over him. "Tell Somers to go," he said. "They'll be breaking in here any minute."

The small garden behind the grocery was a shrubbery, thick with laurels. Somers came down the stairs, white, groaning quietly, holding his broken wrist. Maggie opened the back door cautiously and he stumbled out into the obscurity of the bushes. It was a black night, cloudy, without stars. He seemed at once to be swallowed up. They gave him a few minutes, then followed. Maggie leant forward. Rory hung round her neck. She half-carried, half-dragged him. The six paces between the door and the shrubbery seemed endless. She knew the little twisting path through the bushes and struggled forward towards the spot where it debouched into a ditch. Beyond the ditch was a rising field. The ditch itself ran left, behind the straggle of hedges that were parallel with the village street.

Maggie swayed and tottered between the bushes. Rory bit into his lip so that he might not cry aloud as his dangling wounded leg swayed and flapped.

They reached the ditch. "For God's sake, darling—you're choking me." She lowered him gently till he stood upon his sound leg, and took deep panting breaths. "Where will we make for?" she asked.

"The barn. Can you do it?"

"Do it? Oh, God! We must. We must."

He arranged himself upon her back again and she stumbled forward. A shadow, just darker than the night, rose out of the earth.

"For the love of Mary, don't shoot. 'Tis me—Ken Conroy."

Maggie sobbed with relief. "He's wounded, Ken. He can't walk. We must get him to the barn."

Now it was a little easier. With an arm round the neck of each, Rory hopped forward on one leg. Though he was short, he was heavy, and Conroy was a wisp of a man: the tiny acrobat who would go down the well, standing in the bucket. So they were long about that march of agony, their hearts thundering as their ears reached backwards for the sound of pursuit. There was a moment when simultaneously all three stood in their tracks, sweating with fear. A twig snapped loudly behind them, and for half a minute they stood there with tingling spines awaiting the thump of lead. Then they went on again—shuffle hop, shuffle—but never now separated from the fear of following footsteps.

So they traversed the way through the ditch, behind the blind empty houses, till they were at the street's end, at the cross-roads, behind the priest's house, where unattended by wake or vigil lay the bodies of Father Farrell and young O'Gwyer, who for a sight of Mary Clarke had loosed this agony upon them.

Now from the end of the ditch a rubble of shale gave a slithering access to the high-road, and a groan was wrenched from Rory's lips as he contemplated the horror of that descent. Maggie took him on her back again. Conroy went first, walking backwards, his hands sustaining Maggie's body so that the load might not make her rush or stumble. And thus they came to the high-road and paused there to breathe and listen. There seemed to be nothing in all the night but a bat or two, erratically brushing the heavy-omened air.

Now they slanted over the cross-roads, with the hop-shuffle-hop stabbing its pain through Rory, and they came through a loose-swinging gate to the big field in whose far corner was the dark loom of the barn. So near their refuge, they tried to hurry, Rory swinging out his leg and muttering to them to go quickly. When they were in the gloom of the great building they rested again for a while, drawing deep sobs of joy, fugitives come through ordeal to sanctuary.

Literally, in there, they could not see a step before their faces. But they knew every inch of that way, and unerringly crossed the wide uneven floor to the corner where the ladder went up to the loft. Clinging with both hands, hopping on one leg, Rory could make the ascent alone, every rung gained at the cost of anguish as his loose-hanging leg jarred the ladder. He lay again, half-fainting, at the top. Conroy went warily forward to hold aside the loose boards; Maggie finished the journey as she had begun it, with Rory's strangling arms about her neck.

And now, indeed in sanctuary at last, they chanced a light: the merest glim cast by a small electric torch with a handkerchief tied round its head. They laid Rory upon the pallet, gave him brandy, and then Maggie cut off one leg of his trousers and turned to the box where she kept her bandages and splints.

"My God, there's not a splint in the place," she groaned as the pitiful little light fell upon the box that was her pride. Everything was there, everything she needed, except some pieces of flat wood. She and Conroy gazed with consternation into the box.

"We could smash the box," he said.

"'Tis too strong. I wouldn't dare risk the noise."

"Well, listen, Maggie. You'll find some bits of packing-case wood downstairs behind the door. I brought them myself, intending to smooth them off some day."

"Look after him," said Maggie. "Not an inch must he stir. I'll be back at once."

\*

Sitting on the bench in Richmond Park, with the deer stepping delicately across the grass that was vivid with the green of earliest spring, Maggie paused and looked round in wonder, as though from the horrors she had been recounting she had stepped suddenly into an awareness of the graciousness about her. "I must go on," she said. "It will hurt you." I nodded, and she continued.

"When I got downstairs to the floor of the barn, I was afraid. I had the tiny light with me, and it made the shadows more frightening than if there had been no light at all. I felt as though someone were walking behind me, and someone was. He said suddenly: 'I was sure there were three of you. Where are the others?'

"I stopped quite still. He said: 'Don't move. Don't turn round. There's no reason for you to see me.' Then he took the little light from my hand and stuck the end of the torch in a truss of hay. 'That's excellent,' he said. 'Now I can see you, but I can remain invisible as I have been ever since you left the house. Where are the others?'

"He had a beautiful voice. He spoke so low and so pleasantly that I was almost betwitched into answering.

"'We followed that other fellow, too,' he said 'the one with the broken wrist. We didn't want to lose any of the bonny fighters. There's a matter of a dozen or so dead men to be accounted for, to say nothing of the lot blown up in the lorry last night. Tell me, where are the others?'

"I did not speak. I could almost feel him shrug his shoulders, almost see him smile, standing there behind me in the dark. 'No?' he said. 'No information? Well, my dear, I'm in command of the men here. I feel responsible, you know, after what's happened today. I'm afraid I shall have to find out. Where are the others?'

"This time, he reached out his arm from behind me so that I could see he held a revolver. Then he drew it back, and there was nothing but the voice. It was so different a voice from any that I expected—so smooth and speaking so beautifully.

"'Well, 'pon my soul,' he said at last, 'if you don't speak soon, then by the word of an Essex—'

"And then I knew. All the time he had been speaking, that voice coming out of the dark seemed to be coming out of the darkness of years and years ago. It had been puzzling my memory, and when he said the name everything lit up. I thought of us all sitting that night, singing, when that mad old captain came and we all sang his hymn. And I thought of swimming and sailing and fishing, and he and Rory loving one another. And I thought my heart would break with joy because I knew I had only to turn round and see a face I remembered and say: 'But, Oliver, it's Rory. He's upstairs. You won't want to hurt *him*.'

"And then I turned round, and he said: 'Humph! Inquisitive? Well, here I am.' And with that he turned a strong torch of his own full on his face. And, oh, dear God, it wasn't the face I knew. It was cold and cruel, and the eyes were smiling terribly with wound marks round them, and there were wounds that twisted his lips to a sneer. And my heart dried up, and fear came on me, and suddenly I shrieked.

"And that was how I betrayed Rory.

"There was silence after I shrieked, and then he shrugged his shoulders and said: 'That ought to fetch 'em.' He didn't know me. I could see that he didn't know me.

"And then there was nothing to do but wait. He had snapped out his torch. I could hear a creeping and crawling along the floor of the loft. He could hear it, too. It went on for a long time, till I knew that Rory was at the opening over the ladder. Then suddenly a big electric torch flashed from up there down into the floor of the barn and began searching for us. It was Conroy holding it, so that Rory could shoot. When the shot came I screamed again, and the thunder in my ears drowned the noise of my own cry. Oliver had fired over my head. Rory slipped head first down the ladder, his arms sprawled out, his wounded leg folded up under him when he came to rest. Conroy watched from above. He had no revolver.

"First, Oliver took the revolver out of Rory's hand and put it in his pocket. Then he turned him over. He knew at once. His own revolver fell from his hand. All the marks seemed to go out of his face as though a sponge had cleaned them off. He looked soft and young and gentle. Then they flowed back. There was too much to be wiped away. He picked up his revolver and turned to me, 'Maggie Donnelly?' he said.

"'Maggie O'Riorden.'

"'Christ!' he said. 'Christ?' and ran out of the barn.

"Then Conroy came down the ladder. He stood looking at Rory for a moment with tears streaming down his face. Then he turned and struck me in the mouth. 'You bitch!' he said. He spat in the straw at my feet and stumbled out into the darkness. I knew what he meant. He thought that I had been tortured to make me say where Rory was, and that I hadn't been brave enough to keep my mouth shut, that I had screamed and so brought Rory crawling out to be killed. But it wasn't that. It was Oliver's face."

She began to cry, and I comforted her as best I could, and we got up and walked on a little way.

She had stayed in the barn all night, sitting with her back against a bale of hay, with Rory's head in her lap, her hands stroking his hair. His face was uninjured. Towards dawn she saw through the cracks in the barn a red flickering light. Then she went out and ran across the field which they had traversed so painfully not long before. Half the village was on fire. Great bulging columns of smoke, charged with red light, and dancing volleys of sparks shot up into the darkness from what had been Ballybar. She stood at the cross-roads watching the infernal spectacle till the flames grew paler against the light growing in the east. Then she heard the sound of marching on the road. She crawled behind the hedge, and what was left of the flying column of Black-and-Tans trailed past her in the dawn. Oliver marched at the head of them. Suddenly one of the men began to sing. Oliver turned upon him savagely: "Shut your blasted mouth," he said.

The man protested: "Can't a feller sing?"

Then, Maggie said, Oliver's face went blind with fury. He was carrying a heavy stick and he turned and belaboured the man over the head till he reeled and fell. The others closed about him, muttering. He took a revolver from his belt, formed them into ranks, and marched them off. He walked last, the revolver in his hand. She watched till they were out of sight on the road just grey with morning twilight. Then she went on into Ballybar.

There was nothing to stay for: nothing but the houses foundering in the sea of fire and one or two of the boys' bodies lying in the road. Ken Conroy was there, dead, under the wall of a burning house. She understood the blow he had given her and the reason for it, and she forgave him, and took up his little jockey's body and carried it and laid it under the wall of the graveyard just beyond the end of the street. She kissed the dead face before she laid him in the dust, and that was the last thing she did in Ballybar.

"You see," she said, "Mrs. O'Riorden doesn't understand how it was. She says she would like to have been at the funeral, as though it were something with nice wreaths and singing. But, you see, it was like that. And I couldn't tell her, could I?"

"No, my dear," I said, looking down at the earnest face, so young with its eyes so grey, "I think you were wise and strong to leave it as you did."

"And if I'd talked about it," she said, "it would have been very hard not to mention Oliver. And I didn't want to do that, because Rory was very fond of you, and he loved Oliver once. He wouldn't have wished it. There's sorrow enough in the world, without my coming between friends."

Then I cried, cried as I had never cried before, as I shall never cry again, tears of anguish for the wrong that had been done, tears for Rory lying beyond the reach of tears in a far-off draughty barn, tears for Oliver venting his savage sorrow as he marched hopelessly along the road of twilight, tears of humiliation at the wisdom and steadfastness of the girl at my side. She walked along quietly, embarrassed by the sobs that shook me, looking shyly into my face from time to time.

"You're too good, too good," I managed to say at last. "Why should you protect me like this?"

"Good?" she said. "No, I'm not good. I'm trying to be sensible, that's all. Aren't you sad and lonely like the rest of us? Very well, then."

We walked in silence for a while, and then I asked her: "What are you going to do now?"

"Do?" she asked with surprise. "Why, I must go back."

"Must you?"

"Why, yes. A few more days and I shall be strong enough. There's a lot still to do."

I left her at Eileen's gate.

She wrote to me when she got back, and told me that Rory had been buried at Ballybar. Then she left that part of the country and engaged in I know not what work in Dublin. Her letters continued to reach me irregularly, but never a hint was there as to what she was doing. And then in January, 1922, the Treaty with Ireland was signed, and she wrote me a letter of anguish. She was irreconcilable. With Charles Burgess and de Valera and Mary MacSwiney she turned her back on the old comrades of the long and bloody fight. Then, for the only time, she mentioned Rory's name. "If Rory were alive, his gun would be pointing at Michael Collins now."

She was still in Dublin, and moved by I know not what impulse

I went to see her. She was consorting daily with black rebellious women, indulging in orgies of despair. And soon all this was to issue in a country cleft again, brother turning the knife in brother's wound. When that was over, she sailed for America; and no news ever reached me or Dermot again of Rory's widow.

At the end of that last brief visit to her in Dublin, I sailed for Holyhead in a mood of misery. Ireland and the Irish and the Cause of Ireland and Irish Patriots had haunted my life from that far-off day when Dermot bowed to the memory of the Manchester Martyrs in an Ancoats bedroom. Gladly I watched the coast fade behind me.

At Holyhead my coach was shared by four raffish-smart young men who played cards for high stakes. Their voices had a shrill nervous edge; their eyes were swift yet furtive.

At Chester one of them said: "The Captain'll have to change here for Manchester. Better get out and say good-bye."

They tumbled out on to the platform. I got out, too, to stretch my legs. From farther down the train came a group of men, led by one whose face I felt I ought to know. The two groups mingled, with loud and hearty greetings, back-slapping and nervous laughter.

Then I and my four travelling companions got back into our compartment. The window was down, and the captain and his group gathered there. The train began to move. "Well, boys," the captain shouted, "remember the motto: no work while there's a bank to rob."

He took off his felt hat and waved it, and suddenly I remembered Captain Dennis Newbiggin. Plumage made a spot of bright colour in the band of his hat.

"You boys demobbed at last?" I asked my companions.

None of them answered. They looked at me furtively, suspiciously, as they shuffled the cards and went on playing for high stakes.

## 35

"May it please your Lordship; ladies and gentlemen of the jury. On the first Monday in December last, Percy Lupton, a young man of twenty-seven, went out to his work in the district of Higher Broughton in Manchester. He was a young man who had known a good deal of misfortune. He was gassed during the war, and was something of an invalid thereafter. The consequence was that after leaving the army he was unable to obtain regular employment for a long time. But at last his luck changed—changed, alas! for the worse, as we shall hear—for he was given what promised to be a permanent job. It is one of the most tragic features of this case that on the strength of this promise Lupton married. He had taken a brief honeymoon—a mere week-end—and on that first Monday of December he set out for the first time as a man with work, with hope, with a purpose in life. His young wife's last words to him as he left the house—the last words, as it happened, that she was to speak to him on earth—were these: 'Mind this fog. It will be the death of you.' Words, my lord, and ladies and gentlemen, which seem, as we recall them now, to have had a dreadful prescience and prophecy.

"Lupton's work was this. His uncle was a builder who owned a great deal of house property. There was a small office in the builder's yard, and here Lupton was to take charge of the ordering of builder's material; he was to hear complaints from tenants as to necessary repairs to property; he was to investigate them; and generally make himself useful on the administrative side of his uncle's business. On Monday afternoons, he was to make the rounds of the considerable number of houses which his uncle owned and collect the rents. No one else worked in the office: it was a one-man job.

"You will be told in evidence that Lupton was seen to arrive at the office soon after nine in the morning. The men who came and went in the yard saw him there throughout the morning, and some of them spoke to him. He was seen eating his lunch in the office, and at about two o'clock he was seen to set out on his rounds, carrying a small black Gladstone bag.

"Evidence will be put in, tracing his movements almost to the second of his death. You will hear of the houses he called at and how much money had accumulated in the bag by the time the afternoon was over.

"You will hear that Oliver Essex, who stands there before you accused of the murder of Percy Lupton, lodged in one of the houses at which Lupton collected the rent, that he was aware that Monday was the day for the collection, because his landlady, Mrs. Newbiggin, had once left the money and asked him to pay it, when the collector called. She will tell you that she happened on that occasion to return home earlier than she had expected and that she heard Essex say jokingly to the collector, the predecessor of the murdered man, Lupton, that his little black bag seemed well furnished and might be worth a snatch. The collector replied that he would like to see anyone try a snatch from him; and to that Essex answered: 'I know something of the art.'

"Evidence will be given that Essex had done no work for a long time, that he was in debt not only to his landlady but also to many tradespeople. One of these tradespeople, a tailor to whom he owed fifteen guineas, had pressed him for payment the week before Percy Lupton was killed. He will tell you that Essex said: 'Don't worry. You shall have the money soon if I have to do someone in to get it.'

"Well, now, let us return to what Percy Lupton was doing on that fatal day. Just as he was leaving the last house at which he had to call, he met an acquaintance and old army comrade, Henry Sugden. It was now six o'clock, the fog was thicker than it had been all day, and Sugden will tell you how he and Lupton walked along together, and how Lupton expressed his joy at having found regular work which permitted him to set up a home of his own. Sugden's way home happened to be past the builder's yard where Lupton's office was. Lupton took out his key, opened the office door, and stood for a moment talking to Henry Sugden. He said: 'Don't wait, Harry. I may be ten minutes. I want to enter this money in the books and lock it in the safe.' Sugden then said good-night, and no one saw Percy Lupton alive again.

"Sugden will tell you the exact time at which he parted from the dead man, because when Lupton told him not to wait, he looked at his wrist-watch, and he remembers saying: 'No. I must push off. It's twenty-past six.'

"As it happens, we have a check on time a little later. A young waiter named Daniel Kassassian had arranged to meet his sweetheart, a domestic servant, at a street corner at six-thirty. The corner was on the opposite side of the street from Lupton's office, and about thirty yards farther down. Kassassian, as soon as he arrived there, looked at his watch to see if he were in time for his appointment. He will tell you that he noted he was dead on time—six-thirty; and that at that very moment he heard a terrible cry.

"What happened, my lord, and ladies and gentlemen, in that little office between six-twenty and six-thirty, when Kassassian bounded across the road, it will be for this court, on the evidence submitted, to decide. It is the contention of the prosecution in this case that in those ten fatal minutes Oliver Essex murdered Percy Lupton.

"This is what Daniel Kassassian will tell you. The fog was so thick that he could see nothing. He ran across the road in the direction of the cry, and on the pavement outside the office he collided with a man who seemed—he will go no further than that—who seemed to have come out of the office. The collision was so violent, for both were running, that the man's hat, a black felt hat, was knocked off. Kassassian stooped to pick it up, and when it was in his hand the man snatched it so violently that, to use Kassassian's words, 'it seemed a bit queer to me.' Then Kassassian noticed a peculiar thing: bound round the man's face was a black handkerchief. It was tied over the bridge of his nose, leaving his eyes uncovered, but obscuring the lower half of his face. Kassassian was so startled by this that he retained his hold of the hat and something of a struggle went on for the possession of it. In the course of this struggle, the two swayed within the faint light cast through the fog by a street lamp, and that light was sufficient for Kassassian to see that down the back of one of the man's hands ran a livid scar.

"At last the masked man tired of the struggle, gave Kassassian a push, leaving him in possession of the hat, and ran as fast as he could go into the fog.

"Now Kassassian proceeded to investigate the cry which had brought him to the spot. He entered the office, and to his horror, stretched before the open door of the safe, he discovered the body of a man, later identified as Percy Lupton, with his head battered in. A round ebony ruler, bloodstained, lay alongside him.

"Kassassian placed upon the table the black felt hat, within which, as you will hear from the hatter who sold it to Oliver Essex, were the initials 'O.E.,' and he rang up the police…"

The grey wig surmounting the unmoving blur of scarlet; counsel twitching his gown as he wove mesh after mesh of the net; twelve intent faces of jurors; all about me here in the public gallery the livid eager faces of men and women in at the kill; it all wavered through the foggy air of the court, the phantasmagoric, unbelievable reality upon which I had been waiting. From the moment when Oliver had entered the dock, standing thin and upright as a young poplar, his hand, marked with the scar that Kassassian had seen in the lamplight that foggy night, clutching the rail before him, I had not looked at him. The judge's scarlet was a bloody focus of my vision; all outside it rayed and danced uncertainly like a shimmer of summer heat.

Suddenly it all seemed meaningless, a staged, fantastic show, nothing to do with me, nothing to do with Oliver. I got up and stumbled down the stairs, across the wide tiled hall where a few policemen stood and lawyers went with clicking shoes, their gowns fluttering behind them like black wings. Down the stone steps to the mean and sordid street. And as I looked at the people hurrying by, nothing green, nothing gracious, a wilderness of soot and stone, I knew that this was the phantasmagoria, that the reality was now behind me, and I walked blindly away from its intolerable presence, my heart crying: "O Oliver, my son, my son!"

He had destroyed so much that I had loved: Livia Vaynol, and Maeve, and Rory, and Maggie; but he had called me "Father" again; not "Sir" as in that time when there was ice between our hearts. Oh, why should I sit there and listen to the words and the words and the words, when I knew better than any of them what had happened? He had told me himself, and somehow, God help me, there was comfort in that.

He ran into the fog, and as he ran a voice kept crying in him: "You've left your hat, you fool; you've left your hat." But if he had known incontrovertibly that the hat would hang him, the impulse to run was now stronger than the impulse to go back. "I had killed so many men," he said, with brutal candour; "I had been applauded for killing them, promoted for killing them, given medals for killing them; but don't let any fool tell you there's no difference between killing in peace and war. In three seconds after I had killed that man I knew the difference. I knew that I had killed one man too many."

So, panic in his heart, he ran. There was nobody at home in his lodgings. Dennis Newbiggin had taken his mother to the first house of a music hall. So to calm himself he took a hot bath and changed his clothes. He didn't want to look flustered or unkempt. He was thinking it all out clearly. He left the house feeling fresh, with an overcoat in place of his raincoat, a new hat, well-polished shoes, a few clothes in a small suit-case. He now had a useful sum of money in his pocket. He didn't leave till after nine, and he walked into town. Remembering the tell-tale scar upon his hand, he wore gloves. He habitually wore his hat with the brim tilted forward to hide the scars about his eyes.

To test his nerve, he walked past the builder's yard. The light was on in the office. Two or three people, including a policeman, were inside, and there was another policeman at the door. A knot of curious sightseers had assembled on the pavement. He mingled with them for a moment and asked what the trouble was. Then he went on, his nerves in control, no panic, no haste.

He had a meal at an hotel, spinning it out as late as possible, and then booked a sleeping-berth on the night train to London. The steward who woke him in the morning brought a newspaper with his tea. The death of Percy Lupton was reported in it, though it had not caused much excitement. Kassassian's struggle with the masked man was related, and the paragraph said that "the police are hopeful of tracing this man through the initials 'O.E.' found on the hatband." Well, he was in London now, a big place where O.E. was not likely to be recognised.

What he intended to do was already beginning to take shape in his mind. He set off for Paddington in a taxi, intending to leave his suit-case there, and suddenly panic leapt upon him again. His eye fell on the suit-case, all the initials "O.E." stamped boldly on its side. That was the sort of thing one overlooked! Carrying one's doom about in a taxi!

So at Paddington, instead of putting the bag into the left-luggage office, he hung about for a time and then took another taxicab to

Victoria. It was still early. The police would hardly be looking for "O.E." yet, and if they came looking here and found O.E.'s suit-case, so much the better. Let them hang about and wait till he called for it. They would wait a long time. In the taxi he had transferred pyjamas and shaving tackle to his overcoat pockets. He now bought a new, cheap suit-case, had some bogus initials stamped on it in the shop, put his things into it, and left it at Paddington.

All this, which should have eased his mind, irritated it. He began to be overburdened with a sense of the innumerable small slips that might be made, the innumerable small things that must be done to ensure his safety. He found himself taking off his gloves to pay the taximan, remembering that he must keep them on, fumbling in his pocket, and getting hot and worried.

He intended to travel to Cornwall, but would not do so in the day-time. People in his compartment, people in the dining-car, people in the corridor. Too many people keeping him under observation. Here, among millions, he could move about and be seen by no one twice. In a train it was another matter. So he booked a sleeper on the night train, giving a name that would fit the bogus initials on his suit-case, and then he wandered out to lose himself in London.

Dear God! After all these years Oliver had called me Father again. And again, as when he was a child, we were having "conversations." And this is our conversation: here in the dark bilge of the *Jezebel* his voice is going on and on, telling me of what happened when he had killed one man too many! But there is no ice between our hearts. I do not hate him, and his face, as he looks at me, is not cold. It is old and sleepless and sad, but it is not cold. He has overtaken me in experience. We understand one another. We are easy. There is even a strange happiness flowing between us, as if two ice-floes had melted and come together in an element greater and deeper than either.

*

I read of the murder of Percy Lupton in the *Daily Telegraph* on the morning of the first Tuesday in December, 1922. I read that a black felt hat had been handed to the police by a man named Kassassian, and that the initials "O.E." were on the lining-band. It meant nothing to me. I went into my study and wrote. At eleven o'clock Annie Suthurst brought me my coffee. When she had put it on the table, she went to the window, looked through the parted curtains, and said: "Ah wonder what yon copper wants? Been standin' there gawpin' at t'house all t'mornin'. Looks as though 'e's keepin' us under observation or summat, You 'aven't committed a crime, Mr. Essex?"

I went to the window. "Where? What man?"

"Yon feller walkin' up an' down. He's a plain-clothes man. You can always tell 'em. Look at t'webs on 'im."

"What makes you think he's watching us?" I asked anxiously.

She broke into a laugh. "Nay, get on wi' thy work. Ah'm nobbut jokin'. But there 'e's been sin' nine o'clock."

She left the room and I went back to my desk, but I did not work. I was strangely troubled. I was troubled by thoughts that were monstrous, fantastic. I resisted for a long time the urging to take up the *Daily Telegraph* again; but at last it overcame me.

*"The initials O.E."*

But why should a detective be outside my door?

Well, that's pretty obvious. Suppose they have discovered who O.E. is? Wouldn't they keep an eye on any place he might bolt to—his father's flat, for example?

But this is nonsense—madness. My dear man, you're going off your head.

I suddenly discovered that I was standing before the fire with the paper gripped in both hands, my knuckles standing out white through the skin. My eyes encountered my image in a mirror over the fireplace, a face tense and contorted, with the cheek muscles twitching, out of control.

I sank into a chair lest my trembling legs should drop me. I knew what Oliver had done.

Knew? Yes; in that moment I *knew*, as certainly as if I had been physically present in that little Manchester office and seen the blows raining through the fog-misted light. I knew that now there could be nothing else. Here was a morally logical conclusion. I felt sick to death: old and grey and withered. It was a long time since I had thought of Nellie. Now she was with me, unobtrusive as when she was alive, but persistent and deadly.

*"You're bad for Oliver. You're ruining the boy."*

As though it were being enacted even now before my eyes, I saw the cane lashing down upon the white skin of his young bare back, saw the blue and purple weals start up when, for the only time, she had thrashed him. That day when he had cheated at school, that day when Rory had fled, both to protect Oliver and to test his nerve for torturing ordeals.

*"Love. A great idea you've got of love! D'you call it love to bring a child up to think he can do what he likes without taking the consequences?"*

And as the cane fell on Oliver's back: *"I'm doing your work."*

You ghost of a grey, joyless bitch, leave me alone, leave me alone! I took my hat and coat and almost rushed into the street, but she was there before the gay shop windows, among the hurrying people, in the keen blowing of winter wind and the grind and roar of the traffic: *"You'll know one of these days! You'll know that I was right."*

By the afternoon the murder was a big affair. It was on the front pages. "FAMOUS V.C. AND MURDERED CASHIER."

The hatter had identified O.E. Yes, he remembered selling the hat, only a week before, to Major Oliver Essex.

"The police, making inquiries into Major Essex's movements last night, found that he had not spent the night at his lodgings. His present whereabouts are unknown. Major Essex is the son of William Essex, the well-known dramatist and novelist."

I had remained out till four o'clock. I crept up the stairs to the flat as though I myself were a hunted man. Annie Suthurst brought me some tea. She said nothing. She was as solicitous as a nurse dealing with a patient sick to death. She had seen the papers all right.

Hard on her heels, Dermot came into the room. "Why, Bill," he said, "Bill…" and could say no more. He stood there on the verge of tears.

"For God's sake, get out," I said savagely. "Get out! Leave me alone!"

In the morning I went to Paddington and took the train to Truro.

So far as I knew, there was only one man in England to whom Oliver could turn now, and that was Captain Judas. I didn't know what I intended to do, except that I must get to Heronwater. I told nobody where I was going—not Dermot; not Annie Suthurst. Just to go, just to feel that at this last desperate moment I might get near to Oliver.

It was dark when the train ran over the viaduct into Truro station. I had never before travelled down here by train in the winter. We rumbled slowly over the viaduct, always associated in my mind with tea-time of a summer's day, the children leaning eagerly out of the window: "The viaduct! Look! The cathedral! Look at the green copper roof!" The long journey nearly done, and joy in the morning. And now again, in the dark of the deepening winter night, the long journey was nearly done.

I did not take a taxi from Truro to Heronwater. I walked. No one must know that there was anyone at Heronwater. The shops were lit as I walked through the town. The windows were gay with lanterns and Christmas trees and coloured dainties. But it was a wretched night. A thin rain was drizzling down, and once the main streets were left behind the town seemed like my heart to be bowed beneath a load of misery.

Before I left the town I bought tea and condensed milk, a loaf of bread and a quarter of a pound of butter. That was all I could carry. It was a good four miles to Heronwater, and I did not reach the house till nearly seven o'clock. The big wrought-iron gates were fastened with a padlock and chain. There was a small iron gate at the side: the gate on which Oliver had swung that day when we waited for Dermot who was bringing Donnelly and Maggie to stay with us. I had a key to this small gate, and when I had passed through I locked it behind me. Half a dozen paces took me into the darkness of the rhododendrons. I was alone now in my own little world: a world of blackness and dripping water. I followed the twist of the drive to the front of the house. The place was deserted: not a sound, not a gleam of light. I went on, scrunching over the gravel to the path that led down through the wood to the water. The surface was treacherous with wet leaves and smooth slippery pebbles. Down at last, at the little grassy quay on the water's edge. Here was the shack that had been turned into two rooms for Sam Sawle. That was my objective: the lair in which I could lie hidden and observe all that happened on the *Jezebel*.

I went into the shack, locked the door, saw that the curtains were drawn close across the window, and then ventured to strike a light. Hanging to a hook behind the door was a hurricane lamp that Sawle had used many a time for lighting us to the steps when we came home on dark nights. There was a candle still in it. By this meagre light I looked about the damp and dusty room, filled with relics of the days when Heronwater was alive with happy children. Oars leaned in a corner. Carefully coiled fishing lines, dim with spiders' webs, were on a shelf. There were gaily-coloured cushions for the boats and squares of canvas for repairing sails. A girl's flimsy green bathing-suit was hanging from a hook, and standing along a wall was an assortment of boots and shoes: canvas shoes and rubber shoes and wellingtons. Boat-hooks, bait-tins, a glass jar filled with bright pebbles and cowrie shells from Molunan beach. Over it all, dust undisturbed for years, and a disagreeable musty odour of decay.

Piled in the little hearth was a store of logs. With my booted foot I smashed up a packing-case and managed to start a fire. No one could see the smoke, down there in the darkness alongside the river. Gradually the chill was chased from the room. I sat down in Sam Sawle's sprawling wicker chair and stretched the wet legs of my trousers to the blaze. I opened my overcoat upon another chair. The fag-end of candle in the hurricane lamp spluttered and went out, and in the glow of the firelight I sat there amid the mementoes of so much that had turned to dust. Nellie and Donnelly, Maeve and Rory, Sawle and Martin: all had here come running in and out, dumping this, snatching up that, with the green grass and the green water shining in the sun without. Sitting there isolated from the world, tired to death and grey at the heart, with not a sound reaching me from the night, with the very rain too light and ghostly to make a sound as it dewed the roof, I felt like the survivor of an age that time had done with, and wondered why I myself had been chosen to remain.

I awoke in the first light of the morning stiff and cold. My bones seemed to creak as I got up out of the chair. I was faint for want of food. There was no water in Sawle's shack, so I took the food I had bought in Truro and climbed up the path to the house. I was thankful that we pumped our water; otherwise, the supply would have been cut off. The pump was in the kitchen, and the sound of its clanking in the grey morning light seemed to fill the sheeted house. Sheets everywhere: cold, spectral. Again I had to light a fire to boil the water, and the breakfast, when it came, was nothing but tea and bread and butter. But the hot tea made a great difference. I lit a pipe and felt better. I did not want to enter the ghostly sheeted house again; so I took a few buckets of water, a kettle, a teapot and crockery down to the shack, and then cleared the woodshed of all its logs. I felt, irrationally, but with conviction, that Oliver would come to the *Jezebel*. I did not know how long I should have to wait. Now I could give myself a fire at night, and, if need be, I could live on a loaf for two days. So on that Thursday morning I settled down to wait, looking for hour after hour at the black hull of the *Jezebel* across the river.

I did not see him come. I saw Judas come up on deck once or twice during the Thursday, and his lights burned steadily all through Thursday night. On Friday there was nothing all day, nothing but the blue shimmer of smoke rising from the galley chimney. It was dark by four o'clock; by five the stars were out in a cloudless sky. I shut the door of the shack behind me and walked across the quay, down the steps to the river. I stood there listening to the gentle slapping of the water, looking at the lace-work of bare trees rising above the opposite bank, etched against the star-patterned sky. Then my heart stood still. Leaning over the bulwarks of the *Jezebel*, with nothing to show he was there but a head blocking out a few stars, was a man, and then there were two men. The night was so dark that I could have believed my long vigil had made me ready to see what was not. Then, clearly, two heads moved once more against the stars, and I knew that the waiting was over.

I did not know what to do. I had no boat on the river. I stood there with my heart in a turmoil, trying to form a scheme out of the unco-ordinated swirl of my thoughts. I dared not hire a boat; I dared not show myself.

A *squeak-creak, squeak-creak*, was growing louder on the river. The familiar sound brought me to my senses. Someone was crossing in a dinghy. I moved swiftly and silently to the shadow of the shack. It must be Judas. He knew the river so well. I heard the boat grate gently against the wall at the foot of the steps. A moment later, the white of the old man's hair and beard appeared as a blur in the darkness. He vanished up the path leading to the house.

This was puzzling. For a moment I bothered myself with wondering what Judas was up to. Then I gave up bothering. There was a boat; across the river, if I were not mistaken, was Oliver. I went down the steps, got into the dinghy, untied the painter, and pushed out on to the water.

No light was visible in the *Jezebel*. I tied up the boat to the ring in the hull and pulled on the bell-cord. There was no answer for a long time. At last, gazing up, I once more saw a head outlined against the stars. Down here on the dark water I would be invisible.

"That you, Judas?" The voice was a cautious, fearful whisper.

"No, Oliver. I am your father."

There was no answer.

"Let down the ladder," I said.

I think even at this last minute Oliver must have struggled hard with his obstinacy and pride. The ladder did not come down for a long time. But it came. I climbed up and stood beside him on the deck. He was the first to speak. He said: "I'm glad you've come, Father."

I could not answer him, because I knew I had come too late. He took me by the arm and led me carefully to the stairway. The darkness was intense. But I knew the way pretty well, and when we were down Oliver shut and bolted the door. "Don't move," he said. "Stand where you are."

He struck a match, and I saw that the trap-door was open down to the bilge, where Judas used to keep the dynamite that would blow up the throne of Peter. *Whoosh! Bang! Wallop!* "You go down first," Oliver said.

I gripped the sides with my fingers, hung suspended, dropped. Oliver followed and pulled down the trap-door upon us. Then he lit a lantern. "This is all right," he said. "Quite safe. No one can see the light."

And that was where I came face to face with Oliver again: in a place like a dungeon below water, with the great keel beneath our feet, and the massive ribs rising out of it, and his shadow wavering, fantastic, gigantic, as he moved in the light of the lantern.

For a moment we did not speak. He propped his feet against the keel and leaned back into the concave side of the ship. I looked at him with my heart breaking. He is twenty-six, my thoughts kept saying. Twenty-six...

He looked ageless: haggard, drawn and dissolute. The only fea-ture I knew was the hair. It had grown long again. It was golden, waving over his forehead. He put up his scarred hand and brushed back that youthful banner from the ruins of his face. His eyes were dull with misery. His wounds stood out white and vivid. His cheeks seemed to have collapsed upon his jawbones.

At last he spoke. "Why did you bother?"

"I want to help you. There must be some way to help you."

"For God's sake—why? What am I to you?"

"You are my son."

He said with his lips twisted into a grin: "This is my beloved son in whom I am well pleased."

There was nothing to be said to that. After a while he said: "There is nothing you can do—nothing at all. But I'm glad you came. I suppose this is the moment when I ought to go down at your feet and ask your forgiveness. But I'm not going to do that. I'm glad you came. That's all I can say."

"Why?"

"Because when Judas went out I felt lonely and wretched. And I began to think of the time when I had plenty of friends and was happy. I thought of fooling about on this ship when I was a kid, and out there on the water, just a few inches through these planks." He smacked backwards with his hands at the boards behind him. "Sailing and swimming. And I thought of all the people I knew then and how not one of them knew I was here or cared I was here. And when you came I saw that I was wrong, and that was why I felt glad. It seemed as though I were being told that they would all come if they could: Rory and Maeve, and that chap Donnelly and his daughter—and Mother."

"They were a good lot," I said. "We've been lucky in our friends, Oliver. But nobody you speak of can do anything for you any more. You'll have to make the most of me."

Then I thought of practical things. "What about Captain Judas? What will he do when he finds his boat gone?"

"He won't be back till the morning," Oliver said. "He uses Heronwater as a short cut to Truro. He leaves his boat, climbs up through the woods and takes a bus on the high-road. His friend Jansen is in at Truro, and he's gone to spend the night with him."

"Does he..."

I couldn't say it. The words stuck in my throat. Oliver helped me out. "You mean does he know the police are after me?" He pushed his hand wearily across his brow again. "God knows what the old fool thinks. He expected me. I know that. I didn't surprise him. He swears they shan't take his Lord this time. He'll show 'em whether Judas is a betrayer. And that's all I can get out of him." He grinned uncomfortably. "What a rescuer! I've got myself as far as this, and if I get any farther I'm afraid it won't be with Judas's help."

He sprawled down on the timbers, and I sat beside him. For the first time, our bodies were in close contact. We had not even shaken hands. He hunched himself closer to me, leaned against my shoulder. "That's better," he said. I smiled at him timidly, like a man afraid of making too abrupt an advance to a shy animal.

"Remember our old 'conversations'?" I asked. "You used to sit on the rug. You fitted easily between my feet."

"I call remember much farther back than that," he said. "I'll bet you've forgotten the first thing I can remember."

"What was that?"

"Why, one night when you came home and Mother was bathing me, and it was your turn to do it, and there was a row. That's the first thing I can remember in all my life. I can remember quite clearly feeling sorry for Mother, but thinking that you and I had to stick together."

I took out my tobacco-pouch and pipe. Oliver produced an empty pipe and blew through it. I handed him the pouch. Soon we were both smoking.

"I remember that very well," I said. "Your mother was annoyed because I didn't hear your prayers after the bath. And then you wouldn't say them for her."

"I'd forgotten that part. But I remember thinking about sticking together."

God! How badly we had done about that! As though the same thought were passing through his head, Oliver smoked in silence. "I wish we had," he said simply at last.

I ventured to slip an arm round his shoulders. "Me, too," I said.

"D'you remember writing to me in Germany about Maeve?"

I nodded.

"I got that letter all right. And the tobacco and food later."

And from this I understood him to be saying that he recognised that then I had held out a hand to him, that I had offered the chance of sticking together, and that the fault was his that it had been rejected.

"I wish," he said, "that I had come straight back to you when the war was over. But I was too proud. I wanted to go on hurting you. I wanted to go on hurting everybody. And my God! the job they gave me in Ireland was just made for men who felt like that. There's a chance that I shall hang. I can think about that quite calmly at the moment. I don't know whether I shall later. But what I can't think about calmly is a God-awful government that turns you loose to wreck and murder right and left without any rule or pity, and then slips the hounds at you because you go on being what they made you."

He buried his face in his hands. "I oughtn't to have come here," he said. "This place is too full of Rory." And then, eagerly: "Let me tell you—"

"No, no. Don't distress yourself. I know all about that. Maggie came over to England and told me."

"God, how they must hate me! How they'll be glad to see me swing—Dermot and Sheila—"

"They don't know," I broke in. "Maggie told no one but me. She knew that you didn't know it was Rory when you shot him, and she said that Rory himself wouldn't have wished anyone to know. She seemed to understand."

"I wasn't in their class," he said simply. "I wasn't in the same class as Rory and Maggie. Or Maeve, for that matter. Sorry, Father. God gave you the one bad lot of all the bunch. Why are you bothering with me now?"

Then I told him of all the times I had bothered. I told him of that morning in Holborn when, from the other side of the street, I had watched him come out of Pogson's office and go to meet Livia Vaynol. I told him how I had spent a long winter night in a taxicab outside his lodgings in Camden Town. There was the day when I had watched him marching over Waterloo Bridge with his head up, and the day when, all newly dressed and glittering, he had left Charing Cross for the front. And other times there were: the time when he had come home a hero and Wertheim had played the spotlight on him; and the time when I had come too late to Manchester to prevent his going to Ireland.

I told him of all this, and of how, at any one of those times, I would have laid myself in the mud at his feet.

"Don't!" he said harshly. "Don't say that. You don't know what you're talking about. You're dreaming of a boy who doesn't exist any more. You're dreaming of a son you used to have."

I tightened the arm about his shoulders, but he would not yield himself to me. "I don't deserve you," he said. "I've muddied your name ever since I can remember. Even as long ago as when I was with that old fool Miss Bussell. And then at school. I was never any good. I was always off the rails. Even down here, with Livia Vaynol, that summer you didn't come. And I killed Maeve. I killed Rory. I killed Maggie to all intents and purposes. I've always gone about killing everything that was decent and better than myself. But I've never had the guts to kill myself. I thought of doing it on the way down here, but I hadn't the guts."

He told me of that journey. He had boarded the train to Cornwall on Tuesday night. There were not many travellers and he had a sleeping compartment to himself. His nerves were raddled. He had wandered about London all day, his hat pulled down over his eyes, his gloves never off his hands, watching the crime grow in importance through edition after edition of the evening papers. At the end of the day his photograph was in all of them, with a potted biography. They had it all: the V.C., the Manchester motor company, the work in Ireland, even the "romance" with Maeve, "unfortunately terminated by the death of this talented young actress when at the very height of her popularity."

He felt a hunted man when he reached the train. He didn't dare look anyone in the face. And then, dashing along the corridor to his compartment, he ran into Pogson, actually collided with the man, beyond possibility of evasion.

"I loathed the chap," Oliver said, "and he loathed me. D'you remember that night in Maeve's dressing-room when I shut him up? Yes, I know I didn't look at you, but I saw you there. I never got on with Pogson after that. I'd sucked up to him for years, and he liked me because I was a sucker. No one else had any use for him at all. But you see, during the war I thought I was someone. I wasn't a simple-minded disinterested hero, believe me. I liked it all. I liked bossing people, and I liked the medals and the publicity—all the whole shoot of bunk and ballyhoo. And I thought I was a cut above Poggy, and let him know it. But when I barged into him that night, you'd think we were loving twins."

Pogson recoiled on seeing Oliver, but he quickly recovered and advanced with outstretched hand. You'd think he knew nothing of the hue and cry. "And yet there was an evening paper stuck under the man's arm, with my own picture staring me in the face."

"Well, well, if it isn't old Essex!" Pogson exclaimed. "I thought you'd dropped out of London life completely."

"So I have," Oliver said. "I live in the North. But I've been over-working, and I'm going down to stay with some people in Devonshire. I'll be with 'em till over Christmas. And what about you, Poggy? Why are you bound west?"

"Oh, still in thrall to Pogson's Entire, you know. Just a general business trip round and about to see that the right stuff slakes the nation's thirst. And talking of thirst, come into my compartment. We'll get the waiter to bring a few along."

Oliver excused himself; said he was fagged out and must get straight to bed.

"Well, if you don't sleep, you'll know where to find me," Pogson said. "Only in the next coach."

He went. Oliver got to his compartment, locked the door, and threw himself, fully-dressed, on the berth. He was sweating and shaking with apprehension. "God! You should have seen the people's hero then," he said bitterly. "And that swine knew the funk he'd got me in."

He thought of leaving the train. But it would be like Pogson to be leaning out of the window, keeping an eye along the platform. Oliver looked through the window on the other side. There were empty rails, a platform beyond them, an arc light burning down on a group of porters and taxi-drivers standing there. No; that would look too queer. It must be the other side, and quickly. But if Pogson...

So his mind tossed, tortured by an indecision to which it was not accustomed. At last he leapt up, put on his hat and the overcoat he had thrown across the berth, picked up his suit-case, and laid his hand on the door-knob. At that moment the train started. He threw down bag, hat and coat again, lay on the berth and trembled. Every footstep along the corridor brought him half-way to his feet, listening, watching the door-handle. He didn't trust Pogson. If not now, then at the journey's end, Pogson would have arranged an unpleasant surprise.

With his head down to the pillow, he listened to the wheels drumming over the rails. Words haunted him, attaching themselves to the wheels' rhythm. *Got you at last! Got you at last! Got you at last!* And *hung by the neck, hung by the neck, hung by the neckety, neckety neck.*

It went on for hour after hour. Expresses roared past; they slowed alongside the clacking stutter of shunted trucks; once or twice they stopped in stations, and then he sat upright on the berth, his feet on the floor, grasping the boards with both hands, ready to leap up, fight, run. Then they would move again; he would subside over the rhythm of the wheels, picking up some new diabolical intimation. *Guilty, my lord! Guilty, my lord! Guilty, my lord!*

The wheels were in his head; his head was on the rails; wheels, head, rails—all were one, compounding a threatening iron rhythm. He leapt up, his eyes feeling dry and bloodshot, his nerves twitching, his head splitting. He pulled on his hat and overcoat and gloves, took his suit-case in his hand. At that moment the hurrying rhythm of the train abated. They slowed; they came to an uncovenanted stop.

A moment's relief from that damnable rhythm; and then the silence became as threatening as the wheels' roar had been. For God's sake, *why* had they stopped? He stood rigid at the door, his ear leaning upon it. A footstep hurried along the carpeted corridor. From far-off came the sound of a window let down. There was a hiss of escaping steam; a few voices came gravely out of the darkness. A distant engine whistled. And all this was full of menace in the silence of an hour that was beyond midnight.

He pulled the door open an inch and listened. There was no sound from the corridor. The light out there was dim. The place was deserted and therefore friendly. Through the windows he could see nothing but blackness, and that was friendly, too. He stepped through the door, closed it softly behind him, and stood there for a moment listening intently. Now he was in action again, and he was all right, nerves steady, thinking of everything. He opened the door before him, balanced the suit-case on the running-board outside, stepped out himself, shut the door behind him. "Before I began to do all this," he explained, "I had remembered that you don't have to bang Great Western doors in order to shut them. You can do it by turning the handle." Yes; now that it was action, he remembered everything.

Crouching on the running-board, he shut the door quietly, clutched the board with his fingers, so that he could lower himself without the noise of a jump, then reached down the suit-case. He pushed this between two wheels, and squirmed after it. Hands stretched away in front of his head, clawing at the road-metal, face downwards, he lay on the sleepers. A few minutes passed. "It didn't seem long. I was thinking of Pogson's face when he came to spring his little surprise on me in the morning." Then he heard the deep-chested cough of the engine. The couplings clanked and tautened. The train rumbled forward over his body. It accelerated, and again the rhythm of the rails beat into his head. But he kept his face to the earth, heard it quietening and diminishing, and at last raised his head to see a red eye winking to extinction in the pitch blackness forward.

He did not rise at once. He rolled first to one side, then to the other, using eyes and ears on the darkness. Telling me of it, he actually chuckled. "I'd been caught bending by a Verey light before that." At last he convinced himself that the darkness was uninhabited. Then he rose, took his bag, and stumbled off the track. He didn't know where he was. He didn't know even in what county the train had stopped. The night was not cold, but it was inky dark and misty. Presently his eyes became more accustomed to the darkness. He made out that he was in the vicinity of a small country station. There was a siding with iron beast-pens built upon a concrete ramp, and rising above the pens, looking like a dark oblong blot on the dark sky, was a water-tank, raised on a lattice of iron supports. His mind was still at work, telling him that when he was missed from the train this stopping-place would be remembered. They wouldn't look for him there, on the very spot where the train had stopped. So there he resolved to stay. He clambered up the trellis to the water-tank, dropped the case over the edge so that it stood on end, and, feeling over, discovered that the top of the case was clear of the water.

Listening to Oliver describing these extraordinary proceedings that went forward in the blackness of a December night, his voice here in the boat sounding tranquil and detached, and thinking of that Hampstead house where I had made arrangements so complete for no wind to blow upon him, I felt, for all our proximity, that here was someone I had never known, someone whom now I should never know.

He climbed into the water-tank and sat down upon the end of the suit-case. His feet were propped against one side of the tank, clear of the water. Sitting thus, with his head sunk on his chest, he was invisible. Before an hour had passed he realised that even superhuman resolution would not permit him to keep his legs up, with no support but their own muscular pressure against the side of the tank. Again and again they dropped; again and again he raised them; at last he gave it up, allowed them to rest on the bottom of the tank, under the water. In this position, worn out with anxiety, gnawed by hunger, he dozed through the night.

With the first light of the morning he raised his head and looked about him. As far as he could see, a flat landscape of meadows lay around him. A few elms with a tall church spire pricking through them broke the monotony to the east.

He bowed his head again on to his chest, faced now by the fearful prospect of spending the day doubled up thus in his tin box. He tried to prop up his feet again. They were numb with cold and dropped at once into the water. He cursed himself for not having had the foresight to take off his shoes, stuff his socks into them, and tie them round his neck. He had rolled his trousers up above his knees, but now his shoes would never dry.

The light grew stronger. Men came to work in the station. Trains began to pass through. Now he dared not straighten himself. He had not realised what this was going to mean, but before long he could have cried with the agony of sitting still on a few inches of leather. "It must have been about nine in the morning," he said, "that I suddenly plunged down on my knees, water or no water."

That was a relief, and throughout the day he was now sitting, now kneeling, but never knew a moment's cessation of the strain of keeping his head low.

Sometimes he slept, sitting on the edge of the suit-case, his head hanging towards his knees. The roar of expresses through the station would wake him up, shaking with apprehension, shivering with cold. His legs from the thighs down were blue and pimpled and numbed. He rubbed and rubbed, glad to have something to do.

Men lounged and talked in the beast-pens below him. He could hear the very words of their slow, deliberate country speech. He was glad to have something to listen to.

By noon he could feel no sensation of life in his feet, but his neck and back were strained and burning with the long muscular distortion of his bending. And his stomach was ravening for food. "I could have chucked the whole thing, jumped up and yelled." But he gritted his teeth and told himself that now he had spent more hours in the tank than he had yet to spend.

It was dark by five o'clock, but the station was not yet shut. By now he was down on his hands and knees, moving his head up and down like an animal in a stall in order to loosen the tortured muscles of his neck. For the same purpose, he writhed his back from side to side. His clothes were soaked from head to foot, but now he was long past caring for that. He was whimpering for the deeper dark as a child whimpers for the light.

He left the suit-case when he climbed out of the tank. He could not feel the iron lattice with his feet. He let himself down hand over hand and when his feet touched the ground he collapsed as though he had no bones. He crawled on hands and knees till he was hidden by a hedge. Then he stripped himself naked and worked over his body, slapping life into his legs, harshly massaging his neck. At the end of an hour he was warmer, able to stand and walk. He dressed and made in the direction whence he had seen a light burning an hour ago. It was now extinguished.

He reached the cottage and walked quietly all round it. There was no sign that anyone was awake, but the day and night in the tank had made another hour seem a small matter. He walked up and down on the grass verge of the lane that ran between the cottage and the high-road. He walked for an hour, his legs strengthening all the time.

Then he opened one of the cottage windows. It was a kid's job, he said, that you could do with a pocket-knife. In the cottage kitchen the embers of a fire were still burning. He put on a little more coal, took off his trousers, spread them over a chair, placed his shoes and socks on the fender. Then he found some bread and cheese, ate what he wanted and put the rest in his pocket. When his clothes were fairly dry he dressed again, and then his eye fell on a pair of trouser-clips, such as cyclists use, hanging from a hook screwed into the fireplace. He went out quietly to look for the bicycle, found it in a shed behind the cottage, and five minutes later was cycling west. From that moment the luck was with him, the last luck he was to know.

I woke with a start, not knowing for a moment where I was. The atmosphere in the bilge was disgusting, fetid with our breath and stale tobacco smoke. The lantern had guttered out, my mouth felt stale, my stomach retched. In the pitch darkness I could feel Oliver's head resting against my shoulder. I could hear the slow, gentle drawing of his breath. We had talked and dozed, and waked and talked again, far into the night. Then we had fallen asleep, leaning against the ship's timbers.

I moved my hand and felt his hair, long and silky, the hair I had brushed so carefully that day before taking him down to the birthday party wearing his black silk pyjamas. It felt just the same. I fondled it very softly, fearing to wake him, and tears scalded my eyelids and then began to flow quietly down my face.

O God! Don't let him wake! Don't ever let him wake again. And don't let that lantern ever be lit. I don't want to see his face. I want to feel his hair.

I wished we could both die there, in the darkness below the *Jezebel's* decks, with his head on my shoulder, his soft hair under my hand.

Suddenly his whole body twitched violently and his head was wrenched away. Then, as though he had recollected where he was, he sighed, and leaned back against me. "Hallo, Father," he said.

I could see by the illuminated dial of his wrist-watch that it was seven o'clock. I wiped my eyes furtively. I got up and heard my bones creak. "Gosh! I'm getting an old man," I said, yawning.

"Christ!" he said. "You're not half as old as I am. I feel a million."

He pushed up the trap-door and a faint light fell upon his uplifted face. He looked a million: ashen from the airless night, scarred, dirty, unshaven. His hollow cheek ticked *in, out, in, out,* as regularly as the ticking of a clock. And his eyes were the eyes of a doomed man who knows it. "This might be the bottom of the drop," he said suddenly; and I shuddered from head to foot.

He remained standing there for a moment, one hand resting on the ship's side, his grey face upturned to the grey light. Then he said: "I'd like to go up for some food, but I promised Judas to stay down here."

I knew he was afraid to go up. He was afraid of the light of day. "Give me a hand," I said.

He locked his fingers together. I put one foot upon the palms of his wounded hands, rested one hand in the tangle of his hair. He bore me lightly. He was very strong.

In the body of the ship there was hardly more light than in the bilge. I pulled the curtains back from the windows and swung them open, taking deep breaths of the raw damp morning air. Mist was curling up in little smoky wisps from the river. I could scarcely see the opposite bank.

I lit the galley fire and made some coffee, cut bread and butter. Then I called to him to come up, lay flat on the floor and reached a hand down to him in the pit. He grasped it strongly and I heaved him up, glad to be grovelling on the ground to help him.

We sat at the table with Judas's thin womanly china between us. It was not much of a meal, but it was many years since we had eaten together. He recurred to a thought that had troubled him before. "I don't know why you're doing this," he said.

"Never mind why I'm doing it," I answered. "Don't you know that I'm very happy? I've got a son again."

The wounds round his eyes creased into little puckers of

puzzlement. For the first—and last—time in his life I saw in him a resemblance to Nellie. It was identically her short-sighted bewildered look, and it moved me to the bones.

"I don't understand it," he said. "I don't understand it."

"Never mind," I repeated. "There it is. If you had had a son you might know what I mean."

"I might have had," he said. "Maeve might have had a son... Poor Maeve..."

He buried his face in his hands. I could see the wound in his hand's back and the fair disordered hair falling through his fingers.

"Then it would have been so different," he said, looking up with his white face cupped in his hands. "She became a sweet girl, and very beautiful. Did she speak to you about me? Did she get to like me?"

"She loved you very much," I lied.

I began to clear away the things from the table. "Sit down, and let me do that," he said. "You're as tired as I am. We're both worn out."

That was true. We were both worn out, and not by the events of the last few days. We were a couple of haggard, unshaven old men—my son Oliver and I. Now that the light was stronger, I could see my face in the mirror. I had not shaved for three days. I saw that if I let my beard grow it would be white.

Oliver came out from the galley, and grasping the table edge, looked down on me. "Did you ever see Livia Vaynol again?" he asked.

I shook my head. "Never since the night you left her in Maeve's dressing-room."

"Nor I. I treated her pretty badly." He added after a pause: "But that was a habit of mine. There's only one thing in my whole life that I'm glad about at this moment."

I looked at him questioningly.

"I'm glad Mother didn't live."

Then he dismissed all that with a shrug of the shoulders. "Had we better descend again to the underworld?" he asked.

"It's not necessary. Stay here where the air's fresher. No one can see you, and we can see anyone who approaches the ship. What are you going to do?"

He sat with his hands drooping between his knees. "Hang," he said.

At that, a cry was dragged out of me. "No, no!" I said. "Don't say that! For God's sake don't talk about that, even as a possibility. We must think. We must devise some scheme…"

He looked at me wearily. "Think! Believe me, I've done plenty of thinking. There's just a possibility…just one dog's chance. That's what I came here for."

"Yes?" I prompted him, childishly, pitiably eager.

"I knew I could rely on Judas. I thought that if he could hide me in the bilge till Jansen came in with the *Kay*, I might get away with it."

"Yes, yes!" I cried. "After all, he took you for one voyage, and there's no reason why he shouldn't take you for another."

"Oh, yes, there is," Oliver objected. "Taking a passenger on a honeymoon is one thing. Helping a murderer to escape is another."

The brutal word seemed to strike me between the eyes. "He'll do it," I muttered desperately. "He'd do anything for Judas."

"Yes, I know. And Judas would do anything for me. On paper it's perfect. But paper's thin stuff. You could fall through it on the end of a rope."

He sank his head in his hands again, ruffled his hair. "Jansen's no fool. Why, damn it all!" he shouted, suddenly erect and angry and excited, "don't you see what it might mean to him—losing his name and his ship and his livelihood? Yes! That's what it means now to help a man like me! You'd better clear out, too. It'll do you no good if you're found here. Get out while the going's good. Go on!"

"I'll go and see Jansen myself," I said. "I'll beg him on my hands and knees. Why, good God! I could buy him up, ship and all. I'm a rich man. If he loses over this…"

I had lost control of myself. I was standing up, shouting, quivering. Oliver put an arm round my shoulders, and a strange shudder compounded of joy and repulsion went through me at the touch. "Calm yourself," he said. "I know you would do anything for me. I have always known that, pig-headed swine that I've been. I've always known you were there. There were times when I hated you, but I never doubted you. Is it any consolation to you to know that?"

I nodded my head, unable to speak.

"I'm glad," he said, his grip round my shoulders tightening like a vice, "because now it's too late. You can do nothing more. Look!"

The arm that was not holding me shot out towards the window, the long scar pointing like an arrow. As I looked, his strong arm held me up, or I should have fallen. "That's the end," he said.

He released me, and I gripped the edge of the table for support. My knees were like water. Oliver held out his hand. "We'll say good-bye now," he said.

I took his hand. It closed on mine like iron, not trembling.

"Oliver…Oliver…"

It was a mere quiver of sound, the ghost of all that had been between us fluttering out of the body now dead.

He was not afraid now. I could see that. His face was grey but stern, with the *tick-tick* again pricking the rigid muscles of his jaw.

"Thank you for coming—and for everything," he said. Then he dropped my hand.

We stood face to face at the table, not speaking for a moment, listening to the engine of the motor-boat. The engine dropped to half-speed as the bows pointed in towards the *Jezebel*.

Then he spoke again. "Don't fool yourself with hopes. There's no earthly chance. I want you to make me a promise."

I couldn't speak. I looked at him in anguished silence.

"Don't come to see me in gaol when it's all over. I shouldn't like that. Promise?"

I nodded.

"This is better. We all loved this place—Maeve, Rory, all of us. This is a better place to say good-bye. I'll go and throw the ladder down for those chaps."

He went up the stairs to the deck. I stayed where I was, sunk in misery. I don't know how long I stood there, but at last, footsteps sounding, I looked up. I thought Oliver had come back.

"I'm sorry, Mr. Essex."

I believed it. The man seemed friendly and anxious to help. It was the plain-clothes officer I had seen watching outside my flat a few days before. With a rough gesture of goodwill, he pulled a cigar-case out of his pocket and held it towards me. I shook my head and sank on to a chair.

"There's no need for you to come into this at all," he said. "The fellows in the boat haven't seen you, and for that matter, neither have I. Understand?"

He took my arm and gazed into my face.

I nodded.

"That's all right, then. Good-bye to you."

He held out his hand and I shook it, scarcely knowing what I was doing. I must have lost my senses for a moment. When I recovered, I rushed to the window, in time to see the boat rounding the bend. Oliver was sitting in the stern with the man who had just left me. They had an absurd air of friendship. I might have been watching the *Maeve* setting off for Truro when we were all young and happy, and Maeve and Rory and Oliver...

My hands clutched the window-sill as I crumpled to my knees and wept, for Oliver had turned, and waved his hand, and now I could see nothing but the river, grey and empty, and the trees that had forgotten summer.

I did not remain after the boat had passed from sight. Judas's dinghy was still at the foot of the ladder. I rowed her across to

Heronwater and tied her up where Judas had left her the night before.

There was nothing to wait for, nor any more need to conceal my presence. But I did not want Judas to know that I had been there. Nothing could come of that now. I hid myself in the shack and had not long to wait. He and Jansen came down the path from the house, talking noisily and excitedly together. From behind the curtain I watched them get into the dinghy, saw Jansen pulling across the river with slow powerful strokes, and Judas in the stern pointing to the unusual fact of the dropped ladder.

I sat down for a moment, wondering whether they had come to any decision, whether they had cooked any plot. Jansen was the sort of hare-brained fool who would try anything.

Well, they were too late now, whatever they may have had in mind. I got up to go, saw Jansen step aboard, turn round, and playfully take the little captain by the collar of the jacket and heave him with one hand over the bulwarks. His great laugh came across the water, on which I had heard so much laughter in my time. When they were gone below, I ran up the path and a few minutes later the 'bus was taking me in to Truro.

There is nothing more to be said. They hanged Oliver in Strangeways gaol. I do not know whether a bell was tolled or a flag flown at half-mast or a proclamation nailed to the prison door. I only know that in the desolate street where, so long before, the people had sung and cheered as the Manchester Martyrs went to their doom, I lingered till, almost without seeing, I was aware that the small crowd had broken up and was drifting away.

Then I, too, went, walking in the mournful weather down the squalid road that leads to the heart of the town. The trams crashed by, the pavements were lively with men and women marching in to their accustomed concerns. All the energy of another day was moving to its appointed ends.

Rain was falling as gently as mercy, and a woman, walking with long swift strides, went by me. Her opened umbrella brushed my cheek and she half-turned with a muttered word. It was Livia Vaynol, her quick walk making me think that she was fleeing, as she had fled that day when for the first time she saw Oliver leave for France. Recognition struck instantly between us, but she did not stop. A strong shudder seemed to shake her as she strode ahead of me through the mist. Her hair, I saw, was grey; her hat, her raincoat, were old and shabby.

I knew that she had been saying good-bye, and wondered at her faithfulness.

But this is not the place where I shall say good-bye. I shall go back to London and rest awhile, for I am very tired. Then some day I shall take a train from Paddington. At Fishguard I shall go aboard the little liner that takes you to Cork. I have never been there, but I am told that, having travelled all night, you wake in a wide harbour with a loveliness to make you wonder.

I shall do that, and I shall go ashore and go to Ballybar and find there the grave where Rory lies. Because in my heart you, too, Oliver, will always be lying there. It was not you who went that day with a handkerchief on his face, and struck, and stole, and ran. That was the simulacrum that remained after you had died at Ballybar. You died when you killed your friend. There was nothing for you of good or evil after that. So I shall say good-bye to you by Rory's grave.

Perhaps Dermot will come with me. We shall say good-bye to you together—to you and to Rory—and remember the night before either of you was born when in pride and blindness we told the years what they should do with our sons.

*About the author*

HOWARD SPRING (1889–1965) was born in Cardiff. He began his writing career as a journalist, working for the *Manchester Guardian* and the *Evening Standard* before becoming a full-time writer of novels. His first major success came with *My Son, My Son* (1937), originally titled *O Absalom!*, which was adapted into a successful film in 1940. He is best remembered today for his novel *Fame is the Spur*, a fictional account of a working-class Labour leader's rise to power.